The critics on Stephen Coonts

Fortunes of War

'A stirring examination of courage, compassion, and profound nobility of military professionals under fire. Coonts' best yet' *Kirkus Reviews*

Flight of the Intruder

'[Coonts'] gripping, first-person narration of aerial combat is the best I've ever read. Once begun, this book cannot be laid aside' *Wall Street Journal*

The Red Horseman

'One of the most thrilling post-glasnost thrillers to date' *Publishers Weekly*

Under Siege

'Mr Coonts knows how to write and build suspense. His dialogue is realistic, the story line mesmeric. That is the mark of a natural storyteller'
New York Times Book Review

The Minotaur

'A fast-paced, graphic thriller with harrowing insights into the thankless, razor's-edge world of the navy test pilot and the labyrinth of superpower espionage'
Washington Post

Stephen Coonts is a former naval aviator who flew combat missions during the Vietnam War. He is the author of thirteen published novels. A former attorney, he resides with his wife and son in Las Vegas. He maintains a website at *www.coonts.com*.

The Red Horseman

———

The Intruders

STEPHEN COONTS

ORION

The Red Horseman
First published in USA in 1993 by Pocket Books, a division of Simon and
Schuster, Inc.
First published in Great Britain by Orion Books Ltd in 2003

The Intruders
First published in USA in 1995 by Pocket Books, a division of Simon and
Schuster, Inc.
First published in Great Britain by Orion Books Ltd in 2003

This omnibus edition published in 2006
by Orion Books Ltd,
Orion House, 5 Upper St Martin's Lane,
London WC2H 9EA

A CIP catalogue record for this book is available from the British Library.

ISBN 1 89880 197 5

Printed and bound in Great Britain by
Mackays of Chatham Ltd, Chatham Kent

The author gratefully acknowledges the assistance of the following people on various aspects of this novel: William C. Cohen, Oleg Kalugin, Fred Kleinberg, and George C. Wilson. A special tip of the hat goes to Barnaby Williams, who conceived the idea of personal binary poisons and graciously allowed the author to twist it to his own perverted ends.

And there went out another horse that was red: and power was given to him that sat thereon to take peace from the earth, and that they should kill one another: and there was given to him a great sword.

Revelation 6:4

The Cold War is over; the Soviet Union is no more ... In the past, we dealt with the nuclear threat from the Soviet Union through a combination of deterrence and arms control, but the new possessors of nuclear weapons may not be deterrable.

—Les Aspin,
US Secretary of Defense

CHAPTER ONE

Toad Tarkington first noticed her during the intermission after the first act. His wife, Rita Moravia, had gone to the ladies' and he was stretching his legs, casually inspecting the audience, when he saw her. Three rows back, four seats in from the other aisle.

She was seated, talking to her male companion, gesturing lightly, now listening to what her friend had to say. Now she glanced at the program, then raised her gaze and spoke casually.

Toad Tarkington stared. In a few seconds he caught himself and turned his back.

How long had it been? Four years? No, five. But it couldn't be her, not here. Not in Washington, DC. Could it?

He half-turned and casually glanced at her again.

The hairstyle was different, but it's *her*. He would swear to it. Great figure, eyes set wide apart above prominent cheekbones, with a voice and a touch that would excite a mummy – no man ever forgets a woman like that.

He sat and stared at the program in his hand without seeing it. He had last seen her five years ago, in Tel Aviv. And now she's here.

Judith Farrell. No, that was only an alias. Her real name is Hannah something. Mermelstein. Hannah Mermelstein. Here!

Good God!

Suddenly he felt hot. He tugged at the knot in his tie and unfastened his collar button.

'What's the matter? Are you catching a cold?' Rita

1

slipped into her seat and gave him one of those looks that wives reserve for husbands whose social skills are showing signs of slackness. Before Toad could answer the house lights dimmed and the curtain opened for act two.

He couldn't help himself. When the spotlight hit the actors, he looked left, trying to see her in the dim glow. Too many people in the way. Hannah Mermelstein, but he had promised to never tell anyone her real name. And he hadn't.

'Is something wrong?' Rita whispered.

'Uh-uh.'

'Then why are you rubbing your leg?'

'Ah, it's aching a little.'

That leg had two steel pins in it, and just now it seemed to Toad that he could feel both of them. The Israeli doctors inserted the pins just a day or two before he saw Judith/Hannah for the last time. She came to see him in the hospital.

Toad Tarkington didn't want to remember. He folded his hands on his lap and tried to concentrate on the actors on the stage. Yet it came back as if it had just happened yesterday, raw and powerful – the night he made love to her, that Naples hotel lobby as the man with her gunned down a man in the elevator, the assault on the *United States*, the stench of the ship burning in the darkness . . . that F-14 flight with Jake Grafton. He found himself gripping the arms of the seat as all the emotions came flooding back.

What is she doing here?

Who has she come to kill?

'Come on,' he whispered to Rita. 'I want to go home.'

'Now?' She was incredulous.

'Yes. Now.' He stood.

Rita collected her purse and rose, then preceded him toward the aisle, muttering excuses as she clambered past knees and feet. In the aisle he took her elbow as she walked toward the lobby. He glanced toward where Judith Farrell was sitting, but couldn't spot her.

'Are you feeling okay?' Rita asked.

'I'll explain later.'

The lobby was empty. He led Rita to the cloakroom and fished in his shirt pocket for the claim check. The girl went to fetch the umbrella. He extracted two dollars from his wallet and dropped them into the tip jar, then wiped the perspiration from his forehead with his hand. The girl returned with the umbrella and handed it across the Dutch door counter.

'Thanks.'

When he turned, Judith Farrell was standing there facing him.

'Hello, Robert.'

He tried to think of something to say. She stood looking at him, her head cocked slightly to one side. Her male companion was against the far wall, facing them.

'Rita,' she said, 'I'm Elizabeth Thorn. May I speak to your husband for a few minutes?'

Rita looked at Toad with her eyebrows up. So Judith Farrell knew about his wife. It figured.

'Where?' Toad asked. His voice was hoarse.

'Your car.'

Toad cleared his throat, 'I don't think—'

'Robert, I came tonight to talk to you. I think you should hear what I have to say.'

'The CIA is open eight to five,' Toad Tarkington said, 'Monday through Friday. They're in the phone book.'

'This is important,' Judith Farrell said.

Toad cleared his throat again and considered. Rita's face was deadpan.

'Okay.' Toad took his wife's arm and turned toward the door. The man against the wall watched the three of them go and made no move to follow.

They walked in silence across the parking lot. The rain had stopped but there were still puddles. Toad unlocked the car doors and told Farrell, 'You sit up front. Rita, hop in the backseat, please.'

Once in the car he started the engine and turned on the

3

defroster as the women seated themselves. Then he reached over and grabbed Judith Farrell's purse. Farrell didn't react, but Rita started. Still, she remained silent.

No gun in the purse. That was his main concern. There was a wallet, so he opened it. Maryland driver's license for Elizabeth Thorn, born April 17, 1960. The address was in Silver Spring. Several credit cards, some cash, and nothing else. He put the wallet back into the purse and stirred through the contents. The usual female beauty paraphernalia, a box of tissues, a tube of lipstick. He examined the lipstick tube, took the cap off, ran the colored stick in and out, then replaced the cap and dropped the tube back into the purse. He put the purse back on Farrell's lap.

'Okay, Ms Thorn. You have your audience.'

'I want you to give Jake Grafton a message.'

'Call the Defense Intelligence Agency and make an appointment.'

'Obviously I don't want anyone to know that I talked to him, Robert. So I came to you. I want you to pass the message along, to him and no one else.'

Toad Tarkington looked that over and accepted it, reluctantly. Rear Admiral Grafton was the deputy director at the DIA and Toad was his aide. Both facts were widely known, public knowledge. At the office every call was logged, every visitor positively identified. Admiral Grafton lived in general officers' quarters at the Washington Navy Yard and was guarded by the federal protective service. While it would be easy enough for a professional to slip through the protective cordon, doing so would require the admiral either to report the conversation to his superiors or violate the security regulations. Presumably this way it would be up to the admiral to decide if this conversation had to be reported, a faint distinction that didn't seem all that clear to Toad.

'Rita and I will know.'

'You won't tell anyone. You're both naval officers.' That was also true. Rita was an instructor at the navy's Test Pilot

School at NAS Patuxent River. Both of them hel[...]
of lieutenant commander, both had top secret c[...]
both had seen reams of classified material that they c[...]
even talk about to each other.

Toad turned and looked at Rita, who was staring at the
back of Elizabeth Thorn's head and frowning.

Toad Tarkington gazed out the window at the empty
parked cars as he considered it. 'Why tonight? When I'm
out with Rita?'

'If I had walked up to you when you were alone, you
would have brushed me off.'

That comment irritated him. 'Pretty damn sure of yourself, aren't you?'

Farrell didn't reply.

Toad again glanced over his shoulder at his wife, who
met his eyes. She was going to be full of questions as soon
as they were alone. Now she opened her door and stepped
out of the car. She walked around to the front of the vehicle
where she could watch the other woman's face.

'This better be good,' Toad said. 'Let's hear it.'

It took less than sixty seconds. Toad made her repeat it
and asked several questions, none of which Elizabeth
Thorn answered. From her coat pocket she took a plain
white unsealed envelope, which she passed to Toad. He
opened it. It contained a photo and a negative. The photo
was a three-by-five snap of a middle-aged white man
seated at a table, apparently at an outdoor restaurant, reading a newspaper. There was a plate on the table. His face
registered just a trace of a frown.

'Want to tell me who this is?'

'You find out.'

'Any hints?'

'CIA. You'll talk to Grafton?'

'Maybe, if you'll help me with the caption.' He wiggled
the photograph. 'Like when and where.'

'Jake Grafton can figure it out. I have a great deal of faith
in him.'

'But not much in me.' Toad sighed. 'How about this: just before he took his first – and last – bite of eggs Benedict injected full of arsenic trioxide by beautiful spy Hannah Mermelstein, Special Agent Sixty-Nine realized that the *Sauce Hollandaise* had a pinch too much salt?'

Her face showed no reaction whatever.

Toad Tarkington shrugged. He put the photo back in the envelope and placed the envelope in an inside jacket pocket. 'So how did you know Rita and I were coming to this play tonight?'

Judith Farrell opened the car door and stepped out. 'Thank you for your time, Robert.' She closed the door and walked away. Toad watched her go as Rita came around the car and climbed into the front passenger seat.

'Who is she?'

'Mossad.' The Israeli intelligence service.

'You were in love with her once, weren't you?'

Trust a woman to glom onto that angle. Toad sighed and pulled the transmission lever into reverse.

When the car was out on the street, Rita asked, 'When did you know her?'

'Five years ago. In the Med.'

'Her real name isn't Elizabeth Thorn, is it?'

'No. She got out that name right up front, so I wouldn't call her anything else.'

Rita waited for him to tell her more, but when it became obvious he wasn't going to, she remarked, 'She's very pretty.'

Toad merely grunted.

'Are you going to tell me what she said?'

'No.'

Rita seemed to accept that with good grace. And she had gotten out of the car without being asked. She was a player, Toad told himself, a class act, every inch the professional Judith Farrell was. Perhaps he should have been nicer to Farrell.

This thought was still tripping across the synapses when

Rita remarked, 'I think you're still in love with her. Not like you love me, but you care for her a lot. That was obvious to her, too. If you didn't care you would have been nic—'

'Shut up!' Toad snarled.

'Listen, husband of mine. In three years of marriage neither one of us has told the other to shut up. I don't think—'

'I'm sorry. I retract that.'

'I feel like I'm trapped in a soap opera,' Rita said. After a pause she added, 'And I don't like it.'

No fool, Toad Tarkington decided to let her have the last word.

Later, as they waited for a traffic light, Rita asked in a normal tone of voice, 'So what does Elizabeth Thorn do for the Mossad?'

Toad considered before answering. He decided maybe the truth was best. 'Five years ago she was running a hit squad. Maybe she still is. She's a professional killer. An assassin.'

Toad awoke at dawn on Saturday and took his clothes into the kitchen to dress so he wouldn't wake Rita. After enough coffee had dripped through to make a cup, he poured himself some and went out into the backyard of the little tract home he and Rita had purchased last year near Andrews Air Force Base. The morning was expectant, still, with the diffused sunlight hinting of the heat to come in a few hours. Not even the sound of jet engines of planes from the base. Too early yet. Someone somewhere was burning last fall's leaves, even though it was against the law, and the faint smell seemed to make the coffee more pungent.

Judith Farrell. Here.

Although he would never admit it to Rita, seeing Judith had been a jolt. And Rita knew anyway. Blast women! All that crap about body language and nonverbal speech that

7

they expected men to sweat bullets acquiring was just the latest nasty turn in the eternal war between the sexes. And if by some miracle you got it they would think of something else you needed to know to meet tomorrow's sensitivity standards. If you suffered from the curse of the Y chromosome, Aagh!

He sat sipping coffee and pondering the male dilemma.

After a bit his mind turned to Judith Farrell's message for Jake Grafton. Probably Farrell hadn't tried to contact him when he was home alone because even he and Rita never knew when that would be. This was his first free Saturday this month. That crap about brushing her off . . . Well, it was true, he would have.

Someone told Farrell – told the Mossad – that he and Rita had tickets to that play last night. Who?

He tried to recall just when and to whom at the office he might have mentioned that he and Rita were going last night. It was hazy, but he seemed to recall that the play had been discussed several times by different people, and he may have said he had tickets.

He purchased the tickets over a month ago by calling a commercial ticket outlet and ordering them. And there was no telling to whom Rita might have mentioned the planned evening out. It was certainly no secret.

So that was a dead end. Frustrated, he went inside and poured himself another cup of coffee.

He got out the envelope and looked again at the photo. A very ordinary photo of a very ordinary man. He held the negative up to the light. It was the negative of the photo, apparently. Given to prove the genuineness of the photo. Okay, so what was there about the photograph that made it significant? Toad studied it at a distance of twelve inches. The guy's sitting in front of a restaurant. Where? No way to tell. When? Nothing there either.

Well, Jake Grafton would know what to do with it. Grafton always knew how to handle hot potatoes, a quality that Toad had long ago concluded was instinctive. The guy could be tossed blindfolded into a snake pit and still avoid the poisonous ones.

The water began running in the bathroom. Rita must be taking a shower. He replaced the photo and negative in the envelope and put it into his shirt pocket.

Toad was outside trimming weeds along the fence when Rita appeared in the door wearing a flight suit, her hair braided into a bun that was pinned to the back of her head. 'I'm leaving, Toad.'

He paused and leaned on the fence. 'Back for supper?'

'Yes. Are you going to call Admiral Grafton?'

'I dunno. Haven't decided.'

'You are, then.'

Toad resumed the chore of cutting weeds, trying not to let his temper show.

Rita laughed. He tossed the hedge shears down and turned his back on her.

In a few seconds she appeared in front of him. 'I love you, Toad-man.'

He snorted. 'I'm gonna ditch you and run off with ol' Lizzie Thorn. Won't be nothing here tonight when you get home except my dirty underwear and busted tennis racket.'

She stretched on tiptoe and kissed his cheek. 'See you this evening, lover.'

The numbers . . . the numbers appalled him, shocked him, mesmerized him. He wrote them on the back of an old envelope that he used as a bookmark. The stupendous, incomprehensible quantity of human misery represented by the numbers numbed him, made it impossible to pick up the book again and continue reading.

Jake Grafton stared out the window at the swaying trees in the yard without seeing them, played with his mechanical pencil, ran his fingers yet again through his thinning hair.

And he looked again at the envelope. Fifteen million Russians died fighting the Germans during World War I.

Fifteen million! Dead! No wonder the nation came apart at the seams. No wonder they dragged the czar from his palace and put him and his family against the wall. *Fifteen million!*

The new republic was doomed. The Bolsheviks plunged the land into a five-year civil war, a hell of violence, famine and disease that cost another fifteen million lives. Another *fifteen million!*

Then came Josef Stalin and the forced collectivization of Soviet agriculture. Here the number was nebulous, an educated guess. One historian estimated six million families were murdered or starved to death — another believed at least ten million men, women, and children perished; young and old, vigorous and infirm, those struggling to live and those waiting to die. The Red Army had gone through thousands of square miles robbing the peasants of every crumb, every animal, every potato and cabbage and edible kernel, then sealed the districts and waited for every last human to starve.

Ten million! A conservative estimate, Jake thought.

Then came the purges. Under Josef Stalin — and they had called the fourth Ivan 'the Terrible!' — Soviet citizens were worked as slave labor until they died or were shot in wholesale lots because they might not be loyal to their Communist masters. The secret police murder squads had quotas. And they filled them. Through the use of show trials and extorted confessions, the soul-numbing terror was injected into every nook and cranny of Soviet life. Citizens in all walks of life denounced one another in a paranoid hysteria that fed on human sacrifice. Those who survived the horror had a word for it: *liquidation.*

Over *twenty million* human beings were liquidated, possibly as many as forty million. Only God knew the real number and He had kept the secret.

World War II — the raging furnace of war, famine and disease consumed another twenty-five million Soviet citizens. *Twenty-five million!*

10

The numbers totaled eighty-five million minimum. Jake Grafton added the numbers three times. It was too much. The human mind could not grasp the significance of the numerals on the back of the tattered envelope.

Eighty-five million human lives.

It was like trying to comprehend how many stars were in a galaxy, how many galaxies were in the universe.

'Jake?' His wife stood in the doorway. 'Amy and I are going to the Crystal City mall. Won't you come with us?'

He stared at her. She was of medium height, with traces of gray in her dark hair. She had her purse in her hand.

'The mall . . .'

'Amy wants to drive.' The youngster had just received her learner's permit and was now driving the family car, but only when Jake was in the front seat with her. Callie had announced that her nerves were not up to that challenge and refused the honor.

Jake Grafton rose to his feet and glanced out the window. Outside the sun shone weakly from a high, hazy sky. On this June Saturday all over America baseball games were in progress, people were riding bicycles, shopping, buying groceries, mowing yards, enjoying the balmy temperatures of June and contemplating the prospect of the whole summer ahead.

The envelope and its numbers seemed as far away from this reality as casualty figures from the Spanish Inquisition.

'Okay,' Jake Grafton told his wife.

He eyed the envelope one last time, then slid it between the pages of the book. With the book closed the numbers were hidden; only the top half inch of the envelope was visible.

Eighty-five million people.

But they were all long dead, as dead as the pharaohs. The earth soaked up their tears and blood and recycled their corpses. Only the numbers survived.

He turned off the light as he left the room.

*

Toad Tarkington called after the Graftons returned from the mall. Callie invited him to dinner. Five minutes later she answered the phone again.

'Jack Yocke, Mrs Grafton. I'm leaving for an overseas assignment on Monday and I wondered if I could stop by and chat with your husband this evening.'

'Why don't you come to dinner, Jack? Around six-thirty.'

'I don't want to put you to any trouble.'

Callie was amused. She enjoyed entertaining, and Jack Yocke, a reporter for the *Washington Post*, was a frequent guest. Jake habitually avoided reporters, but Yocke had become a family friend through an unusual set of circumstances. And he had never yet turned down a dinner invitation. Friends or not, he had the most important commodity in Washington – access – and he knew precisely what that was worth. Callie undoubtedly knew too, Yocke thought: she was perfectly capable of slamming the door in his face if she ever thought he had taken advantage of her hospitality.

'No trouble, Jack,' she told him now. 'Where are you going?'

'Moscow! It's my first overseas assignment.' The enthusiasm in his voice was tangible.

Callie stifled a laugh. Yocke had been maneuvering desperately for two years to get an overseas assignment. Other than a short jaunt to Cuba, he had spent most of his five years at the *Post* on the metro beat covering police and local politics. 'Good things come to those who wait,' she told him.

'Actually,' Yocke said, lowering his voice conspiratorially, 'I got the nod because our number two man over there had a family emergency and had to come home. My biggest asset is that I'm single.'

'And you've been asking for an overseas assignment.'

'Begging might be a better word.'

'Moscow? He's going to Moscow?' Jake Grafton repeated when his wife went into the study to give him the news.

12

Callie nodded. 'Moscow. It's dangerous over there, I know, but this is a big break for him professionally.' She left the room to see about dinner.

'He'll certainly have plenty to write about,' Jake Grafton remarked to himself as he surveyed the piles of books, newspapers and magazines strewn over the desk and credenza.

He was reading everything he could lay hands on these days about the Soviet Union, the superpower that had collapsed less than two years ago and was now racked by turmoil. Like a ramshackle old house that had withstood the winds and storms long past its time, the Communist empire fell suddenly, imploded, shattered like old crystal, all in a heap. Now ethnic feuds, runaway inflation, famine and a gradual disintegration of the social order were fueling the expanding flames.

'Plenty,' Grafton muttered listlessly.

Yocke's enthusiasm for his new adventure set the tone at dinner. Almost thirty, tall and lean, he regarded his new assignment as a great challenge. 'I can't stand to go into that District Building one more time. This is my chance to get out of metro once and for all.'

His chance to get famous, Jake Grafton thought, but he didn't say it. The young reporter oozed ambition, and the admiral didn't hold that against him. Ambition seemed to be one of the essential ingredients to a life of great accomplishments. Lincoln had it, and Churchill, Roosevelt . . . Hitler, Josef Stalin.

Grafton played with his food as Jack Yocke talked about Russia. Toad Tarkington seemed preoccupied and quieter than usual. Tonight he listened to Yocke without comment.

'It's hard to imagine the Russian empire without a powerful bureaucracy. The bureaucracy was firmly entrenched by 1650 and became indispensable under Peter the Great. It was the tool the czars used to administer the empire, to run the state. The Bolsheviks just adopted it pen and paper clips when they took over. The problem at the end was that the bureaucracy lost the capability of providing. The infernal machine just ground to a halt and nothing on this earth could get it started again without the direct application of force.'

'Not force,' Jake Grafton said. 'Terror.'

'Terror,' Yocke agreed, 'which the leadership was no longer in a position to supply.'

'Where did they go wrong?' Callie asked. 'After the collapse of communism and the dissolution of the Soviet state, everyone was so hopeful. Where did they go wrong?'

Everyone at the table had an opinion about that, even Amy. 'No one over there likes anyone else,' she stated. 'All the ethnic groups hate each other. That isn't right. People shouldn't hate.'

Toad Tarkington winked at her. Amy was growing up, and he liked her very much. 'How's the driving going?' he asked when there was a break in the conversation.

'Great,' Amy said, and grinned. 'Except for Mom, who sits there gritting her teeth, waiting for the crash.'

'Now, Amy . . .' Callie began.

'She knows it's going to be bad – teeth, hair and eyeballs all over the dashboard.' Amy sighed plaintively. 'I've decided to become a race car driver. I'm going to start in stock cars. I figure in a couple of years I'll be ready for formula one.'

'Amy Carol,' her mother said with mock severity. 'You are not—'

'Talent,' Amy told Toad. 'Some people have it and some don't. You should see my throttle work and the way I handle the wheel.'

After dinner Jack Yocke asked to speak with the admiral alone, so Jake took him into the study and closed the door. 'Looks like you've been doing some reading,' the reporter remarked as both men settled into chairs.

'Ummm.'

'This is my big break,' Yocke said.

14

'That's what you said when the *Post* let you write a column during the '92 presidential primary campaign.'

'Well, that didn't work out. And it wasn't a column – it was just a signed opinion article once a week.'

Jake reached for a scrapbook on a bookshelf and flipped through it. 'Callie saved most of them. I thought some of your stuff was pretty good.'

Yocke shrugged modestly, a gesture that Grafton missed. The admiral adjusted his glasses on his nose and said, 'Let's see – this was written in January, before the New Hampshire primary. You said, "Now Bush admits that he didn't know the country was in a recession. He's the only man in America who hadn't heard the news. The man's a groundhog who only comes out of his hole every four years to campaign."'

'Acceptable hyperbole,' Yocke said and squirmed in his seat. 'A columnist is supposed to be interesting.'

'"If George Bush had been president during World War II, allied troops would have stopped at the Rhine and the Nazis would still be running Germany."'

'Well . . .'

Grafton flipped pages. He cleared his throat. '"The American people don't want George Bush and Clarence 'Coke can' Thomas deciding whether their daughters can have abortions."' Grafton glanced over his glasses at Yocke. 'Coke can?'

'There was a mix-up on that. That comment should not have gotten into the paper. I wrote that as a joke to give the editor something to shout at me about and somehow he missed it. He and I almost got canned.'

Grafton sighed and flipped more pages. 'Ahh, here's my favorite: "Even if Arkansas Governor Bill Clinton is absolutely innocent, as he claims, of having an adulterous affair with bimbo Gennifer Flowers, that by itself would not disqualify him to be president. America has had two presidents this century, perhaps even three, who were faithful to their wives. A fourth would not rend the social

15

fabric beyond repair. It's an indisputable fact that such dull clods rarely seek public office in our fair land and almost never achieve it, so if one does squeak in occasionally, once a generation, how much harm could he do?" '

'A parody of David Broder,' Yocke muttered with a touch of defiance. 'A satire.'

'Everything written in our age is satire,' the admiral said as he closed the scrapbook and slid it back into the book-shelf. When he looked at Yocke he grinned. 'You should be writing for *Rolling Stone*.'

'The *Post* pays better,' Jack Yocke said. 'Y'know, I've written a lot of stuff through the years, yet I still have to spell my name for the guy at the laundry whenever I drop off my shirts. And he's seen me twice a week for five years, speaks English, can even read a little.'

Still wearing a grin, Grafton took off his glasses and rubbed the bridge of his nose. 'Your stuff's too subtle. You should try to give it more punch.'

'Words to live by. I'll remember that advice. But we have a hot tip that I'm going to try to chase down when I get to Russia. The story is that some tactical nukes are on the open market. For sale to the highest bidder.'

'You don't say?' Jake Grafton said. He pushed his eye-brows aloft. 'Where'd you hear that?'

Yocke crossed his legs and settled in. 'I know you won't confirm or deny anything, and you won't breathe a word of classified information, but I thought I'd run this rumor by you. Just for the heck of it.'

Jake Grafton ran his fingers through his hair, pinched his nose, and regarded his guest without enthusiasm. 'Thanks. We'll look into it. Be a help if we knew the source of this hot tip, though.'

'I can't give you that. It's more of a rumor than a tip. Still, if it's true it's a hell of a story.'

'A story to make you famous,' Jake agreed. 'And to think we knew you when. All you have to do is live long enough to file it.'

'There's that, of course.'

Jake stood and held out his hand. 'If worse comes to worst, it's been nice knowing you.'

Jack Yocke looked at the outstretched hand a moment, then shook it. He got out of his chair and smiled. 'One of your most charming characteristics, Admiral, is that deep streak of maudlin sentiment under the professional exterior. You're just an old softie.'

'Drop us a postcard from time to time and tell us how you're doing.'

'Yeah. Sure.'

Jack Yocke opened the door and went out, and Amy Carol came in. She carefully closed the door behind her. 'Dad, I have a question.' She dropped into the chair just vacated by the reporter.

'Okay.'

'It's about sex.'

Jake opened his mouth, then closed it again. Amy was growing up, no question about that. She had filled out nicely in all the womanly places and presumably had consulted with Callie about plumbing, morals and all that. Under his scrutiny she squirmed slightly in her seat.

'Why don't you ask your mom?'

Amy shot out of the chair and bolted for the door. On her way down the hall he heard her call, 'Toad, you owe me five bucks. I *told* you he'd duck it.'

After Yocke said his good-byes, Jake and Toad Tarkington took coffee into the study and carefully closed the door.

'You're not going to believe this, Admiral, but last night at the Kennedy Center Judith Farrell walked up and said hi.'

Jake Grafton took a while to process it. It had been years since he'd heard that name. 'Judith Farrell, the Mossad agent?'

'That's right, sir. Judith Farrell. Now she calls herself Elizabeth Thorn. She had a Maryland driver's license.'

'Better tell me about it.'

Toad did so. In due course he got to the message. 'You remember Nigel Keren, the British billionaire publisher who fell off his yacht a year or two ago while it was cruising in the Canaries?'

Jake nodded. 'Found floating naked in the ocean.'

'Stone cold dead. That's the guy, Nigel Keren. Then his publishing empire went tits up amid claims of financial shenanigans. But nobody could ever figure out how Keren got from his stateroom aboard the yacht over a chest-high rail into the water while wearing nothing but his birthday suit.'

Jake sipped coffee. 'He was a Lebanese Jew, wasn't he? Naturalized in Britain?'

'Yessir. Anyway, ol' Judith Farrell says the CIA killed him.'

'*What?*'

'That's the message she wanted you to have, Admiral. The CIA killed Nigel Keren. Oh, and this photo.' Toad took the envelope from his pocket and passed it to the admiral, who went to his desk and turned on the desk lamp to examine it.

'I know who this is,' he told Toad.

'Yessir. I recognized him too. Herb Tenney, the CIA officer who is going to Russia with us. If we go.'

Jake got a magnifying glass from his desk drawer and examined the photo carefully as he tried to recall what he had read of Keren's death. The financier had been alone on the yacht with its crew until he turned up missing one morning. Several days later his nude body was fished from the ocean. All twelve crewmen claimed ignorance. The Spanish pathologist had been unable to establish the cause of death but ruled out drowning, due to an absence of water in the lungs. So Keren had been dead when his body went overboard. How he died was an unsolved mystery.

Finally Jake laid the glass and the photo on the desk and regarded it with a frown. 'Herb Tenney reading a newspaper.' He sighed. 'Okay, what's the rest of the message?'

'You got it all, Admiral. "Tell Admiral Grafton that the CIA killed Nigel Keren and here's a photo and negative. 'Bye." That's all she said.'

Jake used the magnifying glass to examine the negative. It appeared to be the one from which the print was made. Finally he put both print and negative back in the envelope and passed the envelope back to Toad. 'Take these to the computer center on Monday morning and have them examined. I want to know where and when the photo was taken and I want to know if the negative has been altered or enhanced by computer processing.' He doubted if the negative had been altered, but Farrell had offered it as evidence, so it wouldn't hurt to check.

'Yessir. But what if word of this gets back to Tenney?'

'What if it does? Maybe he can tell us about the photograph.'

'If the CIA killed Keren and Tenney was in on it, maybe they won't want anyone to see this picture.'

'Toad, you've been reading too many spy stories. We'll probably have to ask Tenney about that picture. Farrell knew that. She probably wants us to question Tenney.'

'Then we shouldn't.' Toad said. 'At least not until we know what this is all about.'

Jake Grafton snorted. He had been on the fringes of the intelligence business long enough to distrust everyone associated with it. The truth, he believed, wasn't in them. They didn't know it. Worse, they never expected to learn it, nor did they care. 'Take the print and negative to the computer guys,' he repeated. 'Stick a classification on it. Top secret. That should keep the technician quiet.'

'What about Farrell?' Toad demanded.

'What about her?'

'We could get her address from the Maryland department of motor vehicles and try to find her.'

'She was told what to say and she said it. She doesn't know anything.'

Toad Tarkington flicked the envelope with his forefinger,

then placed it in an inside pocket. He drained the last of his coffee. 'If you don't mind my asking, what did Yocke want?'

'He's heard a rumor that some tactical nukes are for sale in Russia to the highest bidder.'

'*Shee-it!*'

'I know the feeling.' Jake Grafton said. 'The most sensitive, important, dangerous item on the griddle at the National Security Council and Jack Yocke picked it up on the street. Now he's charging off to scribble himself famous. Makes you want to blow lunch.'

CHAPTER TWO

•

Richard Harper was a priest of the High-Tech Goddess. He spent his off-hours reading computer magazines and technical works and browsing at gadget stores. He thought about computers most of his waking hours. There was something spiritual about a computer, he believed. It was almost as if it had a soul of its own, an existence independent of the plastic and wire and silicon of which it was constructed.

So he habitually talked to his computer as his fingers danced across the keyboard. His comments were low, lilting and almost unintelligible, but it was obvious to Toad Tarkington that Harper was in direct communication with whoever or whatever it was that made the machine go. That didn't bother Toad – he had spent years listening to naval aviators whisper to their lusty jet-fueled mistresses: he didn't even classify Richard Harper as more than average dingy.

Just now he tried to make sense of Harper's incantations. He got a word or two here and there. '. . . time for a hundred indecisions, a hundred visions and revisions . . . Do I dare, do I dare?' After a few minutes he tuned out Harper and scanned the posters, cartoons, and newspaper articles taped to the wall. All over the wall. On every square inch. Computer stuff. Yeck!

Tarkington regarded computers as just another tool, more expensive than a screwdriver or hammer but no more inherently interesting. Of necessity he periodically applied himself to making one work, and when required could even give a fairly comprehensive technical explanation of what went on down deep inside. But a computer had no pizzazz, no romance, no appeal to his inner being. This Monday morning he leaned idly on the counter and without a twinge of curiosity watched Harper and his computer do their thing.

But he had a restless mind that had to be mulling something: once again his thoughts went back to Elizabeth Thorn, alias Judith Farrell. He had loved her once. One of the male's biological defects, he decided, was his inability to stop loving a woman. Oh, you can dump her, avoid her, hate her, love someone else, but once love has struck it cannot be completely eradicated. The wound may scar over nicely, yet some shards of the arrowhead will remain permanently embedded to remind you where you were hit. If you are a man.

Women, Toad well knew, didn't suffer from this biological infirmity. Once a woman ditches you her libidinal landscape is wiped clean by Mama Nature, clean as a sand beach swept by the tide, ready for the next victim to leave his tracks like Robinson Crusoe. And like that sucker, he'll conclude that he is the very first, the one and only. Amazingly, for her he will be.

Biology, you old devil.

Ah, me.

Then Toad's thoughts moved from theoretical musings to the specific. He poked around the edges of the emotions that the sight and sound and smell of Elizabeth Thorn created in him and concluded, again, that it would be unwise to explore further. Yet he couldn't leave it. So he circled it and looked from different angles.

He felt a chill and shuddered involuntarily.

'Commander Tarkington?'

It was Harper. This was the second time he had said Toad's name.

'Yeah.'

'Just what is it you want to know about these prints?' Harper flexed his fingers like a concert pianist.

22

'Ah, have they been enhanced? Touched up? Whatever the phrase is.'

'Well, the two prints are identical.' Toad had given Harper two prints, the original that Elizabeth Thorn had handed him Friday night and one he had made yesterday evening from the negative at a one-hour photo shop in a suburban mall. 'I ran them through the scanner,' Harper continued, 'which looks at the light levels in little segments called pixels and assigns a numerical value, which is how the computer uses the information. The prints are essentially identical with only minor, statistically insignificant variations. Possibly caused by dust on the negative.'

Toad grunted. 'Did anybody doctor it up?'

'Not that I can see.' Harper punched buttons. Columns of numbers appeared on the screen before him. 'What we're looking for are lines, sharp variations in light values that shouldn't be there. Of course, with a sophisticated enough computer, those traces could be erased, but then the resultant print would have to be photographed to get a new negative, and that would fuzz everything. I just don't think so. Maybe one chance in a hundred. Or one in a thousand.'

'What can you tell me about the picture?'

Harper's fingers flew across the keyboard. The photo appeared on the screen. 'It's a man sitting at a table reading a newspaper. Apparently at a sidewalk café.'

'Do you know the man?'

'No, but if you like I can access the CIA's data base and maybe we can match the face.'

'That won't be necessary,' Toad Tarkington said. 'Is there anything in the photo that would indicate where it was taken?'

The computer wizard stroked the mouse and drew a box over the newspaper. He clicked again on the mouse button and the boxed area filled the screen. The headline was in English and quite legible, but the masthead was less so.

'We'll enhance it a little,' Harper muttered and clicked the mouse again.

After a few seconds he announced, '*The Times.*'

'*New York Times?*'

'*The Times.* The real one. London.'

'What day?'

'Can't tell. The date is just too small. But look at this.' The whole photograph was brought back to the screen and the cursor repositioned over a white splotch on the café window. Now the splotch appeared. Toad came around the counter and stared over Harper's shoulder. 'It's a notice of the hours the café is open. You can't read the language in this blowup – the picture is too fuzzy – but if the computer uses an enhancement program to fill in the gaps it should become legible.'

His fingers danced. After a minute or two he said, 'It's not English. It's Portuguese.'

'So the photo was taken in Portugal.'

'Or in front of a Portuguese café in London, Berlin, Zurich, Rome, Madrid, New York, Washing—'

'How about the front page of the paper? Can you give me a printout of that?'

'Sure.' Richard Harper clicked the mouse on the print menu and in a moment the laser began to hum. Toad waited until the page came out of the printer, then examined it carefully. There was a portion of a photo centered under the paper's big headline, which contained the words 'Common Market ministers.' He folded the page and put it back into his pocket.

'Well,' he said, 'I guess that's everything. Give me back the prints and erase everything from the memory of your idiot box and I'll get out of your hair.'

Harper shrugged. He put the prints in the envelope that had originally contained them and passed it to Toad, who slipped the envelope into an inside pocket. Then Harper clicked away on the mouse. After a few seconds of activity he sat back and said, 'It's gone.'

'I don't want to insult you,' Toad said, 'but I should emphasize this little matter is a tippy top secret, eyes only. Loose lips sink ships.'

'Everything I do is classified, Commander,' Harper said tartly. He reached for the folder on the top of the pile in his in basket.

'No offense,' Toad muttered. 'By the way, what were those lines you were saying about "visions and revisions"?'

Now Harper colored slightly and made a vague gesture. ' "The Love Song of J. Alfred Prufrock." '

'Umm.'

An hour later in the media reading room in the Madison Building of the Library of Congress Toad found the page of the London *Times* that had been captured in the photo. Several weeks' editions of the newspaper were on each roll of microfilm. He selected the roll that included the date Nigel Keren died, placed it on a Bell & Howell viewing console and began to scroll through the pages. The headline he wanted was on page twenty-three of the scroll, the edition of November 1, 1991.

Rear Admiral Jake Grafton spent the morning in a briefing. As usual, the subject was nuclear weapons in the Commonwealth of Independent States, which was the old Soviet Union. This matter was boiling on the front burner. The locations of the strategic nuclear missiles – ICBMs – were known and the political control apparatus was more or less public knowledge. But the Allied intelligence community had lost sight of the tactical nuclear weapons – weapons that were by definition mobile. They were hidden behind the pall of smoke rising from the rubble of the Soviet Union.

Listening to experts discuss nuclear weapons as if they were missing vases from a seedy art gallery, Grafton's attention wandered. He had first sat through classified lectures on the ins and outs of nuclear weapons technology as a very junior A-6 pilot, before he went to Vietnam for the first time. In those days attack plane crews were each assigned targets under the Single Integrated Operational Plan – SIOP. The lectures were like something from Dr Strangelove's horror cabinet – thermal pulses, blast effects, radiation and kill zones and the like. When the course was over he even got a certificate suitable for framing that proclaimed he was a qualified Nuclear Weapons Delivery Pilot.

But the whole experience was just some weird military mind-bender until he was handed his first target the day after the ship sailed from Pearl Harbor on his first cruise to Vietnam.

Shanghai.

He was assigned to drop a nuclear weapon on the military district headquarters in Shanghai. It wasn't exactly downtown, but it was on the edge of it.

Actually he was not going to drop the bomb: he was going to toss it, throw it about forty-three thousand feet, as he recalled. That was how far away from the target the pull-up point was. He would cross the initial point at five hundred knots, exactly five hundred feet above the ground, and push the pickle on the stick, which would start the timer on the nuclear ordnance panel. The timer would tick off the preset number of seconds until he reached the calculated pull-up point – that point forty-three thousand feet from the target. Then a tone would sound in his ears. He was to apply smooth, steady back-pressure on the stick so that one second after the tone began he would have four Gs on the aircraft. At about thirty-eight degrees nose-up the tone would cease and the weapon would come off the bomb rack and he would keep pulling, up and over the top, then do a half roll going down the back side and scoot out the way he had come in.

He had practiced the delivery on the navy's bombing range in Oregon. With little, blue, twenty-eight-pound practice bombs. The delivery method was inherently inaccurate and the bombs were sprinkled liberally over the countryside, sometimes a couple miles from the intended target. A good delivery was one in which the bomb impacted within a half mile of where you wanted it. With a six-hundred-kiloton nuke, a miss by a mile or two wouldn't matter much.

'Close enough for government work,' he and his bombardier assured each other.

Months later on an aircraft carrier crossing the Pacific with a magazine full of nuclear weapons, the insanity of nuclear war got very personal. Figuring the fuel consumption on each leg of the run-in, working the leg times backward from the hard target time – necessary so he and his bombardier wouldn't be incinerated by the blast of somebody else's weapon – plotting antiaircraft defenses, examining the streets and buildings of Shanghai while planning to incinerate every last Chinese man, woman and child in them, he had to pinch himself. This was like trying to figure out how to shoot your way into hell.

But orders were orders, so he drew the lines and cut and pasted the charts and tried to envision what it would feel like to hurl a thermonuclear weapon into Shanghai. The emotions he would feel as he flew through the flak and SAMs on the run-in, performed the Götterdämmerung alley-oop over a city of ten million people, and tried to keep the airplane upright and flying as the shock wave from the detonation smashed the aircraft like the fist of God as he exited tail-on to the blast – emotions were not on the navy's agenda.

Could he nuke Shanghai? Would he do it if ordered to? He didn't know, which troubled him.

Fretting about it didn't help. The problem was too big, the numbers of human lives incomprehensible, the As and Bs and Cs of the equation all unknown. He had no answers. Worse, he suspected no one did.

So he finished his planning and went back to more mundane concerns, like wondering how he was going to stay alive in the night skies over Vietnam.

That was twenty-three years ago.

Today listening to the experts discuss the possibility that nuclear weapons might be seeping southward from the Soviet republics into the Middle East, the memories of planning the annihilation of half the population of Shanghai made Jake Grafton slightly nauseated.

The voice of the three-star army general who headed the Defense Intelligence Agency jolted his unpleasant reverie. The general wanted hard intelligence and he was a bit peeved that none seemed to be available.

'Rumor, surmises, theories . . . haven't you experts got one single fact?' he demanded of the briefers. 'Just one shabby little irrefutable fact — that's not too much to ask, is it?'

The three-star's name was Albert Sidney Brown. After thirty-plus years in the maw of a vast bureaucracy where every middle name was automatically ground down to an initial, he had somehow managed to retain his.

The briefer was CIA officer Herb Tenney, who briefed Lieutenant General Brown on a regular basis. Today he tried to reason with the general. 'Sir, the place is bedlam. Nobody knows what's going on, not even Yeltsin. The transportation system's kaput, the communication system is in tatters, people in the countryside are quietly starving, armed criminal gangs are in control of—'

'I read the newspapers,' General Brown said acidly. 'Do you spooks know anything that the Associated Press doesn't?'

'Not right now,' Herb Tenney said with a hint of regret in his voice. Regret, Jake Grafton noted, not apology. Tenney was several inches short of six feet. His graying hair and square jaw with a cleft gave him a distinguished, important look. In his gray wool business suit with thin, subtle blue stripes woven into the cloth he looked more like a Wall Street buccaneer, Jake Grafton thought, than the spy he was.

'Congress is performing major surgery on the American

military without benefit of anesthetic,' General Brown rumbled. 'Everybody east of Omaha is tossing flowers at the Russians, and that goddamn cesspool is in meltdown. There are *thirty thousand tactical nuclear weapons* over there just lying around loose! And the CIA doesn't know diddly squat.'

Jake Grafton thought he could see a tiny sympathetic smile on Herb Tenney's face. His expression looked remarkably like the one on the puss of the guy at the garage giving you the bad news about your transmission. Or was Grafton just imagining it? Damn that Judith Farrell!

Tenney's expression seemed to irritate General Brown too. 'I am fed up with you people palming off yesterday's press clippings and unsubstantiated gossip as news. You're like a bunch of old crones at a whores' picnic. No more! I want facts and you spies better come up with some. Damn quick!'

Brown's fist descended onto the table with a crash. 'Like yesterday! I don't give a shit who you have to bribe, fuck, or rob, but you'd better come up with some hard facts about who has their grubby hands on those goddamn bombs or I'm going to lose my temper and start kicking *ass!*'

When the briefers were gone and he and Jake were alone, Albert Sidney Brown rumbled, 'They'll never come up with hard intelligence. Nobody on our side knows anything. Not a goddamn thing. Now *that's* a fact.'

'We just don't have the HUMINT resources, General,' Jake Grafton said. HUMINT was human intelligence, information from spies. The CIA had never had much luck recruiting spies in the Soviet Union. Prior to the collapse the counterintelligence apparatus had been too efficient. It was a different story now, but a spy network took years to construct.

'The world is becoming more dangerous,' General Brown said softly. 'It's like the whole planet is on a runaway locomotive going down a mountain, faster and faster, closer and closer to the edge. The big smashup is waiting around the next bend, or the next. And those cretins in Congress are in a dogfight to divide up the "peace dividend." Makes you want to cry.'

Jake had had numerous wide-ranging conversations with General Brown since he reported to this job six months ago. Brown was convinced that the proliferation of weapons of mass destruction was the most dangerous trend in an increasingly unstable international arena. And Jake Grafton agreed with him.

Recently the United States and other Western nations had agreed to spend $500 million to pay for destruction of the Soviet nuclear arsenal, but the work wasn't going quickly enough. 'They've got bombs scattered around over there like junk cars,' Brown told Jake Grafton. 'They don't know what they've got or where it is, so it's imperative that we get someone over there to keep an eye on the situation and prod them in the right direction. You're that someone.

'The ambassador is talking to Yeltsin right now, trying to sell military-to-military cooperation at the absolute top level. As soon as we get the okay, you're on your way. Keep your underwear packed.'

'Aye aye, sir.'

'Jake, we have got to get a handle on this nuclear weapons situation. I want you to get the hard facts. Ask the Russian generals to their faces – and don't take no for an answer. There isn't time to massage bruised egos. They must be as worried as we are. If their criminal gangs or ragtag ethnic warriors start using nukes on one another, Revelation is going to come true word for word. And if those fanatics in the Middle East get their hands on some . . .' Brown lifted his hands skyward.

Jake Grafton finished the thought. 'This planet will be history.'

'A radioactive clinker,' Brown agreed, and swiveled his chair toward the map of the old Soviet Union that hung on the wall.

'The first day of November 1991,' Toad Tarkington repeated, 'just three days before Nigel Keren went for his long swim.'

Toad fell silent. He had completed his recital of what he learned this morning. Jake Grafton was bent over the photograph on his desk, staring at it through a magnifying glass. Finally he straightened with a sigh.

'We could ask the CIA where Herb Tenney was that week,' Toad suggested.

'No.' Jake squirmed in his chair. He flexed his right hand several times, then let it rest limply on the arm of the chair. 'For the sake of argument, assume that the CIA did kill Keren. Either the president authorized it or someone in the CIA was running his own foreign policy. The Mossad must have concluded the assassination was without authorization or they would not have approached anyone in the American intelligence community, no matter how obliquely. Assuming the CIA did kill Keren. A rather large assumption, but—'

'Sir, we've got to do something about this,' Toad said with a slight edge in his voice.

'What is this evidence of?' Jake gestured toward the photo. 'What?' That was the nub of it. At best this photo might destroy one alibi. 'We've got nothing. Absolutely nothing.'

'Do you think the CIA killed Keren?' Toad asked.

'I have no idea. If the Mossad knows and wanted us to believe, they could have given us real proof. They didn't. Which raises another question – is Farrell still working for the Mossad?'

Toad spent several seconds processing it. 'I can't see her working for anyone else. She . . .'

Toad ran out of steam when Jake Grafton gave him one of those cold glances. With thinning hair and a nose a tad too large, Jake Grafton's face wasn't memorable. It was just another face among the throng. Until he fixed those gray eyes on you with one of those looks that could freeze water,

31

that is – then you got a glimpse of the hard, determined man inside.

'Maybe they wanted to smear Herb,' Toad added lamely.

'That's one possibility. Another is that they want to discredit me.'

'You?'

'I'm not going to be around here very long if I sally forth to slay a dragon armed with nothing but a peashooter and one pea. You see that? The dragon will fry my britches. And if there's no dragon I just immolated myself.'

Jake rooted in his desk drawer for a pack of matches. He found them, then dumped the trash from his wastecan onto the floor. One by one he lit the prints and dropped them into the gray metal wastecan. The negative went last. When the celluloid was consumed, Jake picked up the trash and tossed it back into the can.

Then he picked up a file on the Russian army and opened it. Several minutes later Toad remembered the computer printout of the front page of the London *Times* that was inside his pocket. He wadded it up and tossed it into the classified burn bag.

CHAPTER THREE

June in Washington is very similar to early summer in any
other large city in the northeastern part of the United
States. The days of clouds and rain come regularly, interspersed with periods of sunshine and balmy breezes,
perfect days when it seems the whole world is ripe,
flourishing, vibrantly alive. Weekends are for shopping
expeditions, yard work, an occasional party.

Workdays in the nation's capital begin here like everywhere else. Most people turn on one of the television
morning shows as they dress and drink a cup of hot chocolate or coffee. While they take a quick squint at the
morning newspaper and gobble a fat pill, Willard Scott
tells them about the weather and a lady having her
hundredth birthday. Why supposedly sane people choose
to spend the worst moments of the day with Willard Scott,
Bryant Gumbel and their colleagues on the other networks
is a phenomenon that will probably intrigue archeologists
of a future age.

With the kids shoved out the door to swimming lessons
or other summer activities, working people fire up their
horseless chariots and join the commuting throng. Tooling
out of the subdivision they tune in another set of fools on
their car radios. On each of the morning 'drive shows' one
or two jaded disk jockeys and one syrupy sweet, eternally
cheerful female crank out some combination of pop music,
weather and crude humor interspersed with reports from
a helicopter pilot about the traffic jams that form every
morning around stalls, wrecks and road construction

projects. This mix is occasionally enlivened with a blow-by-blow account of a spectacular police chase of a freeway speeder who suddenly remembered his thirty-two unpaid parking tickets when he saw the cop's flashing light.

And 'news,' lots of it. Usually 'news' is presented in short snippets, 'sound bites,' some of them worth the ten seconds of air time they get, most not. To prevent the working citizen creeping through traffic from getting too down from an overdose of reality, the producers of these shows leaven the mix with the inane doings of show business celebrities and the latest risqué tidbits from the court trials of current cretins. Nothing heavy, nothing in depth, just a once-over-lightly on items that would only interest a heavy metal groupie or a social scientist from planet Zork.

Jake Grafton never listened. Callie had the television going every morning while she fixed Amy's breakfast, but Jake read the newspaper. If the *Washington Post* thought an international story was worth the front page, the American intelligence community was going to be wrestling with it before lunch.

In the car Jake turned off the radio the instant it babbled to life. Amy and Callie always left the squawk box on, he always turned it off.

Today he drove in the usual blessed silence while he reviewed the crises of yesterday and the likely flaps on today's agenda. The Middle East was boiling again: another assassination, more riots protesting ongoing Israeli settlement in the occupied West Bank, more terrorism and murder. Chaos in the Balkans, another wave of Haitians heading for Florida, the usual anarchy in the new Commonwealth of Independent States, or as the bureaucrats had labeled it, the CIS – all in all, this was just another day in the 1990s.

Normally there was little the Americans could do to improve any international situation. Nor, as the optimists noted, was there much they could do that would make things worse. Still everything had to go through the gristmill and be forwarded on to the policymakers for their information. And in the case of the DIA, to the appropriate units of the military to ensure they weren't luxuriating in blissful ignorance.

Besides the usual international crises, the top echelons of the military and civilian policymakers were still trying to formulate America's response to the shape of the post-Communist world. The world had changed almost overnight, yet change was the bureaucracy's worst enemy, the crisis to which it had the most difficulty responding.

This morning Jake Grafton thought about change. The knee-jerk reaction had been to reorganize, to draw more lines on the organization chart. That had been easy, though it hadn't been enough. The brave new world had to be faced whether the policymakers were comfortable or not.

They were uncomfortable. Very uncomfortable. Men and women who had spent their adult lives as warriors of the cold war now had to face the unknown without experience or perspective. Mistakes were inevitable, grievous mistakes that were going to cost people their reputations, their careers. This sense of dangerous uncertainty collided with the extraordinary dynamics of the evolving geopolitical landscape to produce a stress-filled crisis atmosphere in which tension was almost tangible.

This situation is like war, Jake Grafton decided. Every change in the international scene reveals a new opportunity to the bold few and a new pitfall to the cautious many.

He was musing along these lines when the Pentagon came into view. It was a low, sprawling building much larger than it looked.

As he parked the car he was wondering if there was any place at all for nuclear weapons in this changing world. Were they obsolete, like horse cavalry and battleships? He also wondered if he was the only person in the Pentagon asking that question.

*

'Everyone would have been better off if Russia had had another revolution and shot all the Communists.'

General Albert Sidney Brown delivered himself of this opinion and stopped the strategy conference dead. Which was perhaps what he intended. The subject was the growth of virulent anti-Semitism in the former Soviet states.

'General,' CIA deputy director Harvey Schenler said wearily, 'I don't believe fantasies of that type contribute much to our deliberations.'

Brown snorted. 'Most of the problems the new regimes in eastern Europe and the old Soviet Union are now facing were caused by the Communists' grotesque mismanagement, incompetent central planning, believing their own propaganda, lying to everybody, including themselves, cheating, bribery, favoritism – the list goes on for a couple dozen pages. Now that the Commies have become the political opposition, they're preaching hatred of the Jews, trying to blame them for the collapse of the whole rotten system. It's 1932 in Germany all over again. Now you people in the CIA seem to think that if the Communists get back in power, in some magical way this nuclear weapons control problem will just disappear. Bullshit!'

Schenler's tone sharpened. 'I think you owe me and my staff an apology. General. We have said no such thing here.'

'You've implied it. You just stated that we have to keep our lines of communication open to the Commies, treat them as legitimate contenders for power.'

'We're *not* suggesting the United States should aid their return to power.'

Brown cleared his throat explosively. 'Then I apologize. I've become so used to double-talk and new age quackspeak from you people, I'm easily confused. Perhaps today we can dispense with the bureaucratic mumbo jumbo and get down to brass tacks.'

Schenler paused for several seconds as he looked at the page before him. He had an apology and a challenge. He decided to accept the apology and return to the agenda items.

Brown's outburst was the only bright spot in the meeting, Jake Grafton found to his sorrow. These weekly strategy sessions, 'strategizing' the civilian intelligence professionals called it, were usually exercises in tedium. Today was no exception. No facts were briefed that hadn't already circulated through the upper echelons. Most of what ended up on the table were policy options from CIA analysts, career researchers who were theoretically politically neutral. Jake Grafton didn't believe it – the only politically neutral people he had ever met were dead.

So the items discussed here were really policy alternatives that had made their long, tortuous way through the intestines of the Central Intelligence Agency, perhaps the most monolithic bureaucracy left on the planet. Like General Brown, Jake Grafton looked at these nuggets without enthusiasm. Larded with dubious predictions and carefully chosen facts, these policy alternatives were really the choices the upper echelons of the CIA wanted the policy-makers to adopt. The researchers gave their bosses what they thought the bosses wanted to hear, or so Brown and Grafton believed.

Alas, these two uniformed officers well knew they couldn't change the system. So they listened and recorded their objections.

Schenler sometimes argued. Most of the time he just took notes. Grafton never saw the notes. About fifty, with salt-and-pepper hair and an ivy league education, Schenler was an organization man to his fingertips. 'I'll bet the bastard hasn't farted in twenty-five years,' General Brown once grumbled to Jake.

Jake also took occasional notes at these soirées, doodled and watched Schenler and his lieutenants perform the usual rituals.

Today, when he finally concluded that General Brown had given up, he went back to doodling. He used his pencil to doctor up his copy of a reproduction of a current Russian anti-Semitic poster that had been handed around before Brown fired his salvo. The crude drawing depicted two rich Jews – they had to be Jews: guys with hooked noses wearing yarmulkes – counting their money while starving women and children watched. In one corner a man with a red star on his cap observed the scene. Jake penciled a swastika on his chest.

'What is this?' Jake held up a piece of paper and waved it at Toad Tarkington.

'Ah, Admiral, if you could give me a little hint . . .'

'You put this here, didn't you?'

Jake Grafton had been going through his morning mail pile when he ran across Toad's masterpiece, a summary of everything in the computer about the demise of Nigel Keren. It was short, only one page, but pithy, full of facts. Toad knew the admiral was partial to facts.

'Oh,' Toad said when Jake held the paper out so he could see it, 'that's just a little thing I put together for your information.'

The admiral stared at him with humor. 'I know everything I want to know about Nigel Keren.'

Toad had rehearsed this, but looking at Jake Grafton, his little speech went out the window. 'I'm sorry,' he said contritely.

'I know how he was killed,' the admiral said.

Toad gawked.

The admiral put the paper on the desk in front of him and toyed with it. 'A publishing mogul alone on a large yacht, no one aboard but him and twelve crew members, all male. The ship is three days out of the Canaries when he eats dinner alone – the same food that all the crew was served – and spends the rest of the evening walking the deck, then goes to his stateroom. The next morning the crew can't find him aboard. Two days later his nude body is found floating in the sea. A Spanish pathologist found no evidence of violence, no water in the lungs, no heart disease, no burst blood vessels in the brain, no evidence of suffocation. In short, the man died a natural death and his corpse somehow went into the sea. None of the crew members knows anything. All deny that they killed him.'

When Jake fell silent Toad added, 'Then his media empire broke up. Apparently large sums of money, hundreds of millions, may have been taken. If anyone knows, they aren't saying. Keren's son says the deceased father just made too many leveraged deals and the worldwide recession caught them short.'

The admiral merely grunted.

'Perhaps there was a stowaway aboard the yacht,' Toad suggested. 'Or a small vessel rendezvoused with the yacht and an assassin team came aboard.'

'No. The British checked with every ship in the vicinity and interrogated the crew thoroughly. And if he was assassinated, how was it done?'

'You tell me,' Tarkington muttered.

'Remember that top secret CIA progress report that went through here a couple of months ago on the development of binary chemicals?'

Toad nodded once.

'When I saw it then, I thought of the Keren case,' Jake Grafton continued, 'but I forgot all about it until the other day when I was staring at that photo Judith Farrell donated to the cause. And I confess, I used the computer yesterday after you left to reread the Keren file.' He smiled at Toad. 'It would have occurred to you sooner or later.'

'Binary chemicals.'

'That's right. The poisons of the past – arsenic, strychnine, that kind of thing – all had a couple of major drawbacks. If given in sufficient quantity to do the job they killed very quickly, before the killer had a chance to leave the scene of the crime. And there was always the problem of killing too many people, anyone who ingested the poisoned food or drink. Binary chemicals remove those drawbacks. You give your victim one chemical, harmless in itself, perhaps serve it in the punch at a party. Everyone drinks it and no one is the wiser. It's absorbed by the tissues and so remains in the body for a lengthy period, at least several weeks. But it's benign, produces no ill effect. Then at a later date the assassin serves the other half of the poison, also quite benign by itself. And the second half of the brew combines with the first half in the body of the victim and becomes a deadly poison. The victim goes home and goes to bed and the chemical reaction takes place and his heart stops. No one will suspect poison. Even if they do, investigation will reveal that everything the victim ate and drank was also ingested by other people.'

Jake Grafton turned his hand over.

'So Keren could have been given the first drink of the chemical at any time in the preceding few weeks,' Toad said.

'Correct. At a party, a luncheon, a dinner, whatever. It could have been in anything he ate or drank. And that everyone else ate or drank.'

'Then aboard ship . . .'

'The second chemical could have been in the food when it came aboard, maybe in the ship's water tank. Probably the food, which would be consumed or thrown away. When Keren had ingested a sufficient dosage and chemical reaction was complete, his heart stopped. And no one aboard the ship knew anything about it. They were all innocent.'

'Wouldn't this stuff still be in his body?' Toad asked.

'Probably. If the pathologist had known what to look for. Zero chance of that.'

'But why did the body go into the water?'

'That's a side issue,' Jake Grafton said. 'Nothing in life is ever neat and tidy. Someone panicked when they found him dead. You can make your own list of reasons. Maybe the British found out who threw him overboard and kept quiet to protect the dead man's reputation. Extraordinarily wealthy man, pillar of the community, why smear him after he's dead? The British think like that.'

'But later they said Keren committed suicide. That's certainly frowned on by the upper crust.'

'If you have a corpse floating in the ocean and no proof of murder, what would you call it?'

'He was a Jew from the Levant,' Toad said carefully. 'Emigrated to Britain as a young man. Poor as a church mouse.'

'Then he made hundreds of millions and the Mossad was right there when he died to snap a photo of a CIA agent. Makes you wonder, doesn't it?' Toad said, eyeing the admiral.

'Not me,' Jake Grafton said with finality. 'I have no reason to go prying into someone else's dirty little business. And no levers to pry with even if I were foolish enough to try.' He tossed Toad's summary at him. 'Put this into the burn bag and let's get back to work.'

On Friday evening Jake took Callie and Amy to a movie. Afterward they stopped for ice cream. It was a little after eleven before Amy wheeled the car into the driveway and killed the engine. Jake got out of the passenger seat and held the rear door open for Callie.

'Well, Mom, what'd'ya think?' Amy asked.

'You drive too fast.'

'I do not! Do I, Dad?'

'Wasn't that a great movie?' said Jake Grafton.

'Dad!' Amy exclaimed in anguish. 'Don't avoid the issue. Oooh, I just hate it when you do that!'

From the porch – this rambling three-story brick built in the 1920s still had its porch – Jake waved to the federal protective service guard standing on the corner under the light, then opened the door with his key.

'You two are just so narrow bandwidth,' Amy continued, 'so totally random.' Still talking in a conversational tone of voice, she made for the stairs and started up. 'It's like I'm

41

stuck in an uncool fossil movie, some black-and-white Ronald Reagan time warp with all the girls in letter sweaters and white socks and the boys in duck's ass grease-cuts—'

'Amy Carol,' Callie called up the stairs. 'I'll have none of that kind of language in my house.'

Her voice came floating down. 'I'm the last kid in America growing up with Ozzie and Harriet . . .'

'You're very narrow bandwidth, Harriet,' Jake told his wife, who grinned.

'What does that mean?' she asked softly.

'I don't know,' her husband confessed. He kissed her on the forehead and led the way to the kitchen. After Callie made coffee and poured him a cup, he took it upstairs to the study.

He flipped on the light and started. A man was sitting behind the desk. Another sat on the couch.

Automatically Jake's eye went to the door of the safe. It was still closed.

The men were in suits and ties. The man on the couch had blond hair and spoke first. 'Come in and close the door, Admiral.'

Jake stood where he was. 'How'd you two get in here?'

'Come in and close the door. Unless you want your wife and daughter to hear this.'

Jake obeyed.

'Want to tell me who you are?' he said.

Now the man behind the desk spoke. 'You haven't hit the right question yet, Admiral. Ask us why we're here.'

Jake remembered the coffee in his hand and sipped it as he examined the visitors. Both under forty, but not by much. Short hair, clean-shaven, reasonably fit.

'Get out of my chair,' he said to the man behind the desk.

'Admiral, that confrontational tone is not going to get us anywhere. Why don't you sit down and we'll—'

Jake tossed the remainder of the coffee at the man's face.

The liquid hit the target, then some of it splashed on the desk. The man grunted, then wiped his face with his left hand. He stood up slowly. As he got fully erect the blond man on the couch uncoiled explosively in Jake's direction.

Jake had been expecting this. He smashed the coffee cup into the side of the blond man's face with his right hand – the cup shattered – and followed it up with a hard left that connected with the man's skull and jolted Jake clear to the elbow. But then the man had his shoulder into Jake's chest and slammed him back against the bookcase. The other man was coming around the desk.

Jake tried to use a knee on his assailant's body. No. He tried to chop with both hands at the back of the man's neck. He succeeded only in getting himself off balance, so his blows lacked power.

The man from the desk drew back a right and delivered a haymaker to Jake's chin.

The admiral saw stars and lost his balance completely.

When his vision cleared he was on the floor, the blond standing and the other man kneeling beside him. Blondie was using a handkerchief on the side of his face. When he withdrew it Jake could see blood.

'You've had your nose in a matter that doesn't concern you, Admiral. You're not Batman or Jesus H. Christ. This visit was just a friendly warning. You've got a wife and kid and it would be a hell of a shame if anything happened to them. Do you understand me?'

'Jake?' It was Callie's voice. She was outside the door. She rattled the knob. The men had locked it. 'What's going on in there, Jake?'

'What matter?' Jake asked.

'The same thing that happened to Nigel Keren could happen to you. It could happen to your wife. It could happen to your daughter.'

Outside the door Callie's voice was up an octave. 'Jake, are you all right? *Jake, speak to me!*'

'Be a hell of a shame,' Blondie said, 'if your fifteen-year-

43

old daughter died of heart failure, wouldn't it? A hell of a shame. And you'd have only yourself to blame.'

'*Jake!*'

'Think about it,' the first man said, then stood up. He unlocked the door and pulled it open.

'Excuse us, please,' he said to Callie and walked by her for the stairs, the blond man at his heels.

Stunned, Callie stared after them, then rushed to Jake, who was getting up.

He was still dizzy. He leaned on the bookcase. 'Make sure they leave,' he told his wife and pushed her gently toward the door.

He sagged down onto the couch and lowered his head onto the arm. His jaw ached badly. He felt his teeth. One seemed loose.

When Callie came back he was sitting at his desk. 'Jake, who were those men?'

'I dunno.'

She started to speak and he held up his hand. She cocked her head quizzically. He held a finger to his lips. Then he reached for paper and wrote:

The place may be bugged. I'll search it later. Please go downstairs and throw away all the food in the house. Everything except the stuff in sealed cans. All milk, soda pop, beer, frozen food, coffee, everything.

She read it and looked puzzled.

'I'll explain later,' he said. 'Please, go do it.'

She went.

Jake Grafton sat looking out his window for about fifteen seconds, then he knelt by the safe and opened it. His gun was still there, an old Smith & Wesson .357 Magnum that he had carried when he flew in Vietnam. All the classified documents seemed to be as he had left them. After he closed and locked the safe, he rooted through his bottom desk drawer for the box of shells. He loaded the pistol and stuck it in the small of his back, under the belt.

Downstairs in the kitchen he kissed his wife. 'Where are the car keys?'

'In my purse.'

Jake helped himself, then snagged his coat from the hall rack. 'I'll be back in a little while,' he said.

'Where are you going?'

'Tarkington's. There's a chance those guys stopped here first. They're delivering messages tonight.'

'Why don't you call Toad?'

'I want to see these guys again.'

'Jake, be careful.'

'You know me, Callie. I'm always careful.' He kissed her again and let her close the door behind him.

The uniformed guard was walking the beat on the sidewalk. Jake stopped beside him and rolled down his window. 'Did you see two men come out of my house?'

'Yessir. They got into a car parked across the street.'

'What kind of car?'

'I don't know, sir. It was a sedan with government plates. Is there a problem, Admiral?'

'No. No problem. They forgot something, that's all. Thanks.' He took his foot off the brake and got the car in motion before the man could ask any more questions.

The pistol was a hard lump where his back pressed against the seat.

A white Ford sedan with government plates sat in Tarkington's driveway behind Rita's car, which was in the carport. Toad's Honda Accord was parked at the curb. A light in the living room window made the drapes glow. Jake drove past and parked on the next block.

As he walked back he kept looking in parked cars. He saw no one.

These guys were sloppy. No lookouts, no driver waiting behind the wheel, a *government sedan*, for Christ's sake! They were just out putting the fear of God in a few people tonight and not bothering to do it right.

Jake tried the door of the sedan. It was unlocked. He popped the hood latch and eased the door shut. Feeling in the darkness he jerked the leads off the spark plugs, then let the hood down gently. Then he got behind the front of Rita's car, got the pistol out, and waited.

Jake was under no illusions. This was going to be dicey. He was going to have to get control of this situation quickly before these two clowns had a chance to think about it. If he pulled the trigger the cops would be here in short order, someone was going to be arrested, and someone was going to have a lot of explaining to do. And someone – Jake suspected that he might wind up as this someone – would probably find himself in more trouble than he could get himself out of.

He had waited no more than three minutes when he heard the Tarkingtons' front door open.

He got down on his hands and knees in front of Rita's car and looked under it. He saw their feet. They got into the sedan. A muttered oath.

The passenger door opened and a set of feet came around to the front of the car. Grafton straightened and peered through the window of Rita's car.

The sedan's hood was up. The blond man was looking into the engine compartment.

Jake went to his left, around Rita's Mazda. The hood obscured the driver's view and the blond had his back to Jake. He heard Jake coming at the last instant and started to turn just as the pistol butt thunked into his head. He went down like a sack of potatoes.

Jake grasped the butt of the revolver with his right hand and stepped around to the driver's door. He jerked it open.

'Get out.'

The dark-haired man looked slightly stunned.

Jake reached with his left hand and got a handful of shirt and tie. He jerked hard. The man half fell out of the seat. Jake jabbed the gun barrel into his ear and kept pulling.

'Jesus, you can't—'

'Get up and walk or I'll blow your brains out.' He jabbed savagely with the gun barrel.

The man came along.

'Tarkington,' Jake called. 'Get out here.'

The door opened and the stoop light came on.

'Toad, turn off that light and get out here.'

Tarkington came out. He was in his pajamas and they were torn half off his chest. 'That one on the ground,' Jake said, nodding. 'Clean out his pockets. Everything. Put him into the sedan and bring all the stuff inside.'

Rita held the door.

In the living room Jake hooked the dark-haired man's leg and sent him sprawling.

'Search him, Rita, and tell me what happened.'

Rita Moravia was wearing a robe over a nightie. Her hair was down. She began pulling things from the man's pockets as she talked. 'They rang the doorbell and told Toad they were from the DIA and you sent them over here. He let them in. I heard a scuffle out here in the living room and came out and they had knocked him down. They made some threats.'

'How long were they here?'

'Seven or eight minutes. No more.' Rita had finished with the man's rear trouser pockets and side coat pockets. She rolled him over without ceremony and emptied his inside jacket pockets. She turned his front trouser pockets inside out.

'Feel him all over for weapons.'

Rita did so. 'Nope. Just the one wallet, and this.' She held up a card encased in plastic attached to a chain. Jake had seen ones like this before. It was a pass to the CIA's Langley facility.

Jake picked up the wallet and examined it. He extracted the driver's license and held it out so he could read it. 'Okay, Paul Tanana of 2134 North Wood Duck Drive, Burke, Virginia. Want to tell us who sent you on this little errand?'

Rita was finished. She gathered the CIA pass and the change, keys and pens and placed them on a coffee table.

'I asked you a question,' Jake said.

Tanana glowered. 'You'll be sorry for this.'

'I'm sorry I ever laid eyes on you. Who sent you?'

Silence.

'Rita, check on Toad.'

The gun felt heavy in Jake's hand. He kept it pointed at Tanana, who was rubbing his ear. Jake rubbed his fingers back and forth across the stiff plastic of the driver's license.

In a moment Rita and Toad came in. 'Guy didn't have a gun,' Toad said. 'Just a wallet and a CIA pass and a little pack of lock picks.'

'Who sent you to see me tonight?' Jake asked Tanana.

The man snorted. 'You ain't gonna shoot me.'

What's wrong here?

Jake looked again at the driver's license, at the clear plastic, the perfect edges.

He put the license into his pocket and eared back the hammer of the revolver. He approached Tanana. He bent down and placed the barrel of the weapon against the man's temple.

'You're right. I'm not going to shoot you tonight. But if anything ever happens to my wife or kid – if you ever get within a mile of my wife or kid – if I ever see you within a mile of my house – I'll blow your fucking brains out and I'll take a great deal of pleasure in doing it, Paul-baby. Are you getting the message?'

'I got it.'

Jake rose and backed off. 'I jerked the wires off the spark plugs on your car. Put them back on and get the hell out of here.'

Tanana got slowly to his feet. 'What about our stuff? Our wallets?'

'We'll keep them. Maybe I'll frame the CIA passes and display them over at the DIA. They'll be wonderful souvenirs. Now get out.'

Tanana went.

Jake watched from the doorway as Tanana worked on the car. It took a couple minutes. 'Rita, get a pencil and write this down. US government plate, XRC-five-four-five.'

He was wondering if he'd hit the blond man too hard when Tanana slammed the hood down. He got behind the wheel, started the engine and backed out onto the street.

'I think you cracked the other guy's skull,' Toad said as the sedan drove slowly away. Typical Tarkington, Jake reflected. He could almost read his boss's mind.

Jake closed the door and locked it. 'I could sure use a cup of coffee.'

Callie was sitting on the stairs waiting for him when he came through the front door. After he ensured the door was locked behind him, he hung up his coat and took a seat on the step beside her.

'Who were they?'

Jake passed her the wallets. She opened them and looked at the licenses, credit cards, and other items. When she had finished he handed her the CIA passes.

'CIA,' she whispered.

Jake extracted his own wallet from his right hip pocket and took out his driver's license. He held it out so he could see it. 'I got this about a year and a half ago. Look how it's curved from being in the wallet and how the edges have frayed. Now look at those other licenses.'

Callie did so. 'They're like new,' she said.

'They shouldn't be. They were issued a couple years ago. And the credit cards. Notice how the black ink on the raised numbers has yet to rub off. I don't think they've ever been used.'

'So?'

'These two clowns were over at Tarkington's when I got there. I slugged one and we searched the other.'

'They let you do this?'

'That's an interesting question.' Jake pulled the pistol out

49

and showed it to Callie. 'You wave a gun around and everyone does what you tell them, just like in the movies.' And he had had the opportunity to surprise them. A couple of klutzs, or were they?

'What if they had had guns?'

'Then I'd have cheerfully shot the bastards and called the cops.' He stood. 'So they didn't have guns. They were betting I wouldn't panic.' The more he thought about it, the more sure he was that the whole scene was just an act. But why?

'Let's go to bed.'

He helped her to her feet.

'I still don't understand,' she said. 'Were they CIA or not?'

'I don't know,' Jake said slowly. 'Through the years several people have accused the CIA of using agents to deliver warnings – of intimidation attempts. Yet in every case where the accusation was made public, it turned out that the CIA had no agents like the people supposedly involved. Now you tell me – were those two guys CIA agents carrying their own ID, CIA agents carrying false ID, or someone else's hired help using false CIA ID?'

'But the message is clear. Lay off.'

'Precisely. It's from someone very powerful, someone who cannot be reached. And that is part of the message.'

He had the toothpaste on his brush and the brush in his mouth when it hit him.

He took the brush out of his mouth and stared at it. Then he examined the toothpaste tube. Nothing could be easier than poisoning a tube of toothpaste. Merely unscrew the cap and stick a syringe in, then screw the cap back on.

But they had had no syringe on them. At Tarkington's house, anyway. For all he knew they could have thrown it in the gutter or put it in the garbage pail out behind the Graftons' house where it would be hauled away on Tuesday.

A knot developed in his stomach.

He started to put the toothbrush back into his mouth, but he couldn't.

Damn!

He rinsed out his mouth, then threw the toothbrush and the toothpaste into the wastebasket under the sink.

When he and Callie were in bed with the lights out, she asked, 'How do you get yourself into these messes, anyway?'

'You make it sound like I'm a juvenile delinquent.'

'I'm scared.'

'That's what they intended.'

'They succeeded. I'm frightened.'

'Me too,' he told her.

CHAPTER FOUR

On Monday morning at seven-thirty Toad Tarkington opened the door to the DIA computer facility and signed the log. 'Richard Harper, please,' he said to the receptionist when she came over to examine his pass. She had a cup of coffee in her hand and was polishing off the last of a doughnut.

'I'm sorry, but he doesn't work here anymore.'

'Say again.'

She shrugged. 'He doesn't work here now. He's gone.'

'Did he quit or what?'

'I don't know. He didn't come in last Wednesday. Or maybe Wednesday was his last day. Anyway, I heard someone say he transferred to another government agency. Can someone else help you?'

Toad Tarkington leaned his elbows on the counter and gave her a shy grin. 'He was in one of our baseball pools and won a hundred bucks.'

'Maybe he'll call you.'

'He doesn't know he won. We don't roll for the numbers on the grid until Friday.'

She smiled and shrugged. 'I'm sorry. Maybe if you call personnel . . .'

'I'll try that,' Toad said. 'In the meantime, I need a little work done. I need someone to check the CIA data base.'

'Mabel can help you. Right over there.' She pointed.

Mabel's terminal was in a corner. Toad removed a sheet of paper from a manila envelope stamped top secret and laid it in front of her. On it were two names: Paul R.

Tanana and Rodney D. Hicks. 'Please see if these two are on the CIA data base,' Toad asked.

Mabel apparently knew her way around a computer. Thirty seconds later she spoke. 'No.'

'Nothing?' Toad asked.

'*Nada.*'

'Not employees?'

'Nope.'

'How about the FBI data base? Can you access it?'

'It'll take a bit,' she murmured as she whacked keys. Toad watched the words and letters on the screen come and go, come and go. Last week when Harper played with the computer Toad had other things on his mind. Today he was interested.

All this high-tech . . . before it came along you would have just looked in the telephone directory.

The telephone book!

Toad spotted a directory under the desk and reached for it. He should have done this yesterday.

'I don't have any Roger Hicks,' Mabel told him. 'I have a Robert Hicks and a Rose Hicks and two R. Hicks.'

Toad flipped pages. 'Could you print out what you have on the R. Hicks entries?'

'Sure. And you don't have to look in the phone book. We have access to the phone company's files. If they have an account with the phone company, we'll see it. Maybe if you could tell me what you're looking for?'

'Whatever I can get,' Tarkington said. He put the phone book back on the bottom shelf of the desk. 'Check Tanana, then the Virginia Department of Motor Vehicles. And how about the Visa and MasterCard lists. I'll take anything.'

But he already knew what the answers were going to be. When Mabel gave him the printouts there it was in black-and-white. Each man had both Visa and MasterCard credit cards, but they had never made any charges on the cards. These accounts were less than a month old. The driver's licenses were real, but the addresses weren't. Burke, Virginia, had no such street as Wood Duck Drive, where Tanana's license said he lived. Hicks' address was equally bogus. The telephone company had never heard of either man.

So the identities were fake.

'Anything else?' Mabel asked. She was still on the right side of thirty and had a cute, intelligent face.

'Well,' said Toad Tarkington, and grinned conspiratorially. 'There is one little thing. Richard Harper won a hundred bucks in our baseball pool this weekend and we don't know where to get in touch with him. Could you check him on the CIA data base?'

'That isn't official business,' Mabel told him primly.

'I know. But I'll bet Richard would like the hundred.'

'Commander, we're not supposed . . .'

Toad gazed into her eyes and gave her an undiluted dose of the ol' Tarkington charm that had melted panties on three continents. 'Call me Toad. All my friends do.'

Mabel swallowed once and lowered her eyes. 'Okay,' she said and turned back to the keyboard. She punched keys.

'Here it is,' she told him. 'He transferred to the CIA computer facility at Langley. His office phone number is 775-0601.'

'Lemme write that down,' Toad said, and did so on a piece of scratch paper he snagged from beside the terminal. 'Thanks a lot, Mabel. I'll tell Richard he owes you a lunch.'

'You were right,' Toad told his boss. 'Tanana and Hicks are fake identities.'

Jake Grafton just nodded.

'How'd you know?'

Jake shrugged. 'They wanted us to see that ID.'

'And the analyst who worked on the photo of Herb Tenney, Richard Harper, now works at the CIA. As of this past Wednesday or Thursday.'

'So he was probably the leak,' Jake said.

'Yessir.' Toad found a seat. 'What are we going to do now?'

'I don't know,' Jake said.

Toad frowned.

'If you have any suggestions, let's hear them.'

Toad shrugged. 'I'm just the hired help around here, Admiral. You're the guy getting the big bucks.'

'Someone thought this out very carefully,' Jake said after a moment. 'They wanted to scare us, and they did, but there was the possibility that we could be induced to impale ourselves on our own swords. So they came equipped with fake identities and bogus Langley passes. And they drove leisurely from my house to your house to give me time to call you or catch up.'

'I didn't check the passes,' Toad said.

'Oh, they're as fake as the driver's licenses and credit cards. You can bet on it. And if I charged off to the front office with this wild tale about CIA employees threatening us and demanded that General Brown go after someone's head, I would have merely discredited myself, made myself look like a fool. And put General Brown in a difficult position.'

'Too bad we didn't take photos of those clowns.'

'Umm.'

'So what are you going to do?' Toad asked again.

'I'll have to think about it. If I go to General Brown I'm going to have to tell him about that Herb Tenney photo, and I don't know that that's a good idea. We still don't know a goddamn thing.'

'The CIA's reaction to the photo proves that they helped Keren depart for eternity.'

'If those two worked for the CIA. What if Tanana and Hicks were Mossad agents trying to make me suspicious of the CIA?'

'We're going to have to tell General Brown just to cover our fannies,' Toad said.

'Maybe. And that may make General Brown overly

suspicious of the CIA, which might have been the Mossad's goal when they gave us that photo. If it was the Mossad. The whole thing's a mare's nest. A military that stops believing its intelligence service is fumbling around in the dark. As if we had a lot of light now . . .'

Toad was thinking of Judith Farrell. Grafton had implied before that Farrell might have been intentionally trying to harm the United States, but Toad had automatically rejected it. Now he began to consider the possibility seriously.

'I'll bet someone at Langley would like to know where we got that photo,' Jake muttered.

But if that was the case, wouldn't that be the first priority? Why the simple intimidation attempt? It didn't compute. If it were the CIA. But the Mossad angle was even more unlikely.

What was wrong here? He was missing something. It was right in front of him and he couldn't see it. But what?

His eyes came to rest on Tarkington, who was staring at him. Toad looked away guiltily.

What? He went over it again, from Judith Farrell's meeting with Toad all the way through this morning's verification of the false identities of the agents.

Toad said something.

'What?'

'It's like Rubik's Cube, isn't it?' Toad repeated.

Rubik's Cube had a solution, although the solution was complex and one needed a good sense of spatial relationships to figure it out. Jake Grafton had spent a miserable week wrestling with a cube some years back when Amy gave him one for Christmas. Finally his next-door neighbor showed him how the trick was done.

The problems Jake had learned to solve had much simpler solutions: one usually became apparent when you backed off and looked at the forest instead of the individual trees.

Okay, Jake thought, by the numbers – One: if someone at

Langley knows about the photo, why isn't he trying to discover where and how I acquired it?

Maybe he is but I don't know about it.

Unlikely, Jake decided. He and Tarkington were the only people who knew the answers. And Rita and Judith Farrell. But they don't know about Rita. They might know about Judith Farrell or have an agent in the Mossad, but that would be a complex solution, only acceptable if there are no simple ones. There *must* be a simple explanation.

Two: the person who sent the goons on Friday night isn't curious.

Why not? Because he already knows.

How?

Jake Grafton's eyes focused and he looked again at Toad, who was watching him askance.

'No,' Jake said.

'No?'

'Not like Rubik's Cube.'

The admiral pulled around a sheet of paper and picked up a pencil. On it he wrote 'This office is bugged.'

Toad came over and looked at the words. 'You think?' he murmured.

Jake nodded. He got up, removed his jacket and draped it over the back of his chair, loosened his tie and began to look. Toad started on the other side of the room.

In five minutes they had ruled out the obvious, a microphone behind a painting or under a desk. 'Let's go for a walk,' Jake suggested.

'It's nothing obvious,' Jake told Toad as they walked toward the cafeteria. 'Nothing conventional. If it was, the sweeps would have discovered it.' The office was swept for listening devices twice a week at random intervals.

'Maybe it's the telephone. We'll have to take that apart. And how about the window vibrator?' Toad suggested. This device used elevator music to vibrate the glass pane and foil any parabolic listening device aimed at the window. 'What if it isn't a real vibrator?'

'Perhaps our eavesdropper has a parabolic antenna aimed at the window,' Jake said, 'and is unscrambling the tape with a powerful computer, like a Cray?'

'That's a possibility,' Toad admitted after he thought about it. 'Are you sure about the bug?'

'No,' Jake told him. 'But a listening device would explain a lot. And not some simple piece of Radio Shack junk. Something computerized, something so sophisticated we don't see it for what it is.'

'If they're using that window as a sounding board, about all we can do is put another music source near the window, like a portable radio, and complicate the signal. But I think we should search that office until we find a bug or can swear there isn't one.'

'Go down to the maintenance office and get tools. Screwdrivers, pliers, wrenches, and a voltage meter.'

'Aye aye, sir.'

'And a pipe wrench.'

They started on the telephone. They disassembled the plastic box and tested the microphone in the headset and in the desk unit to see if it really went dead when the phone was on the hook. It worked as they thought it should.

Next the light fixtures were removed from their sockets and examined, then reinstalled. The soundproof ceiling tiles were taken down and the overhead and tile framework examined. They moved the furniture and rolled back the carpet. Nothing.

The heating and cooling duct vents were dirty but innocent.

Toad pointed toward the polished walnut molding that framed the door and window and edged the walls.

Jake examined the trim. He rated it because he was the deputy director of the DIA. The nails that held the wood in place were covered with varnish.

He shook his head at Toad and pointed toward the radiator.

The old steam radiator was no longer in use, but the steam pipes were still installed. They used the pipe wrench on the ring nuts.

And there it was.

With the nuts off the steam intake and outlet pipes, they wrestled the radiator out a half inch or so, just enough to reveal the insulated wire that went through the inlet pipe.

So the whole radiator was a sounding board. Inside the cast-iron unit there must be a sensing unit, more likely two or three of them. The signals went out through the wire to God knows where, and there the readings were tape-recorded. An analysis of the tape using the known vibration characteristics of the radiator would produce an electronic signal that could be processed into speech.

There was nothing for an electronic sweep to find. Yet whoever had installed this unit had merely to run the signal through his computer to hear everything said inside the office.

Jake used the pipe wrench to pound a hole in the wall. The pipe made a left turn inside the wall.

'Come on.'

Out in the corridor Toad was ready to pound another hole in the drywall when Jake stopped him. 'Let's find the telephone switchboxes. They probably have it routed through the phone system. Go call the telephone repair people and get someone up here on the double.'

The telephone switching boxes were in the basement. The system technician opened one of the boxes and Jake drew back in amazement. Hundreds of wires. 'How do you know which is which?'

'Well, sir, just tell me the phone number and I'll show you the connection.'

'I don't know the phone number.'

'Well, everything coming into this box has a number.'

Now Jake understood. Somewhere in the building there was a tape recorder or recorders – a monitoring station – hooked up to a telephone. All the eavesdropper had to do was telephone the proper number, punch in a code and the monitoring station would obediently belch forth all its data, which could then be processed by a computer into speech.

The technician was still talking. '. . . they built this building during World War II and have been hooking up telephones ever since. The last big telephone update we did we added more lines and used the old ones where we could. But there's no blueprints or diagrams or anything like that. It's fucking spaghetti.'

They could establish what line it was, of course, by trial and error. Some of the lines were undoubtedly not supposed to be hooked up. But why bother? 'Thanks, anyway,' Jake said. 'I appreciate you showing us this.'

Back in Jake's office Toad Tarkington cut the wire going into the radiator.

'They know everything,' he said disgustedly.

'Apparently.'

'They even got the conversation about binary chemicals.'

'Yep. And one of those goons alluded to it Friday night. He said what a terrible thing it would be if Amy died of heart failure. I should have known right then. Goddamnit!'

The more he thought about the situation the angrier he became.

'Goddamn those bastards!'

General Albert Sidney Brown didn't get angry, he went ballistic. He listened to Jake tell him about the bug in the radiator with an air of disbelief and growing bewilderment, but when Toad used the pipe wrench to disassemble the radiator in the general's plush corner office and he saw *his* wire, he went into an apoplectic rage. He spluttered, his face turned a deep crimson. When he recovered slightly he began to curse. He gave a rich performance at a full-throated volume that would have done the crustiest drill instructor proud.

Only when Brown began to wind down did Jake signal to Toad to cut the wire. If the CIA had someone listening he wanted them to know they had just pissed on and royally pissed off the very upper echelons of the American military. If they cared.

Then the general got on the phone. Sixty seconds after he hung up, the DIA's security officer, an army colonel, was standing in front of Brown's desk. The general led him to the radiator and showed him the wire.

By this point Brown's mood had coalesced into cold fury. 'I want to know how many of these goddamn listening devices are in this agency's offices. I want all the sensors and wire and telephone equipment removed. And take out these' – he whacked the radiator with Toad's pipe wrench – 'fucking antique radiators. I want to know why these bugs weren't detected by your staff. I want to know what it's gonna take to make sure something like this doesn't happen again. And when you have finished with all of that, you and your entire staff are going to stand in this office and swear me a blood oath that there are no more goddamn bugs in any of our spaces.'

The colonel left in a hurry. Brown then eyed Jake Grafton without warmth. 'You and I are going to have a little chat, Admiral. And not in this damned building. Get your hat and let's go see if we can find someplace private.'

They ended up in an exclusive restaurant in Alexandria, Virginia, after a silent ride in Brown's limo. Brown apparently knew the owner, who admitted him after he pounded on the door. After listening to Brown's request she escorted the two officers to the far back corner of the empty dining room.

'I know you don't open until five, but could we please get coffee?'

'Of course, General,' the lady said. 'Make yourself comfortable and we'll bring it out in a few minutes.'

'I appreciate your hospitality, Mrs Horowitz.'

She smiled and left for the kitchen.

'Well?'

Jake told his boss everything, from Judith Farrell's

meeting with Toad to the discovery of the bug. The recitation took thirty minutes and was broken only by the delivery of a pot of coffee and two cups. Brown listened without interruptions.

When Jake finished the general said, 'Admiral, I'll lay it on the line with you. You should have reported the contact by a foreign agent to me as soon as possible. You fucked up.'

'Yessir.'

'You fuck up again, you'll be a civilian by noon the next day.'

Brown refilled his coffee cup and stirred it with a spoon. A slow grin twisted his lips. 'Tell me again about sticking the pistol in that CIA weenie's face.'

When they had finished dissecting Jake's adventure, General Brown began to talk of the CIA and the personalities of the men who ran it. Finally he became philosophical:

'All intelligence services are bureaucracies, of course. The output is always mangled to some extent as it goes through the pipe. But when the people in the intelligence business start editing the raw data to support their policy recommendations, the output becomes fiction. It's worse than worthless – it's fantasy as fact, so it's just plain dangerous. Policymakers think they're getting the big picture and they're making the decisions, but in reality the decision-making function has been appropriated by the person editing the data. The elected policymaker is being manipulated. He becomes a mere rubber stamp.'

'Do you think that is what's happening at the CIA now?' Jake Grafton asked.

Brown grimaced. 'Historically the heads of intelligence services have usually stood right by the throne. Often in Europe the spymasters were the second most powerful men in the government. But not in the United States. The cloak-and-dagger boys have always put the fear of God in our elected politicians, and rightfully so. Are they manipulating our government, now, here?'

He leaned across the table toward Jake. 'They missed the collapse of communism. The biggest political event on this planet since World War II and they missed it. Apparently not a soul at Langley ever predicted it or suggested it as a possibility. They said the Soviet economy was three times larger than it was. They said the Soviet military was much stronger, more capable, more combat-ready than turned out to be the case. They sat there looking at a society in meltdown and never saw a wisp of smoke. The fact is that for the last five years you could have gotten a better picture of what was happening inside the Soviet Union by reading the *New York Times* than you could from reading the CIA intelligence analyses. But was that intentional?

'These damned CIA briefings and intelligence reports give me a queasy feeling,' Brown continued after a moment's pause. 'Nothing I can put my finger on – the stuff is too slickly written for that. Maybe that's the trouble. Maybe it's too slick, every mousehole carefully papered over. I don't know. I just get this feeling. I'd really like to see the raw intelligence, *all* of it.

'What I think . . . what I *think* we're looking at in Russia is merely an interlude between dictatorships, like the 1917 republic after they toppled the czar. The problems are too big, the people are bigots intolerant of dissent and diversity, they are too easily swayed by demagogues spouting bullshit and hate, they readily swallow any hint of a conspiracy, they despise anyone with a ruble more than they've got. The average Russian can't conceive of a loyal opposition: the concept doesn't compute. That's the background for the biggest economic experiment ever tried on this planet, the conversion of a centralized socialized economy into a free market one. But the CIA downplays all that. The folks at the CIA aren't worried. And no one over at the White House seems to be in a sweat. Our politicos have bigger fish to fry, like squabbling over Clinton's tax increases and waggling their fingers at the Japanese.'

Brown rearranged the salt and pepper shakers. 'I'm not

sure what the National Security Adviser thinks. At the CIA briefings sometimes he acts like he smells a rat, other times he sits there like he was getting the gospel in Sunday school.

'What's happening in the former Soviet Union right now may turn out to be the seminal event that determines the course of human life on this planet for the next century. The old union is in the midst of total social and economic collapse. Nothing works. Nothing! No one knows how to make a decision. All look to central authority, which is corrupt, incompetent, self-absorbed. The republics constitute the most highly polluted nation on earth. It's one giant petrochemical sewer, thousands of square miles of soil so radioactive that humans can't survive on it, social systems that have completely collapsed. Doctors are poorly trained and incompetent – they routinely misdiagnose ailments, sick people go to unbelievably bad hospitals where they are butchered by quacks, there isn't enough medicine, equipment, food, clothes, anything . . .

'I could go on for hours.' He picked up a pepper shaker and tapped in on the table, hard. 'I think the pollution is what did in the Communists. Too many people are getting sick. Best guess is at least a million people in the old union are sick with radiation poisoning. Lack of basic sanitation and immunizations causes epidemics of diphtheria, dysentery, polio, influenza – fifty percent of their conscripts are rejected for military service. It's estimated only one in fourteen of the people in uniform could pass a flight physical.

'You can only run a society for the benefit of the elite at the top for so long before the whole thing implodes.' He shrugged.

Jake Grafton found himself leaning forward and lowering his voice. 'So what about those nuclear weapons?'

'CIA hasn't told us the whole story. You can bet your pension on that. Reality has a feel, a texture, that's unique.

It's seasoned with insanity and random chance. This stuff the CIA's selling hasn't got that feel.'

'You sure?' Jake pressed.

'I wish I was. But no, I ain't sure. The key is money. If nuclear weapons are leaving Russia, someone is paying big bucks for them. CIA is looking and says they can't find the trail.'

'Perhaps we should do some looking on our own,' Jake suggested.

'How?'

'Well, we need to draft a computer expert.'

'You say that like you have one in mind.'

Jake did. He just nodded.

'CIA, Treasury, and State won't like it.'

'If we find the trail their objections won't matter much.'

'If it's there to find,' Brown said without enthusiasm.

Jake decided to change the subject. 'What are you going to do about the bugs, General?'

Albert Sidney Brown pushed back his chair and stood. 'I'm going to write a report to the president and send copies to everybody on the list. The CIA will think I'm a patsy if I don't. But just the bugs. Nothing about Nigel Keren or Mossad photographs or intimidation efforts. You were right about that. If we run those shitty rags up the flagpole now, you and I'll be diving headfirst into a foxhole to keep from getting squashed.'

The whole mess was pretty bizarre, Jake Grafton reflected later. It was like climbing a mountain: the higher you got the worse the visibility became, the thicker the cloud. And if it was like this at his level, presumably the president, the man at the top, couldn't see his hand in front of his face. No wonder the government stumbled from crisis to crisis!

That night Jake and Toad searched the Grafton house from top to bottom for bugs. They didn't find any, which merely increased Jake's sense of unease. Then they went over to Tarkington's house and turned it inside out. Rita helped. And they found nothing.

'So what are we gonna do, Admiral?' Toad asked when they had finished and were drinking beer in the kitchen.

Rita flipped on the radio and cranked up the volume.

'Do?'

'Yessir. About Herb Tenney and going to Russia with him and all of this.'

'I dunno,' Jake said. 'Any suggestions?' He glanced at Rita Moravia, who stood with her back against the sink, trying to look deadpan. She wasn't supposed to know about the Russian trip, which was still highly classified. Her hair was pulled back and held with a clasp tonight. Tall for a woman, she had the sleek look of solid, healthy muscle. She colored slightly when she met the admiral's eyes. Feeling a touch of amusement, Jake's gaze returned to Toad Tarkington. 'What would you suggest?'

'I'd like to go over to Langley and sweat somebody.'

'Who?'

'I'd start with Herb.'

'He wouldn't tell you jack, even if he knew anything to tell.' Jake sighed. He drained the last of his beer, then sat the glass out of the way. 'Got a phone book?'

'Sure.'

'Let's go calling. There is a fellow who works at Langley that I'd like to talk to.'

There were fourteen Richard Harpers and eleven R. Harpers listed in the Washington metro telephone directory. Rita did the calling while Toad listened on the living room extension. She worked for a pizza company and they had lost a delivery address.

'This won't work if his wife answers,' Rita pointed out.

'I don't think he's married,' Toad told her. 'He isn't the type.'

'Oh, and what type is that?'

'Sensitive, warm, loving, wholesome, handsome, sharing, caring—'

'Shut up. It's ringing . . . Hello, Richard Harper please . . . Mr Harper, did you order a pizza about a half hour ago? No? Well, a Richard Harper on Gordon Street ordered a large pepperoni and olive and our driver can't find the house . . .'

She fell silent as the man on the phone talked. From the living room Toad signaled no. Rita made her excuses and thanked him for his time.

They got lucky. They found him on the fifth call. An address in Chevy Chase.

'Let's go,' Jake said.

Richard Harper wasn't going to invite them in. Toad shoved the door open and pushed past him. Jake Grafton followed. 'It's two in the morning,' Harper squeaked.

'I know,' Toad Tarkington said. 'But I wanted you to meet my boss, Admiral Grafton. Admiral, this is Richard Harper, late of the DIA and now with Central Intelligence.'

Jake stuck out his hand. Reluctantly Richard Harper took it. While Harper was still wondering how to handle this intrusion, Jake dropped into a chair and turned on the light on the reading stand beside him. 'Let's all sit down and visit a minute.'

Harper moved toward a chair, but he didn't sit. 'This won't take long,' Jake assured him. Harper perched on the front edge of the seat.

Jake displayed his green military ID card and his DIA office pass. Harper refused to touch them. Jake made a show of replacing the cards back in his pocket, then began. 'There's been a security violation at the DIA and we're trying to find the leak. We have to do this after office hours since people don't want to talk about their colleagues at the office. You understand?'

Harper nodded reluctantly.

From Toad's attaché case Jake removed a tape recorder – borrowed from Rita – and placed it on a low table between himself and Harper. He pushed the play button and made sure the tape was turning. 'This is Rear Admiral Jacob L. Grafton. It is now two oh seven A.M. on June eighteen. I am interviewing Richard Harper. Mr. Harper, last Monday did you conduct a computer search of CIA records at the request of Lieutenant Commander Robert Tarkington at the DIA computer facilities?'

'Now wait a minute—'

'No, you wait a minute, Mr Harper. Someone revealed classified information about that computer search to persons without access. Top secret information has been compromised. This is an official investigation. If you fail to cooperate you can be dismissed from government service and prosecuted. Do you understand?'

Harper's face contorted. A tear rolled down his cheek. 'I've already been fired.'

'Say again.'

'The CIA fired me this afternoon. They found out about my record.'

The two naval officers exchanged glances. Jake reached over and turned off the tape recorder. 'Maybe you'd better tell me about it,' he murmured.

The recitation took most of an hour. Periodically there were tears. Richard Harper was twenty-seven and had been fascinated with computers since he was in high school. Just for the challenge of it, he became a hacker, a person who breaks into industry and government computer files for the sheer joy of outwitting the security devices that guard the files. He had been caught once while he was in college and received a suspended sentence. The second time, when he planted a virus program, he had gone to jail.

The computer industry refused to hire him. Computers were his life and he was blacklisted. He had managed to secure a temporary appointment at DIA by lying on his employment application. He knew the FBI would learn the truth sooner or later, so when agents of the CIA approached him about supplying them with information about DIA projects, he had agreed if they would give him a permanent computer job. A month went by, he supplied all the information they asked for, including Toad's bizarre request, and they had him start work at Langley last week. Then today they pretended to have just learned of his previous convictions and fired him. It wasn't fair. He had quit the DIA, the CIA had canned him, the FBI would eventually learn of his record. Computers were his whole life yet he couldn't work in computers.

'Do you have a computer setup here at home?' Jake asked.

It was in the guest bedroom at the back of the little house. There Jake and Toad were treated to a proud recital of hard disk capacity, extended and expanded memory, CPU speed, and all the rest of it as they stared at screens, keyboards and the innards of computers that were scattered everywhere.

'How good a hacker are you?' Jake asked.

'I'm good. Real good. If I hadn't done that virus way back when . . . And it was nothing, just tidbits of zen philosophy that popped onto the screen at holidays and all. It didn't hurt anyone and . . .'

Back in the living room, Jake told Harper, 'I have a job for you. I can't promise a permanent job at the DIA until we get a final FBI check and go over it line by line. But I can pay you by the hour on a temporary basis if you can do this job. It would be here at home, on your own equipment.'

Harper was enthusiastic. Yes. He agreed before he even knew what the job was. Jake felt as if he were throwing a rope to a drowning man. He thought he had the authority to hire Harper on a temporary basis, but if it turned out he didn't he would pay him out of his own pocket.

'I want you to find a river of money,' Jake said, intently watching Harper's face, 'a subterranean river flowing through the world banking systems. The task won't be easy. I'm not even sure that you will be able to recognize the river when you see it. The mouth of the river is in Moscow, but I don't have any idea where it begins.'

'Banks?'

'Banks.'

'I'll need computer access telephone numbers, user names and passwords. If I go after that stuff myself they'll be on to me in hours.'

'I thought—'

'Hackers get into computers by conning the phone number and codes out of somebody. I can do that. But I can't do it three dozen times and get away with it. The National Security Agency has that stuff. They monitor bank transactions on a daily basis.'

'If NSA has it, we can get it,' Jake said, glancing at Toad.

'You give me that stuff, and if the money is there, I'll find it,' Harper said confidently. Too confidently, Jake Grafton thought.

'Don't be so quick to make promises. And I don't want anyone to know you're looking.'

'Maybe you'd better tell me what I'm supposed to be looking for so I'll know it when I see it.'

Fifteen minutes later Harper knew everything Jake did, which was precious little. So Jake devoted another hour to discussing the possibilities and the probabilities. 'The problem,' he told Harper, 'is that I don't know who I can trust. I've got to trust my boss, but who else? I can't call friends in the FBI, in the CIA, people I've known for years. If there is a small cabal in the CIA, only the people involved know it is a cabal. Everyone else thinks they are doing their duty when they report conversations, fill out reports, do what they are told to do. That's the problem.'

'How do you want me to report to you?' Harper asked.

'Well, written reports would be okay. Mail them to my wife. She'll see that I get them wherever I am. I may be out of town for a few weeks.' He gave Harper his address.

When Jake and Toad left at four in the morning, Rita was asleep on the front seat of the car.

Under the streetlight Toad said, 'I have a real bad feeling

about this, Admiral. If Harper steals money or screws up some accounts, you and I will end up in prison.'

'I hope they give us separate cells,' Jake told him. 'A rear admiral ought to rate a private cell.'

CHAPTER FIVE

'Yeltsin said yes. Two hours ago.'

'Sure took him long enough,' Jake Grafton muttered. 'If I were sitting on all those weapons I'd have got a hot seat months ago.'

General Brown consulted his watch. 'Fifteen hours ago two army bases were attacked. The Russian government says the attackers stole machine guns, artillery, APCs and at least ten truckloads of ammunition.'

'Truckloads?'

'Yeah,' General Brown said. 'They killed sixty soldiers at one base, fifty at another, and blew up all but the trucks and APCs they drove out.'

'Who?'

'They aren't sure. Maybe criminal gangs, maybe Armenians again. Maybe some ex-soldiers who are starting their own private army.' General Brown stepped to the map on the wall and pointed. 'Here and here.'

When he had resumed his seat, he said, 'The CIA's man went over yesterday.'

'Tenney?'

'Yes. He'll meet you at the embassy. Ambassador Lancaster will brief you. The president wants the nukes neutralized and the Russian government strengthened. Talk to those people. Let us know what you need to do the job.'

Jake Grafton didn't laugh. It was too ridiculous for that. How in hell had he gotten into the middle of this mess?

'And,' General Brown continued, 'if you can piss on any of those outlaw or rebel gangs, that'll be all right too.'

His stomach felt like there was a rock in it. 'Yessir,' he managed.

'The air force will have a C-141 at Andrews in six hours. Be on it.'

'Aye aye, sir.'

Albert Sidney Brown came around the desk and held out his hand. 'Good luck, Admiral.'

'Don't worry, sir. I'll take my rabbit's foot along.'

'You're going to need more than a rabbit's foot,' Callie told Jake as she passed him aspirin and toilet articles to put in his bag. He had just mentioned his parting remark to General Brown. She didn't think it was very funny. As she watched him stuff underwear around his Smith & Wesson .357 Magnum and shoulder holster, she tartly added, 'You're also going to need more than that little popgun.'

She pushed her hair back out of her eyes. 'Oh, you men! Jetting off into the middle of a revolution. It's so damn pathetic.'

'It isn't really a revolution,' her husband replied as he folded underwear around a box of pistol ammunition and added it to the bag. 'Yeltsin's still in the driver's seat, still in control.'

'For how long? What does anyone think you and Toad can really accomplish?'

'Oh, we'll have some help. Too much probably. But if we can just prod the Russians into—'

'Don't change the subject,' Callie said sharply. 'You know precisely what I mean. Even with the entire United States Army over there you'd still be outnumbered ten to one. Sending you and Toad over there is some kind of insane joke.'

'Umph,' Jake grunted.

Toad Tarkington's opinion had been more colorful but

no more optimistic: 'Once again our politicians are saving the world from foreign politicians stupider than they are. And we nincompoops in uniform smartly salute and grab ankles. BOHICA!' Ah yes, that lovely old acronym, BOHICA—Bend Over. Here It Comes Again.

Callie jerked a pair of trousers away from him that he was rolling up. She folded them carefully and handed them back. 'Not that they'll send the entire army,' she said. 'You'll be lucky to get two privates and a corporal. One of the privates will be the cook and the other will peel potatoes. Presumably the corporal will have a few minutes a day to help you and Toad when he isn't busy supervising the privates.'

She sat heavily. 'Oh, Jake. Why you?'

He sat down beside her and took her in his arms.

'Everything will work out. It always does.'

'No. Everything doesn't always *work out*. I'm really tired of hearing that trite little phrase.'

'You know me, Callie,' Jake Grafton said. 'Trust me.'

'Hey, babe. It's me, Toad. We're leaving today.'

'Now?' Rita asked.

Toad gripped the telephone tightly. 'Plane leaves Andrews at six.'

'I'll see if I can get the rest of the day off,' she said. 'You're at home?'

'Yeah. Packing.'

'If I don't call in ten minutes I'm on my way home.'

'Okay.'

'I have a bad feeling about this, Toad.'

'It'll be okay.'

'I love you.'

'I know that, babe. And I love you.'

'See you in a while.'

The C-141 headed north on the great circle route to Moscow. After it climbed above the stratus clouds covering the East Coast of the United States, it flew in a clear sky illuminated by the sun low on the horizon.

Jake Grafton came up to the flight deck and visited a moment with the pilots, then stood looking at the vastness of the sky. 'It doesn't ever get dark at this time of year at these latitudes,' the copilot told him.

'How many times have you guys flown this route?' Jake asked.

'Couple dozen times for me, sir,' the pilot, an air force major, replied. He nodded at the copilot, a first lieutenant. 'This is his second trip.'

Cold. The sky looked bleak and cold, even with the sun shining. The cockpit was a tiny capsule of life adrift in an indifferent universe.

Jake shivered once, then returned to the little passenger section. There were only eight seats and Toad was asleep in one of them. In the next row the liftmaster, a senior sergeant, also snoozed. The rest of the plane was filled with military rations bound for orphanages and soup kitchens for the elderly. The admiral opened the door to the cargo compartment and stood there looking. Overhead lights illuminated the cargo compartment and the sea of boxes stacked on pallets.

The incongruity of the situation appalled him, filled him with a sadness devoid of hope that seemed to drain the energy from him. Insanity, Callie had said. Yes, that was the word. A nation with enough nuclear weapons to kill half the life on earth and doom the rest couldn't feed its old people, its children.

Jake closed the door and sagged into a seat.

He tried to sleep but it wouldn't come. Finally he turned so he could look out the window at the cold, infinite sky.

At Sheremetyevo Airport near Moscow, the C-141 was parked next to a Soviet military terminal across the field from the regular passenger terminal. Jake and Toad exited the plane through the rear cargo door after it had been opened. Although the plane had been airborne for twelve hours and it was 6 A.M. in Washington, it was two o'clock in the afternoon here on a pleasant summer day. Small puffy clouds floated in a blue sky. They stood on the concrete ramp beside their bags and watched a limo driving toward them. It came to a halt and a man in a US naval officer's uniform climbed out.

'Lieutenant Dalworth, sir,' said the young officer after he had saluted. He pulled open the back door of the car. As Jake and Toad climbed in he added, 'You don't have to go through customs.'

'How come?'

'I arranged it, sir. I've become pretty good friends with several of the customs and emigration guys.'

Jake was taken slightly aback.

'Don't worry, sir. With diplomatic passports, the whole deal is just a formality. I've partied with those guys, given them some sacks of groceries and gotten drunk with them. They know I won't screw 'em.'

Three minutes later, after Jake's and Toad's baggage was loaded in the trunk, Dalworth climbed in and got the car in motion. Toad Tarkington mused, 'Dalworth. Dalworth . . . By any chance, are you Spiro Dalworth?'

A look of discomfort crossed the young officer's face.

Tarkington grinned broadly and seized the lieutenant's hand. He pumped it heartily. 'As I live and breathe.'

Jake Grafton recognized the name too. Lieutenant Dalworth had been assigned to the navy's public relations staff in New York City when he somehow wound up on a television talk show panel discussing 'women in the modern military.' After thirty minutes of weathering abuse from a prominent feminist fanatic who shared the panel with him, Dalworth lost his temper. His parting shot at her had been, 'Oh, Spiro Agnew.'

Three days later someone told the female warrior that the former vice president's name was an anagram for 'grow a penis.'

She charged into the navy's cubbyhole office in the Manhattan federal building with a television reporter and cameraman in tow and proceeded to assault Dalworth with an umbrella while she hurled invective. After she shouted herself out and departed, a stunned Dalworth told the reporter that the feminist had a brain like a prune and a body to match.

The episode was marvelous television.

Alas, Dalworth's new status as a media celebrity interfered with his work and embarrassed the navy, still reeling from the 1991 Tailhook Convention scandal, so now he was a very junior naval attaché at the American embassy in Moscow, eight time zones away from the nearest militant feminist armed with a television camera and umbrella.

'That whole thing was almost eight months ago,' Dalworth muttered. 'You'd think people would at least start to forget.' He was a rangy young man, several inches over six feet, with wide shoulders and bulging biceps. At some point in his athletic past his nose had been slightly rearranged, and the effect was a memorable face. Not handsome, but unique.

'What an honor, Spiro! I sure am pleased to meetcha,' Toad enthused. He playfully tapped Dalworth on the shoulder.

'Did you have a good flight?' Dalworth asked.

'Terrific. Filet mignon over the North Pole and all the free champagne we could drink.'

'The cold chicken box lunch, huh?'

'Yeah. You wonder what the air force does to the chicken to make it taste so bad.'

'Ever been to Moscow before?'

'Neither one of us,' Toad said.

'Sleepy?'

After a glance at Grafton, Toad told him, 'Not too.'

'Drive you around the downtown a little before we go to Fort Apache.' Fort Apache, Jake knew, was the complex behind the embassy where the residents lived, a tag that

77

came straight from the movie *Fort Apache, The Bronx*. 'Give you the hundred-ruble tour.'

The endless rows of concrete apartment buildings were soon in view. Nine and a half million people, Jake knew, lived in Moscow, most of them stuffed into tiny apartments in these crumbling mausoleums. Yet on a sunny June day they didn't look bad. Almost as if he could read Jake's thoughts, Dalworth said, 'Place looks a lot different in the winter. Then it's the devil's own refrigerator, gray and terminally dismal.'

Soon the car was bucketing down a broad boulevard toward the center of the city, a chip afloat in a stream of little sedans and huge trucks, all emitting a noxious miasma that stung the eyes and throat. 'Bad pollution, about like Delhi, India. Sorta like Seoul without the kimchi.'

Dalworth piloted them into the center of the city. Soon they were circling the brick walls and onion-topped towers of the Kremlin. Jake's eye was caught by the cars on the side of the road with their hoods up and people bending over the engines. Someone seemed to be broken down in every block.

Dalworth pointed out the naked pedestals where once statues stood. 'See those? They even tore down the statue of Felix Dzerzhinsky in front of KGB Headquarters, presumably while the KGB types watched out the windows. Now I'll show you my favorite place in Moscow. I found this the other day when I was out walking.'

After three more stoplights, he turned and crossed the Moskva River and went down one of the side streets. In one of the river channels a cruise ship sat listing in the mud, gutted and abandoned. Ahead across the sidewalk was a park. A dirt road for park maintenance vehicles was blocked by steel crowd-control railings. Dalworth drove the car onto the sidewalk, stopped, then got out and moved the railings. He pulled the car through, then replaced them. The park was young trees and grass, but the grass was half weeds and hadn't been mowed. Here and there women with strollers sat taking the sun. After Dalworth drove about a hundred yards, he pulled the car to a stop.

Just to the left, surrounded on three sides by more haphazardly placed crowd-control railings, stood three huge bronze statues amid the dandelions and grass. A smaller marble statue lay on its side in front of the others. Behind them half-hidden by the foliage of the trees one could glimpse rows of apartments.

'This is where they dumped some of the statues,' Dalworth explained. He parked the car and the three men got out.

Jake Grafton ran his hands over the marble defaced with swatches of paint. The lower portion of the statue was broken off and lying in the grass. He moved to the head and stared down into the paint-daubed face of Josef Stalin.

'Who are these others?'

The standing bronzes were three or four times life size. 'They look to me to be three likenesses of the same guy, Admiral,' Dalworth said. 'Dzerzhinsky, I think, but I don't know for sure. Maybe Lenin with hair. For sure he was some big Commie mucky-muck that they were tired of looking at and hearing about. He looks sort of like a Slavic Thomas Jefferson, doesn't he?'

'More like Jefferson Davis,' Jake Grafton murmured, and looked around. 'What's that over there?' He pointed at a huge gray concrete structure three or four stories high a hundred yards away, beside the river. The parking lots were empty, and even from this distance he could see the building was shabby, the facade crumbling.

'Some kind of cultural thing. Just beyond it across that boulevard is the entrance to Gorky Park. See that huge gate?'

'Umm.'

Jake Grafton turned back to Stalin. He ran his hands over the marble and looked again into the stone eyes.

'"Look on my works, ye mighty, and despair,"' Toad Tarkington said.

Lieutenant Spiro Dalworth was more down-to-earth. 'Be fun to have one of these out in the backyard, wouldn't it? To piss on whenever you felt in the mood.'

US Ambassador Owen Lancaster was not a career diplomat – rather he was one of those political insiders who had been repeatedly appointed to key embassies by both Democratic and Republican administrations. His political affiliation was a subject that never seemed to get mentioned by anyone, even the press. In short, he was The Establishment from fingertips to toenails.

And he looked it, Jake Grafton concluded. Tall, lean, patrician and impeccably turned out in a tailor-made wool suit and a handmade silk tie, Owen Lancaster looked exactly like central casting's idea of an heir to a nineteenth century Yankee merchant's fortune, which he was. It seemed as if this room in Spaso House were designed around him: the lighting, color scheme, expensive furniture and carpeting – the room was an exquisite tribute to the interior designer's art. God would have a living room like this if He had the money.

In a chair to the left of the ambassador sat one of the career diplomats, a woman in her mid to late thirties – maybe early forties – it was hard to tell. She wore modest, expensive clothes and no makeup that Jake could see. Her name was Ms Agatha Hempstead, with the emphasis on the Ms. She hadn't yet opened her mouth but Jake Grafton already suspected that she was three or four notches smarter than Old Money Lancaster.

On the other side of the ambassador sat Herb Tenney. He was wearing a suit and tie this afternoon and looked as if he had merely dropped in to pass a few social moments. After he had smiled and nodded pleasantly to Jake and Toad, he devoted his attention to the ambassador's pleasantries.

'I don't pretend to know just what instructions you have been given in Washington, Admiral,' the ambassador was saying, 'or what we Americans can do to improve this situation. I don't know that we can contribute anything to the solution of this particular problem, but it certainly won't hurt to try. The Russians must learn that they can cooperate with us on matters of mutual interest and, indeed, it is in their best interests to do so. I think that's critical . . .'

Jake Grafton twisted in his ornate, polished mahogany chair. Herb Tenney looked *innocent*, Jake concluded. His whole presence radiated comfort, proclaimed to everyone who saw him that here was a man at peace with humanity and his conscience, a man who knew in his heart of hearts that he had nothing to regret, nothing to apologize for, nothing to fear.

All of which somehow irritated Jake Grafton.

'. . . We *can* help,' Ambassador Lancaster was saying, 'solve problems in a constructive way that will . . .'

Toad Tarkington caught Jake's eye with a warning glance. Apparently he could see that his boss was struggling to keep a grip on his temper.

God! Was it that obvious?

The fact that Tenney could probably also see the effect of his innocent act was gasoline on the fire. Jake felt the heat as his face flushed. Herb Tenney and his CIA bugs . . . Sunday op-ed drivel from the ambassador . . . if he had to sit here in this museum exhibit of bureaucratic good taste for another two minutes he was going to be in a mood to strangle them both.

'Mr Ambassador,' Jake interrupted as he struggled to rise from the overstuffed chair. 'I didn't get any sleep on the plane and I've just spent an hour with the naval attaché. I've got to lie down for a few hours. Is there anyplace I can crash?'

'Oh, of course, of course. You must be rested when you meet General Yakolev in the morning. I should have thought of that. Would you like something to eat before you go to bed?'

'No, thank you, sir. Perhaps a light breakfast in the morning?'

'No problem, Admiral. We'll talk again then.'

Jake Grafton shook the ambassador's hand, nodded at Ms Hempstead, then turned and tramped out without even a glance at Tenney.

He woke up at midnight after four hours' sleep and found he was wide awake. He turned on the bedside light and examined his watch. What time was it in Washington? What the hell was the time differential? Eight hours? Four o'clock in the afternoon in Washington. No wonder he couldn't sleep even though he was tired.

From the window he could see the Moscow skyline as the anemic city lights made the clouds glow. And the sky wasn't completely dark – sort of a twilight.

He dressed quickly in civilian clothes and pulled on a light jacket. He picked up the phone and was quickly connected to the enlisted marine at the duty desk. 'Could I get a car and driver? I'd like to do a little sight-seeing.'

'I'll see what I can do, sir.' The marine's voice was matter of fact, held not a trace of surprise. Perhaps these requests were common, Jake mused, from new arrivals suffering from jet lag.

'Okay.'

'It'll be just a few minutes, sir.'

The driver, a sergeant, motored slowly on a journey without a destination as Jake Grafton took it all in from the backseat. The city didn't resemble any city he had ever visited. The streets were poorly lit and had private cars parked everywhere. There seemed to be no shortage of parking spaces. At least there was one thing Russia had enough of. Only because they didn't have many cars. Occasionally he saw a few soldiers at street corners, here and there some civilians.

Now and then the driver told him the name of some public building, softly, almost whispering it.

Yes, Jake too felt like a trespasser.

The public buildings were large and grand, but once away from them the streets were lined with endless blocks of concrete buildings designed without imagination and constructed without craft. What these buildings would look like covered with snow and ice was something Grafton didn't want to think about. Some of the buildings were abandoned, mere shells with sockets where the windows had been.

He always got depressed at first in foreign cities – culture shock, he supposed. Tonight the empty streets and the dark blocks of miserable flats reflected a people devoid of hope. It was a sadness that shook Jake Grafton to the marrow.

Inevitably his mind turned to the eighty-five million. Murder on that scale must have a profound effect on those left behind – an effect beyond anything encompassed by grief or tragedy. To live with evil on such a scale was beyond Jake Grafton's comprehension. These people were all *guilty*, all of them; those who gave the orders and those who pulled the triggers and those who buried them and those who pretended it never happened.

Where does responsibility stop? Is it an exclusive property of these miserable, impoverished people crowded into these miserable, mean buildings, fighting for survival?

Jake Grafton thought not. He rode through the summer twilight streets looking at the new sights with old, tired eyes.

CHAPTER SIX

Herb Tenney arrived at the breakfast table as the orange juice and coffee were served.

'Morning, Admiral. Commander.' He nodded at each of them in turn and gave his order to the waiter.

'Your first time in Moscow?' Tenney asked as Jake Grafton turned his attention back to his coffee cup.

'Uh-huh.'

Tenney launched into a discourse on the city that sounded suspiciously like the text from a guidebook. He looked rested and fresh after a good night's sleep, which wasn't the way Jake felt. He had gotten only one more hour of sleep after the excursion last night. This morning he felt tired, listless.

Tenney poured himself a cup of coffee without missing a beat in his monologue. He added a dollop of cream to the mixture and half a spoonful of sugar, then agitated the liquid with a spoon. He paused in his discourse and took a sip.

'Ahh, nothing like coffee in the morning. Anyway, Peter the Great built . . .'

Jake stared at the black liquid in the cup in front of him. He had already had a sip and the slightly acid taste lingered still in his mouth. Would there be a taste to binary poison? What had that report said?

Tenney took another sip of his coffee, then added another smidgen of sugar and languidly stirred with his spoon while he rambled on about the city of the czars.

When the waiter slid a plate of bacon and eggs in front of him, Jake Grafton could only stare at it.

'Something wrong, Admiral?'

Tenney was looking at him solicitously.

Jake Grafton gritted his teeth. Then his face relaxed into a smile. 'Jet lag.'

'Takes a while to get over,' Tenney said. 'The main thing is to sleep when you're sleepy and not try to fool Mother Nature.'

Jake Grafton slid his chair back. 'I wouldn't dream of it,' he said, then glanced at Toad. 'Come up to my room when you're finished here.'

'Yes, sir.'

General Nicolai Yakolev, the Russian Army chief of staff, was a short, ugly man with bushy eyebrows, a huge veined nose, a lantern jaw, and ears that stuck out like jug handles. The wonder was that he could see anything at all with the eyebrows and clifflike nose obstructing his vision. Still, once you ignored nature's decorations you caught a glimpse of lively blue eyes.

Yakolev squeezed Jake's right hand with a vise grip, then shook hands with Herb Tenney as Jake flexed his right hand several times to restore the circulation and watched that impressive, ugly face.

'Bad news, she rides a fast horse,' the Russian said in easily understandable English.

'So I've heard,' Jake Grafton replied and looked curiously around the room, a vast cavern with ceilings at least eighteen feet high. Mirrors, chandeliers, a massive wooden desk atop a colorful Persian carpet, walls covered with books and several oil paintings – apparently Communists were as fond of perks as Democrats and Republicans. They were on the second floor of the Kremlin Arsenal, a two-story yellow building inside the walls.

'Nice room,' he commented.

The general smiled. 'So, Admiral, what did the American government really send you here to do?'

'Watch you take tactical nuclear warheads apart, General.'

'Sounds very boring.'

'I'm also supposed to count them.'

'Ah, one . . . two . . . three . . . four . . .' Yakolev laughed. 'And you, Mr Tenney?'

'I'm with the State Department, sir. Here to assist the admiral.'

Yakolev nodded and shifted his eyes to Jake. 'Is that true?' he asked.

Jake mulled it for about two seconds, then said, 'He's here to keep an eye on me all right, but he's CIA.'

'Ahhh, a political officer, a commissar. I've known a few of them in my time. But as you gentlemen know, our *zampolits* are at the moment unemployed. The world changes. So, please, Mr Tenney, since I am at the disadvantage, I ask you to let the admiral and me converse alone. Then no harm will be done if we inadvertently make any little political mistakes.'

Tenney glanced at Grafton, then rose and left the room.

Jake got a glimpse of twinkling eyes behind Yakolev's bushy brows, then the general turned his attention to a file that lay before him. 'Your dossier,' he said, indicating the file. 'The GRU is very thorough, one of their few virtues.'

He flipped from page to page. 'Let us see. You had combat experience in Vietnam, the usual tours aboard numerous aircraft carriers, command of two air wings . . . Ah, here is a summary of a regrettable incident in the Mediterranean that we thought would surely end your career – and that involved nuclear weapons, I believe.'

'I can neither confirm nor deny that.'

The general laughed, a hearty roar. 'Very funny. Admiral. You make a little joke, and I like that. We Russians laugh to make the pain endurable. But I tell you frankly, if you expect to work with me, you and I must learn to tell each other the unpleasant truths.' He wagged a finger at Jake. 'Regardless of what our politicians say or the lies they tell, you and I must treat each other as professionals. We must work together as colleagues. No lies. All truth. Only truth. You comprehend?'

Jake studied the Soviet general in front of him. He held out his hand. 'May I see the dossier?'

'It is in Russian.'

Jake nodded.

The general closed the file and passed it across the desk. Jake opened it on his lap. It was thick, contained maybe thirty pages of material. Most of the pages were indeed in Russian, some typewritten, others in script. There was a front page of the *New York Times* with his photo and another photo taken on a street somewhere several years ago. He had been in civilian clothes then. Also in the files were several photocopies of newspaper and magazine articles about the A-12 Avenger stealth attack plane for which he had been the project manager, before full-scale production was canceled. One of the articles was from *Aviation Week and Space Technology*: a magazine commonly referred to as *Aviation Leak* by the American military. The file also contained a photo of Toad Tarkington. Jake closed the file and passed it back.

'I don't read Russian.'

'I know. That fact is in the dossier.'

'You speak excellent English.'

'I spent several years in Washington and two in London. But that was years ago, when I was just a colonel.'

'This is my third trip to the Soviet Union – Russia.' This of course was a lie. It was Jake's first trip.

The general merely nodded and lit a cigarette. The heavy smoke wafted gently across the desk and Jake got a dose. It stank.

Jake looked around the room again. Hard to believe, after all those years of reading intelligence reports about the Soviet military, all those years of planning to fight them, here he was in the inner sanctum talking to a Soviet – now Russian – four-star. And the subject was nuclear weapons. The whole thing had an air of unreality. He felt like an actor in a bad play devoid of logic. Life without reason – that's the definition of insanity, isn't it?

Jake Grafton scanned the room yet again, rubbed his hands over the solid arms of his chair, reached out to touch the polished wood of the desk.

But are these guys on the level? Do they really intend to destroy their tactical nukes? Or is this whole thing some kind of weird chess game with nuclear pieces, something out of one of those wretched thrillers about crazed Communists out to checkmate all their opponents and take over the planet?

'Do you play chess?' Jake Grafton asked the general behind the desk, who was watching him through the drifting smoke.

'Yes,' Yakolev said, 'but not very well.' His lips twisted. This was his grin. After the lie came the grin. Very American, like a used-car salesman.

Jake Grafton grinned back. 'I looked at your dossier in the Pentagon a week or so ago. It says you like to fuck little boys.'

The lips twisted again. 'I like you, Grafton. *Da!*'

Jake cleared his throat. 'We know your politicians are' – he was going to say 'less than accurate' but thought better of it – 'lying about the degree of control they have – the army has – over these weapons. I am here to evaluate the extent of your problems and make a report to my superiors. And to offer suggestions if you are receptive.'

Jake Grafton paused as he eyed the Russian general. 'My superiors want the Yeltsin government to succeed in the revolution that Gorbachev began. They do not want the Communists to regain power, nor do they want to see the Soviet Union balkanized unless there is no other way. Baldly, they want to see a stable government in this country that has the support of the populace, a government that indeed is trying to improve the lot of its citizens.'

'They are humanitarians,' General Yakolev said lightly.

'Don't ever think that,' Jake Grafton shot back. 'They are

damn worried men. Their primary concern is nuclear weapons. They do not want to see nuclear, chemical or biological weapons technology exported. They desperately want you to establish a viable democracy here, but first and foremost – the most important factor – your government must keep absolute control of *all the nuclear weapons that exist on your soil.*'

'Yeltsin is not in control of anything right now. He is at the center but the storm revolves around him. How I say it? – he is like one of your cowboys on a crazy bronco horse. He is still on the saddle but the horse goes his own way. Understand?'

'I will give you the frank, blunt truth, General. I will not repeat the platitudes of the politicians. The Americans will deal with whoever has these weapons, be it a Communist dictator, fascist demagogue, religious fanatic, or a criminal gang leader. Whoever. And I suspect the same is true of the British, the Germans, the French – all the Western democracies. But their liaison officers can tell you that themselves.'

Yakolev came around the desk and pulled a chair closer to Grafton. He sat. 'You and I can work together. We are both military men, both patriots. I serve Mother Russia. You understand?'

Jake nodded.

'I am not blind. Russia must join the world. This planet is too small to sustain an isolated society of three hundred million people. We have tried dictatorship and it failed; now we must try democracy. But I lay out the truth for your inspection: no matter who rules the Kremlin, *I* serve Russia.'

Russia the grand abstraction, Jake thought ruefully. Well, every nation is an abstraction if you stop to think about it. He irritably dismissed the thought and asked, 'And the army? Whom does the army serve?' When the Russian was slow to answer, Jake sharpened the question: 'Will the army obey your orders?'

89

General Nicolai Yakolev spit out the word, 'Yes.'

That, Jake Grafton suspected, was the biggest and baldest lie so far. And mouthed like a pro. And yet . . . 'These weapons distort everything,' he said.

'I know.'

'While they exist, you serve only them,' Jake said.

'Control all the nuclear weapons that exist, you said. I noted your choice of words, Admiral.'

'They must be destroyed,' Jake Grafton said, 'before they destroy you. You asked for truth. There it is.'

The Russian leaned toward Jake. 'You are a soldier, not a politician. I like that. I think we can do business. Come.'

He led Jake to a table under a huge oil painting that should have been in a museum. There was a large map on the table. The Russian general pointed and explained where the weapons were and what might be done with the plutonium after the warheads were disassembled. Through the tall windows Jake could see the soft summer sun sifting down, gently bathing everything in a surreal light.

An hour later the men were back at the general's desk drinking strong, black tea in tall glasses with metal holders. At the general's suggestion Jake had stirred in juice from a slice of lemon and a spoonful of something that looked like blackberry jam.

'Perhaps you could tell me a little about yourself, General,' Jake Grafton said, jerking his thumb at the dossier.

The Russian laughed. 'All the time, effort, and expense that goes into compiling dossiers, and you know what yours tells me? That you are a professional officer. Nothing else. And that I knew before I opened it.

'But it is me you want to know about, even after reading my dossier in the Pentagon. Dossiers are the same the world over. I am old, seventy years. I fought in the Great War. I was young enough to enjoy killing Nazis. In Berlin I saw Hitler's bunker, helped search it. I saw the patio where they burned his body, his and Eva Braun's. I walked through the rubble. All Europe was rubble then, my friend. I tell you that.'

So Yakolev had once been a shooter, a warrior. Maybe down deep under the wrinkles and gray hair he still was. Most of the top men in the world's military organizations weren't: they were bureaucrats and cocktail party politicians.

The general shook his head. 'I was very young then. And that is the only fact about me that would be of interest. The rest is obvious. I survived. I *survived!*'

Ahh, Jake mused, at what cost? How many men have you sold out, General, how many lies have you told, how much of your honor can possibly be left after you clawed and scratched and gouged your way to the top of this squirming snake pile of criminal psychopaths? The scars must be there . . . unless you have become one of them, a man without conscience, a man to whom the end justifies whatever it takes to get there. If so . . .

The general rumbled on. 'But no stories. Old men tell too many stories, stories of a dead past that are of little interest to the young, who think their own problems unique.'

'And I am too young,' Jake Grafton said.

General Yakolev's eyes searched his face. 'Perhaps. Your youth . . .' He shook his head. 'You Americans turn out your officers to fatten in the pasture so very early, just when they grow old enough to have a bit of wisdom, just when they are old enough to understand all the things that they are not, all the things that they can never be, will never be. Just when they are old enough.'

Jake sipped his tea. It wasn't like American tea, weak and insipid. He liked it.

'What do you *know* of Russia?'

Jake drank the last of the tea and set the cup in its saucer. 'The usual, which is not much . . . the bare essentials, twenty years of reading intelligence briefs, a few books.'

'Tolstoy?'

'A little. Chekov I liked. Andreyev's *The Seven Who Were Hanged* was too Russian.' Oops! He should not have said *that!* 'Solzhenitsyn . . .' What could he say about Solzhenitsyn's descriptions of hell on earth? They had horrified Jake Grafton, painted communism as one of the foulest evils ever perpetrated by man upon man. 'I have read him,' he finished lamely.

'Hmmm,' said Yakolev, his face a mask. 'Dinner tomorrow night, yes? The military observers from Britain, Germany, France and Italy will also be here. You know them, yes?'

'No, sir. I've never met them.'

'I will send my car for you at the embassy. About eight.'

'May I bring my aide, sir?'

'If you like. We will take the time to learn to know each other better. I will be interested to learn where you draw the line between Russian and too Russian.'

Jake was led back through the long cold hallways with their dim lights and dark oil paintings that could barely be seen. Herb Tenney was standing near the door, waiting. Outside the summer sun of the Kremlin grounds made Jake squint. The contrast between inside and outside hit him hard. He held his hat on his head as he climbed into the car.

Culture shock, Jack Yocke decided. He felt depressed, alone, listless. He could count on one hand the number of people he had met who spoke English. The constant fumbling with the paperback Russian-English dictionary frustrated him. The heavy, fatty mystery meat and greasy vegetables were clogging his bowels. Culture shock, he told himself, hoping that sooner or later he would adjust.

How good it would be to be back in the *Post* newsroom, talking on the phone to someone who spoke American, understanding the nuances of what wasn't said as readily as he captured the intent of what was. Oh, for a bacon and egg breakfast, with eggs from a lovely American chicken and crisp fried bacon from a handsome American pig! To go across the street to the Madison coffee shop for a hot pastrami on rye! And an American beer, a tall cold American beer in a frosty glass with foam spilling over the top.

He was gloomily contemplating the difference between American beer and the Russian horse piss product when the motorcade came around the corner into view. Three vehicles. Black. Limos.

He was stuck off to one side of the platform where the speakers were going to address the rally. Perhaps a thousand people, mostly men and babushkas, milled around the square and luxuriated in the sun, rolling up sleeves to brown their white arms, drinking juice from glass bottles. The few children were messily eating ice cream bars sold by a sidewalk vendor, who was doing a land office business today. Apparently the vendors, for the city sidewalks seemed crammed with them, were something new, fledgling capitalists trying the new way right here beside a Communist rally. The irony of it made Yocke smile.

The paper's Russian stringer translator was sucking on a foul cigarette and chatting in Russian with his counterpart from the *New York Times*. *The Times* reporter was on the other side of these two and busy scribbling notes, no doubt literate political insights that would form the heart of an incisive think piece. Damn *The Times!*

Jack Yocke took off his sports coat and hung it over one arm. He wiped the perspiration from his forehead. And damn these Commies! Why can't they hire a hall like politicians in more civilized climes?

The senior *Post* correspondent was over at the Kremlin today buttonholing Yeltsin lieutenants, so Yocke was stuck covering this rally of nationalistic Commie retrogrades, people who thought that the Stalin era was Russia's finest hour. Yes, there were still live human beings on this planet who believed that, and here were some of them, waving red flags and posters with slogans. Some of them even wore red armbands, but the red flags were the grabber: to Yocke's

American eye the blood red flags looked like an image straight from a museum exhibit. That there were still people who firmly believed in the gospel of Marx, Engels, and Lenin was a fact that he knew intellectually, yet seeing it in the flesh was a jolt.

These people were obviously committed. Just below the platform four older men were arranged in a circle, shouting at one another. No, it was three against one. Yocke couldn't understand a word of it and thought about asking the stringer what it was all about, then decided against it. He thought he already knew the answer.

Yegor Kolokoltsev was their guru, a man who could rant anti-Semitic filth that would have been too raw for Joseph Goebbels and in the next breath extol the glories of Mother Russia. As Yocke understood Kolokoltsev's message, the Communists never had a chance to purify the Soviet Union and make her great because the Jews had subverted them, stolen the fruit of the proletariat's labor, betrayed the revolution, sucked blood from the veins of honest Communists, etc., etc.

So now he stood sweating as the motorcade drew to a halt and burly guards jumped from the cars and began opening a pathway to the platform. Idly Yocke looked around for soldiers or uniformed policemen. There were none in sight. Not a one.

The bodyguards in civilian clothes had no trouble clearing a path. The crowd parted courteously, as befitted old Communists. And these were mostly old Communists, workers and retired grandmothers. Here and there the mix was leavened by better-dressed younger men, probably bureaucrats or apparatchiks who had lost or were losing their jobs under the new order. Some of the waving signs and red flags partially obscured Yocke's vision of the arriving dignitaries.

The lack of policemen and soldiers bothered Jack Yocke slightly, and he turned to his translator to ask a question about their absence when he heard the noise, a sharp popping audible even above the sounds of traffic from the street.

An automatic weapon!

There was no mistaking the sound.

The crowd panicked. People turned their backs on Yegor Kolokoltsev and his guards and tried to flee. The urge to leave hastily seemed to enter the head of every living soul there at precisely the same instant.

More weapons. The sharp popping was now the staccato buzzing of numerous weapons, but it was strangely muffled by screams and shouts.

Yocke grabbed a handhold on the rail of the speaker's platform and pulled himself up a couple feet so he could see better.

Four people with automatic weapons were shooting at the guards, most of whom were now on the ground. One or two gunmen were pouring lead into the middle limousine.

With all the guards down, two of the gunmen walked toward the car. They were dressed in the usual dark gray suits and wore hats. The crowd was dispersing rapidly now, everyone fleeing for their lives. Several of the elderly were sprawled on the pavement. One or two of them were struggling to rise.

One of the gunmen opened the car door and the other emptied a magazine through the opening from a distance of three feet.

Yocke looked around wildly. The stragglers from the retreating crowd were rounding the corners, probably running down the streets that led away from the square.

The gunmen dropped their weapons and walked away without haste.

No sirens. No more screams.

Silence.

Yocke looked around for the other reporters and their Russian stringers. Gone. He was alone, still clinging to the side of the speaker's platform.

He released his grip and dropped to the pavement. The

whole thing had been like a slow-motion film – he had seen everything, felt everything, the fear, the horror, the sense of doom descending inexorably, controlled by an unseen, godlike hand. Now if he could only get it down!

How much time had elapsed? Minutes? No – no more than forty or fifty seconds. Maybe a minute.

He looked at the backs of the fleeing people. The last of the crowd was hobbling around the corners. Some people had apparently been trampled in the panic; six or eight bodies lay around the square.

Yocke stood and watched the last of the gunmen disappear around the corner where the motorcade had entered the square. A half mile or so down that street was Red Square. The entrance to the metro, the subway that would take them anywhere in Moscow, was only a hundred yards away.

He was alone with the dead and dying. He walked toward the cars. The guards – he counted the bodies . . . seven, eight, nine. He walked from one to the other, looking. All dead, each of them shot at least six or eight times. Blood, one's man's brains, intestines oozing into congealing piles on the stones of the square.

The middle limo was splattered with holes, the door still standing open. Yocke looked in.

The big man was Yegor Kolokoltsev, or had been just a few minutes ago. Now he was as dead as dead can be. Two of the bullets had struck him in the head, one just under the left eye and the other high up in the forehead. His eyes were still open, as was his mouth. Somehow his face still seemed to register surprise. A dozen or more bullets had punched through his chest and throat. There was little blood.

Facing Kolokoltsev was another corpse. The driver of the limo sat slumped over the wheel.

The other two cars were empty. Empty shell casings lay scattered on the street.

Alone in the midst of the vast silence Jack Yocke bent and picked up a shiny shell casing. 9mm.

One of the weapons lay not five feet from him. He merely looked. He couldn't tell one automatic weapon from another.

He turned and looked again at Kolokoltsev. Then he gagged.

He staggered away.

His mouth was watering copiously and his eyes were tearing up. He paused and placed his hands on his knees and spit repeatedly. He had to write *this* too, capture all of it.

Now the sensation was passing.

He walked, working hard at walking without staggering, without succumbing to the urge to run, which was building.

The urge to run became dire. He began to trot. Faster, faster . . .

He saw a narrow street leading away from the square and ran for it. People were standing on the sidewalks looking into the square, but he ran by them without slowing down.

Telephone! He must find a telephone.

'Mike Gatler.' Mike was the foreign editor. He sounded sleepy, and no doubt he was. It was one-thirty in the afternoon here, but five-thirty in the morning in Washington.

'Mike, Jack Yocke. I just witnessed an assassination.'

'Terrific. Send me a story and I'll read it.'

'Right in Soviet Square, Mike. Right in front of Moscow City Hall. They gunned a big Commie weenie when he arrived for a political rally. Crowd there and everything.'

'You woke me up for this?'

'Gee, Mike. It's front page, for sure.'

Gatler sighed audibly. 'What happened?'

'They killed Yegor Kolokoltsev and eleven of his guards. Five gunmen with automatic weapons mowed them down.' The words came faster now, tumbling out: 'It was the goddamnest thing I ever saw, Mike, a cold-blooded execution.

First the guards, then the politician. I'm sure some of the bystanders in the crowd were shot too. Just their tough fucking luck. Like something from a movie. That was my first thought, like something from a movie. Something staged, unreal. But it was real all right.'

'Are you okay?' Gatler sounded genuinely concerned. The contrast between the irritation in Mike's voice at first being awakened and the concern he was now expressing hit Yocke hard.

'I guess so, Mike. Sorry I bothered you at home.'

'It's okay, Jack. Write the story. Take your time and do it right. Kolokoltsev, huh? The Russian nationalist?'

'Yeah. Bigot. Anti-Semite. Holy Russia and all that shit. A Nazi with a red star on his sleeve.'

'You write it. Do it right.'

''Night, Mike.'

''Night, Jack.'

He hung up the phone and stood in the lofty, opulent hotel lobby at a loss for what to do next. Over in the corner a pianist was playing, and the tune sounded familiar. Yocke's heart rate and breathing were returning to normal after the half-mile jog to the hotel, the only place he would find a telephone with a satellite link to call overseas. The Russian phone system was a relic of Stalin's era and couldn't even be relied upon for a call across town. But Yocke was still shook. The surprise of it as much as anything . . . damn!

Soviet Square . . . in front of that statue of Lenin as *The Thinker* . . . with a Pizza Hut restaurant just a block up the street where they serve real food to real people who have real money in their jeans. Hard currency only, thank you. No dip-shit Russians with only rubles in the pockets of their Calvin Kleins . . .

The clerk behind the counter was staring at him, as were several of the guests queued up at the cashier's counter. Now the clerk said something in Russian. A question. He repeated it. He seemed to have lost his English.

98

Jack Yocke shrugged, then headed for the elevator with the clerk staring after him. He should have made the call from the phone in his room. If he had thought about the effect of his conversation on the clerk, he would have.

As the elevator door closed Yocke recognized the music, Dave Brubeck's 'Take Five.' He began laughing uncontrollably.

At the American embassy Jake Grafton spent a few minutes with the ambassador, then was shown to a small office that was temporarily unused. There he began his report to General Brown on the conference today. He wrote in longhand and handed the sheets to Toad to type.

'It went well?' Toad asked.

'Maybe.' *Too Russian.* Jake, you could screw up a wet dream.

He had about finished the report when there was a knock on the door and Lieutenant Dalworth stuck his head in.

'Admiral, I have a message for you.'

Dalworth held out the clipboard with an envelope attached. 'Just fill in the number of the envelope and sign your name, sir.'

Jake did so. As Dalworth left the room Jake ripped open the envelope, which was marked with a top secret classification. It had of course been decoded in the embassy's message center.

FYI LTGEN A.S. Brown died last night in his sleep. News not yet made public.

FYI – for your information, no action required. Without a word Jake passed the slip of paper across to Toad Tarkington.

'Just like that?' Toad asked with an air of disbelief.

'When your heart stops, you're dead.' Jake Grafton folded the message and placed it back into its envelope. It would have to go back to the message center for logging

99

and destruction. He tossed the envelope onto the corner of the desk. 'Just . . . like . . . that.'

'For Christ's sake, CAG, we've got to—'

'No!'

'We can't just—'

'No.'

Toad turned his back for a bit. When he turned around again he said in a flat voice, 'Okay, what are we going to do?'

'I don't know,' Jake said.

What could he do? Write a letter to the president?

'What did Herb Tenney do today, anyway?'

'He went out this morning after you left,' Toad told him. 'Came back about two or three.'

'He's got an office?'

'He's in with the other CIA types. They've got a suite just down the hall and their own radio equipment and crypto gear. They don't use the embassy stuff.'

'Who are the other spies?'

'Well, there are about a dozen, near as I can tell. Head guy is a fellow named McCann who has been here a couple years. I met him at lunch. One of those guys who can talk for an hour and not say anything. A gas bag.'

It was impossible, a cesspool of the first order of magnitude. 'Shit,' Jake whispered.

'Yessir. My sentiments exactly.'

'Have they got a safe in their office?'

'I suppose so. I haven't been in there.'

'Go in tomorrow morning. Look the place over.'

'If I can get in.'

'Tell Herb you want the tour. Gush. Gee-whiz.'

'Yes, sir.'

Toad threw himself into a chair. He sighed deeply, then said, 'Y'know, I really wish you and I had a nice safe job back in the real world – like bungee jumping or explosive ordnance disposal on a bomb squad. Something with a future.'

Jake Grafton didn't reply.

Albert Sidney Brown dead. Damn, damn and double-damn!

Well, it was time to call a spade a spade. The odds that Brown's ticker picked this particular time to call it quits were not so good. Ten to one he was poisoned. Murdered. By the CIA, or someone in the CIA. Christians in Action.

If the CIA really did it, he and Toad were living on borrowed time. Perhaps they had already been served half of the binary chemical cocktail. And any minute now Herb Tenney or one of his agents might get around to serving the chaser.

'You and I are going on short rations as of right now,' Jake told Toad. 'Go down to the kitchen and get us some canned soda pop and some food that we can eat right out of the can.'

'What do I tell the cook?'

'Tell him we're having a picnic. I don't know. Think of something. Tell him I'm sick. Go on.'

After Jake delivered his report to the message center for transmission, he went up to his room. The door that led to Toad's room was open and he was standing in it.

'Someone was in here today,' Toad said.

'You sure?'

'No, sir. But my stuff is a little different.'

Jake felt in his pocket for scratch paper. On it he wrote, 'Look for bugs.'

It took fifteen minutes to find it. They left it where it was.

'Are you hungry, Admiral?'

'No.'

Jake took off his uniform and lay down on the bed. He turned off the light.

Two minutes later he turned it back on, got out of bed and checked the door lock, then asked Toad to come in for a moment. With Tarkington watching, Jake took the Smith

101

& Wesson from his bag, checked the firing pin, snapped the gun through all six chambers, then loaded it.

No doubt the bug picked up the sound of the dry firing. Well, that was fair warning. If anyone came in here tonight Jake Grafton fully intended to blow his head off.

'Night, Toad.'

'Good night, sir.'

Sleep didn't come. Jake tossed and turned and re-arranged the pillow to no avail.

The problem was that he was totally alone, and it was a strange feeling. Always in the past he had a superior officer within easy reach to toss the hot potatoes to. Everyone in uniform has a boss – that is the way of the profession and Jake Grafton had spent his life in it. Now he had nowhere to turn.

He should have, of course. He should be able to just walk upstairs and get on the encrypted voice circuit to Washington. In just a few minutes he would be bounced off a satellite and connected with the new acting head of the DIA, or the Chief of Naval Operations, or even the Chairman of the Joint Chiefs, General Hayden Land. The problem was that the CIA might be monitoring the circuit.

Not the CIA as an organization, but whoever it was that had a grubby hand on Tenney's strings. The agency was so compartmentalized that a rogue department head might be able to run his own covert operation for years before anyone found out. If anyone found out. If the man at the top took reasonable care and kept his operation buried within another, legitimate operation, it was conceivable that it might never be discovered.

The more he thought about it, the more convinced Jake was that he had tripped over just such an operation. Who controlled it, what its goals were, how many people were involved – he had no answers to any of these questions.

So the encrypted voice circuits were out. A commercial line? Every phone in the embassy was monitored.

And if he found a circuit, who was he going to talk to? If

these people could casually squash a three-star general, no one was beyond reach. The ambassador? That Boston Brahman, that man of distinction in a whiskey ad? Yet he *had* to trust someone.

The military was built on trust. Trust and communications. In today's world of high-tech weapons systems and instant communications everyone in the system was merely a moving part. Amazingly, none of the moving parts were critical. As soon as one wore out, was wounded or killed, it was replaced. And the machine never paused, never faltered as long as the communications network remained intact.

Herb Tenney was a soldier too. Staring at the ceiling, Jake told himself he must not forget that fact.

As he began to go over it all for the third or fourth time, his frustration got the better of him. He climbed from the bed and went to the window. The sun hadn't set yet. He tried to visualize what the city must look like in the snow, for snow was the norm. The mean annual temperature here was minus two degrees centigrade. These long, balmy days were but a short interlude in the life of the city and those who inhabited it. In spite of the sun's golden glow he could see buildings in a gray winter's half-light amid the snow driven along by the wind. He could feel the cutting cold.

The Russian winter had killed tens of thousands of soldiers in the past three hundred years, he reflected. No doubt it could kill a few more.

CHAPTER SEVEN

He was going to have to take some chances, run some risks that were impossible to evaluate. As a young man he had learned to stay alive in aerial combat by carefully weighing the odds and never taking an unnecessary chance, so now the unknown dangers weighed heavily upon him. And back then he had only his life at stake, his and his bombardier's. Now . . .

But there was no other way.

When Toad came to the room this morning Jake sent him to get a car. 'You'll drive it,' Jake told him. 'Bring the blanket off your bed.' He put on his short-sleeved white uniform shirt and examined the ribbons and wings insignia in the mirror. All okay.

Three blocks away from the embassy Jake told Toad to stop. They searched the car as traffic whizzed by and the exhaust fumes wafted about them. Not much wind today, drat it.

They opened the hood and examined everything as a crowd of pedestrians gathered, probably attracted by their white uniforms. The two naval officers ignored the curious Russians. It took them five minutes to identify all the wires of the electrical system to their satisfaction. They opened the trunk and lifted out the spare tire and scrutinized every square inch and cranny. Toad put the blanket on the pavement and wormed under the car while Jake opened his pocketknife and took off the door panels. He probed the seat cushions and sliced open the roof liner. They peeled back the carpet on the floor.

Nothing.

When they started the car again they sat staring at the traffic zipping by and the onlookers on the sidewalk, who were drifting away one by one.

'You'd think if there was a bug in this thing we'd find it,' Toad said with disgust in his voice.

'Maybe.' You could never prove a negative to a certainty. All you could do was try to determine the probability.

'Miserable goddamn country,' Toad growled.

After a few moments Jake said, 'If anything happens to me, I'd like you to do me a favor.'

Toad waited.

'Kill Herb Tenney.'

'That,' Toad said with heat, 'will be a real pleasure.'

'Better be quick about it. I've got a feeling that if I die you're going to be knocking on the pearly gate very soon thereafter.'

Toad put the car into gear and pulled away from the curb.

They parked in front of the Hotel Metropolitan amid the taxicabs, right around the corner from Red Square.

Jake left Toad with the car and went inside. 'I wish to speak with one of your guests, an American named Jack Yocke.' And since the man nodded politely, Jake added, '*Pashah'lsta.*' Please.

'Yaw-key?'

'That's right.' Jake spelled it.

As the desk attendant consulted his files Jake surveyed the lobby. He had visited the embassy public affairs office earlier that morning and had gotten the name of Yocke's hotel from the file. He had looked it up himself so the clerk would not see what name he wanted. He felt foolish, paranoid.

'Here it is,' the desk man said, straightening from the files. 'I will telephone him.' The clerk looked natty in a dark suit and tie. Apparently these folks were going after those hard dollars with a vengeance. Jake nodded and went over to one of the plush chairs on the other side of the room to wait. Several of the tourists in line at the counters stared at him. A white uniform certainly had an effect.

Three minutes later the elevator door opened and Jack Yocke stepped out. He was visibly surprised when he saw Jake Grafton. He came over smiling and stopped in front of Jake with his hands held out to his sides.

'Clean and sober, Admiral. In the flesh.' He shook Jake's outstretched hand. 'How goes the war effort?'

'Off the record?'

Yocke laughed. 'You're the last man on earth I expected to see around here.'

'I came to see Lenin. I hear they're selling the body to some outfit in Arizona.'

'Yep. Gonna put the old boy on display right near the London Bridge in Lake Havasu City. Five bucks a head. Old ladies from Moline in stretch polyester and tennis shoes will be filing by the coffin whispering, "Well, I never!"'

'Toad's out in the car. How about coming outside for a minute or two for a chat?'

You had to hand it to Yocke. He didn't even blink. 'Sure,' he said.

'So how's the foreign correspondent gig going?' Toad asked Yocke when they were seated in the car.

'I don't know how I'm holding up,' Yocke said sadly. 'Every day three or four beautiful women, not less than a quart of vodka, meals fit for a czar or local party chief, a ballet or—'

'We've got a little problem,' Jake said firmly, interrupting the litany, 'that we thought you might be able to help with. It's an I'll-never-tell type of problem.'

'No story?'

'Not even a whisper.'

Yocke snorted. 'Do you know how damn tough it is to get a story in this Cyrillic borsch house? I've had exactly one, yesterday, when someone snuffed Yegor Kolokoltsev.'

'We heard about that. Five gunmen in Soviet Square?'

'I was there on the fifty-yard line, six rows back. Just lucky, I guess. I've been upstairs writing it up for the Sunday paper, three thousand sensitive, powerful words that would melt the heart of a crack salesman. The story is what I saw and a bunch of denials from the Russian cops. No, they did not know Kolokoltsev was going to speak. No, they did not keep the police away. That's about it. Lots of on-scene detail and a bunch of denials.'

'So,' Jake asked curiously, 'were they in on it?'

'Something smells, that's for sure. No police or military in the square. Five gunmen drill Kolokoltsev and all his bodyguards. They looked like they were shooting an army qualification course. Just pros punching holes in a professional manner. Then they dropped the guns and walked away. No haste, no waste.'

'It's the wrong feel,' Toad objected. 'The Russians don't do things that way.' He was about to add something when Grafton silenced him with a glance.

The admiral asked Yocke, 'What about that big story that you were so full of back in Washington? People stealing nukes and selling them?'

'Can't smoke it out. The people who were supposed to know something just laughed when I showed up with my letters of introduction and asked. All rumors. So I'm doing features and listening to would-be dictators preach anti-Semitic, fascist poison. I was just lucky to witness a rubout that would make a great movie. BFD.' Jake knew what that meant – Big Fucking Deal.

'Jack, I need to ask a favor. Call your editor and have him deliver a message in person to General Land.'

'This is supposed to make me laugh, right?'

'No joke,' Jake told him. 'Obviously I don't want to use any of the telephones at the embassy, encrypted or otherwise. Nor the embassy's message circuits. And I don't want General Land talking on a telephone in his office, home or car.'

'Why not?'

'Yes or no.'

'Want to tell me about it?'

'No, Jack, I don't. I just want you to say yes.'

'Who don't you want listening in? The overseas lines all bounce off the bird in the sky. Great connection – sounds better than the phone at home – but the people in the telephone office are undoubtedly KGB to a man. You can bet your ass they tape every call. Of course the KGB has a new name, the Foreign Intelligence Service, but a turd by any other name is still a turd. Ten dollars against a ruble they'll be routing a transcript in Cyrillic around Dzer-zhinsky Square before you get back on the sidewalk.'

Jake said nothing.

'So you want to be overheard, huh? By the KGB. Or you don't care.' Yocke writhed in his seat. He glared at both of them. 'You knew I'd say yes. Admiral. Now figure out what I'm going to tell my editor.'

Jake Grafton pursed his lips. 'I'm assuming that this will be a tight little secret over at the *Post*.'

'Like Ted Kennedy's spring vacation plans,' Yocke re-plied sourly. 'You realize that if the KGB wants to know more they will pay me a visit and sweat me.'

'If you have your health . . .' Toad Tarkington said, and gave Yocke a wide grin. 'Jack, I'll never understand you. Where's your sense of adventure? The KGB might put you against a wall and shoot you. You'll be famous! If they just rip out all your fingernails and throw you out of the country the *Post* will probably give you a raise.'

'You macho pinhead! These Russians don't do walls or blindfolds or last cigarettes. No melodrama. They snatch you on the street, strangle you in the car and stuff you into a hole someplace out in the woods so no one else on God's green earth will ever know what became of you. Without muss or fuss you just cease to be. Cease to be *anything!* These people have ruled this country with terror for seventy years and they are real goddamn good at it. If you aren't pissing yourself when you think about them you're a congenital idiot. There ain't no rules but theirs and they keep changing them all the time. This ain't good ol' Iowa, Frogface.'

Toad grinned at the admiral and jerked his thumb at Yocke. 'You may find this hard to believe, but I'm beginning to like this guy.'

Yocke wasn't paying attention. Already he was trying to figure out how to explain this to his editor. He looked at his watch. It was 2 A.M. in Washington. He would call Gatler at home again. Mike was going to be thrilled.

'Let's get something to eat,' Toad suggested. 'For some reason I'm hungry.'

Jake nodded.

'Well, there's a good hard currency restaurant with big prices up the street at the Savoy and a slightly more modest one here at the Metropolitan. It's all Russian grub and the city water system is contaminated, unfit for human consumption. It's Russian roulette – radioactive beef and milk and vegetables full of heavy metals – spin the cylinder and pull the trigger.' He sighed. 'I know you want to treat, so you pick.'

'Here,' Jake said. Toad killed the engine and they climbed out. 'But we call your editor first.'

'Let me get this straight, Admiral. You want me to call Hayden Land right now, at two-twenty in the morning, and ask him to come to the *Post* to call you in the morning?'

Mike Gatler's voice was remarkably clear – the miracle of modern communications technology – and the amazement and disbelief seemed about to leak out of the telephone. Apparently Yocke's call had roused him from a sound sleep.

'No, sir. Tell him you want to meet him at the guard's shack in front of the river entrance to the Pentagon at 8 A.M. *There* you ask him to call me at this number in Moscow as soon as he can. He can use a phone in your office or a pay phone. This is important, Mr Gatler — *no other telephones.* Have him call me here at this number in Moscow. Have you got that?'

'Put Yocke back on the line.'

Jake handed the telephone to the reporter, who mumbled into the instrument and listened intently. After a bit he said, 'Admiral Grafton came over to the hotel this morning and asked for this favor . . . No . . . he hasn't said. He *won't* say . . . Yes.'

Yocke turned and eyed the two naval officers. 'Gotcha,' he told the telephone. 'I understand . . . how did you like my story about—' He bit it off and replaced the instrument on its cradle.

'I'm not to call him again at home in the middle of the night unless I'm dead. And I'm supposed to guarantee you absolute confidentiality.' He sat down beside Jake Grafton on the bed. 'You'll be deep background, never quoted or even referred to. I'm supposed to wring you out like a sponge.'

Jake Grafton grinned. He had a good grin under a nose that was a size too big for his face. When he grinned his gray eyes twinkled. 'Think Gatler will do it?'

'Yeah. The one thing you gotta have in the news game is curiosity — Mike Gatler is chock full of it. He's a helluva newspaperman. I don't know if Hayden Land will agree to see him, but I guarantee Mike will try.'

'He'll see him all right. If Gatler uses my name. Now let's go get some food. I'm starved.'

'Don't they feed you guys at the embassy?'

'Stove isn't working right,' Jake muttered and led the way through the door.

'Hayden Land, Chairman of the Joint Chiefs of Staff,' Yocke said cheerfully as he trailed the naval officers down the hall. 'This is big, huh?'

'So how long you guys been in Moscow?' Yocke asked after they had gone through the buffet line and were picking at the watery scrambled eggs and sampling the fatty sausage.

They had a table in the middle of the room and were surrounded by businessmen and here and there pairs of tourists. Over near the buffet line sat eight Japanese businessmen drinking orange juice and coffee and eating grapes. For twenty US dollars a head. The Russians, Jake Grafton decided, have capitalism all figured out. Charge every nickel the traffic will bear until they quit coming, then drop the price just enough to get them back.

'Couple days.'

'So what do you think?'

'I think a twenty-dollar breakfast is one hell of a way to start a morning,' Jake replied. He managed to choke down his first bite of fatty, greasy sausage and shoved the rest of it to the side of his plate. He tentatively sipped the coffee. It was hot and black, thank God!

'Twenty and ten percent tip,' Yocke said cheerfully. 'Twenty-two American smackeroos to get past that squat lady at the door.'

'These bastards bypassed capitalism and went straight into highway robbery,' Toad mumbled as he stared at the mess on the plate in front of him. 'No wonder Marx was appalled. Twenty-two fucking dollars! Jeeezus!'

Jake looked slowly around at the huge, splendid room in which they sat with the businessmen and tourists, eating nervously. There were just no Russian restaurants that served food a Western stomach could tolerate – none. 'This place is a boom town, like San Francisco during the gold rush. There's no price competition right now.' He shrugged. 'Maybe it'll come.'

Yocke tried to change the subject. 'What are you guys here for?'

Jake Grafton eyed the reporter and this time his gray eyes didn't twinkle. 'Give it up, Jack.'

'You gotta admit, Admiral, this whole thing is curious as hell. The embassy has gotta have enough communications gear to put you in touch with Slick Willie Clinton snarfing gut bombs in a McDonald's.'

111

Yocke shrugged, then leaned back in his chair and assumed his philosophical attitude: 'This whole darn country is curious. Everything is falling apart, nothing works right, yet everybody you meet is a literature expert, a music scholar, or an authority on eighteenth-century Russian poetry. Not a solitary one of them owns a screwdriver or a pair of pliers or even knows what they're for. So the commodes don't work, the light bulbs are burned out, the furnace in the basement crapped out last year, the pipes are busted – and they sit amid the rubble and talk about the nuances in Dostoyevski, the genius of Tolstoy. The whole place is a nuthouse, one giant pyscho ward, some psychiatrist's wet dream.'

'They must have something going for them,' Jake said as he smeared jam inside a croissant. 'They kicked the hell out of Hitler. They're tough, resilient people. They're survivors.'

Jack Yocke rubbed his head and thought about it. He was having trouble getting the right perspective, having trouble seeing the human beings hidden behind the body armor they all wore. 'Maybe,' he muttered. 'Maybe.'

'So what stories have you been working on while you've been here?' Toad Tarkington asked this question.

'Been wandering around trying to get a feel for the place, for the people. They're desperate. It's a scary situation. The people seem to just have no hope. And the Commies are playing to their fears. The anti-Semitism is right out in the open and it's ugly.'

Toad glanced at Jake Grafton, who was looking out the window at the street, now bathed in weak sunshine, as Jack Yocke rambled on about the more prominent Communists and their stump rantings. When the reporter finally paused Jake asked, 'How ugly?'

'What?'

'How ugly is the anti-Semitism?'

'They're prosecuting Jews for hooliganism, profiteering and hoarding. Throwing them into jail. Everyone is doing it but the only people being prosecuted are Jews charged before they changed the law. The persecution is even more blatant outside of Moscow, out in those little provincial towns nobody ever heard of where old Communists are still running the show. To hear some of the Commies tell it, they never had a chance to run this country right because the Jews screwed up everything. It's Hitler's big lie one more time.'

'It worked before,' Jake murmured.

He looked at his watch. Almost eleven. Five or six hours to wait. Maybe Toad could spend the afternoon with Yocke and he could get some sleep in Yocke's bed. He managed only an hour or two's sleep last night. Jet lag. He felt hot and dirty and tired. Or maybe he had caught a dose of that desperation that everyone here seemed to be infected with.

And this would be a good time to call Richard Harper, his private computer hacker, to ask if he had made any progress finding the money. If someone was buying nuclear weapons, then someone was getting paid.

But what will you do when you know?

Hayden Land was the first black man to hold the top job in the American military. A highly intelligent soldier and top-notch political operator, he also had the ability to think very straight when everyone else was panicking. This quality had served him well during the Gulf War several years ago when his sound leadership made him a national hero. Those in the know in national politics even mentioned him as possible presidential timber in 1996, when presumably he would be retired.

Jake Grafton had worked for Land in the past, so the general's calmness on the telephone was no surprise. Hayden Land *never* lost his cool.

'What did you want to talk about, Admiral?'

'Sir, I understand General Brown died a few days ago. I wonder if you have the autopsy results.'

'Well, I don't even know if an autopsy will be performed,'

113

General Land said. 'I thought he died at home of a heart attack.'

'One more question, sir. Have you seen a report from General Brown about listening devices being found in the DIA office spaces?'

Silence. It dragged for several seconds, 'No. Is there such a report?'

'The day I left to come over here General Brown said he was going to write one. We found the bugs a day or so before. Both he and I suspected they were planted and monitored by our friends at Langley, suspected for some very good reasons, but we had no rock-solid proof. One of the things my aide and I had discussed where it could be overheard by those bugs was the death a year or so ago of Nigel Keren, the British publisher. We thought we had some indications that someone from Langley might have killed him with binary poison.'

Jake paused for a moment. Land said nothing.

'Are you still with me, sir?'

'I'm here.'

'General Brown's death might also have been caused by binary poison. Since he apparently didn't write that report of those listening devices, I suggest you ensure that there will be an autopsy, a damn good one.'

'Just what were you and General Brown working on, Admiral?'

'We were discussing Nigel Keren, how he died, who might have killed him. I don't want to go any further into that on this telephone, sir. The KGB is probably eavesdropping. Still, this telephone was preferable to using the embassy communications systems. And I request that you don't use the telephones in your office, car or home to discuss this matter.'

More silence, then a slow, 'I think I see what you're driving at.'

'I don't know what is going on, General, but something is and I'm on the edge of it. So I need some help.'

'What?' That one-word response was pure Hayden Land. No beating around the bush, no questioning of his subordinate's assessment of the situation or demands for further information, just a straight, quick trip to the heart of the matter.

So Jake told him. The two officers talked for another twenty minutes before they spent a few minutes discussing what they were going to tell the *Washington Post* to explain this curious method of communication. Their answer — nothing at this time.

Jake straightened his uniform and put his shoes back on and locked the door behind him.

He found Toad Tarkington and Jack Yocke in the bar drinking espresso and gobbling pretzels. They both stood as Jake walked toward them.

'Thanks a lot, Jack,' Jake said.

'He called you?'

'Yes.'

'One word?' Yocke looked incredulous. 'That's all you're going to give me?'

Jake grinned. He extended his hand and the reporter took it.

As Toad and Jake were walking toward the main entrance, Yocke called, 'You owe me a steak when I get back to Washington.'

Jake lifted his hand in acknowledgment.

Out in the car Toad asked, 'Are you thinking what I'm thinking about that Yegor Somebody killing?'

'Not the Russians' style, you told Yocke. You can't hand Yocke a bone like that with meat on it, Toad — he's too smart.'

'Yeah. I'm sorry.'

'The whole thing looks like a classic in-your-face Mossad hit. Like Paris, Rome, Frankfurt, and a dozen others you could name. The KGB makes you disappear, the Mossad makes you a wire-service example.'

'Maybe the Russians are changing tactics.'

'Maybe.'

'Then again . . .'

For a while Grafton rode silently, looking out the window. Then he said, 'Say the Mossad decided to wipe a struggling young Hitler protégé and dropped a hint to someone in the Yeltsin government. Maybe some of Yeltsin's lieutenants thought the idea up. Whatever. Someone thought that Kolokoltsev's departure to Communist heaven wouldn't be an unmitigated disaster and called the cops off. That much is obvious, yet there's no way in the world to prove a damn thing on anybody. None of these clowns are ever going to breathe a word. Yocke is wasting his time asking embarrassing questions through an interpreter who is trying to keep from wetting his pants. All he'll do is irritate people who don't like to be irritated.'

Tarkington grunted. He was thinking about General Brown, smacked like a fly. 'Are you just speculating about the Mossad, Admiral, or was that a power think?'

Jake Grafton growled irritably. 'I don't know a damn thing.'

'I don't like any of this.'

'Write a letter home to mama,' Jake told him.

At least Judith Farrell is somewhere in Maryland, Toad told himself. She's mowing grass and watching baseball games on television and going to the theater on Friday nights. But even as he trotted that idea out for inspection he threw it back – he didn't believe it. He had seen her in action once, eliminating a terrorist in a Naples hotel. That memory came flooding back and he felt slightly ill.

'The Russians have their own rules,' Jake Grafton said. 'The language is different, the heritage is different, the mores are different, they don't think like we do. It's hard to believe this is the same planet we live on.'

Jake Grafton had listened for over twenty years to stories about all-male Russian dinners and vodka celebrations. They were always thirdhand or fourthhand, and the parties described sounded rather like something one might find in a college fraternity house on a Saturday night after the big football game.

And that, he thought ruefully, would be a good way to describe the festive atmosphere of which he was a reluctant part.

The problem was quite simple – he hadn't had this much to drink in years. He was sweating profusely and feeling slightly dizzy.

Across the table from him Nicolai Yakolev was telling another Russian joke, one about a high party official and a simple country girl. He had to tell it loud to be heard over the noise of the piano.

Jake had told a few of these jokes himself earlier in the evening, before the level of the fluid in the vodka bottle had gone down very far. He had never been very good with jokes – couldn't remember them long enough to find someone to tell them to – but he did recall several of those crude riddles that had been popular years ago, the so-called Polish jokes. So he transformed the bumblers into Communists and delighted the general and his guests with questions such as, How many Communists does it take to screw in a light bulb? Twelve – one to stand on the chair and hold the bulb, eleven to turn the chair.

Before dinner he had had a chance to meet the allied officers one on one.

Lieutenant Colonel West of the Queen's Own Highlanders was a deeply tanned trim man, about five feet six inches, with dark hair longer than US military regulations allowed. He seemed quite relaxed with the Russians and Jake heard him murmur a few phrases in the language.

'Delighted to see you, Admiral,' West said when they shook hands. 'Met you one time in Singapore years ago. No reason you should remember. Think you were a commander then.'

Jake seemed to think he did recall the man. 'A party with the Aussies?'

'Righto. About ten years ago. Jolly good show, that.'

Now he remembered. Jocko West, a specialist on guerrilla warfare, terrorism and jungle survival. 'You seem to have picked up a little of the local lingo, Colonel.'

West leaned closer and lowered his voice. 'Afghanistan, sir. A bit irregular, I dare say. Sort of a busman's holiday. These lads were the oppo.' He sighed. 'Well, the world turns, eh?'

The Frenchman was Colonel Reynaud, impeccably uniformed. He spent dinner chatting with two Russian officers in French. Prior to dinner, when he and Jake were introduced, he used English, which he spoke with a delicious accent. 'A pleas-aire, Admiral Grafton.'

'How did you manage to wrangle a trip to Moscow in the summertime, Colonel?'

'I am a student of Napoleon, sir, you comprehend? Think, had Napoleon arrived in the summer, perhaps history would have been so different, without these Communists. I came to see where it went wrong for him, for France. So I will do a little of work, a little of the seeing of the sights.'

'The people at my embassy told me you are an expert on nuclear weapons.'

Reynaud smiled. 'Alas, that is true. I study the big boom. In a way it is unmilitary, *n'est-ce pas?* The nuclear weapons will make *la guerre* so short, it will not be *la guerre*. They leave us without honor. It is not pretty.'

Jake managed to shake hands with Colonel Rheinhart, the German, and Colonel Galvano, the Italian, but he didn't get to visit with them until after dinner. They both impressed him as extremely competent officers of great ability. Rheinhart was the smaller of the two, a man whom the American embassy said had a doctorate in physics from the University of Heidelberg.

'Herr Colonel, or should I address you as Herr Doctor?'

The German laughed easily. One got the impression that Rheinhart would be a valuable officer in anyone's army.

Galvano was not as easy to read, perhaps because Jake had difficulty understanding his English. Still, he looked fit and highly intelligent, as all four of the colonels did. Their nations had sent the best they had, Jake concluded, and that best was very good indeed.

As he surveyed these officers at dinner he had wondered about his own selection. He was certainly not a weapons expert or diplomat. Could he get the job done? Looking at the foreign officers, he had his doubts. Then his eyes came to rest on Herb Tenney and the doubts evaporated. He had met a few slick bastards in his career and he thought he knew how to handle them, or at least get them sidetracked where they wouldn't do anyone any harm. He reached for his glass and had it almost to his lips when he remembered General Albert Sidney Brown. His hand shook slightly. He lowered the glass to the table without spilling any of the liquid.

Two hours after dinner General Yakolev still seemed fairly sober considering how much he had had to drink – at least two for every one of Jake's. He was sweating and having some trouble forming his English words, yet he looked pretty steady nonetheless.

A miracle.

Right now Jake Grafton felt like he was going to be sick. He excused himself and made for the rest room, where he found Toad Tarkington.

'What in hell do they put in that Russian moon-shine anyway?' Toad demanded. 'It tastes like Tabasco sauce.'

Jake upchucked into a commode, then used his hand-kerchief to swab his face with cold water. His hands were shaking. Fear or vodka?

'You okay?' he asked Toad.

'About three sheets to the wind, CAG. I'm ready to blow this pop stand anytime you say.'

'A red hot night in Po City, huh?'

'I'm ready to go back-ship.'

'Give me another fifteen minutes or so. In the meantime get out there and mix and mingle.'

Jake led General Yakolev over to a corner where they wouldn't be so easily overheard. 'General, you impress me as a professional soldier.'

Yakolev didn't reply to that. His smile seemed frozen. God, his eyes seemed completely hidden behind those brows!

'I think you have brains and balls,' Jake added.

'The balls yes, but the brains? I have doubts. Others have doubts also.'

'I have a little problem that I need some help with,' Jake said as he fought the feeling that he wasn't handling this right. Why had he drunk those last two shots of vodka? This just wasn't going to work! He turned away with a sense of defeat, then turned back. What the hey, give it a shot. 'I'd like to ask a favor.'

Yakolev made a gesture that might have meant anything.

'I've had too much of your vodka. I'm having a little trouble saying this right. But I honestly need a favor.'

The general looked as foreign as an Iranian ayatollah. Jake pushed out the words. 'I want you to have a man arrested tomorrow.'

Now he could see Yakolev's eyes. They were locked on his own. 'Let's go into my office,' the Russian said. 'It's quiet there.'

The following day was overcast and gloomy when the contingent of foreign military observers gathered in the large room adjacent to General Yakolev's office where they had dined the night before. None of them looked the worse for wear, Jake thought as he surveyed them through eyes that felt like dirty marbles. He tried to slow the rate of blinking and swallowing, but he couldn't seem to affect it much.

The six aspirin had helped. At least he felt human again. Last night around midnight he had cursed himself for being a damn fool. After he and Yakolev had closeted themselves in the general's office, the old Russian had produced another vodka bottle from his desk drawer.

The last thing Jake remembered was a promise from the general that he would talk to the Foreign Intelligence Service, a name that gave the general a good laugh. Jake had laughed Like hell too because he was drunk.

Stinking drunk. God, how long had it been since he got so stinking, puking, deathly drunk? Fifteen . . . no, almost seventeen years. Make that eighteen.

Toad had driven him back to the embassy. He had passed out by then. He woke up in the bathroom hanging over the commode.

This morning he tried to pay attention as the Russian Army briefing officers used maps and charts to explain how the tactical warheads were being shipped to the disassembly site at an army base on the eastern side of the Volga river.

Herb Tenney was supposed to be here, but he wasn't. Jake and Toad had skipped breakfast and driven to the Kremlin in their own car, one of the black Fords the embassy used. Toad said Herb was coming on his own.

The briefing was an hour old when a soldier slipped into the room and handed General Yakolev a note. He read it, then interrupted the briefers and suggested a pause. He motioned to Jake.

'As you requested, your friend has been arrested.'

'Where is he?'

'KGB Headquarters. The soldier waiting outside will drive you there.'

KGB Headquarters on Dzerzhinsky Square was an imposing yellow building – the Russians seemed fond of yellow on public buildings. No doubt it made a nice contrast with the red flags that had hung everywhere in the not too distant past. Still, even with the cheerful yellow facade the building seemed to dominate the naked pedestal and traffic in the square below.

The driver steered the car to an entrance in the back and showed a document to the uniformed gate guard. Parked in the semidarkness under the building under the scrutiny of several armed soldiers, the driver remained behind the wheel of the car.

Jake and Toad were escorted through endless dark corridors by a slovenly man in an ill-fitting blue suit. The corridors had a smell, a light, foul odor. Jake was trying to place it when they went around a corner and there they were – the cells. They were small, dark. Some of them contained men. At least they looked like men, shadowy figures in the back of the cells who turned their backs on the visitors.

Terror. He had smelled terror, some evil mixture of sweat, stale urine, feces, vomit and fear. Looking at the forms of the men behind the bars and trying to see their faces, Jake Grafton felt his stomach turn.

He was perspiring when the guard opened a door at the end of the corridor, and unexpectedly they were in an office. There was a man in uniform behind the desk, the green uniform of the Soviet army, only this one wasn't in the army. He was a KGB general. He didn't rise from behind his desk, although he did look up. The escort left the room and closed the door behind him.

'Admiral Grafton.'

'Yes.'

'I am General Shmarov.'

Jake Grafton just nodded and looked slowly around the room. A large framed print of Lenin on the wall, which had once been green and was now merely earth-tone dirty. There was a window behind the general and it was even dirtier than the walls. Three padded chairs in poor condition. The desk. A telephone. And the KGB general.

Shmarov's bald head gleamed. Even with his mouth shut you could see that his teeth were crooked. Now he spoke again and Jake caught the gleam of gold. 'General Yakolev asked for a favor, so I was glad to help.'

Grafton couldn't think of a thing to say.

'Nicolai Alexandrovich is a friend.'

'Thanks,' Jake managed.

'Here is the passport.' The Russian held it out and Jake took it. It was a US diplomatic passport. He flipped it open. Herbert Peter Tenney. Jake thumbed the pages, which were festooned with entry and exit stamps. Tenney certainly got around. He passed it back to the general.

'Now if you'll just check it to see if it's genuine.'

'But of course.' A flash of gold.

The door opened and the escort in the blue suit was there waiting. Shmarov nodded his head. Grafton returned the nod and wheeled to follow the escort. Toad trailed along behind.

The room where the two Americans ended up contained only a table and a few chairs. On the table were clothes and shoes, a coat, a briefcase.

'His things,' Blue Suit said, and gestured.

'Everything?' Toad asked.

'Everything. He is being X-rayed. To see that nothing inside, then back to cell.'

'Thank you.'

Blue Suit gestured to the table, then pulled up a chair and sat down to watch. He took out a cigarette and lit it.

Jake took the briefcase while Toad started on the shoes.

The briefcase was plastic, with a plastic handle. It was unlocked, so he opened it and removed the contents, a legal pad, paper and pencils. Nothing else was inside. He examined the pens, cheap ballpoints, then disassembled them.

The padded handle of the briefcase showed wear but seemed innocuous. Jake used his penknife to cut it open. Nothing. Then he used the knife to slice out the padding that coated the interior of the case.

Their escort left the room for a moment, then returned with pliers, a screwdriver and a magnifying glass. Jake used the screwdriver to take off the tiny metal feet of the case.

Finally he turned his attention to the shoes. The laces, the heels, everything was examined closely and minutely with the magnifying glass.

When Toad began looking at the case, Jake turned his attention to the clothes – trousers, shirt, underwear, socks, tie, jacket and coat. He felt every seam and probed every questionable thickness with his pocketknife.

The suit wore a label from Woodward & Lothrop, a well-known department store in the Washington, DC, area. Jake shopped there himself on occasion. The belt was cut from a single piece of cowhide and had a hand-tooled hunting scene on it. The buckle was a simple metal one. A Christmas or birthday present, probably. After scrutinizing every inch of it as carefully as he could with the glass, he began leafing through the contents of the prisoner's pockets, which were contained in a cardboard box. A couple of keys, a wallet, a handful of loose ruble notes and American dollar bills, a fingernail clipper, a piece of broken shoelace, an odd white button that looked as if it was off a dress shirt, a key very similar to the one in Jake's pocket that probably opened Herb Tenney's room at Fort Apache – that was the crop.

Toad watched him examine everything under the magnifying glass, then helped him spread the contents of the wallet on one end of the table. Driver's license, credit cards, a library card, a folded *Far Side* cartoon torn from a newspaper, several hundred American dollars in currency, a receipt from a laundry in Virginia.

Toad perched on the edge of the table. 'Agent 007 always had a pocketful of goodies. I'm disappointed in our boy.'

'What should be here and isn't?'

Toad glanced at the Russian. 'What do you mean?'

'Is there anything you would expect to find him carrying around that isn't here?'

Toad surveyed the little pile, then shook his head. 'I can't think of anything. Except maybe an appointment or memo book with some phone numbers. A bottle of invisible ink, a suicide pill, I don't know.'

'All his phone numbers are in his head.'

Jake picked up the keys, held them where the Russian could see them, then stuck them in his pocket.

'Let's go do the car,' he told Blue Suit as he handed back the magnifying glass and hand tools. 'We'll keep the keys and bring them back in a few hours.'

The man nodded and pulled the door open.

Back at Fort Apache one of the keys opened the door to room 402. The room number was right on the key. Jake Grafton turned on the lights. 'Go find Spiro Dalworth. I want screwdrivers, pliers, a magnifying glass, a big sharp knife from the kitchen. My pocketknife is too small.'

'Yes, sir.' Toad left.

Jake went into the bathroom and picked up all the toilet articles. He spread them out on a table and examined each of them.

The problem was that he didn't know what form the binary poison would be in, if it were here at all. A liquid would be the easiest to administer but the hardest to transport. Pills or powder would be easier to carry and almost as efficient. But any water-soluble solid would do, he thought, so even an object like a button or a pencil eraser might be the object he sought.

Now he sat looking at some tablets. A small plastic aspirin bottle with a child-proof lid contained the usual small white pills. He counted them. All of them had the word *aspirin* impressed into the surface. On one side. No, wait a minute. Some had the word on both sides. Huh! He separated the pills into two piles. Eight one-side-only and six both-sides, fourteen tablets total.

He put them back into the bottle and slipped the bottle into his pocket.

When Toad and Lieutenant Dalworth arrived, he put them to searching. 'I want to see any pills or powder or

125

liquid you can find. Anything that might form a hidden container. Look carefully.'

Dalworth looked puzzled, but he asked no questions.

An hour later they decided that everything had been examined by all three of them.

'Mr Dalworth, thank you for your help. We'll sort of straighten everything out and lock the door when we leave. Of course, I'll appreciate it if you would keep this little adventure to yourself.'

Dalworth's eyes went to Toad, then back to Jake. 'I don't suppose this would be a good place to ask questions.'

'You're very perceptive, Spiro,' Toad said.

When the door closed behind him and Toad had checked to make sure that Mr Dalworth didn't have his ear against it, Jake removed the aspirin bottle from his pocket and spread out the tablets on the desk. 'Take a look at these, Toad.'

Tarkington used the magnifying glass. 'Well, they look like aspirin, but I dunno.'

'I have some aspirin on the bathroom sink in my room. Will you get them, please.'

They filled a tumbler with water and dropped one of Jake's aspirin in it. In twenty seconds the tablet had dissolved to a mound of white powder. After thirty seconds had passed they swirled it and the powder covered the bottom of the glass. After a minute it was still there.

Now Jake took one of the tablets with the double-sided label and dropped it into a fresh glass of water. It too dissolved rapidly, but without leaving the powder residue. The entire tablet went into solution.

'Thank God for the scientific method,' Toad muttered. 'When I was a kid I got a microscope one year for Christmas.'

Jake saved six tablets from his bottle and dumped the rest down the toilet. Those six he put in Herb Tenney's bottle. Herb's five remaining pills went into Jake's bottle.

As they folded clothes and replaced them in the suitcase

and dresser, Toad said, 'He's going to know someone was in here.'

'I suspect so.'

'Dalworth may blab.'

'He might.'

'You sure you got this figured out, CAG?'

'No.'

Toad touched Jake's arm. 'You're betting both our lives, you know.'

Jake just looked at him. 'I'm aware of that,' he said finally. 'If you have any ideas I'm always open to suggestions.'

Toad went back to straightening the closet. After a moment he said, 'I suggest we shoot friend Tenney and find a hole to stuff him and his aspirin bottle into.'

When Jake didn't respond, Toad added in a tight little voice, 'Of course you have carefully calculated all the possible reasons why there were two less of those pills marked on both sides than there were of the other kind.' His voice was sarcastic. 'No doubt you've weighed it, pondered on it, considered every possible aspect and come to some intricate, subtle conclusion that a mere junior officer mortal like me couldn't possibly appreciate.'

'What do you want me to say?' Jake replied patiently. 'That Herb probably took two for a toothache? We both know he probably fed them to us. Us and half the people in this embassy.'

'We really oughta take this guy out into the forest and make him dig his own hole. I kid you not.'

'KGB Headquarters must have really gotten to you.'

'Yes, sir. It sure as hell did. I admit it. I about vomited all over that fucking general's desk.'

'Hurry up. Let's get this done. We have to get back for the afternoon briefing.'

'How do you know,' Toad asked, 'that those are all the binary pills Herb has access to?'

'I don't.'

'He could have some in his desk in the CIA office, he

could have some stashed in any hidey-hole he thought handy. He can just ask Langley for more.'

'What a deep thinker you are! Let's hope he doesn't find out we took a few.'

'What if he runs short? What if he's embarked on a major urban renewal project?'

'You ask too many questions.'

'You and I are going to end up dead,' Toad said sourly.

'Sooner or later,' Grafton replied. What was there to say? Herb and his colleagues must have killed General Brown so that he wouldn't make waves. The job was only half done as long as Jake and Toad were wandering around upright.

'The whole fucking CIA can go to fucking hell for all I care,' Tarkington said crossly. When he got no reply, he muttered something to himself that Grafton didn't catch.

CHAPTER EIGHT

Butyrskaya Prison looked like something from a Kafka nightmare, Jack Yocke decided, and jotted the thought on a blank page of his notebook as he sat in the waiting room.

The Russian interpreter sitting on the bench across from him was as nervous as a pickpocket at a policeman's ball. He gnawed on a fingernail already into the quick, then stared at the sliver of nail still remaining. He pushed on the raw quick experimentally and grimaced. He crossed and recrossed his feet and stared morosely at the filthy paint on the wall and the dirty floor. He carefully avoided looking at any of the other people slumped on the wooden benches.

Yocke wondered about this desire to avoid even eye contact. After sweeping each of the other eight people in the room, his gaze returned to the uncomfortable interpreter, Gregor Something, Gregor followed by five or six Slavic syllables that sounded to Yocke's American ear like a pig grunting. Two days ago Gregor jackrabbited away from Soviet Square, yet the following morning he showed up at Yocke's hotel as if nothing had happened.

Still glowing with the virtuous warmth of his new-found heroism and curiously eager to make this gutless wonder squirm a little, Yocke asked, 'Why did you run?'

'My wife was ill.'

Gregor didn't blink or blush, didn't look away, even when Yocke sneered.

To be able to lie outrageously and shamelessly was an asset, Jack Yocke told himself, one that would of course stand Gregor in good stead here in this workers' paradise of poverty and desperation, but it would also be a cheerful bullet for his résumé even in brighter climes, such as the US of A. Across the pond in the land of the free and home of the brave he could lie like a dog to clients and customers, cheat on his spouse, steal from his employer, write creative fiction for the IRS, and in the unlikely event he ever got caught he could fool the lie detector and skip away with a happy smile. This multilingual grunter would fit right in, as red, white and blue as a telephone solicitor hyping penny stocks to shut-in geriatrics. Once he got his fastball high and tight he could even become a politician.

This morning in the waiting room of Butyrskaya Yocke asked Gregor, 'Have you ever thought of emigrating to America?'

'My wife's cousin lives in Brooklyn.'

Yocke stared.

'Brooklyn, New York.'

'I'm trying to recall if I ever heard of Brooklyn. It's out west, isn't it? With cowboys and Indians and tumble-weeds?'

'Perhaps,' Gregor said softly. 'I don't know. My wife's cousin drives a taxi and earns many dollars. He likes America.' He shrugged.

'America is a great country.'

'He drives a Chevrolet. Only five years old.' He glanced at the other people in the room to see who was listening. One or two had glanced up at the sound of a foreign language, but now all but one had retreated into their self-imposed isolation.

'Umm,' said Jack Yocke, looking hard at the young man who was looking at them. He had longish hair and an air of quiet desperation. His gaze wavered, then fell away.

'Petrol is cheap there, my wife's cousin says. Every day he drives many many miles. All the streets are paved.'

A door opened and a man passed through the waiting room. Jack Yocke caught a whiff of the prison smell. He had smelled it before in the jails of Washington, a devil's brew of urine, body odor and fear. Yocke delicately inhaled a thimbleful as Gregor regaled his listener with the adventures of his wife's cousin in his Chevy on the paved boulevards of Brooklyn.

Two minutes after Yocke reached saturation, a man came through one of the doorways and spoke to Gregor, then led the way along endless dingy corridors. The warden's corner office was big and had a carpet. A dial phone straight out of the 1930s sat on the wooden desk.

The warden came around the desk to shake hands, then trotted back around the desk and arranged himself in his chair. He was a sloppy fat man with a heavy five-o'clock shadow that made his skin look dingy gray.

Gregor and the warden nattered a while in Russian, then Gregor turned to Yocke. 'He welcomes the correspondent for the American newspaper *Post* to Butyrskaya.'

'Thank him for taking the time to see me.' Of course Yocke had an appointment, arranged by an official with the Yeltsin government, but he was willing to pretend this was a social call.

More Russian.

'Ask your questions.'

'I am here today at the request of the editor of my newspaper, the most influential newspaper in the United States. Everyone in Washington reads my newspaper every day, from Hillary Clinton right on down. Everyone, including all the people in the Senate and House of Representatives. Tell him that.'

After an Uzi-burst of Russian, Yocke continued. 'I am here to interview Yakov Dynkin, a Jew who was convicted of arranging the sale of a private automobile for profit. I understand he was sentenced to five years in the gulag at hard labor.'

The warden's face lost its friendliness as Gregor translated. Yocke didn't understand the words, but he understood the tone. The interpreter said, 'Yakov Dynkin is not here. No Jews are here.'

'Has he been shipped to the gulag?'

'No,' was the answer that came back. Just no.

Yocke thought about it. Dynkin wasn't here and he hadn't been shipped to the gulag. 'Have they turned him loose with a pardon or probation?'

The warden merely frowned.

Yocke extracted a press clipping from his jacket pocket. He handed it to Gregor and pointed at the appropriate paragraph. 'Two weeks ago Tass said Dynkin was here. There it is in black and white.' Gregor stared at the clipping. 'Go on! Show him that and tell him I wish to see Dynkin and write about what wonderful treatment he is receiving here at Butyrskaya even though he was convicted of violating a law that was repealed a week before he was arrested.'

Slowly, as if this were costing him a major portion of his pension, Gregor passed the piece of paper across the desk. The warden refused to touch it, so it came to rest in the empty spot on the desk in front of him. He bent over and looked at the English words without showing the slightest glimmer of comprehension.

After a few seconds the warden picked up the offending paper and handed it back to Yocke, who accepted it. Another spray of words.

'He says you are wrong. Dynkin is not here. No Jews are here.'

'Where are they?'

'He doesn't know. Is there anything else he can help you with?'

'Couldn't he consult his records or something and tell me if Dynkin has ever been here? Or when he left. Or where he is.'

Gregor considered.

'These people do have records, I assume, something scribbled somewhere to tell them who is rotting in what hole . . .'

Gregor spoke to Yocke as if he were a small boy incapable of understanding the obvious. 'He is not here.'

'Who are you working for? Him or me? Ask him the question.'

'But he has told you the answer. What more could he possibly say? The warden is a powerful senior official. If he says the man is not here, then he is not. That is all there is to that.'

Jack Yocke smiled at the warden. He then turned the grin on Gregor. 'This fat geek is lying through his teeth. These greasy Commie bastards railroaded Dynkin for making an honest ruble just because he's a Jew. They've got him locked up somewhere in the large intestines of this shit factory. This pompous son of a bitch knows the whole prosecution was a farce to fuck Jews and embarrass Yeltsin and his people, make them look like lying hypocrites when they go begging in America and Europe for foreign aid. Dynkin sold a car for a profit and these old Commies are grinding him into hamburger.'

Gregor's face was frozen, immobile. Even his eyes were blank.

'Ask him if it's true that about a hundred and twenty thousand people are still imprisoned in labor camps for doing business that is legal in Russia today. Ask him.'

Gregor put his tongue in motion. After a few syllables from the warden, the translator told Yocke, 'He doesn't know.'

'Ask him how Russia can establish a free market-economy if it keeps all these people in prison for earning a profit.'

Gregor looked at his shoes.

'Ask him!'

The translator's head moved from side to side, about a millimeter.

Yocke flashed another broad grin at the warden. 'Come on, Gregor. There's a story here. These Commies ain't got religion. They're still the same filthy, diseased assholes they always were. They screwed Dynkin to get at Yeltsin. You can see *that*, can't you? They can't get away with it if we tell it to the world.'

Gregor's face looked as bad as Lenin's, who had been dead for over sixty years.

'Don't chicken out on me again,' Yocke pleaded. 'Think up something that will open up this pig's . . .'

But Gregor was leaving. He stood and nodded obsequiously to the warden while he jabbered away like a parrot with a hard on. The warden expended the effort to get to his feet. He tugged his jacket down over his gut and adjusted his tie. He grinned at Yocke and thrust out his hand.

At a loss for what to do next, Yocke closed his mouth, gave the warden's soft hand a token pump, then followed the retreating Gregor.

Going down the corridor Yocke demanded, 'What did you tell that fat screw?'

'Screw? What is a screw?'

'A prison guard. A power pervert.'

Gregor gave Yocke a look that was about an equal mixture of contempt and amazement and kept walking.

Outside in the street, Gregor exploded. 'You can't talk to a powerful person like you did in there. This is *Butyrskaya!* Are you *insane?* Do you know *nothing?*' He sprayed saliva.

'My newspaper sent me to get a story,' Yocke snarled. 'That asshole was lying! He didn't even look at the records. What a crock! You people have held your nose so long that you can't smell shit when you're in it up to your ears. You've been fucked by these people for seventy-five years because you bent over and grabbed your ankles and held the position. You gutless wonders will—'

Gregor spit at Yocke's feet. 'You are a little boy throwing pebbles at a great bear. The chain holding the bear is very rusty, very weak. If you arouse him you will end up in his belly and no one at your rich newspaper in Washington USA will ever know what became of you.' He snapped his fingers. 'Like that. You will be gone. You and your dirty words and stupid questions and your notebook where you write your words making fun of us. Gone forever, Mister Jack Yocke. Think about that if you have any brains to think with.'

They went to Gregor's tiny Soviet sedan and shoe-horned themselves in. Sitting there with his knees jammed against the dashboard, Yocke said, 'Why don't you drop the *kru-lak* act and stop feeding me bullshit?'

'Why don't you stop acting like stupid Yankee billionaire looking down his nose?'

'I will if you will.'

Gregor inserted his key in the ignition, then glanced sideways at Yocke. 'Standing in Soviet Square while gunmen shoot bullets was the most grotesque' – he had to search for words – 'the most dumbest stupid thing I have ever in my life seen. Everyone ran because those who shoot don't want anyone to see their faces. We stupid Russians think of that real quick.' He bobbed his head once and snapped his fingers. 'Even if stray bullets don't kill you the gunmen will if you stand there like you are watching old men play chess. And *you* hung there on the side of the speaker's platform, an ape in the zoo. *You* weren't shot – a miracle, like an immaculate conception. Truly there is a God and he looks after grotesque stupidly Americans.'

Jack Yocke's embarrassment showed on his face. 'Well, that was sorta . . .'

Gregor pointed at the prison. 'In there, you shot your mouth.'

'Shot my mouth off.'

'Yes. Off. Shot mouth off. Can warden speak English?' Gregor shrugged grandly. 'Was the office bugged by people who tape and listen?' He shrugged again. 'Can the people who tape and listen speak English?' Another shrug. 'Will the warden tell something he has been told not to tell to *you*, an American reporter to write in your glorious important foreign newspaper God knows what?' He lifted his hands and raised his eyebrows.

'Rub it in.'

'Okay.' He used his knuckles to rub Yocke's head. 'There. It's rubbed in. You Americans!'

'So what happened to Yakov Dynkin?' Yocke asked as he tried to smooth his hair back into place with his fingers.

'We could spend the afternoon thinking possibilities. He is dead. Moved to another prison. Maybe sick. Maybe released. Maybe in Siberia. Maybe used to clean up mess at Chernobyl. Whatever, for us he is no more.'

'Then why did the warden say no Jews were here? Most liars don't expand the tale beyond what is necessary.'

'Oh?'

'Why tell a whopper if a little lie will do? If Dynkin's dead—'

'I don't know.' Another shrug.

'Let's try to find Dynkin's wife. I have her address written down here someplace.'

Gregor turned the key and the engine caught after only three seconds of grinding.

The apartment building was one of dozens in a sprawling area outside the second Moscow loop. They all looked alike, five stories high, splotchy plaster, flat roofs, not a tree in sight. They found the one they wanted because it had a number painted on one corner.

Yocke looked it over and began to compose his story in his head. The adjectives, nouns and verbs came effortlessly as he looked at the appalling, dreary buildings and tried to imagine what it would be like to call one of these concrete cell blocks home.

But he kept his thoughts to himself. Gregor probably lived in an apartment house like this. Or wished he did.

When Gregor parked and killed the engine, Yocke laid a hand on his arm. 'Let's see if we can reach an understanding between us. I'm a foreigner, a stranger. I'm here because the American people are interested in Russia and my newspaper wants to print the stories. All I want to do is understand. If I can understand what is going on, I can write it. But I need to get the truth. I need to get it anyway I can.'

Gregor stared straight ahead. 'In Russia there is no such thing as truth. There is only what you write, and it is good for someone and bad for someone else.'

That comment seemed to give Yocke no opening, so he attacked in another direction. 'Are you for democracy?'

Gregor considered. 'Maybe.'

Yocke frowned. Aloud he said, 'For democracy to work, people have to know what is really happening. My job is to find out.'

Come on, Jack! You sound like a candidate for county sheriff. Even you don't believe *that* treacle. You are employed by the owners of the newspaper to make them money, to write stories that sell newspapers. To keep the long green flowing they aren't too picky about who they screw, an attitude they share with hundred-dollar, have-a-nice-day hookers. Now that is *truth* as red, white and blue as a Harley tattoo.

'This isn't America,' Gregor explained patiently, damn him!

The reporter grasped his door handle and pulled. 'It's a hell of a lot closer than you think,' he muttered through clenched teeth.

Jake Grafton and Toad Tarkington sat in General Yakolev's car in the alley behind KGB Headquarters while they waited for the driver to return the keys. Toad was in the front beside the driver's seat. He stared at the cut-stone walls morosely. Herb Tenney was in the belly of the beast and that was a good place for him, he told himself. Unfortunately Herb would be out dancing in the sunbeams in about an hour.

Jake Grafton had properly rejected his spur-of-the-moment proposal to send Herb on to his next incarnation. The complexities of the proof problem troubled Toad not a whit: he *knew* Herb was guilty – but there undoubtedly were other people involved in Herb Tenney's slimy little mess; there *had* to be. Maybe as few as three or four others, maybe

137

the whole damned CIA, all sixteen thousand of them slopping through kimchi right up to their plastic photo ID badges. As usual Grafton was right. Why trade the devil you knew for heaven knows how many you didn't?

And just what was Herb's mess? If the CIA were merely squashing billionaires like stinkbugs, that could be forgiven as some kind of kinky weekend sport, sort of like tennis with live grenades. If they switched to American billionaires they could probably get a TV contract and sell tickets. No, if that were the game they wouldn't be so twitchy.

So what *was* going on?

Keren was a newspaper mogul, wasn't he? Perhaps his papers had uncovered something the CIA didn't want uncovered. Now that made sense. Arms for Iran? Cocaine for guns? Maybe something to do with the last American election.

But all of this was pure speculation. He was trying to guess what the puzzle looked like after getting a fuzzy glimpse of one small piece.

Toad glanced over his shoulder at the admiral in the backseat. He too was looking at the grim secret police headquarters and the grotesquely ugly buildings across the street, but his face showed no emotion.

You're never gonna be an admiral, Toad-man. Never! You don't have the cool for it.

His mind turned from that happy subject to his serious contemplation of the murder of a fellow human being. He had been serious, he reminded himself guiltily. What if Grafton had said yes? Then it would have been his responsibility. No, Toad told himself, then it would have been the responsibility of both of you.

Are you that frightened of Herb? Toad asked himself.

Yes!

In spite of the mild temperature, Toad Tarkington shivered.

Toad almost went to sleep in the afternoon briefing, a technical seminar on how properly to dispose of nuclear warheads. The speakers were physicists and chemists and weapons designers, all of whom were in love with their subjects as far as Toad could tell.

When Herb Tenney slipped in and dropped into an empty seat, Toad came wide awake. Herb looked none the worse for his ordeal and sat listening as if he could actually understand this technical mumbo jumbo.

Toad tried to ignore Herb, which was difficult. He well knew that some people could sense when they were being watched, and he didn't want Herb to get the idea that he and Grafton were responsible for his recent unpleasantness, at least not for a while.

Still, when the break in the presentation came and he saw Jake Grafton angling through the crowd for Herb, Toad managed to be within earshot.

'Herb, I thought you were going to be here this morning,' the admiral said.

'I'm sorry, sir. Something came up unexpectedly.'

'*This* is important,' Grafton replied.

'I'm aware of that.' Toad thought this reply had just a trace of disrespect in it, which would be typical of the Herb Tenney he had come to know and love.

'We're supposed to be working together on this, Mr Tenney,' Jake said, his voice so low Toad had to step closer to catch the words. 'I don't know what else you have going on here in Moscow and I don't really care, but if you can't give this assignment the attention required then I'm going to have to report you to Washington. I expect you to be at official functions clean and sober and on time.'

'It won't happen again,' Tenney replied matter-of-factly, without a trace of rancor.

'Fine,' Jake said, and walked away.

That evening back at the embassy Toad Tarkington dug into his luggage. A couple years ago at a Virginia pawnshop he had purchased a Walther PPK, a slick little automatic in .380 ACP caliber. It had probably once belonged to a cop who had used it as a hideout gun because it had a spring-steel clip spot-welded onto the left side of the slide. The clip allowed the pistol to be slipped behind the waistband in the small of the back and hooked onto the top of the trousers. It rode there quite nicely, such a small package that it would usually escape notice, yet it could be drawn easily with the right hand.

He had brought along only enough shells to load the magazine once, so he did that now and slipped the magazine into the pistol. He cycled the slide to put a round in the chamber, then lowered the hammer. He tucked the pistol into the small of his back, checking carefully to make sure the clip engaged his waistband, then fluffed his shirt out over the protruding grip.

It wasn't much of a gun. Still, it felt good to have it.

He had brought more gun along, a 9mm Browning Hi Power, but it was too bulky to tote around unobtrusively. Toad got out the Browning and cycled the slide and sat on the bed thinking about Herb Tenney and his little white pills.

He pointed the gun at the mirror above the dresser and squeezed the trigger. The hammer fell with a metallic thunk.

He lay back on the bed and closed his eyes. Now he remembered the little square of paper he had found in the pocket of the shirt he was wearing when he unfolded it this morning. He fished it from his wallet and held it up where he could read it.

> *Your touch, your kisses*
> *open the pathways to my heart*

Rita was fond of writing little love notes and putting them where he would find them at a moment when he least expected it. He wondered when she had written this one.

Perhaps when she was ironing the shirts, the afternoon he was packing. Or days before.

Rita . . .

Funny, but when he was dating and playing the field he had never realized how much he could love a woman. Or how much a woman could love him.

Strange how life reveals its mysteries. Just when you think you have the game scoped out, that you know all the rules and all the intricacies, all it has to offer, a new rich vein of truth reveals itself.

Rita is what you have to lose, Toad Tarkington. Death is not the threat. That's coming sooner or later any way you cut the cards. The richness of life with Rita and the extraordinary gift of *what might be* – that is what Herb Tenney and his little white pills can deprive you of.

He held the Browning up where he could see it. Without realizing it he had eared back the hammer.

He pulled the trigger and listened again to the thunk as the hammer slammed down.

The embassy residents were at dinner when Herb Tenney dusted his bathroom sink with fingerprint powder. Yes, there were fingerprints there, most of them smeared but a couple fairly nice. He used tape to lift the best ones and placed the tape on a white file card.

Back at his desk he compared the prints to those on the fax he had received an hour ago on the CIA's private com equipment. One of them was a perfect match.

So Jake Grafton had personally searched the place. That dweeb Tarkington was probably with him when he did it. The fax also supplied him with a copy of Tarkington's fingerprints, but developing more raw prints for comparison hardly seemed worth the effort. Herb Tenney sighed and stowed the bottle of powder and the brush and tape in the fingerprint kit.

That arrest this morning had been a farce. They had stopped his car a block from the embassy and handcuffed him. Then a Russian had driven him and his car to KGB Headquarters. There he was escorted to a cell and stripped and X-rayed.

He had spent three hours sitting stark naked in an isolation cell before they returned his clothes. Throughout the entire experience no one had asked him a single question. Not when they picked him up, during the ride to the prison, nor while they were holding him.

After he was dressed, a man in a blue suit led him through the corridors to an office. Sitting behind the desk pawing through the stuff that had been in his pockets was General Shmarov.

'Find anything interesting?'

Shmarov held up the white button that came off yesterday's shirt and looked from it to the CIA officer. 'Maybe the cleverest transmitter I have yet seen, Tenney.'

Then he grinned and tossed the button on top of the currency and passport lying there. 'Sorry for the inconvenience today.'

'Was this supposed to be funny? Should I laugh now?'

Shmarov shrugged. 'You know how these things are. I was asked to do a favor by a very high officer in the Defense Ministry. He wanted your passport checked. How could I refuse? He had been asked to do this by an American naval officer.'

'Rear Admiral Grafton? He was here?'

'Yes. Grafton. With an aide. Did he leave any of your seams intact?'

Tenney found a chair and dropped into it. 'I think I caught a cold in your dungeon. I never realized how drafty these damned places are.'

'They searched your car and took the keys that were in your pocket. They brought them back a few minutes ago.' General Shmarov displayed the keys and placed them beside the button on top of the rubles and dollars. He lit a cigarette, took a deep drag, and filled the room with smoke. Then he said, 'Want to tell me what this is about?'

142

'I'm as mystified as you are, General,' Herb Tenney told him.

Shmarov displayed his gold teeth in a grin and puffed some more on his cigarette.

'Who rubbed out Kolokoltsev?'

The golden grin disappeared. Shmarov stubbed out the cigarette and stared through the dissipating smoke at his visitor. 'Someone who wanted to make a lot of trouble. They succeeded.'

'Hard to believe that something like that could happen here in Moscow, almost under your nose. Soviet Square is what, a half mile from here? A kilometer?'

'What do you know about it, Tenney?'

Herb Tenney got up and approached the desk. He picked up his things and placed them in his pockets. Then he put his knuckles on the desk and stared into Shmarov's face. 'I think it looks as if you people killed your own guys so you could set up Yeltsin. They'll think that over at the Kremlin. They'll think it in Washington too. Whoever pulled the cops out of that square really screwed the pooch.'

'We are not that stupid.'

'I'll tell them that at Langley. But if I were you I'd find someone to hang it on, and damn quick.'

The ringing phone woke Jake Grafton. He had thrown himself on the bed and just dozed off.

'Grafton.'

'Admiral, this is Jack Yocke.'

'Hey.'

'I was wondering if you could come over for a drink.'

'Well, I don't think—'

'See you within an hour, Admiral, in my room.' And Yocke hung up.

Jake cradled the receiver and swung his feet over onto the floor. He looked at his watch. Eleven at night. He was still fighting the jet lag and hangover and he felt lethargic, unable to concentrate. He put on his shoes and splashed some cold water from the sink onto his face.

Yocke's room was on the fourth floor of the hotel. He opened the door at Toad's knock. 'Come in.'

When he had the door closed Yocke said, 'General Land called a little while ago. You're to wait here with me.'

'For what? Another phone call?'

Yocke shrugged. 'I just take messages and deliver them.'

Jake sank into the one stuffed chair.

'How's the foreign correspondent these days?' Toad asked Yocke as he dropped onto the bed.

'He's right in the middle of the biggest story in Russia and he can't make heads or tails of it,' Yocke replied, staring at Jake Grafton. 'Can't print it either.'

'I guess assassins can be tough to interview if you can't find them.'

'That isn't the story I meant. Anyway, my editor took me off that and gave it to the senior man. I'm doing political stuff. Y'know, "Today the Russian Ministry of Economics announced a new stabilization policy for the ruble." Drivel like that.' He sighed. 'Other than that, the food here is barely edible and grotesquely expensive, the vodka tastes like rubbing alcohol, my bed is lumpy, the pillow's too big, and I had a devil of a time yesterday getting a roll of toilet paper from the maid. Had to give her a US dollar for it. I've got to find an apartment by next week and get out of this hotel or the bean counters at the *Post* are going to get testy. What's new with you?'

Tarkington just made a noise and stretched out on the bed. In a moment he said, 'This pillow is too big.'

'Would I lie to you?'

'I don't think the bed's lumpy though.'

Before Yocke could think of a reply, Jake Grafton asked, 'How would you like to tag along with me and Toad for a while?'

The question startled Yocke. Toad opened his eyes, sat

up and stared wide-eyed at Jake for a few seconds, then flopped back on the bed and groaned.

'Sort of like Washington a couple of years ago, eh?' Yocke said with a grin. 'Same rules?'

'Well, not exactly.' Jake frowned. 'I guess I don't know precisely what the rules should be. So I'd want some sort of promise that you won't print anything on any subject without my okay.'

'I assume that you're working with the Russians. Do they know I'll be there? A reporter?'

'I've talked to General Yakolev about it. I told him I could trust you.'

Toad groaned again. 'Spreading it a little thick, aren't you, sir? I'd trust Jack the Hack with parking meter money, but . . .'

'Yakolev? Isn't he the chief of staff for the new Commonwealth Army?'

'That's the guy. Nicolai Yakolev.'

'Soaks up vodka like a sponge,' Toad tossed in.

'I agree.' Yocke grinned broadly and offered Jake his hand. After the admiral shook it, he grabbed a steno pad and a pencil and plopped onto the edge of the bed, forcing Tarkington to scoot over. He flipped the pad open to a fresh page and said, 'Shoot.'

'No notes. None.'

'I *have* to take notes. I got a good memory but it ain't Memorex. Only way to ensure accuracy later on when I write the story.'

Grafton appeared unmoved, so Yocke steamed on. 'We're talking the *Washington Post* here, not the Alfalfa County *Clarion*.' Yocke added confidentially, 'I'll use my own private shorthand. No one can read it but me. Honest.'

'Not even if you write in Swahili.'

Tarkington chortled.

Yocke tossed the steno pad on top of the dresser. 'No notes.'

'The other part of it is that the CIA may try to kill you.'

Yocke's mouth fell open. He glanced at Toad, then back at Jake. 'The CIA? *Our* guys? You're kidding, right?'

'No.'

'I can't write a story if I'm dead.'

'That thought may occur to them too.'

'Them? The whole CIA or a couple of bad apples or who?'

'I dunno.'

Yocke lost his temper. 'Jesus Christ, Admiral! You don't give a guy much. What say we do this the conventional, tried-and-true traditional way? You tell me whatever you want to tell me and I'll write and publish it, just like a real working reporter. You'll be an anonymous, reliable source, an unnamed high government official. I won't reveal your name to another living soul, even if they throw me in jail. I'll stay alive and out of your hair. Anytime you want to talk, just give a shout.'

'Be like having your own psychotherapist on the cheap, CAG,' Toad said unctuously, 'but you could skip the messy details about your sex life unless you wanted our modern Dr Freud to make you famous.'

Jake Grafton shook his head. 'Won't work that way,' he told Yocke. 'You either come along for the ride on the chance that someday you may get to write a story or you stay at home. It's up to you.'

'Just what do you get out of this arrangement?' Yocke demanded.

'I get an independent observer who has the power to reach the American public. I'm not sure what that will be worth because I don't know how things will shake out. But . . . if Toad and I get killed and you somehow manage to live to tell the tale, it might make very interesting reading in some quarters. I don't know. Too many ifs. I just don't know.' He eyed Yocke. 'At the very least you're an unknown quantity added to the equation.' He shrugged.

A knock sounded on the door.

'Well?' Jake asked. 'Yea or nay?'

'I'm in.'

Yocke went to answer the door. The man who came in was wearing a suit and overcoat and had a hard case that looked as if it contained a videocamera handcuffed to his wrist. The case displayed a diplomatic tag.

'Admiral Grafton?'

'Yes.'

'I'm Master Sergeant Emmett Thornton. I need to see your ID, sir.'

Jake took out his wallet and extracted his green military ID card. Thornton gave it a careful look, then handed it back. 'Thank you, sir.' He extracted a piece of paper from his inside coat pocket and held it out. 'Now if you will just sign for this equipment, it's all yours.'

Jake scribbled his name. 'How much is this going to cost me if I lose it, Sergeant?'

'About a hundred grand.'

Toad snapped his fingers. 'We'll put it on our Amoco card.'

Thornton glanced at Yocke.

'He's okay,' Grafton told him.

Thornton laid the case on the bed and used a key to open it. They gathered around for a look as he began unpacking items. 'What we have here is a TACSAT – tactical satellite – com unit with built-in encryption device. The signal goes right up to the bird, which rebroadcasts it to the Pentagon com center. Ni-cad batteries and a universal recharger. All you do is set the encryption code and use it like a two-way radio. General Land wanted me to remind you that the codes were generated by the National Security Agency.'

Jake examined the switches and buttons on the device. 'We'll need a brief and the codes.'

'Yessir. I'll come to that. This other item is simpler. It's a tape recorder with an encryption device attached. You merely record a message, anything you want up to thirty minutes. Then you punch up a six-digit code in this window here. Find a telephone, call the party you want, and when they are ready, you hit the play button. The garbled sound goes out at high speed. Takes about sixty seconds to play a thirty-minute message. If the other party has a message for you, you then put your machine on record and hold it up to the phone. Later on you can play the message and the machine will decode it into plain English. This thing works with telephones or TACSAT.'

The TACSAT came with a set of codes on water-soluble paper. Since it was possible the codes could fall into the wrong hands, 'unauthorized personnel' was Thornton's phrase, each authentic message should start with a code word that the admiral was to make up. Now. After a moment's thought Jake wrote a word on a matchbook and showed it to the sergeant, who then burned the matchbook in the wastepaper basket.

'The code for the telephone encrypter is a little more difficult. If you other gentlemen would like to step out of the room for a minute?'

'No, Sergeant,' Jake told him. 'Let's you and I go for a walk.'

Out on the sidewalk in front of the hotel the evening breeze was picking up. The sergeant explained: 'General Land suggested this code. Take the date, multiply it by the year in which you were born, then divide by the hour of the day in which you sent the message.' He produced a sheet of paper. 'Try it. Today is the second of July here so write that as seven oh two. And use local time in the military format. It's now twenty-three fifty, so use twenty-three hundred.'

Jake got a pen from his shirt pocket and did the math. 'I get five nine three point six four seven – something.'

'You were born in 1945, right?'

'Yes.'

'Okay, Admiral. You would just punch that six-digit number into the encrypter and place the decimal in the proper place. Always start with a positive integer and carry out any fractions so that you have six digits. Add zeros to the right of the decimal as necessary.'

'Who has this code, besides you and me?'

'Just General Land.'

'We'll always use Moscow time?'

'Moscow date and time.'

'Okay. Come upstairs and give Toad and me a complete brief on the gear and we'll be all set. Did you just get in from Washington?'

'I came here straight from the airport, sir. They're waiting to take me back.'

'Long flight.'

'I'm used to it. I sleep on the plane.'

Jake Grafton stared at the communications devices with a sinking feeling. After a moment he screwed up the courage to ask, 'Just how secure is this techno-junk?'

The sergeant faced him squarely. 'Admiral, this stuff is like a padlock on a garage. It'll keep honest people honest. But with a good computer a competent cryptographer could break any message in a couple hours.'

All Jake Grafton could manage was a grunt.

'The good news,' the sergeant continued, 'is that the ruskies don't have many good computers. They do most of their crypto work by hand, so it'll take them a couple weeks. Then one hopes the report will get routed here and there through the bureaucracy and a couple more weeks will pass before it lands on the desk of someone who may or may not decide to believe it.'

'A couple hours. With a good computer.'

'That's about the size of it, sir.'

And the CIA has the best computers in the world. Jake Grafton took a deep breath and thanked the sergeant for his trouble. Being an army man, the sergeant saluted.

CHAPTER NINE

The plane was the personal transport of the Minister of defense and still the rest room smelled like an outhouse and no water came out of the sink taps. No paper towels. So much for personal hygiene!

Jake opened the door and stepped out into the aisle that led to the cockpit. There was no cockpit door and he could see the instrument panel between the pilots.

The warning placards were in Cyrillic and the instruments had funny labels. He stood there looking over their shoulders for several seconds before the pilot realized he was there and looked over his shoulder. He said something in Russian and Jake replied in English.

'Good morning,' the pilot managed.

'Good morning,' Jake echoed. 'Nice plane you got here.'

When the pilot tapped his watch and made half a circle on the face with his finger, Jake nodded sagely and returned to his seat.

General Yakolev was in a seat across the aisle conferring with his aide. They were going over documents. Toad sat in the next row with Jocko West, who was broadening the American's horizons. Behind them sat the other foreign military representatives.

Today they were making a trip to a Russian nuclear weapons depot to see how warheads were disassembled. The name of the base they were going to was Petrovsk, on the Volga watershed. Jake glanced at the map again. The place was a hundred miles or so north northeast of

Volgograd, formerly Stalingrad, where the Soviet army shattered Adolf Hitler's ambitions.

Jake Grafton hadn't even been born then, but Yakolev was a young soldier in the Soviet army. Once again Jake pondered the twists of fate that had lifted Yakolev to the top, wondered again about the man who wore that uniform.

The window was scratched from being repeatedly wiped with dirty rags, but Jake managed to get a look through it at the land sliding by thirty thousand or so feet below. Forests, occasional small villages, roads that followed the contours of the land.

It just didn't look like America, or even western Europe. Those landscapes had their own distinct look that an experienced air traveler would recognize at a glance. Part of the problem, Jake decided, was that Russia was just too big. Great distances were the blessing that caused Napoleon and Hitler to founder and the curse that had stymied generations of Communist economic planners.

Soon Jake heard the power being reduced and felt the nose drop a degree or two as the pilot began his descent.

All this talk about weapons . . . it would be good finally to see some of the damned things.

The weapons were being disassembled in a makeshift clean room that didn't look any too tight. This was the scene of Yakolev's show-and-tell session. The Western visitors gathered in front of a plate-glass window and watched white-robed technicians use mechanical arms to manipulate the warhead parts while an interpreter translated Yakolev's comments, which were in Russian. Amazingly, when they entered the facility no one had offered them film badges to record the level of radiation to which they might be exposed, nor was anyone working here wearing one.

Beside the general stood a man in civilian clothes who looked nervous. Jake assumed he was the manager of this facility. Occasionally Yakolev asked him a question and pondered the reply, but the interpreter didn't translate these exchanges.

From the clean room an army truck took the party to a large hangar where row after row of missiles sat on their transporters. Against one wall were stacked wooden crates of pallets – nuclear warheads. The small party stood in silence taking it all in.

Yakolev stood beside Jake. Finally he spoke, in English. 'Impressive, yes?'

'That it is.'

'Russia shook the world with these missiles,' Yakolev said. 'And now we take them apart.'

Jake Grafton searched the older man's impassive face.

'We become another poor country without a voice in the world's affairs,' the general continued after a moment, still looking at the row upon row of missiles decorated with huge red stars. 'The television brings us news of the great things that are happening in Washington, New York, London, Paris, Bonn . . . We learn the thoughts of the great men of our age. The world's leaders ponder the future of mankind and debate how much money to give Russia while we eat our potatoes and borsch.'

Yakolev slapped Jake on the back. 'That is progress, no? No more bad old Communists! Now Russians buy televisions and watch CNN and the BBC and bet on world cup soccer and tennis matches at Wimbledon. They worry about stock prices in Tokyo and London and New York. No more bad old Russians! They are *just like us.*'

Yakolev turned away and Jake Grafton watched his retreating back. Then he stood looking at the missiles.

General Yakolev excused himself for a few hours' work, so Jake asked for a tour of the base. This disconcerted the civilian interpreter, but within a few minutes a military guide-interpreter was provided. 'What want to see?' the man asked with a heavy accent, wearing a perplexed look.

'The enlisted barracks, the mess hall and the hospital,' Jake told him.

The guide was in uniform, with a rank designation that Jake didn't recognize, and now he looked around in bewilderment. Jake guessed that he was in his early twenties. Seeing no one handy to voice his concerns to, yet unwilling to refuse the request of this important foreign visitor in the strange uniform, he slowly led Jake and Toad out the door of the hangar office and set a course across the packed dirt toward a distant building.

'What's your name?'

'Mikhail Babkin, sir.'

'You speak excellent English.' Jake Grafton mouthed the complimentary lie easily, without a twinge of conscience. English is different than all other languages, he reflected. Most Frenchmen listening to badly spoken French will pretend that they cannot understand or ignore the offender entirely. Yet any American meeting a goatherd in sub-Sahara Africa or on the windswept steppes of Mongolia who knows a word or two of pidgin English will compliment that worthy on his command of the language.

The barracks was of concrete construction, the usual Russian mix of too little cement, too much sand. The soldiers lived in one large, smelly, musty room with wooden bunks without springs. In the middle of the room stood a wood stove with an exhaust pipe leading to the roof. The bathrooms were communal, with no seats on the filthy toilets and one large shower with five drippy heads. There was no hot water heater. The smell . . .

'No hot water?'

'Hot? No.'

For an American naval officer who had spent half his adult life aboard ship where men were forced to live together in close quarters, this barracks was an appalling sight. The men who lived here must be constantly sick.

The mess hall was even worse. It was filthy, without refrigeration facilities or hot water. Jake asked how the dishes were washed and was told that each man dips his plate into a large drum of cold water. He was shown the drums.

At the hospital he wandered the corridors and looked at the soldiers in the beds. They stared back at him. He peeked into one empty operating room with little equipment.

'Where do you sterilize the instruments?' They are boiled, he was told. There was a sink in the anteroom, the taps dripping. He turned them on full and let them run. Uh-oh.

'Hot water?'

'Hot? No. Want see X-ray machine?'

Stunned, Jake left the dimly lit building meekly when an officious person, presumably the administrator or doctor in charge, fired a volley of Russian at their escort and pointed at the door.

'The sewage treatment plant . . . I want to see the sewage treatment plant.'

The translator had great difficulty understanding the request. Toad got into the act. Finally Jake realized that there was no sewage treatment plant. Eventually it became clear that the sewage was piped straight to the local river. The translator led them to the bank where they could look down upon the discharge pipes.

And nearby was the garbage dump. Above ground. The wind brought a whiff of it to where Jake and Toad and the translator were standing. Some small creature darted toward the pile, birds wheeled above, clouds of flies . . .

For all these years, Jake thought savagely, we have been told about the vast capabilities of the Soviet military machine. And it's all a lie. The shiny missiles and pretty tanks are the whole show. The men who must operate these weapons are poorly housed, in ill health, live in unsanitary conditions and eat food a Western health inspector would send to a landfill. It's all a lie.

What was it General Brown had said? *The Soviet Union is*

a nation in total social and economic collapse. Nothing works. Nothing!

He was in a subdued mood when he boarded the plane for the return flight to Moscow. General Yakolev made some comment but he paid no attention.

Toad Tarkington had a drink in each hand, and he held out one to Jake Grafton, who looked but didn't reach.

'It's Scotch on the rocks,' Toad said. Seeing the look on Grafton's face, he added, 'I broke the seal on the bottle myself and poured it.'

Jake accepted the glass and tried to grin.

'I know,' Toad said.

Around them the Fourth of July reception at Spaso House, the United States' ambassador's residence, was in full swing. Jake Grafton estimated the crowd at four or five hundred people. They were everywhere, in every room, in every hall, bumping into one another, nibbling delicacies from the trays of passing waiters, and drinking champagne by the gallon. In one corner a combo played light music by American composers. The light from the chandeliers cast a warm, soft glow over everything.

Ambassador Owen Lancaster was mixing and mingling. Agatha Hempstead hovered discreetly, ready to whisper a name into the ambassador's ear yet far enough away that she was not a party to his conversations. It was a delicate balancing act but she seemed to pull it off without effort.

A few minutes ago Jake had seen Herb Tenney talking to the British Army officer, Colonel Jocko West. In rumpled civilian clothes that somehow didn't quite fit, West looked like the caterer's husband dragged away from the television to help with the snack tray.

On the other hand Colonel Reynaud, the French officer, looked like a millionaire standing in the casino at Monte Carlo waiting for the baccarat tables to open. He was impeccably turned out in full dress uniform with medals.

Just now he seemed to be discussing a wine with one of the embassy staffers – he was holding the glass up to the light, now sniffing it, paying close attention to what the State Department employee had to say.

Colonel Galvano, the Italian, was in a corner with a Russian diplomat. They were deep in conversation but weren't grinning.

'Jack Yocke here yet?' Jake asked Toad.

'Not yet, sir. Dalworth is waiting for him at the door.'

Toad reached out and flicked a piece of lint off the left shoulderboard of Jake's white dress uniform. With medals and sword. Toad was similarly decked out. He squared his shoulders and adjusted his sword.

'We look sorta spiffy, don't we, sir? What say you go stand over next to that South American general or policeman or postal inspector and let me get a photo for posterity.'

'Dalworth know what to do?'

'Yessir. I briefed him. Stick like glue all evening.'

'Even in the head.'

'All evening,' Toad repeated. Jake wanted Herb Tenney and his CIA colleagues to see Yocke and learn who he was, but he didn't want them moving in on him. So Spiro Dalworth had been carefully briefed.

'Okay,' the admiral said. Toad wandered off.

Dalworth seemed like a bright, capable junior officer. Just how the navy managed to keep attracting quality young people was one of the modern mysteries. It wasn't the pay or career opportunities, not in this era of red tape, budget cuts, politically correct witch hunts and reductions in force.

Jake was sipping his drink and musing about the hundreds of men like Dalworth he had known through the years when the ambassador rendezvoused on his right elbow. 'Good evening, Admiral.'

'Good evening, sir. Are all the Fourth of July whingdings like this?'

'Well, this is my first, and the staff said I was going to be surprised. I think for a lot of the Russians the invitations were a welcome relief from the ordinary. I don't think we'll have many leftovers, if you know what I mean.'

Jake knew. He had already glimpsed several Russians by the hors d'oeuvre table surreptitiously wrapping food items in napkins and pocketing them. He had pretended not to notice.

'Haven't had a chance to chat with you the last day or two. Everything going, okay?'

Jake Grafton nodded thoughtfully. 'So far.'

'Anything I or my staff can do . . . What do you think of General Yakolev?'

'I'm not sure yet.'

'He's as Russian as Rasputin. When you figure him out, I'd be interested to hear what you think.'

'Yessir. If I may ask, who are these four or five Americans that arrived this afternoon?'

'Eight of them, I think,' Lancaster said. 'They're investigators who are going to go through the files of the KGB, the Apparat . . .' Lancaster waved vaguely. 'When Yeltsin invited the Americans over to look at the files, we took him up on it. They're FBI, CIA, some military investigators, one each from the House and Senate Foreign Relations Committees.'

'Will there be anything left in the files to find?' Jake asked, musing aloud.

'Depends on how hard they look,' Lancaster said sourly. 'I doubt that shredder technology has arrived here yet but the Russians have matches and garbage dumps. Still, one never knows. A lot of these people thought they were in the vanguard of the march of history and wanted to preserve their place in it with written records. Then there's the bureaucratic imperative, what I believe you military types crudely refer to as CYA.'

CYA – Cover Your Ass. Jake Grafton knew about that!

'Is Yeltsin here yet?' he asked the ambassador.

'No. He didn't come last year either, which is a diplomatic faux pas that no European prime minister or president would ever commit. But this is Russia.'

Agatha Hempstead brushed against the ambassador's elbow, and he raised one eyebrow at Jake. Then he was on his way to the next group. Jake smiled at Agatha as she passed and got an expressionless nod in return.

He looked at his watch. What was the time in Washington? About ten in the morning. If it were not a holiday Callie would be at the university holding office hours. She had an eleven o'clock class this semester. Amy was on summer vacation, going swimming and flirting with the Jackson boy, who had long hair and pimples and a learner's permit. Since it was a holiday, they had probably gone to the beach. Jake wished he were there with them.

General Yakolev was here tonight with his boss, Marshal Dimitri Mikhailov. The head of the Russian military looked every inch a curmudgeon used to getting his own way. He was playing with a champagne glass and listening to an interpreter explain what the British ambassador was saying.

Apparently not that enthused with diplomacy, Yakolev wandered to the buffet table and helped himself. Soon Ambassador Lancaster had him cornered, but the Russian was eyeing Ms Goodbody Hempstead as he munched Swedish meatballs. Hempstead favored him with a demure smile. And there was Herb Tenney, handing them champagne from a tray. Herb Tenney, champagne waiter . . . Those CIA guys had all the social graces.

Jake looked at the drink in his hand. What if Tenney slipped his damned stuff into the embassy's water purification system? Spaso House's system? Moscow tap water was heavily polluted and the Americans ran it through a purifier before they made it available for human consumption. Perhaps the kitchen staff uses tap water to cook with. People brush their teeth with it. Ice cubes are made from it.

He had had what? – one or two sips?

Hell, Jake! Quit sweating it. This stuff is safe as holy water until Herb slips you the second half of the cocktail.

But it was no use. Even if he were dying of thirst he wouldn't touch it. He put the glass with its two ice cubes on the table behind him, on a magazine so it wouldn't leave a ring, and stuffed his hands into his pockets.

There was Yocke now, escorted by Spiro Dalworth. He came wandering over to where Grafton was parked and waggled his eyebrows in greeting. 'How's the booze?'

'Free.'

'Jack Daniel's and water, a double,' the reporter told Dalworth. 'And anything you want for yourself.'

After a glance at Grafton, Dalworth turned and headed for the bar.

'So what's new on the Soviet Square murders?'

'Damn if I know,' the reporter replied. 'They had me chasing human interest today. Tommy Townsend, our senior guy, took over the assassination since it's so hot, but the poor bastard is probably hanging out at the Kremlin waiting for a press release. The cops over here won't tell you diddley squat. I'm going to try to milk them tomorrow.'

'What human was of interest today?'

'Yakov Dynkin, a Jew that these enlightened democrats stuffed into a crack for selling a car for more than he paid for it. Funny thing, the warden of Butyrskaya Prison says he isn't there. No Jews are there, according to him. And I can't find Dynkin's wife.'

'You have her address?'

'Yeah. One of our people interviewed her a couple months ago. But the people at her apartment house say they never heard of her. Someone else has her apartment. No forwarding address. The people at the post office look at me like I'm a terrorist spy. The concept of giving a Russian's address to a foreigner doesn't compute.'

Jake Grafton rubbed his eyes.

Jack Yocke looked around at the expensive furniture and

original art on the walls and the cheerful people sipping champagne and Perrier. A sour look crossed his face. 'I wish to God I was back in Washington on the cop beat, back looking at street-corner crack dealers shot full of holes and interviewing their parents – even covering the District Building.'

'Well, look at all the material standing here tonight. Bring your notebook?'

'Tommy Townsend's here. Though maybe I can go down to the kitchen and get enough for a Style section piece on how they do the canapés with a Russian twist . . . Say, isn't that General Yakolev standing over there ogling that broad?'

'That's him.'

'I hear he wants to get rich. He signed a book contract the other day with a New York publisher to write a nonfiction treatise on the former Soviet armed forces. For a cool half a million. Dollars. That ought to keep the old fart in rubles until the middle of the next century.'

'Huh!'

'Yep. They've signed up Yakolev and about six other old Commies. One of them's in the KGB, one in the Politburo, a couple of Gorbachev's old lieutenants, a former ambassador to the United States and an ex-foreign minister. This time next year we'll know more about the goings on in the Kremlin than we ever knew about the Reagan White House.'

'Money talks.'

'It sings, but I don't have any to salt around. If I ever paid a nickel for an interview the *Post* would have my *cojónes*.'

'I didn't know reporters had ethics.'

'Ha ha ha and ha. I ask my little questions and smile brightly and these Russians look at me like I'm some sort of low-life slime.'

'Good luck.'

'Thanks.'

Dalworth returned with Yocke's drink, and with the lieutenant at his elbow, the reporter drifted off to mix and mingle.

Jake Grafton had just greeted the naval attaché, Captain Collins, when a face he recognized from *Time* magazine approached, Senator Wilmoth from Missouri. 'I thought I recognized you, Admiral. You're Grafton, aren't you?'

'Yessir. I don't believe I've had the pleasure of meeting you before, Senator.'

'You testified in front of one of my committees several years ago about the A-12 Avenger attack plane. We were never introduced. You were a captain then, I seem to recall.'

'Yessir.'

'Are you permanently assigned here to Moscow?' Wilmoth actually seemed interested, which surprised Jake a little.

'It's a temporary thing, Senator. I work for the DIA now.'

'Well, what's your slant on fledgling democracy?'

'Don't have one, I'm afraid, sir. Is this a working vacation for you or a business trip?'

'Business. I'm going to be digging through the KGB files too.' He looked at the crowd. 'I just wish there was some concrete thing America could do to help the Russian people. Our foreign aid is just a drop in the bucket and it's all we can afford.'

'I've got an idea,' Jake Grafton told him, then wished he hadn't. 'You'll think it's nuts,' he added tentatively.

Wilmoth eyed him speculatively. 'Well, I could always use a laugh.'

Oh, well. What's the harm? 'Buy Siberia. Russia could use the money and we could use the resources.'

Wilmoth looked slightly stunned. He was apparently trying to decide if Jake was serious when Tarkington appeared at the admiral's elbow.

'You have a telephone call from General Land, sir,' he

whispered. 'You can take it upstairs in the ambassador's office.'

As Tarkington retrieved Jake's attaché case from beside the credenza behind him, Jake said good-bye to the senator, who had decided to be amused at Jake's suggestion. The admiral followed Toad through the crowded room toward the stairs in the hall.

Three minutes later he picked up the telephone in the ambassador's office. The operator came on. 'Admiral Grafton? Please wait while I connect you with General Land.'

In seconds he heard Land's voice. After the usual greetings, Land asked, 'Got your gadget handy?'

'Yessir, but I don't have the code set.'

'You can do that afterward.'

'Just a moment, sir.'

The message took about twenty seconds to tape. The two men said their good-byes, then broke the connection.

Jake used a pocket calculator to compute the code, which he set into the device. Then he took it outside. A small garden in the back of the structure had some nice trees, some scraggly grass and flowers. No one was around. After a scan of the windows above him, he pushed the play button and held the device up to his ear.

Amazingly enough, the damned thing worked.

The second sentence was the essence of the message. 'Albert Sidney Brown was poisoned.' That thought was expanded and various chemical compounds were discussed, but there was no doubt. The corpse contained lethal amounts of a synthetic compound not found in nature.

When Jack Yocke got back to the Metropolitan Hotel that evening, he asked the desk clerk if he had any messages. Assured that neither his editor nor his mother had seen fit to invest in a call halfway around the world this evening, he strolled for the elevator.

He checked his watch. Only ten-thirty. What the hey, why not a cup of coffee before bed?

He detoured into the bar, nodded at Dimitri, the night barman, and ordered.

With his coffee in front of him, he sat contemplating the painting on the wall opposite the bar. It looked as if it were old and the varnish had darkened, but maybe it had been painted to look old. The wall of the Kremlin was on one side of the picture and St Basil's Cathedral on the other. But Red Square wasn't there – merely mud and a few shacks and a giant ditch along the Kremlin wall to make things tough for touring Mongols and visiting Poles. Just slightly left of center stood a nobleman listening to a peasant. Yocke looked at this painting at least three or four times a week and often wondered what the serf was saying.

His idle musings were derailed when he realized a woman had seated herself at the bar with only one stool between them. She greeted the barman pleasantly and ordered coffee in American English.

'A fellow Yank, as I live and breathe. What brings you to Sodom on the Moskva?'

She turned her head toward him and grinned. She had dark brown eyes, almost black, set wide apart. Dark brown hair tumbled to her shoulders. Her chin was the perfect size, her lips just right. With the exception of one prostitute who visited the hotel occasionally, she was the prettiest woman Yocke had yet seen in Russia, which was saying something since Russia had its fair share of beautiful women. Best of all, she was about his age and wasn't wearing a wedding ring. Or any ring.

'I live in Moscow,' she told him.

'Is that a Boston accent?'

'Actually Vermont, but four years at Brandeis ruined me, I'm afraid.'

'Name's Jake Yocke.'

'Shirley Ross.'

She wasn't cover girl *Cosmo* gorgeous, Yocke concluded, but she had perfect bones: the forehead, the cheekbones, the chin. Her face was a feast for the eyes.

She had been here over a year, she told Yocke, first as an interpreter for an American telecommunications company, then as a journalist for an English-language monthly magazine published here.

'Small world. I scribble for a living too. *Washington Post.*'

'The *Post*?'

'The one and only.'

'Do you know Sally Quinn?' Sally was a *Post* reporter, columnist and all-around original character. She had even written a novel or two.

'Uh-huh.'

Shirley Ross grinned.

Twenty minutes later they were sitting in the corner sipping Bailey's. 'So how is this borsch batch going to come out?' Yocke asked her.

'You want a prediction?'

He nodded.

'Yeltsin, democracy and where to place your bets for the coming civil war.'

Yocke tasted his drink again. She was working on her second but he was still nursing his first. After the whiskey at the embassy and the coffee here the liqueur was too sweet. And he was feeling the alcohol. This woman in front of him was also stimulating his hormones.

Her discussion of the political situation struck Jack Yocke as enlightened and well informed. She got her tongue around the names of these Russian politicians without a single slip. Jack Yocke felt slightly deflated. Shirley Ross knew more about Russian politics than he ever hoped to know. When she fell silent he told her that.

She grinned again. 'Not really. It's my job. You'll pick it up. Wow your friends back home when they get tired of talking about TV shows and movies. People will avoid you at cocktail parties.' She mugged with a suspicious glance out of the corner of her eyes, then joined him in laughter.

He looked into those deep brown eyes and felt completely at ease. American women are the very best. 'This Soviet Square killing — what are people saying about that?'

Her eyes flicked around the room and came to rest on him. 'Do you want Sunday op-ed bullshit or do you want the truth?'

Dimitri was loading the German-made dishwasher and making the usual noises. Jack and the woman were the only people in the bar. 'Without surrendering my right to later argue that op-ed pieces are an attempt to write the truth, I choose the second alternative. What truth do you know?'

She toyed with her swizzle stick while he studied her face. At last the eyes came up to meet his. 'The truth will never come out.'

'Perhaps,' he said, and relaxed. He looked at his watch. Tomorrow was going to be a long day hunting for cops willing to talk while he listened to Gregor's tales of Brooklyn. He took a deep breath, exhaled and scooted his chair back. 'Do you come here often, Shirley?'

'The KGB is setting up Yeltsin.'

'How do you know that?'

'I can't tell you.'

Yocke squared off to face her. 'What can you tell me?'

'Nothing that you can print.' She lay down the swizzle stick and hunted in her purse. She extracted a pack of Marlboros and a pack of matches. After she lit one she examined Yocke's face through the smoke.

'You came here tonight to meet me, didn't you?'

Her eyes stayed on his face. She smoked the cigarette in silence. The dishwasher behind the bar lit off with a rumble.

'Anything you tell me I have to confirm. Someone else must confirm every fact or I can't print it.'

'If you ever tell anyone where you got this or who I am you will ruin me.'

'We never reveal sources who request anonymity.'

'This is Russia.'

She didn't know anything. Perhaps she thought she knew something, but what the hell could it be? She's an American, for Chrissake!

'Three KGB officers . . .' She stubbed out the cigarette and looked at Dimitri, who was working on receipts on an IBM computer terminal. Her eyes came back to Yocke.

'Three KGB officers . . .' He had to lean forward across the table to hear her voice above the noise of the dishwasher.

She swallowed and fumbled for another cigarette.

'Three KGB officers went to police headquarters a half hour before the assassination. They ordered the police away from Soviet Square.'

'How do you know this?'

A whisper: 'The order was transmitted over the radio. The police in the square heard it on their little radios. You've seen those little radios they wear, haven't you?'

'I've seen them.' The police here were wired up just like the cops in Washington and Detroit.

'Kolokoltsev was a pawn sacrifice. It's the king they want.'

'Who's they?' To his chagrin, Yocke's voice came out a whisper. He raised it a notch and repeated the question. 'Who's they?'

She just shook her head.

'I need some names.'

She leaned back and sucked fiercely on the cigarette. Her eyes went to Dimitri and stayed there.

'He can't hear us.'

'He's KGB. All these hard-currency hotel people are.'

'He can't hear us over that dishwasher,' Yocke insisted. 'You're going to have to point me in the right direction. Give me a name. One name. Any of them. Any one of them.'

She stabbed the cigarette out in the ashtray and drained her drink.

'I have to have someplace to start looking, Shirley, or your trip down here was a waste of time. You must know how goddamn tough it is to get Russians to open up to an American reporter. It's like asking a dope dealer if he's got a load coming in anytime soon.'

Her lips twisted into an attempt at a grin as she stood up. Now the lips straightened. Gripping her purse tightly she leaned across the table and whispered, 'Nikolai Demodov.'

'Was he one of the three?'

But she was walking out. She went through the door and turned left and was gone.

Up in his room Jack Yocke wrote the name on his computer screen and sat staring at it. Nikolai Demodov.

Well, it was a pretty story. No getting around that. A pretty story. He didn't know enough to even guess how much truth there might be to the tale, if any, but his instinct told him some truth was there. You develop that instinct in this business after you have listened to a lot of stories. Maybe it's their eyes, the body language.

He tapped aimlessly on the keyboard for a few moments, then turned the computer off.

He brushed his teeth and washed his face and hands and stared at his reflection in the mirror over the sink while he thought about Shirley Ross and the three KGB agents.

If only he could have gotten more out of her. How should he have handled it? She must have known all three of the names. At the minimum she knew how the hell Nikolai Demodov fits in. Where had he lost her? And where did she get her information?

Aaagh! To be tantalized so and have the door slammed in your face! Infuriating . . .

Most people are poor liars. Oh, every now and then you meet a good one, but most people have not had the practice it takes to tell a lie properly. Cops can smell a lie. So can some lawyers and preachers. And all good reporters. Even if you can't put your finger on why it plays right, you know truth when you find it.

Just now Jack Yocke decided he had seen some of it. And the glimpse excited him.

CHAPTER TEN

Sergi Pavlenko was dozing in the guard shack when the noise of a helicopter brought him awake. He was nineteen years old, a conscript from a collective farm, and he was not used to helicopters. He came immediately awake and went outside where he could see better.

It was one in the morning, the middle of the summer night, which was still short here three hundred miles southeast of Moscow at the Serdobsk Nuclear Power Plant.

The lights of the helicopter were curious, a red, a white and a light that flashed and made the machine look like some unearthly thing, some vision from a vodka-drenched nightmare. When it became obvious that the machine was going to land here, Sergi Pavlenko straightened his uniform tunic and resettled his hat on his head at the correct angle. He eased the strap that held his rifle into the correct position and stood erect with his heels together, as a proper soldier should.

Now the helicopter's landing light came on, a spotlight that shone downward and slightly ahead. Pavlenko started. He had never before seen a helicopter flying at night and the landing light was unexpected.

As the light moved toward him, the thought suddenly occurred to him that he might be in the place where the descending machine was going to alight. Galvanized, he scurried back toward the guardhouse at the entrance to the power plant.

Safe in his refuge, he looked across the enclosure at the

guard kiosk at the main gate, where he could just see his friend Leonid under the light pointing with one hand and covering his mouth with the other. Leonid would laugh and tease him; he must have looked like a frightened rabbit running from the helicopter.

And now it was there in front of him, roaring like an enraged bear and stirring up a hurricane as it settled onto the grass.

The engines died immediately. The pilot obviously had no fuel to waste.

Five men climbed out. One of them, wearing a dark suit and dark tie, came toward him. Sergi straightened to attention.

'Where is the manager?'

'I don't know. No one said you were coming.'

'I'm accustomed to being met by the manager of the facility.'

'The telephone from the outside is out of order. It has not worked all night.'

'Well, tell the manager I am here.'

Sergi was at a loss for words. *Who* was here? Should he ask for identification? The panic must have shown on his face, for the man's expression softened and he growled, 'Just get him out here.'

There was a telephone in his guardshack, a little wooden building that looked as if it had been added as an afterthought right by the concrete wall of the reactor building. It was a rotary dial instrument. Sergi wiped his hands on his trousers before he picked up the handset and checked the list of telephone numbers taped to the wall. The list was so dirty as to be almost unreadable. Control room, number 32. That was the only place in the complex where there would be people this time of night.

The first time Sergi dialed nothing happened. No ringing in the earpiece. The equipment was old and the electrical switches were worn out, like every other telephone system in the former Soviet empire. Still, the only telephone on Sergi's collective farm had belonged to the manager, an important person, and Sergi had never used it. Having a telephone waiting for him to pick up to call someone – just within the facility, this instrument could not be used to call elsewhere – made Sergi proud. To complain about the quirks of the instrument was an impulse that had never crossed his mind.

Now he used his thumb on the hook to break the circuit, then lifted it and listened for the dial tone. There it was. He carefully dialed the number again. This time he heard the ringing. As he waited he turned and looked at the helicopter and the big red star on the fuselage. One of the passengers was over at the kiosk at the main gate talking to Leonid: Sergi could see them standing together under the light.

A man's voice answered the telephone.

'This is the main door guard,' Sergi Pavlenko said loudly into the mouthpiece. 'A helicopter has arrived. An important person wishes to see the manager.'

'The manager is home in bed. I'm the watch officer.'

'Yes, yes. He is waiting here to talk to someone in authority. It is a big helicopter with many rotor blades.' This fact impressed Sergi; it should impress the man inside too.

Apparently it did. 'I'll be right out,' the voice told him.

Sergi Pavlenko hung up the telephone and turned to report to the man from the helicopter. As he did so the man used a silenced pistol to shoot him once in the head, killing him instantly.

The five men worked fast. The main door had a lock that worked only from the inside. When the watch officer opened it they herded Leonid from the main gate, the watch officer and everyone in the building into an empty office and gunned them down with silenced submachine guns. They didn't bother to pick up the empty brass cartridge cases strewn about.

171

They blocked the front door open with a piece of wood and carried in bags from the helicopter.

The reactor was operating at 50 percent power. The man who had shot Sergi examined the control panel carefully, then led the way through the lead-lined door that led to the reactor space.

A nuclear reactor is, when explained to schoolchildren, a very simple piece of machinery – a large tea kettle is the common analogy. True, the first reactor, Enrico Fermi's pile under the University of Chicago's football stadium, was indeed simple. But there was nothing simple about the Serdobsk reactor, a liquid-metal-cooled fast breeder. The core was made up of five tons of metallic oxides of uranium-235, plutonium-239, and uranium-238, the breeding material that would be converted into plutonium during the course of the reaction. This material was fashioned into twelve thousand long pins, each less than six millimeters in diameter and arranged with extraordinary precision inside a small core, a hexagonal container only three feet across each face.

The core sat in a cylindrical stainless-steel pot filled with molten, liquid sodium that was cycled through the core by three pumps. Unavoidably the sodium flowing through the core absorbed some neutrons and was converted into sodium-24, a highly radioactive gamma ray emitter, so the radioactive sodium was run through an exchanger where it gave up some of its heat to the secondary cooling system, also liquid sodium. The unpressurized stainless-steel vat that contained the core and the primary and secondary cooling systems was forty feet high and forty feet in diameter. Between the surface of the liquid sodium and the top of the vat was a cloud of argon, an inert gas. Lead shielding surrounded the entire vat. Surrounding the lead was a concrete vault with walls about three feet thick.

Pipes brought the secondary sodium out of the vat near

the top and took it to a second heat exchanger, where it was used to boil water for steam to turn turbines, then returned it to the vat. The pipe holes in the vat and the lead and concrete shields were all above the level of the liquid sodium.

The nuclear reaction itself was controlled by dozens of graphite rods that absorbed radiation. These rods were withdrawn from the core to start the reaction and pushed into it to kill it.

The men from the helicopter began with the rods. Standing on top of the concrete vault, they planted a series of small explosive charges designed to shatter the rod mechanisms before they had a chance to slide down into the core. This job took about half an hour.

Still on top of the concrete biological shield, they used tape measures and chalk while the man in charge consulted a sheet of paper in his hand. When the chalk marks were precisely where he wanted them, he personally began placing six shaped charges that would vent their explosive force down into the vat. While he was at it several of the men climbed up the ladder and wandered out into the hallway for a smoke.

One of them came running back. 'Colonel, the helicopter is starting!'

'What?'

'Listen.'

Yes, he could faintly hear the whine as the engines spooled up. He stumbled and almost fell running for the ladder. He hurried up and raced along the catwalk toward the control room. He arrived outside just in time to see the helicopter transition into forward flight and move away into the darkness.

Two of the men came out behind him and one aimed his submachine gun at the departing machine.

'Nyet,' the colonel cried. 'That won't do any good.' The fool! If he successfully shot down the helicopter the noise of the crash would bring everyone in the army camp over here. And it would be damned hard to fly out of here in a crashed helicopter.

The colonel stood listening to the noise of the machine as it faded. When all he could hear were the night noises of frogs and insects, he still stood undecided. He had expected problems, but not this – to be abandoned by the helicopter pilot! Betrayed!

The pilot was a Ukrainian. He should have demanded a Russian pilot. The colonel choked back his rage and frustration and wondered what to do. He had, he well knew, miserably few options.

'What do we do now, Colonel?' one of the men asked.

The query decided him.

'Let's set the charges.' He was surprised at his own voice. It sounded calm, in control, which wasn't the way he felt at all. Usually when he was enraged his voice became a hoarse croak.

'If we hadn't cut the telephone lines we could call for another helicopter,' one of the men said disgustedly. 'We certainly can't blow this damn thing up unless we have transport out of here.'

'Back inside,' the colonel said. 'Let's finish the job while I think.'

They were reluctant but the habit of obedience was strong. The colonel followed them back into the building.

It took forty-five minutes to finish setting the charges atop the biological shield. Forty-five minutes of sweating an impossible situation.

He should have had a backup chopper, should have brought a two-way radio. But there was no time. *No! Do it now! Do it tonight!* the general had said.

All the careful planning, all the preparations that didn't get done, all the backups that weren't quite ready. That was the trouble with the Soviet system – the remorseless pressure to make 'it' happen always forced shortcuts, compromises in quality and safety. It was infuriating when you saw the disasters everywhere you looked but goddamn catastrophic when it was your life on the line. How easy it was for a bureaucrat or general to shout 'Now!'

He forced himself to work slowly, with meticulous care, as he set the shaped charges. There would be no second chance. This had to be done right the first time, which, he told himself furiously, would be the only recorded instance of the accomplishment of that feat in Russia since the czar impregnated his bride on their wedding night.

He was perspiring heavily when he finished. He stood back and used a rag to wipe his face and hands. 'Insert the detonators.'

'Colonel, how are we going to get away from here?'

'I said insert the detonators. Wire them up but don't arm the triggering device. I'll go find us some transport. Give me a submachine gun.'

One of the men passed his weapon over.

'Get busy.'

The colonel slung the weapon over his shoulder and climbed the ladder.

When he left the cavernous room two of the men were inserting detonators and wiring them to the firing device as the other two watched.

The army camp was three kilometers up the road. The colonel cooled off as he walked in the darkness. He was unwilling to use the flashlight, so he stumbled occasionally over uneven places in the road. Still he walked quickly. Only two hours until dawn.

He stopped when he was still fifty meters from the circle of light above the gate and looked the camp over. It was surrounded by a sagging, rusted wire fence. A guard kiosk stood by the open gate. No doubt a sentry was there, the only man awake in the camp. He hoped that no one else was awake.

There, by that building in the back, wasn't that a truck? Yes. It had grass growing around it to the top of its wheels. Perhaps there was a car or another truck in the garage.

The colonel moved toward the sentry's kiosk, staying in the shadows, making as little noise as possible. He kept the submachine gun over his shoulder but held the pistol with the silencer in his right hand.

He was still fifteen feet from the kiosk, just coming into the light circle, when the sentry inside the unpainted wooden shack saw him and jerked in surprise.

The colonel pointed the pistol at the soldier and said, as calmly as he could and just loud enough to be heard, 'Don't move. Just stay exactly as you are and you won't get hurt.'

The man froze. He was young, in his late teens.

'Now very carefully, step outside.'

The soldier complied. He was trembling.

'Where is the other sentry?'

The soldier merely shook his head.

The colonel pointed his weapon and repeated the question.

'I'm the only one, sir.'

'If you are lying you will be the first to die. Do you understand?'

'Yes, sir.'

'Let's go look at the truck.' The colonel snapped on his flashlight and used it to point the way. He followed the soldier, who had now decided to raise his hands a little.

The truck was a rotting hulk. The tires were flat, the glass was broken from several windows, weeds peeked through the radiator grill.

'Where is the other truck?' he demanded, his voice a forced whisper.

'In the garage.'

'Open it, quietly. If anyone wakes up . . .'

The truck in the garage was fairly new, painted olive drab and had air in all the tires. Keeping the weapon pointed at the soldier, the colonel eased the driver's door open and shone the flashlight on the instrument panel. No ignition key was required. Merely switch on the electrical system and push the starter button. The colonel reached in and flipped the electrical switch. The proper lights came on. He examined the fuel gauge. The needle rested on the left side. Empty! The colonel flipped the switch off.

'Where's the gasoline?'

'We haven't had any gas for a month.' The young soldier's hands were down and his voice unnaturally loud.

The colonel lowered the barrel of the pistol and fired a round into the dirt at the soldier's feet. The report was merely a soft pop. 'You'd better find some.'

'Over there.' The gesture was quick, jerky.

There were some cans against the wall, beside a motorcycle. The colonel hefted one. Half full. The others were empty – all eight.

'This motorcycle – does it work?'

'Oh yes. The captain rides it every day over to the reactor. And into town on Sundays. He—'

'Shut up!'

The colonel quickly checked every other fuel can in the garage. All empty. He examined the controls on the motorcycle, the tires, then opened the cap on the fuel tank. At least half full. He made the trembling soldier fill the tank from the only can containing fuel.

'Okay, push it out of here and down to the kiosk at the gate.'

Under the light at the gate the colonel examined the machine. He turned the petcock and let gasoline flow to the carburetor, twisted the throttle, checked the chain and the clutch.

The only way to see if it would run would be to start it. But not here.

'Start pushing.' He gestured to the northwest, toward the reactor facility. The soldier did as he was told.

It was hard work pushing the motorcycle along the dirt road in the darkness. The machine fell once and the soldier went on top of it. The colonel waited while he righted the thing and got it going again.

When they had gone about half a kilometer the colonel told the soldier to stop and put down the kickstand. Then he shined the flashlight into the soldier's eyes and shot him while he stood blinking helplessly.

The man went down without a sound. The colonel dragged the corpse off the road into some weeds.

With his gun in one pocket and the flashlight in another, he climbed aboard the motorcycle and eased the kick starter down until he felt compression. Then he raised himself up and gave a mighty kick.

No.

Again.

Nothing.

Again.

The fourth time the machine chugged once, but he fed it too much gas and it died.

This time he got all of his body weight into the down-stroke of his leg and the machine gurgled into life. As he sat astride the saddle and waited for the engine to warm, the colonel used the flashlight to check his wristwatch. Almost an hour gone. One hour of darkness left.

Carefully he disengaged the clutch, popped the transmission into gear, and eased the clutch out. The engine almost died but he caught it with the throttle and let the clutch engage. The sound the engine made was well-muffled since the machine was fairly new.

The colonel brought it to a stop a hundred meters short of the gate to the reactor facility. He walked from there.

Two of his men were waiting by the door.

'We thought we heard an engine a few moments ago,' one told him.

'You did. A car. I parked down the road in case someone comes by. Are the detonators set?'

'Yes, sir. All you need to do is set the timer. Do you want us to go on down and sit in the car until you come?'

'Okay. I need maybe ten minutes. I'll send the others along.'

When these two were about twenty-five feet away with their backs to him, he used the silenced submachine gun.

It wasn't fair, but there it was. He had transport for one. The reactor had to be destroyed. After he had shot them he walked over to where they lay and put a bullet into each man's skull.

One of his men was in the control room. 'I've got a car parked down the road out of the light,' he said. 'Go sit in it until I get the device armed.'

'How much time are you going to give us?'

'What's the maximum possible time?'

'One hour.'

'Then that's what we have.'

'That would be a lot if we had a helicopter,' the man objected reasonably, 'but we don't. What if we have a flat tire or this car breaks down?'

The colonel wasn't in the mood. 'We take our chances. Where's Vasily?'

'In the reactor space checking the wires and detonators one more time.'

'Go wait in the car.'

Just before the man reached the door the colonel took the submachine gun off his shoulder and shot him. As he was lowering the weapon the door to the reactor clicked shut.

He heard a noise, running feet. Damn! Vasily.

The colonel popped the magazine from the weapon and replaced it with a full one. After he had checked to ensure it was seated properly, he opened the heavy, lead-lined door to the reactor space and slipped in.

A bullet smacked into the wall.

What else can go wrong? Sweat broke out on his face. A more dangerous place for a gunfight would be hard to imagine. One stray bullet could sever a critical wire or punch a hole in a pipe carrying molten sodium or water or steam or . . .

179

He was inside against the wall, the door on his right side. Another bullet whapped against the wall.

The silenced pistol was in his left hand, the submachine gun in his right. Where was—

A bullet caught him in the hip and half turned him around. He tossed the submachine gun and fell heavily on his face, his right hand palm up at an odd angle.

The trick was old and hoary and he was a fool to try it. If he had had a moment to think he wouldn't have. If Vasily kept his wits about him or used a smidgen of sense . . . But he didn't. He didn't even shoot the colonel a second time, a mistake the colonel certainly wouldn't have made.

The colonel lay like a sack of very old potatoes. He felt the catwalk vibrate from Vasily's footsteps and he even got a glimpse of one foot. Still he lay absolutely motionless, muscles slack, scarcely breathing, his left hip on fire as the numbing shock of the bullet wore off. When he heard the door begin to open beside him he moved – rolled and instantly triggered the pistol into Vasily's foot, then his leg, then as the man fell, into his body. He fired again and again as fast as the pistol would work. When it was empty he stopped shooting.

Vasily sighed once as the spent cartridges tinkled on the concrete far below. He didn't inhale again.

The colonel got slowly to his feet and examined the location of the bullet hole in his clothing. Blood was oozing out. The catwalk where he had lain was smeared with it.

He put his weight on the injured hip. Well, the bone wasn't broken, although the wound hurt like hell. He looked at Vasily to ensure he was dead, then popped the empty clip from the automatic and inserted a full one from his jacket pocket. When that was done he retrieved the submachine gun. He hung it over his shoulder on its strap.

He made his way along the catwalk and descended the ladder onto the top of the reactor shield.

Thank God the charges were there, still properly

installed and wired up. He got out his dirty handkerchief and wiped his face and hands as he examined the timer mechanism.

One lousy hour.

He pushed the test button on the battery, verified that the green light came on, then released the button.

One stinking, tiny, miserable little hour.

For it came to him then that his luck had gone very bad. Everything had gone wrong. All of his experiences in life had taught him that luck runs in cycles – sometimes good things happen for a while, then bad. And he was deeply into the bad just now. Was this hole in his hip the last of the bad things, or only the next to last?

He was not a religious man. Nothing in his forty-four years of life had even suggested possible resources other than his own skill, courage and endurance. Yet just now as he stared at the detonator he sensed that his own resources probably weren't going to be enough.

He twisted the knob that turned the needle on the clock face. He turned it to the maximum reading, sixty minutes. He consulted his watch.

Now he looked about, again tested his weight on his injured hip, savored the sharp edge of the pain, wiped his hands one more time.

This was necessary. They would not have sent him if it weren't.

Oh, hell. Everyone has to die sooner or later and he wasn't afraid of it. Dying is the easy part, like going to sleep. Getting to that moment can be a real bitch, though.

He looked again at the sweep second hand on his watch. When it swung by the straight-up position he pushed the button to start the timer on the detonator. Exactly one hour from now, at 5:07 A.M. If this clock keeps good time.

He watched it tick for a few seconds, then crossed to the ladder and went up it, favoring his bad hip only a little.

In the control room the colonel scanned the dozens of gauges and dials. With a sure hand he reached for the master control and began inching the rods out of the core while he kept a careful eye on the temperature gauges. Another five minutes passed before he was satisfied with the new stabilized readings. The reactor was now at almost 80 percent power.

When he left the building he removed the wooden door-jamb and let the outside door close and lock.

Fifty-three minutes.

He limped past the bodies sprawled near the gate and turned right on the road. The breeze cooled the sweat on his face but he didn't notice as he hurried along.

He got on the motorcycle and checked that the fuel was on. When he tried to shift his weight to his left hip and push up to get some leverage for the kick start lever the pain was so bad he almost fell over.

Gritting his teeth, he tried again. This time he managed to kick the bike through but it didn't start.

Again with no luck.

The third time it fired and he gave it just enough gas to keep the engine going. He almost collapsed onto the seat. His leg was wet with blood. How long before he passed out? He fumbled for the headlight switch. There. But the headlight didn't come on.

He hadn't checked the headlight. Burned out, probably.

Somehow he got the bike into motion.

This road led off to the northwest, he remembered, up-wind, so he stayed on it. When he went by the gate to the reactor facility he got a fleeting glimpse of his watch from the light on the pole. Forty-one minutes to go.

Riding a motorcycle on a rutted dirt road on a dark night takes intense concentration and high physical effort. The colonel found that even at a slow speed he was always on the verge of losing control. Still, with every minute he gained confidence. When his eyes were fully adjusted to the darkness he could see the road easily enough, so he eased on more throttle and shifted to a higher gear. This meant he was going faster when he fell. The nose wheel hit a rut, the handlebars twisted violently and he was instantly flying through air.

The impact with the ground stunned him.

When his wits returned he levered himself upright and groped for the motorcycle. He *had* to put some miles between himself and that reactor. He tried to see the hands on the watch but it was impossible. He felt for the flashlight. It didn't work. Broken by the fall.

The submachine gun on his shoulder was gouging him, so he took it off and threw it away into the darkness.

Getting the bike upright took all his strength.

Kick. No start. Kick again.

He lost count of the number of times he tried to start the motorcycle.

How long had it been? How much blood had he lost?

Flooded. He had probably flooded the damn thing.

He sat wearily on the bike gathering his strength.

Are you beaten?

No!

Throttle off. Kick, a real high arch off the bad hip so all his weight would come down on the kick lever under his right foot.

The engine caught. Slowly he twisted the throttle and brought the engine up to a fast idle. Now the shift lever.

He kept the bike at a slow pace, maybe four or five miles per hour. The wind in his face was the only bright spot. If he could just get a little distance and get behind something solid, some earth perhaps, he could survive the blast. The wind would carry the radioactivity in the other direction.

He was climbing a hill. He could tell by the amount of throttle necessary. And the sky was getting lighter to the northeast. He realized then that he could see the road and the ruts better, so he eased on more throttle.

How much time?

Couldn't be much. If he could just get over the hill. There on the other side, with the hill between him and the reactor, there he would be safe.

Every bounce, every jolt was another second past.

How many more did he have? He took his left hand from the handlebar and tried to see the watch. The bike swerved dangerously and he grabbed the handlebar again.

How far had he come? Was he far enough . . . ?

The shock wave almost knocked him off the motorcycle. Then intense heat. He felt intense heat on his neck, on the back of his head, even through his jacket. And he wasn't under cover, wasn't . . .

Behind him a cloud of dirt and debris blown aloft by the explosion formed in the darkness above the reactor. In seconds it began to glow. The radiation intensified. The sensation of furnace heat was the last thing the colonel felt as a virulently radioactive ball of fire rose from the melted remnants of the steel, lead and concrete shielding.

In seconds he was dying even as the motorcycle continued away from the blast, dying like the sleeping soldiers at the army base on the other side of the reactor, dying like every other mammal within four miles of the now-glowing nuclear plant. Four miles, that was how far the colonel had traveled. The motorcycle continued upright with his dying weight for a few seconds, then the front wheel kicked against a rut, and the machine and the corpse upon it skidded to a stop in the road.

The engine of the motorcycle choked to a stop as a mushroom cloud formed over the reactor and the wind on the ground strengthened markedly as air rushed toward the intense heat source.

People and animals a few miles farther away from the reactor had several minutes of life left, amounts varying depending on the amount of material shielding them from the runaway nuclear inferno. By the time the sun came up in the northeast only a few insects were still alive within seven miles of the plant. Other people were also dying as a cloud of ferociously intense radioactivity drifted southeast on the prevailing wind.

CHAPTER ELEVEN

As Jack Yocke dressed the following morning his mood was gloomy. The euphoria he felt last night had completely evaporated. He had managed only two hours' sleep and spent the rest of the night tossing and turning.

At about four in the morning the implications of being sought out by Shirley Ross finally sank in. Why Jack Yocke? He wasn't a famous personage, not a known face. And how had she known to find him at the Metropolitan? Now the significance of her evasion of that question grew. Maybe this was a setup.

He was in way over his head, chasing an impossible story. He didn't speak the language, he didn't have an ongoing professional relationship with a single, solitary soul in this goddamn hopeless Slavic morass. He was a foreigner in a country deeply suspicious of all foreigners. He didn't know the politics in a capital where politics was the staff of life, played for blood and money. Nobody would talk to him. Nobody would trust him to tell the truth. Nobody.

Except Jake Grafton, and he didn't count. He wouldn't know beans about the Soviet Square killings. Even if he did and were willing to share it, Yocke couldn't print it. He needed something he could publish.

Gregor was standing beside his battered tan Lada when Yocke came out of the hotel. The sixty-degree morning air was heavy with pollution and the sky looked like rain. The best the reporter could manage in reply to Gregor's cheerful hello was a nod. He sagged onto the passenger's seat and stared morosely though the windshield at a beggar woman arranging herself for a day on the sidewalk while Gregor got himself situated behind the wheel and coaxed the car to life.

'Sleep well?' Gregor asked.

'Not really.'

'Where would you like to go this morning?'

Yocke sighed and ran his fingers through his hair. 'Police headquarters.' No, on second thought, the district attorney was the place to start. What did they call the prosecutor over here? 'Make it the public prosecutor's office.'

'No interview with Yeltsin? Well, maybe tomorrow.'

'Boris will have to wait. Tomorrow we do Gorby's proctologist.'

'Procto . . .?'

'Can the corn and drive.'

The foyer was crowded with reporters. Yocke's heart sank. He looked around for Tommy Townsend, the *Post's* senior correspondent, and didn't see him. At least a dozen people from the international press crowded around the desk man, who was grunting surly Russian and scowling. A television team had lights on and a camera going. What a way to start a day!

Gregor elbowed his way to the desk, and in two minutes came back with the word. A press conference in fifteen minutes. Jack Yocke stared at the TV reporter putting the final touches on his hair and nodded. If Townsend showed up, Jack was going to have to make a critical decision since the Soviet Square Massacre was now Tommy's story. Should he share the Shirley Ross tip with Tommy?

Thank heavens he didn't have to. Tommy never showed, even though the press conference started late, as do most things in Russia. It went about as Yocke expected. In the glare of the television lights the prosecutor's spokesman made a statement about the ongoing investigation – no leads yet on the identities or whereabouts of the killers that could be announced publicly, no arrests imminent, the

Russians had asked for Interpol assistance. The questions from the floor were asked in a respectful tone, merely for clarification of the spokesman's points. No one asked about anything he had not mentioned. Yocke edged toward the door behind the podium and pulled Gregor along.

When the farce was over he buttonholed the spokesman on his way out, a husky man who tried to breeze by.

'I need to speak with the prosecutor for one minute.'

Through Gregor came the answer: 'He is busy. He cannot see you.'

'The *Washington Post* has a story about why the police left the square that the prosecutor needs to confirm or deny.'

The spokesman eyed him suspiciously. 'Wait,' was his answer.

Yocke waited. The other reporters drifted out, the television crew packed up lights and extension cords and cameras and departed, Gregor lit a cigarette and lounged against the podium. Yocke looked at his watch.

Fifteen minutes had passed when he looked again. Gregor was on his third cigarette.

The prosecutor bustled into the room. '*Washington Post?*'

'Yes.'

'What is your story?'

Yocke took a deep breath and stared the man straight in the eye. He had but two lousy bullets to fight the war with and here goes shot number one: 'The police were pulled out of Soviet Square by a transmission over the police radio system.' He paused for Gregor to translate.

The prosecutor's eyebrows knitted, but that was his sole reaction.

Yocke continued: 'The police left because three KGB agents appeared in police headquarters and demanded that the police be removed from the square.'

Now the prosecutor's eyes widened in surprise. He spewed Russian. 'Where do you get this story? We announce nothing. Who talk to you?'

Yocke had counted on the man being a novice at dealing with Western reporters. He was new at the game, all right. Yocke decided to try a shot in the dark.

'Why have you relieved the police chief from his duties?'

The attorney's face darkened a shade. He chewed on the back of his lower lip while his eyes scanned Yocke's face. The reporter tried to remain deadpan, but it was difficult. 'We are investigating,' the prosecutor finally said.

Jack Yocke bit his own lip to keep from smiling. 'Will he be prosecuted?'

The man shrugged. 'Maybe.'

'For obeying the KGB?'

'Who has talked to you? No one should talk during an investigation.'

'Was the police chief in conspiracy with the killers?'

'Certainly not.'

'But he should not have obeyed the KGB?'

The prosecutor took a deep breath and adjusted the jacket on his shoulders. He frowned. 'This is a complex matter with many facets. We want no stories written just now. Surely you can understand that an accusation not later supported by facts would do great damage. To people's rights. To human rights. To right to a fair trial. Surely you see that, *Washington Post*.'

Jack Yocke couldn't believe his luck. He had expected stony denials and the prosecutor had denied nothing. And he had implicitly confirmed that the police chief had obeyed the orders of KGB officers, technically now Ministry of Security officers. The reporter decided to fire his last bullet and pray for a hit.

'Was Nikolai Demodov one of the KGB officers?'

The reaction was an explosive '*Nyet.*' Gregor translated the rest of it. 'That's a lie. Who told you this lie?'

'It was just a rumor. But you deny it?'

'Absolutely. It's a lie.'

'Who is Nikolai Demodov?'

But the prosecutor was leaving. He turned his back and stomped away.

Jack Yocke whipped out his steno pad and furiously began taking notes.

In the car he asked Gregor, 'Who is Nikolai Demodov?'

'Big man in KGB. Deputy to General Shmarov.'

'And who is Shmarov?'

'Number two man, I think. Little is printed about top Ministry of Security officers. They are Old Guard, old Communists loyal to the past. No-goodniks, most of them.'

'Shmarov is a no-goodnik? That means he's anti-Yeltsin, antidemocratic, doesn't it?'

The Lada squealed loudly as Gregor braked to a stop at a red traffic light. He sat hunched over the wheel staring at the red light on the pole. 'I want more money,' he said with finality. 'You told me you wished to write stories about life in Russia. Human being interest. You must pay me more.'

Jack Yocke rolled down the passenger window and dragged a half-bushel of pollution down into his lungs.

'You have no idea what it means to be Russian,' Gregor remarked.

The light changed and he popped the clutch and revved the tiny engine of the little sedan. Beside the car an army truck kept pace and poured noxious fumes through Yocke's open window. The American gagged and hastily spun the crank.

'Where are we going?' he asked Gregor.

'I don't know. You haven't told me.'

Soviet Square, Yocke decided, and informed his colleague. Gregor just nodded.

It was a broken-down car with the hood up that gave Yocke the idea. Cars with open hoods and the drivers bent over engines that refused to run were commonplace in Moscow. In a society without spare parts, without mechanics, without garages, without service stations, you either fixed it yourself on the side of the road with parts from junked vehicles or you left it there to be mined for parts by other motorists.

He explained what he wanted to Gregor, who again demanded more money. Yocke explained about his editor's parsimony and getting the expense approved in Washington, Moscow on the Potomac. Reluctantly Gregor agreed to help.

As they neared Soviet Square on Gorki Street Gregor turned the ignition off and let the car coast to the curb. Both men got out and raised the hood. Gregor disconnected the spark plug leads and took the top off the air filter. They put their elbows on the fender and their butts in the air and waited.

A policeman in gray uniform and white hat, carrying a white traffic baton and wearing a brown leather holster from which the butt of a small automatic protruded, arrived in three minutes. Yocke got busy under the hood and Gregor did the talking. Two minutes later, when the policeman wandered away, Gregor summed it up in a short sentence. 'He was on duty in Red Square the day of the assassination.'

They tried it again around the corner. The cop this time smoked one of Gregor's cigarettes and offered mechanical advice. They finally got the engine running and drove away waving.

'He heard the transmission over the police radio. He was one of the ones that left. The name of the policeman in charge of the radio is Burbulis.'

'We'll make a reporter of you yet. Police station.'

It took a lot of talking and cigarettes all round from the Marlboro carton, but Gregor and Yocke got in to see Burbulis. He was a chain smoker with steel teeth. He eyed Yocke suspiciously.

'I write for the *Washington Post*, a great American newspaper,' Gregor translated. 'I am following up a report that your chief is in trouble with the prosecutor because of the Soviet Square killings.' While Gregor translated this, Yocke tried to decide how much Burbulis liked the chief of police. He was praying for a little professional loyalty even if Burbulis loathed the man personally.

'Not his fault. I know the men. Good KGB men. We have worked together many times.'

'Names and addresses,' Yocke told Gregor, trying to keep the excitement out of his voice. 'Get names and addresses.'

They got three names and one address. And a lecture about the duty of the police to cooperate with the proper authorities. 'This questioning of police doing their duty by the prosecutor would never have happened in the old days,' Burbulis summed up, and sneered. 'Yeltsin has no courage. No respect. He understands nothing.' Burbulis smashed his fist on the table and glowered.

Out on the street Yocke carefully wrote down the names as Gregor spelled them in English. The address was merely a street. 'Do you know this street?'

'Yes. Off Arbat.'

He had it! A sure-fire page one barn burner that implicated the KGB in the murders of Communist ultranationalist Yegor Kolokoltsev and his henchmen! He jabbed his fist in the air and let out an exultant shout. The story would be picked up by the wire services and papers that reprinted *Post* stories and run worldwide. By Jack Yocke. Send the best, fire the rest!

He ignored the staring pedestrians and did a little hot-damn shuffle.

He had it all right, but first he had to write it. And if these KGB Commie assholes got a whiff of what was going down, he would write it ten years from now when he got out of the gulag in the middle of the Siberian winter.

He dove into the passenger seat of the Lada. 'Back to the hotel, James, and don't spare either of your beasts.'

Up in his room he packed the laptop in its padded case and confirmed that he had his passport and travel papers. He added a change of underwear to the case and his toothbrush and razor. He decided an extra pair of socks wouldn't hurt and stuffed them in. Then he zipped the case closed and stood staring at the rest of his stuff, taking inventory. His wallet and credit cards were in his pocket. He had a couple hundred on him. The rest of his cash and travelers checks were in the hotel safe; they could stay there.

He made sure his two suitcases were unlocked. If and when those guys came to look, he didn't want them breaking the locks.

He looked at his watch. Ten minutes before two. He had had no lunch. He wasn't hungry. Too excited.

He rode down in the elevator with a smile on his face. He even sang a few bars to himself in the mirror, a little James Brown: 'I feel good, da da dada dada da, like I knew I would, da da dada dada da.'

Gregor unlocked the trunk and Yocke laid the computer on top of a pile of engine parts and fan belts.

'We gotta go find these three KGB guys and see if they'll finger Demodov.'

Gregor sat behind the wheel and stared at him. 'Then what? Will you want to go see Demodov? In Dzerzhinsky Square?'

'I'll just call him, or try to anyway. He'll deny everything. Not worth the wear and tear on your car.'

'Idiot.'

'His denial in the last paragraph of the story will be the icing on the cake. Every last living soul will know he's guilty as hell.'

'Idiot,' Gregor repeated.

'Hey, this is the *Washington Post*, not the Slobovia *Gazette*. We always run the denials. About one time in a hundred the asshole is telling the truth, then we're covered. The lawyers like it like that.'

Gregor put both hands on the wheel and sat staring stonily ahead.

'Come on. Let's go.'

'I don't know what hole you will dive into when the story is printed, but I live here. I don't have any holes.'

'I told you I would talk to my editor about a raise. I meant that.'

Gregor snorted.

'What are they going to do to you? Is this your fault? Are you a reporter? You just drove me around and translated, for Christ's sake! Yeah, they may sweat you a little, and you can tell them everything. You have absolutely nothing to hide or apologize for. You're an interpreter! Then what? They'll let you go. You know that and I know that. The world has changed. Joe Stalin is rotting in some hole in the ground.'

Gregor started the car and put it in motion. 'I wish I were driving a taxi in Brooklyn with my wife's cousin.'

It took an hour and a half to find the only address they had, one for a KGB agent named Ivan Zvezdni. His apartment was on the top floor of a ten-story building and they had to walk up. The smell of grease and dirt and cabbage hung like a miasma in the crumbling concrete stairwell.

The woman who opened the door was in tears. Gregor had barely gotten out Yocke's identity and profession when she began to wail. 'They took him away. Just minutes ago,' Gregor muttered to Yocke. 'Men from the public prosecutor's office.'

Yocke eyed the only soft chair and eased himself into it. He wasn't leaving until he had it in spades.

It took half an hour to get the whole story, but it was worth it. Two mornings ago Zvezdni received a telephone call from Nikolai Demodov ordering him to go to police headquarters and tell the chief to pull the officers out of Soviet Square. Zvezdni knew it was Demodov because he knew his voice. Demodov specialized in political matters.

Although Demodov didn't explain the order, Zvezdni told his wife that the boss probably didn't want the police presence tarring the Old Guard with the wrath that

Kolokoltsev's message usually brought forth from Yeltsin's aides, especially since Yeltsin's people had denied Kolokoltsev a rally permit. Mrs Zvezdni didn't pretend to understand any of it, and she claimed her husband didn't. Ivan was a good officer, a loyal servant of the state. He always did as he was told, she said.

Whatever Ivan Zvezdni thought of Demodov's reasons, he obeyed orders this time too. He did, however, take two other agents along to protect himself. Mrs Zvezdni named them. Now he was under arrest. For doing his duty. For obeying orders. Life was just not fair. Mrs Zvezdni was reduced to silent tears.

It was damn thin, Yocke thought, but looking at Mrs Zvezdni he bought it. Well, if you were a KGB agent and your boss called and gave you an order, wouldn't you obey it?

The apartment was crowded but neat. There was no refrigerator. The family's food supply sat on a sideboard under a window. The furniture was old, scarred and spotlessly clean. The carpet was clean and threadbare.

'Make sure,' Yocke told Gregor, 'that she understands I write for an American newspaper.'

'She knows that. She does not care.'

He wanted to touch her arm, pat her head, but he refrained. She was using a scrap of white cloth to wipe her tears. 'Tell her I am sorry,' he said.

He was going to have to work fast. This story was too hot to wait. On the way to the car he told Gregor, 'Find a phone.' Gregor didn't protest.

Gregor made the call to the KGB. After repeated waits and spurts of Russian, he motioned to Yocke and handed him the receiver. They were standing at a pay phone on a sidewalk somewhere near Arbat Street. The phone was mounted on a wall and had a little half booth arranged around it.

'Hello. My name is Jack Yocke. I'm a reporter for the *Washington Post.*'

The voice on the other end said 'wait' in a heavy accent. At least it sounded like 'wait.'

Another minute passed before a guttural voice pronounced a name: 'Demodov.'

'Mr Demodov, do you speak English?'

'Yes.'

'My name is Jack Yocke. I'm a reporter for the *Washington Post*. We have a story that we are going to run that says that three National Security agents went to police headquarters this past Tuesday and asked the police chief to pull the police out of Soviet Square. The chief complied and Yegor Kolokoltsev was murdered minutes later. According to our information, you were the person who sent them to police headquarters. Do you wish to comment?'

Silence. Finally the voice again. 'I did not do that.'

Yocke scribbled the answer in his private shorthand.

'Have you been questioned by the public prosecutor about this matter?'

'No.'

'Are you aware that Ivan Zvezdni, one of your subordinates, was arrested by men from the public prosecutor's office just about an hour ago?'

'No. How do you know all this?'

'Do you wish to make any other comment about this story?'

'I know nothing about it. What more can I say?' And the connection broke.

Yocke replaced the phone on the hook and turned to Gregor.

'We got it. He denies everything.'

CHAPTER TWELVE

'Admiral Grafton, this is Jack Yocke. I've got a little problem and need your help.'

'What kind of problem?' The tone of the admiral's voice on the telephone made it clear that he didn't have time for a social call.

'It's a long story, sir, and I'd like to tell it to you in person.'

'I'm really swamped right now. Where are you?'

'Down here in the little reception office in front of the embassy compound.'

Grafton sighed. 'Okay. I'll send Toad down.'

'Thanks.'

Yocke hung up the telephone and went back outside. Gregor was sitting in the car, double-parked in the street. The reporter bent down so he could talk through the passenger window. 'I'll need the computer out of the trunk.'

Gregor killed the engine and climbed out. He opened the trunk without a word and let Yocke reach in and get the computer case. 'So it's good-bye then.'

'You're still on the payroll, Gregor. And I will talk to the editor about that raise.'

Gregor closed the trunk, locked it, then got back into the car. Yocke pulled a roll of bills out of his pocket and peeled off five twenties. He stood by the driver's door. 'Here. This is for you.'

Gregor stared up at him. He tried to smile but it didn't come out that way. 'No.'

'This isn't charity, Gregor. You've earned it. Feed your family.'

The Russian started the car and put it in gear. Yocke tossed the bills in his lap as the car got under way. 'I'll call you,' he shouted.

He adjusted the strap of the computer bag and watched the Lada go down the street trailing a thin blue cloud of exhaust fumes. After it disappeared from sight he turned toward the embassy gate. Toad Tarkington was standing there watching him.

'What have you been into this time?'

Yocke glanced at the gate guard, a Moscow policeman wearing the usual gray uniform. He went past him into the reception office and turned to face Tarkington.

'The KGB was waiting for me at my hotel.'

Toad snorted. 'You sure?'

'We drove by. There were a dozen police cars out front, a dozen or so guys in dark suits around the entrance. Three or four at every other door. It looked like Al Capone's garden party. I tripped over a hornet's nest.'

Toad snorted. 'Kicked it over, you mean. Then you come charging over to the Hotel Grafton with your hair on fire and a rat in your mouth.'

'Dammit, Toad, I've got to write this story and file it.'

'Story on what?'

'The Soviet Square killings.'

Toad pursed his lips as he examined Yocke's face. 'Better come up and tell it to the admiral,' he said, and made a hi sign to the receptionist behind the safety glass. After she pushed her button Toad opened the door for the reporter.

Jake Grafton was surrounded by computer printouts and maps. He was curt. 'Let's hear it.'

So Toad told it. Quickly and concisely. When he had completed his recitation the admiral glanced at Tarkington, who was leaning back against the wall with his eyebrows up as far as they would go.

'So the KGB set up their stooge, Kolts-something,' the admiral said. 'Why?'

'Well, there are several possible reasons why they might have done it, like—'

'You're going to write this story without *knowing* why they did it?'

'Yep.' Yocke glanced at his watch. 'It'll run on tomorrow's front page.' Seeing the look on Grafton's face, the reporter went on: 'Gimme a break, Admiral. If we had waited to get Lee Harvey Oswald's reasons before we reported Kennedy's assassination, we'd still be waiting.'

'That's a real argument stopper, but it's hardly germane to this case.'

'Facts are facts.'

'If you've got any.'

Jack Yocke's face flushed. 'Jesus! You're worse than my editor.'

'I'm just pointing out the obvious. If I were a reporter I'd want it in spades before I accused someone of murder. But you're the guy they pay the big bucks.' Grafton cleared his throat while Jack Yocke figured out how to handle his face.

When the reporter spoke his voice was carefully under control. 'I'm not accusing anyone of anything. I've got a story about how the police were pulled out of that square and in my professional opinion, it's solid. I—' He stopped speaking because Jake Grafton had waved his hand, cutting him off.

The admiral toyed with a pen, clicking the point in and out a few times. 'Yeltsin is going to be one happy man when he hears about this,' he said finally.

'I suppose.'

Toad cleared his throat. 'How about describing this woman you met in the bar.'

'Now wait a minute. It doesn't really matter who she is. She merely gave me a tip and I verified it by an independent investigation.'

Yocke hadn't given the woman's motives a thought and

Toad's question irritated him. In America people routinely sought out reporters to put them onto a story. Reporters knew these people were driven by a variety of motives, including revenge. Yet if the story checked out as true and newsworthy, the tipster's motives didn't really matter. And Jack Yocke knew damn well he had latched onto a big, true story. A huge story. The dimensions of it slightly awed him. And it was solid. There was no way in hell those people today were acting, feeding him a line. After questioning a few thousand people, he knew the truth when he heard it. If he heard it. And by God, today he had heard it.

The problem was Tarkington. He was a good man, but at times he was tough to swallow. Jack Yocke took a deep breath and added, 'The public prosecutor has the three KGB agents who went to the police station locked up right now. They want to jug me.'

'Yeah, yeah, I know all that. You've scooped everybody and you're gonna be famous. Now tell me what this broad looked like.'

'Well, she was about five eight or so, dark brown shoulder-length hair, dark brown – almost black – eyes set wide apart, a classic bone structure.'

'Good figure?'

'Well, I suppose so.'

'You queer or what?' Tarkington asked sharply.

'She was wearing modest clothes, a good wool suit. Underneath it all she was probably built like a brick shithouse. Is that what you want to hear, sailor boy?'

Toad met Jake Grafton's gaze. His eyebrows went up and down once in reply to Grafton's silent question.

'You know her?' Yocke asked Toad.

'Just curious, Jack. What I'm trying to figure out is why you.'

'Because she knew I was a reporter.'

'This town is full of reporters. Why you?'

'You two sailors are a real pair. I thought you'd let me hole up here.' His voice rose: 'But no, Jack, you might write something that embarrasses the good ol' US of A. and we probably can't handle—'

'That's enough,' Jake said disgustedly. 'You can sleep on the couch. Right now you go into Toad's room' – he nodded toward the bedroom door – 'and write your story. When you're ready to send it in let me know. In the meantime don't pick up the phone even if it rings.'

Jack Yocke stood and hoisted the computer. He had half a mind to tell these two clowns where to go and what to do to themselves when they got there, but . . . He mumbled his thanks, then his eye fell on the maps and computer printouts. 'Say, what is all this paper?'

'Not a word to your editor about this one,' Jake told him. 'But you ain't the only guy with problems. The Russians just had another nuclear power plant meltdown.'

'*Holy* . . . *!* Like Chernobyl?'

'Maybe worse.'

'Where? Around here?'

'Someplace called Serdobsk, about three hundred miles southeast of here. Now go in there and shut the door and let us work.'

After the door closed Toad turned on the radio. Classical music came out.

'Judith Farrell?' Jake asked.

'I'd bet the ranch, CAG.'

Jake Grafton went to the window and stood looking out. He rubbed the back of his neck, then moved his shoulders up and down. Finally he stretched.

When he turned around he told Toad, 'The Israelis sure get their money's worth out of that woman.'

'Uh-huh.'

Toad was looking at the map spread upon the floor. The wind was going to spread that radioactivity over hundreds of square miles. He was looking now at the villages in the fallout zone. He couldn't even pronounce the Russian names upon the chart. A great many people from a culture he didn't know were about to die, and it sickened him.

'Do you believe in God?' he asked Jake Grafton.

'Only on Sundays,' the admiral replied.

'There's a military base here in this footprint, sir. Petrovsk. Here, take a look. Wasn't that the base we visited a couple days ago?'

Jake Grafton looked. 'Yes. Petrovsk. Missiles with nuclear warheads.'

'They'll have to evacuate that base, if they haven't already.'

Evacuate. That meant airplanes, fuel. And what percentage of the base personnel could be carried on the planes?

'Wonder if Moscow will even tell those people that a lethal cloud of radioactivity is coming their way?'

'If only five or ten percent of them could possibly escape, would you tell them?' Jake Grafton mused, his voice so low that Toad almost missed the comment. '*What* would you tell them?'

A little later he muttered, 'A lot of that radioactivity is going to go into the Volga.'

He looked again at the predicted radioactivity levels. The numbers were two or three times worse than Chernobyl. How did people manage to make such horrible messes on this tiny, fragile planet? His finger moved on the map, down the Volga past Saratov and Engels, past Kamyshin, all the way to Volgograd, formerly Stalingrad. The water supplies of those cities would be grossly contaminated. The land. The food supply. Jake Grafton picked up the estimate of the various isotope levels and their half-lives and stared at it, trying to take it in.

And on down the Volga to the Caspian Sea. How much radioactivity could that closed inland ocean tolerate before it became a dead sea?

This was worse than a disaster — it was a nightmare. When the Russian people finally learned the truth, what would be their reaction?

The telephone rang and Toad picked it up. After saying 'Yessir,' several times, he replaced the receiver and told

Jake, 'The ambassador wants you to go with him to the Kremlin. In a couple hours our president will announce that the United States will assist Russia any way it can.'

Jake Grafton took a deep breath and let it out slowly. 'So when is the Yeltsin government going public on this?'

'The ambassador's aide didn't say. Soon, apparently.'

Yeltsin had no choice. Gorbachev had waited for days to tell the world of Chernobyl and had been excoriated for it. But Gorbachev had been a Communist and Yeltsin swore he no longer was. 'Umm,' Jake Grafton said.

'Maybe you'd better wear your uniform, sir,' Toad said gently. 'It looks like it's going to be one of those days.'

'Jack Yocke has just been had by a pro. She conned him good and he's so anxious for a story – any story – that he swallowed it without even tasting it.'

Toad Tarkington nodded. 'I'll buy that.'

'She may try again.'

'Naw. She's not that stupid. Too big a risk.'

'When the stakes get this large any risk is justified. *Any risk!* We've got to get to her before Jack Yocke does.'

Captain Herbert 'Tom' Collins was the naval attaché. As the senior naval officer he supervised a staff of just three other officers: one a marine lieutenant colonel, one a navy commander, and the other the politically impure lieutenant, Spiro Dalworth. A surface warfare officer with a destroyer command behind him, Collins had acquired a degree in Russian from the US Naval Postgraduate School in Monterey, California, while he was still a lieutenant. Tonight Jake recalled with a jolt that Collins' first assignment after the Naval Academy had been to nuclear power school. After graduating, he then spent his first tour tending a reactor aboard a nuclear-powered frigate.

These days Collins tried to keep track of what was happening in the former Soviet Navy as the ships, planes and sailors were divided between the newly independent republics. The job was impossible. In the past the naval officers had subsisted on a mere trickle of information, mainly what the Soviets wanted them to see and hear – now they were drowning in it. The Russians were showing them everything, telling everything, talking openly about weapons capability, maintenance problems with ships, engines, radars, planes, problems with personnel, training, recruitment, supply, food . . . everything. If there were any secrets left in the new Commonwealth, Collins had yet to bump into one of them.

Two nights ago he told Jake Grafton, 'Today the Russian Navy would lose a fight with the Italians. Honest to God, since the collapse they can't get food or fuel to steam with. They can't feed the sailors; they can't maintain the ships; they got 'em tied up rusting at the pier. A couple more years of this and most of those ships will be beyond salvage.'

Tonight in the courtyard Tom Collins turned up the volume on his portable radio, which was tuned to a Russian station playing American jazz. They were standing in the shadow of the new embassy complex, empty and condemned because it was hopelessly infested with bugs – the electronic kind.

'Isn't one of your chiefs a communications specialist?' Jake asked.

'One of my two, sir. Senior Chief Holley.' Collins was eyeing Jake's uniform and the ribbons displayed there. The admiral had just returned from the Kremlin with the ambassador.

'I need to borrow him for a while. Holley and Dalworth.'

'We're drowning in my shop, Admiral. I've got them working twenty hours a day.' Collins and the other military people were using every contact they had to try to discover what the Russian military knew about the extent of the damage from the Serdobsk meltdown. Jake had spent the day helping, trying to analyze information received in dribbles from all quarters.

'I understand. This is important.'

'Aye aye, sir.'

Jake Grafton felt like a jerk. He merely needed two people he could trust – anyone really – and Collins had an important job to do. Still, if he could get to Judith Farrell . . .

'So what are the Russians saying?' Jake asked.

'Same old story. It's all Yeltsin's fault.'

'Is it?'

'Well, there's no money to maintain reactors and they're all in terrible shape. An American inspector from the Nuclear Regulatory Commission would have a heart attack if he saw one of those plants, but they've been like that for years. This country is too poor to properly build or maintain or operate nuclear power plants. They just don't have the technical expertise or the trained people.' Collins' shoulders sagged. 'They're like monkeys with a computer.'

'Nobody over at the Kremlin will even hazard a guess about why that thing melted.'

Collins grunted. 'There are meltdowns and there are meltdowns,' he said. 'The accidents at Three Mile Island and Chernobyl could be classified as radiation leaks. This one was a real whing-ding, snap-doodle of a meltdown – there isn't much left out there. The satellite sensors show unbelievable temperatures. The first reading they got was thirty minutes after the thing went. We got a fax of a satellite photo half an hour ago and you wouldn't believe it. Looks like the damn thing was hit with a ten-ton block-buster. The structure is gone – steel, concrete, everything. Nothing left but some rubble and a hole in the ground.'

After a bit Collins added, 'Of course, there's not a chance in a zillion that anyone survived it.'

Grafton whistled. 'You're saying it's almost like it blew up.'

'That's precisely what it did. In the argot of the trade, "a power excursion," or a runaway. In lay terms, the son of a bitch blew up.'

Jake was stunned. Today no one had mentioned an

explosion, nor had the word passed the lips of anyone at the Kremlin. 'I thought nuclear reactors couldn't explode.'

'A popular misconception. Fast breeders can. This one did.'

Jake was still trying to take it in. 'Exploded?'

'The core exploded.'

'A nuclear explosion?'

'Boom.'

'How could that happen?'

Collins rubbed his face. He looked around, then by reflex turned up the volume on the radio. 'Serdobsk was a liquid metal fast breeder reactor, one of the first ones the Russians built. The core is made up of uranium-235, which is surrounded by rods of uranium-238, which breed into plutonium. In a water-cooled pressure reactor, bleeding off the water causes the core to melt and fission to stop. Of course the hot core can melt the containment vessel and release radioactivity, but fission stops. In a breeder, loss of coolant has the opposite effect: the fission reaction increases. The more rapid the coolant loss, the worse the effect. As the temperature rises the core melts and fills the spaces between the rods. When the material is compact enough, it can detonate in a nuclear explosion.'

Collins waved a hand impatiently. 'It's been years since I studied this stuff, but as I recall, theoretically you could get an explosion about the equivalent of ten tons of TNT if the core is really cooking when the coolant goes. That looks to me about what they had. An explosion like that would blow maybe half the core material into the atmosphere – that's tons of really filthy uranium, plutonium, iodine, strontium-90, that kind of crap.'

Jake Grafton felt like a sinner listening to God's verdict. 'Tons?'

Collins was merciless. 'If you want all the trade words, a liquid-metal-cooled breeder is autocatalytic – it's its own catalyst for manufacturing power excursions. The process of compaction and excursions that result in more compactions is a little like what happens in a collapsing star at the end of its life. Power melts the core, it crashes down, more power, more rebound or crashdown, poof! Think of it like a little supernova. The nuclear reaction stops only when the core disassembles – blows itself to smithereens.'

'What could cause this . . . core compaction?'

'Well, I'm no expert, but—'

'You're as close to an expert as I've got.'

'As I recall, there are a bunch of theoretical possibilities. Basically any event that causes the core to be compacted can start the process. The reactor is cooled by liquid sodium, which is hotter than hell: molten steel could cause the sodium to vaporize and explode. A sodium vapor explosion is the most likely way, but fuel vaporizing could trigger it. Or an external explosion that damages the core and compacts it, or coolant loss or surges that damage the core—'

Jake had had enough. He stopped the recitation with a raised hand. 'So how bad is it?'

'Bad?' Collins stared at him as if he were a dense child. 'This reactor was old, full of plutonium and really raunchy crud. Plutonium is the deadliest substance known to man. It has a half-life of twenty-four thousand two hundred years. One would have to wait for about ten half-lives, call it two hundred and fifty thousand years, for the stuff to cool off to the tolerable level.'

'Forever.'

'Essentially forever.'

'How much land will have to be permanently abandoned?'

'I dunno. They're trying to figure that out in Washington. And I'm trying to make some estimates. Depends on the winds and how much atmospheric mixing there was, how much rain, all that stuff.'

'So guess,' Jake Grafton said.

'Maybe fifty thousand square miles. Maybe twice that.' Collins shrugged.

'Yeltsin's fault,' Jake Grafton said slowly.

'It's somebody's.' Collins weighed his words. 'You know, I got out of nuclear power after my first tour. Oh, I was a gung-ho little nuke all right – had my interview with that troll Rickover and did my time in Idaho and thought we had the fucking genie corked up tight. But this stuff – he looked around again, searching for words – 'God uses fusion to make the stars burn. We use fission now and we're working up to fusion. We're playing God . . . toddlers sitting in the dark playing with matches. The consequences . . . I just decided I wanted no more of it.'

'Serdobsk blew. Man's hubris? Or did someone help this supernova compaction along?'

'What do you want, Admiral? Probability theory?'

'Yes.'

'Never bet on God. Go with the main chance. Men build 'em, men screw 'em up.'

'If you were going to blow a breeder, how would you go about it?'

Collins was in no mood for what-if games, yet a glance at Grafton's face made him concentrate on the question. 'Shaped charges on top of the vessel. Blow down and in. Put some hot molten steel into that sodium stew. The charges wouldn't have to be very big since the containment vessel is unpressurized. With luck I'd get a little sodium vapor explosion that would send a shock wave down into the core. The first shock wave would lead to a power excursion and another – bigger – shock wave, and so on. If I were willing to meet my maker with that on my conscience, that's the way I'd do it.'

Jake Grafton just grunted.

The telephone rang at midnight. 'Admiral Grafton.'

'This is Richard, Admiral. I've got it.'

Jake came wide awake. Richard Harper. 'This isn't a secure line, Richard.'

'Okay.' Two seconds of silence. 'It was a hell of a trail

and they were damn cute, but I *got it*. How do you want it?'

'I'll have someone call you. Can you write it out?'

'Sure.'

CHAPTER THIRTEEN

The storm broke in Russia the next morning. The speaker of the Congress of People's Deputies managed to call the house to order, but that was the last thing he accomplished. While the world watched on television the deputies brawled. Finger pointing and shouting gave way to shoving and fists. Before the camera was turned off several deputies were seen to be on the floor being kicked and pounded with fists by their colleagues.

A huge, angry crowd gathered in Red Square. Conspicuous today were the red flags, the ugly mood. Then, as if someone struck a match, the crowd exploded. A truck was overturned and set on fire. Policemen were beaten, several to death. Then the rioters spilled out of the square and headed for the nearby hard-currency hotels and restaurants, which they looted. One hotel was set ablaze. Foreigners were attacked on the streets and beaten mercilessly. Somehow CNN managed to televise most of the riot live to a stunned, angry, frightened world.

Although the sense of fear and betrayal was strongest in Russia, the rest of the world felt it too. Nuclear power plants stood throughout the Western world. Their safety had long been an issue, but the debate seemed esoteric to electorates concerned with the mundane issues of jobs, wages, education and housing. The massive, catastrophic pollution from the Serdobsk accident was something the public could understand. They were seeing the consequences of an accident that advocates of nuclear power said would never happen.

In Italy the coalition government fractured and the premier resigned. The French president addressed a crowd estimated at ten thousand people and was forced to stop speaking when a riot broke out on the edge of the crowd. Across the channel the British prime minister was questioned sharply in Parliament from both sides of the aisle about the dangers of Britain's nuclear reactors. Here too a significant percentage of the lawmakers were immediately ready to shut down all the reactors.

By the time Americans began to wake up with their coffee, newspapers and morning television shows, the fat was in the fire. The television played scenes of rioting in Russia and the political crises in Europe while people read the front pages of their newspapers with a growing sense of horror. Jack Yocke's story on the KGB's involvement in the Soviet Square massacre – it was dubbed a massacre by an inspired headline writer and the name stuck – made the front page of the Washington *Post*, at the very bottom. The rest of the page was devoted to the Serdobsk meltdown.

Experts were stunned by the extent of the disaster. It was as if none of the redundant safety systems in the reactor had functioned. Initial estimates on the level of radioactivity at ground level where the reactor had stood were hastily developed from satellite infrared and other sensors. 'It will be three hundred thousand years,' one physicist declared, 'before an unprotected human can safely walk upon that site.'

In the Capitol in Washington congressmen elbowed one another vying to get in front of the cameras in the press briefing rooms. Every one of them swore he would support a critical review of the American nuclear power program. A significant minority was ready to shut down all the reactors right *now*. Among this minority were several of the legislators who had fought hardest on behalf of the utilities that operated reactors – the same people, incidentally, who had accepted the most PAC money from those utilities.

The antinuclear lobby was having a great day. Triumphant

and exultant as the tide lifted their boat, they excoriated senators and congressmen who had consistently pooh-poohed safety concerns. They damned the Nuclear Regulatory Commission as an industry puppet, vilified every public official who ever said that nuclear power was safe, and demanded the immediate resignation of the secretary of the Department of Energy.

While the antinukes danced and pranced in television studios in New York and Washington, a huge crowd gathered outside the Capitol and were harangued by impromptu speakers. After an hour the crowd became unruly and police used tear gas to break it up.

When the sun rose in Japan the antinuclear, anti-technology forces arrayed in helmets and plastic body armor were ready to do battle with club-wielding riot police. The battle surged through downtown Tokyo, commuter trains were literally overturned, power lines were dragged down while still hot, and a mob broke through the fence at Narita airport. Outnumbered riot police turned and ran as the demonstrators charged for the Boeing 747s at the terminal gates. Most of the giant planes suffered minor damage, mostly to their tires, but two were set on fire.

The chaos brought the city to a choking halt while legislators in the Diet crafted a hasty plan to shut down Japan's nuclear power plants. The power loss would stun the economy, but in a small nation that had never forgotten Hiroshima or Nagasaki, this was the only possible political choice. As uncomfortable, perspiring physicists sat before television cameras and tried to assess the Serdobsk melt-down damage based on fragmentary information, Japan got out of the nuclear power business.

At stock exchanges around the world the value of stocks in electrical utilities that owned nuclear power plants fell disastrously before trading was halted because of the huge disparity between buy and sell orders.

But Serdobsk was in Russia, and it was there that the situation got completely out of control as the evening shadows lengthened. The development 'at any price' mentality of the post-World War II years was revealed for what it was — a grotesque miscalculation that had bankrupted the nation, left the people paupers on the brink of starvation, and now had made huge portions of the nation uninhabitable. Raging mobs roamed the core of Moscow and no foreigner was safe. Three hotels were now ablaze. The entrances to the Kremlin were blocked with barricades, and police hid behind them to fire into the enraged crowds. Several tanks appeared on the streets, only to be surrounded and disabled. The crews were dragged out and beaten to death as television camera crews broadcast the scenes from the safety of the rooftops.

A mob surrounded the American embassy complex and probably would have stormed it if the ambassador hadn't ordered the marines to use live ammunition and shoot to kill. They did. By the time the summer sun had set, over a dozen bodies lay on the streets around the embassy. One of the bodies was of a young woman who had tried to get close enough to the wall to hurl a Molotov cocktail. When a corporal shot her, the bottle shattered beside her and her corpse was immolated. This vignette would have made great television, but unfortunately the CNN crew on the rooftop across the boulevard was having trouble with their satellite feed.

Jack Yocke saw the incident and used it to lead off a story for the *Post*. He knew he had something. The woman's hair blowing in the wind as she lay dead in the street, the burning gasoline igniting the asphalt, her clothing, and finally that wispy brown hair — he could still see the scene in his mind's eye as he tapped on the laptop and tried to capture the insanity of infuriated, berserk people charging marines behind a brick wall armed with M-16s. Blood and guts were what he did best, so he wrote quickly and confidently.

As he wrote he could still hear the occasional sharp crack of an M-16. Now and then through the open window he got a whiff of the acrid smoke of a burning car that the locals had torched this morning. It was a Ford with diplomatic plates – just which embassy employee it belonged to Yocke didn't know. When he was finished he checked his work over for spelling and punctuation, then called the *Post* on Grafton's telephone and sent the story via modem.

After Yocke had sent off his story, he locked the door of the apartment and went looking for Jake Grafton. He found him against the southwest corner of the compound wall busy with the TACSAT gear and encoder. The admiral merely glanced at him and continued to punch buttons, so Yocke sat down beside him.

Above them, standing on some empty furniture crates so he could see over the wall, was a marine with a rifle. He was scanning the windows of a Russian apartment house just across the alley. Fortunately no rioters had chosen to get up there and shoot down into the compound, probably because none of them had guns. The Communists had made damn sure that the civilian inhabitants of their workers' paradise were unarmed and stayed that way.

'Hell of a day, huh?' Yocke said.

Grafton finished with the number sequence. He diddled a bit with the dish and high-gain antenna on top of the box and finally got the voice echo in sync with his voice. He pushed another button, then leaned back against the wall with the telephone-style handset cradled on his shoulder and glanced at the reporter. 'Yeah,' he said.

After a moment be spoke into the mouthpiece. 'General Land, please. Admiral Grafton calling.'

More waiting. Grafton nodded at Yocke's trousers. 'Toad loan you those?'

'His are too small. He bought me some stuff at the embassy store.'

Grafton merely nodded and played with the handset cord.

Almost a minute passed before he spoke again:

'Admiral Grafton, sir. Calling from the embassy compound in Moscow . . . Yessir . . . Ambassador Lancaster talked to Yeltsin about a half hour ago on the satellite phone. Called Washington and they called Yeltsin and patched him through . . . I think the local phone system is overloaded, everybody calling everybody . . . Yessir . . . Yeltsin told the ambassador that the generals won't bring in troops to put down the rioting. They want him to resign and appoint a junta . . . That's right, a junta — seven of them . . . Marshal Mikhailov, General Yakolev, a KGB guy named Shmarov — those three I've heard of. There're a couple more generals and one admiral. The seventh guy is some civilian . . . Yessir.'

Grafton eyed Yocke, who had raised his eyes and was watching the marine on the crates.

'I don't know,' Grafton said, then listened some more.

Grafton was in civilian clothes — Yocke noticed that the trousers were none too clean. Neither was the shirt. Then he realized the clothes were Russian, not American. So were the shoes.

'I wonder if you could order some photos for me. I want satellite photos of the Russian base at Petrovsk.' He listened a moment, then spelled the name of the base. 'That's right. It's in the footprint of the Serdobsk fallout. Should be too hot for humans. I want a shot at least a month old, one maybe last week and one now. And some of that Serdobsk nuke plant.'

The admiral listened a moment, then went on. 'Well, I would like about six antiradiation suits . . . No, better make that ten suits, with oxygen-breathing apparatus. Fly them in on a C-141. We'll get out to the airport somehow . . . Ten . . . Yessir . . . Self-contained breathing apparatus, the whole shooting match. Geiger counters, film badges, everything . . . Yessir, I'd like to get down to Serdobsk if I can.

'Well, I don't think Yakolev is going to lift a finger. He's busy trying to take over the government . . . Not a soul, sir. No, I don't think he'll do anything to obstruct us, but the worse this gets the worse Yeltsin and the democrats look . . . I know, that occurred to me too. That's one reason I want to get to Serdobsk.'

Grafton fell silent for a moment and eyed Yocke. It wasn't a pleasant look. 'We'll steal one,' he told General Land. 'Send me a couple pilots that can fly anything, and I mean anything. And just to be on the safe side, could you send a marine recon team with all their gear and hot suits?'

They talked about that for a moment, then Jake said, 'And one more thing, sir. I've had a man named Richard Harper trying to find the money trail to whoever it is here in Russia that is selling weapons. He called last night and said he has it. I asked him to write a report. He's supposed to mail it to my wife, but I wonder if you could send someone from your office over to his house in Chevy Chase to pick it up? Make a copy for yourself and send me a copy.' Jake gave him Harper's address.

'Thank you, sir,' he said finally and hung up the receiver. He punched buttons and the lights on the gadget went out.

'Needless to say, you don't want me to print a word of that,' Yocke said conversationally.

'Needless to say.'

'What are you going to steal?'

'A helicopter.'

'Can I go too?'

'I'll think about it.'

Yocke nodded. Grafton packed the com gear into a soft carrying bag. He was zipping it closed when Yocke asked, 'Think Yeltsin will resign?'

'Maybe.'

'Well, by God, after—'

'He may not have a choice,' Grafton said. 'In case you haven't noticed, Russia is a Third World shithole. The rule in Third World shitholes is that the head of government serves at the pleasure of the guys with the guns.'

Jack Yocke wasn't paying much attention. His mind was in high gear ruminating on Nikolai Demodov and the KGB general, Shmarov, who it turned out wanted to be one of the magnificent seven. And Demodov denied he had been involved in the Soviet Square rubout . . . Shit! Those assholes must have been biding their time, waiting for just the proper moment to dump Yeltsin. They just didn't want that xenophobic neo-nazi Kolokoltsev around to embarrass them when the puck went down. But how could he tie those Commies to Kolokoltsev's killing?

Grafton stood and arranged the strap of the com gear bag over his shoulder. He looked up at the marine. 'Did you hear anything, Corporal Williams?'

'Not a word, sir.'

'Fine.'

Grafton took a couple steps, then paused and looked back at Yocke. 'Well, you coming or are you going to sit there in the dirt contemplating your navel?'

The reporter got up and dusted his trousers. 'You oughta see my navel. Got a ruby in it. Arab belly dancer gave it to me when I was sixteen. She was my first piece of ass.'

Yocke's attempt at humor fell flat with Jake Grafton. He too had seen the girl shot and her corpse burned. And he was trying to understand what must have moved her to pick up a bottle filled with gasoline with a burning rag stuck in the mouth and run across that street at the American embassy.

Betrayal? The Russian people had been betrayed by the Communists, all right, who had promised much and delivered little.

But the American embassy?

Perhaps she felt a profound anger at a system that for fifty years had paid any price to acquire technology, yet in the end the technology betrayed them all. The Americans were the gurus of high-tech, the master alchemists.

Musing thus, Jake was still unsure. A great disgust at technology and technicians was motivating much of the political unrest worldwide, he thought, but still . . . Serdobsk was a Russian reactor. Perhaps mixed with those emotions was the age-old Russian suspicion of all things foreign. The Russians weren't as bad as the Chinese in that regard, but they did fear the outside world, some sort of a national inferiority complex that they soaked up with their mother's milk.

He would like to have asked that young woman, but that chance was gone forever. She was a heap of charcoal and bone now, out there on a spot of melted, charred asphalt.

Jake Grafton wondered if the dead woman had had any relatives at Serdobsk or out there in that radioactive footprint.

He was opening the door to the apartment building when Jack Yocke asked, 'Did General Land say what America's response to the meltdown was going to be?'

Now Jake saw it. He let go of the door handle and turned to face Yocke. He could almost hear her voice. *You are America. You are not stupid and venal and corrupt, yet you did nothing to help us. You let the stupid, venal, corrupt men tell their lies and build their poisonous monuments to our ignorance and so destroy us, the helpless. You, America.*

Jack Yocke repeated his question.

'No,' Jake Grafton muttered, shaking his head. 'He didn't.' And he turned back for the door handle.

Upstairs in the apartment, which of necessity was also Jake's office, Yocke had more questions. 'Just how much nuclear material was in that reactor, anyway?'

'About four and a half tons.'

'Tons?'

'Yeah. Maybe three or so tons of uranium and a ton and a half of plutonium.'

'Gee, that sounds like a lot. I guess I always thought those things used just a couple of hatfuls.'

'This was a fast breeder. A typical water-cooled reactor would have maybe three times that amount.'

'So this time they got off lucky?'

Jake Grafton snorted. 'Not hardly. The goddamn stuff

blew up, went nuclear. Probably half the core went into the atmosphere. We don't know enough yet to even make an intelligent estimate. And a breeder like that – it figures they had three or four tons of plutonium in the pipeline, just lying around. Some of that probably got swept up into the atmosphere and scattered all over too. No, these Russians just had no luck at all.'

After a bit Yocke asked, 'So how bad is it?'

'Bad?' Grafton looked perplexed.

'Compared to Chernobyl.'

Grafton shrugged. 'A hundred times worse? Two hundred times? "Bad" is a ridiculous understatement. The stuff that went into the air is really filthy . . .' He groped for words, then gave up. 'Really filthy,' he repeated. 'Serdobsk is way the hell and gone away from everything, so no cities were poisoned immediately, but by the time all that fallout hits the rivers and streams and lakes . . .' He shrugged. 'I wouldn't be surprised if this incident ultimately kills a million people.'

Jack Yocke just stared.

'*Another million,*' Jake Grafton roared savagely. 'God in heaven, when will it ever stop?'

Yocke got out his laptop and pecked aimlessly until Jake suggested he do that in the bedroom, so he went in and closed the door. The muffled crack of a rifle penetrated the room and Jake half-rose off the couch before he thought better of it.

He needed time to think. One of the most trying things about a military career, he thought, was that so many decisions had to be made immediately with the best information available, which used to be precious little and fragmentary at best. Then came computers and the highly touted information age; the trickle of information became a raging torrent of facts and numbers endlessly pouring from laser printers that no one had time to look at. Who could drink from a fire hose?

Jake Grafton knew that if he merely picked up a telephone

and asked, he could have more information in an hour than he could read in a year. Better to go with what he had. He leaned his head back onto the couch, closed his eyes and tried to assess his meager collection of facts and impressions.

The most important fact . . . impression maybe . . . was one he wasn't sure he had right. Most people automatically assume that people everywhere are all alike – *'they think like we do!'* Jake knew better. But he thought he could see the viewpoint of the professional soldiers like Yakolev who saw their place in Russian society slipping out from under them. Without the American enemy to stimulate the allocation of damn scarce resources and keep the ranks filled and people motivated, the military was crumbling. They had tried to fashion a new mission to protect ethnic Russian minorities wherever they might be and had been out-maneuvered by Yeltsin and his allies. The nukes were being taken away while the Americans and Europeans kept their conventional forces, there was no money, not even to feed the troops, the industrial establishment necessary to support a modern military was disintegrating, all at a time when the values the leaders had devoted their lives to were belittled or rendered politically meaningless. The Soviet Union was gone. Mother Russia was collapsing from within, there were no more secrets to guard, there was no place for men of integrity and honor. So the generals were going to save Russia in spite of politicians.

How far would these men go?

How far had they already gone?

Yakolev: *'I serve Russia!'* A uniform for a patriot or a bloody rag to hide a tyrant's nakedness?

Someone was shaking him. He opened his eyes with a start. It was Tarkington, holding a finger to his lips for silence. He seized Jake's arm and nodded toward the hall door, which was partially open. His lips moved, a silent word: 'Come.'

When they were in the hallway Toad eased the door

shut behind them until it clicked, then led Jake down the hall. He passed Jake his pistol, which was sheathed in its shoulder holster. The gun had been under the pillow in Jake's bedroom, and Toad had retrieved it before he woke the boss.

'Yocke has an outside call,' he whispered. 'The senior chief stalled and told her he's trying to find him. When we get back to the switchboard he'll ring the phone. Yocke's in there, isn't he?'

'Uh-huh.' Jake glanced at his watch. Almost two in the morning.

Toad broke into a trot.

'Is it her?' Jake wanted to know.

'I didn't hear her voice. But I got this feeling.' After all, Toad thought, how many women could there be in Moscow who want to talk to Jack Yocke?

When the two officers came through the door, Senior Chief Dan Holley flipped a switch on the switchboard. 'Still there, ma'am?' he asked. Then he said, 'He's staying with some folks. I'll ring now.' Then he toggled the switch again and handed the headset to Jake Grafton.

'The mike won't work, but you'll hear everything.'

Jake donned the headset and listened to the ringing. The telephone in the apartment was in the small living room and Yocke was probably asleep, so this was probably going to take a moment.

The phone rang and rang.

Oh, damn. Two nights ago when Yocke arrived at the embassy, he had told him not to answer the phone. What if he doesn't?

Toad and the senior chief were watching. More ringing.

C'mon, Jack. You're supposed to be a curious reporter!

'It's ringing,' Jake told his audience. And then the door opened and Spiro Dalworth slipped into the room. Jake had had Spiro, Toad and the senior chief alternating shifts on this switchboard since Captain Collins gave his approval.

221

The regular operator supervised and gave them directions, but the navy men listened to the voice of every caller and waited for someone to ask for Jack Yocke.

Now it had happened.

Ten rings. Eleven. *Dammit, Jack! Answer the phone!*

'Hello.' Yocke was still half asleep.

'Jack?' A woman's voice. An American woman. Was it her?

'I think so.' He sounded almost petulant.

'This is Shirley Ross. I'm glad I reached you. I tried half the hotels in town and was about to give up when I thought of the embassy.'

'Hmm. What time is it?'

'It's late I know, but I just had to talk to you.'

'Glad you called.' Yocke's voice was crisp and alert. He was wide awake now. 'How are you weathering the riot?'

'I heard about your story,' she gushed. 'I'm so thrilled! It's so important that people know the truth.' She was laying it on too thick, Jake Grafton thought, and he bit his lip. 'I never thought you would get it,' she finished.

'Luck.'

'And . . . I don't know just how to say this, but . . . I didn't think you had the courage to write it.'

'Balls like a bull. What's on your mind tonight, Shirley?'

'There's more. A *lot* more. They're counting on the fact that no one will ask the right people the right questions.'

Yocke merely grunted.

'They're playing for keeps, and they don't really care who gets hurt.'

'Shirley, I'll never get inside that place, even if anyone inside would talk to me, which they won't. Oh, I could do some follow-up on the guys who followed orders and got arrested – when they get out of the can – if they ever get out – but the story has hit the wall. These things happen.'

'It's something else.'

Silence as Yocke digested it.

When the silence had gone on too long, she said, 'Some-thing really important . . .'

'I'm listening.'

'The Rizhsky subway station.'

'Gimme a fact, Shirley. One little fact and the promise that you know more.'

'Have I lied to you?'

'Jesus! How many times have I heard that line! Yeah, baby, I love you no shit.' Yocke sighed audibly. 'A subway station. Are the subways still running?'

Jake Grafton's eyes widened in surprise. He hadn't thought she could pull it off.

'Amazingly enough, yes. An hour from now. Come alone. And be careful.'

'Where is that, anyway?' Yocke asked, but she had already hung up.

Jake pulled off the headset and tossed it on the table.

Geez, she calls on the local phone system, which is only working because it's the middle of the night, and she tells him where to meet her! She might as well have put it in the newspaper. So it'll be Judith Farrell, Jack Yocke and enough KGB agents to arrest the Presidium.

'She told him he had courage,' Jake reported to the little group. 'He told her he had balls like a bull.'

Toad Tarkington grinned broadly.

She'll meet him on the way. Or someone will. That's the way she'll work it. She just wants him out on the street and moving in the right direction. That means she'll probably pick him up quick, not long after he leaves the embassy.

'She set up a meet at the Rizhsky subway station,' Grafton told his audience. He rubbed his face to ease his fatigue. 'As curious as Yocke is, it's hard to see how the sucker lived this long. Unbelievable.'

He had three guys plus Yocke. No radios. Clandestine surveillance in a foreign city was Judith Farrell's game, her profession, how she lived – none of his people had any training or experience, including Jake.

'Okay,' Jake said finally. 'Toad, go see how many of those rioters are still outside and figure out how we can get out of here without getting beaten to death. Then get back here quick. Spiro, go get Yocke. Senior Chief, go find the marine captain and get a couple more pistols, three M-16s, four of those infrared binoculars, and some ammo. Go.' He shooed them out.

There was no way he could trap Judith Farrell. He was going to have to send Yocke out into the streets and pray that Farrell found him before the KGB did, and that the reporter could somehow convince Farrell to play the game Jake's way.

'Amateur night in Moscow,' he muttered disgustedly.

The switchboard lights were blinking again. Jake went into the office next door to find the regular operator and ask him to return to the board.

CHAPTER FOURTEEN

Jake was in the empty office next to the switchboard when Toad Tarkington returned. 'Looks pretty deserted out there, Admiral, all things considered. A few people gawking at the bodies but that's about it.'

'They haven't picked up the bodies?'

'No, sir.'

'Any Russian cops around?'

'Not a one in sight. They split early this morning.'

'Go get a car. Open the gate and bring it into the compound. No, get two cars. Go.'

Toad went. One of his great virtues was that he never had to be told anything twice. Nor did he ask foolish questions or want directions clarified. He just grabbed the ball and ran with it.

Spiro Dalworth came in leading Jack Yocke, who looked grim.

'Go help the chief with the maps and weapons,' Jake told the lieutenant, who closed the door behind him.

Yocke glanced at his watch. 'What's up?' he asked.

'Sit down.'

Yocke did so. 'Dalworth said you wanted to see me.'

Jake just nodded. Yocke was wearing jeans, moderately dirty tennis shoes, and a nondescript sweater. Jake dimly recalled seeing Tarkington in that sweater a few days ago. Yocke must have helped himself. He still looked as American as a ball park hot dog. Jake Grafton pulled out the lower drawer of the desk he was sitting behind and parked his feet on it. A muffled report of a gun penetrated into the room. Jake closed his eyes and massaged his forehead.

'Admiral,' Yocke began impatiently, 'I really—'

'How long do you think you'll last out there before the KGB picks you up?'

Jack Yocke's face first showed surprise, then darkened into anger. 'You were listening! Damned if I will—'

'*Shut up!*' Grafton's voice cracked like a whip. He softened it a little and continued, 'You aren't naive enough to think it's possible to have a private conversation on a telephone in this country, are you? They tell me that sometimes there are so many eavesdroppers on the line that there isn't enough juice left to ring your phone.'

Yocke leaped to his feet, grabbed a bound report off the desk and hurled it against the far wall. He planted his feet in front of the desk where Jake sat and glowered down at the admiral. 'I'm about fed up to here with this cra—'

'Sit down and we'll talk this over.' Jake nodded at the chair Yocke had vacated.

When Yocke was back in his chair, Jake continued. 'You're a good reporter, Jack. Somewhere deep inside that polished chrome *Post* ego I think you really do give a teeny-tiny damn about the people you write about. But, honest to God, when are you going to see that you are in about ten miles over your head?'

Yocke merely stared at the admiral.

'I want you to keep your date with Shirley Ross. We're going to help you.'

'Thank you, thank you, thank you. The US government wants to help *little ol'* me, praise the Lord! I don't know whether to shout hosannas or just let the pee trickle down my leg.' He took a long deep breath and exhaled slowly while he examined his hands. Finally he said, 'What do you think she wants to talk to me about?'

'I don't know.'

Yocke thought that over. 'Her name isn't Shirley Ross, is it?'

'No.'

'Why don't you level with me, Jake?'

'I am leveling with you,' Jake Grafton said, the soul of reason. 'The truth is that you can't tell the wrong people what you don't know. I suggest you take a little comfort from that fact. There are people in Russia who could make a stone sing – they've had a lot of practice.'

'Boy, they'd be wasting their talents on this kid. You still haven't even told me why you want me to go out there tonight. For some strange reason I have this sneaky suspicion it ain't got nothing to do with writing stories for the *Washington Post*.'

'I want to have a private chat with Shirley Ross. You're going to get her for me.'

Jack Yocke didn't reply. He worried a fingernail and glanced at Jake Grafton from time to time, but he had nothing more to say.

Senior Chief Holley and Spiro Dalworth returned carrying maps and guns. Jake Grafton selected a map of the city and spread it out on the desk. Then Toad came breezing in. 'Cars are ready,' he announced and glanced at Yocke, who ignored him.

'Gather around.' Jake leaned over the map. He pointed out the embassy and the Rizhsky subway station, which was a transfer point for the adjoining train station.

'The first assumption is that the KGB listened to the call. They monitor all calls to the embassy. Shirley Ross knows that. So she will have to pick Jack up before he gets to the rendezvous. Now there are two ways to figure the KGB – either they think Shirley and Jack are who they seem, two neophytes playing games, so they merely go to the subway station and wait for them to arrive, or they figure that these are two pros and the meet will occur on the way, so they try to follow Jack from the embassy. My guess is they'll play it both ways, try to follow Jack and have people at the station, just in case.'

'Third possibility, sir,' Toad said. 'Maybe they'll think

the subway station was just a blind and the meet is on for someplace else.'

'So they follow Jack,' the admiral said. He looked at the reporter. 'The second assumption is that they really want Shirley. Want her alive or dead. You're just bait.' Jake Grafton shrugged. 'I may be wrong. They may try to grab you as soon as they lay eyes on you. Are you in?'

'Want her alive or dead? Why?'

Jake thought about it. How much could he tell Yocke? 'By this stage of the game the folks in Dzerzhinsky Square may have gotten an inkling or two that Ms Ross is the source of some of their painful difficulties.'

Yocke's face was flushed. 'You've assumed all along that I was going to help you. I haven't decided.'

Jake Grafton had had enough. 'Don't get pissy with me, kid. You've got ten seconds to decide. Yes or no.'

The pistols that the senior chief had put on the desk were 9mm automatics. Jake picked one up, popped out the magazine and reached for a box of cartridges on the desk.

'Why do you want Shirley?' Yocke asked.

Jake Grafton's open palm descended onto the desk with a vicious smack. 'In or out?' he snarled.

'Fuck! I'm in.'

'We'll meet you here.' He stabbed his finger at the map and everyone bent over to look. 'It's that park on the south bank of the Moskva River where the statues are, about four hundred yards east of the entrance to Gorky Park.' He looked at the reporter. 'You're going to have to find it in the dark. Study this map carefully. When Shirley picks you up, you bring her here. If you're followed there will probably be shooting. I want Shirley Ross alive and uninjured. She's *your* responsibility.'

'What if she doesn't want to meet you?'

'Make sure she does. Tell her anything you want.'

Jack Yocke looked from face to face. He swallowed once. 'I don't get paid anywhere near enough to do this shit.'

'When this is over we'll get you a tattoo.'

Toad Tarkington slapped Yocke on the back. 'Relax, Jack. Everybody has to contribute their mite. And under our enlightened system of government you only have to die once. That's right in the Bill of Rights along with all the freedoms — freedom of religion, freedom of the press, freedom of sexual satisfaction, freedom from ex-wives, free—'

'Kiss my ass, you silly son of a bitch.'

'Do this right and I'll kiss your ass at high noon on the front steps of the *Washington Post*.'

'I want a story out of this,' Yocke told Grafton.

'You know the rules,' the admiral replied mildly. 'If and when I say.'

Jack Yocke bit his lip. He was going to write a story about this whether Jake Grafton liked it or not. Grafton knew damn well who Shirley Ross was — probably an American agent: he had known from the moment Yocke first mentioned her name. And Grafton didn't even cheep. And Tarkington — always with the smart mouth and shit-eating grin because he knows something you don't. Yocke's slow burn began to sizzle.

Jesus, what if that story she gave him about the Soviet Square killings wasn't true? Could it have been a setup? The possibilities swirled in Yocke's mind as he examined the admiral through narrowed eyes. He looked at the nose a touch too big, the short salt-and-pepper hair, the cold gray eyes. *Grafton could have set it up!* Sure.

Say Shirley's story was all true except for the identity of the person who made the telephone call to the KGB agents. Say the agents thought they were talking to Demodov and it wasn't really him. What if Demodov was the fall guy? What if Demodov's denial was *true?*

Was Jake Grafton capable of a stunt like that?

Like what? Faking the phone call to set up Kolokoltsev? Or killing that neo-Nazi and his aides? Kolokoltsev was no great loss to anybody. In fact, his demise was one of the few bright spots in a Russia trying to come to grips with a sordid past and an uncertain future. That bigoted demagogue . . . was . . .

Staring at the admiral now, Jack Yocke felt the cool hard shape of truth as rigid as steel. Jake Grafton was capable of doing whatever he thought was right. God help the poor bastard who wandered into the way! Jake Graf—

'You want a gun?' Jake was holding out an automatic. Dalworth and the senior chief were loading M-16s.

The reporter stared at the pistol, his train of thought broken. A gun. He shook his head. 'If I get caught with a gun the *Post* will fire me.'

Toad was incredulous. 'I knew civilian jobs were hard to get, but . . . You'd rather be dead than unemployed?'

'If I'm unarmed they may not shoot me. Killing reporters is damn poor PR. Sooner or later they'll get tired of feeding me and ship me home to the bony bosom of my editor.'

Jake Grafton shrugged and tossed the pistol on the table. 'Your choice.'

'And I thought you'd decided to get into the game,' Toad Tarkington said.

'Been a lot of reporters buried because they knew too much,' the senior chief remarked.

Yocke flipped a hand in acknowledgment but refused to change his mind.

Jack Yocke walked out of the embassy with nothing but his passport in one pocket and a wad of rubles in another. He had studied the map for fifteen minutes and thought he knew where he was going. He had exactly six minutes to make the subway station rendezvous and there was no way. He had pointed out to Grafton that he was going to be very late, but the admiral said, 'They'll wait for you,' and made him take the time to study the map carefully.

He scurried out the main gate past the bodies lying in the street, pathetic little piles of rags with all the life smashed out. His course inadvertently took him by the body of the woman incinerated by her own Molotov cocktail. He tried not to look, looked anyway and almost vomited.

Moscow was not lit up like an American or European city. Occasional weak streetlights enlivened the gloom and gave enough light to see, but they offered little comfort.

Yocke wasn't alone on the street. People were watching from doorways and alleys, people staying well under cover. Yet they made no move to interfere with him. There was no traffic at all.

He walked as fast as he could and had to resist the urge to break into a trot.

If his editor ever heard about this evening's expedition he would be fired within two heartbeats for taking foolish risks. So why had he agreed to this anyway?

Grafton had laid out the route, the most direct way to the rendezvous. His course took him north on Tchaikovsky Street, through Vosstanija Square and onto Sadovaja-Kudrinskaja Street, which was really the same boulevard as Tchaikovsky Street. The names of the streets of Moscow changed at every major intersection, a European tradition designed to baffle tourists and keep taxi drivers fully employed.

He was getting into the rhythm now, his heart and lungs pumping as he swung along with a stride that ate up the distance.

Once he heard running footsteps and ducked into a doorway. The street was empty. Trying to stay calm, he stood stock-still for several seconds as his heart thudded like a trip-hammer.

Were they watching? Waiting for him?

'Someone will meet you long before you get there,' Jake Grafton had said.

Of course someone is watching.

For the first time that evening Jack Yocke felt the icy fingers of true fear. Unsure of what he should do now, he finally stepped back onto the sidewalk and resumed his journey. Where in hell was Shirley Ross?

His head was swiveling uncontrollably. When he realized that he was really seeing nothing because he was trying to see everything, he locked his head facing forward. Still his eyes swept nervously from side to side and he couldn't resist an occasional glance behind him. But he wasn't being followed.

They *must* be watching. Of course!

They. Whoever *they* were. Watching him hump along like a bug scurrying across a stone floor. Any second the shoe would come smashing down and—

He could smell himself. He was perspiring freely and he stank. He wiped the sweat off his forehead and rubbed his hand against his trousers, which left a wet spot.

A little car came around the corner and drove past him. The two heads – two male heads – didn't turn his way. The car went up the street and turned right at the next corner. A black car.

He was tiring. The nervous energy was burning off and the pace he was making was too fast. He slowed to almost normal speed.

Ahead of him on the right a door opened. Unconsciously he swerved left toward the street and picked up his pace.

God! He should have accepted that pistol Grafton offered. Grafton knew what the score was and offered it – why didn't he have the sense to—

'In here, Jack.'

It was her voice, a conversational tone.

'Don't just stand there,' she said. 'Come in here *now!*'

He went through the door into a darkened hallway. She was there, with a man. The man closed the door and she took his arm. 'Through here, quickly. We have a car out back. Hurry.' She broke into a trot.

'Jake Grafton wants to see you.'

'Where?'

'A park on the south side of the Moskva. He said—'

'Quiet.' She went through a door and they were in an alley. 'Into the car.' She dove into the passenger seat and

232

Yocke climbed into the back. Before he could get the door completely closed the car was in motion. He opened it partially and slammed it shut.

'Lie down,' she said.

He did so.

The car swerved and accelerated with a blast from the exhaust.

'Jake Grafton said that—'

'Wait.'

With his head against the seat Yocke tried to look out the windows. The car was accelerating down a narrow street, now braking and swerving around another corner.

'When the car stops,' Shirley Ross said, 'I want you to quickly get out. The same side you got in on. Be sure to close the door. There will be a panel truck right beside the car. You go into the truck and I'll be right behind you.'

'Okay.'

And almost immediately the car swerved sideways again. In seconds the driver applied the brakes.

'Now.'

He sat up and grabbed the door handle and got out as fast as he could. There were four vans there, but only one with the rear doors open. Shirley pushed him toward it. He scrambled in and she followed and someone closed the door and the vehicle began to move.

'Where?' she said.

'A park on the south side of the river four hundred yards east of the entrance to Gorky Park. They put the statues there after they tore them down.'

'I know where it is.' She moved forward in the van's interior and said something to the driver in a language Yocke didn't know.

When she returned to his side she devoted her attention to a small device she held in her hand. Then she held it up to her ear. A radio. Yocke could hear the voices.

'Are we being followed?'

'They are following three of the vans.'

233

'This one?'

She held up a hand to silence him. After a minute she went forward to confer with the driver.

How in hell had he gotten himself into this mess anyway? Hurtling though the streets of Moscow in a van that smelled like a garbage truck, being trailed by the KGB – he braced himself against the swaying of the vehicle as it darted around a corner.

She was back beside him. 'In a few minutes we will switch vehicles again. Stay with me.'

'Okay.'

She listened intently to the radio.

'What's your real name?'

She didn't reply.

'What did you want to tell me?'

'You? Nothing. I need to talk to Jake Grafton and the telephones are all tapped. He figured it out.'

Jack Yocke opened his mouth again but now her fingers were against his face, feminine fingers that brushed his cheek and remained against his lips.

Jake Grafton sat in the grass with his back against one of Felix Dzerzhinsky's bronze legs, facing in the direction of Gorky Park. About seventy-five yards to the north, his right, was the south bank of the Moskva River. Farther ahead on the right, between where he sat and the boulevard in front of the Gorky Park entrance columns, was a vast low building, a cultural institute, with its empty parking lots. Farther to the west the Grecian columns of the park entrance gate were visible behind streetlights on the boulevard. Several hundred yards away to the south, on Jake's left, were block after block of drab apartment buildings. Behind him to the east the park went for a quarter mile until it reached a street.

Toad Tarkington was on Jake's left lying on his belly amid some scrub trees and weeds. Spiro Dalworth was against the corner of the cultural building. Senior Chief

Holley was behind Jake, watching his back. All three men had M-16s.

The city seemed abnormally quiet tonight, Jake Grafton thought. Perhaps the day of rioting had drained the energy from the Moscovites and they were home in bed worrying about their future. They certainly had a bucketful of troubles to fret about.

Ambassador Lancaster had telephoned as Grafton was walking out the door of his apartment, five minutes after dispatching Jack Yocke. Toad took the call and made some excuse. Whatever was on the ambassador's mind would have to wait a few hours.

Tonight Jake's .357 Magnum revolver lay beside him in the grass. All he had to do was drop his hand to it. In his hands he held a stick that he had picked up before he sat down. He was whittling upon it with his pocketknife while he speculated about what Lancaster had wanted. Lancaster didn't seem the type to invite him to Spaso House for an evening of poker.

No stars tonight.

Another high overcast that might or might not bring rain.

How long had it been? Twenty minutes?

Over on the boulevard in front of Gorky Park several trucks rumbled by. The noise carried oddly, sounding abnormally loud. The city was too quiet.

Looking the other way, toward the northeast, Jake could see the turrets and spires of the Kremlin, lit up tonight as usual. It was eerie, in a way, how for centuries that old fortress had housed czars and czarinas in extraordinary opulence. Favored by accidents of birth, they had lived out their lives in that palace and the one in St Petersburg while the mass of Russians struggled just to stay alive. When the Communists came along they moved right in. Yet like the czars, the days of the Reds were over, so tonight Yeltsin and his allies were in there trying to figure out how to ride the tiger. And out here amid the discarded, smashed statues the Russians were still struggling to stay alive, just as they always had.

Bracing his elbows against his knees, Jake scanned the area again with what appeared to be heavy binoculars. Unlike regular binoculars, this set picked up infrared light.

He could see Spiro against the corner of the building. He had told the lieutenant to stay down, but he was up against the wall, peering this way and that.

Do the Russians have infrared binoculars?

Toad was nearly invisible – all Jake could see was the faintest indication of a glow where he must be lying. The senior chief seemed equally well hidden.

No one else in sight. Not a dog, not a prowling cat, not a drunk or pair of lovers. Well, it's not a good night for drunks or lovers.

Jake raised the glasses and scanned the buildings to the south and east.

Somewhere in the city Yocke was playing secret agent. That guy! Always sure he knew everything when in reality he was just stumbling along in the dark with everyone else.

Maybe he shouldn't have let Yocke go. If something happened to him . . .

Finally he lowered the glasses and zipped up his jacket. The evening was getting chilly. Wondering about Yocke, worrying about Yeltsin and his grand experiment, Jake Grafton went back to his whittling.

Jack Yocke couldn't see any of the features of the man behind the wheel of the van, even looking in the rearview mirror. He had dark hair and wore a dark jacket and whispered with Shirley Ross in a foreign language that Yocke tried in vain to identify in the deep silence that had fallen once the van's engine was turned off. This was the third van he had been in tonight. Shirley Ross apparently had access to a motor pool.

The driver and the woman consulted a map, made more whispered comments, stared out the window to the left.

The driver had a hand-held radio that now sounded startlingly loud. He turned down the volume and held it close to his ear.

Finally she turned back to Yocke. 'The statues are over there about a hundred yards or so, through the little trees.'

'Who are you?'

'You and I will get out and walk across the grass. Stay with me. If anything goes wrong, just fall down on your stomach and stay there.'

'If what goes wrong?'

'Anything.'

The man in the front seat handed back a submachine gun. Shirley Ross put the strap across her left shoulder, tucked the butt under her right armpit and grasped the pistol grip and trigger assembly with her right hand.

The driver got out of the van and closed the door. In seconds the rear doors of the van opened.

'Let's go,' she said, and went first.

Jack Yocke took a deep breath, then followed.

The van was sitting in front of a huge slab of apartments. Across the street was the park. She was already moving. Yocke followed. As they crossed the sidewalk and entered the weeds and longish grass, it occurred to him that he had never even got a glimpse of the driver's face.

There was just enough light for him to pick up the vague outline of tree trunks and bushes. He tripped twice, then had to take several long strides to catch up to Shirley Ross, who was just a vague black shape moving quickly away from him.

Once she stopped and he almost bumped into her, then she was moving again, though in a slightly different direction.

Just as Jack Yocke was beginning to wonder if she knew where she was going, she slowed down and spoke softly: 'Good morning, Admiral.'

'Hello, Judith. Come sit over here by Stalin's head.'

'I don't think we were followed, but they might have

fooled me. They've been running spot surveillance on you since you arrived and they're hunting really hard for me.'

Yocke almost fell over the marble statue that lay on its side. He sat down with his back against it. Shirley sat on his right. Sitting facing them, with his back against one of the huge bronze statues, the reporter recognized Jake Grafton. He had a pair of heavy binoculars in his hands.

'I brought your reporter back,' Shirley told Jake. 'Where can we put him so that you and I can have a private conversation?'

'Oh, I think he's earned a little piece of the truth. He won't print anything without my permission.'

'You trust him?'

Jake Grafton chuckled. 'Beneath that polished, ambitious facade beats a pure and noble heart.'

'Shmarov blew up the Serdobsk reactor.'

'Sure,' Jake Grafton said. 'And the KGB killed Kolokoltsev in Soviet Square. If we're going to tell each other fairy stories, Judith, let's go find a warm bar that serves good whiskey.'

'Oh, you know we killed Kolokoltsev. After we did it the KGB breathed a collective sigh of relief – the man was an embarrassment to the Old Guard heavy hitters – and so I thought why not get some PR mileage out of it, muddy the water.'

'How do you know about Serdobsk?'

'The helicopter pilot that flew them down there is one of ours. He helps us pay off the authorities and smuggle Jews out. Then a few nights ago he was called at home and told to come in for a priority flight. Five men and their equipment to the nuclear power plant at Serdobsk. When he got there he realized things weren't going right when his passengers shot one security guard and herded the other inside. So he waited a bit, then started the engines and got out of there. The reactor blew up about two hours later.'

After a few seconds of silence, Jake Grafton asked, 'Who does your man work for?'

'KGB.'

'And the passengers?'

'Also KGB. The man in charge was a Colonel Gagarin.'

'How do you know Gagarin blew the thing up?'

'Obviously I'm adding two and two.'

'Where's Gagarin now?'

'I don't know. He never came back.'

'He blew himself up?' Jake asked incredulously.

'Well, he didn't shoot the guard at the front gate for sport, then carry bags full of equipment inside to equip the local baseball team. But he and his men could have gotten out somehow and the KGB then eliminated them. I don't know.'

'And Shmarov?'

'Gagarin was one of his lieutenants. He didn't do anything that Shmarov didn't know about and approve.'

'It's damn thin, Judith.'

'Admiral, in this business you are never going to get sworn affidavits.'

Jake Grafton could see her silhouette but not her face. She sounded tired. How many years had it been since he last saw her? He counted. Five. Five years running clandestine, covert operations, five years of false identities, deceit, risks calculated, chances taken, five years of stalking enemies of the Jewish state, five years of secret warfare . . . and she had been a covert operations professional when he first met her in Italy.

'Let's talk about Nigel Keren,' Jake Grafton said.

'You guarantee that this reporter . . . ?'

'If he writes a word that I don't approve of, you can shoot him anywhere you find him.'

Jack Yocke didn't think that was a joke.

The woman was answering Jake: '. . . Keren was financing our efforts to get Jews out of Russia. He gave us about a billion dollars.'

'A *billion?* That much money—'

'Bribes,' she told him. 'Expenses. We had to pay off the

authorities, pay for everything.' She turned slightly, toward Yocke. 'You were looking for Yakov Dynkin? He's in Israel now. We'll get his wife there as soon as we can. We bought him out of prison, bought a false passport and visa. He left from Sheremetyevo.'

'Keren was a Jew,' Jack Yocke said.

'Keren wanted to help. The CIA finally found out about it through the KGB and decided to stop Keren's contributions. The Arabs want Jewish immigration to Israel stopped and the CIA was trying – is trying – to play all sides in the Middle East. Iraq and Syria are buffers against Shiite fundamentalism, but they are bitter enemies of Israel. Give everybody a little, preserve the status quo. They—'

A shot rang out. Then another.

A stream of muzzle flashes from the darkness. Jack Yocke threw himself sideways as a surge of adrenaline shot through him and tried to burrow under the marble statue of Stalin. Vaguely he was aware of a silenced, guttural buzzing beside him, more shots, then a weight fell across his legs. A heavy report sounded just beside him. More shots.

And as suddenly as it began, it was over. In what, ten or fifteen seconds?

'Judith? Judith?' Jake Grafton's voice.

Yocke tried to move but the weight on his legs held him. It was a body. 'I've got her,' Jake Grafton said. 'Get up, Jack.'

Grafton had a small penlight. 'She's been shot. Judith, can you hear me?'

Someone else was there. 'Two CIA guys from the embassy.' Toad Tarkington's voice. 'They're both dead. We've got to get the hell out of Dodge.'

'Judith's been shot,' Jake told him. Now Toad saw the revolver in his hand. 'You and Yocke take her to the car and I'll get the other guys.' He took the M-16 from Toad and slung it over his shoulder.

She was heavy. Jack Yocke got her legs and Toad her shoulders. Toad wanted to go faster than Yocke could manage. 'Come on, you son of a bitch,' Toad swore. 'Move it!'

They had to carry her a hundred yards. She seemed to weigh a ton and several times Yocke thought he might drop her. She was limp, unconscious. Somehow his savage grip on her bare, shaved legs seemed obscene, an invasion of her womanhood that added embarrassment to the stew of emotions surging through the reporter.

'What happened?' Yocke asked Toad between breaths as they stumbled along.

'Two men. I got one with the first shot and the other charged and exchanged shots with Judith. I think they shot each other or else Grafton or somebody drilled him. Hell, maybe I got him too, not that it matters a damn. I got a look at their bodies. Both CIA guys from the embassy.'

CIA? Jesus, Yocke swore under his breath, he thought that story this Shirley or Judith or whatever her name is had told was all crap!

'What did you say?' Toad demanded.

'Jesus!'

She groaned once, just before they maneuvered her into the backseat. Toad jumped in back. 'You drive, Jack. Keys are under the floormat.'

Yocke got behind the wheel and fumbled with the keys.

'Come on, Yocke! Let's get her to the embassy before she bleeds to death.'

Somehow Yocke got the right key into the ignition and the engine started. He pulled the lever into drive and tried to resist the urge to floor the accelerator.

In the backseat Toad was trying to see where she was hit. Three bullet holes, as near as he could tell, all into the left lung area. He had his arm around her and could feel the warm, sticky wetness. Damn! One of them must have punched into her heart.

She whispered something. He put his ear almost against her lips. 'Hello, Robert.'

'We'll get you to the doc at the embassy, Hannah.' Without thinking, he had used her real name. He almost bit his tongue.

Her pulse was fluttering, her muscles slack.

And Toad knew. She was dying. Fury welled in him, all the frustrated bitterness accumulated through the years from loving a woman when the love wasn't returned, couldn't be returned – now it washed over him as a wave of pure rage, then as suddenly dissipated, leaving an emptiness in its place.

'Judith Farrell,' he whispered, his lips right next to her ear. 'I have loved two women in my life. You were the first.'

Whether or not she heard him he didn't know. A moment later he realized she had no pulse. He hugged her tighter and sat watching the buildings as the car sped through empty streets.

CHAPTER FIFTEEN

.

'Somebody sold us out.' Toad Tarkington was in a fine fury, his face dark, his eyes narrowed to slits. Unconsciously Jack Yocke took a step backward.

Senior Chief Holley and Spiro Dalworth took the full brunt of Tarkington's anger. They stood their ground as Toad continued in a low, intense voice: 'Someone here in this room told the CIA where the meet was, who was going to be there. They didn't get it over the phone, they didn't get it from a wiretap, they didn't follow anybody there. Someone talked, whispered into a spook's ear, and because of that, Judith Farrell *died*.'

Spiro Dalworth's face was a study as he tried to keep it under control. Toad Tarkington zeroed in, put his face inches from that of the lieutenant. *'Somebody broke the faith.'* He said the words slowly, like an Old Testament prophet pronouncing the doom of a king. 'Somebody betrayed his shipmates, sold out to the spook fucks playing power politics. Why don't you tell us about it, Dalworth.'

'Commander, I—'

'You *shit!*'

'Listen, we're on the same team. I—'

The back of Toad's hand flicked across Dalworth's face with a whiplike smack. Dalworth staggered and almost fell.

'That's enough, Toad,' Jake Grafton said.

Tarkington stepped back and stood glowering at Dalworth, who rubbed the side of his face and looked at the admiral. 'Sir, I'm *sorry!*' the lieutenant said. 'I thought—' His voice broke. He was near tears.

'Who'd you tell?' the admiral asked in a tired voice.

'Herb Tenney. We've talked before about an agency job when I get out. My naval career—'

'When did you tell him?'

'Before we left to go to the park.'

Jake Grafton looked out the window at the fountain in front of the complex cafeteria. On the other side of the square was the empty new embassy riddled with electronic listening devices. KGB bugs, CIA bugs, maybe Mossad, MI-5, German bugs, you name it. Was there anybody anywhere in this uncertain world who was willing to sleep in blissful ignorance of what the US ambassador said to his aides? Or his assistant? Or his wife?

'Admiral, I—'

'No.' Jake Grafton thought he knew what Tarkington was going to say. Toad would desperately love to go find Herb Tenney and shoot him dead.

Let's assume Judith was telling the gospel truth. The CIA learned of the Nigel Keren operation through the KGB. And the KGB has just blown up the Serdobsk power plant, contaminating thousands of square miles and killing thousands of people, thereby triggering a leadership crisis that might result in a new dictatorship of the Old Guard, some of whom lead the KGB. Assume also that this development would not be frowned upon by the rogue clique in the CIA that controlled Herb Tenney. In some crazy way it fitted. Jake Grafton got that hollow feeling in the pit of his stomach again.

The Middle East, eastern Europe, the horn of Africa, southeast Asia . . . Every major event affects every person in this interdependent world. The collapse of communism in the Soviet Union upset the equilibrium. No, the collapse of the shah in pro-Western Iran was the triggering event. Like shock waves radiating from the epicenter of an earthquake, these events triggered other events, upset the balance of power that kept a world with too few resources and too many greedy men from coming apart at the seams. And now the seams were ripping.

He turned from the window. 'Toad, you and Jack take Farrell's body back to the park.'

'Why not the Israeli embassy, sir? She ought to have a decent funeral and burial. She deserves that.'

Jake Grafton thought the white-collar crowd at the Israeli embassy would be extremely embarrassed if they received the body of a covert soldier killed in an operation that the government of Israel would deny all knowledge of. He merely repeated his order: 'Take her to the park.'

'Aye aye, sir. Come on, Yocke.'

'Senior Chief, go to bed.'

Jake Grafton and Spiro Dalworth were standing alone in the room when Toad Tarkington closed the door.

Out in the car Judith Farrell's body lay under a pile of jackets on the backseat. Toad got behind the wheel and Jack Yocke got in beside him.

The sky was just beginning to gray when Toad turned the corner and sped south on the wide, empty boulevard that ran toward the river.

Jack Yocke was still trying to fit together all the pieces. 'How well did you know her?' he asked Toad.

Toad didn't answer immediately. 'Pretty well,' he said finally.

'Shirley Ross, Judith Farrell . . . aliases?'

'Yep. And she had others.'

'Do you know her real name?'

'She told it to me once.'

'To die like that . . .'

'In her line of work it was bound to happen sooner or later.'

As they crossed the Moskva bridge, Jack Yocke asked, 'Do you think her team really killed Kolokoltsev in Soviet Square?'

Toad said, 'You told me that one of the gunmen held the

door to the limo open and one stood there cool as a cucumber squirting bullets into the people inside? Well, the shooter for the *coup de grâce* was undoubtedly Judith Farrell. That was the payoff — those people were putting their lives on the line to kill that anti-Jewish hate merchant. You can bet your last kopek that Judith Farrell was right there at the trigger to make damn sure there was no slipup. That was the way she operated.'

Jack Yocke glanced into the backseat, then looked back at Toad. 'She was an assassin?'

'She fought for her people.'

'Well . . .'

'*Asshole!*' Toad roared. '*I* killed a man tonight. *I* am not in the mood for moralizing from the editorial page pulpit. This ain't a cocktail party in Georgetown! They slaughter people by the millions on this fucking continent! Mass murder is the European sport. Got a social problem, kill another million!'

'Sorry,' Yocke said contritely.

Toad snarled, 'They oughta make you the fucking wine editor at the *Post.*'

The two men sat in the car looking at the park as the night faded into a gray dawn. They had nothing else to say to each other. Each was occupied with his own thoughts.

If there was anyone watching, Toad didn't see them. Finally he opened his door and stepped out. 'Help me with her,' he muttered to the reporter.

They left Judith Farrell under the nearest tree. Toad tried not to look at her face. As he straightened up he could see the body of the man he had shot still lying just as he had fallen.

On the way back to the car Jack Yocke glanced over his shoulder at the body of the Israeli agent. Toad Tarkington didn't.

A Russian army detail was picking up the bodies around the American embassy compound when Toad and Jack returned. The soldiers were piling the corpses in a large truck. They weren't carrying weapons.

A marine opened the gate and Toad drove through. As he got out of the car he saw her walking toward him. She wore khakis and a leather flight jacket and her hair was in a bun. When he held out his arms she broke into a run.

'Rita!'

'Hello, Toad-man.' She gave him a fierce hug, then stepped back. 'I brought you a present,' she said. She unzipped the jacket and held it open. 'Me!'

He took her in his arms. 'When did you get here?' he asked finally.

'An hour ago.'

'Why?'

'Admiral Grafton asked for three pilots. I volunteered.'

Toad tried to frown. 'I told you never to volunteer.'

'Ah, Toad-man, you do it all the time.'

'Yeah. And look at me. God, I'm glad you're here.'

The marine recon team commanding officer was Captain Iron Mike McElroy. His broad shoulders tapered to a trim waist and a flat stomach that was probably corrugated like a washboard under his camo shirt. He saluted crisply and introduced himself. He and Jake had just started to get acquainted when Agatha Hempstead came marching across the sidewalk straight at them.

'Ambassador Lancaster didn't know or approve of this decision to bring in a marine recon team.' She ignored Captain McElroy.

'General Land talked to the president about it,' Jake Grafton said mildly. 'The president approved it.'

'Owen – Ambassador Lancaster should have been consulted. This request should have gone through the State Department. We can't have the military making foreign poli—'

'Ms Hempstead,' Jake said firmly, cutting her off. 'I apologize to Ambassador Lancaster. I did not intend to cut

247

him out of the loop. But time and urgent operational considerations required that I communicate directly with General Land in the Pentagon.'

'What considerations? What considerations do you consider to be nonpolitical? Here in Russia everything is political! Everything! I don't think you understand Ambassador Lancaster's position!'

Jake cocked his head and eyed Ms Hempstead. 'You're the one who seems to be having the difficulty understanding who is responsible for what, ma'am. I suggest we stop this little turf war before it goes any further and start cooperating.'

'What considerations?'

Jake Grafton was ready to use a dirty word or two, but he swallowed it and rammed his fists into his pockets. 'The situation here in Russia is a bit out of control. I'm sure you've noticed.'

'The marine guard is quite capable of defending the embassy compound from a riot, Admiral.' Jake had never heard a flag officer's rank pronounced quite this way. Antipathy, derision, disrespect – Goodbody Hempstead got a lot of mileage out of one little word. 'The decision to augment the marines is for Ambassador Lancaster to make. A reconnaissance team armed to the teeth is *not* going to help matters very much!'

She paused, so Jake said, 'The team is not here to augment the marine guard.'

But she was merely marshaling her arguments, not entertaining replies. 'I'm sure the Yeltsin government will be making a diplomatic protest within hours. A recon team ready for combat strikes me as a very serious stretch of the military cooperation agreements that we have been operating under these last few weeks. Ambassador Lancaster—'

'Maybe I'd just better have a talk with the ambassador.'

'What *are* you going to use the team for?'

'I'll tell it to the ambassador.'

So seven minutes later he was standing in the ambassador's office. Boris Yeltsin was on television addressing the nation. Jake and Hempstead stood silently while the ambassador listened to a translator. When the broadcast was over, Lancaster muttered, 'Well, at least he's not resigning.'

'These seven people that want to take over, this junta, any mention of them?' Jake asked as the translator left the room.

'No. That's a good sign, I think. But the situation is very fluid.' Lancaster sat down behind his desk and turned to Jake again. He went straight to the point: 'What's the recon team for?'

'I haven't decided yet, sir. I thought they might come in handy.'

'Admiral, I don't want you or Hayden Land starting a war. Before any of those gung-ho special warriors dons his warpaint or steps outside of this compound, I want a complete briefing. In writing.'

'Yessir.'

'We'll put them in the gymnasium. They can sleep there. But so help me, Admiral, the secretary of state is not going to be a happy little camper. Foreign policy is the prerogative of civilians under our system of government. It's a tried and true system and we're going to ensure the United States sticks with it. If Land shoved the president out onto thin ice the shit is going to hit the fan.' The cuss word sounded weird coming from the New England Brahmin. Jake would have bet money the old man had never even heard the word.

'Before you even scratch yourself,' the ambassador continued, 'I want a complete briefing.'

'I should have discussed my concerns with you, sir, but the press of events didn't seem to allow the time. I apologize. In a few hours I'm going to steal a couple helicopters from the Russians and fly down to Serdobsk for a look. I want to see that power plant.'

Lancaster sat back in his chair. 'They tell me that site is too hot for humans.'

'The marines brought some antiradiation suits. And we probably won't land. But I want to see what the place looks like and we need to get some better data on radiation levels.'

Lancaster digested that with a sour look on his face. Apparently he came to the conclusion that the less he knew the better. '*Steal* helicopters?' he asked mildly.

'Steal.'

Jake reached across the desk for an envelope, turned it over and wrote: Today I will steal two helicopters and fly to Serdobsk.

He signed his name, wrote the date, then passed the envelope to Lancaster, who looked at it and sighed. He ran his fingers across his scalp. 'You don't let much grass grow under your feet, do you, Admiral?'

'One other thing you should probably be aware of, sir. I would suggest you and Ms Hempstead keep this to yourself, not report it to Washington, not discuss it with anyone else on the embassy staff.'

'The ambassador will make that decision,' Agatha Hempstead said tartly.

Jake Grafton shrugged. 'Last night my aide and I had a little shooting scrape with a couple armed men near Gorky Park. They were killed. I think they might have been CIA agents.'

'Who were they?' Lancaster asked.

Jake gave him the names.

Owen Lancaster and Agatha Hempstead just looked at each other, then transferred their stunned gaze to the admiral.

'If you'll excuse me, sir,' Jake said and got to his feet. 'I have to go see about those helicopters.' The diplomats watched him go without recovering their voices.

Jack Yocke tapped listlessly on his computer. He had found

that having the keyboard under his fingers was therapeutic. When his mind was wandering his fingers merely tapped out disjointed phrases, but when he was thinking about something specific his fingers strung words together into sentences as his thoughts rolled along.

The secret is to think in logical, coherent sentences, which most people don't do. Yocke did, most of the time. As he witnessed an event or thought about a subject the words scrolled through his mind. If he had a keyboard under his fingers the words became text.

Now he glanced at the screen. 'Nigel Keren' was written there.

Ah yes. The headline flashed through his mind and the words appeared on the screen. 'British billionaire Nigel Keren murdered by CIA.' That headline could get him a story in every newspaper in the world.

And he couldn't write the story.

Frustrated, he got up from the computer and went to the window. He was still in Admiral Grafton's apartment in the embassy complex, and unless he was willing to head straight back to the land of Diet Coke and hot dogs, he was going to have to stay here.

A great end to your first foreign correspondent assignment, Jack! Write one good story that blames a political murder on the wrong crowd, the local secret police, who promptly jump on your case like stink on Limburger.

Maybe he should call his editor. He glanced at the phone and even took a step in that direction, then returned to the window.

Yocke knew his editor. Gatler would pretend to be incredulous, thunderstruck: you're hiding out and missing the *great* stories, the big, stupendous, attack-on-Pearl Harbor, war-declared stories – world's worst nuclear accident kills zillions, democracy collapses in Russia, military dictatorship ousts Yeltsin? If you don't get a piece of those stories, his editor would shout, you'll go back on the cop beat for the rest of your natural, miserable life.

251

Jack Yocke had no intention of informing his editor that he had made a tiny little mistake on the Soviet Square Massacre story. That the KGB were innocent lambs, victims of a foul Israeli plot to besmirch their honor. He wasn't going to call that one in, even if Grafton gave him permission to print the truth, which he wouldn't.

The fact is that he had been set up by someone who knew just how much truth he could uncover and how to twist it into the story she wanted told. *Now* he knew, and he couldn't tell. Wouldn't tell, even if he could.

But everyone manipulates the press, don't they? Politicians and cops, athletes and movie stars do it all the time.

Moscow seemed quiet out there beyond the brick wall topped with two strands of barbed wire. Yocke could see the marine opening the front gate and letting cars go in and out.

As he watched he saw Toad Tarkington, Rita Moravia and Spiro Dalworth pile into a car with a couple of marines armed with M-16s. Two more marines and the other two pilots got into a second car. Away they went, out the gate. His curiosity piqued, Yocke wondered about their errand and destination.

When the second car turned the corner and was out of sight, Yocke turned back to his computer.

No, the story he wasn't getting was *KGB blows up Serdobsk reactor! Zillions Die!* Now that would be a story that would make Jack Yocke as famous as Michael Jackson, a story to launch a hell of a career, a story to get him his own column, maybe even an investigative team like Bob Woodward had. And what did Woodward dig out from under his rock? Richard Nixon with a coverup dripping from his fingers – a popcorn fart compared to this little beauty.

But he hadn't missed it yet. Oh no! Jake Grafton had it and no other reporter was going to get a sniff. Sooner or later Jack Yocke would mine that ore. He could feel it in his bones.

Zillions die. Not zillions, but maybe tens of thousands.

The import of those words struck home as Yocke stared at them on the computer screen. Tens of thousands, men, women, children – the lame, the halt, the blind, the virtuous, the guilty, the oh so very human. All. Everyone in the fallout zone.

And that Mossad killer Judith Farrell told Jake Grafton the KGB did it intentionally. On purpose. Murder. Political murder. The ends justify the means. Kill them all.

Was she lying again?

Suddenly Yocke had had enough of the computer. He turned it off and went to the window and looked out for a while.

Then, since he was tired, he laid down and tried to sleep. After a while he did.

Jake Grafton was also thinking about the people in the fallout zone, thousands who were already dead or dying or sick as a human could be. If this were America or western Europe there would be no helicopters to steal. Those machines the networks hadn't commandeered to carry their insta-cams, satellite feed gear and blow-dried reporters would all be in use for evacuation and relief efforts. If this were America or western Europe.

One of the interpreters was watching Russian television and periodically summarizing what she heard, and she had not gotten a single hint that any relief efforts were under way.

'It's too early,' Captain Collins said uneasily. 'It'll take them a while to figure out what they need to do, then another while for anyone to decide he has the authority to set things in motion, then a third while for anybody to get off his ass and actually do something. The only certainty is whatever they do will be too little, too late, and completely ineffective.'

Jake nodded. He had had only an hour's sleep last night and was very tired. He tried to concentrate.

'How hot is the fallout zone?' he asked Collins.

The nuclear engineering officer just shrugged. 'At one of these Russian nuke facilities a few years ago,' he said, 'they didn't know what to do with the hot waste, so they dumped it into a pond a hundred feet deep. Kept doing that. Then one summer the pond partially dried up and the mud turned to dust and blew away. Contaminated an area of four hundred eleven square miles. Contamination level of six hundred roentgens an hour, which is a fatal dose. Spend one hour anywhere in that area unprotected and you're history.'

'So what did the Russians do after Chernobyl?'

'They lied about the extent of the accident, they lied about the radiation dosages people got and the number of victims, they ordered in troops to clean up the mess and lied about the dosages they got, they lied about the extent of food contamination, the relief money was stolen by corrupt officials, they misdiagnosed the cancers . . . they basically fucked it up from end to end.'

Collins searched for words. 'Maybe lie is the wrong word. These people have always operated on the premise that no one should ever be told bad news, so they are incapable of effectively dealing with any problem at any level. Bad news doesn't go up the ladder and doesn't come down, which means that *no one ever knows the truth.*'

On that note Collins felt silent. When Jake failed to ask any more questions, Collins had a question of his own. 'What do you want me to do with Dalworth, Admiral?'

'Did he tell you about the fracas in the park?'

'Yessir. And about whispering to Herb Tenney.'

It was Jake's turn to shrug. 'Don't do anything.'

Collins picked at a discolored place on his uniform trousers.

'Did Dalworth tell you those two guys we killed were CIA?'

'Uh, yessir.'

'I may need Dalworth,' Jake said slowly. 'I don't know what the hell Herb Tenney is up to, but whatever it is, it's going to get him burned. I intend to light the fire.'

CHAPTER SIXTEEN

What was Herb Tenney up to? Jake worried the question as he lay inert on a couch with a throbbing headache. He had downed four aspirin and now had a wet washcloth draped across his forehead. Droplets of water trickled through his hair and wet the miserably thin pillow.

It was hard to keep the proper perspective. Somehow, some way, a group within the CIA was embedded in this Russian mess up to its hidden microphones. Perhaps Toad's reaction was the proper one – absolute outrage. But Toad would surrender to that emotion and lose sight of the other aspects. That was the thing about Toad . . . passionate sincerity was the steel buried under that flippant shell he wore to ward off the bumps and abrasions of everyday life.

He still loved Judith Farrell, Jake was positive of that. Toad had given himself to her once, years ago, and he was the type of man for whom there could never be any emotional retreat. Love once bestowed could never be withdrawn. Oh, he could love another woman, and did – he was desperately in love with Rita Moravia. Now he must hide the hurt of the loss to avoid injuring another – only the Toad-man would get himself into that pre-dicament. And Jake could only guess how badly he was hurting.

Yakolev, Shmarov . . . He had met those two and come away confused. Yakolev at least wore the face he thought the foreigners wanted to see: maybe all he did was wear it. Shmarov looked like some hideous apparition from a Boris

Karloff movie, ready to jerk out fingernails and slice off testicles.

Money. Somehow he had missed the money connection between Nigel Keren and the Mossad, and it was right there in plain sight. *Billionaire* publisher and industrialist Nigel Keren . . . Money, money, money . . .

Richard Harper said he had *it*. But what did he have? Is money the connection between the CIA and the KGB?

The salient feature of communism that made it different from every other system of government man has yet devised was that it made everyone poor. All one could hope for under communism was access to more perks, to the right schools, a dacha in the Lenin Hills, a car, shopping in the party stores, party hospitals, and a plot in a party cemetery when the party doctors could do no more. But money? No. Today Boris Yeltsin was only paid the ruble equivalent of a hundred dollars a month.

What do desperate comrades do when the tide goes out and leaves them stranded on a mud bar?

What have they done?

Everyone must be dead at the Petrovsk Rocket Base. Collins said it was in the center of a fallout pattern, a mere eighty miles downwind. The men and women there must have died quickly, almost in their tracks. Perhaps the people in the clean rooms lasted a little longer. Perhaps not.

But the missiles and their warheads would be unaffected. They would be sitting there in the hangars on their transports and the clean room would be full of partially disassembled warheads.

How do you dispose of plutonium warheads? This was the question that had bedeviled the foreign experts and the Russian military. Simply taking them apart wasn't the answer – they could be assembled again by anyone with the know-how.

Atomic weapons were the ultimate curse, Jake told himself once again. Their very existence warped space and time and human affairs like little black holes.

There must be some solution, something that rendered the warheads incapable of harming anyone. But what?

'Admiral. Admiral Grafton.'

It was Senior Chief Holley.

'Commander Tarkington called on the scrambled hand-held.' At least the marines had brought com equipment! 'They've found some choppers. He said to tell you it'll be a couple more hours before they're fuelled and checked out.'

'Thanks, Senior Chief.'

He tried again to turn off the muscles, to relax completely into sleep. So Toad found some choppers . . .

He was drifting in a late afternoon sky filled with giant white clouds over a blue landscape, clouds with tops shot with fire and bases hidden in deepening shadow.

He saw the clouds the other day from the window of the jet as they flew back to Moscow from the missile base, saw them from above, from the angle that God sees them. What does *He* think, watching the clouds drift across the landscape, watching the humans grapple in the mud, poisoning one another in the deep purple shadows?

The question flitted across a tired mind, then was gone, leaving only the clouds and the blue land below and the dark shadows of the coming night.

They looked like garbagemen in the one-size-fits-all baggy NBC (nuclear, biological, chemical) suits. American servicemen called these things hot suits because there was no provision to cool the wearer. Britain's Jocko West helped the French and German officers into their suits, then donned his own. The Italian officer, Colonel Galvano, couldn't be reached at this hotel or the Italian embassy.

Although normally the suits merely provided filtered air, these were the latest models with a limited self-contained oxygen supply. When the oxygen was gone they would have to go on filtered air, and in an environment as hot as the one Tom Collins predicted, the filters were going to get quickly contaminated.

Before they came out to the airport, a heliport on the southeastern side of the city, Jake had spent twenty minutes talking with General Hayden Land on the scrambled telephone. 'Do what you think best,' Land said. What else could he have said?

'Can you fly this . . . thing?' Jake asked Lieutenant Justin 'Goober' Groelke, one of the pilots who came to Russia with Rita and the marines. Goober was already decked out in his hot suit.

'I think so, sir. I got a couple thousand hours in big choppers.'

'How much fuel do we have?'

'Not enough. We'll all ride in this one. Toad's loaded the other machine with fuel in drums. All we could find was a hand pump. We'll fly in formation as far southeast as we can, land the other machine in a clean area. Then we'll refuel this chopper and fly on. When we come back from the hot zone we'll fuel up again.'

'Or abandon this machine.'

'Yessir. If it's too contaminated.'

'What kind of condition are these machines in?'

Here Groelke paused. 'These are fairly new machines, Aeroflot Mi-8s, with very low times on the tachs. They've been sitting outside without engine covers for a couple months, apparently. We cleaned the dirt and bird shit out of the intakes as best we could, drained the sumps, checked all the systems we could, all the fluid levels, the hubs . . . The hydraulic fluid may have some water in it and the engine oil doesn't look good on either machine. The batteries were dead. We used a power cart to start the engines and we hovered both machines. There's no telling how much dirt was in the engines before we turned them up. I assumed that you were willing to run some risks . . .' His voice trailed off as Jake's head bobbed once.

Both men were professional aviators – they well knew

the risks of flying in unknown machines that had been essentially abandoned. The weeds were now flattened by the rotor downwash where Goober hovered, but they had been up to the belly of the machines when the Americans found them. One of the tires of the helicopter carrying the fuel had been flat. A half hour was spent getting an air compressor from the hangar to start. A family of birds had nested in one cooling intake, but Goober didn't think that worth mentioning.

'How are you going to get these engines started out there' – Jake nodded toward the southeast – 'if they run long enough to get us there?'

'We loaded two power carts into the other chopper, sir. That cut the amount of extra fuel we could carry.'

'I don't want to walk back.'

'I think we'll be all right, sir.'

Well, Goober was his pilot. He could go over the figures with him or take his word for it. 'Okay,' Jake told him and turned to his little group. 'Let's get out of these suits after Captain Collins checks each one. Be careful with them. These are the only hot suits we have.'

'How did you get permission to borrow these machines, Admiral?' Colonel Rheinhart asked as he worked his zipper down.

'It's a standard midnight requisition, Colonel,' Toad put in, but his smile never arrived. Jake Grafton saw that and wondered if Rita did. She was helping Captain Collins check the suits. 'Common procedure in the American Navy,' Toad assured him.

'Oh, you're stealing them?'

'We showed the guards at the gate a personal note from Boris Yeltsin.' The colonel looked at him askance, so Toad added, 'An interpreter at the embassy wrote the note. We gave it to the sergeant of the guard as a souvenir, along with two cartons of cigarettes and a bottle of bourbon.' Actually Spiro Dalworth had done the talking and Toad had watched. Dalworth was trying hard to please Tarkington, who had little to say to him. Just now Dalworth stood watching this exchange. He wasn't trying on a hot suit since he was going to remain with the fuel chopper.

'What if the Russians shoot us down?' Jack Yocke whispered to Jake Grafton, who pretended not to hear him. The admiral walked over to Rita and had some final words with her.

'If I may, gentlemen,' Colonel Reynaud offered, 'I believe it is time to "mount up"? As zhey say in ze western movies, we are burning ze daylight.'

Jake rode beside Goober Groelke in the copilot's seat for the first leg. He was impressed by Groelke's flying ability: he handled the large Russian helicopter like he had flown it for years. Jake examined the faces of the instruments that were telling him God-knows-what and watched the pilot at work for the first five minutes, then his mind wandered.

More puffy clouds this afternoon. And they had a late start.

They soon left the heavily industrialized suburbs of Moscow behind and followed a two-lane road for a while, then the road turned more to the east and the helicopters flew across wood lots and fields and here and there small villages. The land didn't look prosperous, Jake decided. From a thousand feet the fields looked weedy and unattended, the occasional house just a shack, the villages collections of shacks. At random intervals the machines crossed above power lines and railroad tracks, incongruous fixtures that ran across the gently rolling countryside from one hazy infinity to the other.

The helicopter flew from sunlight into the random cloud shadow, back to sunlight again while Jake Grafton thought about radioactivity and nuclear warheads.

The noise was loud but not painfully so. Oh, to be able to fly on forever and never have to arrive. His eyelids grew heavy. To fly on and on and never have to arrive at the radioactive hell embedded in the haze and puffy clouds somewhere beyond the horizon, beyond the blighted promises and twisted dreams . . .

Fueling the helicopter that was to take them on to Serdobsk and Petrovsk was a nightmare. The hand pump leaked and took the best efforts of two men. Everyone took turns. Three or four minutes of intense effort reduced most of them to puffing. The marine captain was in the best shape, but after five minutes even he needed a break.

They were in a pasture several miles from the nearest village, but no one came to see who they were or why they had landed. Two scrawny steers watched from the safety of some trees at the far end of the field.

'How's the machine flying?' Jake asked Goober.

'Left engine is running a little hot,' he was told, 'but the oil levels seem okay. And the pressure in the primary hydraulic system fluctuates occasionally, but it's nothing we can't live with.'

'And the other machine?'

'A bunch of circuit breakers popped. The stab aug is out. Several hydraulic leaks.'

The refueling took over an hour while Tom Collins rigged his radioactivity detection equipment, which he described to Jake as advanced Geiger counters. The sensors were on small winches so they could be lowered from the open rear door of the chopper to get readings at ground level. In the meantime Groelke and the other pilot climbed all over the two helicopters, checking everything.

When fueling was complete, everyone stepped behind the helicopter to relieve themselves, then took long drinks of water. The party that was flying on donned the hot suits.

'Toad,' Jake said, 'you ride with Goober in the cockpit.' Toad would do the navigation. He had several charts which he got out and stacked in the order in which he would need them. Most of the officers had cameras. They checked them carefully before they donned their helmets and zipped the gloves into place.

They were going to breathe filtered air as long as the radiation levels were not too high. Collins would tell everyone when to switch on their oxygen systems.

Jack Yocke walked over to Jake and said, 'If anything goes wrong, we're dead men. You know that?'

Jake Grafton was tempted to make a flippant reply, but after a look at the reporter's face, he refrained. 'I know, Jack,' he said patiently, and pulled his helmet on.

He knew the dangers better than the reporter did. No one in the other machine had hot suits and the machines would be too far apart for radio reception. If this machine had a serious mechanical problem and was forced down, everyone abroad was doomed. Even in well-maintained helicopters with excellent equipment and thorough, careful planning, this mission was too dangerous for anyone but a desperate fool. Which was, he told himself scornfully, why the Russians weren't here and he was.

He had given the other pilot explicit orders: if we don't come back after six hours, you are to return to Moscow.

The hour-and-forty-five-minute flight from Moscow had put a sufficient charge on the helicopter's batteries that Goober got a start without using the external power cart. They had wrestled one of the carts into the passenger bay and Spiro Dalworth was outside standing beside the other, just in case.

Jake strapped himself into the crewman's seat by the rear door. He surveyed the compartment. Some of the other people had strapped in, some hadn't. Yocke was playing with his buckle, toying with the adjustment catch. Perhaps each of them in his own way was pondering his karma.

Jake looked forward and saw Toad looking back at him. He gave Tarkington a thumbs up.

When the engine RPM had stabilized, Goober lifted the tail and the machine left the ground.

All that remained of the Serdobsk fast breeder reactor was rubble arranged around a shallow hole in the ground. From a hover two hundred feet above the plant it was obvious that no one had survived the blast. Jake Grafton lay on his belly with his helmeted head poking out the open helicopter door. Seventy-five feet below him the radioactivity sensor was inscribing little circles in the air. Beside him people were taking turns snapping cameras.

Jake felt a hand pulling him. It was Collins. They put their helmets together and Collins shouted, 'We can't stay here more than a couple minutes. It's hotter than holy hell down there.'

'What's that stuff over there?' Jake pointed to the wreckage of a building several hundred yards away from where the reactor had stood. Numerous drums were visible amid the concrete rubble, some of them split open. The contents looked dark, almost black.

'Plutonium. They probably had tons of the shit stored there.'

'The containers have ruptured.'

'Yeah, and the stuff is going to get blown away on the wind or washed into the creeks and rivers or soaked into the soil. Come on, Admiral, let's get the hell outta here.'

Jake went forward to the cockpit and tapped Goober on the shoulder. The pilot eased the stick forward and the helicopter left the hover.

'Circle over that KGB troop facility.'

Groelke did so. One of the buildings had burned and several bodies were visible, but nothing moved. Nothing.

The helicopter flew in a gentle circle until it was pointed southeast toward Petrovsk. Goober Groelke climbed to several thousand feet to minimize their radioactivity exposure.

Now the noise of the engines became mesmerizing, Jack Yocke thought. One listened carefully, anxious not to hear any change, any burble or hiccup or unexplained sound. With your life depending on the continued smooth running of these two engines, the sound captures your attention and holds you spellbound. The ruins of the reactor had been horrifying, but the sound of these engines was the promise of continuing life, a drug more powerful than anything a doctor could prescribe.

Yocke tried to put his emotions into words, tried to string the words together as he sat with closed eyes and concentrated on that perfect humming.

On the floor of the passenger compartment Tom Collins fiddled with his equipment and made notes of radioactivity readings from which he could extrapolate estimates of the levels present on the surface. Jake Grafton watched him. At times Collins shook his head. Finally he folded up the notebook and sat hunched, staring at the needles on the dials in front of him

The helicopter flew over a village, then a small town, then farther along another village. Cattle lay dead in the fields. Not a sign of life below, not even buzzards. They were dead too.

All those people went to bed one evening and at dawn, or just after, the radioactive fallout arrived, an invisible rain that fell without noise, without beauty, without warning, and brought quick, gentle death. Most of the victims probably died in their sleep.

Is that the fate of civilization? Is that the end that awaits our species? No bang, no warning, just death for every last man, woman and child as they lay sleeping on the dawn of the last day?

Jake Grafton felt his eyes tearing over and blinked repeatedly.

Collins had given up on the instruments and was standing beside Grafton looking aft, out the open door, when they saw the river, the Volga, broad and deep, the water reflecting the blue of the sky and the white of the clouds.

'Let's go down and hover just above the surface.'

Goober turned the machine and went back. After twenty seconds of hovering, Collins signaled to fly on. Toad saw him and waved his hand at Groelke.

Jake bent down to where Collins was making notes.

He was not writing down radiation levels, but a sentence: 'The Volga is now a river of radiation carrying poison to the sea.'

They circled the Petrovsk Rocket Base while Collins took more readings. Jake looked out the window. The barracks and offices and hangars were all intact, but nothing moved. From this altitude the scene reminded Jake of a model railroad setup, complete with cars, trucks and several airplanes parked on the mat just off the runway, and a locomotive and flatcars near the biggest hangar.

But his attention was captured by the empty transporters parked on the mat. There were three of them, green tractors with green flat trailers hooked behind them, all empty.

Jocko West and the two European officers stood in the door looking at the transports, then Rheinhart began snapping pictures.

'I think we can land, Admiral,' Collins shouted.

'How long?'

'As little time on the ground as possible.'

'How hot is it?'

'Unprotected, you'd be fatally ill in a half hour. Maybe less.'

Groelke put the chopper near the main hangar and killed the engines to save fuel. Breathing pure oxygen, the people got out of the machine carefully, gingerly, conscious of anything that might rip or damage their antiradiation suits.

'Goober, stay with the machine. Toad, stay with him.'

Jake Grafton led the little party toward the open hangar door.

The giant missiles riding on their transporters were stark, functional sculptures with the red star prominent upon their flanks.

There was open space near the door, apparently enough for the three transporters that sat a quarter-mile away across the concrete. Impressive as the missiles were, the little group was soon standing gazing at medium-size wood crates arranged on pallets.

One of the boxes had been ripped open, revealing a cylindrical-shaped device about twelve inches in diameter. Wires and electronic devices covered it like spaghetti. Yet just visible between some of the wire bundles was a dull black substance arranged in the shape of a ball. This black stuff, Jake knew, was the conventional explosive trigger. Upon detonation it would squeeze the plutonium in the core – the center of the ball – into a supercritical mass. There in that tiny space the plutonium atoms would have their electrons stripped away, an instantaneous rape that would release stupendous amounts of energy. $E = MC^2$.

Jake Grafton counted quickly. Four warheads on each pallet, how many pallets? Almost a hundred.

The visitors were wandering away from the warheads when they saw the bodies stacked in one corner. Jake went over for a look, then found that only Jack Yocke had followed him.

Blood everywhere. Blood? Jesus, these people were shot! Lined up and gunned down.

Now he saw the spent cartridges that lay scattered around. He picked one up. Soviet. Not that that meant anything. The Soviets sold military equipment all over the world, just like the Americans, Germans, French and British. Superpowers do that, right? To keep the factories humming and the diplomats employed.

How many people? Fifteen or so.

There was a telephone on the wall and he went toward it. He held the handset against his helmet and tried to hear a dial tone. Nothing. He played with the buttons. Finally he replaced the instrument on its hook.

He left the building and headed for the clean room.

More bodies, all with bullet wounds. Some had died quickly, others bled a lot. There were bullet holes in the protective shield that sealed the room from the raw plutonium on the other side of the window. Even the flies were dead on the floor. Jake Grafton looked, then turned to find Jack Yocke staring at him through his faceplate. Yocke had a camera but he wasn't taking any pictures. Jake brushed past him and headed for the door.

He had seen all he wanted to see. The others were ahead of him, walking toward the helicopter. Yocke trailed behind. Jake counted. Everyone here.

He climbed through the door and found Goober and Toad in the cockpit. 'Crank it up,' he shouted. 'Let's get outta here.'

Goober manipulated switches. Nothing happened. 'Battery's dead,' he announced.

It took all of them to manhandle the power cart out of the helicopter. After looking all the controls over carefully, Toad Tarkington set the choke, turned on the battery, and pushed the start button. Nothing happened.

'Fuck,' Toad said, loud enough for Grafton to hear. 'Nothing in this fucking country works,' he announced, then turned back to Jake.

Grafton looked at his watch. They had been on the ground for fourteen minutes. 'Those transporters probably have jumper cables and some hand tools. Maybe. Go see.'

Toad went trotting off, a silver figure laboring through the heat waves rising from the concrete.

Time passed. Jake Grafton stared at the sky.

There was a jet up there. He could see the contrail. There it was, a silver gleam coming out from behind that cloud.

The mirror was in his pocket. Inside the hot suit.

Well, there was no other way. He gingerly unzipped the suit enough to admit his hand, reached inside and snagged the mirror. Then he zipped the suit closed.

The mirror was rectangular, about two inches by four inches, with a hole in the middle. Jake looked above him for the jet, then raised the mirror and tried to get the refracted spot of sunlight to come into the crosshair. Then he realized that a cloud had drifted between him and the sun. He put the mirror down and studied the clouds.

A few minutes.

'Those people were murdered.'

Jack Yocke was beside him.

'Everyone southeast of Serdobsk was murdered,' Jake Grafton said. 'Those folks in there just happened to be shot.'

'Why?'

Jake flipped a hand at the empty transporters.

'Somebody stole some missiles?'

'Looks that way, doesn't it?'

'How are we going to get this helicopter started?'

'I don't know that we can.'

Then the sun came out. And there was the jet, still high up there against the blue. Jake raised the mirror to his eye and moved it carefully to focus the light.

Yocke began to understand. 'Is that Rita up there?'

'Maybe. I hope so.'

'Goddamn it, Grafton,' Yocke began. 'Why didn't—'

'We'll get out of this or we won't, Jack. That's the whole story.' He was working the mirror. The sunspot was right on the crosshair. 'Those people in there look like they are at peace.'

'That's a peace I'm not ready for yet.'

'They probably weren't ready either, but it came regardless. The one thing I can promise you – this is going to be one of the most peaceful spots on this planet for a couple hundred thousand years.' Jake removed the mirror from his eye and turned to face the reporter. 'The peace that death brings is all any of us can count on.'

Yocke was watching the jet high in the sky above. 'I think maybe she saw you,' he said.

One of the transporters rumbled into life. With diesel smoke pouring from the exhaust pipe, it slowly rolled toward the helicopter. 'There's a set of jumper cables in it,'

Toad told Jake when he got down from the cab, 'but no tools. The fucking Russians stole 'em or never put them in.'

'Try to hook the cables up and get that power cart started. Rita's coming but we may still need this chopper.'

The jet was a three-holer, a Tupolev 154 with Aeroflot markings, a Russian ripoff of the Boeing 727 design. It wasn't until it turned off the runway that Jake realized there was no hot gas coming from the center engine exhaust.

Rita taxied up and gestured to him from the cockpit.

'Everyone, we're taking the jet,' Jake roared. 'Help Captain Collins with his gear. Then get on the back of the transporter. Toad, when everyone's on it, back that thing up to the door of the jet.'

Two US marines opened the door for them and they scrambled aboard. Toad came in last. 'Do we need to move the transporter?'

Rita was standing there. 'No,' she told him. 'I'll back us out with thrust reversers. Close the door and let's go.'

They took off the hot suits and threw them into the back of the passenger cabin. Jake made his way to the cockpit and dropped into the copilot's seat. 'You got an engine out?'

'Yessir. It was overheating. Maybe a bad thermocouple, but I don't know. We got a heck of a takeoff roll without it, but I think we can make it.'

'How much runway we got?'

'About nine thousand feet. We're light, nowhere near max gross weight. We'll make it if the tires don't blow. There's no tread left and I could see cord in a couple places.'

Jake Grafton looked down the runway at the trees beyond. Relatively flat terrain, thank the Lord! 'Well, I guess we'll find out soon enough.'

Toad stuck his head in. 'Rita, you get more beautiful every time I see you.'

She flashed him a wide grin.

'Did you see the mirror okay?' Jake asked.

'Yessir. I had a little trouble finding this place. Most of the Russian nav aids don't work. I circled for about a half hour and had about decided you were going out on the chopper.' She was all business, relating it crisply, a matter of fact just to be reported.

'There's the gear handle and the flaps.' She touched each lever. 'We'll begin our takeoff roll with the flaps up so we'll accelerate a little faster. I'll call for takeoff flaps at about a hundred eighty kilometers per hour – the airspeed is calculated in clicks so don't get excited. You put them down to the first detent, takeoff. When we're airborne I'll call for the gear, then the flaps.'

'Let's do it.'

She taxied to the very end of the runway and held the brakes while she ran her two good engines up to full power. Then she released the brakes.

The jet accelerated slowly. Jake could hear the thumping as the wheels passed over the expansion joints.

Rita Moravia made no attempt to rotate, merely sat monitoring the engine instruments and the airspeed indicator between glances at the end of the runway, which they were stampeding toward at an ever increasing pace.

'Flaps,' she called.

Jake moved the handle to takeoff. The indicator moved. 'They're coming!'

The airspeed needle kept rising, but oh so slowly. The end of the runway came closer, closer.

Jake was reaching for the control wheel to rotate the plane when Rita eased it back and the nose came off, then the main wheels just as the end of the runway flashed by. 'Gear up,' she called, and Jake Grafton raised the handle.

When the gear was fully retracted the plane accelerated better. Still Rita kept the nose down and let the airspeed increase. 'Flaps up,' she said at last, and Jake moved the handle.

When they were climbing through three thousand

meters – the altimeter was calibrated in meters – Rita told Jake, 'This is the biggest plane I've flown. Handles better than I thought it would.'

CHAPTER SEVENTEEN

When the airliner was level at cruising altitude, Captain Collins checked everyone for radiation. Jake had to part with his shirt. Colonel Rheinhart lost his trousers. 'As soon as we get to Moscow,' Collins told them, 'I want each of you to take a long shower. Wash your hair thoroughly. The stuff you want to get rid of is radioactive dust and dirt. Stay in the shower as long as you can stand it and don't come out until you're as clean as a new penny.'

When Jake had settled into a seat, Yocke came over and sat beside him. 'Where'd you guys get this airliner?'

'Aeroflot.'

'Who'd you have to kill?'

'Nobody. Toad told them we wanted to charter an airliner and waved American money. He got this one full of gas for seventeen hundred dollars cash and two bottles of mediocre whiskey that he stole out of Spaso House on the Fourth of July. The Aeroflot man insisted a Russian pilot come along, but he came down with something and got off when Rita gave him a hundred. She flew it out of Sheremetyevo.'

'What about air traffic control?'

'One of the enlisted marines speaks tolerable Russian. He's up in the cockpit with Rita now.'

Yocke shook his head. 'It's amazing what real money will buy.'

'Ain't it, now.'

'Think that's what happened to those missiles?'

'Your guess is as good as mine.'

'Now, Jake! Don't start that crap! I've risked my butt this afternoon right along with you and Rita and all these other military heroes. It wouldn't hurt an iota for you to come clean and tell me the whole truth. For once.'

Jack Yocke got the gray eyes full face. There was no warmth in them. 'That's the second time you've called me Jake. You aren't old enough or wise enough. Don't do it again.'

'Yessir. No offense. But I mean it about leveling with me. I feel like a kid in a haunted Halloween house. I've paid my buck and I keep getting the shit scared out of me even after it ceases to be fun. How about telling me what you know?'

'I don't know what happened to those weapons. I was as surprised as you were when I saw those empty transporters and the bodies.'

'The story I heard that got me over to this country was that the Iraqis were trying to buy some nuke weapons. I heard they had three billion to spend for the right toys.'

'Where'd you hear that?'

Jack Yocke scratched his nose, then rubbed his face good. It went against the grain to reveal a source but he didn't see any way out of it. Finally he said, 'One of the ICB executives told me, off the record. He was sitting in a New York jail awaiting trial when I interviewed him.' The International Commerce Bank had recently been shut down worldwide for money laundering on a stupendous scale, that and a garden variety of other financial crimes.

'Did you believe him?'

This was the crucial question. A professional reporter hears a lot of stories, every now and then a true one. The good reporters can smell a lie a block away. 'I thought he was telling the truth,' Yocke told the admiral. 'Or what he believed to be the truth. It had the right feel.'

'I don't mean to insult you, but did you get that feel when Judith Farrell told you her Soviet Square tale?'

'Yeah, I did. I've been thinking about that. In the first place she was a professional liar and damn good, and second, most of the story was true, in fact all of it except who was ultimately responsible. So it played well. There was nothing fancy or hyped. I bought it.' He shrugged.

Jake Grafton visibly relaxed. 'Don't feel like the Lone Ranger. I bought one of her stories one time too.'

Jack Yocke got the feeling he had just passed some kind of test. 'Well, the ICB tip didn't pan out over here. I had the names of two former ICB execs who had run to earth in Moscow that my source swore knew the ins and outs − if they could be persuaded to talk. These two birds supposedly shuffled the money every which way to Sunday to make it impossible to trace. That made sense, so I looked for them for four straight days but couldn't get a sniff. Not that I'm any great shakes at finding people in Moscow, but still . . .'

'I heard about the money going through ICB too,' Jake said softly. 'Maybe from Iraq. Maybe from an Iraqi working for Iran.'

'Heard any names? Which Russian might have gotten the dough?'

'A name or two. That much money, it's impossible to keep it secret. Oh, they've tried. But that much money . . .' He had repeated the rumors to Richard Harper in the hope that he could find the trail. Did he?

He heard the power being reduced. 'I'd better go talk to Rita,' Jake said. 'We'll land at another airport and Toad can call Aeroflot. No use letting the manager see who was on his chartered airplane.' Yocke got out of his seat, then Jake maneuvered himself into the aisle and walked forward to the cockpit.

Three billion dollars. That wasn't pocket change anywhere, but in Russia it was a stupendous amount of money. Too much, really. Jack Yocke moved to the window seat and sat staring out, wondering where the money could be, what a Russian could use it for. In Russia there were no stocks to buy, no bonds, no office buildings to invest in, no art masterpieces for sale, no private oil syndicates setting out to drill up Siberia or the Gulf of Mexico. It was amazing, really. Here was a whole nation with not a god-damn thing to invest money in, unless you were looking to throw your bucks into worn-out factories producing obsolete, shoddy goods that no one on the planet except starving, penniless Russians wanted.

However, one possibility did come to mind. He looked toward the cockpit, started to get out of the seat and go that way, then decided against it. If he thought of it, the idea must have already occurred to Jake Grafton.

He sighed and scratched himself and turned his attention back to the window.

It was dark when the Tupolev 154 landed at Domodedovo, a huge field for domestic airliners thirty miles southeast of Moscow. Rita taxied to the corner of the airport most remote from the terminal and shut down the engines. Jake went back to find Captain Collins. He wiggled a finger at Iron Mike McElroy, the marine captain, who came over. 'I want this airplane washed before we call Aeroflot. I don't want any radioactivity overdoses on my conscience.'

McElroy agreed to use his people to find some tank trucks and hoses and to do the washing, and Collins agreed to use his equipment to ensure they got the hot spots and diluted the runoff as much as possible.

'Do the best you can,' Jake told them, and left it at that.

An hour later Jake was in Ambassador Lancaster's office in the embassy complex. Ms Hempstead sat on the couch with a notepad on her lap.

'Yeltsin refused to resign,' Lancaster said. 'The anti-Yeltsin forces have forced a no-confidence vote in the Congress of People's Deputies. The best Yeltsin could do was get it delayed until Friday.'

This was Monday evening. Jake glanced at the calendar on the ambassador's desk to make sure. Three days.

'Yakolev and Shmarov have been on television,' the

ambassador continued. 'They and the rest of the junta seem to have a lot of support. People are hungry, unemployed, the factories don't have raw materials or markets, this Serdobsk disaster may have been the last straw.'

'Yeltsin was popularly elected. I didn't know the legislature could throw him out.'

'Technically they can't. But over here they're still making up the rules as they go along. If he loses on the no-confidence vote he can either call for a new election of deputies or resign and let the congress choose a successor. The problem is that his support is melting away.'

'What's the American position?'

'We've got to let the Russians sort it out for themselves. We'll recognize any government that gets in without resort to violence.'

'How about blowing up the Serdobsk reactor? Would Washington classify that as a violent act?'

Lancaster goggled. Hempstead came off the couch and floated toward the desk. 'Blew it up? Who?'

'I'm not accusing anyone of anything. I'm merely asking a question.'

'This isn't the time for soaring hypotheticals, Admiral,' Hempstead said acidly, 'or cute questions about when someone stopped beating his wife.' She stalked back to the couch and snatched up her notepad.

'I assume you do have some basis for your question,' Owen Lancaster said uneasily. 'Exactly what did you find out on your helicopter trip to Serdobsk?'

'The reactor and containment vessel are gone, sir, nothing left but a crater and some rubble. The entire control building was destroyed. A storage building a hundred yards or so from the reactor was severely damaged and the plutonium containers that were inside ruptured.'

Lancaster merely nodded. Like most people, he had only the vaguest idea of what a meltdown was or what the physical effects might be. He expected something terrible of course, but just what was rather hazy. This description sounded properly catastrophic, so he murmured 'horrible' and shook his head. 'Nobody survived, I suppose?'

'No, sir,' Jake Grafton said, and paused for a few seconds to gape at the vastness of the great man's ignorance.

Then he continued: 'The fallout zone is huge and extraordinarily hot. Collins will have some numbers in a few hours. We won't know the exact dimensions of the fallout zone until aerial surveys are conducted. But to return to my question – I guess I didn't phrase it right. Please excuse me. I'm just curious about how willing the United States government might be to get into a shooting scrape over here if the junta looks like it might be coming out on top.'

'That's a decision for the president,' Hempstead piped from her ringside seat, her tone suggesting Grafton was a few cards short of a full deck.

Lancaster spoke more slowly. 'I seriously doubt if anyone in Washington will be very enthusiastic about a military adventure in Russia, Admiral, even if Yakolev himself personally blew up a dozen reactors and CBS News has a videotape of him pushing the plunger. Speaking hypothetically, of course.'

Jake Grafton wondered what the administration's reaction would be to medium-range ballistic missiles armed with nuclear warheads in Iran or Iraq. He didn't ask the diplomats though. He wanted to talk to Hayden Land before he set Lancaster's pants on fire.

While Senior Chief Holley was checking the navy's minuscule office for bugs and rigging the telephone scrambler, Jake went to find Jack Yocke. 'I want you to write a story about what you saw today. Get the radiation numbers and isotopes and all that from Collins when he gets back. Write an eyewitness account, just what you saw. Leave out the bit about the transporters and the missiles. And let me see the story before you call it in.'

Jack Yocke had just completed his shower. He was tired and looked longingly at the couch in the small apartment that Grafton and Tarkington shared. Now Grafton was ordering up journalism like a fried-to-order hamburger. Yet he barely paused before he said, 'Yessir. I'll have the story for you in about an hour. When Collins gets back I can just insert a few paragraphs.'

'I'll be down in the office.'

Back in the office Holley was still looking for electro-magnetic fields that shouldn't be there. 'What did Herb Tenney do today?' Jake asked.

'He left the embassy about eleven, sir, and returned in time for dinner.'

The admiral grunted and began to think about what he was going to say to Hayden Land. When Holley pro-nounced the office clean, Jake punched his code into the scrambler and placed his call. It took seven minutes before the Pentagon operator got them connected.

'Let's go secure,' Land told him after he heard Jake's voice.

Jake pushed the proper button and waited while the two encrypters talked to each other with chirps and clicks, then he heard Land's voice. 'Richard Harper is dead.'

'How?'

'Apparent heart attack.'

'Do you have the report?'

'No. The house was ransacked.'

Jake didn't wait for the effect of that to numb him. He immediately began to report the events of the day.

While Jack Yocke tapped away on his laptop in the small living room, Toad and Rita took a long shower together and then crawled into bed. With the lights out and her head cradled on Toad's shoulder, Rita said, 'On the ride over here from the airport Yocke was telling me some wild tale about some women he met, a Shirley Ross and a Judith Farrell. I listened for about five minutes before it dawned on me that he was talking about Elizabeth Thorn.'

'She had a lot of names.'

'And she's dead.'

'Yes.'

'You loved her, didn't you?' Rita whispered.

'Yes.'

'Yocke needed someone to share it with.'

'Uh-huh.'

'He's a good guy underneath.'

Toad Tarkington didn't want to talk about Jack Yocke. Judith Farrell was on his mind, and this extraordinary woman beside him. 'It wasn't—' Toad began.

'Hush,' she told him. 'I'm not jealous. I know what I mean to you.'

He thought about that, tried to get the round peg into the square hole. Women are really amazing creatures – just when you think you've got their brain structure figured out, they stun you by revealing a feature of genetic engineering that you never expected, not in your wildest –

'Still,' she added, 'I think you should have told me about her. Oh, you married me and all that, but I didn't realize that you had all these torrid romances stacked in the closet that I am going to have to keep dealing with.'

It dawned on Toad that the peg wouldn't fit. 'You aren't the first woman I ever shook hands with.'

'You did a lot more than shake Elizabeth Thorn's hand, or Judith Farrell, or whatever her name was. Don't sugar-coat it and don't deny it.'

'Rita, I'm not denying anything! And I'm not going to lie to you about Judith. She was one hell of a fine woman. I loved her very much. She went her way and I went mine and eventually I met you. And I'm damn sorry she's dead.'

'Just how many more of *these women* are out there?'

The ol' Horny Toad knew the ice was damn thin. He carefully weighed his answer. 'You're the woman I married. You're the woman I want to spend my life with. Why are you jealous?'

'I am *not* jealous! Answer the question.'

'What question?'

'How many?'

'I dunno for sure. I didn't carve notches on the bedstead. Not counting you, let's see . . . maybe ten thousand, more or less.'

'Go ahead and count me, Romeo,' she growled. There was acid in her voice.

'Well, I'd have to consult my little black books. All of us Romeos have those. I did ratings, on a one-to-ten scale. I can probably use those records to come up with a fairly accurate count, although of course I didn't rate casual encounters. As I recall you scored a ten. It's sorta sad, but there weren't many tens, not more than one a month. All those books . . . it'll be a big job.' He took a deep breath and exhaled audibly, laced his fingers across his chest and stared at the ceiling, apparently contemplating the vast quantities of time and effort that were going to be involved in rooting through his voluminous files.

When she remained silent, he decided to take the offensive. But carefully. 'How many of your old boyfriends are you gonna torture me with?'

She thought about that. Finally she began counting on her fingers. At last she said, 'One hundred ninety-three. The first was a boy named Freddy that I had a crush on in kindergarten. He had blond hair and dimples and I desperately wanted him for my very own. The second was—'

'I missed you,' Toad told her.

'Oh, Toad, I missed you too.'

And then she sat up and he could see her whole face, her eyes, her nose, her mouth spreading into a smile. 'You're going to be a daddy,' she said softly.

'*What?*'

'It's too early to be absolutely sure, but I think so.'

He was horrified. He shoved her out to arm's length. 'You're pregnant and you flew that jet into that radioactive hell this afternoon? Are you out of your mind?'

One of her eyebrows arched. 'Not so loud. Let's not discuss this with Jack Yocke.'

'Rita,' he hissed, 'if you're pregnant you can't—'

'I can do what has to be done. Like every kid ever conceived, Toad Junior is going to have to take his parents as they come. Flying is what I do.' She stroked his eyebrows with a fingertip. 'Relax. I'll be careful. I pulled his father out of the fiery furnace today. Someday the Toadlet will understand and thank me.'

Toad needed time to digest it. After a while he said, 'Do you think it's a boy?'

Rita grinned and shrugged.

'Well, you ought to go back to the States. You shouldn't even have come over here. This place is too goddamn polluted for a pregnant woman.' Herb Tenney and his binary poisons crossed his mind. 'And—'

She wrapped her arms around him and pushed him backward. With her face just inches from his, she told him, 'Toad Tarkington. The women you fall in love with aren't housewives. If I become one I risk losing you. That's a risk I have no intention of taking.'

'But—'

'But nothing! This baby is mine too. You just stifle your male instincts and start thinking up names. I'll handle the rest of it.'

Toad tried to sort it out. Perhaps she was right, he decided. Probably. Women! If it floats, flies or fucks, rent – don't buy! Great advice but impossible to follow. After a bit he asked, 'Can you still make love?'

This question drew a giggle from the mother-to-be, who grasped him in a very intimate way and lowered her mouth onto his.

Senior Chief Holley woke Jake at five in the morning. The sun was already up. 'The helicopter made it back a couple hours ago. The guys just got here.'

'Fine,' Jake said, and the senior chief closed the door behind him. Jake had left orders that he be awakened when they returned, now he had trouble getting back to sleep.

282

He couldn't eat, not with Herb Tenney in the same city, and he was only getting a few hours' sleep a night. This regimen wasn't good for him – he would soon have trouble concentrating. Maybe he was already feeling the effects.

He lay in the darkness staring at the ceiling. Soon his thoughts were on Callie and Amy. What time was it in Washington? What would they be doing today?

When he came awake again the chief was shaking him. 'Admiral, we have a call from General Land. I've set up the encrypter in the living room.'

Jake got out of bed and pulled on his pants. In the living room Jack Yocke was drinking coffee.

'What time is it?'

'Almost noon.'

'Toad up?'

'Still in bed.'

'Let him sleep.'

'Want me to leave?'

'You can stay, but everything you hear is classified. You can't print anything.'

'I know the ground rules,' Yocke said mildly and sipped at the coffee. 'Take your call. I'll get you a cup.'

'Admiral Grafton, sir.'

'Land. I got yesterday morning's satellite photo and the one the bird got at seven local time this morning over Petrovsk. How many empty transporters were there outside when you were there?'

'Three, sir.'

'This morning there were four. There were also two bodies there this morning.'

'Dead bodies?'

'They're lying down. The photo interpreter's labeled them dead. They look dead to me. One is right by a transporter, the other is near the abandoned helicopter.'

'Much cloud cover at Petrovsk this morning?'

'About thirty percent or so. There was a decent hole over the field when the bird went by.'

'We're lucky.' Jake had asked for the daily satellite shoot, but he hadn't expected anything this dramatic. 'Sounds like someone went back to the gold mine.'

'The morning after the meltdown was overcast, so nothing that morning. The next day the transporters were there. And yesterday. This morning four.'

'Who was it?' Jack Yocke handed Jake a cup of coffee and sat down on the couch.

'An AWACS bird over the Persian Gulf picked up three transports leaving a military airfield near Samarra, northwest of Baghdad, at a few minutes after nine last night. They tracked them flying just a little west of north until they departed the area. Then three transports came back this morning a few minutes after dawn. One crashed fifty miles north of the air base, the other two landed there.'

'They didn't have the right gear to withstand the radiation.'

'Looks that way.'

'General, somebody is going to have to destroy those missiles before any more of them are carried away. Those missiles are too big a temptation.'

'I'm going over to the White House in about fifteen minutes. I've already talked to the secretary of defense. He and the national security adviser will meet us there. Why don't you be in Ambassador Lancaster's office an hour and a half from now? Someone will call you.'

'Aye aye, sir.'

Jake hung up the phone and switched off the crypto device.

'Someone went back?' Yocke asked.

'Apparently. They carried off at least three missiles before the meltdown. That night. The radiation was supposed to cover up the fact the missiles were missing, for a while anyway. But someone got careless and left the transporters outside.'

'Why didn't they take the transporters too?'

'Too big. Too heavy. Oh, maybe they took one or two,

284

but they opted to leave at least three behind and take the missiles instead.'

'And someone went back last night?'

'And maybe got a couple more missiles. Left at least two dead people on the mat and one more empty transporter.'

'Satellite?'

'Uh-huh.'

'Just how good are those satellites?'

'They can see something the size of a pack of cigarettes. The problem is that we only have so many satellites. Right now we're trying to monitor every base in Russia where nukes are stored.' Jake started to add something, then just shook his head.

'So what are we going to do?'

'If you mean the United States, Land is going to see the president now.'

'Who got the missiles?'

'Saddam Hussein.'

'Oh, hell.'

'That isn't the worst of it. Remember all those warheads stacked around? Those are highly portable. Odds are that for every missile they carried away, they took half a dozen warheads.'

Jake Grafton headed for the bathroom to shower and shave. He decided to put on his uniform. It looked like it might be that kind of day.

'What?' said Ms Hempstead, her brows knitted.

'I expect the ambassador will be getting a call in a little while from the White House. General Land asked me to be here when it comes.'

'Have a seat, Admiral. I'll talk to the ambassador. He's on the telephone right now with Yeltsin's aide, trying to arrange an appointment.' She whirled and marched for the door to the inner sanctum.

Jake Grafton picked a seat and settled in. The secretary thought she could spare him a smile, then thought better of it and went back to pounding the keyboard of her computer terminal. Jake picked up a three-month-old copy of *Southern Living* and began to leaf through it. There were articles there on a couple of houses he wouldn't mind living in if he ever inherited five million dollars.

Ten minutes later he tired of the magazine. He checked his watch. The ambassador's door was firmly closed. The secretary was pretending to work on something on her desk.

He was examining the paintings on the wall thirty minutes later when the door opened. 'Would you come in, please, Admiral Grafton,' Hempstead said. She stood aside and he walked in.

The ambassador was on the telephone. He was listening. Every now and then he said, 'Yessir.' Finally he said, 'He's here now with me, sir . . . Yessir . . . If you think . . . I'll let you know immediately. Yessir. Good-bye.'

Lancaster hung up and looked around blinking. His eyes settled on Grafton, then moved to Hempstead. 'Agatha, please use the telephone in the other room to get me an appointment with Yeltsin. Tell the aide I have an oral message from our president that I must deliver immediately. Have a seat, Admiral.' Jake did so.

When Hempstead was gone, Lancaster said, 'It would have been nice if you had given me some warning about this last night.'

'I thought I'd better talk to my boss first, sir.'

'So you didn't level with me. I've been an ambassador on and off for over twenty years. I was talking to presidents about affairs of state when you were a lieutenant filling out fitness reports on drunken sailors. I was helping prevent World War III when our new president was smoking pot without inhaling.'

Owen Lancaster got out of his chair and walked around the desk. He leaned against the mantel of the fireplace, then half-turned so he could see Jake.

'I'll tell you right now that the United States has no

business taking sides in the Russians' political battles. We have no money to offer them. We have no bottled cure for all the problems they face. All our crowd knows how to do is jack the interest rate up or down a half a point and hire another ten thousand bureaucrats to manage the social problem de jour. These people are going to have to solve their own problems.'

When Jake said nothing, Lancaster came over and dropped into the adjacent chair. 'The president wants me personally to brief Yeltsin on the goings on at the Petrovsk military base. I am to give him two options. A – he may order an air strike on the missiles and warheads still in the hangars at Petrovsk. The weapons must be destroyed by noon tomorrow, or B – the United States will do the job for him. His choice.'

'I doubt if he will accept either option,' Jake murmured.

'That is also my opinion. He doesn't have enough clout with the Russian military to enforce an order telling them to blow up their own base, and it would be political suicide to allow American warplanes to fly across Russian territory to make an attack on a Russian military installation. The president and national security adviser see this the same way. So . . . if he refuses both options, I am to give him a third, a compromise. He will supply two airplanes and weapons and two of your test pilots will fly to Petrovsk and destroy the base.'

'I see.'

'I wish you did, Admiral.' Owen Lancaster levered himself from the chair and went to the window. With his back to Jake he said, 'The Russians are a proud people. We are going to force Yeltsin into doing something that will probably sink him politically. To get rid of what? – a hundred or so nuclear warheads? – we are going to run a serious risk of putting a military dictatorship into the Kremlin. A hundred weapons – a drop in the bucket. Our president made this decision in less than an hour after talking with only Hayden Land and the national security adviser, who six months ago was preaching the big ideas to pimple-faced fraternity boys at a college in New England, kids who are still carrying their first condom in their wallets.'

'Yeltsin is no liberal Little Rock Democrat, sir. He's half dictator. Any government Russia gets will be a dictatorship to some degree.

'Admiral, I quit listening to that isolationist apologia when my hair started falling out. The Russians have gone from tyrant to tyrant since the dawn of time. They *like* tyrants — someone to do the thinking for them. But Yeltsin . . . he's trying to force these isolated wood hicks into the world economy, the world culture. Boris Yeltsin may be Russia's last hope. And ours.'

Lancaster headed for the door. As he went he muttered, 'You knotheads don't seem to understand that you can't go off half-cocked when the whole goddamn planet is at risk.'

CHAPTER EIGHTEEN

It was three in the afternoon when Lancaster informed Jake by telephone of Yeltsin's decision. 'He'll make two Su-25s available at the Lipetsk air base.'

'Where is Lipetsk?'

'About two hundred miles south. There will be a helicopter waiting for your pilots in two hours at Domodedovo. It will take them there.'

'Yes, sir.'

'And, Admiral . . . I don't know what story he is telling the air force.'

'Uh, are you trying to say we're on our own?'

'Precisely.'

Jake hung up the telephone and looked around at his little staff. 'Okay, gang. Here's the plan. Rita and I will catch a chopper in two hours at Domodedovo that will take us to a Russian air base. They'll make two Su-25 Frogfoots available. Rita and I will bomb the base at Petrovsk. Any questions?'

'Uh, CAG,' Toad began, glanced at Rita and cleared his throat. 'Why Rita?'

Jake was genuinely surprised. Toad was not in the habit of questioning Jake's decisions. 'Well, she flew F/A-18s for several years before she went to test pilot school. Goober Groelke has a helo background, and Miles' – the third test pilot – 'came out of antisubmarine warfare. This job is dropping bombs and getting hits the first time around.'

'Oh.'

Jake looked expectantly at Toad.

'Just curious, that's all.'

Rita was looking at her husband through narrowed eyes. A domestic matter, Jake decided, and forgot about it.

'Frogfoots. Those will be good planes for this job,' Groelke said.

'Should be,' Jake acknowledged. 'We'll find out.' He knew the Frogfoot from its reputation. A Russian close-air support and antiarmor weapon, the plane was a close copy of the Northrop A-9, which had lost the US Air Force's competition for a tank killer when flying against the A-10 Warthog. The Soviets used Frogfoots in Afghanistan and supposedly they were good airplanes.

'Brunhilde Tarkington,' Toad said to Rita when they were alone.

'What?'

'A name for the kid. If it's a girl.'

'Don't you ever, *ever* do that to me again, Toad. I don't question your professional assignments. Don't you question mine.'

'I'm not pregnant. Nor am I ever likely to be.'

'And don't get cute with me, Bub!'

'I just love it when you talk dirty.'

She gave him her coldest stare. 'I wear the uniform, I got the training, I take the pay – I *will* fly the missions when they come.'

'Brunhilde.'

'Not on your life.'

He watched her walk away with her shoulders slightly hunched, her head down, as if she were walking into a strong wind.

This fatherhood bit . . . it was awful sudden. Of course, when you're married and do all the conjugal things, parenthood is one of the risks. Or rewards. Whichever. Still, it would have been nice to have a few years to think about it before it became a fact. Why didn't she say, Maybe we ought to think about being parents? Why didn't she say that?

Perhaps, he thought, she assumed I was thinking about it all along. Women are big assumers. The biggest assumption of all is the one they routinely make, that men think just like they do. And they are tortured by disappointment when it is proven for the umpteenth jillion time that men *don't*.

Because he hadn't been thinking about it. In fact, the possibility had never once crossed his mind. Kids are little people who wail in supermarkets, get beaned by baseballs at Little League, and ride in the back end of station wagons making faces at people in other cars. Other people have them. Usually other older people. The fact that he had been a kid once upon a time had never inspired him to want one of his very own or to even contemplate the prospect.

Of course he knew the theory that sex causes kids, but he had assumed Rita was taking care of everything. After all, she never got pregnant before.

Surely Rita would not have made a decision like that on her own. Would she?

Maybe there had been an accident. Toad Tarkington, professional naval flight officer, knew a great deal about accidents. A little dollop of carelessness could cause you to crash, burn and die. Sometimes even without the careless-ness you crashed, burned and died – at a level too deep for philosophers, luck was involved. Life is a grand game of chance. This kid must have been an accident, he decided. Not that it mattered.

Diapers. They were extremely messy and smelled to high heaven. Of course he had never actually seen or smelled a loaded diaper or wiped a baby's bottom – he knew from listening to adults who had taken the parental plunge. As he contemplated the messy prospect now, he shuddered. And washing clothes in the same machine used for diapers! Do people get two washing machines? His mom had never owned but one . . . Funny, he had never thought of that before. He would have to ask somebody.

He wondered if Rita would want to nurse. There's something . . . not obscene . . . jarring, yes, jarring, about watching a woman open her blouse and do something to her bra and plug a kid in. Seeing a woman nurse gave Toad the same sensation he got watching a sword swallower: the sight jolted him right to his toenails. These modern women have waited so long for kids they do it everywhere – in cars, restaurants, theaters, stores, hair places – not just in the ladies' room like their grandmas used to do.

And somebody once said that babies don't just eat three square meals a day – they are hungry every two hours. That seemed like a lot, and he frowned. Every two hours couldn't be right. That guy must have had a fat kid.

His kid wouldn't be fat. He would speak to Rita about that. Eat right and get plenty of exercise, throw the ol' ball around, climb trees and play tag and all that stuff. He would see to it.

Boy or girl, he would raise this kid right. Help with the homework and stories at night, lots of sports . . .

How in the heck had his parents done it?

He recalled some spankings and flashes from holidays and picnics, and some run-ins with the little girl who lived next door – Becky or Rebecca or something like that – but it was precious little when he tried to add it up. That stunned him. Shouldn't he remember more? God, he hadn't tried to dredge up this stuff in years, not since . . . well, he had never tried.

And now he needed it. Slam bam thank you ma'am and he was going to be a father.

Maybe he ought to write to his mom and get some sort of operator's manual, something in writing.

Rita wouldn't like that, might get all huffy.

Did she remember more about being a kid than he did?

Probably not, but she would confidently assume that since she wasn't cursed by the Y chromosome she would instinctively know the right things to do.

Why couldn't he remember?

Jake Grafton used the phone in the office after the senior chief had rigged the scrambler. He reached General Hayden Land at the Pentagon.

'The real problem is Iraq,' Land told Jake after he had related Ambassador Lancaster's little speech. 'Missiles armed with nuclear warheads in Saddam Hussein's arsenal is something these people in Washington don't want to face.'

'The Iraqis only took a few missiles,' Jake informed him. 'Apparently they elected to take warheads instead.'

'I think so too. The president didn't have any problem putting the wood to the Russians to destroy Petrovsk. He was ready to use US assets to bomb it if the Russians refused. Almost too ready.'

'What do you mean, General?'

'He hasn't got burned yet by one of these military adventures blowing up in his face. So he's ready to damn the torpedoes and full speed ahead.'

'What did CIA say to all this?'

'They told the president to go slow. That he risked making an enemy of Russia. They were about to threaten World War III but he shut them up before they got it out.'

'General, now is the time to go get those weapons in Iraq. Every day that passes means we are one day closer to a desert Armageddon.'

'I'm listening,' Land said.

'We're going to have to go into Iraq. An airborne assault. We'll go into Hussein's backyard, take or destroy the missiles and warheads, and leave as quick as we can. We're going to have to do it before he uses those weapons.'

Silence. 'That won't be easy.'

'Yes, sir. I know that.'

'Saddam may bag the whole lot of you.'

'That's a possibility. But we'll destroy the missiles first. General, we're going to have to pay a little now or pay a lot later – there are no other options. Any way you cut it, we've got to get the jump on him. We *have* to take the initiative while there is still time.'

'I don't like it. It's too risky. Too many things can go wrong, then you'll be stuck on the ground with a lot of casualties. The Iraqis may bag the whole lot of you, then we have a political prisoner situation. No, the way to do this is an air strike. We'll bomb that base into powder and that will be the end of Saddam's nuclear arsenal. We might lose a few pilots, but not a whole bunch of people.'

'If destroying the missiles were the only objective, I would agree with you,' Jake told the chairman. 'But it's not. We must prove to the world that Saddam has the weapons. We've got to show the world these missiles and warheads. Here's what I want to do.' Jake laid it out. His explanation took almost five minutes.

When Jake was finished, Land didn't say anything for several seconds. Finally he said, 'Well, maybe. I'll think about it. Present it to the president. As a soldier, I'll tell you right now that all that is too complicated.'

'It's our best shot, sir.'

'I'll think about it. What time frame are you thinking about for this operation?'

'As soon as humanly possible, sir. As soon as we can plan it. The sooner the better. I'm going to be flying one of these Russian jets down to Petrovsk tomorrow. We're flying out of the Lipetsk air base. We leave here in about an hour. I figure we'll get a checkout on the planes tonight, then fly first thing in the morning. Tomorrow night I can go to Arabia.'

'The weather people say that you can expect scattered to broken stratocumulus in the Petrovsk area, maybe fifty percent coverage, bases around three or four thousand feet, occasional rain showers.'

'That'll be good enough.'

'Who is the other pilot?'

'Lieutenant Commander Moravia, sir.'

'Okay. Take your scrambler with you and call me from Lipetsk before you take off. I'll go back to the White House and see what they think about Saddam Hussein.'

'Yessir.'

'Good luck, Jake.'

'Thanks, General.'

Only two options left to stop Saddam Hussein – an air strike or an airborne assault. Jake thought about that after he broke the connection. When you are down to just two options in this dangerous world, you are in deep and serious trouble. He knew that and Hayden Land knew it, but did the president?

She was in the apartment rolling her hair into a bun, with her mouth full of bobby pins. She was already wearing her flight suit and steel-toed flight boots.

'Gertrude Murgatroyd Tarkington,' Toad told her. 'Or Tarkington-Moravia or Moravia-Tarkington. Do you want the kid hyphenated?'

'Tarkington is okay,' she said, grinning around the bobby pins and eyeing him in the mirror.

He rammed his hands into his pockets and stood looking at this and that, avoiding meeting her eyes. 'Have you told your folks?' he asked finally.

'Of course not. Just you. We'll wait until the rabbit dies before we tell anyone.'

'Does a rabbit really die?'

'Not anymore. Used to though.'

Toad thought about that for a moment, about rabbits giving their lives to let women know they were pregnant – really! There was a *whole lot* about this baby business that he didn't know.

He glanced at her reflection in the mirror and said, 'You be careful out there.'

'I will.'

He came over and stood right behind her. 'This is supposed to be a little day jaunt down to Petrovsk, roll in and make a couple of runs with live ordnance, then back to the barn. But it may not go like that.'

'What do you mean?'

'The other night we were sitting in a park when people started shooting. Some people here and there would probably like to see Jake Grafton dead. Somebody wants those missiles pretty badly. Keep your head on a swivel. Watch your six. If anybody looks cross-eyed, blow 'em out of the sky.'

Rita got her hair the way she wanted it and inserted bobby pins.

'Grafton's been shot at by experts,' he told her. 'Anybody that straps him on is in big trouble. Just stick to him like glue. Stay with him. No matter what, fly your own airplane.'

'I will, Toad.'

She finished with her hair and turned around to face him. He put his hands on her shoulders. 'I want you back in one piece.'

'I know, lover.'

'We're in a helluva fix when we send pregnant women to fight our battles.'

'Shut up and kiss me.'

Jake took Spiro Dalworth along because he spoke Russian. Unfortunately he knew next to nothing about aviation or airplanes or weapons, so the terms didn't translate very well. Yet somehow Jake and Rita found out what they had to know. They took turns sitting in the cockpit of an Su-25 asking questions. Dalworth translated and a Russian pilot supplied the answers.

The pilot was young, a lieutenant. He was in culture shock. 'Who flies?' he asked Dalworth.

Spiro pointed to Jake and Rita.

'The woman?'

'Yes, she will fly.'

'A woman? *She* will fly?'

'Yes.'

When Rita asked a question, the answer was short, curt. When Jake asked one Dalworth had trouble finding a pause to translate amid the Russian's verbal flood. Rita saw the problem and addressed her comments to Jake, who then asked the questions. The process seemed to work better that way.

The olive-drab airplane with a red star on the tail seemed an excellent piece of military equipment. With two internal engines generating over eleven thousand pounds of thrust each, ten external weapons pylons under a wing designed to haul a big load of ordnance, an adequate fuel supply, and a twin-barrel 30mm cannon mounted internally, the airplane seemed just what the doctor ordered for ground attack. The avionics were not state-of-the-art, however. The plane lacked a radar and had no computer to assist the pilot, who had to do his own navigation with a minimum of electronic help. Jake and Rita would have to find the target with their Mark I, Mod Zero eyeballs and attack it with dumb weapons. The plane contained a laser ranger and could deliver laser-guided weapons, but it lacked a laser designator. The bombsight was strictly mechanical.

The cockpit and pilot chores were straightforward enough, yet the switches and gauges were scattered throughout the cockpit with apparently no forethought given to ease of operation or minimizing the pilot's work-load.

Visibility from the cockpit wasn't great either. Although the pilot sat well forward of the wing, the view aft was nonexistent and the view downward was restricted by the sides of the airplane.

The electronic warfare (EW) panel was simple and passive. Lights illuminated when the plane was painted by radars on certain bandwidths, but after receiving that quiet warning the pilot was on his own.

'It's no A-6 or F/A-18,' Rita remarked.

'More like an A-7,' Jake muttered.

The only officer they met was the lieutenant who had led them to the hangar for their briefing. The CO of the base and the CO of the air wing were conspicuously absent. They were cooperating on orders from Moscow, but that was all.

The officers' quarters were a barracks. Rita tossed her stuff on a bunk and stared back at the Russian pilots, who were whispering among themselves.

They were offered food. Jake declined for everyone – he didn't want to risk a case of the trots. Hunger was preferable.

After Jake had used his satellite com gear for another long talk with General Land in Washington, he sat on a bottom bunk with Rita and examined the charts they had brought from Moscow. With only these charts they had to find the Petrovsk base, then find their way back here. Most of the Russian nav aids were inoperable and the Su-25 might not reliably receive the ones that were transmitting.

There was a minor flurry in the bathroom when Spiro insisted all the Russians depart so that Rita could use it, but the lights went out without fanfare after Rita disappointed a little knot of onlookers by crawling under her blanket fully dressed.

Jake Grafton lay under his blanket staring into the darkness, tired but not sleepy. The hangar where the missiles and warheads were housed was priority number one tomorrow morning. Then, if there were any bombs or cannon shells left, they would attack the clean room with its warhead parts stacked everywhere. And they had to do it on the first flight. There was no way they could ask Yeltsin to let them fly another mission, not with the outstanding cooperation and friendly attitude these uniformed folks here had displayed.

And then there was the problem of the missiles in Iraq. Just how long did mankind have before Saddam Hussein decided his new arsenal was operational? Had the dictator reached that point already? How could the Americans plan an airborne assault into Iraq that minimized the hundreds of possible things that could go wrong and yet gave them a reasonable chance of grabbing or destroying the weapons before the Iraqi military massively retaliated? Were the odds good enough to order people into action, or should they be asked to volunteer? They would volunteer to a man, Jake was convinced, but he wanted no part of asking anyone to commit suicide. Nor did he plan on doing it himself.

What was Herb Tenney up to these days? Did the CIA tell him of this bombing mission? What could he do about it? Why would he do anything? More to the point, what could Yakolev and his cohorts do, assuming they were so inclined?

Dozens of questions, no answers. But first things first. The mission tomorrow – Jake knew how tough it would be. Using contact navigation to get to Petrovsk would be tough enough. Flying there in a type of aircraft he had never flown before was a helluva challenge. The task would be huge even if he were current on jet aircraft, which he wasn't. How long had it been since he had flown a tactical aircraft? Three years? No, four. Actually four years and three months.

And Rita had never been in combat. Oh, this wasn't supposed to be combat, but what if someone started shooting? How would Rita handle it?

Maybe he should have said something to her.

What? Knowing Rita Moravia, anything he could come up with would wound her pride. Oh, she wouldn't let on, would say yessir and nosir with the utmost respect, but . . .

So what could go wrong tomorrow?

Only a couple million things. He began to list them, to sort through the possibilities and try to decide now what he would do if and when he was faced with real problems.

He was still mulling contingencies an hour later when he

finally drifted into a troubled sleep filled with blood and disaster.

He was preflighting the ejection seat and removing the safety pins when he realized that one pin was already out. This one here, attached to the others with this red ribbon, that went where? He looked. Must be somewhere here on the side of the seat, to safety the drogue extraction initiator mechanism.

He found the place. A steel pin protruded from the hole. He tried to pull it out with his fingers.

Nope. It was in there to stay.

Someone hammered this steel rod into that hole. Oh, the ejection seat would still fire, but the drogue chute would not deploy and so the main chute would stay in its pack as he sat in the seat waiting, all the way to the ground.

Jake Grafton climbed back down the ladder to the concrete. Spiro Dalworth was standing there with the Russian lieutenant, the only officer on the base who had talked to them.

'Spiro, tell this clown to take me to the base commander.'

Dalworth fired off some Russian. When it didn't take, he repeated it.

The Russian pilot's eyes got large, but he whirled and started walking. Jake Grafton and Spiro Dalworth stayed two steps behind him.

The base commander had his office in a crumbling concrete building with the Russian flag on a pole out front. He was a rotund individual with a lot of gold on his epaulets. A general, probably.

'Someone sabotaged my airplane, hammered a steel pin into the ejection seat so that it will not function properly. Tell him.'

Dalworth did so. The general looked skeptical.

'I want two different airplanes. And I want his people to arm them while we watch.'

300

This time the general fired off a stream of Russian and gestured widely.

'He says that you are mistaken. You know nothing of this airplane, which is a fine airplane. Combat-tested in Afghanistan. His men are all veterans and take excellent care of their equipment. This is a front-line fighting unit, not—'

'Pick up his telephone. Call the Kremlin in Moscow. Ask for Yeltsin.'

To his credit, Dalworth didn't hesitate. He reached for the telephone as if he were going to order a pizza. When he asked the operator in Russian to get him the Kremlin operator, the general came out of his chair with a bound.

Jake was ready. He pulled the .357 Magnum revolver from his armpit holster and fired a round through the top of the general's desk. The gun went off with a roar that the walls of the room concentrated into a stupendous, soul-numbing thunderclap. The bullet punched a nice hole in the top of the wooden desk and a long splinter came loose. Dalworth almost dropped the telephone.

The general froze, staring at Jake, who looked him straight in the eye as he returned the pistol to the holster under his leather flight jacket.

The door flew open and a soldier with a rifle appeared. Dalworth said something to the general and made a shoo-ing motion to the soldier, who finally backed out of the room and closed the door.

Dalworth started talking on the telephone. After three or four sentences and a wait, he looked at Jake expectantly.

'Tell them that this general doesn't understand that he is to cooperate.

'Tell them that the two airplanes he wants us to fly have been sabotaged.

'Tell them that I want two good airplanes armed to the teeth, and I want them *now*, as President Yeltsin promised the president of the United States.'

Dalworth translated each sentence in turn and listened a

moment, then held out the instrument to the Russian general, who accepted it reluctantly.

When the general finally hung up the phone, he stood, straightened his uniform jacket as he snarled something at Dalworth, jerked his hat on and headed for the door.

'We are to follow him, Admiral. From what I could tell, he was bluntly told to cooperate or face the music.'

Jake grunted and strode after the general.

The Russian general stood in the middle of the parking mat and gave orders fast and furiously. He pointed, first at the planes Jake and Rita were to fly, then at the row of Su-25s still sitting in their revetments.

The general was in fine form, with officers and enlisted saluting and trotting obediently when Rita approached Jake. She held out her hand. In it were five coins, rubles.

'I found these glued to the stator blades inside the intakes of the plane I was to fly.'

Jake nodded. The coins would have stayed glued while the engines were at idle, but when the engines were accelerated to full power for the takeoff roll the coins would have come unstuck and been sucked through the compressors, which would have started shedding blades seconds later. The predictable result would be catastrophic engine failure and perhaps fire just as the aircraft lifted from the runway with a full load of weapons. It would be a spectacular way to die.

The airplane switch took an hour. New planes were pulled forward with a tractor and topped off with fuel. Two arming crews took the 250-kilogram bombs off the sabotaged planes and manhandled them onto the racks of the new ones. Another arming crew serviced the 30mm cannon on each plane with belts of ammo. While all this was going on, Rita inspected each aircraft, examined the fuses on the bombs, looked at each arming wire.

She was still at it when the general told Dalworth the planes were ready, and he translated this message for Jake.

Grafton turned his back on the airplanes and stood looking toward the office building. The telephone lines went to a pole that also carried the lines from the hangars. These lines went off to the east until they disappeared behind some buildings that looked like enlisted barracks.

Above them clouds floated southeast. Patches of blue were visible in the gaps. The clouds were puffy, full of moisture.

When Rita was finished, she came over to Jake. 'Whenever you're ready, sir.'

The Russians had G-suits, torso harnesses, oxygen masks and a variety of helmets arranged upon the hood of a tractor. The two fliers donned the flight gear carefully and tried on helmets until they found ones that fitted snugly.

'I'll lead,' Jake told Rita. 'You follow me as soon as I begin my takeoff roll and rendezvous in loose cruise. I want you above me. We'll spend the day below two hundred feet and only climb when the target is in sight. The radio has four channels – we'll use channel one. Get a radio check on the ground and then stay off the radio except for emergencies.

'When we're airborne, I'm going to arm my gun and shoot out the telephone box on the edge of the base. Once you arm your weapons, don't de-arm them. Our old equipment would always chamber a round on arming and leave the round in the chamber when you disarmed it, so the gun jammed the second time you hit the arming switch. I don't know how these guns are wired but let's take no chances.'

'Yessir.'

'Got any advice on how to fly this thing?'

'Be smooth,' Rita Moravia said. 'Let the plane fly itself. No sudden control inputs – don't force it to do anything. Stay in the center of the performance envelope as much as possible. Visually check every switch before you move it. Be ready every second. Don't ever relax.'

'You got your mil setting for the bombsight?'

'One hundred ten mils.'

'Okay.'

'Rita, if anything happens to me, bomb that missile storage hangar. No matter what.'

'Aye aye, sir.' She said it matter-of-factly, without inflection.'

Jake Grafton wanted to ensure that he was properly understood. 'I guess what I'm trying to say is, do whatever you have to do to destroy those missiles.'

'I understand.'

He examined her face. She was a beautiful woman, but right now she wore a look of confidence and determination that would have set well on any man Jake had ever flown with. Satisfied, Jake turned to Dalworth.

'Stay with the helicopter. Don't let the pilot wander off. Wave money at him if you have to. And don't let anyone here touch that machine. If we aren't back in three hours, get the hell out of Dodge.'

'Aye, aye, sir.'

'Let's get at it,' Jake Grafton muttered to Rita as he pulled his helmet on.

'Oh, Admiral,' Rita said. 'Thanks.'

Jake looked at her, not quite clear on what she meant. She drew herself to attention and saluted.

He nodded at her and a puzzled Spiro Dalworth and, with his charts in one hand and his oxygen mask in the other, walked toward his plane.

CHAPTER NINETEEN

Jake's aircraft didn't want to come unstuck from the runway. With the engines at full power it was accelerating nicely, but the nose wheel remained firmly planted. He tugged experimentally on the stick.

The trim! He had guessed at the takeoff setting. He blipped the trim button on the stick with his thumb and eased the stick back. Now the nose came up. And the mains were off. He was flying. The wings rocked and he over-controlled with flaperons as he reached for the gear handle.

It wouldn't move. He pushed it in, then pulled it out. *Now* it moved. Had to be pulled.

Trimming nose down, airspeed increasing. Gear indicates up. When he felt comfortable he looked for the flap handle, then moved it to the up position. Here they come . . .

At a thousand feet he retarded the throttles some, lowered the nose a little and dropped the left wing about fifteen degrees. The plane stabilized in a level left turn. No warning lights, no gauges with pegged needles. He hit the switch to segment the hydraulic system.

He glanced over his shoulder and caught sight of Rita's plane.

His aircraft was decelerating. Not enough power. He added a little, readjusted his nose attitude, cursed himself for being so far behind the plane.

His oxygen mask didn't fit right. It was leaking oxygen around his cheeks, making flatulent noises that he could hear above the background roar of the engines. He tried to tighten the retaining straps with his left hand, and finally gave up.

Another glance at Rita, who was turning with him and closing.

She's a good stick. Don't worry about her. Fly your own plane.

When Rita was stabilized behind him and out to the right side, Jake began looking at the ground. The base was small by US standards, the buildings grouped tightly together, probably to keep everything within walking distance. Surrounding it were miles of forests.

There was the telephone line leading off, and there by the road intersection, wasn't that some kind of junction box mounted on that pole?

He reversed his turn, and when the plane stabilized, reached for the master armament switch. He lifted it. There was no locking collar like US planes possessed. Now the gun switch.

As he turned it on he felt a thud. That would be the gun charging. He hoped. Bombsight on, reticle lit. What had that Russian pilot said? Ten mils deflection for the gun? He twisted the adjustment knob.

Now into a left turn, looking again for the road intersection. It was several miles away off the left wing, slightly behind it, so he turned steeply to get the nose around.

More power in the turn, as the wings come level back off some. This will be a nice slow pass, plenty of time to aim.

He was too fast. Throttles back more, nose down a smidgen and trim.

He concentrated on finding the pole in the bombsight.

Small target. Too goddamn small . . .

There!

Damn, he was too close. He slewed the nose a tad with rudder, adjusted the nose attitude with stick, then quickly centered the rudder and squeezed the trigger.

The gun vibrated hard and he saw the muzzle flashes through the sight. At night the muzzle blast would be blinding.

Now off the trigger and stick back smartly. With the nose well above the horizon he rolled the plane ninety degrees and looked. *Careful, boy*, you're carrying a hell of a load low and slow!

Pole and box down!

Level the wings . . . raise the nose. More power. Safely away from the ground, let's turn on course 130.

He craned his neck. Rita was back there, stepped out and up. As he watched she eased in a little closer and gave him a thumbs up.

Okay!

Airborne and still alive. *Okay!*

The two Su-25s soon left the last of the forest behind and found themselves over the steppe. Jake had descended to about two hundred feet above the rolling terrain, which meant that he was constantly jockeying the stick and adjusting the trim as the plane rose and fell with the land contours. Below them the grass spread from horizon to horizon, broken only by stands of wheat and an occasional dirt road.

This broad valley of the Volga had been peopled since ancient times, yet now the fallout would deny it to future generations. The enormity of the Serdobsk tragedy intruded into Jake's thoughts even as he worked on holding course and altitude.

Farther south, below the radioactive fallout zone, stood the city of Volgograd, formerly Stalingrad, the city built in the 1920s and 1930s as a civic monument to the new Communist way of life. In the last half of 1942 it had been the site of the stupendous battle with the German army that marked the turning of the Nazi tide. The battle destroyed Stalin's city, of course, and nearly everyone in it. When the Red Army counterattacked and trapped the German Sixth Army, Hitler sacrificed over a quarter million men rather than give up that pile of rubble. Stalingrad, that shattered monument to a generation sacrificed in a titanic struggle between two absolute despots, was rebuilt after the war. Soon the radioactive particles and mud carried by the Volga would make the city a deathtrap once again.

He had loved this type of flying when he was younger. Racing low across open country, working the stick and throttles to make the airplane dance gracefully, sinuously, in perfect rhythm with the rise and fall of the land – this was flying as it ought to be, a harmonious mating of man, machine and nature.

Today the magic of it never occurred to him. He was thinking of shattered dreams and tyrants and a people poisoned as his eyes scanned the terrain ahead and occasionally flicked across the instrument panel. On one of these instrument checks his eye was caught by a light, a small bulb that flicked on, then off, then on again.

He looked carefully, identifying it. He was being painted by a fighter's radar. Perhaps they had not located him yet, but the fighters were looking.

Damn!

He and Rita were flying two subsonic attack planes, and somewhere up there above the clouds fighters were stalking them. *Oh, yes, they're after us.* Jake Grafton assumed the worst. That was the only way to stay alive. Automatically he tugged at the straps that held him to the ejection seat, tightening them still more.

Without warning the warplanes crested a low rise and the great river lay before them, with clouds and swatches of blue sky reflecting on its wide, brown surface.

The planes cleared a power line and then shot out over the water. The sky reflections on the water drew Jake Grafton's eyes upward. He scanned, and saw contrails . . . two pairs. In seconds the eastern shore swept under the nose and Jake Grafton eased into a gentle climb to stay just above the rising land.

Contrails in pairs . . . they could only be made by fighters in formation. Fighters. Looking for . . . ?

This eastern shore of the Volga was heavily eroded into

308

corrugated ravines and streambeds. Jake Grafton picked a decently large creek and dropped into the valley it had cut flowing west toward the river.

He was down here in the weeds hiding from radars that sat on the surface of the earth. These radars would provide vectors to the fighter-interceptors when they found him. If he stayed below their horizon, they couldn't.

But fighters aloft – the new generation of Soviet fighters possessed pulse Doppler radars that allowed them to look down and identify a moving target amid the ground clutter. And the new missiles would track a target in the ground clutter. 'Look-down, shoot-down' the techno-speak guys called it.

The light blinked on and off several more times.

What's the worst airplane that could be up there? The MiG-29? It was sure deadly enough, but no. The absolute worst plane that he could think of was another masterpiece from the design bureau of Pavel Sukhoi, the Su-27 Flanker. Designed in the mid-1980s to achieve air superiority against the best planes the West possessed, the Su-27 was thought by some Western analysts to be able to outfly the F-14, F-15, F-16 and F-18, plus every fighter the French, British and Germans have – all of them.

If those were Flankers up there, they were probably carrying AA-10 'fire and forget' antiaircraft missiles with active radar seekers.

And a missile could be on its way down right now.

He lowered the nose and dropped to fifty feet above the rocky creek. Rita was still with him, in tighter now, only forty or so feet away and a little behind.

The warning light was on steady.

They've found us. Missile to follow. Or a lot of missiles.

The land was a rough wilderness devoid of trees. Rock outcroppings, meandering creeks in rocky draws, sandy places – Jake Grafton was working hard holding the attack plane in the draw. Several times he couldn't make a turn and lifted the plane across the rim with only several feet of clearance, then banked hard and slipped the plane back into the draw.

Vaguely he was aware that Rita had slipped into trail behind him where she could ride just above his wash.

'We have fighters above us,' he told her on the radio.

No response. Radio silence meant radio silence to Rita Moravia. If she heard——

A flash on his left. He glanced over and saw a rising cloud of dirt and debris as it swept aft out of his field of vision. A missile impact!

'They're shooting,' he announced over the radio.

He lifted the nose of the plane and cleared the little valley, then dropped the left wing. Throttles to the stop, stick back – the Gs tugged him down into the seat.

Another flash, this time on his right side.

Jesus, each Flanker can carry up to *eight* missiles! How many have they fired?

When he had completed about ninety degrees of turn he rolled wings level, eased the nose back down. He was running only twenty feet above the high places in the lumpy ground, which gave him a tremendous sensation of speed. The warning light was blinking.

A pulse Doppler radar identified moving targets by detecting their movement toward or away from the radar. If he could fly a course perpendicular to the searching fighter, its radar could not detect him. When it lost him the searching fighter would probably turn to alter the angles and try to acquire him again. Still . . .

Trying to ensure he didn't inadvertently feed in forward stick, he craned his head to see aft.

The missiles will be coming at three or four times the speed of sound, fool! You'll never see them. But you will kill yourself looking for them.

He concentrated on the flying. After twenty seconds on this heading, he rolled into a right turn, then leveled the wings after ninety degrees of heading change. Back on his original course, southeast. The warning light went out.

A small miracle. A temporary reprieve. Jake Grafton was under no illusions – he was flying a plane designed to destroy tanks and provide close-air support to friendly troops: those Sukhoi masterpieces above were designed to shoot down other airplanes. The Russians couldn't make a decent razor or even an adequate toothbrush, but by God they could built great airplanes when they put their minds to it.

He looked for Rita.

Not there.

Did they get her?

How much fuel have those guys got? He and Rita were late getting off. Maybe the fighters were already airborne and are running out of fuel. There's a maybe to pray for.

The warning light was blinking again.

He rolled into enough of a turn that he could look behind him. Visibility was truly terrible out of this Soviet jet! Clear right. He rolled left and twisted his body around. Uh-oh. Up there at the base of that cloud, coming down like an angel on his way to hell – a fighter!

And Jake was still toting ten 250-kilogram bombs, about 5,500 pounds of absolutely dead weight. He was going to have to get rid of the bombs or he would be meat on the table for the fighters.

He turned hard left to force the fighter into an overshoot, make him squirt out to the right side because he couldn't hack the turn. As he did so, Jake worked the armament switches. In a strange plane he had to look to check each one, all the time pulling Gs and hoping the fighter was doing what he wanted him to do.

He couldn't just pickle off the bombs, not this close to the earth: they would hit the ground almost under him and might detonate. If they did the shrapnel and blast would destroy his aircraft, and him with it.

When he had the switches set, he rolled hard right and stabilized in an eighty-degree bank, four-G turn. Then he pickled the bombs. The G tossed them out to the left. The instant the last one went he tightened the turn to six Gs.

Where was that fighter?

There – crossing over above in an overshoot.

And Lord, there's another one at eleven o'clock honking around hard.

These guys weren't first team – they came in too fast and scissored the wrong way. Pray that they don't learn too fast!

He checked the compass. He was headed southwest. He brought the nose more west and punched the nose down. He wanted to run right in the weeds until he found those ravines and valleys that led down to the Volga. If he could just hide in those . . .

The fighter high on his left was pulling so hard vapor was condensing from the air passing over his wing – he was leaving a cloud behind each wing. Damn – it *was* an Su-27! He had to be in afterburner. That guy was aggressive enough, no question about that.

And the other one – Jake twisted his body halfway around, risked flying into the ground just to get a glimpse – at six-thirty, thirty degrees angle off, nose already down, accelerating.

How much fuel do these clowns have?

The rough ground ahead was his only chance. These guys could go faster, accelerate faster, and probably out-maneuver him. A stand-up dogfight with two of them would be suicide.

Jake was down to fifteen or twenty feet above the ground now, going flat-out with the throttles against the stops, doing maybe five hundred knots – the damn airspeed indicator was calibrated in kilometers and only God knew the conversion factor.

He was too close to the ground to look behind him. In fact, he was too close to the ground – he was sure he had hit a rocky outcrop but somehow managed to avoid it by inches. To kiss the ground at this speed would be certain death, yet his only hope to stay alive was to fly lower than those two fighter pilots would or could.

There – on the right! The ground dropped away into an eroded valley.

Quick as thought he had the stick over and was skimming down into the valley. Turn hard – pull, pull, pull! – to keep from hitting the sides that rose steeply above him.

Well into the winding valley, Jake Grafton eased over to the left side as he pulled the power levers back and deployed the speed brakes.

His speed bled off quickly. If one of those guys came into the gorge after him . . .

Cannon shells went zipping across the top of his right wing like orange pumpkins.

The right wing fell without conscious thought. Speed brakes in. Throttle full forward.

The fighter slid by on his right side, the pilot climbing and trying to slow.

As the sleek fighter went in front Jake pulled up hard and squeezed the trigger on the 30mm cannon. No time to aim! Just point and shoot!

The cannon throbbed and Jake hosed the shells in front of the twisting fighter, which flew into them. A piece came off the Su-27. Fuel venting aft. A flash.

Jake released the trigger and rolled away as the fighter exploded.

Where was the wingman?

A blind turn to the right coming up. Jake pulled hard to make it and got the nose coming up. As he went around the turn he climbed the side of the little valley and popped out on top. He swiveled his head.

There! Coming in from the left side, shooting.

Nose down hard. Back toward the valley.

The second fighter was going too fast and overshot. That's the problem when you've got a really fast plane: you want to use all that speed the designers gave you and sometimes it works against you.

313

This guy pulled Gs like he had a steel asshole. The fighter tried to turn a square corner, the down wing quit flying and the plane flipped inverted. In the blink of an eye the Su-27 hit the ground and exploded.

Jake got into the valley, retarded his throttles to about 90 percent RPM and stayed there.

He examined the electronic warfare panel. Goddamn light still blinking.

He rammed his left fingers under his helmet visor and swabbed the sweat away from his eyes.

They would find him again. How many more? He had seen four up there when he and Rita crossed the Volga a lifetime ago. Two were down, two still flying, perhaps off chasing Rita, perhaps now up there somewhere in the great sky above examining their track-while-scan radars and looking for him, perhaps calling on the radio to their comrades who would never answer again.

Could they find him in this valley, which was fast ceasing to be a steep gorge and was spreading out as the creek flowed its last few miles to the Volga?

There – on the left – another valley coming into this one. Jake dropped the left wing and pulled the plane around. He went back up the new valley, still seeking shelter as the EW light blinked intermittently.

Jake Grafton had flown his first combat mission in Vietnam over twenty years ago. He knew the hard, inescapable truth: in aerial combat the first pilot to make a mistake is the one who dies. The two men who had died in the Sukhoi fighters had each made fatal mistakes. The first man pursued too fast, so he had overshot when his victim unexpectedly slowed down. The second was overanxious, had pulled too hard and departed controlled flight too close to the ground. He was dead a half-second later, probably before he even realized what was happening.

The next time Jake might not be so lucky.

He swabbed more sweat from his eyes as he examined the fuel gauge. Still plenty. Like the A-6, the engines of this

Russian attack bird were easy on fuel and the plane carried a lot of it. That was the only advantage he possessed when compared to the fighters, which sacrificed fuel economy to gain speed and range to gain maneuverability.

Where were the other two fighters? Chasing Rita?

A flicker of concern for Rita crossed his mind, but he forced it away. Rita was a professional, she had been an F/A-18 Hornet instructor pilot for two years before she went to test pilot school – she could take care of herself.

He hoped.

No time to worry about her. If only he knew where she was . . .

They came in shooting from the rear quarter on each side. His first inkling that they were there was the sight of glowing cannon shells passing just in front of the nose, from left to right. He rammed the stick forward and his peripheral vision picked up shells passing just above the canopy from right to left. Just streaks really, but he knew exactly what they were.

The negative G lasted only for an instant before he had to jerk the stick back to avoid going into the ground. But it was enough. Even as he fought the positive G he saw the pair of fighters flash across above his head and arc tightly away for another pass.

He wouldn't survive another pass.

Slamming the throttles full forward, he kept the nose coming up and topped the cliff on the right side of the valley, then ruddered the nose down. He pulled hard in a tight turn, trying to turn inside the faster fighter.

And the fighter pilot wasn't looking!

The idiot had his head in the cockpit – he was worried about flying into the ground. That was a serious threat this close to the earth, the brown land whirling by at tremendous speed just scant feet below the right wingtip.

The nose of Jake's plane passed the fighter and he began to pull ahead. Range closing as the aspect angle changed. The fighter was turning into Jake. Angle off about seventy degrees, now eighty, ninety as the two planes flashed toward each other. Jake eased out some bank. A full deflection shot –

Now!

He triggered the cannon. The tracers passed in front of the fighter's nose, then in an eyeblink the fighter flew through the stream, which stitched him nose to tail. His nose dropped and his right wing kissed the earth.

Jake raised his nose a smidgen to ensure he didn't share the same fate, banked and pulled.

If he could get around quickly enough, he would present the second fighter with a head-on shot, and if that guy had any sense he would refuse the invitation and pull up into the vertical, where Jake lacked the power to follow.

And that is what happened as the two planes flashed toward each other nose to nose. Jake wanted to take a snapshot but couldn't get his nose up fast enough. He slammed it back down and was pulling hard to get the plane's axis parallel to the canyon when he flashed over the rim. He let the plane descend on knife edge until the rock wall shielded him.

His heart was threatening to thud its way out of his chest. Talk about luck! Three mistakes, three dead men who would get no wiser.

But this last guy – he was no overeager green kid who thought he was bulletproof. He had pulled his nose up the instant he saw the head-on pass developing. This guy would take a lot of killing.

And Jake Grafton didn't know if he had it in him. Somehow he got his visor up and swabbed away the sweat that poured into his eyes when he pulled Gs, this while he threaded his way up the valley and looked above and aft to see what the Russian was up to.

What would you do, Jake Grafton?

I'd slow down to almost coequal speed and follow along, getting lower and lower, and when my guns came to bear I'd take my shots. And he would fall.

Jake got a glimpse of his opponent. He was high up and well aft, on a parallel course, his nose down. He must have lost sight for a moment and allowed Jake to extend out. But now he was closing.

You've had a good life, Jake. You've known some fine men, loved a good woman, flown the hot jets. Maybe your life has made a difference to somebody. And now it's over. That man up there is going to kill you. He's going about it just right, slowly and methodically; he isn't going to make any mistakes. And you are going to die.

The Russian was throttled back, coming down like the angel of doom.

What's ahead? I'll out-fly the bastard. I'll fly that son of a bitch into the ground.

Even as the thought raced through his mind, he knew it wouldn't work. This guy wasn't going to make any mistakes unless Jake forced the action. If he were allowed to play his own game he would win.

Jake Grafton risked another over-the-shoulder glance to see if he had room. Maybe. It was going to be tight.

He kept the wings level and pulled the stick straight aft. The throttles were up against the stops. A nice four-G pull so he would have something left on top. If this guy were wise and had plenty of fuel, he would light his burners and climb, avoid the head-on that was developing. A head-on pass that gave each guy a fifty-fifty chance – that was the best Jake could play for when the other pilot had every performance edge.

But the Russian pilot accepted the challenge!

Upside down at the top of the loop, Jake fed in forward stick and placed the pipper in the reticle high to allow for the fall of his shells, then pulled the trigger. The Russian was already shooting. Strobing muzzle blasts enveloped the nose of the opposing fighter as Jake pulled his trigger.

Jake felt the trip-hammer impacts as cannon shells ripped into his plane. Then the Russian blew up.

Jake knifed through the falling debris and tried to right his machine. Fuel was boiling out the left wing and the left engine was unwinding. He shut it down. A big red light on the left side of the bombsight was illuminated – fire. He needed a lot of right rudder to control his plane.

Now he was level. And alive.

For how long?

That depended on the fire warning light. It flickered several times, then went out. Maybe he had a chance after all.

He glanced at the compass. He was heading east. He dropped the right wing into a gentle turn and let the nose drift down as he juggled the rudder to maintain balanced flight. He had to get low again, avoid the radar that was probing this sky.

He steadied up heading south, descending. One of the Russian's cannon shells had impacted the second weapons pylon on the left wing, shattering it and twisting it so badly fuel was coming out of the wing. Even as Jake stared at the damaged pylon the last of the wing fuel rushed away into the slipstream. Primary hydraulic pressure was on its way to zero. If that was the primary system gauge.

The warning lights seemed predictable. The damaged engine hadn't blown up – if it did there was nothing he could do but die. His heart was still beating, thud, thud, thud. He was still *alive!*

That Russian must have been low on fuel. In a hurry. Too bad for him.

Jack Yocke tapped aimlessly on his laptop computer and from time to time glanced at Toad Tarkington sitting in the big chair. Toad had a pistol in his hand and kept looking at it, turning it this way and that, wrapping his fist around the grip and hefting it.

Herb Tenney lay on the couch with his hands taped together behind his back, his ankles taped together, and a strip of tape over his mouth. Herb seemed calm.

Jack Yocke had done the taping with a roll from the first aid kit when Toad brought him into the room at gunpoint.

Now the three of them sat – Herb calm, Yocke full of questions, Toad playing with that goddamn pistol.

'Did he come willingly?' Jack asked, breaking the silence.

'Uh-huh.'

'Where did you find him?'

'In the cafeteria. Waited until he had finished his coffee and followed him out.'

'Would you have shot him if he didn't come along?'

Toad merely glanced at Yocke, then turned his gaze back to the pistol in his hand. The reporter saw the same thing that Herb Tenney must have seen fifteen minutes ago. Toad would have pulled the trigger with all the remorse he would have had swatting a fly.

Jack Yocke had another question, but he didn't ask it. Did Jake Grafton tell you to corral Tenney? Toad didn't do anything unless Jake Grafton told him to, Yocke told himself, and once told, Toad would do literally anything. The asshole was like a Doberman, ready to rip the throat out of the first man his master sicced him on.

Yocke sighed and went back to tapping. He was listing what he knew about Nigel Keren, about the Mossad bribing Russians to get Jews out of the country and assassinating Russian politicians, about the KGB blowing up the Serdobsk reactor, about a hangarful of nuclear-armed mobile missiles and warheads that were going south into Iraq a planeload at a time. He was sitting on at least four huge stories, any one of which would win him a Pulitzer prize, and all he could do was tap on this frigging keyboard and pray that someday soon he could telephone something to the *Post*. If he still had a job!

He felt a little like the prospector who has spent his whole life looking for traces of color when he finally stumbles onto the mother lode. And doesn't know where the vein leads.

All he really had were pieces of stories. Jack Yocke had

spent five years chasing stories and he knew that he didn't have all of any one of them. Oh, he had some great pieces, but he didn't know where the roots led.

Jake Grafton knew. Of that he was convinced.

Damn, he was getting as goofy as Tarkington. Toad sat there playing with his pistol and if you asked, he would tell you that Jake Grafton knows everything. What's your problem? Grafton will tell you what he wants you to know when he wants you to know it. If that time ever comes. And if it doesn't, then you shouldn't know.

Jack Yocke didn't think Jake Grafton knew all the answers. He thought Jake was feeling his way along, examining the trees, trying to size up the forest. Jack Yocke didn't have Toad's faith.

The truth, he decided, was probably somewhere in the middle.

He jabbed the button to save what he had written and then turned off the computer. He closed the screen over the keyboard and pulled the plug out.

'You done?' Toad asked.

'What's it look like?' Yocke snarled. He was extremely frustrated, and Toad marching in a big CIA weenie at gunpoint hadn't helped.

'Would you like to help me?'

'Do what?' Jack asked suspiciously.

'Well, you gotta sit here with this pistol and watch our boy Herb. I have an errand. If Herb twitches, blow his fucking head off. If anybody comes through that door besides me, blow their fucking head off. Think you can handle it?'

'No.'

'You ought to be the pro-choice poster child, Jack. If your mother only knew how you were going to turn out she would have grabbed a rusty old coat hanger and done it herself.'

'Any time you get the itch, Tarkington, you can kiss my rosy red ass. I am not about to get mixed up in the middle of a war or shoot anybody. And no more goddamn cracks about—'

Toad tossed the gun at him. Yocke snagged it to prevent it from hitting him in the face.

Toad stood up. He looked over the items from Herb's pockets that were spread on the low coffee table and selected a ring of keys, then faced Yocke. 'Anyone besides me comes through that door, they'll kill you if you don't kill them first. And you can bet your puny little dick that Herb would cheerfully do the job if he had his hands free. Think about it.'

With that Toad went to the door and carefully opened it. He looked out. Now he checked to ensure the door would lock behind him, passed through and pulled it closed.

Jack Yocke looked at Herb Tenney to see if he had any big ideas. Apparently not. He then examined the pistol in his hand. This thingy on the left side looked like the safety. Is it on? Yocke kept his finger well away from the trigger, just in case.

He had had a journalism professor who once told the class that the problem with the profession was the company a reporter had to keep to get his stories. Truer words were never spoken, Jack told himself ruefully.

'If I get out of this alive,' he informed Herb Tenney, 'I'm going to get a job washing beer mugs in a bikers' saloon. Associate with a better class of people. Keep better hours. Make more money. Get laid more.'

Out in the hallway Toad slowed to talk to the marine sergeant sitting at the head of the stairs with an M-16 across his knees. He also wore a pistol in a holster on a web belt around his middle. 'Everything okay?'

'Yessir. Not a soul's been around.'

Toad glanced down the hall at the marine on the other end, who was looking his way.

Satisfied, Toad said, 'He's in there with Jack Yocke. If he

comes out shoot him in the legs. Whatever you do, don't kill him.'

'Aye aye, sir.'

When he was inside Herb's room, Toad scanned it, then went straight to the bathroom and Herb's shaving kit above the sink. Yep, the shit still had that plastic pill bottle with the child-proof cap. Toad glanced at them to ensure they were what he wanted, then pocketed them. He considered taking Herb his toothbrush. Naw. His fucking teeth could just rot.

Out in the bedroom Toad got Herb's suitcase and opened it. Well, ol' Herb was a neat packer. His mother would be proud.

Toad dumped everything into a pile in the middle of the bed and examined the lining of the suitcase. He and Jake Grafton had been through Herb's stuff once before, but it wouldn't hurt to do it again. Carefully and thoroughly.

Underwear, socks, shirts, trousers, a sweater. A spare can of shaving cream. Toad squirted some onto the carpet. Yep, shaving cream.

The closet held several suits, ties, white shirts and a spare pair of shoes. Toad examined the shoes. He got out his penknife and pried off the heels. Nothing. He felt the suits carefully and threw them on the floor. Except for a spare pen and a pack of matches that Herb had overlooked, the pockets were empty.

Now he turned his attention to the room, systematically taking everything apart. As he worked he thought about Rita.

Pregnant. Refusing to stop flying.

If he were her, he would . . . But he wasn't Rita. Rita was Rita and that was why he married her.

You just have to take women as they come. It's hard to do at times, considering. Amazing that hormone chemistry could make such a big difference in the way men and women's brains worked. It was like they were a different species, or creatures from another planet.

He threw himself into the chair and sat staring morosely at the mess in front of him. There was nothing here to be found, of that he was sure. So he thought some more about Rita in the cockpit of that jet, flying through a strange sky over a radioactive landscape, nursing the stick and throttles and dropping bombs and fighting the Gs.

There were so many things that could go wrong. And a Russian jet for chrissake, designed, built and maintained by a bunch of vodka-swilling sots.

She can handle it, he told himself, wanting to believe. She'll get back all right. She's with Jake Grafton. I mean, she's good and he's great. They're a good team. They'll make it.

Fuck, they'd better! He wasn't up to losing Rita just now. She had damn near died in a crash a few years back – just the memory of those days made him nauseated.

And he didn't want to lose Jake Grafton either. Grafton told him to snag Herb Tenney, and if Grafton didn't come back, Toad was going to have to figure out what to do next. Not that he had a lot of options. One thing sure, though – Herb was going to be finishing off his supply of happy pills if Jake Grafton didn't make it.

When he opened the door to the apartment, the first thing he saw was Jake Yocke's pasty face, then the Browning Hi-Power which he held with both hands. It was pointed askew at nothing at all.

Toad locked the door behind him and took a look at Herb, who was pretending to sleep.

Yocke held the pistol out to Toad butt-first. Toad took it and stuffed it into his waistband. 'Thanks,' he said. 'I kept waiting to hear the shots.'

Yocke didn't think that comment worth a reply.

'Would you have used this?' Toad wanted to know.

'I don't know.'

After they had sat Herb Tenney on the ceramic convenience in the bathroom, then fixed a can of chili for lunch, Yocke asked, 'How can you just walk around stick-ing pistols in people's faces?'

Toad looked mildly surprised. 'I'm in the military. Jake Grafton gives orders, I obey them.'

'This isn't a movie, you know. That's a real gun with real bullets.'

Toad helped himself to another spoonful of chili. When it was on its way south he said, 'You keep looking for moral absolutes, Jack. There aren't any. Not in this life. All we can do is the best we can.'

'But how do you know you're doing the right thing?'

'I don't. But Jake Grafton does. It's uncanny. He'll do the right thing regardless of the consequences, regardless of how the chips fall. I'll take that. I do what I'm told knowing that the CAG is trying to do right.' Even as he said it his mind jumped to Rita. He had bowed to Rita's decision to fly while pregnant based on faith in her judgment. Now the chili made a lump in his stomach. He dropped the spoon into the bowl and shoved it away. 'You gotta believe in people or you're in a hell of a fix,' he said slowly.

'You answer a question, Toad, by evading it. What is *right*? Why do you think Grafton knows what *right* is?'

Toad was no longer paying attention. He was staring at his watch, watching the second hand sweep. They should be on the ground by now . . . if they were still alive. Why hadn't they called? Did he really trust her judgment, or was he a coward not to assert himself? If anything happened to her . . .

Jake Grafton saw the smoke column twenty miles away. The black smoke towered like a giant chimney at least three thousand feet into the atmosphere. As he got closer he could see that the wind had tilted the column, which was visibly growing taller, mushrooming into the upper atmosphere.

Creeping up to two hundred feet to avoid the dust being sucked into the inferno raging at the base of the smoke, he bounced in turbulence even here on the up-wind side of the fire. The turbulence made his bowels feel watery: that damaged wing might have a broken spar. As the plane bucked the stick felt sloppy and the secondary hydraulic system pressure dropped. He must be oh so careful.

The hangar was ablaze. Rita.

Ten or fifteen minutes ago?

Something silver on the mat? A wing?

It couldn't be a wing from Rita's plane, could it? *Could it?*

He edged in for a closer look. No. It was a big wing, attached to a transport that was also on fire. She caught someone parked on the mat and shot them apart.

He turned away from the blaze and consulted his fuel gauge. Fuel would have been okay plus a bunch if he hadn't spent all that time maneuvering at full throttle and let that jerk shoot up his plane. Going to be tight.

Right engine was still alive and pulling hard – no more warning lights. The slop in the controls when operating on the backup hydraulic system was acceptable as long as he didn't have to defend himself, as long as the secondary pump held together, as long as he could make his aching right leg work. The plane flew okay on one engine if he held in forty pounds or so of right rudder. The rudder trim wasn't working. Sorry about that!

He had about forty miles of radioactive terrain to cross before he could get out and walk. It was a little like flying over a shark-infested ocean – you prayed for the engine to keep running, counted every mile, watched the minute hand of the panel clock with intense interest.

Jake Grafton's eyes scanned the vast distances between the horizon and the bottom of the cumulonimbus clouds. He gazed up into the gaps between the clouds, searched behind him and out to both sides. The sky appeared to be empty. Because he knew how difficult another aircraft was to spot in a huge, indefinite sky, he kept looking. And occasionally his eyes came inside to check the clock.

So she made it to here and took out the hangar and that transport on the mat. He hadn't seen any craters on the mat that would mark misses. Apparently she put all her ordnance into the bucket, a neat, professional job.

Thank you, Rita, wherever you are.

He listened to the engine. He watched the clock hand sweep. He unhooked his oxygen mask and swabbed the sweat from his eyes.

Forty miles of terrain required about ten minutes of flying to cross. When the ten minutes had passed Jake began to relax. His right leg was hurting since he had to maintain constant pressure on the rudder, but he felt better. It was goofy when you thought about it – Captain Collins said *about* forty miles, and of course the fallout zone had no definite boundary. The intensity of the radiation would just decrease as the miles went by. Knowing all this and feeling slightly silly, Jake still felt better with each passing mile.

If this shot-up jet would just hold together . . .

When the city of Lipetsk appeared in the haze at ten or twelve miles, Jake Grafton eased the nose of his Su-25 into a climb. He went across the city at several thousand feet and made a gentle turn to line up for the northwest runway about eight miles away.

Nothing happened when he lowered the gear handle. He found the little emergency switch and held it in the down position. The gear broke free of the wells and fell into the slipstream – he could feel the drag increase.

His numb right leg refused to put the right amount of pressure on the rudder. The nose wandered a little from side to side. Carefully playing his single engine, Jake Grafton tried to keep the speed up and fly a flat approach. Only when he was sure he could make the field did he use the electrical switch to drop ten degrees of flaps.

He cut the engine immediately after he felt the tires squeak. Without brakes this thing would roll forever; he had no idea how to engage the emergency system. He had tried turning the parking brake handle ninety degrees and it didn't want to rotate.

When the jet was down to about twenty mph it began to drift toward the edge of the runway. There was nothing he could do. It rolled off the edge and came to rest in the grass.

For the first time in over an hour, Jake Grafton relaxed his right leg. It was numb, shaking.

Jake used the battery to open the canopy. As the huge silence enveloped him he took off his mask and helmet and wiped the sweat from his hair. He was drained.

Somehow he managed the energy to get his gloves off and begin unstrapping. When he got the fittings released he sat there massaging his right thigh.

'Admiral! Admiral Grafton!' It was Rita, running across the grass toward him.

'Hey, kid. Am I glad to see you!'

She slowed to a walk, just fifty feet or so away. She glanced at the shattered wing pylon, then looked up at Jake. 'I got the hangar, sir.'

'I know,' Jake said, and wiped his eyes with his fingers. 'I know.'

CHAPTER TWENTY

The helicopter's two radios were mounted on a shelf on the bulkhead between the cockpit and passenger compartment. The leads had a collar that allowed them to be unscrewed when the radio needed to be removed for servicing. Jake Grafton used his fingers to twist the collars and pull out the plugs. Then he told Spiro Dalworth to tell the pilot to land at the Lipetsk railroad station.

Not a single Russian had come out to look the Su-25s over when Jake landed at the army airfield fifteen minutes ago. He climbed down from the cockpit and followed Rita toward the helicopter.

'What happened at Petrovsk?' Jake asked.

'There was a four-engine jet transport on the mat, sir, and they were loading a missile aboard. I looked on the first pass and shot on the second. On the third the transport caught fire. I then bombed the hangar and it caught fire. I fired out the gun on the clean room.'

He wondered what thoughts went through Rita Moravia's mind when she saw live humans and knew they couldn't be allowed to get on that plane and leave. What had she thought when she lined up the cargo plane in her sight and pulled the trigger? All things considered, it was probably better not to ask. 'Did you see any markings on the plane?'

'Arabic script, sir. They must have wanted those missiles pretty badly to risk a trip in daylight.'

'Lot of cloud cover. They might have pulled it off.'

'Saddam sent his people on a suicide mission. One man I saw on the ground wasn't wearing a hot suit.'

The wars of the kings were much more civilized, Jake reflected. No wonder Churchill preferred the nineteenth century over this one.

The Russian chopper pilot was already in the cockpit and started the engines as they climbed aboard. Within a minute he lifted the machine from the parking mat.

Staring now at the disconnected radio leads, Jake concluded he needed a knife. He didn't have one. He wedged the lead between the hammer and frame of his revolver and used that to strip off the collar. Now the lead could not be reconnected. He did the same with the lead to the second radio.

Someone wanted him dead. Perhaps those dead fighter pilots had orders to concentrate on the lead plane or were so ill with buck fever that they lost track of Rita at a crucial moment. Whichever, both he and Rita were fortunate to be alive. Still, with only a telephone call more fighters could be launched to shoot down this unarmed helicopter and convert their earlier escape into an alarmingly brief reprieve.

A prudent man would find another form of transportation. Jake Grafton was a prudent man.

Very prudent. After the chopper settled into the street in front of the railway station, he asked Dalworth, 'What's the pilot's name?'

'Lieutenant Vasily Lutkin, sir.'

'Tell him to fly on to Moscow after we get off.'

He watched the helo pilot lift the collective and feed in forward cyclic. The pilot glanced once at him, then concentrated his attention on flying his machine.

Jake watched the helicopter until it crossed the rooftops heading just a little west of north.

Vasily Lutkin might make it. Maybe. If his luck was in.

Those four fighter pilots were trying to kill you, Jake, but not this guy.

Okay, so now you know how Josef Stalin did it. Just give the order and watch them go to their doom.

With sagging shoulders he followed Dalworth and Rita into the cavernous station.

And how much luck do you have left in your miserable little hoard, Jake Grafton? *Not much, friend. Not much. Guilt and luck don't mix.*

There was a vending booth inside the terminal building selling Pepsi in tiny paper cups, about an ounce of the soft drink for a ruble. Jake laid a ten-ruble note on the counter and while Dalworth went to buy tickets, he and Rita each drank five cupfuls of the sticky sweet liquid. Then Jake wandered off for the men's room, burping uncontrollably.

The train was full to bursting. There were no empty seats in the car they found themselves in so the three Americans wedged themselves into a little space on the floor. Men, women, and children with everything they owned filled the car. One man had a goat. Several women had baskets that contained live chickens. A man lay in the floor between the aisles vomiting repeatedly while a woman periodically gave him something to drink from a bottle.

'Radiation sickness, I think,' Dalworth whispered.

Jake just nodded. After a half hour Rita went over to help, dragging Dalworth along to translate.

The air was thick with a miasma of odors. Smoke from Papirosi cigarettes made a heavy haze.

The train stopped about once an hour for ten minutes or so. Each time Jake stayed seated in his corner with his hand under his jacket on his gun butt watching the people fighting their way aboard. The scrambler was wedged under his legs.

No one got off the train. Moscow was the universal destination. Some of the people who clamored aboard were soldiers in uniform, but they were wrestling bags of personal articles. No one in uniform or out paid any attention to the Americans. Finally the train got under way again and all the struggling humanity somehow found a place to ride.

330

These Russians had endured so much, yet there was so much still to endure. When he had replayed the morning's flight for the twentieth time and the adrenaline had finally burned itself from his system, Jake sat looking at his fellow passengers, trying to fathom their stories and their lives as snatches of Russian swirled on the laden air. Finally his head sagged onto his knees and he slept.

Every minute passed slower and slower for Toad Tarkington. He paced, he stood at the window from time to time and stared out, occasionally he turned on the television and stood gazing at the images on the screen for minutes at a time without seeing them, then snapped it off. He paced some more.

When he could stand it no longer he picked up the phone and dialed. 'Captain, this is Toad. Heard anything?'

Then he hung up and went back to pacing, and fidgeting, and gazing gloomily at Herb Tenney and Jack Yocke.

'What did Collins say?' Yocke asked.

'Nothing.'

'What are you going to do if Grafton and Rita don't come back?'

Toad didn't answer. He didn't want even to acknowledge the possibility out loud, let alone discuss it with Jack Yocke. Jake Grafton and Rita Moravia were the two most important people in his life. He felt as if he were teetering on the edge of a dark abyss. Every minute that passed made the gaping horror more probable, and more unspeakable.

After a while Yocke said, 'Surely we ought to discuss it.'

'They'll be back.' End of conversation.

They were on the ground somewhere. Tactical jets carry a limited supply of fuel, and when it's exhausted . . . no one ever ran out of gas and floated around up there unable to get down. So where were they? In the fallout zone? Shot down! Why *hadn't* they called? Any way you figured it, something had gone seriously wrong. And our boy Herb probably had something to do with that something.

Toad found himself glowering at the CIA agent asleep on the couch. Sleeping! He forced himself to look away.

By six o'clock in the evening Toad had reached the breaking point. For lack of something better to do, he decided to go find Collins. 'I'm going out,' he announced to Jack Yocke, who looked up from the paperback novel he was reading. 'Keep an eye on Herb.' Toad hoisted himself erect and walked toward the door.

'Aren't you going to give me your pistol?' Yocke asked.

'Nah. There's marines outside.'

'Outside?'

'In the hallway. You have any trouble, just shout and they'll come running.'

The reporter was speechless.

Toad pulled the Browning from his waistband. 'This thing wouldn't do you any good anyway.' He thumbed off the safety and pulled the trigger. Click. 'It's empty.'

Yocke found his voice. '*Empty!*'

One of Jack Yocke's endearing qualities – and he had precious few, in Toad's opinion – was that sometimes he was extraordinarily slow on the uptake. Maybe it was an act. Whatever, Toad Tarkington savored the moment. 'You don't think I'm stupid enough to give a loaded gun to a trigger-happy thrill-killer like you, do ya? If you didn't shoot off your own toe, you'd probably go berserk and murder everybody north of the Moskva.'

'You dirty, rotten, slimy, retarded stumblebum, you—'

That was the high point in a long, dreary day of merciless tension and uncertainty. Toad stepped through the door and pulled it shut behind him before Jack Yocke got really wound up. He mumbled a greeting to the marine sitting at the top of the stairs as he went by.

It was after 7 P.M. when a pale, exhausted Rita Moravia sagged onto the floor beside Jake. Her flight suit reeked of vomit.

'How is that sick man?' Jake asked.

'Dead. Radiation poisoning, dehydration I think – oh, I don't know. His heart stopped and we just . . . gave up.' She brushed a wisp of hair out of her eyes and hugged her knees.

Several platitudes occurred to Jake, but he held his tongue.

'How did you evade those fighters this morning?' Rita asked. 'This morning! God, it seems like another lifetime ago.'

'One guy stalled and went in, I shot down the others.'

'You were lucky.'

'That's all life is: luck – some good, some bad, most indifferent. Some of it you make yourself, most of it you just have to take as it comes.'

'What's going on here, Admiral? Why did the Russians blow up their own reactor?'

'To hide the fact that nuclear weapons were gone.'

'You aren't serious?'

'Oh, but I am. Somebody – let's postulate a small group of somebodys – collected a lot of money from Saddam Hussein for some nuclear weapons. Saddam took delivery at Petrovsk the evening before the reactor blew up. Everyone there who wasn't in on the sale was killed. Then the reactor exploded and the usual prevailing wind delivered a lethal concentration of fallout on Petrovsk. Eventually someone would visit Petrovsk, but the way things work in Russia, that visit was a long way off. Maybe years. When it eventually came to pass, our small group of somebodys were sure they could control the dissemination of the news of what happened at Petrovsk because long before then Boris Yeltsin would be driven from power. And they would be in.'

'How could they be sure of that?'

'The reactor explosion would cause a political crisis. They would escalate the event to a crisis if it didn't happen naturally. And they had done their homework with

Saddam's money. A lot of money. Real money, hard currency. The people at the top in Russia are just like the people at the top everywhere else – they want good food, nice clothes, adequate housing, an education for their kids, decent medical care. The Communist party used to deliver all that, but those days are gone. Whoever can deliver that life-style to the people in power will rule.'

'Money.'

'Hard currency – US dollars. For bribes. To dole out to the faithful. To buy votes in the legislature. There's a flourishing dollar economy in Moscow – just how on earth does an honest Russian come by dollars?'

'Oh, my God,' Rita whispered. 'To murder all those people! I can't believe it.'

'This is *Russia*,' Jake told her, his voice low. 'Even the stones are guilty. See that old man over there, the one with the campaign ribbons on his lapel? He's a veteran of World War II. He probably has a hundred stories about how he and his fellow soldiers fought to the last ditch and saved Russia from Hitler. What he won't tell you about are the penal battalions – every division had one. These were unarmed battalions of political prisoners – Russians who had said something unwise about Stalin or the NKVD, people who appeared to be less than happy living in the new Communist paradise. The men in the penal battalions were herded ahead of the tanks before every attack to step on the land mines and clear the way. And German machine gunners slaughtered them and revealed their positions to the Red Army troops. Then the tanks and gallant soldiers like that old man killed Nazis and won glorious victories. They saved Mother Russia. Ah yes, that old man is proud of his ribbons.

'Yet this is the amazing part – *the Commies never ran out of recruits for the penal battalions*. That maniac Hitler gassed and shot and starved his domestic enemies – all at his cost. Stalin killed his enemies just as dead but he turned a nice profit doing it. And Stalin didn't bother cremating the corpses: he let the body parts rot right where they lay to fertilize the soil.

'Yes, Rita, a group of ambitious people intentionally blew up the Serdobsk reactor. If a half million humans had to die to get them to the top, so be it. Like that old man over there with the ribbons, these people have paid their dues. *They have created a hell on earth and they are going to rule it.*'

'Stalin's children,' Rita murmured.

Twenty minutes later the train entered the outskirts of Moscow. 'Where's Dalworth?' Jake asked Rita.

'I don't know. He wandered off when that man died.'

'Find him. We're going to have to hop off this train fast and try for a taxi. If our luck is in, no one will be looking for us at the railroad station.'

She was very tired. 'You sent that helicopter pilot off to be shot down.' It was just a statement of fact, without inflection.

Jake Grafton merely glanced at her. 'Go find Dalworth,' he told her patiently.

If there were any security men scrutinizing the crowd, Jake didn't see them. The three Americans went through the station unaccosted, found the exit with Dalworth's help, and walked out onto the sidewalk. There were taxis. Jake and Rita climbed into the backseat of one while Dalworth negotiated the fare.

The streets looked normal to Jake's eye with the usual traffic and strolling pedestrians, here and there a policeman. At ten o'clock in the evening the sunlight, diffused by a thin layer of cirrus, came in at a very low angle and gave the city a soft, almost inviting look.

Dalworth sat in the front seat chatting with the taxi driver, and in a few moments he turned around and said to Jake, 'This fellow says that troops have road blocks around the embassy. They're checking everyone's papers.'

The taxi proceeded for several blocks before Jake spoke. 'We need to find something else to ride in.'

'Like a tank,' Rita said gloomily.

About a quarter mile from the embassy they passed a line of armored personnel carriers parked by the curb. 'One of these might do,' Jake said. 'Could you drive one, Rita?'

'It doesn't have wings,' she pointed out.

'Yes or no?'

'Yes.'

'Spiro, tell the driver to pull over.'

He dropped them at the head of the line. One soldier with a rifle stood on the curb. There were at least a dozen APCs in the line and another soldier lounged at the far end, almost two hundred feet away. Apparently the concept of vehicle theft hadn't caught on here yet.

'Walk by this guy,' Jake told his companions, and the three moved. Jake kept talking. 'Rita will drive. Dalworth will take the soldier's rifle and I'll assist him into the vehicle.'

The Russian soldier remained relaxed as they approached, his rifle held in the crook of his left arm. He watched them disinterestedly. As the trio passed him Jake drew his revolver and stuck it into the Russian's ribs as Dalworth neatly seized the rifle. The door to the APC stood open, so Rita merely climbed in.

Jake nodded toward the vehicle and the soldier, wearing a look of uncertainty and fear, went willingly enough. Jake glanced toward the other sentry. He was facing in the other direction. Really, these kids shouldn't be guarding anything more valuable than a garbage dump!

When everyone was inside, Dalworth closed the door and dogged it down.

'Any time, Rita.'

'Give me a minute, sir.' She was looking at the controls.

The seconds dragged by. Finally she adjusted a lever and pushed a button. The engine turned over but didn't catch.

More fiddling.

'Maybe our guy here knows how to drive,' Dalworth suggested.

'Ask him.'

Dalworth did so. The soldier's eyes got big, but he held his tongue. He was young, about twenty. Not a trace of beard showed on his face.

Rita ground some more with the starter. Then the diesel caught. She wrestled with the shift lever, ground the gears, then engaged the clutch. The thing lurched, then got under way.

'Empty his rifle,' Jake told Dalworth, 'and throw it in the back.'

Dalworth popped out the magazine and handed it to Jake, who tossed it into the back of the vehicle. The rifle followed.

The APC lumbered along at a stately pace. Rita steered it toward the center of the street. Two blocks later they saw a line of cars waiting in front of a roadblock with several dozen soldiers milling about.

'Drive right through,' Jake told his pilot. 'And don't run over anybody.'

'Admiral!'

'They'll get out of your way.'

She floored it and the soldiers ahead scattered. Amazingly, no shots were fired.

'Maybe they would have let us through,' Dalworth remarked.

'Maybe,' Rita agreed.

Jake kept his maybes to himself.

The APC rumbled the two blocks to the embassy along an empty street. She turned the corner from the boulevard and dropped down the street to the main entrance of the embassy, where she braked to a stop.

At least the stars and stripes were still flying.

The Russian soldier sat glued to his seat staring dumbfounded as the trio walked past four armed US marines in battle dress and entered the little brick reception building.

The marine on duty behind the desk punched the button to let them in and spoke through the window. 'The ambassador wants to see you, sir, and so does Captain Collins. And welcome back!'

He was rewarded with a grin from Rita.

The security door hadn't even closed behind the trio as the sergeant at the desk dialed Toad's telephone number. Lieutenant Commander Tarkington had been down here three times this evening – the sergeant was delighted that he had some good news to deliver for a change.

Toad came thundering down the stairs as Rita started up.

'Hey, Babe!'

'Hello, Toad-man,' she said as she was lifted from her feet in a fierce bear hug.

CHAPTER TWENTY-ONE

'General Shmarov is dead,' Tom Collins told Jake.

'Are you kidding me?'

'Nope. Apparently had a heart attack last night. Died in bed. At least that's what I hear from the Defense Ministry and Yeltsin's office. Of course, someone might have taken him for a ride last night and pumped a lead slug into his chest. Lead poisoning is a leading cause of heart attacks among the upper echelons in this neck of the woods.'

'Humph,' Jake Grafton replied, trying to visualize how Shmarov's demise fitted in. 'So what is CIA up to today?'

'Nothing, as near as I can tell. Toad escorted Herb Tenney upstairs right after breakfast this morning. Harley McCann' – McCann was the ranking resident CIA officer – 'went to his office and did the usual. I think he's still there.'

'At nine-thirty at night? He's got to know we have Tenney under lock and key.'

'Well, even if he's the worst spy we have, you'd think he'd find an event like that hard to miss. We've had armed marines guarding your apartment all day.'

'Shmarov had a heart attack.' Jake Grafton shook his head. 'What's the ambassador want?'

'He's been on the phone to Washington all day. Probably has some instructions, wants to know what happened at Petrovsk . . .'

'I'll have a little visit with Herb first. Then you and I will go see the ambassador.'

'Yes, sir.'

'In the meantime get the marine, Captain McElroy, and

have him stand by outside my apartment. Have him wear his sidearm.'

Herb Tenney's color wasn't good when Jake entered the apartment. His shirt was wet with sweat and his forehead was shiny. He looked as if he hadn't shaved in days.

'Where's Toad?' Jake asked Jack Yocke.

'In the bedroom with Rita.'

'Ask them to come out here, will you please?' Jake pulled a chair around to face Tenney, who was still on the couch.

While the reporter knocked on the bedroom door, Jake ripped the tape from Herb's mouth, wadded the strip up and tossed it toward a wastepaper basket. He missed. Rita and Toad came out of the bedroom holding hands.

'I want to go to the bathroom,' Herb said belligerently.

Jake weighed it for two seconds, then nodded. Toad and Jack hoisted him to his feet and carried him. When they got their guest settled on the throne with his pants down, Toad came out and shut the door.

'It went okay today. He hasn't said a word, we haven't questioned him. He's eaten a little and had a couple naps. Maybe I misread him, but I thought he looked slightly stunned when the gate guard called and said you and Rita were back. I told Yocke, and Herb had trouble controlling his face, I thought.'

'No questions today even when you had the tape off?'

'No, sir. The man knows how to keep his mouth shut.'

'A truly rare talent in this day and age. Find anything in his room?'

Toad took the pill bottle from his shirt pocket and handed it to Jake. 'There's four of each left in the bottle – eight pills.'

'Get my pill bottle from my bag.'

Rita asked, 'Admiral, do you want me here?'

'Yep. You and Toad and Jack and Spiro Dalworth. But everyone keeps their mouth shut, no matter what. Toad, take Jack into the bedroom and tell him if he says one word, he'll be ejected. Then rig up Jack's cassette tape recorder just out of sight under the couch.' Toad went and Jake turned to Rita. 'Call Captain Collins and ask him to send Dalworth up.'

'Aye, aye, sir.'

In the bedroom Toad delivered the message to Yocke, who merely nodded. Toad popped the magazine from the Browning and removed a handful of cartridges from his pocket. He pushed the shells into the clip one by one.

'Why didn't you have your pistol loaded today?' Yocke asked.

Toad was tired, emotionally drained. His mind wasn't working fast enough to come up with a quip, so for once he told Jack Yocke the unvarnished truth. 'Jake Grafton wanted him alive. Sitting there looking at him with a loaded gun, waiting . . . I don't know if I could have resisted the temptation to kill him.'

Yocke watched as Toad finished loading the magazine and snapped it into the handle of the pistol. He worked the slide, thumbed the safety into position. Then he slid the pistol into the small of his back.

'Why are you loading it now?'

'Maybe I'll get lucky.'

In the bathroom Jake filled a dirty glass of water and examined the white tablets from Herb's bottle. He selected one marked Aspirin on one side and dropped it into the water.

It all came down to this. If Herb knew Jake had substituted aspirin for half the binary cocktail, he was too many steps ahead for Jake to catch him now.

He held the glass up to the light and swirled the water as the tablet slowly disintegrated. Into a pile of white powder.

Aspirin.

Thank God!

*

Out in the living room Herb Tenney was back on the couch. Jake Grafton emptied the pill bottle onto the table. He picked up each tablet and examined the markings. When he was finished he had two small piles of tablets.

'General Shmarov died last night,' he remarked conversationally. 'Tell us about that.'

Herb had watched Jake examine the white tablets. Now he looked at the faces of the other people in the room, then back at Jake. 'I don't have anything to say.'

'Tenney, I don't think you understand how tight the crack is that you're in. You are going to talk or we're going to force these pills down your throat. All of them.'

'Now you listen, Admiral. I don't know what the fuck you think you're doing, but I know my rights. I have the right to an attorney and I have the right to remain silent. You're an agent of the government.'

'You think there's going to be a trial? You're joking, right?'

Jake Grafton hitched his chair closer to Tenney and leaned forward so his face was only a foot or so from Herb's. 'Let me say it again – either you answer my questions with God's truth or I'm going to stuff these pills into your mouth and tape it shut. The pills will dissolve in your mouth even if you don't swallow.'

Herb Tenney looked at the tablets and he looked at Jake Grafton. He was perspiring. Everyone was looking at him except Jack Yocke, who was staring at the tablets on the table.

Herb cleared his throat. 'Get these other people out of here.'

'They stay.'

'All this is classified.'

'Yeah, and if you tell me your pals will have to kill me. I've heard that crap before.'

'What do you want to know?'

'Who made the decision to kill Nigel Keren?'

Herb Tenney licked his lips. Sweat formed a little

rivulet down his cheek and a drop coalesced on his chin. Then it fell away.

'Who?' Jake repeated. He picked up a tablet and examined it. Finally he placed it back on the table and stood up.

'Toad, Spiro, hold him down. Rita, get the tape and tear off a strip.'

Toad came flying across the room like a linebacker. He slammed into Tenney and knocked him flat on the couch, then sat on his chest. Dalworth was just a step behind. Rita charged for the bathroom to get the tape roll.

Herb tried to scream. He couldn't get air with Toad sitting on his chest. Then Jake held his nose until his mouth popped open. Herb's skin was slippery with sweat and he was still trying to scream. Jake stuffed the tablets in as Herb bucked and writhed, even with Toad on his chest and Dalworth on his legs. Jake used both hands to hold his jaw shut.

'Where's the damn tape?'

'Jesus H. Christ, Grafton!' Yocke's voice, from somewhere behind.

'Let me in there,' Rita said, elbowing her way into the pile. She slapped a strip of tape over Tenney's mouth. Then they released him.

The naval officers stood back, breathing hard. Herb was snorting through his nose, his eyes wild.

'Can you feel them dissolving, Herb?' Jake leaned over until his eyes were only a few inches from those of the CIA agent's. 'The poison will be absorbed through the sides of your mouth into your bloodstream. You know more about the effect than I do. How long will it take? How long before your heart stops? An hour? Five hours? Twelve? Maybe you have a whole day. I hate to see you die like this, Herb, but it was your choice.'

Tenney was moaning in his throat.

Jake let him moan. Now Herb managed to get into a sitting position. He was bobbing his head.

'You want to talk now?'

Tenney's head bobbed vigorously.

Jake reached over and ripped the tape away from Herb's mouth.

Herb spat the pills onto the floor. He sobbed convulsively. Then he vomited.

'Who?'

'Let me wash my mouth out.'

'*Who?*' Grafton roared savagely.

'Schenler.'

'Harvey Schenler? Deputy director of the CIA?'

Herb Tenney nodded.

'*Answer me, goddamnit!*'

'Yes.'

'Why?'

'I don't think—'

'I don't give a fuck what you *think!* Why?'

'Keren was giving the Israelis money to get Soviet Jews to Israel. The Arabs don't want them there. We're trying to stabilize the Mideast.'

'So you poisoned Nigel Keren. How'd you do it?'

Tenney rubbed his mouth, then bent at the waist and wiped his tongue on his trousers. When he straightened he looked from face to face. 'It was in his aspirin bottle,' he said finally.

'You murdered a man and stabilized the Mideast. Everything's okay down at the corner gas station. Congratulations.'

'Now look here, Admiral,' Tenney said heatedly. 'The world is a cesspool and you know it. We need oil. The Arabs have it. We have enough troubles with the ragheads without idiots like Nigel Keren using their fat wallets to cause more. The situation is volatile.'

'Albert Sidney Brown? Did he stick his fat wallet somewhere it didn't belong?'

'I don't know anything about General Bro—'

'*Don't lie to me!*' Jake thundered. He could really roar when he wanted to; this time he rattled the windows. 'You are one answer away from the grave. I've killed four men today, maybe five, and believe me, I won't lose any sleep if I have to kill you.' Jake Grafton paused, then shook his head with annoyance. 'In his aspirin bottle! Well?' he demanded.

'Brown was about to cause serious problems.'

'What kind of problems?'

'He sent a written report of the bugs to Schenler. Demanded an investigation. There was no other way to cork him.'

Jake changed direction. 'General Shmarov – why'd you kill him?'

'I am not—'

'Sit on him, Toad.'

Tarkington stiff-armed Tenney on the shoulder and he toppled. 'No,' he sobbed. 'For Christ's sake, no!'

'Answer the question.'

'Shmarov set up the weapons sale to Iraq. He arranged everything, the transfer of the money, the reactor explosion – everything. He was in the junta but he was hedging his bets, showing the American delegation KGB files, files that they shouldn't see, just in case Yeltsin came out on top after all.'

'Didn't he bribe the deputies?'

'Yeah, but you know how it is. Those kind of swine won't stay bought.'

'What kind of files?'

'You're so fucking smart, you tell me.'

Jake opened his mouth to say Toad's name, but he refrained. Another episode with the pills and Tenney might indeed die, even if one-half the binary cocktail were aspirin. Perhaps he already had the missing chemical in his system.

'Okay,' Jake said slowly. 'The CIA and the KGB have cooperated on numerous matters in the past. Those were the files Shmarov was going to hand to the senator and the people with him. Those files would inevitably lead the

345

Americans to Harvey Schenler and his cronies, people like you, people who have been running their own foreign policy within the CIA. So Shmarov had to die. And all along I thought you were just trying to poison me. Ha! You were sent here to make sure Shmarov didn't spill the beans either. How many people in Moscow were on your shit list, Tenney?'

'Kiss my—'

'Richard Harper.'

'Who?'

Jake Grafton bent down and began picking up the tablets from amid the vomit on the floor. Several of them were soft but intact.

'Don't fuck with me, Tenney. I'm out of time and patience.'

'We caught Harper in some of the computer files and tracked him down,' Herb Tenney said, his voice rising slightly. 'He wasn't a very good hacker, nowhere near as good as he thought he was.'

'He found the money trail, didn't he?'

'What money trail?'

'*The* money trail, you simple shit.' Jake Grafton unzipped a large chest pocket on his flying suit and extracted an envelope. He removed the contents. 'Here is a letter to me written by Richard Harper. Look at it. It's in Harper's handwriting. Look at it!'

Tenney looked.

'Harper sent it to my wife,' Jake continued, his voice like broken glass. 'She took it to Hayden Land and he sent it here by diplomatic pouch. You got to Richard Harper too late!'

'I don't know what you are talking about.'

'I'm talking about Saddam Hussein's three *billion* dollars. I'm talking about the Mideast Palm Oil Import Corporation, a CIA front. I'm talking about J. W. Wise Organic Commodities, Inc., another CIA front. I'm talking about seven more corporations controlled by the CIA that shuffled Saddam Hussein's money back and forth all over the world until it ended up in Moscow – in the hands of General Shmarov and his allies in the military and in the legislature. Money for nuclear weapons. Money to buy friends. Money to overthrow Yeltsin. Blood money! Tell me about *that* money!'

'I don't—'

'If you tell me you don't know just one more time we're gonna do the pills. This time the tape stays on.'

Tenney shook his head and sweat flew. 'I didn't know he wrote a letter.'

'I guess not. If you had, my wife would be dead now, huh?'

'Listen, Admiral. We—'

'So now Saddam Hussein has nuclear weapons? Is *that* right?'

'We helped possible friends in high places in crucial nations with money! Okay? We've done it before. We'll do it again. Jesus, where do *you* think you are? Oz? Never-never land? We—'

'Answer my question!' Jake roared. 'Saddam Hussein has nuclear weapons?'

'Israel has them. Russia is in meltdown. We need a stable government in Russia or the world is facing a new dark age. Hussein wants to be a regional power. A couple dozen nuclear weapons – shit! We have tens of thousands. He knows that. So he can be a big frog in a little pond and we can make damn sure he doesn't get out of line.'

'You think you can control him? What about the Gulf War?'

'Let's call a spade a spade, Admiral. We can control him or kill him. America needs a stable government in Russia. That's priority number one. With Russia on its feet and in our corner, the two of us can keep Saddam on a short leash or knot the noose.'

'So you let Shmarov and Yakolev murder a half-million Russians. No, let me rephrase that – *you helped them murder a half-million Russians!*'

'We *didn't*—'

'Harper found that the money went through CIA dummy corporations, didn't he? *That's* why you killed him.'

'You make it sound as if we're the bad guys. We aren't. We're trying to keep the peace in an unstable world. Surely you can see that? We had no choice. Yeltsin is failing: he's doomed. He can't possibly succeed, not a chance in a million. Either we have an in with his successors or we get the door slammed in our faces. *That's* the only goddamn choice we have.'

'How long have you and Schenler been running your own foreign policy?'

'Huh?'

Jake's voice was almost a whisper. 'How long has the CIA been running its own foreign policy? That's a simple question.'

Tenney looked bewildered, as if he didn't understand what was being asked. And then the truth dawned on Jake. Presidential administrations came and went but the professional spies soldiered on regardless. The CIA had been doing what the CIA leaders believed necessary for as long as there had been a CIA, almost fifty years. It still was.

'All you people, you bottle-sucking lollipop *amateurs* — fucking around in national security matters,' Herb raved, becoming more and more infuriated. 'You're all gonna *die!* This ain't a fucking football game. This is real, for keeps. *America* is at stake here.'

He's coming apart, Jake Grafton decided. He's been through too much.

Jake averted his eyes as Tenney ranted on: 'Those ten-cent codes you use on the scramblers — they've been reading the messages thirty minutes later. They even fax me hard copies. *They* know what the fuck you traitors are up to. *They know!'*

Jake and Toad taped Herb Tenney's mouth and put him in the bedroom. When the door was closed, Toad asked, 'So he wasn't trying to poison us?'

'Sure he was,' Jake muttered. He put the tablets into the bottle and dropped it into his shirt pocket.

'What are those tablets, some kind of suicide pills?' Spiro Dalworth asked.

'Binary poison,' Toad told him. 'It's medicine for people you don't want to see anymore.'

Jack Yocke sat over in the corner with his chin resting on one hand. He glanced at Jake Grafton, who was staring at the floor, then leaned back in his chair and closed his eyes.

Toad reached under the couch for the cassette recorder and pushed the rewind button. When the rewind was complete, he placed the recorder on the table and pushed the play button. He thumbed up the volume. Several minutes went by as they listened to feet shuffling, someone coughing, then finally Jake Grafton's voice: 'General Shmarov died last night. Tell us about that.'

The little machine had caught it all. The confusion and muffled comments as they poisoned Tenney were brutally plain, as was the sound of Tenney retching afterward. The listeners studiously avoided looking at one another.

When Tenney got out Harvey Schenler's name, Jake motioned to Toad to turn off the tape. 'Get the senior chief and fire up the TACSAT,' Jake told him. 'Send that tape to General Land.'

'You heard Herb, CAG. They'll crack the code.'

'Send it. Use the TACSAT. In the meantime we'll deliver a message of our own to Harley McCann.'

'What about the ambassador? He wanted to see you.'

Jake glanced at his watch. 'The night's young.'

Jake was still in his flight suit when he entered the ambassador's outer office and encountered Agatha Hempstead. She sniffed gingerly, no doubt slightly appalled at Jake's aroma, then opened the door to Lancaster's office.

The ambassador looked coldly across the top of his glasses at Jake Grafton and said, 'I asked to see you when you returned to the embassy, Admiral.'

'Yessir. I apologize. I didn't have much to tell you two hours ago, except to report that Lieutenant Moravia destroyed the weapons at the Petrovsk facility and a transport that was probably Iraqi. We were intercepted by four Russian fighters on the way down there.'

'But you evaded them. Obviously.'

'Yessir. Is Senator Wilmoth still in Moscow?' Wilmoth was the US senator who wanted a peek at the KGB files.

'He's staying at the embassy, but he's leaving tomorrow. The KGB slammed the door today after Shmarov died. I'm afraid Yeltsin doesn't have a lever big enough to pry it open.'

'I might be able to help. Could you ask the senator to come here to your office now? I have a tape I would like for you both to listen to. Then we're going to have to have a lengthy chat.'

Lancaster looked dubious, but he picked up the telephone. Jake took the cassette player from his pocket and sat it on the desk. Hempstead helped him find a plug.

When Wilmoth arrived, Jake started the tape. He had to stop it at numerous places and explain. Lancaster wanted to know what in the world Admiral Grafton was forcing into Herb Tenney's mouth, so Jake displayed the two pill bottles, even dumped the tablets onto Lancaster's polished mahogany.

After the first run-through, Jake played the tape again without interruptions. Then a third time at Senator Wilmoth's request.

It took some digesting. The fact that the Old Guard junta had blown up the Serdobsk reactor infuriated Wilmoth, who swore in a manner that Jake Grafton found most gratifying. Finally he said, 'Wait until the president hears this!'

'I suspect he's listening to it right now, sir,' Jake told him. 'I've already sent this via a TACSAT unit to General Land at the Pentagon. He said he would take it to the White House immediately.'

'What about Harley McCann?' the ambassador said. 'Was he in on this?'

'Captain McElroy has him outside in your waiting room. Why don't you ask him?' McElroy had taken four marines with him to the CIA spaces. They had found McCann and his deputies merely sitting at their desks, waiting. 'Apparently after Toad snatched Herb Tenney this morning, they talked it over and decided that they didn't want any part of whatever was going down. They appear to be quite ready to talk.'

'I have a few questions to ask them,' Wilmoth said heatedly.

'I suggest, Senator, that you send a team of your investigators to the CIA office and impound the files. I don't know what the CIA puts on paper, but some of that stuff might be interesting reading.'

Wilmoth grabbed for the telephone.

Lancaster reached for the white tablets on the desk and examined them. Finally he put them back on the desk next to the pill bottle.

When Wilmoth got off the phone, Jake said, 'Perhaps, Mr Ambassador, tonight would be a good time for President Yeltsin to call on the American Embassy. We can made a duplicate tape for him to keep. He might be able to find a good use for an artifact like that.'

Lancaster nodded. 'And?'

'Well, I need a plane to get to Saudi Arabia. I need to get there without being intercepted and attacked by Russian fighters. Perhaps after Yeltsin listens to the tape, we can discuss that problem with him.'

'On the tape you said you killed four men today. Who?'

'We were intercepted by fighters. Rita and I are still alive.' Jake Grafton shrugged.

Lancaster grinned wolfishly. 'I'm beginning to understand why General Land holds you in such high regard, Admiral. Agatha, while we're talking to Mr McCann, would you see if you can get President Yeltsin on the telephone?'

'Start scribbling.'

'Scribble what?' Jack Yocke was down on his hands and knees with a sponge and a bucket trying to clean Herb Tenney's vomit from the carpet. He leaned back on his heels and looked up at Jake Grafton.

'How the Old Guard blew up the Serdobsk reactor and murdered a half-million human beings. How the Old Guard sold nuclear weapons to Saddam Hussein. How they used the money to bribe elected Russian politicians to vote Yeltsin out. *That* story. Write it.'

'An agent of the US government tortured for information can hardly be quoted as a "reliable, high-placed government source,"' Yocke pointed out acidly. He dabbed at the wet place in the rug. 'I don't know if there was a single word of truth in what he said.'

'I thought you were a red-hot reporter.'

Yocke threw the sponge in the bucket and got to his feet. He sat down in the chair he had occupied during Tenney's interrogation. He dried his hands on his trousers. 'I don't want to write it.'

Grafton gazed at Yocke for a moment, then found a chair. 'Maybe you'd better explain.'

'The world is full of bad people. I write about them every day. They rob, steal, cheat, take drugs, bribes, beat their kids to death, kill their spouses in drunken rages or gun the bitches on the courthouse steps when they're stone-cold sober. Those people I can understand. They're human. These people here, people like Tenney, Shmarov, Yakolev . . .' Yocke's voice trailed off.

'They're human too. Their crimes are just worse.'

'No. They aren't human. They are *evil*. They have no humanity.' Jack Yocke shuddered.

'They're human all right,' Jake Grafton told him. 'If anything, too human. What you don't want to face is that everyone has a little Hitler, a little Stalin in him. Given the means and motive, a lot of people could become absolutely corrupt. What's the difference between killing a man and ordering his death? What's the difference between ordering one death or a half-million? Or a million? Or five million. Or ten million. With a stroke of a pen you can kill all the Jews – all the educated people – all the rich people – all the poor people – all the homosexuals . . . whoever. Evil and sin are exactly the same thing – you just need to convince yourself that the ends justify the means. *Every human alive is capable of that little trick.*'

'I don't want to write it.'

'You don't have a choice. I'm making the decisions around here. Get out your computer and plug the damn thing in. If necessary, I'll write the story for you.'

'Just who the fuck do you think you are, Grafton?'

'I'm a public servant trying to do his job. You are a newspaper reporter who wants to get famous by writing the truth. We've got a bucketful of truth here and you are going to write it because people need to come face-to-face with it. What they do with the truth is beyond my control: I'm not taking responsibility for the human condition. But by God they are going to see it smeared all over the front page of every newspaper in the world. Then if they refuse to face it they are just as evil and just as guilty as the men you're writing about.'

Jake Grafton stood. 'You're going to have to name names. Lancaster is in his office right now playing the tape for Yeltsin. Put that in your story.'

Jack Yocke gnawed on a fingernail as he thought about it. Finally he said, 'You want me to say how you got the information from Tenney?'

'You can do it like an interview, if you want. Don't mention binary poisons. I think that little problem is going to solve itself. Just quote Herb. Don't forget to mention that the interview was recorded and the president got a copy of the tape.'

' "That little problem is going to solve itself." God-damnit, Admiral, shit is shit! If we're going to nail the Commies to the cross we ought to nail our own bastards up there with them.'

'Oh, we will, Jack. We will. But one set of bastards at a time.'

'Who authorized you to release this story? The president?'

'I authorized myself.'

Yocke couldn't think of a reply, which infuriated him since he had known what Grafton's answer would be before he asked the question.

'Wake me up in two hours,' the admiral said, 'and let me read your story. I'm not much of a writer but maybe I can help you with the commas.'

And with that Jake Grafton stretched out on the couch. He turned so his back was to Yocke. In moments, as Jack Yocke stared, he was breathing deeply and regularly. By the time Yocke got his computer plugged in and running, Jake was snoring lightly.

CHAPTER TWENTY-TWO

Boris Yeltsin was a bear of a man, a burly, fleshy Russian with a bulbous, veined nose that one hoped did not indicate the condition of his liver. He shook Jake Grafton's hand and waved toward a chair as he traded Russian with an aide who didn't bother to translate. The interpreter who had led Jake into the room also remained silent.

The sun streamed between the drapes of the tall window on Yeltsin's left. Blinking in the glare, Jake Grafton looked around curiously. It was a good room, a man's room, tastefully decorated and heaped with piles of paper.

Yeltsin kept glancing at Grafton as he spoke. Finally one of the aides said, 'President Yeltsin wishes to thank the American government for its help in this crisis.'

Jake Grafton nodded pleasantly and glanced at his watch. The first edition of the *Post* carrying Jack Yocke's story was probably hitting the streets of Washington just about now. If the *Post* editors placed the story on the wires it was going to be on CNN and every other television and radio station in the Western world within an hour. Yeltsin's phone should start ringing in very short order.

After Yocke sent the story to the *Post* in the wee hours this morning via modem, his editor, Mike Gatler, called back and questioned him for ten minutes. When Yocke was about to lose his temper, he passed the telephone to Jake Grafton, who told Gatler, 'Yeah, I read the story. Every word's true.'

'Saddam Hussein has two *dozen* nuclear weapons?'

'At least that.'

Gatler whistled. 'Can this CIA source – what's his name?—'

'Herb Tenney.'

'Yeah. Can Tenney be trusted?'

'I don't know that I trust him, but I think he told the truth on this matter.'

'Can we quote you on that?'

'If you spell my name right.'

'Rear Admiral, right?'

'Yes.'

'And you and Yocke both saw the base where Hussein got the weapons? Weapons sold to him by the Russians?'

'Yes. Name of the place is Petrovsk. Yocke has it in the story. We went there in a helicopter.'

'This is a *big* story,' Gatler said.

'That's what Jack said.'

'Put him back on, please.' Jake held out the telephone.

'This story just scratches the surface,' Gatler complained to Yocke.

'I know that, Mike. I'm getting all I can. I'll send you more as soon as possible.'

'I want you to work with Tommy Townsend on this. Call him at his hotel.'

Yocke decided to call Townsend in the morning. He went to the bathroom, washed his face and hands, and was just stretching out on the floor with a pillow when Gatler called back. 'The State Department refuses to confirm or deny this story.'

'Nothing I can do about that,' Yocke said, waving frantically to Jake Grafton. The admiral sat up on the couch and rubbed his head.

'Yocke, this is the biggest story since the Japs hit Pearl Harbor,' Gatler said. 'Our White House guys can't get any confirmation, State refuses to confirm or deny, the people at the Pentagon refuse to comment, the CIA press people refuse to confirm that they've ever even heard of this Tenney guy. And CIA says that none of their people would ever talk to the press – violation of security regs and all that crap. So we've got your story and a voice on the telephone who claims he's Rear Admiral Jake Grafton. That's all.'

'I heard the Tenney interview, Mike. I was there in person. I saw the tape being made. I saw the rubble of the Serdobsk reactor, I visited the base at Petrovsk. I saw some bodies. I saw some weapons. I talked to Jake Grafton on the record – he's the deputy director of the Defense Intelligence Agency, for Christ's sake! He explicitly agreed to be quoted. I talked to an Israeli Mossad agent who's now dead – she was shot in my presence. I've got all that I can give you. If you haven't got the balls to run the story, then don't run it.'

'Don't get testy with me, Jack. I'm just explaining how far out on the limb we are with this story.'

'I'm sorry, Mike, but it's a good story. Every fucking word is true. I guarantee it. I don't give a shit what anybody else says, General Shmarov sold Saddam Hussein those bombs and blew up the Serdobsk reactor to cover up the fact that the weapons were gone.'

'Shmarov is dead.'

'I know that, Mike.'

'Heart attack.'

'No, he was poisoned by Herb Tenney.'

'*What?*' Gatler roared, '*Poisoned! By a CIA agent? That isn't in this story!*'

'I know that too, Mike. I can't get any confirmation for that from anybody. But Tenney confessed to the killing in my presence. I didn't put that in this story because I don't know that anyone will ever confirm that Shmarov was even murdered, much less that Tenney did it. I'm telling you that the stuff that *is* in that story is confirmed gospel. I've got a mountain of stuff that isn't in there because I haven't yet got it confirmed.'

Gatler thought that over for five seconds, then said, 'I want a copy of the tape of Tenney's confession.'

'Grafton won't release it. The White House might, but I doubt it. It covers a lot of ground, all of it classified up the wazoo.'

'I want more stories when you get confirmations.'

'I understand. When and if, you'll be the first to hear.'

They said their good-byes and Yocke told Jake, 'He's gonna print it.'

Jake Grafton had grunted from his position on the couch and pulled his jacket around him. He was asleep again in minutes.

This afternoon Jake idly wondered what Boris Yeltsin would do when he heard the story was out. Oh well, he was a politician, experienced in converting lemons into lemonade.

He settled back into the chair and crossed his legs. This afternoon President Clinton was supposed to call to talk to Yeltsin about the mess in Iraq. Last night Yeltsin invited Jake to come here to answer any questions his staff might have.

Now the telephone rang. One of the aides picked it up, said something, then Yeltsin took the other line. Jake looked at his watch. He wondered if the airplanes coming in from Germany would be on time.

But this wasn't President Clinton's call. The interpreter hung up his phone and Yeltsin fell into his chair as he listened intently on his own instrument. Occasionally his eyes swung to Grafton. This went on for several minutes with Yeltsin grunting occasionally. Finally he replaced the telephone on its hook and swiveled his chair to face Grafton. He wiggled his finger at the interpreter and spoke.

The interpreter said, 'A news story has appeared in the *Washington Post*. You are quoted. Did you release a story to the newspaper?'

Jake nodded. 'I did.'

Yeltsin listened to the answer and swiveled his chair nervously. He toyed with a pencil, then stared at it, finally replaced it. He said something to the interpreter.

'The president wishes to know why you released the story.'

'As we discussed last night, it is of critical importance that those weapons be recovered or rendered harmless. We cannot go after those weapons without a public explanation of our actions. So the truth must be told. The truth is that a small group of individuals here in Russia sold weapons to get money to overthrow the elected government. They murdered hundreds of thousands of people to cover up their crime. *This* is the story. The sooner the world knows it, the better – for Russia, for the United States, for the people of the Middle East.'

'*You* released this story?'

'Yes.' Of course he had discussed it with General Hayden Land, but both men had agreed it would be best if Jake took the responsibility. If the story came from Jake it was deniable in Washington, and that might well be the first reaction of panicky politicians with a genetic aversion to telling the public about disasters. In the ordinary course of things weeks might pass before they screwed up the courage to talk publicly about this one. Yet Hayden Land and Jake Grafton knew they didn't have weeks to clean up this mess: at best, they had hours.

'What is going on, Admiral?' In Washington, Yeltsin meant.

'Sir, we discussed this matter last night. Nothing has changed. US Air Force planes are flying in from Germany to take me and the other foreign military observers to Arabia. From there we will go to Iraq to recover the weapons. You agreed that Marshal Mikhailov and General Yakolev would accompany our group on behalf of the Russian Republic.'

'I don't want *them* talking to reporters.'

'I understand. I promise that they won't.'

'I should have been consulted before you talked to the press.'

Jake acknowledged this. He apologized, though not very convincingly.

Yeltsin didn't look too put out – the story Yocke wrote couldn't have been more favorable to him even if he had written it himself. Complete innocence was a rare commodity, one to be savored. Being the unwounded target of a cutthroat power play that misfired was even nicer.

'I have a suggestion,' Jake added. 'In an hour or so you, Mr President, are going to be besieged by reporters wanting your comments. The reporter who wrote this morning's story for the *Washington Post*, Jack Yocke, is downstairs. Why not get him up here, give him an interview, and get your side of this on record before the spin doctors in Washington and Baghdad get into the act? Mr Yocke is knowledgeable about this matter and sympathetic to your government.'

The mention of Baghdad did the trick. Saddam Hussein would be on camera as soon as he heard about the *Post* story. Hussein had just two options, as far as Jake could see: deny he had nuclear weapons or admit it and claim that the government of Russia sold them to him. That government, of course, was Boris Yeltsin. Which option Hussein picked would depend, Jake suspected, on the amount of time he still needed to get the nuclear weapons operational. The nearer he was to being ready to push the button the more likely he was to admit that he had them. But this was speculation, and just now Jake was trying to cover all the possibilities.

In minutes Jack Yocke was being ushered into the president's office. He glanced at Rear Admiral Jake Grafton seated at an oblique angle from Yeltsin's desk, then turned his attention to the Russian president.

Yocke knew exactly what his editor, Mike Gatler, wanted – a gold-plated confirmation of the first story – and he went after it without making any detours. Point by point he led Yeltsin through the story and scribbled his answers on a small steno pad.

Yes, it was true that Shmarov had used the KGB to collect money from Saddam Hussein. He sold things that belonged to the nation that he had no right to sell. That was a crime. Such a thing would be a crime in any nation on earth.

Yes, Shmarov allowed the removal of planeloads of weapons from the base at Petrovsk the day before the Serdobsk reactor was destroyed. Yes, Shmarov ordered Colonel Gagarin of the KGB to destroy the Serdobsk fast breeder reactor. And yes, Gagarin committed the crime. Yeltsin was not yet prepared to say what Shmarov did with the money he collected for the weapons – the government was investigating. The new fact to lead off this story – Yeltsin had ordered Marshal Mikhailov, commander of the Russian armed forces, and General Yakolev, commander of the Russian army, to accompany Rear Admiral Jake Grafton and a group of officers from Germany, Britain, France and Italy on a trip to Iraq to recover the stolen weapons.

'Stolen?' Yocke asked, looking up at Yeltsin.

'Stolen,' the interpreter repeated after a burst from Yeltsin. 'The government of Russia has never sold and will never sell or give away nuclear weapons. We have given our solemn promise on that point to numerous governments throughout the world. We have signed treaties.'

Jack Yocke then asked the next logical question: what would Russia do to get the stolen weapons back if Saddam Hussein wasn't gentleman enough to return them? The answer: 'We are cooperating with the United States and the governments of other nations to secure the return of the stolen weapons.'

That should have been the end of it, but Yocke was Yocke and couldn't resist asking one more. After a glance at Grafton, whose face showed no emotion whatever, he said, 'General Shmarov allegedly died of a heart attack the night before last. Was it a heart attack?'

'I don't know,' Boris Yeltsin said. 'An autopsy is being performed.'

Yocke opened his mouth, glanced again at Grafton, then

thanked President Yeltsin for the interview. He was ushered from the room. Jake Grafton remained seated.

Out in the waiting area Yocke grabbed his computer from the chair where he had placed it and opened it on his lap. In seconds he was tapping away while the US marine captain, McElroy, watched over his shoulder.

When Yocke finished and looked up, McElroy and the four enlisted marines with him were no longer in the room. But there was a secretary behind the desk and she had a telephone in front of her. 'May I make a collect telephone call?' he asked.

She merely grinned nervously at him.

'Use the phone?' He reached for it and raised his eyebrows.

She nodded. Yocke snagged the instrument and when he heard a voice addressing him in Russian, asked for the international operator.

The C-141 was somewhere over the Black Sea when Jack Yocke tired of looking out the window at the four F-15 escorts, their KC-135 tanker and the electronic warfare E-3 Sentry that formed this aerial armada. Jake Grafton obviously intended to make it to Arabia regardless of who had other ideas.

As they were boarding the airplane in Moscow, Yocke had asked, 'You don't really expect the Russian air force to try to shoot us down, do you?'

'With the story out, probably not. But we have Mikhailov and Yakolev. Who knows how that will play? It's like trying to figure prison politics.'

Yocke had watched with growing wonder as the F-15s occasionally slipped in behind the tanker for fuel, then slid away afterward. The planes seemed to hang motionless in the sky, a perspective Yocke found unique and fascinating. The noise of their engines was masked by the background noise inside the C-141, so the show outside was a silent, effortless ballet.

He had already tried to interview Lieutenant Colonel Jocko West and the three bird colonels from Germany, Italy and France. None of them wanted to talk, on or off the record. They did spell their names for him, for future reference. Then they shooed him off. As he turned to go back to his seat, West told him with a grin, 'Reporters are like solicitors and doctors – the less you see of them the more tranquil your life.'

Marshal Mikhailov and General Yakolev were in the back of the compartment surrounded by four armed marines. Captain McElroy was seated nearby; he had merely moved his head from side to side about half a millimeter when Yocke looked his way.

Up front Jake Grafton was in conference with Toad Tarkington and Captain Tom Collins. Yocke stood in the aisle and stretched. Even after that hassle with the story last night and just two hours sleep, he wasn't a bit tired. How often is it that you get to interview the president of a big nation and write a story that will make every front page on the planet, then jump on a plane and jet off to do another? Ah, he could get used to this.

Better enjoy it while it lasts, he told himself, because when it's over it'll be really over. He would be back scribbling crime stories and the city council news that was fit to print all too soon.

Yocke passed by Grafton and his colleagues and went forward to the cockpit. Rita Moravia was in the left seat. She turned and flashed him a grin.

'She's not really a pilot, you know,' Jack told the air force major standing behind Rita. 'She was Miss July of 1991.'

'Careful, friend,' the major rumbled. 'This is the new modern American military. Comments with any sexist content whatsoever have been outlawed.

'Sorry.'

'You want to remain politically correct and ideologically pure, don't you? No more male and female pronouns. Everything is *it*. During the transition period you may say *hit* and *sit* instead of *it*, but no *shit*. One slip and the sexual gestapo will be on your case.'

'After they gets finished with you,' the copilot told him gravely, 'you'll have to Spiro Agnew.'

'Actually,' Rita Moravia said, patting her hair to ensure it was just so, 'I was Miz July.'

'Where are we?' Yocke asked when the three stooges had calmed down. All he could see out the window was sea and sky.

'Thirty-three thousand feet up,' the copilot told him, and laughed shamelessly at his own wit.

The reporter groaned. Look out, Saddam! The Americans are coming again. Yocke left the flight deck and went back to the cabin.

Jake Grafton was seated beside Tarkington. Collins was back in his own seat reading something, so Jack sat on the arm of the seat across the aisle from the admiral. 'How's planning for the war?'

Jake Grafton examined Yocke's face. 'Our agreement is still in effect, right?'

'Oh, absolutely.'

'I mention it because last night you flapped your mouth to your editor about General Shmarov's death. That subject was and is off limits.'

'Admiral, Gatler was on the fence over whether or not to run the story. I had to give him a hot off-the-record fact so he would think I had a lot more, that we were scraping the icing off a very big cake. And that tidbit about Shmarov was the only hot fact I could think of just then. I assumed you wanted the story in the paper or you wouldn't have bothered to order it' – Yocke snapped his fingers – 'like a ham and cheese on rye.'

'Then you tried to inch onto that subject with Yeltsin this afternoon with that last question, on the off chance he might spill his guts on the spot.'

'Admiral I—'

Jake cut him off. 'I saw you give me that guilty look,

364

should I or shouldn't I, just before you put your mouth in motion. Either you play the game my way or you can zip right over to the commercial airport when we land and ride your plastic right on back to Moscow. We are playing with my ball, Jack.'

'Yessir. Your ball, your rules. But for my info, are you ever going to let me loose on the CIA's creative use of binary poisons?'

Grafton shrugged. 'I don't know. Doubtful. That situation will probably solve itself.'

' "Solve itself," ' Yocke repeated sourly, and drew in air for an oration on the hypocrisy of not airing our dirty linen while we launder other people's.

He never got the chance. Jake jerked his thumb aft. 'Those two are a part of our international team.'

'The two Russian prisoners, you mean?' Yocke said, and instantly regretted it. Jake Grafton's gray eyes looked like river ice in winter.

'This may be just a story for you,' Grafton said, almost a whisper, 'but there's a bit more at stake for everybody else.'

'I'm not writing fiction, Admiral. Not intentionally, anyway.'

'I'm not asking you to. But no interviews with them until I say so, if and when.'

'Aye aye, sir.' Yocke tried to keep the sarcasm out of his voice and succeeded fairly well. Tarkington gave him the eye, though.

Grafton went back to studying the photographs that lay in his lap. He used a magnifying glass.

'Aerial photos?' Yocke asked.

'Satellite.'

'May I look?'

Grafton passed him a couple. They looked like shots from just a couple thousand feet above an airfield. He could see the aircraft clearly, the power carts, the revetments, even people and the shadows they cast. 'These are really clear,' he murmured. 'Are the missiles here at this base?'

'I think so. The trouble with satellite surveillance is that you can rarely be absolutely certain of anything. It's true, at times the resolution is so good that you can read license plate numbers, and if people like Saddam think we can see everything all the time, that's just fine with us. But we can't. There are very real technical limitations. The art is in the interpretation of what you *can* see.'

'So are we going to hit this base with an air strike?'

'That would be the easy way,' Jake acknowledged, then selected another photo and bent to examine it. When he finally straightened he added, 'Nobody ever accused us of doing anything the easy way.'

Jack Yocke returned the photos and went back to his seat by the window. He sat staring at the two fighters he could see. They were in loose formation, so loose one was over a mile away.

The sun was setting, firing the tops of the clouds below with pinks and oranges. Beneath that the sea was a deep, deep purple, almost black. He stared downward, between the clouds. That looked like . . . maybe it was land. Were they over Turkey? Or was that ocean down there in the gloom?

He finally reclined his seat and tried to sleep.

Up forward Toad Tarkington muttered to his boss, 'You may trust that jackass, but I don't.'

'To which of our jackasses are you referring?'

'Yocke.'

'Oh, he's got his rough edges,' Jake said, 'but he's an honest man. Rather like you in that regard.' When he saw that Toad was at a loss for a reply, Jake grinned and added, 'You guys are Tweedledum and Tweedledumber. Amy says you're both fun to have around. She's still trying to decide which of you is Tweedledumber.'

'Thanks, CAG.'

'Anytime, Toad.'

CHAPTER TWENTY-THREE

The command bunker at the sprawling military base outside of Riyadh looked like a *Star Wars* movie set. A long rack of television monitors mounted above a huge wall chart of the region displayed everything from the current CNN broadcast to real-time satellite ambient light and infrared views of selected areas inside Iraq, computer presentations of Iraq and UN troop positions, computer presentations of the vehicles moving near Baghdad and Samarra, aircraft aloft over Iraq, Arabia, Kuwait, and the Persian Gulf, ships at sea in the Gulf – everything a commander might want to know was on one of those screens. At computer stations facing the screens were the men and women who punched the keys that made it all work.

Just now all eyes in the room were on the CNN monitor. Jake Grafton and the European colonels stood together in a knot staring upward at the jowly visage of Saddam Hussein, who was busy calling the *Washington Post* and Boris Yeltsin liars. 'Iraq does not possess nuclear weapons. Lies have been told. Yeltsin is desperate, attempting to use Iraq as a scapegoat to prevent political collapse in Russia.'

'What do you think?' Jake asked Jocko West.

'If he has trained Russian technicians, I think he can shoot the missiles on launchers any time. At best, within hours. But he probably only has two or three missiles on their Russian Army launchers. The launchers were just too bulky and heavy to transport. He took as many missiles as he could, probably intending to put them on launchers he already has. And he took warheads, which are small and could be loaded quickly onto his planes. I suspect that he's playing for time in order to load the missiles he stole on old Scud launchers and adapt the warheads for use on his missiles.'

Colonel Rheinhart agreed. 'If he has the people and the proper tools, he can begin placing nuclear warheads on the Scuds in a few days, arm perhaps thirty Scuds in ten days or so. Five or six ready-to-shoot weapons are not enough for a war.'

The Italian and Frenchman nodded at this assessment. Jake Grafton wasn't so sure. A lunatic might start a war even if he had only one bullet.

As Jake Grafton stared at Saddam's image on the monitor, he reviewed what he knew about the Iraqi dictator. Born poor, poor as only an Arab can be, in a squalid village a hundred miles north of Baghdad, he went to live with an uncle in the capital at the age of ten, about 1947. His uncle was the author of a screed entitled *Three Things That God Should Not Have Created: Persians, Jews, and Flies.* This tract became young Saddam's *Mein Kampf.* Within months, according to his official biography, he killed his first man.

When he was twenty, the young thug joined the Iraqi Baath party, where he became a triggerman disposing of the party's enemies, of whom there were many. One of the people he murdered was his brother-in-law. Two years later, in 1959, he bungled an assassination attempt aimed at the current Iraqi dictator, General Abdul Kassem, and was shot by Kassem's guards. Somehow he escaped and fled to Egypt.

In 1963 the Baath party successfully murdered Kassem and took power. Saddam returned to Iraq and ended up in prison nine months later when the Baathists were overthrown by an army junta.

When the Baathists seized power again in 1968, Saddam

was there in the councils of power. In a stunning parallel to the career of Josef Stalin, he took control of the secret police and systematically set out to murder everyone he could not control, thereby becoming the real ruler of Iraq. Before long he took personal control of the nation's foreign policy. The nominal president of the country soldiered on under Saddam's orders until 1979, when he retired, thereby becoming the first ruler of Iraq not to die in office within the memory of living men. Saddam anointed himself dictator and gave himself a new title, The Awesome. Perhaps it loses something in translation.

Yet Saddam never forgot how he got to the top, never lost touch with his roots. New title and all, he still liked to use a pistol to personally execute cabinet officers, generals, and relatives who had the temerity to argue with him or whom he suspected of harboring a nascent seed of disloyalty.

From any possible viewpoint, Jake Grafton thought, Saddam appeared as the master thug, a self-centered man without conscience or remorse capable of any crime. In other words, a perfect dictator.

Oh, he had screwed up badly a time or two — the eight-year war with Iran cost Iraq a hundred thousand lives and $70 billion it didn't have, and the little fracas over Kuwait didn't turn out quite the way Saddam thought it would. But the man wasn't a quitter. After those debacles he had ruthlessly shot, gassed and starved his domestic enemies into oblivion. Iraq was still his: he was hanging tough, arming himself with nuclear weapons. Then he would find who still wanted to play the game and who was willing to kneel at his throne.

Saddam's tragedy was that he ruled such a small corner of the world. If only he could have had a stage the size of Germany or Russia!

A naive person might wonder why the civilized nations of the earth continued to deal with miserable vermin like Saddam, but Jake Grafton didn't. *Realpolitik* kept him alive.

He was part and parcel of the forces in dynamic tension that kept the Middle East from exploding into religious and race war. And Iraq had oil.

Jake wondered if now, finally, the fearful politicians of the 'civilized nations' had had enough. He was still pondering that question when he was called into a room with General Frank Loy, the UN commander. General Loy was talking on the satellite link. He handed the telephonelike handset to Jake.

'Rear Admiral Grafton, sir.'

'Hayden Land. Glad you arrived.'

'I just watched Saddam on the tube.'

'Yeah. They're in a dither here. They're pissed that you gave the story to the *Post* and I had to admit I authorized it. So they're peeved at me. If I weren't black they would have fired me.' He indulged himself in an expletive. 'Anyway, Saddam isn't cooperating. He denied he has nukes, so now the fact that there is no independent confirmation has them in a sweat.'

'So no air strike?'

'No air strike,' Land said wearily.

'Saddam has put his forces on alert,' Jake said. 'It'll take four or five days to bring them up to full alert, so whatever we're going to do we must do quickly. Every hour that goes by is going to cost us lives.'

'I know that,' Land said.

'The German expert thinks that Saddam could have the stolen missiles ready to launch in hours, if they aren't ready to go now.'

Land didn't respond. In a moment he said, 'These people here are trying to figure out a way to blame this mess on George Bush. He had his chance to stomp this cockroach and didn't, so now they have to dirty their shoes with it.'

'Yessir. Should Yocke do another story?'

'Your staff reporter? No. Not right now. They would lock me out of the White House if that happened. Soooo . . . I want you to plan an assault on that airfield.

370

Figure out what it will take, when you can do it, what it will cost.' Jake knew that when Hayden Land talked cost, he wasn't talking dollars: he was talking lives. 'Then call me back. If you and Loy think an assault is feasible, my idea is for you to take some network camera teams along. If we treated the world to a live broadcast showing the Russian missiles and warheads that Saddam says he doesn't have, these people here will be off the hook. Then you can fly the weapons out.'

'We try to fly the weapons out, General, this is going to be a big operation and damned risky.'

'I know that. But these people inside the Beltway don't have the balls to take any flak from the Sierra Club about nuclear pollution. They'd rather take US casualties than Iraqi casualties. It's not that they're callous, it's just the fact that they got in with a plurality of the votes. We're dealing with a president that sixty percent of the American people didn't want. He knows it, his staff knows it – and they won't risk alienating the support they do have. That's political reality. So plan for an airlift.'

'Don't we have a carrier battle group in the Gulf of Oman? If she ran west through the Strait of Hormuz into the Persian Gulf that would help.'

'We'll send her in. Now let me talk to Loy again.'

Jake passed the handset to General Loy and walked out of the room.

'They're in Samarra.' The air intelligence staff officer said it positively.

Jake Grafton needed to be sold. 'A fifty-fifty chance, sixty-forty, what?'

'No, sir. They're there. We saw the planes come in from Russia and nothing big enough to transport a missile has left. We've got round-the-clock real-time satellite surveillance. They're there.'

'The missiles?'

'The missiles are there, yessir.'

'And the warheads?'

'I don't know,' the staff officer said, and shook his head. 'They're so small . . .'

'Have they been moving Scuds around?'

'No. We would have seen that. They've tried to keep them under cover since the war. We know where some of them are, but certainly not all.'

'Let me see if I have this right: the Russian missiles are in Samarra, but we only know where some of the Scuds are. If the Iraqis are mating nuclear warheads to the Scuds, they must have taken the warheads to the missiles, because they haven't brought the missiles to Samarra.'

'Yessir.'

'Then we're fucked.'

'Yes, sir. That's a very apt description. I couldn't say it any better myself.'

'Find the Scuds.'

'Sir, we've been trying to do that for eighteen months.'

'Have the Iraqis taken warheads to the sites of the Scuds we know about?'

'I don't know, sir. We've been trying—'

'You're not trying hard enough,' Jake Grafton said coldly. 'Track every vehicle leaving the Samarra base and see where it goes. If the vehicle visits the site of a known Scud, you've just found one.' Jake lowered his voice. 'They tell me you people are the very best. Your equipment is the best. Find those warheads. I don't care what you have to do, but find them. Now!'

A modern joint military operation is extraordinarily complex and requires extensive planning. The myriad of details cannot be worked out in hours, not even by competent, experienced professionals. Days, even weeks, go into the planning of a successful joint operation.

Jake Grafton was demanding this one be put together and be ready to launch in eighteen hours, by 20:00 local time tomorrow. He would have gone sooner, even in daylight, if the planning could have been completed, but even he had to admit there was no way. As it was there would be no time for a run-through with the commanders involved, no time to sort things out before the starting gun fired, so there were going to be snafus – people getting in one another's way, people who didn't go at all, busted equipment, too many people at one place, too few at others, things that had to happen but didn't . . . He expected all that. But it could get worse – there could be good guys shooting at good guys. He and the troops would have to live with it. Or die with it. Being Jake Grafton, he didn't think much about the dying part, except to ensure that the medical support would be there, all that could be fitted in.

Fortunately General Loy named a competent professional to plan and command the operation, Major General Daniel Serkin, a whipcord-tough soldier with only one pace – fast.

Jake Grafton stood and watched, walked the floor and listened to the planners, perused op orders, conferred repeatedly with General Serkin. And worried that while the allies fretted over call signs and radio frequencies Saddam would start spraying nuclear warheads at his enemies.

At dawn he called General Land and gave him a preliminary overview. The operation would start with a navy SEAL team delayed parachute drop from thirty thousand feet. Chutes would open under two thousand feet. The team would secure the airport perimeter, wipe out anti-aircraft resistance and machine gun emplacements. A battalion from the 101st Airborne Division (Air Assault) would then arrive in helicopters escorted by electronic warfare aircraft – Wild Weasels – and fighters, with helicopter gunships providing close air support. The idea was to quickly overpower any resistance, make the airfield safe for transports. These would come in with their own aerial escort, which would orbit overhead and prevent Iraqi forces from counterattacking. With all the Russian weapons aboard, the transports would leave and the American and allied troops would pull out under air cover. If everything went according to plan, the raid would be over before the Iraqis could bring overwhelming military power to bear.

Fortunately Saddam Hussein seemed to be expecting an air strike. The radars in the Baghdad and Samarra area were almost constantly on the air and mobile antiaircraft guns were moving into the area. But not troops.

Toad Tarkington suggested a name for this operation, Operation Appointment. Jake told him the name lacked pizzazz, but he too had read John O'Hara so he recommended the name to General Land, who accepted it without comment.

'So it all depends on how deep the Iraqi forces are at the airfield?' Land said finally, when Jake was finished.

'Yessir. Intelligence says we'll be facing a battalion of Republican Guard.'

'Armor?'

'Yessir. We have a choice – try to wipe out the tanks with Apaches prior to the SEAL drop, or drop the SEALs and try to achieve surprise, then bring in the Apaches.'

'Has General Serkin made a decision?'

'Not yet.'

'Found the Scuds?'

'Not yet, sir.'

'What if you don't find them?'

'We'll go anyway.'

'And the antiaircraft defenses?'

'We'll use missiles, chaff, and jamming, then A-6s and A-10s.'

'Call me back later.'

Jake went to find a place to sleep. One office had a couch. He was pulling off his shoes when Toad Tarkington tracked him down. 'Here's a message from Ambassador Lancaster in Moscow, for your eyes only.'

Jake tore open the envelope. Herb Tenney was dead. In his sleep.

Half the pills Jake put in Herb's mouth were aspirin, but some of them were part of the binary cocktail. Perhaps Herb already had the other half in his system. *Damn!* Or someone just poisoned him.

Jake replaced the message in the envelope and passed it back to Toad. 'Herb Tenney died in his sleep.'

Toad snorted. 'His tough luck.'

Jake balled his fist and started to pound his thigh, then opened his hand and ran it through his hair. 'I am really sick of this mess.'

'I know,' Toad said. 'I know.'

'Turn the lights out and close the door. Let me sleep for three hours.'

'Yessir.

'And question General Yakolev. Find out if they shot down that Russian helicopter pilot, Vasily Lutkin.'

'CAG, you aren't responsible for that. Yakolev is. You can't—'

'Just do it, Toad.'

'Aye aye, sir.'

He lay in the darkness trying to relax. Too many details ran through his mind, too many questions were still unanswered.

Saddam Hussein was down to his last trick, but it was a dilly this time. He had tried to take the Iranian oil fields and lost, tried to take Kuwait and found out that a second- or third-rate military power could not win on a modern conventional battlefield. So now he was playing the nuclear card. And it would be a winner unless allied forces arrived in time.

In time.

What was happening in Washington?

When Toad woke Jake up, he had a message. 'The president said Go. You're to call General Land.'

For some reason he didn't quite understand, Jake felt refreshed and relaxed after his nap. He followed Toad to the com center and sat drinking coffee while the technicians placed the call to Washington.

Hayden Land's voice had a note of optimism this morning, actually midnight or after in Washington. 'The White House crowd finally faced up to the fact they have no choice.'

No choice! The words echoed in Jake's mind. It's almost as if the grand smashup is preordained, he thought.

'Where are the Scud missiles?'

'They aren't moving on the roads, sir,' the air intelligence officer told Jake Grafton. 'And we can't find any vehicles leaving the Samarra base that go to any of the Scud sites we know about. None. We've used computers to analyze satellite imagery and side-looking radar to track their vehicles. We've come up dry.'

'Maybe most of the warheads are still at the Samarra base.'

'Reluctantly, I come to that conclusion too, Admiral.'

It is never safe to assume that your opponent is doing what you want him to do. Jake Grafton was well aware of that pitfall, and yet . . . 'Perhaps,' he murmured, 'Saddam is having his trouble adapting the warheads to the missiles.'

'It's possible,' Colonel Rheinhart agreed. 'The Iraqis reduced the payload capability of their missiles several years ago in order to carry more fuel.'

'So where is Saddam?' Jake asked the intelligence staff.

'He rode out the Gulf War in '91 in a camping trailer that moved randomly around Baghdad. We told the press we knew where all the command and control facilities were, which was a serious stretcher. Then we blew up a few of them with smart bombs and he concluded we were telling the truth.'

'And now?'

'Well, we've refined our satellite capability since the Gulf War. We have side-looking radar in the air that tracks moving vehicles so that we can find Scud sites. Now we do have all the command and control facilities spotted and we can follow Saddam for five days at a time. Unfortunately, right now we seem to have lost track of him.

'Could he be at the Samarra base?' Jake asked.

'Sir, he could be anywhere.'

General Loy, Major General Serkin, and Jake Grafton reviewed the final plan together. They set H-Hour for 24:00 this night. Serkin said he didn't think they could go sooner, and with yet another glance at his watch Jake acquiesced.

Then he went to find Toad. 'Did you get anything out of Yakolev?'

'He refused to say a word. When he heard the question he looked at me like I was crazy.'

Jake Grafton sighed. 'I'm jumping tonight with the SEALs,' he said after a bit. 'I want you to bring the nuclear weapons experts in on choppers. Get chopper transport for Jack Yocke and a network camera team and as many other print and television reporters as you can cram in. Have Captain McElroy and the marines bring our two Russian friends and Spiro Dalworth. Bring Colonel Rheinhart, Jocko West and the other international observers. You're in charge of that operation.'

'No, sir. I'm going with you.'

Jake Grafton did a double take. 'Toad, I want you to get the press and the international people there. This is the key to the whole deal.'

'Rita can handle it, CAG. I'm going with you.'

'Maybe I didn't make myself clear, Commander. You—'

'CAG, you can court-martial me if you like. But I'm going with you to watch your back. *You* are the key to this operation and if you get zapped, the rest of us are in big fucking trouble. I'd never forgive myself if that happened and Rita wouldn't forgive me either. Now that's *that.*'

'Have you ever made a delayed parachute drop?'

'I've done as many as you have, sir.'

'Okay, smart-ass. We'll hold hands all the way down.'

Jack Yocke had a request of his own when Toad told him he was going in on a chopper with Rita. 'I'd like to go with you and the admiral.'

'Yeah, I bet you would,' Toad said. 'Forget it, pencil pilot. We'll give you a window seat on the executive helicopter if you promise not to pee your pants.'

'No, I want to jump with you guys. It'll be a great story.'

'You don't seem to understand, Jack. We'll be the first guys in. *This is a twenty-eight-thousand-foot free fall at night into a concentration of enemy troops who are probably on full alert.* There'll be bullets flying around, helicopter gunships blasting tanks, the whole greasy enchilada. Get serious! Your mother wouldn't even let you play with a cap pistol when you were a kid.'

'Let me ask the admiral.'

Grafton listened to Yocke state his case, gave Toad an evil glance, and said, 'Sure you can come. Why not? The more the merrier.'

They started sweating during the suiting up at 20:00, after dinner in the main cafeteria. Camo clothing, insulated one-piece jumpsuit, jump boots, helmet, silenced submachine gun, ammo, knife, radio, canteen, flak vest – 'The bullets will bounce off like you're fucking Superman' – parachute harness, parachutes, oxygen mask, oxygen supply system, gloves, jump goggles, night vision goggles for on the ground . . . almost eighty pounds of equipment. They waddled when they were finally outfitted.

'I don't want a gun,' Yocke said.

'No weapon, no jump,' Jake Grafton told him curtly. 'Your choice. I'm not taking a tourist into a firefight, and that's final.'

So they hung a submachine gun and ammo on Yocke and he kept his mouth shut. As a final indignity, Toad Tarkington smeared his face with black camouflage grease.

It was bizarre. The SEALs looked like extras from an

Arnold Schwarzenegger action flick. Zap, boom, pow! No doubt he did too. And they were all grown men!

Yocke began really sweating in the lecture that followed. A chief petty officer explained each piece of gear, explained about the wrist altimeter, how they should check it occasionally but wait for the main chute to deploy automatically – 'It'll work! Honest! It's guaranteed. If it doesn't, you bring it back and we'll give you another' – how they would run out of the back of the C-141 in lines, lay themselves out in the air to keep from tumbling, steer in free fall, steer when the chute opened, how they should land.

And when all the questions had been answered from the three neophytes, the final piece of advice: 'Don't think about it – just do it.'

Jake Grafton had too many things on his mind to worry about the jump. As the C-141 climbed away from the runway, he adjusted his oxygen mask, ensured the oxygen was flowing and let the jumpmaster check his equipment, all the while trying to figure out what Saddam Hussein had done with the weapons. Were they still at the Samarra base, or had The Awesome outsmarted the Americans?

Sitting beside the admiral, Toad Tarkington thought about the upcoming jump as the air inside the plane cooled. The red lights of the plane's interior and the noise gave it the feel and sound of flight deck control, the handler's kingdom in the bottom of a carrier's island. And he had that night-cat-shot rock in the pit of his stomach.

He looked at the blank faces and averted eyes of the SEALs around him and thought about Rita. Would she be all right? Had he made the right decision coming with Grafton? If they shot Rita down she had no parachute, no ejection seat – if that woman died Toad wanted to die with her. This thought had tripped across his synapses when he was weighing his request to accompany Grafton. Nuclear weapons to murder millions – with Jake Grafton alive and thinking, they had a chance to pull off this crazy assault. With him dead it would be just another bloodletting and probably end up too little, too late. Although racked with powerful misgivings, Toad had elected to go with his head and not his heart.

The oxygen, he noted now, had a slightly metallic taste.

Maybe, Toad decided, a little prayer wouldn't hurt. He didn't bother the Lord often, just checked in occasionally to let the man – or woman – upstairs know he was still down here kicking, but now, he thought, might be a good time to put in an earnest supplication from the heart.

Dear God, don't let anything happen to Rita.

Jack Yocke was thinking exclusively about the upcoming free fall. Unlike Grafton and Tarkington, he had never ejected from an airplane, nor had he ever jumped out of one. He knew people whose idea of a perfect Saturday was to leap out of an airplane with six of their buddies and free fall, then float down in sport parachutes, those colorful flying wings. He had never had the slightest desire to join the macho brigade. Maybe those folks had maladjusted hormone levels or were trying to spice up dull, boring existences, but Jack Yocke was perfectly happy with his feet upon the ground. He still got dates when he wanted them and his dick got stiff at the right time, so why spit in the devil's eye?

Part of the reason he was here, he admitted to himself, was Tarkington. The Toad-man had a knack of rubbing him the wrong way. That coolest-of-the-cool, studlier-than-thou attitude, that . . . asshole! So now here he was, getting colder and colder, about to fall over *five fucking miles* through the night sky, then ride a parachute – if that contraption of bedsheets and fishing lines opened – right smack into the middle of a goddamn war with a bunch of raghead Nazis.

What if the chute doesn't open? I mean, really! You gotta lay there in the air like a store dummy for two minutes and forty seconds waiting . . . waiting . . . waiting . . . If you panicked and pulled the manual ripcord too high you might run out of oxygen, or drift away from the landing area and the support of your fellow soldiers. Or you might find yourself hanging up there when the helicopter gunships and troop transports came in with their blades whirling around, flak searching the darkness, cannon fire, machine gun bullets . . . No, Jack, don't take a chance on pulling the ripcord too early. Wait for this seventy-nine-cent gizmo from Woolworth's to do the job for you.

He would wait. Under absolutely no circumstances would he panic. He told himself that yet again, trying to believe it. He would close his eyes and wait until the chute opened. It *would* open. He assured himself of that for the fiftieth time. If it didn't, by God, they would scrape him off the asphalt in the middle of the runway, his eyes scrunched shut, his hands and legs outstretched, still waiting.

Now, fifteen minutes after takeoff, Yocke was *ready.* He was properly psyched and ready to leap straight into hell. Then he looked at his watch and saw that they had over an hour to go.

Oh, Jesus!

Rita Moravia sat in almost total darkness with her back against the forward bulkhead of the Blackhawk's passenger compartment. Sharing the compartment with her but quite invisible were the four European colonels 'observing' and the two Russian flag officers.

The Russians also had escorts, Captain Iron Mike McElroy and one of his sergeants. Rita had briefed them carefully.

Right now she wasn't thinking about the other passengers. She was listening to the muffled roar of the engines through her headset and thinking about her husband, Toad.

He would be okay, she assured herself. When she heard he was jumping she thought of the two steel pins in his leg and wondered if he should. When she mentioned his leg he glared at her.

Isn't that just like a man? If the man is concerned he's thoughtful, chivalrous, gallant. If a woman voices her concern she's a nag.

So life isn't fair. Tell it to Yocke and let him put it on the front page.

The navy had been a tough row to hoe. First the Naval Academy, then flight training, the squadrons, test pilot school — Rita had encountered subtle covert and overt discrimination every step of the way. Oh, the senior officers thought it would be fine to have women in the navy as long as the pretty ones wanted to be executive secretaries to those said senior officers, but women shouldn't be on ships! Or in cockpits. Or where men were shooting. Or drinking. Or telling dirty jokes. Heaven forbid!

Jake Grafton didn't think like that. Because he didn't Rita had found herself riding the tip of the arrow, slaughtering doomed men with a 30mm cannon.

Here in the darkness inside this helicopter over the desert, Rita Moravia remembered that moment. She remembered the feel of her airplane, the look of the clouds, the look of the Iraqi plane on the parking mat as she dove at it, the Gs tugging at her as she maneuvered, the lighted reticle in the sight glass, the vibration as the cannon vomited out its shells, the smoke billowing skyward as she pulled up and banked away . . . Everything was crystal clear, engraved on her memory.

She had killed.

Oh, it had to be done . . . but *she* had done it.

She thought now that she understood those senior officers she had met through the years, understood that look in their eyes. It had been a tired look, a weary look.

Now she forgave them. Yet they were wrong.

Jake Grafton was right.

You can't avoid it or wash it off your hands just because you didn't get a Y chromosome and a penis. Oh no.

Little Toadlet inside of me, this world you will come into isn't just flowers and teddy bears. Male or female, you are going to have to live, endure, survive, do the best you can. You must be strong, little one. Somehow, some way, you must find the strength to do what you believe to be right. And the strength to live with it afterward.

CHAPTER TWENTY-FOUR

The cruisers were on the western side of the task force, arranged in a broad semicircle over five miles of ocean. The Tomahawk missiles popped out on cones of flame, rising and accelerating, then nosing over and descending to just a hundred feet above the sea as their turbo-fan engines took over. Missile followed missile, a total of fifteen in all. Their targets were five radar sites between Samarra and the southern border of Iraq, with each radar being the target of three missiles.

The last missile had just disappeared into the darkness when the carrier to the east of the cruisers turned into the wind and the first tow of her aircraft rode the catapults into the night sky, one off the waist, one off the bow. The launch took seven minutes. The planes were still climbing away from the carrier when more Tomahawk missiles rippled from the cruiser's launchers.

Meanwhile a half-dozen AH-64 Apaches were approaching their targets, two more Iraqi radar sites, at just forty feet above the desert sand. Apaches from the 101st Airborne Division had made a similar attack against radar sites only a few miles from these on the opening night of the Gulf War in 1991. The Iraqis had worked for two years to build these replacement sites, which now met the same fate as their predecessors. They were turned into twisted junk by a blizzard of Hellfire missiles, 2.75-inch rockets, and 30mm cannon shells.

Wild Weasel antimissile aircraft were already orbiting over Baghdad. Under their wings were the radar-killing beam-rider missiles that would take out Iraqi fire-control radars when they began transmitting. Since the Gulf War allied aircraft had routinely patrolled the skies over Iraq and they were there again tonight, waiting.

The two C-141s carrying navy SEALs crossed the border at thirty thousand feet on a direct course for the Iraqi air base at Samarra. Someone had suggested a feint toward Baghdad, but Jake Grafton vetoed that. The most valuable target in Iraq was at Samarra. Feints were merely a waste of fuel and precious time.

The Iraqi command center duty officer in Baghdad noticed on his radar presentations the flight of aircraft crossing the Kuwaiti border and another flight coming in from Arabia, all converging on Samarra. This was unusual, the deviation from the standard allied patrolling tactics that he had been briefed to look for. He was about to pick up his telephone when the first of the navy Tomahawk cruise missiles struck its target and one of his radars went blank. Then a second, and a third. Frantically he jiggled the hook on the telephone. The operator came on the line. Alas, Iraq's fiber-optic, state-of-the-art military communications system was heavily damaged during the Gulf War and was still under repair. So the duty officer had to use the civilian telephone system.

'The air base at Samarra, quickly.'

What he would have said to the people at Samarra we will never know, for at that moment a Tomahawk missile penetrated the reinforced concrete wall of this command and control center and six-thousandths of a second after the initial impact its thousand-pound warhead detonated. The people inside the structure never felt a thing – they merely ceased to exist.

The battle had begun.

Flights of A-10 Warthogs and A-6 Intruders raced into the area around Baghdad and Samarra and began attacking antiaircraft missile sites. They were protected by electronic warfare jamming planes and a curtain of chaff that a flight of B-52s was dumping from thirty-six thousand feet.

The SEALs in the C-141s were up and in line. Silent, tense, they watched the red jump light high in the rear of the compartment, above the open ramp that led into cold, black nothingness. Jake Grafton, Toad Tarkington and Jack Yocke were in the middle of the line against the starboard side of the aircraft.

Jack Yocke had switched his mind off. He was running now on adrenaline and instinct.

It was like being back on the high school basketball team waiting for a tipoff, all hot and sweaty, ready to go whichever way the ball bounced.

Once his eyes caught a glimpse of the blackness yawning beyond the lead men, but he ignored it. Then the jump light turned yellow. The man behind him crowded him forward, so he took a step, nudging up toward Toad's back.

He was chanting into the oxygen mask: 'Come on, baby, let's do it! Let's go, go, go, go,' so when the light turned green his muscles surged and he was charging right behind Toad and shouting 'Go, go, go,' and the ramp wasn't there anymore and he was falling, falling, falling into the infinite eternal darkness.

Jake lay spread-eagle in the sky and waited for his eyes to adjust to the near-total darkness. It would have been great if they could have worn the night-vision goggles, but those bulky headsets would have been torn off by the wind blast. In seconds he was up to terminal velocity, 120 miles per hour.

He was still getting oxygen. Fine. So how many seconds had it been?

He scanned, trying to pick up the men who were falling with him. He saw a few shapes in the darkness, but that was all. He concentrated on staring into the blackness below. Nothing was visible, of course, since there was a thin cloud layer at twenty thousand feet. After they were through that the lights of Samarra should be visible underneath, perhaps the air base lights if they were still on, and to the south, the lights of Baghdad.

So he lay there in the sky feeling the cold wind tear at him, maintaining his balance. That was important, and extremely difficult to do in the darkness without a visual reference. All you could do was pray you didn't tumble, and if that happened of course you would know it. Even though the wind was cold, he wasn't freezing. His jumpsuit and clothes seemed to be enough. And as he fell the air would become warmer.

What was down there? Were the Iraqis on full alert, or would the surprise be enough?

Toad Tarkington had a problem. His goggles had somehow come off in the scramble out and now he was squinting against the wind. There was nothing to see, so he scrunched his eyes tightly closed and began counting. 'One, one thousand, two, one thousand, three . . .'

He was falling at the rate of two miles a minute, a mile every thirty seconds. At the end of a minute he should be through the cloud layer. Then he would open his eyes.

This fall was a whole hell of a lot different than the last time he jumped, that time in Nevada when he and Rita had nearly bought the farm.

Actually this wasn't bad. He could feel the cold but he wasn't freezing. And nobody was shooting.

They were going to be shooting on the ground. Toad was certain of that. The most dangerous part of this whole jump was the last few hundred feet, when any Iraqi draftee who could lift a rifle would have a free shot.

The thing to do was to get the weapon out when the parachute deployed and be ready. He rehearsed the moves that he would make, how he would get the weapon free and cycle the bolt. Ahmad the Awful might get his shot at the ol' Horny Toad, but it wouldn't be free.

*

Yocke wasn't counting. He was trying to stabilize himself in the spread-eagle position. He could feel the dizziness of rotation, and try as he might, he couldn't seem to stop it. Damn!

And he had lost track of the time. Well, two minutes and forty seconds was an entire lifetime. He would still be falling like this in the middle of next week if he didn't get stabilized.

He forced himself to spread his arms and hands to full extension. According to the chief who had briefed them, that should stop the tumbling.

But he wasn't spread out. Now he realized that he was almost doubled up at the waist. He was so pumped up he couldn't even tell what position his body was in!

He forced himself to full extension. The rotating feeling slowed. And stopped.

And he was still chanting. 'Go, go, go . . .' He stopped and took a deep, ragged breath.

He stared straight ahead, which must be down. The wind was in his face, trying to pull his arms and legs backward, so straight ahead must be down.

Thirty years of life, and all of it led up to this. School, work, family, women, good moments and bad, and all of it was mere prelude for *this* moment, this free fall into a cold, black eternity.

Jack Yocke began to laugh. He laughed until he choked, then decided he might be getting hysterical, and stopped himself.

How long has it been?

Does it matter?

And the answer came back. *No.*

He fell on toward the waiting earth.

Jake knew he was through the cloud layer when lights suddenly appeared in the velvet blackness below. There was Samarra, and the base almost directly under him. He twisted his head so he could see Baghdad. The navy and air force were doing their job, he noted. In the blackness he saw the wink and twinkle of explosions, here and there jeweled strings of tracers streaking through the darkness at odd angles. No sounds, just muzzle blasts and flashes of warheads and those twinkling strings of tracers.

He tried to steer toward the center of the air base below, that black spot where the runways must intersect.

Now the two-miles-per-minute rate of fall was quite discernible. The lights below were coming up at sickening speed. Even though he had spent years flying tactical aircraft at night, the visual impact of his rate of descent was disconcerting. Would the parachute open?

This question must run through the mind of every free fall parachutist. Jake Grafton had a pragmatic faith in military equipment – through the years he had occasionally witnessed the spectacular, usually fatal, outcome when vital equipment failed.

He pulled his left wrist in, and examined the luminous hands of the wrist altimeter. Three thousand feet still to fall!

How many seconds?

The math was too much. He waited, noting the absence of muzzle flashes. Maybe they had achieved surprise!

Toad's eyes were slits, staring at the lights rushing up at him. He reached for and grasped the manual ripcord. And waited.

The runways were plainly visible, and the hangar. There was a plane!

How high was he? Still a couple –

The opening of the chute almost tore his boots off.

Toad took off the oxygen mask and threw it away, then began checking his equipment. He still had it. All right! He got the submachine gun unslung and checked the magazine.

Still no muzzle flashes on the airfield directly below. Please God, let them be asleep!

*

Jack Yocke was chanting again, some mindless sound he repeated over and over as he fell toward the lights on the earth below.

The air was warmer here. In one corner of his mind he took note of that fact, but the flashing, twinkling lights embedded in the velvet, Stygian blackness claimed the rest of his attention. The lights were coming closer, growing larger. He could even hear muffled explosions. They were having a war down there, and he was falling into it at two miles per minute.

He caught himself fumbling for the ripcord. No. No! *No!*

The lights were rushing toward him now, faster and faster and fast – a tremendous jolt jerked his head up and tore at his crotch.

He yelled. Into the oxygen mask.

And he was hanging by the harness, the fierce wind now a zephyr. He tore at the oxygen mask and succeeded in freeing one side of it.

He was drifting. Where? What was that lighted complex there?

The city! God, he was coming down into the city of Samarra, not the airfield, which was over there to the right. Buildings below, streets . . .

He pulled on the left side of the parachute risers and felt himself slowly turn in the air. Now he was going toward a street. Good! He looked up, trying to see the parachute. He could just make out its vague, winglike shape. Where are those cords that you use to steer it? He fumbled, trying now to find them. Oh well, he was coming down into that street –

Something tore at his feet and he tumbled forward all in a heap, the wind knocked out of him.

He rolled over on his back, gasping.

Alive! Thank God!

Something tugged at his shoulders. The chute was on the ground, tugging in the gentle breeze. Clumsily he got to his feet and fumbled in the darkness for the Koch fittings that held the parachute on. He got them released. The chute began to move away.

He let it go as he stood there staring all about him at the buildings, the windows, the empty street lit by the occasional streetlight. No one about. No Iraqis, which was wonderful, but no SEALs either.

In the pregnant gloom of an Arab street his euphoria gave way to fear.

He scuttled to the doorway of a building and stood sheltered there, looking and listening as the sounds of battle echoed off the buildings. The swelling, fading, then swelling sound of jet engines set his teeth on edge. His hands were shaking, he realized, and he was biting his lip.

Which way was the airfield?

He had no idea. It had been on his right as he descended but he had hit the street and tumbled and lost all sense of direction, so now he gazed upward at the three- and four-story buildings, trying to decide in which direction the airfield lay as the fear congealed into a lump of ice in his chest.

He found that he had the submachine gun in his hands. The hard coolness of the plastic and metal should have comforted him somewhat, but if it did he didn't feel the effect.

As he tried to remember what the map had looked like when he studied it several hours ago surrounded by SEALs – in his former life, before he leaped through that extraordinary threshold from the airplane into the void – he drew a total blank. He had absolutely no idea where in the city he was or in which direction the airfield lay.

He stood paralyzed. He was panting and he was desperately afraid, a freezing, numbing fear that left him unable to think, unable to move.

The parachute finally brought him out of it. The white silk had draped itself around a car and fluttered ever so gently in the wind. Anyone looking out a window would see it. Anyone who came along, anyone who –

Jack Yocke stepped from the safety of the doorway and started along the sidewalk. His steps quickened. He ran.

He had gone several blocks and just crossed a fairly wide street at a hell-bent gallop when he heard the truck. The noise of a big engine at full throttle boomed off the buildings and penetrated his fear-soaked brain. He dove into a doorway as a large army truck thundered across the intersection he had just crossed.

Follow it! Yes. It must be going toward the base.

He waited until the engine noise died away, then willed his legs to move.

He was in the middle of the street when a jet streaked overhead just above the housetops – the thunder of its engines arrived all at once and temporarily deafened Yocke. The glass in several windows broke and fell to the sidewalk. The roar faded almost as fast as it came and left a terrifying silence in its wake.

Someone was looking out a window. He caught a glimpse of a face. He kept going. His pace was slower now, more sure. He wiped the sweat from his face with his right hand, then grasped his weapon again. He held it in front of him, ready.

He had walked for five minutes or so when he heard the first rifle shots. Single shots, then the staccato ripping of an automatic weapon. The reports seemed loud.

When Jake Grafton's chute opened, he bounced once in the harness and breathed a tremendous sigh of relief.

He quickly took off the oxygen mask and grabbed for the steering cords on the parachute risers. He was directly over a big hangar. He didn't have a lot of options, so he steered for the dark area behind it. He seemed to be covering ground quickly. Going downwind. There was no help for it.

The breeze carried him well clear of the hangar. He tried to make out the terrain where he would be coming down. Vague shapes – was that a truck? Then his feet struck something and he took a vicious rap on the left shin.

He smacked into something else, then was on the ground with a thump.

Opening his eyes, he found he was in a parking lot. He had bounced off two trucks before he got to the ground. His shin felt like it was on fire.

He rolled over and tried to get up. His leg took his weight but the pain brought tears into his eyes. Holy—!

He pulled the chute down with the risers. Only then did he unfasten his Koch fittings.

Aagh, his shin! He sat down heavily and felt his left leg. It was swelling rapidly and maybe bleeding, but it didn't seem to be broken.

He got the goggles off, the helmet off, then donned the infrared night vision goggles. He found the switch and adjusted the sensitivity. After replacing his helmet, he wiggled out of the parachute harness and the unopened backup chute. Now for the silenced submachine gun. He tilted the goggles up and made sure it was loaded, with the safety on.

Massaging his shin, he sat there trying to recall where the truck parking area was on the field.

Yes, the hangar he wanted was that big one he had floated over, that one over there.

Jake Grafton got to his feet and gingerly hobbled to the gate. It wasn't locked. He stood there scanning with the goggles.

He could see figures moving out beyond the hangars. These blobs of red stayed low, moving swiftly and surely, then stopped to reconnoitre. SEALs! But closer in . . . there! A sentry by a guard shack, looking out into the darkness. Even as he watched, the sentry contorted and collapsed onto the concrete. Jake scanned. The shooter who had drilled the sentry with a silenced weapon from almost a hundred feet away began to creep along the side of the hangar toward the door.

Jake opened the gate and hobbled toward the hangar as fast as he could go.

The shooter by the hangar wall watched him come. When he was five feet away, the man said, 'Jesus, CAG, what happened to your leg?'

Toad Tarkington!

'Banged it up. You okay?'

'Yeah, I think so. Landed on some concrete. But I don't think this hangar is the one we want. Aren't we on the wrong side of the airfield?'

'You're assuming this is the right airfield.'

'Don't tell me.' Toad Tarkington pulled a compass from his shirt. He consulted it. 'This has got to be the right airfield, but the wrong hangar. Ours is over there.' He pointed.

Missiles streaked overhead before they could react. They heard the explosions of the warheads detonating, then the roar of jet engines at full military power.

More jets. One went over with his cannon spitting bursts.

Jake Grafton sat on the ground. He pulled his map and a pencil flash from a leg pocket and studied it while the jets worked over the Iraqi armor beyond the field perimeter. Finally he replaced the map and flash in his pocket. 'Help me up.'

'How bad's your leg?'

'Ain't broke. Come on. Let's go.'

With Toad leading and Jake hobbling along behind, the two of them headed into the darkness of the center of the field toward the distant hangars on the other side.

They had gone no more than a hundred feet when they heard the small-arms fire. It seemed to be coming from the perimeter.

'Well, they know we're here,' Toad muttered.

They came to a drainage ditch and were wading through the mud in the bottom when they heard the first chopper. It swept across the field only a few feet above the ground without a single light showing. Somewhere off to the left it slowed, almost a hover, then kept going toward the airfield perimeter.

*

Jack Yocke heard the background hum of the chopper engines, and he heard several more of the machines coming across the city. These were the Apaches, he assumed, the gunships that were to act as heavy artillery under the direction of the SEALs on the ground.

But he was on the wrong side of the flight. He was supposed to be inside the airfield perimeter, under cover.

Goddamnit!

Nothing in war ever goes the way you planned it. Wasn't that what Jake Grafton told him as they waited to board the plane?

Explosions ahead. Flashes, and after a few seconds, the noise, which swept down the night streets in waves that could almost be felt. And the roar of automatic gunfire. Burst after burst.

A man opened a second-story window and stuck his head out. He saw Yocke and ducked his head back in.

That lump in the pit of Yocke's stomach turned cold. He was sweating profusely now. Unable to do anything else, he kept going, toward the gunfire.

He came to a corner and approached it carefully. The firing was loud now, no more than a block away. Close against the side of a building and sheltered in darkness, he waited until a helicopter swept over and eased his head around. And found himself staring straight into the face of a man just a few feet away.

Yocke swung the weapon and pulled the trigger. Nothing. *Mother of God! The safety! He tried to find it.*

There was no time. The Iraqi came for him in a rush.

Yocke swung the gun barrel, still trying to find the safety, and literally pushed the man away with the barrel. But he kept coming.

Galvanized, Yocke pushed him again, this time using his left hand.

He felt the bite of the knife on his arm. It stung.

The knife gleamed in the man's right hand as he crouched, then flung himself at the reporter.

Yocke was at least six inches taller than the Iraqi and twenty pounds heavier and his terror gave him tremendous strength, which probably saved his life. Somehow he got hold of the Iraqi's right wrist and began to twist. As the two men fell to the ground the knife came loose.

Yocke got it.

And rammed it into the Iraqi's body. Twice, three times, jabbing with all his strength.

The Iraqi groaned once, almost a scream, then the strength drained from him.

Yocke stabbed him three or four more times, then rolled away.

He lay beside the dead man, trying to get his breath.

Sticky. His hands were sticky and wet.

His arm was burning.

Horrified, he looked at the blood. On his hands, his arm, his clothes, the gear he wore. On the Iraqi. Smeared on the sidewalk.

Jack Yocke managed to get to his feet and stood swaying as the sounds of battle came echoing down the empty street. Amazingly, he discovered he still had the knife in his hand. He opened his fingers. The knife made a hollow sound when it bounced on the sidewalk.

Sobbing, Yocke examined the submachine gun still slung around his shoulders and found the safety. He flicked it off.

The Apache helicopters were pouring fire into an area by the main gate, about two hundred yards away, as Jake Grafton and Toad Tarkington lay in the darkness on the edge of the concrete parking mat and studied the hangar looming ahead of them. Lights mounted above the center of the main door and by a sentry box at the left corner were still illuminated.

What the lights revealed were bodies. Jake counted. Eight. Even as he watched, one of the men lying near the hangar moved, and drew immediate fire from out of the darkness on Jake's right. With the goggles on, Jake could see the prone figure who had just fired.

'The SEALs are here,' Toad whispered. 'Isn't this Saddam's safety-deposit box, the Treasure Chest?'

'I think so.'

'There's a personnel door over behind that sentry box. We might be able to get in there.'

'Let's check in first. Keep an eye peeled.'

Jake extracted his radio and fumbled with the switches. Then he held it to his ear and keyed the mike. 'Snake One, this is the Doctor.' Snake One was the commanding officer of the SEALs team, Commander Lester Slick. Slick was a hell of a name for a naval officer but if anyone snickered they did it well away from Lester, who had the body of a professional wrestler and the scarred face of a man who liked to fight and had done far too much of it.

'Snake One, aye. Say your posit.'

'By the target hangar, west side.'

'Wait one.'

They waited in the darkness, listening to the battle. Jake removed his night vision goggles and let his eyes adjust.

The radio squawked. 'Snake One, this is Snake Four. There's four of us out here in the middle of a whole god-damn raghead platoon.'

'Fight your way in, Snake Four. You're behind schedule.'

That was Lester Slick. If you wanted sympathy, write home to mama.

'Roger.'

Jake looked at his watch. In six minutes the first of the Blackhawks was scheduled to arrive.

'Okay, gang, this is Snake One. Let's start moving in on the Treasure Chest.'

Jake and Toad rose from the ground and scuttled toward the hangar. As they came into the light he saw five other men, SEALs, coming at a trot. 'Let's get inside,' Jake told Toad, and went for the personnel door by the sentry box.

Jake opened the door and stepped into a foyer, a dead

space to keep out blowing sand. Toad was right behind him. They paused and listened, then Toad opened the inner door several inches while Jake peeked through the opening. He stepped back and motioned for Toad to close the door.

'Over a dozen men. Some armed,' Jake whispered.

'The nukes?'

'A lot of them.'

'Whoo boy!'

'There's a door in the east side, by the aircraft door,' Jake said. 'It's open. I'm gonna step out and look around the corner. Open the door for me.' His heart was hammering, he was perspiring freely, and he was breathing hard, as if he had run ten miles, but when Toad opened the door he slipped back outside.

The light over the doorway outside had to go. Jake reached up and broke it with the silencer on the end of the submachine gun. Then he inched his head around the corner of the hangar. Just bodies visible. He ran the length of the building as fast as his sore leg would allow and paused at the next corner by the sentry box, then cautiously inched his head out.

There was a trailer or something, a dozen or so armed Iraqis, some of them looking this way. He jerked his head back.

The fat was in the fire. They must have seen him. A grenade!

He got one from his web belt, pulled the pin, then threw it as hard as he could around the corner. When it blew he leaned out a few inches and let go with the silenced weapon.

Three men were down. The nearest man was picking himself up off the concrete, just twenty feet away. Jake's slugs smacked him and he went over backward, his weapon flying. Jake sprayed another burst at the men by the trailer, then ducked back into shelter.

Bullets splattered into the metal of the hangar just above his head as the ripping of a weapon echoed off the clustered buildings. Jake crouched, looking for the muzzle blasts. There! He squeezed off a burst as he scuttled sideways for the dubious safety of the sentry box.

More bullets spanged in.

Now he took his time, sighting carefully: this was what the Iraqi hadn't done. He squeezed the trigger and held the muzzle down. And saw the Iraqi fall from behind a barrel where he had taken cover.

Quickly he took the empty magazine from his weapon and inserted another. Now back to the corner. Another burst at figures now trying to get behind the trailer.

There was a car there. A car? A limo, it looked like.

Shots from inside the hangar. Toad must have gone in.

Jake heaved another grenade.

After it exploded, he looked again. The car was right beside the trailer, the passenger door open. Two men were hosing lead in this direction. The car was also facing this way.

Jake got down on his belly and aimed his weapon at the front tires of the car. The two men who were upright now went down, dropping their weapons. Jake gave the tires a whole clip.

New magazine inserted.

Even though its front tires were flat, the limo started to move. Grafton pumped a burst into the engine compartment and watched as a cloud of steam came out. The limo stopped.

The gunfire on the western side of the base was building into a sustained racket. Grafton looked around. A SEAL was running toward him, his weapon at the ready.

The SEAL flopped down behind Jake. 'Go into the hangar and help out,' Jake said. 'One of our guys is in there. Be careful where you shoot.'

Without a word the other man got up and went into the hangar.

Jake lay where he was, watching the limo and the trailer by the hangar wall. No one moved.

A helicopter swept over. Then another. Running without lights. Rockets rippled from a third machine and streaked away to the west. Now Jake heard the roar of a 30mm cannon. This machine was barely moving, pouring fire at several tanks just outside the perimeter fence. The wash from the rotors of this machine fanned Jake.

Two figures rose from a low place out on the airfield and came slowly this way, bent at the waist. They stopped and crouched occasionally. They approached the car.

'Don't shoot him,' Jake shouted during a momentary lull in the gunship barrage going on just behind him. 'Take him into the hangar.'

With that he got up and opened the hangar door.

Inside the foyer he wiped the perspiration from his eyes, got a good grip on the submachine gun, then jerked open the interior door and dived through.

He slid right into the body of an Iraqi soldier. His throat had been cut. More bodies lay near the eastern door, the one that led to where the trailer was parked. Jake inched forward and looked carefully around. A group of Iraqis was standing near the west wall of the hangar with their hands up. Three missiles on trailers sat against the north wall, and here and there, several compact, cylindrical devices – warheads. Piles of wooden crates sat in one corner. A Scud on its launcher sat against the west wall.

'Toad?' Jake made it loud, because the noise from outside was reverberating inside the large metal building.

'Over here, CAG.'

'Everything under control?'

'Seems to be.'

'Are you behind something?'

'Yes, sir.'

'Stay there. I'm gonna take a look out this east door.'

Jake walked across the hangar warily. He didn't take time to count the warheads, but there were a lot of them.

Approaching the door he stepped to one side. The door was ajar. He eased it open and inched his head around the jamb for a look. This was, of course, an excellent way to get his brains blown out, but right now didn't seem to be the time to play it safe.

Three bodies were lying near the door. Four more were visible to the right, toward the south. And fifty feet away the limo still sat, the two SEALs kneeling behind it. Jake stepped out and walked toward them.

'There were about a dozen men here when I first saw them. Did you guys see where the others went?'

'They went hoofing it toward the north. There's a network of trenches over there, I think. You'll find their bodies about fifty yards up that way.'

As helicopters crossed above and the whuff of Hellfire missiles and rockets being launched washed over them, one of the SEALs seized the front door of the car and jerked it open. The driver sat with his hands on the steering wheel, offering no resistance. 'This guy's been watching too many American cop movies. Okay, Ahmad, outta there.'

The rear door on Jake's side of the car opened. He stood ready, the submachine gun leveled, his finger on the trigger. First a leg came out, a leg clad in uniform trousers. Then an arm and head, then the man was standing there. He was bareheaded, wore a long-sleeved uniform shirt without a tie or jacket, and had a thin brush mustache on his upper lip.

Jake gestured with his gun. 'Raise 'em.'

The man obeyed.

'Okay, Saddam,' Jake said, stepping aside and jerking his left thumb at the door, 'let's join the others at the party.'

Jake stopped outside the door and got out his radio. He selected the proper channel and checked in. 'The weapons are here. The dance is on.'

He waited for an acknowledgment, then turned down the volume of the radio to save the battery. He kept it in his hand though.

Right now the SEALs were establishing a perimeter around this building and locating the remainder of the Iraqi Republican Guard troops. The Apaches were working over the Republican Guard camp and the nearby barracks. Yet this was makeshift, a temporary expedient until the helicopters with the 101st Airborne Air Assault troops and their heavy weapons arrived. Outside the base fighter-bombers would attack the Republican Guard without mercy and hopefully prevent Iraqi troops from amassing sufficient combat power to retake the base or hinder the American buildup. As usual in modern war, timing, mobility, and firepower were the key.

Commander Lester Slick came striding in. His radio was also squawking in his hand. 'Admiral, we have four dead that I know of and about twenty men unaccounted for. One of them is the reporter.'

Jake merely nodded.

'We've scouted out most of the base and neutralized some of the opposition, but the bulk of my men are setting up lights for helo landing zones. The choppers should be here in about a minute, sir.'

'Runways intact?'

'Appear to be, sir.'

'So how are we doing?'

'We're right on schedule. Less resistance than we anticipated from the Republican guard, which is a blessing.'

'Let's stay on schedule. When you can, send me a couple more men to guard these prisoners. And if you come across the reporter, send him in here.'

'Aye aye, sir.'

The buildings of the town ended abruptly. Beyond was a sandy area, then the fence that encircled the airfield. And the fence had a hole in it, a fairly big hole that was just visible in the muted light from the town. The edge of the wire was curled and one post was awry. Beyond the hole was nothing, just darkness.

Jack Yocke lay against the side of a building facing the fence. From where he lay he could see the body of a man lying facedown, half-buried in the sand. Yocke could see the entire length of the body, which lay about twenty feet away. The US style helmet was quite plain, the parachute pack on the back, the weapon, the desert camouflage trousers, the desert boots.

From the angle of the head against the shoulders, it was obvious that the man's neck was broken. And probably half the other bones in his body.

Yocke shifted his gaze. He watched the muzzle blasts of the helicopters making runs on the Iraqi troops outside the base and the streaks the Hellfire missiles made.

To the east pulsing fingers of antiaircraft fire was rising into the night sky. The strings of tracers seemed to be probing randomly, without purpose. Even as he watched he saw the flashes of bombs exploding on the horizon, where the guns must be. The guns fell silent.

He picked up a handful of sand and idly let it run through his fingers. Then he studied the hole in the fence some more.

Well, there it was – a way into the air base. All he had to do was run for it.

It was too good to be true, really. And that was why he was lying here looking.

He concentrated on the problem, tried to think objectively about the hole in the fence. Why was it there? Perhaps the Iraqis were just sloppy. Well, that made sense. The streets and buildings he had come through were certainly Third World ratty.

He looked left. No one in sight.

Right. The same.

But . . . it didn't feel right. Something was wrong.

His contemplation of the problem was interrupted by a chopper that came from over the city behind him and swept across the fence, merely a black, fast-moving shape, then laid into a right turn. He was watching as the streak

403

came in from the right and intersected the chopper. Then it exploded. A white flash registered on his brain, then a red-yellow fireball, then the wreckage was angling downward. It hit the ground and fire splashed forward in the direction the machine had been traveling.

Even from this distance, Yocke could faintly feel the heat against his cheeks.

The fire burned fiercely for several minutes, then subsided. Finally it winked out, leaving the darkness beyond the fence even blacker than before.

Yocke looked right and left again, then began to crawl. Across the street onto the sand, toward the dead American sailor. Murphy. That was the name on his clothes.

After one more look around, Yocke got to his feet. Hunched over to present the smallest silhouette possible, he made for the fence.

He was twenty feet from the hole in the wire when he saw the helmet. He took two more steps before he saw that the helmet still had a head on it. And there on the wire, a piece of cloth. No, an arm, with a hand attached.

Jack Yocke froze.

Now he saw the hole in the ground under the tear in the fence.

Mines!

He was standing in a minefield.

He looked wildly around, trying to see the triggers. All he could make out in the gloom was sand and trash.

Off to the right – there, something moving. Only Yocke's eyes moved. A soldier, coming this way. An Iraqi!

In front of him was the hole that led into the beckoning darkness. More pieces of the American sailor who must have tripped the mine. Fifteen feet. No more. Tracks.

Tracks! He could see where the doomed man had stepped.

Yocke moved. One step. Two. Three.

A bullet sang over his head. And another.

He ran. Straight through the hole in the wire and on for

fifty or sixty feet as bullets cut the air near him and one tugged at the equipment on his back.

Finally he threw himself down and spun around facing back the way he had come. The land was so flat that through the fence he could still see the Iraqi who had been shooting at him. The helmeted man was bent over, working with the action of his rifle. A bolt action rifle!

Jack Yocke's weapon was in his hands. He sighted it carefully, as carefully as he could as he struggled to control his breathing. Now he pulled the trigger. He held the trigger down as the weapon vibrated in his hands.

The last shell flew out and he wrestled the empty magazine out of the gun and slammed in a new one.

Now he saw that the Iraqi was down. Lying on the sidewalk, barely visible in the half-light.

Yocke sighted carefully at the prone figure. Again he pulled the trigger and held it down. He fired the whole magazine, then lay still in the darkness listening to his heart thudding. Only then did it come to him that the man he had just killed had probably been even more scared than he was. A bolt-action rifle – missing bang, bang, bang . . . at that range! Probably a recent draftee, maybe militia.

Yocke began sobbing again.

CHAPTER TWENTY-FIVE

Rita was wearing the headset and listening to the radio traffic and conversation between the two pilots as they approached the Samarra air base through the southern corridor. Two sanitary corridors had been hacked through the Iraqi defenses by the allied jets and attack helicopters, which had pulverized every antiaircraft weapon and fire-control radar that they could locate.

Still, there was no way that the gunships could kill every Iraqi with a rifle, so Rita and the people in the chopper with her were wearing flak vests and sitting on extra ones. They were also trying to make themselves very small.

You hunch up, move self-consciously into the fetal position, and you wait. You wait for that random bullet to find your flesh.

Those bullets were out there zinging through the darkness. Occasionally one struck the helicopter. Several times Rita thought she could feel the delicate thump and once the pilot commented. Fortunately the helicopter was flying perfectly with all its equipment functioning as it should.

Still you draw your legs up and tuck your hands under the flak vest and wait for random death. The seconds tick by. You become aware of the beating of your heart. Stimulated by adrenaline, your mind wanders uncontrollably.

Violent death happens to other people — it won't happen to me. No bullet will rip my flesh or open arteries or smash bone or tear through that delicate mass of neurons and brain cells that makes me me. No.

She was focused inward, waiting, when she heard the pilot gag and felt the chopper pitch abruptly sideways. The copilot cursed.

'Let go of the stick, Bill! Goddamn, *let go of the fucking stick!*'

Standing in the door, Rita reached over the pilot slumped in the right seat. He had a death grip on the stick. The bucking chopper threw her off balance.

'Unstrap him,' the copilot urged Rita over the ICS. 'Get him out of the seat. Bill, leggo the fucking stick!'

She released the shoulder Koch fittings of the pilot's harness and leaned forward for the lap fittings. The cyclic stick and his hand were right there. The copilot was wrestling the cyclic with both hands. The chopper was bucking. Rita grabbed.

'Get him outta the seat,' the copilot demanded.

She released one lap fitting and fumbled for the other. The dying man was jerking the cyclic stick and the machine was obeying. Rita lost her footing. She regained it and hung herself over the back of the seat.

There. He was no longer attached to the seat.

'Get him *out!*'

Rita grabbed his shoulders and pulled. Oh God, he was heavy.

She braced herself and gave a mighty heave.

The pilot came half out of the seat but he still kept his death grip on the cyclic stick.

His helmet, with the wires. She tore it off his head.

She grabbed him again, two handfuls of harness, braced her right leg against the back of the seat and pulled with all her strength.

He came out of the seat and Rita kept pulling and the two of them tumbled backward into the passenger compartment, the wounded pilot on top.

She fumbled for her flashlight. The beam showed blood. He was shot in the face. His eyes were unfocused, blood flowing.

'He took a bullet in the face,' she told the copilot.

'Five minutes. We'll be on the ground in five minutes. Keep him alive.'

How do you keep a man alive who has been shot an inch under the right eye?

Then she realized that the convulsions had stopped. He was limp. Rita Moravia found a wrist and felt for his pulse. Still a flicker.

Since there was nothing else to do, she cradled him in her arms and hugged him.

How long Jack Yocke lay in the sandy dirt he didn't know. The noise of the helicopters and the explosions and concussions that reached him through the earth finally subsided, so he levered himself from the ground and began walking. He walked until the exhaustion hit him, then he sat down in the sand beside a runway. He was sitting there unable to summon the energy to move when he heard the crunch of a boot in the sand.

Yocke grabbed his weapon and ran his fingers over the action, trying to brush off the sand.

'Hey, shipmate! What're you doing out here?'

'Uh ...' Relief flooded Yocke and he tried to collect his thoughts. He gestured toward the fence, back there somewhere behind him. 'His chute didn't open. Murphy. His name was Murphy.'

The man came over for a look.

'You're one of the SEALs, right?'

'No, but I jumped with them.'

'Better get over to the hangar. We're setting up a perimeter along the fence.'

'There's mines on the other side.'

'You came down in town?'

'Uh-huh.'

'How bad are you hurt? You got a lot of blood on you.'

'Most of it isn't mine.'

'Medic over by the hangar. Move along now, buddy.'

'Where?'

The sailor pointed.

'Thanks.'

Yocke placed his weapon in the crook of his arm and began walking. He had gone about ten paces when the man behind him called, 'Better move it on out, shipmate, because the main wave of Blackhawks are overdue. They're going to land right here. Fact is, I can hear 'em now.'

In spite of his exhaustion and all the gear he was still wearing, Jack Yocke dutifully broke into a trot. When he too heard the swelling whine of the oncoming engines his gait became a run.

Yocke paused by the door of the hangar and watched four Blackhawks settle in and disgorge more troops. The men came pouring out just before the wheels hit the runway, then the choppers were gone in a blast of rotor wash and noise. Choppers with underslung artillery pieces were next. When the slings were released, these machines also kissed the earth and more men came out running, then they were gone.

The choppers brought machine guns, ammo, artillery, antitank weapons, com gear, and men, many men. By the time the fourth wave came in, the artillery pieces from the first wave were banging off rounds toward the east.

Above him three huge choppers materialized in the darkness – Sky Cranes, with pallets under their bellies.

Jack Yocke turned his back and went through the hangar door.

The first things he saw inside were the missiles. The long, white pointed cylinders still wore red stars on their flanks. He stood for several seconds staring before he saw the warheads – yes, those things were warheads – sitting on wooden forklift flats. He began to count.

Thirty-two of them. And missiles sporting red stars.

And against the far wall, a missile on another truck, but

this one was different – it had Arabic script on the side near the nose and sported a black, white and red flag. A Scud!

In front of the Scud launcher stood a row of Iraqis with their hands up. Several SEALs and US soldiers guarded them.

He was still standing there inspecting the warheads, taking it all in, when a group of people came trotting through the door with Captain Collins in the lead. Yocke recognized the British soldier, Jocko West, who was carrying a box of something. Another of the men was Rheinhart. West and Rheinhart immediately opened and began unpacking the box they had slung between them. Jack stayed behind Collins and watched as the muffled noise of war thudded through the hangar.

'The hot stuff is still in these warheads,' Collins said to Colonel Galvano, who was busy with a radiation counter.

'There is much background radiation, *Comandante*.'

'I'll bet these idiots didn't even hose down these weapons when they brought them here,' Jocko West muttered, then added, 'Let's open the hangar doors and start loading these things.'

Yocke wandered over to look at the prisoners. Most of them were Iraqis, but several were Russians. They didn't look happy. One of the Russians was trying to talk to an American soldier in English. 'I go, *da*? With you? You take us?'

'Keep your hands where I can see them, Boris.'

'Seen Admiral Grafton, soldier?' Yocke asked.

'He's in one of those offices behind the missiles,' the soldier said.

Yocke thanked him and walked in the indicated direction. One of the office doors was open. Yocke stepped in.

'Didn't fit. They're too big,' Spiro Dalworth was telling Jake Grafton. Three Russians sat in chairs. 'They cannot be made to fit without completely altering the structure of the missile.' More Russian. 'Hussein shot two of our men. Shot with a pistol, one bullet each. In the head. He told us we would make the warheads fit.'

'Are these all the warheads and missiles? Have the Iraqis taken any of the warheads anywhere else?' Jake asked this question and Dalworth spewed it out in Russian.

'*Nyet.*'

'All the weapons are here.'

Toad moved over beside Yocke. 'You look like one of Dracula's afternoon snacks,' Toad whispered. 'If all that blood is yours you must be a couple quarts low.'

Jack Yocke just shook his head. 'What's happening?'

'It was screwed up from the beginning,' Toad muttered. 'The warheads are out of bigger, heavier Soviet missiles. Saddam wanted them installed in the Scuds but they wouldn't fit. World-class problem solver that he is, he wouldn't take no for an answer.'

'So he shot two Russians?'

'To motivate the others. Terrific leadership technique, huh?'

'How about the missiles they have sitting out there? Why didn't he roll them out and tell the world to kiss its ass good-bye.'

Toad leaned closer to Yocke's ear. 'Those missiles don't have any guidance systems. Oh, the warheads are there, the fuel and all the rest of it. But without guidance systems . . .'

And Jack Yocke nodded. Russia, the land where nothing works, where shortages are endemic. It was sort of funny, really. Saddam, The Awesome, makes a sharp deal and the Russians give him the shaft.

'Can I print this?'

'That's up to the admiral.'

'This whole . . . thing, a goddamn fuck-up?'

'Sometimes the best-laid plans . . .'

A half-million Russians dead, another half-million or million or two million doomed, Americans dying outside, Iraqis . . . all because some Russian politicians desperately needed money and Saddam Hussein wants to be the Arab Stalin!

And he himself had just killed two men. So he could go on breathing and write the big stories . . . about how fucked up the world is!

Yocke walked over to a corner and plopped down. Suddenly he had a raging thirst. He got out his canteen and took a long drink, then another. He was nursing the water and listening to the translators when the first television crew arrived. The camera man was dragging the end of a cable, which went out the door. Another man set up some lights.

'Can we film in here?' the reporter asked Grafton.

'Have right at it,' the admiral said, and got out of his chair. 'Interview these Russians.' Jake gestured at Toad. The two of them left the room together.

There was a massive steel beam that formed an angle with one of the upright supports on the wall. Staring at it and listening to the CNN reporter's breathless delivery into the camera, Jack Yocke got an idea. He removed the magazine from his weapon. Then he wedged the silencer and barrel of the piece into the junction of the beam and angular support. Now he pulled with all his might. He paused, braced his feet, then put his weight into it. The barrel bent. With sweat popping on his forehead he made a supreme effort. The bend got bigger. When the barrel had bent about thirty degrees the stock shattered. Yocke removed the remains of the submachine gun from the joint, inspected it, then tossed it on the floor.

Everyone was watching the television reporter interview the Russian technicians.

Jack Yocke wandered out of the room with his hands in his pockets, lost in thought.

The air base was secure. For the moment. Approximately a hundred casualties, about thirty of them fatal. The 101st Airborne assault commander wanted to be gone in three hours, at least an hour before he estimated that the Iraqis could put together an armored assault. Although he had real-time communications via satellite with headquarters in Arabia and thought he had the air power available to stop any conceivable Iraqi military effort, he didn't want to take any more chances or casualties than he had to.

Jake Grafton listened to the report and nodded. He had no questions. The little knot of officers stood in one corner of the hangar watching technicians load the warheads onto pallets with forklifts. Through the open doors came the whine of helicopter engines at idle and the pulsating thud of turning rotors. This noise almost drowned out the distant bark of artillery, which was shelling known remnants of Iraqi forces to prevent their concentration. Almost drowned it out, but not quite.

Someone handed Jake Grafton a paper cup full of coffee. Beside him someone else lit a cigarette.

'Can you spare the rest of that pack of cigarettes?'

'Sure, Admiral.'

'And the lighter.'

The staff officer handed it over. 'I didn't know you smoked, sir.'

'I don't.'

As he walked across the hangar Jake saw Jack Yocke standing with his hands in his pockets. He looked tired and pensive, the flesh of his face tightly drawn across the bones. 'You okay?' Jake asked.

'Yes, sir.'

'Come with me,' Jake said and walked on.

'I've seen enough,' Yocke told the admiral's back. Jake Grafton acted like he hadn't heard. Yocke quickened his pace to catch up. 'I've had enough.'

The admiral didn't even look at him. 'Who hasn't?' he muttered.

The marine guard outside the door of the room where General Yakolev and Marshal Mikhailov were being held saluted Jake as he approached. Rita Moravia was standing beside him, and she also saluted.

'Are you injured?' Jake Grafton asked. She had blood on the front of her flight suit.

413

'No, sir. We arrived fifteen minutes ago. Our pilot was killed by small-arms fire.'

'Is the machine airworthy?'

'I think so, sir. We took a couple of other hits, but nothing vital. They're refueling now from a bladder that one of the Sky Cranes brought in. We'll be ready to leave in another fifteen minutes or so.'

'Fine. Have the Russians had anything to say?'

'No, sir. Lieutenant Dalworth is inside with them now, just in case.'

Jake nodded and opened the door. Jack Yocke followed him into the room. Dalworth stood up. 'Thank you, Lieutenant. Let me have a few minutes alone with these gentlemen.'

'Yessir.'

When the door closed behind Dalworth, Jake sat down at the table across from Yakolev and passed him the pack of cigarettes and the lighter. Yocke took a chair in a corner.

'A last cigarette, Admiral?' Nicolai Yakolev muttered. He took one and offered the pack to Mikhailov, who also stuck one in his mouth.

'Perhaps. We'll get to that.'

'At least these aren't Russian cigarettes.'

Yakolev glanced at Yocke, who was getting out his notebook. Mikhailov concentrated on savoring his cigarette and ignored Jake. He looked exhausted, shrunken, the lines around his eyes and mouth now deeply cut slashes. He looked old. The marshal didn't speak English, Jake remembered.

'Who is he?' Yakolev inclined his head an eighth of an inch at Yocke.'

'A reporter.'

'A *reporter?*'

'That's right. His speciality is news that isn't fit to print.'

Yakolev closed his eyes. He took an experimental drag on the cigarette, sucked the smoke deep into his lungs, then exhaled through his nose.

'So explain to me, General,' Jake said, 'how the hell you got yourself into this fucking mess.'

'You want the history of Russia in the twentieth century? For an American newspaper? Will this be deep background or a Sunday thinkpiece?'

'Just curious.'

'Another philosopher,' Yakolev said heavily.' I give you some good advice, Admiral. While you wear that uniform you cannot afford to be a philosopher, to ponder the nuances of good and evil. You do the best for your country that you can and live or die with the results. That's what the uniform means.'

'Blowing up a reactor? Poisoning hundreds of thousands of your own countrymen? You did *that* for your country?'

Yakolev smoked the first cigarette in silence, then lit another off the butt of the first one and puffed several times to ensure it was lit. Under his heavy eyebrows his eyes scanned Jake Grafton's face carefully.

'Russia is disintegrating,' the Russian general said finally. 'Very soon it will be like Somalia, without government, without law, without civilization, without food for its people. We are not talking about a return to the Dark Ages, Admiral, but a return to the Stone Age. Roving bands of armed thugs, mass starvation, epidemics, a complete breakdown of the social order – to survive, future Russians will become vicious, starving rats fighting on the dung heap.'

Yakolev glanced at Mikhailov, then continued. 'Already it has begun in the countryside, in the republics, in little towns in Russia that your news media does not cover, on the farms where there is no one to see the babies and old people starve, no one to watch or care as people die of pneumonia and tuberculosis. No agriculture, no food, no fuel, no transportation, no medical care, no electricity, no one to protect those who cannot protect themselves, violence leading to ethnic warfare, feuds building toward genocide – it is here *now!*

'In Moscow the ministries are corrupt from top to bottom. A small number of bureaucrats trade in dollars and live well while the rest of Russia – the rest of the Soviet Union – sinks deeper and deeper into the morass of starvation. *This* is what the future looks like when this grand scheme you call civilization collapses.'

He shifted his weight in his chair. Mikhailov said something, to which Yakolev gave a short reply. Then he turned his attention back to Jake. 'You Americans, with your television eyes. You look at Yeltsin and expect him to create miracles with his mouth! Those political swine – hot air is all they are good for.'

Yakolev leaned forward and reached for another cigarette. 'That is why.'

In the silence that followed, the sounds of a helicopter going overhead penetrated the room, followed by distant explosions.

'Do you have any regrets?' Jake Grafton asked when it became obvious Yakolev felt his explanation was sufficient.

'Regrets?' Yakolev said the word bitterly. 'Oh, yes!' His head bobbed. 'I wish the God the Communists swore did not exist had given this stupid sack of shit sitting beside me some balls. If he had had some balls we would have shot Yeltsin. We would have thrown the selfish swine out of the Congress of People's Deputies. We would have gone through the ministries and shot every corrupt bastard that we could lay hands on. We would have hunted down the thugs terrorizing the countryside and slaughtered them like rabbits. Then we would have made the farmers grow food and the trains run and people would have had food to eat. Regrets? To watch your country die while the politicians argue and the cowards wring their hands? Yes, Admiral, I have regrets.'

'Why didn't you shoot him first?'

'That is what I should have done.' Yakolev leaned back in his chair and rubbed his face. 'Ahh, I am old and tired. I have lived too long. I have seen too much. I am ready to die.'

'The world is going to hell, so you played God.'

'You Americans have a phrase that seems a perfect reply to sanctimonious comments like that: fuck you.'

'You won't get off that easy,' Jake Grafton said. His voice had an edge to it. 'Russia is in the mess it's in because of people like you, because czars and dictators and administrators used pens to authorize murder. "It had to be done." "*I* had to do it." "*I am responsible and I know the way things have to be, so they have to die!*"

'You Commie messiahs think your people are pigs. For them you have the profoundest contempt. They are too ignorant, too stupid, too blind to see what's good for them, so they must be taken care of by wise men like you. You feed, clothe, and house them, keep them warm in the winter, and slaughter them when necessary. All for their own good. It's just too goddamn bad they don't understand how wonderful it is that learned, wise, responsible men like you are willing to get their hands dirty running the hog farm.'

Jake Grafton leaned forward in his chair. '*What if you're wrong?*'

'We weren't wrong.'

'Don't give me that *shit!*' Grafton roared. 'Lenin was wrong, Stalin was wrong, you're wrong! I'm sick to death of you self-anointed messiahs willing to murder half the people on earth to save the other half, the half you're in. You make me want to vomit!'

Yakolev said nothing, merely reached for another cigarette.

'We have another one out there' – Jake pointed toward the hangar bay – 'ready to slaughter everyone alive who doesn't agree with him. Now I tell you this – it's time for all of us little people to take a page from the book of you prophets of doom and damnation.' He stared at Yakolev.

The Russian sneered. 'So you brought two Russian villains to Iraq to parade in front of your cameras. The folks at home can see the dirty devils on CNN, prisoners of the victorious, virtuous Americans.'

'No. I brought you here to help me solve a problem. I need your help.'

'Help?' Yakolev laughed, a dry, vicious bark.

'As one soldier to another.'

The laughter died. Nicolai Yakolev's face twisted again. 'You tell me I have no honor, then you appeal to it.' He spit on the table, in Jake's direction. 'I am not a coward! I am not afraid of death. I do not fear a bullet.'

'I know that,' Jake said gently.

'I have two sons and a daughter. They have children.'

'A trial . . .'

'When?'

'You'll know when the time comes.'

Yakolev glanced again at Jack Yocke, then shrugged. 'I'll think about it. For you personally I would do nothing.'

Jake Grafton rose from the chair and started for the door. 'Come on, Jack.'

Out in the hangar bay Yocke wanted to know, 'What was that all about?'

'About doing the right thing, for a change.'

'Like what?'

'You'll figure it out.'

The room had a table in it about eight feet long. And chairs. At one end of the table sat Saddam Hussein, who glowered at Jake Grafton and Jack Yocke when they came in. He roared something in Arabic. The translator said to Jake, 'He wants to know if you are in charge, sir.'

'I'm one of the officers in charge, yes,' Jake said as he motioned to the two soldiers on guard duty to leave the room.

Hussein ignored Yocke, who leaned against the wall opposite the translator, and directed his remarks at Jake.

'The United States makes war upon Iraq,' the translator said. 'You meddle in affairs that are none of your business.'

Hussein's hands were bound with a single plastic tie in front of him, so he waved them, now stopped and shook his doubled-up fists: 'How long, how long, until you nonbelievers stop raping our daughters? How long until you stop defiling the sacred places? How long until you leave the children of God to worship as the Prophet taught us?'

Toad came over to Jake and handed him a pistol, a 9mm automatic. 'We took this off him.'

Saddam thundered on: 'You violate the sovereignty of this nation, of this people. You shoot down Iraqi airplanes over Iraq, you send inspectors to hunt through our offices, you—'

Jake Grafton fired the pistol into the ceiling. The deafening report stopped the flow of words.

The spent casing slapped against the wall and fell to the floor with a tinny, metallic sound.

'I have a question,' Jake said softly to the translator. 'Ask him how many Iraqis he has killed with this pistol.'

The translator did so.

Hussein sat in silence, saying nothing.

'How many Iranians?'

Silence.

'How many Kuwaitis?

'How many Kurds?

'How many Shiites?

Unbroken silence.

'If you don't know or can't remember how many men you have personally murdered, perhaps you can tell me how many have died at your orders?'

Saddam Hussein's eyes were mere slits.

'When you are dead will they hold a great funeral, or will they drag your corpse through the streets and burn it on a dung heap?'

When he heard the translation Saddam Hussein opened

his mouth to speak, then apparently decided not to. He looked at the translator, at Jack Yocke, then let his gaze return to Jake Grafton.

The automatic was heavy. Jake Grafton stared at it, examined the safety, the hammer, the maker's name stamped into the metal. Then slowly he removed his own pistol, a .357 Magnum Smith & Wesson revolver, and hefted it thoughtfully.

He laid the revolver about a foot from his right hand, then gave the automatic a gentle shove with his left. It slid down the table and came to rest about a foot or so in front of the Iraqi dictator, the barrel pointing out to one side.

'Let's settle this right there,' Jake said. 'You have killed many men – one more certainly won't matter on Allah's scales. And an unbeliever to boot. Go ahead! You grab for yours and I'll grab for mine and we'll kill each other.'

As the translator rattled this off Jake studied the Iraqi's face. It had gone white. Beads of sweat were coalescing into little rivulets that ran down beside Hussein's nose and dripped off his mustache. Stains were rapidly spreading across his shirt from under each armpit.

'You've seen cowboy movies, haven't you? Let's shoot it out, you simple, filthy son of a bitch.'

Hussein sat frozen. He didn't even glance at the automatic within his grasp.

'*Pick it up,*' Jake Grafton roared.

Hussein sat silently while Jake regained his composure. He took several deep breaths, then said, 'This is your last chance to go out like a man. The next time you will get the same chance you gave your minister of health, the same chance you give the people you send your thugs to kill, the same chance you were going to give the people those bombs out there were meant for, which is none at all. *This* is your *only* chance!'

Seconds passed. A tic developed in Hussein's left eyelid. As the twitching became worse, he raised his hands and rubbed his eye. Finally he lowered his hands back to his lap.

Jake reached for the revolver. As he grasped it the Iraqi started visibly. The admiral rose from his chair, and holding the revolver in his right hand, retrieved the automatic. He stuck it into his belt.

After one last look at the dictator, Jake Grafton turned and left the room.

Jack Yocke had stood throughout this exchange. Now he pulled a chair away from the table and dropped into it. He got out his notebook and mechanical pencil and very carefully wrote the date on a clean sheet of paper. Beside it he wrote the dictator's name.

He looked at Hussein, who was staring at the open door. An armed American soldier stood there gazing back at him.

Jack Yocke cleared his throat and caught the attention of the interpreter, who had also pulled up a chair. 'I was wondering, Mr President,' Yocke said, 'if you'd care to grant me an interview for the *Washington Post.*'

Fifteen minutes later Jake Grafton came back through that door, followed by the two Russian generals. Captain Iron Mike McElroy was behind them, cradling a submachine gun in his arms. Then came a television reporter and cameraman and two technicians with lights and cables in coils over their shoulders.

Jack Yocke got out of his chair and leaned against a wall. Toad Tarkington eased in beside him, but he said nothing. Then Jack realized that Toad was holding a pistol in his hand, down beside his leg, hidden from sight.

Spiro Dalworth was also there. As the television reporter gave orders to his cameraman and the technicians discussed where to put the lights, Yocke heard Jake say to Dalworth, 'Ask General Yakolev if Lieutenant Vasily Lutkin is still alive.'

'Lutkin?'

'Lutkin, the helicopter pilot. Ask him.'

Dalworth stepped over to where the general sat and asked the question in a low voice. Yakolev glanced at Jake, then shook his head from side to side. Mikhailov, Yocke noted, sat staring at the top of the table in front of him.

The television types opened a discussion of lighting and camera angles. Later, when he tried to recall exactly what had happened, Jack Yocke was never sure of the sequence. He remembered that someone else from a television crew came in carrying a floodlight and several people began looking for plugs. Another cameraman came in and his helper began unrolling cable.

The television reporter was talking to Admiral Grafton about the possibility of moving the news conference out into the hangar bay so they could use one of the missiles for a backdrop when Toad went over to where General Yakolev sat. Yocke caught that out of the corner of his eye, but he didn't pay much attention.

Toad must have laid the pistol on the table in front of Yakolev, because he was standing there opening a pocket-knife – probably to cut the plastic ties around the Russian's wrists – when Yakolev elbowed him hard and he fell away, off balance.

'No!' Yocke yelled, almost as the first shot hammered his eardrums. Mikhailov's head went sideways – a bullet right above the ear. Then Yakolev was shooting at Saddam Hussein.

Boom, boom, boom – the pistol's trip-hammer reports were painfully magnified in the confines of the room.

The Iraqi dictator came half out of his chair on the first shot into Mikhailov, so he took the next three standing up, at a distance of about ten feet. A burst of silenced sub-machine gun fire followed the pistol shots almost instantly. Yakolev went face forward onto the table as Saddam Hussein fell back into his chair and the chair and the body went over backward with a crash. The whole sequence didn't take more than three or four seconds.

'Shit, I think they're all dead.' Tarkington's voice. He stood and slowly looked around.

Jake Grafton got up from the floor and examined the Russians. Yocke tried to recall when Jake went down and couldn't.

'Yakolev is dead,' Jake said. 'Mikhailov is still breathing. One right above the left ear. I don't think he's gonna make it, but . . . Dalworth, go get a medic.'

Yocke pushed by the horrified Iraqi interpreter, who stood frozen with his hands half-raised. Toad was bending over the body of the dictator, which was lying on its side. Toad rolled him over. Saddam had three holes in his chest, one in the left shoulder, one dead center, and the other a little lower down. His eyes were fixed on the ceiling. Toad released a wrist and announced, 'No pulse.'

Saddam Hussein was as dead as Petty Officer Murphy . . . and that Iraqi Jack Yocke had knifed in Samarra, the soldier with the rifle he had mowed down. Dead.

Toad Tarkington stood looking down at Saddam's face as he folded his pocketknife and dropped it into a pocket. He held the pistol Yakolev had used with his left hand wrapped around the action, so the barrel and butt were both visible. That looks like Saddam's pistol, Yocke thought, but he couldn't be sure.

Toad glanced up and met the reporter's gaze.

Jack Yocke took a last look at the Iraqi dictator, then walked for the door. McElroy was replacing the magazine in his weapon. He didn't bother to look at Yocke as he went by.

Out in the hangar bay the reporter ran into another television crew, this one still shooting footage of soldiers loading nuclear warheads onto pallets and the pallets into helicopters.

'Were those shots we heard in there? What happened?' The reporter shoved a microphone at him.

'Saddam Hussein is dead,' Jack Yocke said slowly. 'A Russian general killed him.'

'*Holy* . . . ! C'mon, Harry, grab the lights. Ladies and gentlemen, we are broadcasting live from the Iraqi base at Samarra and we have just learned that Saddam Hussein is *dead!* Stay with us while—'

Yocke walked on through the hangar and went outside. One of the Sky Cranes was lifting off with a Russian missile slung beneath.

The rotors created a terrific wind that almost lifted Yocke's helmet off. He watched the machine transition into forward flight and disappear into the darkness.

CHAPTER TWENTY-SIX

Jake Grafton was asleep when he heard the knocking on the door. 'Just a minute.' He pulled on his trousers and opened it.

Yocke walked in lugging his computer. 'I've written a story and I need to phone it into the paper. You'll have to read it on the computer.'

He turned on the desk lamp and set up the machine.

Jake seated himself in front of the screen and put on his reading glasses. 'You push the buttons.'

'Okay.'

As Jake finished each page, he nodded and Yocke brought up the next one. The story was an eyewitness account of the air assault on Samarra, the recovery of the nuclear weapons, and the death of Saddam Hussein. Yocke got down to cases on the third page.

Just before the news conference was to begin, General Yakolev seized a pistol from an American officer and shot Marshal Mikhailov and Saddam Hussein before he himself was shot by a guard. Hussein was shot three times and died instantly. Mikhailov suffered a severe head wound and died approximately an hour later. Yakolev was dead at the scene.

Jake got out of the chair and switched on more lights.

'I thought you weren't going to write fiction,' he said to the reporter.

'There isn't a word in there that isn't true.'

'Well . . .'

'Look, you're doing the best you can with your weapons, I'm using mine.'

'You know, Jack,' Jake Grafton said softly, 'that's the nicest thing you've ever said about me, but I don't know that it's true. Arranging that little shoot-out was the dirtiest thing I ever did.'

'You were going to shoot Saddam yourself, weren't you?'

Jake Grafton ran his fingers through his hair. 'Well, not at first. After that talk with Yakolev I thought he'd do it, and I felt dirty. *I* wanted Saddam dead! But if I killed him the political implications would be unpredictable, and perhaps profound. Then in that room listening to him spout bullshit, I thought what the hell, maybe we'll kill each other.'

'He wouldn't play, so you let Yakolev shoot him.'

'Something like that.'

'I'm not ever going to print this.'

'I know, Jack.'

'But did someone in Washington want Saddam dead?'

'If they did they never said it to me.' Jake met Yocke's eyes. 'I learned a long time ago in the military that you can have all the authority you are willing to use, but God help you if you screw up.'

'Did you know Yakolev was going to shoot Mikhailov?'

'No. I'm sorry he did. That was his decision.'

'So what are you going to do now?'

'Hell, what is there to do? I'm going to live with it.'

'Do you feel guilty?'

Jake Grafton made a gesture of irritation.

'You did what had to be done.'

Jake Grafton rubbed his face. 'I thought so then, and I thought so when I sent Lieutenant Lutkin on to Moscow in a chopper that I suspected was going to be shot down, when I stuffed those damn poison pills into Herb Tenney's mouth . . . but!' He gestured helplessly. 'When all the

426

preachers have shouted themselves out, the bottom line is that people shouldn't kill people who aren't trying to kill them.' His gaze shifted to Yocke's face. 'The easiest lie ever told is that old nugget you tell yourself, *I'm doing what has to be done.*'

'You're not feeling sorry for Saddam Hussein and Yakolev and Herb Tenney, are you? They were *guilty.*'

Jake Grafton laid a hand on Yocke's arm. 'I'm feeling sorry for myself, Jack. They got what they deserved all right, but what do I deserve? I'm not God. I don't want his job.'

'This is the real world, Admiral, not some class in metaphysics. Herb Tenney murdered people with poison and died of it himself. An absolute despot and two wantabes are dead – they did it to each other. *You* didn't pull the trigger.'

'That's sophistry, Jack. You should have been a lawyer.'

Jack Yocke exploded. 'Goddamnit, Admiral! I've had it with all these people who tut-tut over the state of the world and won't *do* anything. Mass murder, starvation, tyranny – it's damn near two thousand years since Christ and . . .' He gestured helplessly. 'Guilt seems to be the in drug of the nineties. Okay, I'll drink my share. I'm *glad* Saddam's dead . . . and those two Russian gangsters in uniform. Looking back, I wish I had pulled the trigger.'

Yocke swallowed hard. 'I killed a man last night with a knife. Honest, there was no other way. I had to do it. It was him or me. Then I panicked and gunned a soldier or militiaman who was banging at me with a bolt-action rifle. I wish I hadn't shot him. I shouldn't have shot him.' he wiped the perspiration from his face. 'I knew at the time that he was no threat, but you know . . . I *wanted* to kill him. Do you understand?'

Jake Grafton nodded.

'I've been thinking about those two men all day,' Yocke continued. 'Thinking about guilt, about what I should have done, what . . .' He took a deep breath and exhaled audibly.

Now he looked at his hands. '. . . what I wish I had done. But it's over. And *I* have to live with it.'

Jake Grafton cleared his throat. 'I can live with it too.' His voice became softer. 'Maybe that's why it worked out the way it did.'

Jack Yocke bobbed his head.

'How's your arm?'

'Fifteen stitches, but the cut wasn't deep.'

Grafton stood. 'Call your story in. I'm going back to bed.'

'Toad says you always try to do the right thing. I think he's right.'

'I hope he is,' Jake said. He extended his hand. Yocke took it and squeezed.

Yocke closed the door behind him and walked down the hallway of the makeshift BOQ. He called his story in as it was written, not changing a word.

Then he stood looking out the window at the desert. The sun was overhead and heat mirages distorted the horizon.

After his return to the United States from Saudi Arabia, Jack Yocke threw himself at the word processor. His articles on the upheaval in the former Soviet states were well received and widely reprinted. He called the Graftons and invited them out on two occasions, but the first evening he had to cancel and the second time the admiral got tied up at work.

Yocke understood. Jake was the new director of the Defense Intelligence Agency and was busy trying to stay on top of rapidly changing events in the former Soviet states and the Middle East.

As Jake Grafton had predicted, the CIA problem took care of itself. As September turned into October Jack found the obituary of Harvey Schenler buried on a back page. Although the story didn't say so, by Yocke's count Schenler was the fourth high-ranking CIA officer to die since mid-

August. According to the press release, all died of natural causes. In their sleep.

Jack called Admiral Grafton at the office, and got him.

'Congratulations on the new job.'

'Thank you, Jack. How are things going for you?'

'Oh, just sitting here reading the obituaries. Seems that a deputy director of the CIA died in his sleep last night. Guy named Schenler. Heart failure.'

'Well, all things considered, it's not a bad way to go,' Jake Grafton told him.

'Fourth CIA bigwig in the last six weeks. Must be something in the water over at Langley.'

'It was their choice. Protects their families and the institution.'

'How is the Toad-man?'

'Doing fine.'

'Think I'll ever get to write anything about Schenler and his pals?'

'I doubt it,' Jake said promptly. 'Certainly not anytime soon.' He paused, then continued with a hint of concern in his voice: 'You aren't running out of stuff to write about, are you?'

'We're managing to keep the paper full – turmoil in the Middle East, a revolution in Iraq, Yeltsin still riding the tiger and trying not to get eaten. Same old song, different verse. How's Callie and Amy?'

'Doing fine, Jack. Doing fine. I'll tell them you asked.'

'Well, I'll let you go, Admiral. But the reason I called – I just wanted to say thanks.'

'For what?'

'For taking me along, for keeping me alive, for making me a part of the team. Thanks.'

'Take care, Jack.'

In October Jack was notified by the Russian embassy that his request for an in-depth interview with Boris Yeltsin had been granted.

When he checked into the Metropolitan Hotel in

Moscow there was some difficulty about the bill from his previous visit – they had held his room for a week after his hurried departure to the US embassy. He had a tense conference with the manager. After a call back to Washington, he agreed to pay the disputed amount.

Once again the barman greeted him by name. The oil painting of the nobleman outside the Kremlin walls hadn't been cleaned. Jack Yocke sat staring up at it and thinking of Shirley Ross, or Judith Farrell, as Toad and Jake had called her.

After his interview with Yeltsin, he took a taxi to the entrance to Gorky Park, then walked east. The statues of Stalin and his henchman now lay in the early winter snow surrounded by naked trees. The branches swayed in the bitter wind.

Jack found where a bullet had scarred the last bronze standing upright. He fingered the mark as he took in the scene one last time, then buried his hands in his pockets and walked back to the waiting taxi.

In November Yocke was invited to speak on the problems facing Russia at a symposium at Georgetown University. He was seated on the stage near the podium nervously fingering his notes and waiting for the lights to dim when he saw them come in: Rita Moravia, Toad Tarkington, Amy and Callie and Jake Grafton. They found seats along the left side of the auditorium.

Rita looked pregnant, Yocke noted with surprise.

Amy Carol waved, so he waved back. Jake and Toad returned his grin. Both the women smiled at him.

A warm glow settled over Jack Yocke. It's good to have real friends, he told himself, and he was very fortunate – he had five. Perhaps they would like to go out for coffee and ice cream later this evening when the lecture was over. He would ask.

Jake Grafton put the bottle containing the tablets of binary

430

poison into a desk drawer at his office and forgot about them. Through the winter and the rains of spring, through meetings, briefings and staff conferences, through turmoil and upheaval in Iraq and Russia, through coups in South America, through wars in the Balkans and another round of mass starvation in the horn of Africa, the pills stayed in the drawer.

He found them one evening in late May as he rooted in the drawer for a fresh pen. He fingered the bottle, then pried off the cap and dumped the white tablets on the desk in front of him. As he looked at the pills, the whole experience came flooding back.

Toxic waste. That's what these pills were. If he dumped them down the toilet the man-made chemical compounds would go through the sewage treatment plant into the Potomac. Too dangerous to just toss them into the garbage for burial in a landfill. Can't throw them into the ocean. If he burned them . . . but Lord knows what that might do to the active ingredients. And the resultant fumes might be poisonous.

These things were like plutonium pellets, their components deadly in the most minute quantities, difficult to dispose of safely.

That evening on the way home he bought a new battery for the car and asked if he could bring in the old battery in the morning for recycling. Sure.

After he had the new battery installed, he opened one of the plastic cell caps on the old one and dropped the tablets into the acid. Then he quickly screwed the cap back on.

When he looked up he found Callie was standing there in the garage with her arms folded across her chest, watching him. 'What was that stuff you put in there?'

'Ahh . . .'

She stood looking at him with raised eyebrows.

What the hell! 'Binary poison. This was what all the hassle was about last summer.' He told her about Herb Tenney.

'Do you think putting that stuff in there is safe?'

'Should be. They'll drain this battery into a huge vat of acid and that will dilute the poison. Whatever they do to the acid should destroy the compound, I think.'

'It's a risk then.'

'Life's a risky business,' he told her as he wiped his hands on a rag.

'Jake, what really happened in Iraq?'

'That was ten months ago, Callie. Does it matter?'

She shrugged. 'I suppose not, but on some level it does. Last fall when we went out for ice cream with Jack Yocke after that lecture, he and I talked. I read his story in the *Post*.'

'And?'

'Well, I never understood exactly what happened. Why did Saddam get killed? The Russian generals?'

'Yocke talked to you about that?' The words came out sharply, and Jake regretted it.

Callie didn't seem to notice. 'No,' she said slowly, recalling that conversation. 'He said his story covered it. That was the problem. The story just explained what happened, not why. I kept the clipping. I was looking at it again last week. You usually never talk about things like that – which I can understand, although at times it seems hard, unfair even. There's a whole side of you I don't know about.'

'Why did you wait until now to bring this up?'

'I wasn't going to,' Callie said. 'Then you brought that poison home. So I'm asking. If you don't want to tell me, I understand.'

Jake Grafton stared at his wife. After a moment he said, 'Yocke's story is true. He reported what he saw.'

'But not everything he saw.'

'No, not everything.' Jake ran his fingers through his hair. 'We were in the hangar at Samarra. Toad put the gun he was holding on the table in front of Yakolev and bent over to cut the plastic tie that held his hands. Yakolev grabbed the gun and killed Mikhailov and Hussein.'

432

'Toad wouldn't make a mistake like that. You set it up?'

My wife knows me very well, Jake reflected. Too well. 'Yes,' he said softly.

'And the marine captain killed Yakolev?'

'Yes.'

'Shot him in the back?'

'Yes.'

Callie thought about it. 'Why?'

'I thought the world would be a lot better place if Saddam Hussein wasn't in it. My responsibility. But if I shot him he would be a martyr. So I had a talk with Yakolev. We both knew that if he went back to Russia he would be shot. He said he was a soldier, he didn't fear a bullet. I told him I knew that and wanted his help.'

'And what was his reply?'

'He just looked me in the eye and said he would think about it. So I set it up. When Yakolev saw the pistol placed on the table within his reach, he knew what it was I wanted. And he knew how it would end. He made his choice. Mikhailov didn't know what was going on but perhaps he would have wanted it to end the way it did. Maybe. He was old and tired and wanted to die . . . that was my impression, anyway.'

She stepped toward him and touched his cheek. 'Why didn't you tell me about this sooner? You shouldn't have carried this by yourself.'

'Yakolev and Mikhailov were soldiers. They screwed up big-time. I think they realized that toward the end.'

'And Hussein?'

'Saddam Hussein was a thug who clawed his way to the top of the neighborhood dung heap, like Al Capone, Joe Stalin, Adolf Hitler, Attila the Hun and a hundred others. I have no regrets.'

'General Land? The president? What did they think afterward?'

'They liked Jack Yocke's version. After they put down the newspaper they probably said, Next problem.'

He flipped off the garage light as he followed her out the door into the late spring evening.

'How many times,' she asked, 'can you take on the Herb Tenneys and Saddam Husseins of the world and come out alive?'

He looked at her with raised eyebrows. 'Gimme a break, Callie. I lead a very sedentary life. I'm a bureaucrat, for heaven's sake. You know me!'

'I know you better, Jacob.'

He examined her face, pushed a stray lock back from her forehead. 'I'll fight the good fight as long as I have any fight left in me.'

She smiled, then brushed her lips across his cheek as she took his hand. 'Come eat your dinner,' she said as she led him toward the house. 'You can't fight on an empty stomach.'

left in me.

She smiled, then brushed her lips across his cheek as she
took his hand.

THE INTRUDERS

AUTHOR'S NOTE

For their kindness in assisting with the technical aspects of this novel, the author wishes to thank Captain Sam Sayers, USN Ret., and Captain Bruce Wood, USN.

The in-flight emergencies featured in this novel are based on actual incidents. Where necessary I have simplified the complexities of cockpit switchology, emergency and air traffic control procedures in the interest of readability and pacing. I have also altered the outcome of some of the incidents. It was not my intent to write an aviation safety treatise or a manual on how to do it, but to entertain.

I also hope that you, the reader, develop a better understanding of the pride, skill, professionalism and dedication of the men and women of US Navy and Marine Corps Aviation. As you read these words, they are out there on the oceans of the earth working for all of us. This book is dedicated to them.

Eternal Father, strong to save,
Whose arm does bind the restless wave,
Who biddest the mighty ocean deep,
Its own appointed limits keep;
O hear us when we cry to thee
For those in peril on the sea.

– *The Navy Hymn*,
William Whiting

CHAPTER ONE

The huge ship towered above the pier that projected into the bay. The rain falling from a low, slate-colored sky made everything look dark and wet – the ship, the pier, the trucks, even the sailors hurrying to and fro.

At the gate at the head of the pier stood a portable guard shack where a sailor huddled with the collar of his pea coat turned up, his hands thrust deep into his pockets. There was no heater in the wooden shack so the air here was no warmer than it was outside, but at least he was out of the wind. Raw and wet, the swirling air lashed at unprotected flesh and cut like a knife through thin trousers.

The sailor looked yet again up at the projecting flight deck of the great ship, at the tails and wing butts of the aircraft sticking over the edge. Then his eyes wandered back along the ship's length, over a thousand feet. The gray steel behemoth looked so permanent, so solid, one almost had to accept on faith the notion that it was indeed a ship that could move at will upon the oceans. It looked, the sailor decided, like a cliff of blue-black granite.

Streams of water trickled from scuppers high on the edge of the flight deck. When the wind gusted these dribbles scattered and became an indistinguishable part of the rain. In the lulls the streams splattered randomly against the pier, the camels that wedged the hull away from the pilings, and the restless black water of the bay.

The sailor watched the continuous march of small swells as they surged against the oil containment booms, swirled trash against the pilings, and lapped nervously against the hull of the ship. Of course the ship didn't move. She lay as motionless as if she were resting on bedrock.

Yet she was floating upon that oily black wet stuff, the sailor mused. This 95,000 tons of steel would get under way tomorrow morning, steam across the bay and through the Golden Gate. All of her eighty aircraft were already aboard, all except the last one that was just now being lifted by a crane onto the forward starboard elevator, Elevator One. This past week had been spent loading bombs, bullets, beans, toilet paper – supplies by the tractor-trailer load, an endless stream of trucks and railroad cars, which were pushed down tracks in the middle of the pier.

Tomorrow.

Carrying her planes and five thousand men, the ship would leave the land behind and move freely in a universe of sea and sky – that was a fact amazing and marvelous and somewhat daunting. The carrier would be a man-made planet voyaging in a universe of water, storms, darkness, maybe occasionally even sunlight. And on this planet would be the ants – the men – working and eating, working and sleeping, working and sweating, working and praying that somehow, someday the ship would once again return to the land.

And he would be aboard her. This would be his first cruise, at the age of nineteen years. The prospect was a little strange and a little frightening.

The sailor shivered involuntarily – was it the cold? – and looked again at the tails of the planes projecting over the edge of the flight deck. What would it be like to ride one of those planes down the catapult into the sky, or to come across the fantail and catch one of the arresting gear wires? The sailor didn't know, nor was it likely he would ever find out, a fact that gave him a faint sense of disappointment. He was a storekeeper, a clerk. The aviators who would fly the planes were officers, all older and presumably vastly more knowledgeable than he – certainly they lived in a world far different than his. But maybe someday. When you are nineteen the future stretches away like a highway until it disappears into the haze. Who knows what lies ahead on that infinite, misty road?

The sailor wasn't very interested in that mystical future: his thoughts turned glumly to the here and now. He was homesick. There was a girl at home whom he hadn't been all that serious about when he joined the Navy after high school, but the separation had worked its insidious magic. Now he was writing her three long letters per week, plus a letter to his folks and one to his brother. The girl . . . well, she was dating another guy. That fact ate at his insides something fierce.

He was thinking about the girl, going over what he would say in his next letter – her last letter to him had arrived three weeks ago – when a taxi pulled up on the other side of the gate. An officer stepped out and stood looking at the ship, a lieutenant, wearing a leather flight jacket and a khaki fore-and-aft cap.

After the cab driver opened the trunk, the officer paid him and hoisted two heavy parachute bags. One he swung onto his right shoulder. The other he picked up with his left hand. He strode toward the gate and the guard shack.

The sailor came out into the rain with his clipboard. He saluted the officer and said, 'I'm sorry, sir, but I need to see your ID card.'

The officer made eye contact with the sailor for the first time. He was about six feet tall, with gray eyes and a nose that was a trifle too large for his face. He lowered the bags to the wet concrete, dug in his pocket for his wallet, extracted an ID card and handed it to the sailor.

The sailor carefully copied the information from the ID card to the paper on his clipboard as he tried to shield the paper from the rain. LT JACOB L. GRAFTON, USN. Then he passed the credit-card-size piece of plastic back to the officer.

'Thank you, sir.'

'Okay, sailor,' the lieutenant said. After he stowed the card he stood silently for several seconds looking at the ship. He ignored the falling rain.

Finally he looked again at the sailor. 'Your first cruise?'

'Yessir.'

'Where you from?'

'Iowa, sir.'

'Umm.'

After a last glance at the airplanes on the flight deck above, the officer reached for his bags. He again hoisted one of the parachute bags to his right shoulder, then lifted the other in his left hand. From the way the bags sagged the sailor guessed they weighed at least fifty pounds each. The officer didn't seem to have any trouble handling them, though.

'Iowa's a long way behind you,' the lieutenant said softly.

'Yessir.'

'Good luck,' the lieutenant said, and walked away down the pier.

The sailor stood oblivious to the rain and watched him go.

Not just Iowa . . . everything was behind. The ship, the great ocean, Hawaii, Hong Kong, Singapore, Australia – all that was ahead. They would sail in the morning. Only one more night.

The sailor retreated to the shack and closed the door. He began to whistle to himself.

An hour later Lieutenant Jack Grafton finally found his new two-man stateroom and dumped his bags. His room-mate, a Navy pilot, wasn't around, but apparently he had moved into the bottom bunk.

Jake climbed into the top bunk and stretched out.

Just five months into his first shore tour – after three years in a fleet squadron with two combat cruises – his tour was cut short. Now he was going to sea again, this time with a Marine squadron.

Amateur hour! Jarheads!

How had he gotten himself into this fix anyway?

Well, the world started coming unglued about three weeks ago, when he went to Chicago to see Callie. He closed his eyes and half-listened to the sounds of the ship as it all came flooding back.

'Do you know Chicago?' Callie McKenzie asked.

It was 11 A.M. on a Thursday morning and they were on the freeway from O'Hare into the city. Callie was at the wheel.

Jake Grafton leaned back in the passenger's seat and grinned. 'No.'

Her eyes darted across his face. She was still glowing from the long, passionate kiss she had received at the gate in front of an appreciative audience of travelers and gate attendants. Then they had walked down the concourse arm in arm. Now Jake's green nylon folding clothes bag was in the trunk and they had left the worst of O'Hare's traffic behind.

'Thank you for the letters,' she said. 'You're quite a correspondent.'

'Well, thank you for all the ones you wrote to me.'

She drove in silence, her cheeks still flushed. After a bit she said, 'So your knee is okay and you're flying again?'

'Oh, sure.' Unconsciously Jake rubbed the knee that had been injured in an ejection over Laos six months ago. When he realized that he was doing it, he laughed, then said, 'But that's history. The war's over, the POWs are home, it's June, you're beautiful, I'm here – all in all, life is damn good.'

In spite of herself Callie McKenzie flushed again. Here

5

he was, in the flesh, the man she had met in Hong Kong last fall and spent a bittersweet weekend with in the Philippines. What was that, seven days total? And she was in love with him.

She had avidly read and reread his letters and written long, chatty replies. She had told him she loved him in every line. And she had called him the first evening she arrived back in the States after finishing her two-year tour in Hong Kong with the State Department. That was ten days ago. Now, here he was.

They had so much to talk about, a relationship to renew. She was worried about that. Love was so tricky. What if the magic didn't happen?

'My folks are anxious to meet you,' she said, a trifle nervously Jake Grafton thought. He was nervous too, so nervous that he couldn't eat the breakfast they had served on the plane from Seattle. Yet here with her now, he could feel the tension leaving him. It was going to be all right.

When he didn't reply, she glanced at him. He was looking at the skyline of the city, wearing a half-smile. The car seemed crowded with his presence. That was one of the things she had remembered – he seemed a much larger man than he was. He hadn't changed. Somehow she found that reassuring. After another glance at his face, she concentrated on driving.

In a moment she asked, 'Are you hungry?'

'Oh, getting there.'

'I thought we'd go downtown, get some lunch, do some sightseeing, then go home this evening after my folks get home from the university.'

'Sounds like a plan.'

'You'll like Chicago,' she said.

'I like all American towns,' he said softly. 'I've never yet been in one I didn't like.'

'You men! So hard to please.'

He laughed, and she joined in.

He's here! She felt delicious.

She found a parking garage within the Loop and they went walking hand in hand, looking, laughing, getting re-acquainted. After lunch with a bubbling crowd in a pub, they walked and walked.

Of course Callie wanted to hear an account from Jake's own lips about his shootdown and rescue from Laos, and they talked about Tiger Cole, the bombardier who had broken his back and was now undergoing intensive phys-ical therapy in Pensacola.

When they had each brought the other up-to-date on all the things that had happened to them since they last saw each other, Callie asked, 'Are you going to stay in the Navy?'

'I don't know. I can get out after a year in this shore tour.' He was a flight instructor at Attack Squadron 128 at NAS Whidbey Island, Washington, transitioning new pilots and bombardier-navigators (BNs) to the A-6 Intruder. 'The flying is fun,' he continued. 'It's good to get back to it. But I don't know. It depends.'

'Oh what?'

'Oh, this and that.' He grinned at her.

She liked how he looked when he grinned. His gray eyes danced.

She thought she knew what the decision depended on, but she wanted to hear him say it. 'Not finances?'

'No. Got a few bucks saved.'

'On a civilian flying job?'

'Haven't applied for any.'

'On what then, Jake?'

They were on a sidewalk on Lake Shore Drive, with Lake Michigan spreading out before them. Jake had his elbows on the railing. Now he turned and enveloped Callie in his arms and gave her a long, probing kiss. When they finally parted for air, he said, 'Depends on this and that.'

'On us?'

'You and me.'

The admission satisfied her. She wrapped her hands around one of his arms and rested her head on his shoulder. The gulls were crying and wheeling above the beach.

The McKenzies lived in a brick two-story in an old neighborhood. Two giant oaks stood in the tiny front yard between the porch and the sidewalk. After apparently struggling for years to get enough sunlight, most of the grass had surrendered to fate. Only a few blades poked through last autumn's leaf collection. Professor McKenzie appeared to be as enthusiastic about raking leaves as he was about mowing grass.

Callie introduced Jake to her parents and he agreed that he could drink a beer, if they had any. The professor mixed himself a highball and poured a glass of wine for each of the ladies. Then the four of them sat a few minutes in the study with their drinks in hand exchanging pleasantries.

He had been in the Navy for five years, liked it so far. He and Callie had met in Hong Kong. Wasn't this June pleasant?

Callie and her mother finally excused themselves and headed for the kitchen. Jake surveyed the room for ashtrays and saw that there weren't any. As he debated whether he should cross his legs or keep both feet firmly on the floor, Callie's father told him that he and his wife taught at the University of Chicago, had done so for thirty years, had lived in this house for twenty. They hoped to retire in eight years. Might even move to Florida.

'I was raised in southwestern Virginia,' Jake informed his host. 'My dad has a pretty good-size farm.'

'Have you any farming ambitions?'

No, Jake thought not. He had seen his share of farming while growing up. He was a pilot now and thought he might just stick with it, although he hadn't decided for certain.

'What kind of planes do you fly in the Navy?' Professor McKenzie asked.

So Callie hadn't mentioned that? Or the professor forgot. 'I fly A-6s, sir.'

Not a glimmer showed on the professor's face. He had a weathered, lined face, was balding and wore trifocals. Still, he wasn't bad looking. And Mrs McKenzie was a striking lady. Jake could see where Callie got her looks and figure.

'What kind of planes are those?' the professor asked, apparently just to make conversation.

'Attack planes. All-weather attack.'

'Attack?'

'Any time, anywhere, any weather, day or night, high, low or in the middle.'

'You . . . drop . . . *bombs?*' His face was blank, incredulous.

'And shoot missiles,' Jake said firmly.

Professor McKenzie took a deep breath and stared at this young man who had been invited into his house by his daughter. His only daughter. Life is amazing – getting into bed with a woman is the ultimate act of faith: truly, you are rolling cosmic dice. Who would have believed that twenty-five years later the child of that union would bring home this . . . this . . .

'Doesn't it bother you? Dropping bombs?'

'Only when the bad guys are trying to kill me,' Jake Grafton replied coolly. 'Now if you'll excuse me, sir, maybe I should take my bags upstairs and wash my face.'

'Of course.' The professor gestured vaguely toward the hallway where the stairs were and took a healthy swig of his highball.

Jake found the spare bedroom and put his bags on a chair. Then he sat on the bed staring out the window.

He was in trouble. You didn't have to be a genius to see that. Callie hadn't told her parents *anything* about him. And that look on the old man's face! 'You drop *bombs?*'

9

He could have just said, '*Oh, Mr Grafton, you're a hit man for the Mafia? What an unusual career choice! And you look like you enjoy your work.*'

Jesus!

He dug in his pocket and got out the ring. He had purchased this engagement ring last December on the *Shiloh* and carried it with him ever since, on the ground, in the air, all the time. He had fully intended to give it to Callie when the time was right. But this visit . . . her parents . . . it made him wonder. Was he right for this woman? Would he fit into her family? Oh, love is wonderful and grand and will conquer all the problems – isn't that the way the songs go? Yet under the passion there needs to be something else . . . a *rightness*. He wanted a woman to go the distance with. If Callie was the woman, now was not the time. She wasn't ready.

And he wasn't if she wasn't.

He looked disgustedly at the ring, then put it back into his pocket.

The evening sun shone through the branches of the old oak. The window was open, a breeze wafted through the screen. That limb – he could take out the screen, toss down the bags, get onto that limb and climb down to the ground. He could be in a taxi on the way to the airport before they even knew he was gone.

He was still sitting there staring glumly out the window when Callie came for him thirty minutes later.

'What's wrong?' she asked.

'Nothing,' he said, rising from the bed and stretching. 'Dinner ready?'

'Yes.'

'Something is wrong, isn't it?'

There was no way to avoid it. 'You didn't tell me your Dad was Mr Liberal.'

'Liberal? He's about a mile left of Lenin.'

'He looked really thrilled when I told him I was an attack pilot.'

'Dad is Dad. I thought it was me you were interested in?'

Jake Grafton cocked his head. 'Well, you *are* better looking than he is. Probably a better kisser, too.' He took her arm and led her toward the stairs. 'Wait till you meet my older brother,' he told her. 'He can't wait for the next revolution. He says the next time we won't screw it up like Bobby Lee and Jeff Davis did.'

'How would you rate me as a kisser?' she asked softly.

They paused on the top stair and she wrapped her arms around him. 'This is for score,' he whispered. 'Pucker up.'

That night when they were in bed Professor McKenzie told his wife, 'That boy's a killer.'

'Don't be ridiculous, Wallace.'

'He kills people. He kills them from the air. He's an executioner.'

'That's war, dear. They try to kill him, he tries to kill them.'

'It's murder.'

Mary McKenzie had heard it all before. 'Callie is in love with him, Wallace. I suggest you keep your opinions and your loaded labels to yourself. She must make her own decision.'

'Decision? What decision?'

'Whether or not to marry him.'

'*Marriage?*'

'Don't tell me you didn't know what was going on?' his wife said crossly. 'I swear, you're blind as a bat! Didn't you see her at dinner tonight? She loves him.'

'She won't marry him,' Professor McKenzie stated positively. 'I know *Callie!*'

'Yes, dear,' Mrs McKenzie muttered, just to pacify the man. What her husband knew about young women in love wouldn't fill a thimble. She herself was appalled by Callie's

11

choice, believing the girl could do a whale of a lot better if she just looked around a little.

Callie was inexperienced. She didn't date until college and then couldn't seem to find any young men who interested her. Mrs McKenzie had hoped she would find a proper man while working for the State Department – apparently a futile hope. This Grafton boy was physically a good specimen, yet he was wrong for Callie. He was so . . . blue-collar. The girl needed a man who was at least in the same room with her intellectually.

But she wasn't going to say that to Callie – not a chance. Pointed comments would probably be resented, perhaps even resisted. In this new age of liberated womanhood, covert pressure was the proper way, the only way. One had to pretend strict neutrality – 'This is *your* decision, dear' – while radiating bad vibes. She owed her daughter maternal guidance – choosing a mate is much too important to be left to young women with raging hormones.

Secure in the knowledge that she was up to the task that duty had set before her, Mrs McKenzie went peacefully to sleep while her husband stewed.

At breakfast Professor McKenzie held forth on the Vietnam War. The night before at dinner he had said little, preferring to let the ladies steer the conversation. This morning he told Jake Grafton in no uncertain terms what he thought of the politicians who started the war and the politicians who kept the nation in it.

If he was expecting an argument, he didn't get it. In fact, several times Jake nodded in agreement with the professor's points, and twice Callie distinctly heard him say, 'You're right.'

After the senior McKenzies left the house for the university, Jake and Callie headed for the kitchen to finish cleaning up.

'You sure handled Dad,' Callie told her boyfriend.

'Huh?'

'You took the wind right out of Dad's sails. He thought you were going to give him a bang-up fight.'

She was looking straight into his gray eyes when he said, 'The war's over. It's history. What is there to fight about?'

'Well . . . ,' Callie said dubiously.

Jake just shrugged. His knee was fairly well healed and the dead were buried. That chapter of his life was over.

He gathered her into his arms and smiled. 'What are we going to do today?'

He had good eyes, Callie thought. You could almost look in and see the inner man, and that inner man was simple and good. He wasn't complicated or self-absorbed like her father, nor was he warped with secret doubts and phobias like so many of the young men she knew. Amazingly, after Vietnam his scars were merely physical, like that slash on his temple where a bullet gouged him.

Acutely aware of the warmth and pressure of his body against hers, she gave him a fierce hug and whispered, 'What would you like to do?'

The feel and smell and warmth of her seemed more than Jake could take in. 'Anything you want, Miss McKenzie,' he said hoarsely, mildly surprised at his reaction to her presence, 'as long as we do it together.' That didn't come out quite the way he intended, and he felt slightly flustered. You can't just invite a woman to bed at eight-thirty in the morning!

His hand massaged the small of her back and she felt her knees get weak. She took a deep breath to steady herself, then said, 'I'd like to take you to meet my brother, Theron. He lives in Milwaukee. But first let's clean up these dishes. Then, since you so coyly suggested it, let's slip upstairs in a Freudian way and get seriously naked.'

When Jake's cheeks reddened, Callie laughed, a deep, throaty woman's laugh. 'Don't pretend you weren't thinking about that!'

Jake dearly enjoyed seeing her laugh. She had a way of throwing her head back and unashamedly displaying a mouthful of beautiful teeth that he found captivating. When she did it her hair swayed and her eyes crinkled. The effect was mesmerizing. You wanted her to do it again, and again, and again.

'The thought did flit across my little mind,' he admitted, grinning, watching her eyes.

'Ooh, I want you, Jake Grafton,' she said, and kissed him.

A shaft of sunlight streamed through the open window and fell squarely across them in the bed. After all those months of living aboard ship, in a steel cubicle in the bowels of the beast where the sun never reached, Jake thought the sunlight magical. He gently turned her so their heads were in the sun. The zephyr from the window played with strands of her brown hair and the sun flecked them with gold. She was woman, all warm taut sleek smoothness and supple, sensuous wetness.

Somehow she ended up on top and set the rhythm of their lovemaking. As her hair caressed his cheeks and her hands kneaded his body, the urgency became overwhelming. He guided her onto him.

When she lay spent across him, her lashes stroking his cheek, her breath hot on his shoulder, he whispered, 'I love you.'

'I know,' she replied.

Theron McKenzie had been drafted into the Army in 1967. On October 7, 1968, he stepped on a land mine. He lost one leg below the knee and one above. Today he walked on artificial legs. Jake thought he was pretty good at it, although he had to sway his body from side to side to keep his balance when he threw the legs forward.

'It was in II Corps,' he told Jake Grafton, 'at the base camp. And the worst of it was that the mine was one of

14

ours. I just forgot for a moment and walked the wrong way.'
He shrugged and grinned.

He had a good grin. Jake liked him immediately. Yet he
was slightly taken aback when Theron asked, 'So are you
going to marry her?' This while his sister walked between
them holding on to Jake's arm.

Grafton recovered swiftly. 'Aaah, I dunno. She's so
pushy, mighty smart, might be more than a country boy
like me could handle. If you were me, knowing what you
know about her, what would you do?'

Both men stared at Callie's composed features. She
didn't let a muscle twitch. Theron sighed, then spoke: 'If I
were you and a woman loved me as much as this one loves
you, I'd drag her barefoot to the altar. If I were you.'

'I'll think about it.'

'And what about you, Sis? You gonna marry him?'

'Theron, how would you like to have you throat cut?'

They ate lunch at a sports bar around the corner from
the office where Theron worked as a tax accountant. After
a half hour of small talk, Theron asked Jake, 'So are you
going to stay in or try life on the outside?'

'Haven't decided. All I've got is a history degree. I'd have
to go back to school.'

'Maybe you could get a flying job.'

'Maybe.'

Theron changed the subject. Before Callie could get an
oar in, Theron was asking questions about carrier aviation
– how the catapults worked, the arresting gear, how the
pilots knew if they were on the glide slope. Jake drew
diagrams on napkins and Theron asked more questions
while Callie sat and watched.

'God, that must be terrific,' Theron said to Jake, 'landing
and taking off from an aircraft carrier. That's something
I'd love to do someday.' He slapped his artificial legs. 'Of
course, I can't now, but I can just imagine!'

Callie glowed with a feeling of approaching euphoria.

She had known that these two would get along well: it was almost as if they were brothers. Having a brother like Theron was hard on a girl – he was all man. When you have a real man only a year and a half older than you are to compare the boys against, finding one that measures up isn't easy.

Jake Grafton did. Her cup was full to overflowing.

'Is he going to stay in the Navy?' Mrs McKenzie asked her daughter. They were in the kitchen cutting the cherry pie.

'He hasn't made up his mind.'

Grafton's indecision didn't set well with Mrs McKenzie. 'He probably will,' she said.

'He might,' Callie admitted.

'The military is a nice comfortable place for some people. The government feeds and clothes and houses them, provides medical care, a living wage. All they have to do is follow orders. Some people like that. They don't have to take any responsibility. The military is safe.'

Callie concentrated on getting the pie wedges from the pan to the plates without making a mess.

'Would he continue to fly?' Mrs McKenzie asked. 'If he stayed in?'

'I suspect so,' her daughter allowed.

Mrs McKenzie let the silence build until it shrieked.

When Callie could stand it no longer, she said, 'He hasn't asked me to marry him, Mom.'

'Oh, he will, he will. That's a man working himself up to a proposal if ever I saw one.'

Callie told her mother the truth. 'If he asks, I haven't decided what the answer will be.'

Which was, Callie McKenzie suspected, precisely why he hadn't asked. Jake Grafton was nobody's fool. Yet why she hadn't yet made up her mind, she didn't know.

I love him, why am I uncertain?

Mrs McKenzie didn't know much about Jake Grafton,

but she knew a man in love when she saw one. 'He's an idiot if he throws his life away by staying in the Navy,' she said perfunctorily.

'He's a pilot, Mom. That's what he does. He's good at it.'

'The airlines hire pilots.'

'He's probably considering that,' Callie said distractedly, still trying to pin down her emotional doubt. Had she been looking for a man like Theron all this time? Was that wise? Was she seeking a substitute for her brother?

Her mother was saying something. After a moment Callie began to pay attention. '. . . so he'll stay in the Navy, and some night they'll come tell you he's crashed and you're a widow. What then?'

'Mother, you just announced that some people stay in the military because it's safe, yet now you argue it's too dangerous. You can't have it both ways. Do you want whipped cream on your pie?'

'Callie, I'm thinking of you. You well know something can be physically dangerous yet on another level appeal to people without ambition.'

Callie opened the refrigerator and stared in. Then she closed it. 'We're out of whipped cream. Will you bring the other two plates, please?' She picked up two of the plates and headed for the dining room.

She put one plate in front of Jake and one in front of her father. Then she seated herself. Jake winked at her. She tried to smile at him.

Lord, if her mother only knew how close to the edge Jake lived she wouldn't be appalled – she would be horrified. Jake had made light of the dangers of flying onto and off of carriers this afternoon, but Callie knew the truth. Staying alive was the challenge.

She examined his face again. He didn't look like Theron, but he had the same self-assurance, the same intelligence and good sense, the same intellectual curiosity, the same easy way with everyone. She had seen that in him the first

17

time they met. And like Theron, Jake Grafton had nothing to prove to anyone. Perhaps naval aviation had given Jake that quality – or combat had – but wherever he acquired it, he now had it in spades. He owned the space he occupied.

He *was* like Theron! She was going to have to come to grips with that fact.

'The most serious problem our society faces,' Professor McKenzie intoned, 'is the complete absence of moral fiber in so many of our young people.'

They had finished the pie and were sipping coffee. Jake Grafton let that pronouncement go by without bothering to glance at his host. He was observing Callie, trying to read her mood.

'If they had any sense of right and wrong,' the professor continued, 'young men would have never fought in that war. Until people understand that they have the right, nay, the duty, the obligation, to resist the illegal demands of a morally bankrupt government, we will continue to have war. Murder, slaughter, rapine, grotesque human suffering, for what? Just to line the pockets of greedy men.'

After the prologue, the professor got down to cases. Jake had a sick feeling this was coming. 'What about you, Jake? Were you drafted?'

Jake eyed the professor without turning his head. 'No.'

Something in his voice drew Callie's gaze. She glanced at him, but his attention was directed at her father.

'Wallace,' said Mrs McKenzie, 'perhaps we should—'

'You volunteered?'

'Yes.'

'You volunteered to kill people?' the professor asked with naked sarcasm.

'I volunteered to fight for my country.'

The professor was on firm ground here. He lunged with his rapier. 'Your country wasn't under attack by the Vietnamese. You can't wrap the holy flag around yourself

18

now, Mister, or use it to cover up what you people did over there.'

Now the professor slashed. 'You and your airborne colleagues murdered defenseless men, women and children. Burned them alive with napalm. Bombed them in the most contemptible, cowardly manner that—'

'You don't know what the hell you're talking about.'

'Gentlemen, let's change the subject.' Mrs McKenzie's tone was flinty.

'No, Mary,' the professor said, leaning forward with his eyes on Jake. 'This young man – I'm being charitable here – is courting our daughter. I think I have a right to know what kind of man he is.'

'The war's over, Mr McKenzie,' Jake said.

'The shooting has stopped, no thanks to you. But you can't turn your back on all those murdered people and just walk away. I won't allow it! The American people won't—'

But he was orating to Jake Grafton's back. The pilot walked through the doorway into the hall and his feet sounded on the stairs.

Mrs McKenzie got up abruptly and went to the kitchen, leaving Callie alone with her father.

'You didn't have to do that, Dad.'

'He's not the man for you, Callie. You couldn't live with what he did, he and those other criminal swine in uniform.'

Callie McKenzie tapped nervously on the table with a spoon. Finally she put it down and scooted her chair back.

'I want to say this just right, Father. I've been wanting to say this for a long time, but I've never known just how. On this occasion I want to try. You think in black and white although we live in a gray world. It's been my experience that people who think the dividing line between right and wrong is a brick wall are crackpots.'

She rose and left the room with her father sitting openmouthed behind her.

In the guest room upstairs Jake was rolling up his clothes

19

and stuffing them into his folding bag. The nylon bag, Callie noticed listlessly, was heavily stained. That was the bag he had with him in Olongapo last autumn.

'I've called a cab,' he told her.

She sagged into a chair. 'My father . . . I'm sorry . . . why do you have to go?'

Grafton finished stuffing the bag, looked around to make sure he hadn't forgotten anything, then zipped the bag closed. He lifted it from the bed and tossed it toward the door. Only then did he turn to face her.

'The people I knew in the service were some of the finest men I ever met. Some of those men are dead. Some are crippled for life, like your brother. I'm proud that I served with them. We made mistakes, but we did the best we could. I won't listen to vicious slander.'

'Dad and his opinions.'

'Opinions are like assholes – everybody has one. At his age your father should know that not everyone wants to see his butt or hear his opinion.'

'Jake, you and I . . . what we have might grow into something wonderful if we give it a chance. Shouldn't we take time to talk about this?'

'Talk about what? The Vietnam War? It's *over*. All those dead men! For *what*? For fucking nothing at all, that's for what!' His voice was rising but he didn't notice. 'Oh, I killed my share of Vietnamese – your father got *that* right. They are dead for nothing. Now I've got to live with it . . . every day of my life. Don't you understand?'

He slammed his hand down on the dresser and the photo on top fell over. 'I'm not God. I don't know if we should have gone to Vietnam or if we should have left sooner or if the war was right or wrong. The self-righteous assholes who stayed at home can argue about all that until hell freezes. And it looks like they're going to.

'I took an oath. I swore to uphold the Constitution of the United States. So I obeyed orders. I did what I was told to the absolute best of my ability. Just like your brother. And what did it get us? Me and your brother? You and me? Jake and Callie – what did it get *us?*'

He took a ragged breath. He was perspiring and he felt sick. Slightly nauseated. 'It isn't your father. It's *me.* I can't just *forget.*'

'Jake, we must all live with the past. And walk on into the future.'

'Maybe you and I aren't ready for the future yet.'

She didn't reply.

'Well, maybe I'm not,' he admitted.

She was biting her lip.

'You aren't either,' he added.

When she didn't answer he picked up the folding bag and carry-on. 'Tell your mom thanks.' He went out the door.

She heard him descend the stairs. She heard the front door open. She heard it close.

Then her tears came.

Almost an hour later she descended the stairs. She was at the bottom when she heard her mother's voice coming from the study. 'You blathering fool! I'm *sick* of hearing you sermonize about the war. I'm *sick* of your righteousness. I'm *sick* of you damning the world from the safety of your alabaster pedestal.'

'Mary, that war was an obscenity. That war was wrong, a great wrong, and the blind stupidity of boys like Grafton made it possible. If Grafton and boys like him had refused to go, there wouldn't have been a war.'

'Boys? Jake Grafton is no boy. He's a *man!*'

'He doesn't *think*,' Professor McKenzie said, his voice dripping contempt. 'He *can't* think. I don't call him much of a man.'

Callie sank to the steps. She had never heard her parents address each other in such a manner. She felt drained, empty, but their voices held her mesmerized.

'Oh, he's a man all right,' her mother said. 'He just doesn't think like you do. He's got the brains and talent to fly jet aircraft in combat. He's got the character to be a naval officer, and I suspect he's a pretty good one. I know that doesn't impress you much, but Callie knows what he is. He's got the maturity and character to impress *her*.'

'Then she's too easily impressed. That girl doesn't know—'

'Enough, you *fool!*' said Mary McKenzie bitterly. 'We've got a son who did his duty as he saw it and you've never let him forget that you think he's a stupid, contemptible fascist. Your *only* son. So he doesn't come here anymore. He *won't* come here. Your opinion is just *your* opinion, Wallace – you can't seem to get it through your thick head that other people can honorably hold different opinions. And a great many people do.'

'I—'

His wife raised her voice and steamed on. 'I'm going to say this just once, Wallace, so you had better listen. Callie may marry Jake Grafton, regardless of our wishes. In her way she's almost as pigheaded as you are. Jake Grafton's every inch the man that Theron is, and he won't put up with your bombast and supercilious foolishness any more than Theron does. Grafton proved that here tonight. I don't blame him.'

'Callie won't marry that—'

'You damned old windbag, *shut up!* What you know about your daughter could be printed in foot-high letters on the head of a pin.'

She shouted that last sentence, then fell silent. When she spoke again her voice was cold, every word enunciated clearly:

'It will be a miracle if Jake Grafton ever walks through that door again. So I'm serving notice on you, Wallace, here and now. Your arrogance almost cost me my son. If it costs me my daughter, I'm divorcing you.'

Before Callie could move from her seat on the steps, Mrs McKenzie came striding through the study door. She saw Callie and stopped dead.

Callie rose, turned, and forced herself to climb the stairs.

CHAPTER TWO

After a miserable night in a motel near O'Hare, Jake got a seat the next day on the first flight to Seattle. Unfortunately, the next Harbor Airlines flight to Oak Harbor was full, so he had two hours to kill at Sea-Tac. He headed for the bar and sat nursing a beer.

The war was over, yet it wasn't. That was the crazy thing.

He had tried to keep his cool in Chicago and had done a fair job until the professor goaded him beyond endurance. Now he sat going over the mess again, for the fifteenth time, wondering what Callie was thinking, wondering what she felt.

The ring was burning a hole in his pocket. He pulled it out and looked at it from time to time, trying to shield it in his hand so that casual observers wouldn't think him weird.

Maybe he ought to throw the damned thing away. It didn't look like he was ever going to get to give it to Callie, not in this lifetime, anyway, and he certainly wasn't going to hang on to it for future presentation to whomever. He was going to have to do *something* with it.

He had been stupid to buy the ring in the first place. He should have waited until she said yes, then taken her to a jewelry store and let her pick out the ring. Normal guys got the woman first, the ring second. A fellow could avoid a lot of pitfalls if he did it the tried-and-true traditional way.

Water under the bridge.

But, God! he felt miserable. So empty, as if he had absolutely nothing to live for.

He was glumly staring into his beer mug when he heard a man's voice ask, 'Did you get that in Vietnam?'

Jake looked. Two stools down sat a young man, no more than twenty-two or -three. His left hand was a hook sticking out of his sleeve. His interrogator was older, pushing thirty, bigger, and stood waiting for the bartender to draw him a beer.

'Yeah,' the kid said. 'Near Chu Lai.'

'Serves you right,' the older man said as he tossed his money on the bar and picked up his beer. He turned away.

Jake Grafton was off his stool and moving without conscious thought. He laid a heavy hand on the man's shoulder and spun him around. Beer slopped from the man's mug.

'You *sonuvabitch!*' the man roared. 'What do you think you're doing?'

'You owe this guy an apology.'

'My *ass!*' Then the look on Grafton's face sank in. 'Now hold on, you bastard! I've got a black belt in—'

That was all he managed to get out, because Jake seized a beer bottle sitting on the bar and smashed it against the man's head with a sweeping backhand. The big man went to the floor, stunned.

Grafton grabbed wet, bloody hair with his right hand and lifted. He grabbed a handful of balls with his left and brought the man to his feet, then started him sideways. With a heave he threw him through the plate-glass window onto the concourse.

As the glass tinkled down Jake walked out the door of the bar and approached the man. He lay stunned, surrounded by glass fragments. The glass grated under Jake's shoes.

Jake squatted.

The man was semiconscious, bleeding from numerous small cuts. His eyes swam, then focused on Grafton.

25

'You got off lucky this time. I personally know a dozen men who would have killed you for that crack you made in there. There's probably thousands of them.'

Slivers of glass stuck out of the man's face in several places.

'If I were you I'd give up karate. You aren't anywhere near tough enough. Maybe you oughta try ballet.'

He stood and walked back into the bar, ignoring the gaping onlookers. The ex-soldier was still sitting on the stool.

'How much for the beers?' Jake asked the bartender.

'Yours?'

'Mine and this gentleman's. I'm buying his too.'

'Four bucks.'

Jake tossed a five-spot on the bar. Through the now-empty frame of the window he saw a policeman bending over the man lying on the concourse.

Jake held out his hand to the former soldier, who shook it.

'You didn't have to do that.'

'Yeah I did,' Jake said. 'I owed it to myself.'

The bartender held out his hand. 'I was in the Army for a couple years. I'd like to shake your hand too.'

Jake shook it.

'Well,' he said to the one-handed veteran, who was looking at his hook, 'don't let the assholes grind you down.'

'He isn't the only one,' the man murmured, nodding toward the concourse.

'I know. We got a fucking Eden here, don't we?'

He left the bar and introduced himself to the first cop he saw.

It was about four o'clock on Monday afternoon when a police officer opened the cell door.

'You're leaving, Grafton. Come on.'

The officer walked behind Jake, who was decked out in a

blue jumpsuit and shuffled along in rubber shower sandals that were several sizes too big. He had been in the can all weekend. He had used his one telephone call when he was arrested on Saturday to call the squadron duty officer at NAS Whidbey.

'You're *where?*' that worthy had demanded, apparently unable to believe his own ears.

'The King County Jail,' Jake repeated.

'I'll be damned! What'd you do, kill somebody?'

'Naw. Threw a guy out of a bar.'

'That's all?'

'He went out through a plate glass window.'

'Oh.'

'Better put it in the logbook and call the skipper at home.'

'Okay, Jake. Don't bend over to pick up the soap.'

This afternoon he got into his civilian clothes in the same room in which he had undressed, the same room, incidentally, in which he had been fingerprinted and photographed. When he was dressed an officer passed him an envelope that contained the items from his pockets.

Jake examined the contents of the envelope. His airline tickets were still there, his wallet, change, and the ring. He pocketed the ring and counted the money in the wallet.

'Don't see many white guys in here carrying diamond rings,' the cop said chattily.

Grafton wasn't in the mood.

'Dopers seem to have pockets full of them,' the cop continued. 'And burglars. You haven't been crawling through any windows, have you?'

'Not lately.' Jake snapped his wallet shut and pocketed it.

'Bet it helps you get laid a lot.'

'Melts their panties. Poked your daughter last week.'

'Sign this receipt, butthole.'

Jake did so.

They led him out to a desk. His commanding officer,

27

Commander Dick Donovan, was sitting in a straight-backed chair. He didn't bother watching as Jake signed two more pieces of paper thrust at him by the desk sergeant. One was a promise to appear in three weeks for a preliminary hearing before a magistrate. Jake pocketed his copy.

'You're free to go,' the sergeant said.

Donovan came out of his chair and headed for the door. Jake trailed along behind him.

In the parking lot Jake got into the passenger seat of Donovan's car. Donovan still hadn't said a word. He was a big man, easily six foot three, with wide shoulders and huge feet. He was the first bombardier-navigator (BN) to ever command the replacement squadron, VA-128.

'Thanks for bailing me out, Skipper.'

'I have a lot better things to do with my time than driving all the way to Seattle to bail an officer out of jail. An *officer!* A bar brawl! I almost didn't come. I shouldn't have. I wish I hadn't.'

'I'm sorry.'

'Don't shit me, Mister. You aren't *sorry!* You weren't even drunk when you threw that guy through that window. You'd had exactly half of one beer. I read the police report and the witnesses' statements. You aren't sorry and you've got no excuse.'

'I'm sorry you had to drive down here, sir. I'm not sorry for what I did to that guy. He had it coming.'

'Just who do you think you are, Grafton? Some comic book superhero? Who gave you the right to punish every jerk out there that deserves it? That's what cops and courts are for.'

'Okay, I shouldn't have done it.'

'You're breaking my heart.'

'Thanks for bailing me out. You didn't have to do it. I know that.'

'Not that you give a good goddamn.'

'It really doesn't matter.'

28

'What should I do with you now?'

'Whatever you feel you gotta do, Skipper. Write a bad fittie, letter of reprimand, court-martial, whatever. It's your call. If you want, I'll give you a letter of resignation tomorrow.'

'Just like that,' Donovan muttered.

'Just like that.'

'Is that what you want? Out of the Navy?'

'I haven't thought about it.'

'*Sir!*' Donovan snarled.

'Sir.'

Donovan fell silent. He got on I-5 and headed north. He didn't take the exit for the Mukilteo ferry, but stayed on the freeway. He was in no mood for the ferry. He was going the long way around, across the bridge at Deception Pass to Whidbey Island.

Jake merely sat and watched the traffic. None of it mattered anymore. The guys who died in Vietnam, the ones who were maimed . . . all that carnage and suffering . . . just so assholes could insult them in airports? So college professors could sneer? So the lieutenants who survived could fret about their fitness reports while they climbed the career ladder rung by slippery rung?

June . . . in the year of our Lord 1973.

In Virginia his dad would be working from dawn to dark. His father knew the price that had to be paid, so he paid it, and he reaped the reward. The calves were born and thrived, the cattle gained weight, the crops grew and matured and were harvested.

Perhaps he should go back to Virginia, get some sort of job. He was tired of the uniform, tired of the paperwork, even . . . even tired of the flying. It was all so absolutely meaningless.

Donovan was guiding the car through Mount Vernon when he spoke again. 'It took eighty-seven stitches to sew that guy up.'

29

Jake wasn't paying attention. He made a polite noise.

'His balls were swollen up the size of oranges.' The skipper sighed. 'Eighty-seven stitches is a lot, but there shouldn't be any permanent injuries. Just some scars. So I talked to the prosecutor. There won't be a trial.'

Jake grunted. He was half listening to Donovan now, but the commander's words were just that, words.

'The prosecutor walked out from the Chosin Reservoir with the Fifth Marines,' Donovan continued. 'He read the police report and the statements by the bartender and that crippled soldier. The police file and complaint are going to be lost.'

'Humpf,' Jake said.

'So you owe me five hundred bucks. Two hundred which I posted as bail and three hundred to replace that window you broke. You can write me a personal check.'

'Thanks, Skipper.'

'Of course, that jerk could try to cash in on his eighty-seven stitches if he can find a lawyer stupid enough to bring a civil suit. A jury might make you pay the hospital and doctor bill, but I doubt if they would give the guy a dime more than that. Never can tell about juries, though.'

'Eighty-seven,' Jake murmured.

'So you can pack your bags,' Donovan continued. 'I'm sending you to the Marines. Process servers can't get you if you're in the middle of the Pacific.'

With a growing sense of horror Jake realized the import of Commander Donovan's words. 'The *Marines?*'

'Yeah. Marine A-6 outfit is going to sea on *Columbia*. They don't have any pilots with carrier experience. BUPERS' – the Bureau of Naval Personnel – 'is looking for some Navy volunteers to go to sea with them. Consider yourself volunteered.'

'*Jesus H. Christ*, Skipper!' he spluttered. 'I just completed two 'Nam cruises five months ago.' He fell silent, tongue-tied as the full implications of this disaster pressed in upon him.

Shore duty was the payback, the flying vacation from two combat cruises, the night cat shots, the night traps, getting shot at, shot up and shot down. Those night rides down the catapults . . . sweet Jesus how he had hated those. And the night approaches, in terrible weather, sometimes in a shot-up airplane, with never enough gas – it made him want to puke just thinking about that shit. And here was Tiny Dick Donovan proposing to send him right back to do eight or nine more months of it!

Aww, fuck! It just wasn't fair!

'*The gooks damn near killed me over North Vietnam a dozen times! It's a miracle I'm still alive. And now you feed me a shit sandwich.*'

That just popped out. Dick Donovan didn't seem to hear. It dawned on Jake that the commander probably couldn't be swayed with sour grapes.

In desperation, Jake attacked in the only direction remaining. 'The jarheads maintain their planes with ball peen hammers and pipe wrenches,' he roared, his voice beyond its owner's control. 'Their planes are flying death-traps.'

When Donovan didn't reply to this indisputable truth, Jake lost the bubble completely. 'You can't *do* this to me! I—'

'Wanna bet?'

There were three staff instructors seated at stools at the bar nursing beers when Jake walked into the O Club. The afternoon sun streamed through the tall windows. If you squinted against the glare you could see the long lazy reach of Puget Sound, placid in the calm evening, more like a pond than an arm of the sea. If you looked closely though, you could see the rise and fall of gentle swells.

Jake broke the news that he was on his way to the

31

Marine squadron going aboard *Columbia*. He could see by the looks on their faces that they already knew. Bad news rides a fast horse.

Heads bobbed solemnly.

'Well, shore duty gets old quick.'

'Yeah. Whidbey ain't bad, but it ain't Po City.'

Their well-meaning remarks gave Jake no comfort, although he tried to maintain a straight face. Not being a liberty hound, the whores and whiskey of Olongapo City in the Philippines had never been much of an attraction for him. He felt close to tears. *This* was what he wanted more of – the flying without combat, an eight-thousand-foot runway waiting for his return, relaxed evenings on dry land with mountains on the horizon, the cool breeze coming in off the sound, delicious weekends to loaf through.

The injustice of Donovan's decision was like a knife in his gut. It was his turn, yet he was leaving all the good stuff and going back to sea!

'Lucky you aren't married,' one of the barflies said. 'A little cruise in the middle of a shore tour would drive a lot of wives straight to the divorce court.'

That remark got them talking. They knew four men who were in the process of getting divorces. The long separations the Navy required of families were hell on marriages. While his companions gossiped Jake's thoughts turned morosely to Callie. She was a good woman, and he loved her. He could see her face, feel her touch, hear her voice even now.

But her father! That jerk! A flash of heat went through him, then flickered out as he surveyed the cold ashes of his life.

'Things happen to Marines,' Tricky Nixon was saying when Jake once again began paying attention to the conversation.

Tricky was a wiry, dark, compact man. Now his brows

knitted. 'Knew a Marine fighter pilot once. Flew an F-4. He diverted from the ship into Cecil Field one night. Black night. You guys know Cecil, big as half of Texas, with those parallel runways?'

His listeners nodded. Tricky took another swig of beer. After he swallowed and cleared his throat, he continued: 'For reasons known only to God, he plunked his mighty Phantom down *between* those parallel runways. In the grass. Hit the radar shack head-on, smacked it into a million splinters.'

Tricky sighed, then continued: 'The next day the squadron maintenance officer went into Cecil on the COD, looked the plane over pretty good, had it towed outta the dirt onto a taxiway, then filled it with gas and flew it back to the ship. It was a little scratched up but nothing serious. Things happen to Marines.'

They talked about that – about the odds of putting a tactical jet with a landing weight of 45,000 pounds down on grass and not ripping one or more of the gear off the plane.

'I knew a Marine once,' Billy Doyle said when the conversation lagged, 'who forgot to pull the power back when he landed. He was flying an F-4D.'

His listeners nodded.

'He went screeching down the runway with the tires smoking, went off the end and drove out across about a half mile of dirt. Went through the base perimeter fence and across a ditch that wiped off the landing gear. Skidded on across a road, and came to rest with the plane straddling a railroad track. He sat there awhile thinking it over, then finally shut 'er down and climbed out. He was standing there looking 'er over when a train came along and plowed into the wreck. Smashed it to bits.'

They sipped beer while they thought about forgetting to pull the throttle to idle on touchdown, about how it would feel sitting dazed in the cockpit of a crashed airplane with the engine still running as the realization sank in that you had really screwed the pooch this time. *Really* screwed the pooch.

'Things happen to Marines,' Billy Doyle added.

'Their bad days can be spectacular,' Bob Landow agreed in his bass growl. He was a bear of a man, with biceps that rippled the material of his shirt. 'Marine F-8 pilot was trans-Pacing one time, flying the pond.'

He paused and lubricated his throat while his listeners thought about flying a single-seat fighter across the Pacific, about spending ten or twelve hours strapped to an ejection seat in the tiny cockpit.

Landow's growl broke the silence. 'The first time he hit the tanker for gas, the fuel cells overpressurized and ruptured. Fuel squirted out of every orifice. It squirted into the engine bay and in seconds the plane caught fire.

'At this point our Marine decides to eject. He pulls the face curtain. Nothing happens. But not yet to sweat, because he has the secondary handle between his legs. He gives that a hell of a jerk. Nothing. He just sits there in this unejectable seat in this burning aircraft with fuel running out of every pore over the vast Pacific.

'This is turning into a major-league bad day. He yanks on the handle a couple more times like King Kong with a hard on. Nothing happens. Gawdalmighty, he's getting excited now. He tried jettisoning the canopy. Damn thing won't go off. It's stuck. This is getting seriouser and seriouser.

'The plane is burning like a blowtorch by this time and he's getting *really* excited. He pounds and pounds at the canopy while the plane does smoky whifferdills. Finally the canopy departs. Our Marine is greatly relieved. He unstraps and prepares to climb out. This is an F-8, you understand, and if he makes it past that tail in one piece he will be the very first. But he's going to give it a try. He starts to straighten up and the wind just grabs him and whoom – he's out – free-falling toward the ocean deep and blue. *Out,* thank God, *out!*

'He falls for a while toward the Pacific thinking about Marine maintenance, then decides it's time to see if the parachute works. It wasn't that kind of a day. Damn thing streams.'

'No!' several of his listeners groaned in unison.

'I shit you not,' Bob Landow replied. He helped himself to more beer as his Marine fell from an indifferent sky toward an indifferent sea with an unopened parachute streaming behind him.

'What's the rest of it?' Tricky demanded.

Landow frowned. There is a certain pace to a good sea story, and Tricky had a bad habit of rushing it. Not willing to be hurried, Landow took another sip of beer, then made a show of wiping his lips with a napkin. When he had the glass back on the bar and his weight lifter's arms crossed just so, he said, 'He had some Marine luck there at the end. Pulled strings like a puppeteer and got a few panels of the rag to blossom. Just enough. Just enough.'

He shook his head wearily and settled a baleful gaze on Jake Grafton. 'Things happen to Marines. You be careful out there, Jake.'

'Yeah,' Jake told them as he glanced out the window at the reflection of small puffy clouds on the limpid blue water. 'I will.'

CHAPTER THREE

Jake Grafton was dressed in khakis and wearing his leather flight jacket when he stepped onto the catwalk around the flight deck. The sun was out, yet to the west a layer of fog obscured the higher buildings of San Francisco and all of the Golden Gate Bridge except the tops of the towers. The gentle breeze had that moist, foggy feeling. Jake shivered and tugged his ball cap more firmly onto his head.

The pier below was covered with people. The pilot rested his elbows on the railing of the catwalk and stood taking it all in. listening to the cacophony of voices.

Sailors, Marines, officers and chiefs stood surrounded by their families. Children were everywhere, some clinging to their mothers, others running through the crowd chasing one another, the smaller ones being passed from hand to hand by the adults.

A band was tuning up on Elevator Two, which was in the down position and stuck out over the pier like a porch roof. Even as Jake watched, the conductor got the attention of his charges and whipped them into a Sousa march.

On the pier near the stern another band was assembling. No doubt that was the Naval Air Station band, which tooted for every ship's departure. Well and good, but *Columbia* had a band too and apparently the ship's XO thought there couldn't be too much music.

Above Jake's head the tails of aircraft stuck out precariously over the edge of the flight deck and cast weird shadows on the crowded pier. Occasionally he could see people lift their gaze to take in the vast bulk of the ship and the dozens of aircraft. Then the people turned their attention back to their loved one.

Last night he had stood in line at one of the dozen phone booths on the head of the pier. The rain had subsided to occasional drips. When his turn for the booth came, he had called his folks in Virginia, then Callie. It was after midnight in Chicago when she answered.

'Callie, this is Jake.'

'Where are you?'

'On the pier at Alameda. Did you get my letters?'

'I received three.'

He had written the letters and mailed them from Oceana, where he had been sent to do field carrier qualifications with a group of students from VA-42. He had completed his field quals, of course, but didn't go to the ship. There hadn't been time. He would have to qual aboard *Columbia* after she sailed. He needed ten day and six night traps because it had been over six months since his last carrier landing.

'Another letter is on the way,' he told Callie, probably a superfluous comment. 'You'll get it in a day or two.'

'So how is the ship?'

'It's a ship. What can I say?'

'When do you sail?'

'Seven-thirty in the morning.'

'So when I wake up you'll be at sea.'

'Uh-huh.'

They talked desultorily for several minutes, the operator came on the line and Jake fed in more quarters, then he got down to it. 'Callie, I love you.'

'I know you do. Oh, Jake, I'm so sorry your visit was such a disaster.'

'I am too. I guess these things just happen sometimes. I wish . . .' And he ran out of steam. A phone booth on a pier

37

with dozens of sailors awaiting their turn didn't seem the place to say what he wished.

'You be careful,' she said.

'You know me, Callie. I'm always careful.'

'Don't take any unnecessary chances.'

'I won't.'

'I want you to come back to me.'

Now Jake stood watching the crowd and thinking about that. She wanted him to come back *to her*.

He took a deep breath and sighed. Ah me, life is so strange. Just when everything looks bleakest a ray of sunshine comes through the clouds. Hope. He had hope. She wouldn't have said something like that unless she meant it, not Callie, not to a guy going on an eight-month cruise.

He was standing there listening to the two bands playing different tunes at the same time, watching the crowd, watching sailors and women engage in passionate kisses, when he saw the Cadillac. A pink Cadillac convertible with the top down was slowly making its way down the pier. People flowed out of its way, then closed in behind it, like water parting for a boat.

Cars were not allowed on the pier. Yet there it was. A man in a white uniform was driving, yet all of his passengers were women, young women, and not wearing a lot of clothing either. Lots of brown thighs and bare shoulders were on display, several truly awesome bosoms.

In complete disregard of the regulations, the car made its way to the foot of the officers' gangway and stopped. The driver got out and stretched lazily as he surveyed the giant gray ship looming beside the pier. The women bounded out and surrounded him.

It's Bosun Muldowski! Who else could it be? No sailor could get a car past the guards at the head of the pier and few officers under flag rank. But a warrant officer four? Yep.

Muldowski.

He had been the flight deck bosun on *Shiloh*, Jake's last

ship. Apparently he was coming to *Columbia*. Now Jake remembered – Muldowski never did shore duty tours. He had been going from ship to ship for over twenty-five years.

Look at those women in hot pants and short short skirts!

Sailors to the right and left of Jake in the catwalk shouted and shrieked wolf whistles. Muldowski took no notice but the women waved prettily, which drew lusty cheers from the onlooking white hats.

With the bosun's bags out of the trunk of the car, he took his time hugging each of the women, all five of them, as the bands blared mightily and spectator sailors watched in awe.

'The bosun must own a whorehouse,' one sailor down the catwalk told his friends loud enough for Jake to hear.

'He sure knows how to live,' his buddy said approvingly. 'Style. He's got *style*.'

Jake Grafton grinned. Muldowski's spectacular arrival had just catapulted him to superstardom with the white hats, which was precisely the effect, Jake suspected, that the bosun intended. The deck apes would work like slaves for him until they dropped in their tracks.

All too soon the ship's whistle sounded, bullhorns blared and sailors rushed to single up the lines holding the great ship to the land. The men on the pier gave their women one last passionate hug, then dashed for the gangways. As seven bells sounded over the ship's PA system, cranes lifted the gangways clear and deposited them on the pier.

The last of the lines were released and the ship began to move, very slowly at first, almost imperceptibly. Slowly the gap between the pier and the men crowding the rails widened.

Sailors tossed their Dixie cups at the pier and children scurried like rats to retrieve them. The strains of 'Anchors Aweigh' filled the air.

When the pier was several hundred feet away and aft of the beam, Jake felt a rumble reach him through the steel on which he stood. The screws were biting. The effect was noticeable. The pier slid astern slowly at first, then with increasing speed.

Now the pilot climbed to the flight deck and threaded his way past tie-down chains toward the bow, where he joined a loose knot of men leaning into the increasing wind. Ahead was the Bay Bridge, then the Golden Gate. And the fog beyond the Golden Gate was dissipating.

The ship had cleared the Bay Bridge and was steaming at eight or ten knots past Alcatraz when the loudspeaker sounded. 'Flight Quarters, flight quarters. All hands man your flight quarters station.'

The cruise had begun.

Jake was in the locker room donning his flight gear when a black Marine in a flight suit came in. He had railroad tracks pinned to the shoulders of his flight suit, so he was a captain, the Marine equivalent of Jake's Navy rank of lieutenant. He looked Jake over, nodded to a couple of Marines who were also suiting up to get some traps, then strolled over to Jake.

'They call me Flap. I guess we're flying together.'

The BN had his hair cut in the Marine Corps' version of an Afro – that is, it stuck out from his head about half an inch and was meticulously tapered on the sides and back. He was slightly above medium height, with the well-developed chest and bulging muscles that can only be acquired by thousands of hours of pumping iron. He looked to be in his late twenties, maybe thirty at the most.

'Jake Grafton. You're Le Beau?'

'Yep.'

'How come you weren't at the brief?'

'Hey, man. This is CQ!' CQ meant carrier qualification. 'All we're gonna do is fly around this bird farm with the wheels down, dangling our little hook thingy. Where is *your* bag. You can hack it, can't ya?'

Jake decided to change the subject. 'Where you from?'

40

'Parris Island. Get it? Le Beau? French name? Parris Island?'

'Ha ha.'

'Don't let this fine chocolate complexion fool you, my man. It's French chocolate.'

'French shit,' said one of Le Beau's fellow Marines.

'Eat it, butt breath,' Flap shot back. 'I'm black with a seasoning of Creole.'

'Sorta like coffee with cream,' Jake Grafton remarked as he zipped up his torso harness.

'Yeah man. That's exactly right. There was a planter in Louisiana, Le Beau, with a slobbering craving for black poontang. After the Civil War he took personal offense when his former slaves adopted his last name. They did it 'cause most of them was his sons and daughters. But Le Beau didn't like the thought of being recognized in history as a patriarch, didn't want to admit his generous genetic contributions to improving a downtrodden race. Hung a couple of his nigger kids, he did. So all the blacks in the parish adopted the name. More damn black Le Beaus in that section of Louisiana than you could shake a stiff dick at. Now that redneck Cajun planter bigot was one of my many great-great-grandpappys, of whom I am so very proud.'

'Terrific,' said Jake Grafton, who checked to see that the laces of his new G-suit were properly adjusted.

'We heard you were coming. The Nav just didn't think us gyrenes could handle all this high tailhook tech. So we heard they were sending an ace Navy type to indoctrinate us ignorant jarheads, instruct us, lead the way into a better, brighter day.'

Grafton didn't think that comment worth a reply.

'It'll be a real pleasure,' said Flap Le Beau warmly as he grabbed his torso harness from his locker, 'flying with a master hookster. Just think of me as a student at the fount of all wisdom, an apprentice seeking to acquire insights into the nuances of the arcane art, appreciate the—'

'Are you always this full of shit or are you making a special effort on my behalf?' Jake asked.

Le Beau prattled on unperturbed. 'It's tragic that so many Navy persons are dangerously thin-skinned in a world full of sharp objects! One can infer from your crude comment that you share that lamentable trait with your colleagues. It's sad, very sad, but there are probably gonna be tensions between us. None of that male-bonding horse pucky for you and me, huh? Tensions. Stress. Mis-understandings. Heartburns. Hard feelings. Ass kickings.' He sighed plaintively. 'Well, I try to get along by going along. That's the Cajun in me coming out. I am so very lucky I got this white blood in me, ya know? Lets me see everything in a better perspective.'

The Marine bent slightly at the waist and addressed his next comment to the deck: 'Thank you, thank you, Jules Le Beau, rotting down there in hell.'

Back to his locker and flight gear – 'Lots of the bros ain't as lucky as I am – they can't tell trees from manure piles, and—'

'Oh, for Christ's sake, Flap,' someone in the next row said. 'Turn off the tap, will ya?'

'Yeoww,' Flap howled, 'I feel *great!* Gonna get out there and fly with a Navy ace and see how it's *done* by the best of the best!'

'How did I wind up with this asshole?' Jake asked the major two lockers down.

'No other pilot wanted him,' was the reply.

'Hey, watch your mouth over there,' Flap called. 'This is my rep you're pissin' on.'

'Pisson' on, *sir!*'

'Sir,' Flap echoed dutifully.

The sun shone down softly through a high thin cirrus layer. The wind out of the northwest was heaping the sea into long windrows and ripping occasional whitecaps from

42

the crests as gulls wheeled and turned around the great ship.

Two frigates and four destroyers were visible several miles away, scattered in a haphazard circle around the carrier. These were the carrier's escorts, an antisubmarine screen, faithful retainers that would attend the queen wherever she led.

On the eastern horizon land was still visible. It would soon drop over the earth's rim since the carrier would have to spend the next several hours running into the northwest wind, then the universe would consist of only the ships, the sea and the sky. The land would become a memory of the past and a vision of a hazy future, but the solid reality of the present would be just the ships and the men who rode them. Six small moons orbiting one wandering planet . . .

Jake's vision lingered on that distant dark line of earth, then he turned away.

The ship rode easily this morning, with just the gentlest of rolls, which Jake noticed only because he didn't have his sea legs yet. This roll would become a pitching motion when the ship turned into the wind.

Sensing these things and knowing them without really thinking about them, Jake Grafton walked slowly aft looking for his aircraft. There – by Elevator Four.

She was no beauty, this A-6E Intruder decked out in dull, low viz paint splotched here and there with puke green zinc dichromate primer. An external power cord was already plugged into the plane. Jake lowered the boarding ladder and opened the canopy, then climbed up and placed his helmet bag on the seat. He ensured the safety pins were properly installed in the ejection seat, let his eye rove over the cockpit switches, the gear handle, the wing position lever and the fuel dump switches, then checked the fuel quantity. Ten thousand pounds. As advertised. He toggled the seat position adjustment switches, noted the whine and felt the seat move, then released them. Jake climbed down the ladder to the deck and began his preflight inspection.

In Vietnam he had flown A-6As, the first version of the Intruder. This plane was an A-6E, the second-generation bomber, the state-of-the-art in American military technology. Most of the updates were not visible to the naked eye. The search and track radars of the A-6A had been replaced with one radar that combined both search and track functions. The A's rotary-drum computer had been replaced with a solid-state, digital, state-of-the-art version. The third major component in the electronics system, the inertial navigation system, or INS, had not yet been updated, so it was now the weak point in the navigation/ attack system. The new computer and radar were not only more accurate than the old gear, they were also proving to be extraordinarily reliable, which erased the major operational disadvantage of the A-6A.

The E had been in the fleet for several years now, yet it had not been used in Vietnam, by Pentagon fiat. Had the updated E been used there, the targets could have been hit with greater accuracy, with fewer missions, thereby saving lives and perhaps helping shorten the war, but inevitably some of these planes would have been lost and the technology compromised, i.e., seen by the Soviets.

So lives had been traded to keep the technology secret. How many lives? Who could say.

As Jake Grafton walked around this A-6E looking and touching this and that, the raw, twisted Vietnam emotions came flooding back. Once again he felt the fear, saw the blood, saw the night sky filled with streaks of tracer and the fiery plumes of SAMs. The faces of the dead men floated before him as he felt the smooth, cool skin of the airplane.

It seemed as if he had never left the ship. Any second Tiger Cole would come strolling across the deck with his helmet bag and charts, ready to fly into the mouth of hell.

Jake felt his stomach churn, as if he were going to vomit. He paused and leaned against a main-gear strut.

No!

Six months had passed. His knee had healed, he had visited his folks, done a little flight instruction at Whidbey Island, visited Callie in Chicago . . . thrown that asshole through the window at Sea-Tac . . . why was he sweating, nauseated?

This is *car quals*, for Christ's sake! It's a beautiful day, a cake hop, a walk in the park!

He stood straight and, looking out to sea, took several deep breaths. He should have popped the question to Callie – should have asked her to marry him. And he should have resigned from the Navy.

He shouldn't even be here! On the boat again! He had done his share, dropped his share of bombs, killed his share of gomers.

For God's sake – another cruise – with a bunch of jack-off jarheads!

He took his hand off the strut and stood staring at the plane, his face twisted into a frown. Primer splotches everywhere, dirt, stains from hydraulic leaks . . . And it was a fairly new plane, less than a year old!

Camparelli would have come screaming unglued if they had sent a plane like this to *his* squadron. Screaming-meemy fucking *unglued!*

Somehow the thought of Commander Camparelli, Jake's last skipper in Vietnam, storming and ranting amused Jake Grafton.

'Looks like a piece of shit, don't it?'

Bosun Muldowski was standing there staring at the plane with his arms crossed.

'Yeah, Bosun, but I ain't looking to buy it. I'm just flying it this morning.'

'Sure didn't expect to find you aviatin' for the jugheads, Mr Grafton.'

45

'Life's pretty weird sometimes.'

The bosun nodded sagely. 'Heard about that shithead that went through the window at Sea-Tac.'

Jake nodded and rubbed his hand through his hair. 'Well, I guess I lost it for a little bit. I'm not the smartest guy you ever met.'

'Smart enough. Thanks.'

With that, the bosun walked forward, up the deck, leaving the pilot staring at his back.

'Hey, my man! Is this mean green killing machine safe to fly?' Flap. He came around the nose of the plane and lowered the BN's boarding ladder.

'We'll find out, won't we?'

'It's an embarrassing question to have to ask, I know, yet the dynamics of the moment and the precarious state of my existence here in space and time impel me to ponder my karma and your competence. No offense, but I am growing attached to my ass and don't want to part with it. What I'm getting at, Ace, is, are you man enough to handle the program?'

The pilot slapped the fuselage. 'This relic from the Mongolian Air Force is going off the pointy end of this boat in about fifteen minutes with your manly physique in it. That's the only fact I have access to. Will your ass stay attached? Will sweet, innocent Suzy Kiss-me succumb to the blandishments of the evil pervert, Mortimer Fuck-butt? Stay tuned to this channel and find out right after these words from our sponsors.' He turned his back on Flap Le Beau.

'I have no doubt this thing will go *off* this scow, but can *you* get it back aboard all in one piece?'

Jake Grafton shouted back over his shoulder: 'We'll fly together or die together, Le Beau. None of that macho male bonding crap for hairy studs like us.'

The bosun – he didn't have to say that. And it was a beautiful day, the sun glinting on the swells, the high, open sky, the gentle motion of the ship . . .

The plane would feel good in his hands, would do just as he willed it. She would respond so sweetly to the throttles and stick, would come down the groove into the wires so slick and honest . . .

As the sea wind played with his hair the pilot found himself feeling better.

CHAPTER FOUR

Wings spread and locked, flaps and slats to takeoff, Roger the weight-board – it all came back without conscious thought as Jake followed the taxi director's hand signals and moved the warplane toward the port bow catapult, Cat Two. Flap didn't help – he didn't say or do anything after getting the inertial aligned and flipping the radar switch to standby. He merely sat and watched Jake.

'Takeoff checklist,' Jake prompted.

'I thought you said you could fly this thing, Ace.'

Jake ran through the items on his own as he eased the plane the last few feet into the catapult shuttle and the hold-back bar dropped into place.

The yellow-shirt taxi director gave him the 'release brakes' signal with one hand and with the other made a sweeping motion below his waist. This was the signal to the catapult operator to ease the shuttle forward with a hydraulic piston, taking all the slack out of the nose-wheel tow-launching mechanism. Jake felt the thunk as he released the brakes and pushed both throttles forward to the stops.

The engines came up nicely. RPM, exhaust gas temperatures, fuel flow – the tapes ran up the dials as the engines wound up.

The Intruder vibrated like a living thing as the engines sucked in rivers of air and slammed it out the exhausts.

'You ready?' Jake asked the bombardier as he wrapped the fingers of his left hand around the catapult grip while he braced the heel of the hand against the throttles.

'Onward and upward, Ace.'

The taxi director was pointing to the catapult officer, who was ten feet farther up the deck. The shooter was twirling his fingers and looking at Jake, waiting.

Oil pressure both engines – fine. Hydraulics – okay. Jake waggled the stick and checked the movement of the stabilator in his left-side rearview mirror on the canopy rail. Then he saluted the cat officer with his right hand. The shooter returned it and glanced up the cat track toward the bow as Jake put his head back into the headrest and placed his right hand behind the stick.

Now the cat officer lunged forward and touched the deck with his right hand.

One heartbeat, two, then the catapult fired. The acceleration was vicious.

Yeeeaaaah! and it was over, in about two and a half seconds. The edge of the bow swept under the nose and the plane was over the glittering sea.

Jake let the trim rotate the nose to eight degrees nose up as he reached for the gear handle. He slapped it up and swept his eyes across the instrument panel, taking in the attitude reference on the vertical display indicator – the VDI, the altimeter – eighty feet and going up, the rate of climb – positive, the airspeed – 150 knots and accelerating, all warning lights out. He took in all these bits of information without conscious thought, just noted them somewhere in his subconscious, and put it all together as the airplane accelerated and climbed away from the ship.

With the gear up and locked, he raised the flaps and slats. Here they came. Still accelerating, he stopped the climb at five hundred feet and ran the nose trim down. Two hundred and fifty knots, 300, 350 . . . still accelerating . . .

To his amusement he saw that Flap Le Beau was sitting upright in his ejection seat with his hands folded on his lap,

49

just inches from the alternate ejection handle between his legs.

At 400 knots Jake eased the throttles back. Five miles coming up on the DME . . . and the pilot pulled the nose up steeply and dropped the left wing as he eased the throttles forward again. The plane leaped away from the ocean in a climbing turn. Jake scanned the sky looking for the plane that had preceded him on the cat by two minutes.

He had four thousand pounds of fuel – no, only three thousand now – to burn off before they called him down for his first landing, in about fifteen minutes.

Better make it last, Jake. Don't squander it. He pulled the throttles back and coasted up to five thousand feet, where he leveled indicating 250 knots in a gentle turn that would allow him to orbit the ship on the five-mile circle.

Flap sighed audibly over the intercom, the ICS, then said, 'Acceptable launch, Jake. Acceptable. You obviously have done this once or twice and haven't forgotten how. This pleases me. I get a warm fuzzy.'

There the major was, almost on the other side of the ship, level at this altitude and turning on the five-mile arc. Jake steepened his turn to cut across above the ship and rendezvous.

'I almost joined the Navy,' Flap confided, 'but I came to my senses just in time and joined the Corps. It's a real fighting outfit, the best in the world. The Navy . . . well, the best that can be said is that you guys try. Most of the time, anyway.'

He talked on as Jake got on the major's bearing line and eased in some left rudder to lower the nose so he could see the major out the right-side quarter panel. Rendezvousing an A-6 with its side-by-side seating took some finesse when coming in on the lead's left because the pilot of the joining aircraft could easily lose sight of the lead plane. If he let himself go just a little high, or if he let his plane fall a little behind the bearing line – going sucked, they called it – and attempted to pull back to the bearing, the lead would disappear under the wingman's nose and he would be closing blindly. This was not good, a situation fraught with hazard for all concerned.

This morning Jake stayed glued to the bearing. If Flap noticed he gave no indication. He was saying, '. . . the closest I ever came to being in the Navy was the wife of some surface warrior I met at MCRD' – Marine Corps Recruit Depot – 'O Club on a Friday night. She rubbed her tits all over my back and I told her she was going to give me zipper rash. She was all hot and randy so I thought, Why not. We went over to her place . . .'

When he was fifty feet away from the major's plane Jake lowered the nose and crossed behind and under. He surfaced into parade position on the right side, the outside of the turn. The BN gave him a thumbs-up.

Jake's BN talked on. '. . . I just put the ol' cock to her . . .'

After a frequency shift that the major's BN signaled and Jake had to dial in because Flap wasn't helping at all, they made two more turns in the circle, then started down.

'She had those nipples that are like strawberries, you know what I mean? All puffed up so nice and sweet and red and they're just made for sucking on? I like them the very best. Can't understand why God didn't equip more women with 'em. Only about one broad in ten has 'em. It's a mystery.'

They were descending through patches of sunlight interspersed with shadow. The occasional golden shafts played on the planes and made the sea below glisten, when Jake could steal a second from holding position on the lead plane and glance down.

His plane handled well. Slick and tight and responsive. He contented himself with moving his plane a few inches forward on the lead, then a few inches back, staying in absolute control. When he felt comfortable he moved in on the bearing line so that the wing tips overlapped. He stopped when he could feel the downdraft off the lead's wing and the tip was just two feet from his canopy. He held it there for a moment or two to prove to himself that he could still do it, then eased back out to where he belonged.

Flying is the best that life offers, Jake Grafton thought. *And carrier flying is the best of the flying. These day traps and cat shots are going to be terrific.* He fought back the sense of euphoria that suffused him.

'. . . as close as I ever came to being in the Navy, I'll tell you that.'

If Flap would just shut up!

But he won't. So no sense making a scene.

The two warplanes came up the ship's wake at eight hundred feet glued together. There were already two other planes in the pattern with their gear and hooks down, two A-7 Corsairs, so the major delayed his break. Then the BN kissed him off and the major dumped his left wing and pulled. Jake watched the lead plane turn away as he counted to himself. At the count of seven he slammed the stick sideways and pulled as he reached for the gear handle with his left hand and slapped it down. Then the flaps.

Turning level, three G's . . . gear coming, flaps and slats coming . . . seven thousand pounds of fuel.

Stable on the downwind he toggled the main dump and let seven hundred pounds squirt out into the atmosphere. He wanted to cross the ramp of the ship with precisely six grand.

Precision. That's what carrier flying is all about. That's the challenge. And the thrill.

'. . . just don't see why anybody would want to float around in the middle of the ocean on these bird farms. Eight months of this fun. The Navy is full of happy masturbators . . .'

Hook up for the first pass, a touch-and-go. Let the LSO get his look and learn that I'm not suicidal.

Coming through the ninety, on speed, exactly 118 knots

with a three-o'clock angle-of-attack . . . there's the meat-ball on the Fresnel lens. Cross the wake, roll out, coming in to the angled deck, watch the lineup! There's the burble from the island . . . power on then off fast. Keep that ball in the center . . .

The wheels smacked into the deck and the nose came down hard as Jake Grafton shoved the throttles to the stop and closed the wing-tip speed brakes with the throttle-mounted switch. The Intruder shot up the angled deck and ran off into the air. He brought the stick back and got her climbing.

'The amazing thing is that the Navy finds so many of you masturbators to ride these floating aviaries. You wouldn't think there were this many jack-off artists in the whole world. Not if you just looked at the world casually. I mean, most people like their sex with *somebody else*, y'know? No doubt a lot of you guys are queer. Gotta be.'

On the downwind Jake lowered the hook and checked that his harness was locked. Normally he flew with it unlocked so that he could lean forward if he wished or wiggle in the ejection seat.

He toggled the seat up a smidgen and adjusted the rheostat that brightened the angle-of-attack indicator.

The interval between Jake and the major was good, and the major trapped on his first pass as Jake was reducing power at the 180-degree position. Down and turning, on speed, looking for the ball crossing the wake, wings level and reducing power, now power on for the burble, watching the lineup and flying that ball . . .

The Intruder swept across the ramp and slammed into the deck. As the throttles went forward the tailhook caught a wire and dragged the plane to a dead stop.

Then the plane began to roll backward. Jake jabbed the hook-up button and added power to taxi out of the gear. The director was giving him the come ahead as Flap said, 'The whole concept of having five thousand guys crammed together without women is unnatural. Everybody horny, jacking off in the shower, into their sheets – this boat is a floating semen factory! In nineteen seventy-three! My God, haven't we humans made any progress in understanding man's sexual needs in all these years of . . .'

Queued up waiting for Cat Two, checking the gear and flap settings, the fuel, then following the yellow shirt's signals as he brought the plane into the shuttle – Jake was doing the things he knew how to do, the things that made the hassles worthwhile.

Throttles up . . . the salute – and wham, they were off to do it again. This time Jake left the gear and flaps down. He flew straight ahead upwind until the major passed him on the left going downwind.

Jake banked for the crosswind turn. The plane entered a shaft of sunlight and the warmth played on his arms and legs. Inside his oxygen mask Jake grinned broadly.

After four traps Jake was directed to fold his wings and stop near the carrier's island with the engines running while the plane was refueled, a 'hot' turnaround. He opened the canopy and took off his oxygen mask. His face was wet with sweat. He swabbed away the moisture and watched the planes making their approaches.

Flap Le Beau also sat watching, silent at last.

Heavenly silence. Except for the howl of jet engines at full power and the slam of the catapult and an occasional terse radio message. The flight deck of an aircraft carrier was the loudest place on earth, yet oh so pleasant without Flap's drivel.

In a few minutes Jake had 6,500 pounds of fuel and gave the purple-shirted fuel crew the cut sign, a slice of the hand across his throat. Mask on, canopy closed, parking brake off, engage nose-wheel steering and goose the throttles a smidgen to follow the director's signals. Now into the queue waiting for the cat . . .

All too soon it was over. Jake had the ten day traps the law required and was once more day qualified as a carrier pilot. He shut the plane down on the porch near Elevator Four and climbed down to the deck still wearing his helmet. After a few words with the plane captain, he descended a ladder to the catwalk, then went down into the first passageway leading into the 0-3 level, the deck under the flight deck.

Flap Le Beau was behind him.

'You did okay out there this morning, Ace,' Flap commented.

'You didn't.' Jake stopped and faced the bombardier-navigator.

'Say again?'

'I got an eighty-year-old grandmother who could have done a better job in the right seat than you did today.'

'Kiss my chocolate ass, Ace. I didn't ask for your opinion.'

'You're going to get it. You flew with me. I expect a BN to help me fly the plane, to act as a safety observer at all times, to read the checklists.'

'I just wanted to see if you could—'

'I *can!* While you were sitting there with your thumb up your butt and boring me to tears with the story of your miserable life, you could have been checking out the computer and radar for the debrief. You never even brought the radar out of standby! Don't *ever* pull that stunt again.'

Flap put his face just inches from Grafton's. 'I ain't taking any shit from the Navy, swabbie. We'd better get that straightened out here and now.'

'Le Beau, I don't know if you're senior to me or I'm senior to you and I really don't give a rat's ass which way it is. But in that cockpit I'm the aircraft commander. You're going to do a solid, professional job – there ain't no two ways about it. If you *don't*, your career in the grunts is gonna go down the crapper real damn quick. You won't be able to catch it with a swan dive.'

Flap opened his mouth to reply, but Jake Grafton snarled, 'Don't push it.' With that he turned and stalked away, leaving Flap Le Beau staring at his back.

When Jake was out of sight Flap grinned He nodded several times and rubbed his hand through his hair, fluffing his Afro.

'Flap, my man, this one's gonna do,' he said. 'He's gonna do *fine.*' And he laughed softly to himself.

Jake was seated in the back of the ready room filling out the maintenance forms on the airplane when the air wing landing signal officer, the LSO, and the A-6 squadron LSO came in. The A-6 guy Jake knew. He was an East Coast Navy pilot who had been shanghaied like Jake to provide the Marines with 'experience.' His name was McCoy and by some miracle, he was Jake's new roommate. If he had a first name Jake didn't learn it last night, when the LSO came in drunk, proclaimed himself to be the Real McCoy, and collapsed into his bunk facedown.

'Grafton,' the senior air wing LSO said, consulting his notes, 'you did okay.' His name was Hugh Skidmore. 'Touch-and-go was an OK, then nine OKs and one fair. All three wires. You're gonna wear out that third wire, fella.'

Jake was astonished. OKs were perfect passes, and he thought he had five or six good ones, but nine? To cover his astonishment and pleasure, he said gruffly, 'A *fair?* You gave me a *fair?* Which pass was that?'

Skidmore examined his book again, then snapped it shut. 'Seventh one. While you were turning through the ninety the captain put the helm over chasing the wind and you went low. You were a little lined up left, too.' He shrugged, then grinned. 'Try a bit harder next time, huh?'

56

Skidmore went off to debrief the major but McCoy lingered. 'Geez, Real, you guys sure are tough graders.'

'Better get your act together, Roomie.'

'What did you do to rate a tour with the Marines? Piss in a punch bowl?'

'Something like that,' the Real McCoy said distractedly, then wandered off.

After lunch Jake went to his stateroom to unpack. He had gotten the bulk of his gear on hangers or folded when McCoy came in, tossed his Mickey Mouse ears on his desk, and collapsed onto his bunk.

'I threw a civilian through a plate glass window,' Jake told the LSO. 'Just what did *you* do?'

McCoy sighed and opened his eyes. He focused on Grafton. 'I suppose you'll tell this all over the boat.'

'Try me.'

'Well, I made too much money. I got to talking about it with the guys. Then I had the Admin guys draft up a letter of resignation. Before I could get it submitted the skipper called me in. He said a rich bastard like me could just count his money out on the big gray boat.'

'Too much money? I never heard of such a thing. Did you loot the coffee mess?'

'Naw. Nothing like that.' McCoy sat up. He rubbed his face. 'Naw. I just got to playing the market.'

'What market?'

'*The* market.' When he saw the expression on Jake's face, he exclaimed, 'Jesus H Christ! The *stock* market.'

'I never knew anybody who owned stock.'

'Oh, for the love of . . .' McCoy stretched out and sighed.

'Well, how much money did you make, anyway?'

'You're going to tell every greasy asshole on this ship, Grafton. It's written all over your simple face.'

'No, I won't. Honest. How much?'

McCoy regarded his new roommate dolefully. Finally he

57

said, 'Well, I managed to save about sixteen thousand in the last five years, and I've parlayed that into a hundred twenty-two thousand three hundred and thirty-nine dollars. As of the close of business in New York yesterday, anyway. No way of knowing what the market did today, of course.'

'Of course,' Jake agreed, suitably impressed. He whistled as he thought about $122,000, then said, 'Say, I got a couple grand saved up. Maybe you could help me invest it.'

'*That's* what got me shipped out here with these jarheads! All the guys in the ready room wanted investment advice. Everybody was reading the *Wall Street Journal* and talking about interest rates and P/E ratios and how many cars Chrysler was gonna sell. The skipper blew a gasket.'

McCoy shook his head sadly. 'Ah well, it's all water under the keel. Can't do nothing about it now, I guess.' He looked again at Jake. 'Tell me about this guy you threw through the window.'

When they had exhausted that subject, Jake wanted to know about the officers in the squadron.

'Typical Marines' was the Real's verdict, spoken with an air of resigned authority since he had been with this crowd for three whole weeks. 'Seems like three months. This is going to be the longest tour of my life.'

'So how many are combat vets?'

'Everyone in the squadron, except for the three or four nuggets, did at least one tour in 'Nam. Maybe half of them did two or more. And six or eight of them did tours as platoon leaders in Vietnam before they went to flight school. Your BN, Le Beau? He was in Marine Recon.'

Grafton was stunned. Le Beau? The San Diego cocks-man? 'You're pulling my leg.'

'I shit you not. Recon. Running around behind enemy lines eating snake meat, doing ambushes and assassinations. Yeah. That's Le Beau, all right. He's a legend in the Corps. Got more chest cabbage than Audie Murphy. He ain't playing with a full deck.'

Jake Grafton's face grew dark as he recalled Flap's rambling cockpit monologue. And that aura of bumbling incompetence that he exuded all morning!

Seeing the look, McCoy continued, 'God only knows why the Marines made him a BN. HE went back to Vietnam in A-6s. Punched out twice, the first time on final to DaNang. Walked through the main gate carrying his parachute and seat pan. The second time, though, was something else. His pilot got his head blown off and Le Beau ejected somewhere near the Laotian border. Maybe in Laos or Cambodia – I don't know. Anyway, nobody heard anything. Just nothing, although they looked and looked hard. Then seventeen days or so later a patrol stumbled onto him out in the jungle in the middle of nowhere. He was running around buck naked, covered with mud and leaves, carrying nothing but a knife. Was busy ambushing the gomers and gutting them. They brought him back with a whole collection of gomer weapons that he had stashed.'

From the look on Grafton's face, McCoy could see that he was not a happy man.

'That ain't the amazing part, Jake,' the Real McCoy continued. 'The amazing part is that Le Beau didn't *want* to get rescued. Two guys have told me this, so I'm assuming that there's something to it. He didn't want to come back because he was having too much *fun*. The grunts on that patrol almost had to tie him up.'

'Why me, Lord?'

'His last pilot didn't cut the mustard,' McCoy continued, 'not to Le Beau's way of thinking. Was having his troubles getting aboard. Oh, he wasn't dangerous, but he was rough, couldn't seem to get a feel for the plane in the groove at night. He might have come around, then again he might not have. He didn't get the chance. Le Beau went to the skipper and the skipper went to CAG and before you could whisper "Semper Fi" the guy was transferred.'

'*Le Beau* did that?'

'Whatever it takes to make it in the Corps, that dickhead has it. He just got selected for promotion to major. Everyone treats him with deference and respect. Makes my stomach turn. Wait till you see these tough old gunnies – they talk to him like they were disciples talking to Jesus. If he lives he's going to be the commandant someday, mark my words.'

'Strangers in a strange land,' Jake murmured, referring to himself and McCoy.

'Something like that,' the Real agreed. He pulled off his steel-toed flight boots and tossed them carelessly on the floor. 'This tour is going to be an adventure,' he added sourly.

'Uh-huh.'

'We've got an all-officers meeting in the ready room in about an hour. I'm going to get fourteen winks. Wake me up, huh?'

'Okay.'

McCoy turned over in his bunk and was soon breathing deeply.

Jake snapped off the overhead light, leaving only his desk lamp lit, the little ten-watt glow worm. He tilted his chair back against McCoy's steel foot locker and put his feet up on his desk.

Thinking about Le Beau, he snorted once, but his thoughts soon drifted on to Callie. The gentle motion of the ship had a tranquilizing effect. After a few moments his head tilted forward and sleep overcame him.

The skipper of the squadron was Lieutenant Colonel Richard Haldane. He was a short, barrel-chested, ramrod-straight man with close-cropped black hair that showed flecks of gray. In this closed community of military professionals his bearing and his demeanor marked him as an officer entitled to respect. He took Jake aside after the all-officers meeting – boring administrative details in a crowded, stuffy room filled with strangers – and asked him to sit in the chair beside him.

Haldane had Jake's service record on his lap. 'We didn't get much of a chance to talk last night, Mr Grafton, but welcome aboard. We're glad to have someone with your carrier experience.'

'Thank you, sir.'

'We're going to assign you to the Operations Department. I think your experience will be the most help to us there.'

'Yessir.'

'During this transit to Hawaii, I want you to put together a series of lectures from CV NATOPS.' CV NATOPS was the bible on carrier operations. The acronym stood for fixed-wing carrier naval air training and operation procedures. 'We've been through it several times while working up for this deployment,' Colonel Haldane continued, 'but I'd like for you to lead us through the book again in detail. I want you to share with us everything you know about A-6 carrier operations. Do you think you can do that?'

'Yes, sir.'

Richard Haldane nodded his head a millimeter. Even sitting down he exuded a command presence. Jake sat a little straighter in his chair.

'I see from your record that you have plenty of combat experience, but it's experience of the same type that most of the officers in this room have had – bombing targets ashore.'

'Single-plane day and night raids, some section stuff, and Alpha strikes, sir, plus a whole hell of a lot of tanker flights.'

'Unfortunately our combat experience won't do us much good if we go to war with the Soviets, who are our most likely opponent.'

This remark caught Jake by surprise. He tried to keep his face deadpan as Haldane continued: 'Our part in a war with the Russians will probably involve a fleet action, our ships against their ships. Mr Grafton, how would you attack a Soviet guided-missile frigate?'

Jake opened his mouth, then closed it again. He scratched his head. 'I don't know, sir,' he said at last. The truth was, he had never once even thought about it. The Vietnam War was in full swing when he was going through flight training, when he transitioned into A-6s, and during his three years in a fleet squadron. The targets were all onshore.

'Any ideas?'

Jake bit his lip. *He* was the naval officer and he was being asked a question about naval air warfare that in truth he should know something about. But he didn't. He decided to admit it. 'Sir, I think the answer to that question would depend on a careful analysis of a Soviet frigate's missile and flak envelope, and to be frank, I have never done that or seen the results of anybody else's look. I suspect the Air Intelligence guys have that stuff under lock and key.'

'So what weapons does a Soviet frigate carry?'

Jake squirmed. 'Colonel, I don't know.'

Haldane nodded once, slowly, and looked away. 'I would like for you to study this matter, Mr Grafton. When you think you have an answer to the question, come see me.'

'Aye aye, sir.'

'That's all. Good luck tonight.'

'Thank you, sir.' Jake rose and walked away, mortified. Well, hell, the stuff he had spent his career attacking was all mud-based. Of course he *should* know about ships, *but* . . .

What Haldane must think — a *naval* officer who doesn't know diddly-squat about *naval* warfare!

Congratulations, Jake. You just got your tour with the Marines off to a great start.

CHAPTER FIVE

There was still a little splotch of light in the western sky and a clearly discernible horizon when Jake Grafton taxied toward the catapult that evening. This first shot would be a 'pinky,' without severe sweat. He needed six landings to attain his night qualification, which meant after this twi-light shot there would be five more . . . in stygian darkness. A pinky first one was just dandy with him.

He carefully scanned the evening sky. The cloud cover was almost total, with the only holes toward the west, and low, maybe seven or eight thousand feet. Wind still out of the northwest, but stiffer than this morning. That was good. Tonight the ship could steam slower into the wind and yet still have the optimum thirty knots of wind over the deck. Since every mile upwind took her farther from the coast and the airfields ashore, the fewer of those miles the better.

Car quals are always goat-ropes, Jake thought, some-thing going wrong sooner or later, so there is at least a fifty-fifty chance I'll have to divert ashore once tonight. And if my luck is in, maybe spend the night in the Alameda BOQ, call Callie . . .

No matter how long you've been ashore, after a half hour back aboard one of these gray tubs you're tired, hungry and horny. No way to cure the horniness, but a night ashore in a real bed would work wonders on the other syndromes, with real food and a long, hot shower and Callie's voice on the phone—

His reverie was interrupted by Flap Le Beau's voice on

the intercom system, the ICS. 'Don't do nothin' cute tonight, huh? My internal table ain't so stable when we're out here flyin' through black goo.'

'You and Muhammad Ali. How about laying off the monologue. When I want comedy I watch TV.'

'Golden silence to practice your pilot gig. You got it. Just fly like an angel flitting toward paradise.'

'You do the radio frequency changes and I'll do the transmissions, okay?'

'Fine.'

'Takeoff checklist,' Jake said, and Flap began reading off the items. Jake checked each item and gave the appropriate response.

And soon they were taxiing toward the cat. Automatically Jake leaned forward and tugged hard on the VDI, the televisionlike display in the center of the instrument panel that functioned as the primary attitude reference. It was tight, just as it should be.

'Flashlight on the backup gyro, please,' Jake said to Flap, who already had it in his hand. If both generators dropped off the line, the little gyro would continue to provide good attitude information for about thirty seconds, long enough for Jake to deploy the ram-air turbine, called the RAT, an emergency wind-driven generator.

Of course a double generator failure was rare, and if it happened on a launch with a discernible horizon there wouldn't be a problem. Yet on a coal black night . . . and all nights at sea were coal black. Jake Grafton well knew that emergencies were quirky – they only happened at the worst possible time, the time when you least expected one and could least afford it. Then you would have to entertain two or three.

The A-7 on the cat in front of Jake was having a problem with the nose-tow apparatus. A small conference was convening around the nose wheel, but nothing obvious seemed to be happening.

Jake looked again at the sky. Darkening fast.

Automatically he reviewed what he would do if he got a cold cat shot – if the catapult failed to give him sufficient end speed to fly. From there he moved into engine failure. He fingered the emergency jettison button, caressed the throttles and felt behind him for the RAT handle. Every motion would have to be quick and sure – no fumbling, no trying to remember exactly what he had to do – he must just do it instinctively and correctly.

They were still screwing with the A-7. *Come on, guys!*

He felt frustrated, entitled to a pinky. These guys had better get with the program or this shot will be like being blasted blindfolded into a coal bin at midnight.

'Gettin' pretty dark,' Flap commented, to Jake's disgust. The pilot squirmed in his seat as he eyed the meeting of the board under the Corsair's nose.

'Why did you stay in the Navy anyway?'

What a cracker this Le Beau is! 'I eat this shit with a spoon,' Grafton replied testily.

'Yeah, I can see you're loving this. Me, I'm too stupid to make it on the outside. It's the Marines or starve. But you seem smarter than me, so I wondered.'

'Put a cork in it, will ya?'

Jake smacked the instrument panel with his fist and addressed the dozen men milling around the Corsair: 'For Christ's sake, let's shoot it or get it off the cat. We gonna dick around till the dawn's early light?'

And here came Bosun Muldowski, striding down the deck, gesturing angrily. 'Off the cat. Get it off.'

And it happened. The Corsair came off the cat and Jake eased the Intruder on. Into the hold-back, the thump as the shuttle was moved forward hydraulically, off the brakes and full power, cat grip up, cycle the controls, check the flaps and slats, now the engine gauges . . .

Time to go.

Jake flipped on the external lights, the nighttime

equivalent of the salute to the cat officer. He placed his head back into the rest, just in time to catch Flap giving Muldowski the bird.

Wham!

As the G's slammed them back into their seats Jake roared into the ICS: '*Yeeeeoooow*,' and then they were airborne. A pinky! *All right!* Not very pink, but pink enough.

Engines pulling, all warning lights out, eight degrees nose up – his eyes took it all in automatically as he reached for the gear handle and slapped it up.

With the gear coming, the bird accelerating nicely, the pilot keyed the radio transmitter: 'War Ace Five One One airborne.'

'Roger, Five One One,' the departure controller said from his seat in front of a large radar screen in Air Ops, deep in the bowels of the ship. 'Climb straight ahead to six thousand, then hold on the One Three Five radial at sixteen miles. Your push at One Seven after the hour.'

'Five Eleven, straight up to Six, then hold on the One Three Five at Sixteen.' Jake moved his left thumb from the radio transmit button to the ICS key and opened his mouth. He wanted to say something snotty to Flap about the gesture to the bosun, but the bombardier beat him to the switch.

'Hey, I damn near ejected on the cat stroke. What in hell was that squall you gave back there?'

'I—'

'You damn fool! I came within a gnat's eyelash of punching out. I coulda *drowned!* If I got run over by the boat you wouldn't be so damn happy. Yelling on the ICS like a wildcat with a hot poker up your ass – that's the stupidest thing I ever . . .'

Jake Grafton waited until the flaps and slats were safely in, then he reached over and jerked the plug on Flap's mask.

Silence. Blessed silence.

Damn you, Tiny Dick Donovan. Damn you all to hell.

The night quickly enveloped them. The world ended at the canopy glass. Oh, the wing-tip lights gave a faint illumination, but Jake would have had to turn his head to see them on the tips of the swept wings, and he wasn't doing much head turning just now. Now he was flying instruments, making the TACAN needle go where it was supposed to, holding the rate-of-climb needle motionless, making the compass behave, keeping his wings level. All this required intense concentration. After five minutes of it he decided enough was enough and reached for the auto-pilot switch. It refused to engage.

Maybe the circuit breaker's popped. He felt the panel between him and the bombardier. Nope. All breakers in.

He punched the altitude-hold button three more times and swore softly to himself.

Okay, so I hand fly this monument to Marine maintenance, this miraculous Marine Corps flying pig.

He hit the holding fix, sixteen miles on the One Three Five radial, and did a teardrop entry. Established inbound he pulled the throttles back until he was showing only two thousand pounds of fuel flow per hour on each engine. This fuel flow would soon give him 220 knots indicated, he knew from experience, the plane's maximum conserve airspeed. Would as soon as the speed bled off.

Hit the fix, start the clock, turn left. Go around and around with the tailhook up, because this first one is a touch-and-go, a practice bolter.

The second time he approached the fix the symbology on the VDI came alive and gave him heading commands from the plane's onboard computer. Flap. He glanced over. The BN had his head against the black hood that shielded the radar scope and was twiddling knobs. Sure enough, the mileage readout corresponded with the TACAN DME, or distance measuring equipment.

'You plugged in?' Jake asked.

'Yep.'

'Thanks for the help.'

'No sweat.'

'Autopilot's packed it in.'

'I noticed.'

Just like an old married couple, here in the intimacy of a night cockpit. There are worse places, Jake thought, than this world of dials and gauges and glowing little red lights. Worse places . . .

At exactly seventeen minutes after the hour he hit the fix for the third time, popped the speed brakes and lowered the nose. This was the pushover. The A-7 that had been holding at five thousand feet was inbound in front of them a minute earlier.

Jake keyed the mike: 'Five One One is inbound at One Seven, state Seven Point Six.'

'Roger, War Ace Five One One. Continue.'

At five thousand feet Jake shallowed his descent as Flap called on the radio: 'Five One One, Platform.'

'Roger, Five One One. Switch button One Seven.'

Flap changed the radio frequency. Jake watched the TACAN needle carefully and made heading corrections as necessary to stay on the final bearing inbound. Soon he was level at 1,200 feet, inbound. At ten miles he dropped the gear and flaps. This slowed the plane still more. He checked the gear and flap indications and soon was stabilized at 120 knots. Flap read the landing checklist and Jake rogered each item.

Seventy-five hundred pounds of fuel. He toggled the main dump and let a thousand pounds bleed overboard into the atmosphere. If this worked out, he should cross the ramp with exactly six thousand pounds remaining, the maximum fuel load for an arrested landing.

Jake adjusted the rheostat on the angle-of-attack indexer, a small arrangement of lights on the left canopy bow in front of him. These lights indicated his airspeed, now a smidgen fast. One hundred eighteen knots was the speed he wanted, so he eased off a touch of throttle, then eased it back on. The indexer came to an on-speed indication. He checked his airspeed indicator. Exactly 118. Okay.

There – way out there – the ship! It appeared in the dark universe as a small collection of white and red lights, not yet distinguishable as to shape. Oh, *now* he could see the outline of the landing area, and the red drop lights down the stern that gave him his lineup cues. The ball on the left side of the landing area that would give him his glide slope was not yet visible.

The final approach controller was talking: 'Five One One, approaching the glide slope, call your needles.'

The needles the controller was referring to were cross-hairs in a cockpit instrument that was driven by a computer aboard the ship. The computer contrasted the radar-derived position of the aircraft with the known location of the glide slope and centerline. It then sent a radio signal to a box in the aircraft, which positioned the needles to depict the glide slope and centerline. The system was called ACLS, automatic carrier landing system, and someday it would indeed be automatic. Right now it was just the needles. Jake had to fly the plane.

'Down and right.'

'Disregard. You're low and slightly left . . . Five One One, slightly below glide slope, lined up slightly left. Come a little right for lineup, on glide path . . . on glide path . . .'

At the on-glide path call Jake squeezed out the speed brakes and concentrated intently on his instruments. He had to set and hold a six-hundred-foot rate of descent, hold heading, hold airspeed, keep the wings level and this plane coming down just so delicately so.

'I've got a ball,' Flap told him at two miles.

The controller: 'Left of course. Come right.'

The pilot made the correction, then glanced ahead. Yes,

69

he could tell from the drop lights he was left. When he was properly lined up again he took out most of the correction. Still his nose was pointed slightly right of the landing area. This correction was necessary since the wind was not precisely down the angled deck, which was pointed ten degrees left of the ship's keel. Except for an occasional glance ahead, he stayed on the gauges.

'Five One One, three-quarter mile, call the ball.'

Now Jake glanced out the windshield. There's the meatball, centered between the green datum lights. Lineup looks good too. Jake keyed the mike and said, 'Five One One, Intruder ball, Six Point Oh.'

'Roger, ball. Looking good.' That was the LSO on the fantail, Skidmore.

The ball moved in relation to the green reference or datum lights that were arranged in a horizontal line. When the yellow 'meatball' in the center moved up, you were above glide path. When it appeared below the reference line, you were low. If you were too low, the ball turned red, blood red, a stark prophecy of your impending doom if you didn't immediately climb higher on the glide slope. The back end of the ship, the ramp, lurked in red ball country, waiting to smash a plane to bits.

Yet as critical as proper glide slope control was, lineup was even more so. The landing area was 115 feet wide, the wing span of the A-6, 52. The edges of the landing area were defined by foul lines, and aircraft were parked with their noses abutting the foul lines on *both* sides of the deck. Landing aircraft were literally sinking into a canyon between parked airplanes.

And Jake had to monitor his airspeed carefully. The angle-of-attack indexer helped enormously here, arranged as it was where he could see it as he flew the lineup and glide slope cues. Any deviation from an on-speed indication required his immediate attention because it would quickly affect his descent rate, thereby screwing up his control of the ball. Running out of airspeed at the ramp was a sin that had killed many a naval aviator.

Meatball, lineup, angle-of-attack – as he closed the ship Jake's eyes were in constant motion checking these three items. Nearing the ship he dropped the angle-of-attack from his scan and concentrated on keeping properly lined up, with a centered ball. As he crossed the ramp he zeroed in on the meatball, flying it to touchdown.

The wheels hit and the nose slammed down. Jake Grafton thumbed the speed brakes in as he smoothly and quickly shoved the throttles forward to the stops. The LSO was on the radio shouting, 'Bolter, bolter, bolter,' just in case he forgot to advance the throttles or to positively rotate to a flying attitude as he shot off the edge of the angled deck.

Jake didn't forget. The engines were at full song as the Intruder left the deck behind and leaped back into the blackness of the night. Jake eased the stick back until he had ten degrees nose up and checked for a positive rate of climb. Going up. Gear up. Accelerating through 185 knots, flaps and slats up.

Now to get those six traps.

The radar controller leveled him at 1,200 feet and turned him to the downwind heading, the reciprocal of the ship's course. He was stable at 220 knots. Jake reached for the hook handle and pulled it. Hook down.

The controller turned him so that he had an eight-mile groove, which was nice. As soon as the wings were level he dropped the gear and flaps. Once again he concentrated intently on airspeed and altitude control, nailing the final bearing on the TACAN, retrimming until the plane flew itself with only the tiniest of inputs to the stick to counter the natural swirls and currents of the air. This was precision flying, where any sloppiness could prove instantly fatal.

'Five One One, approaching glide slope . . . Five One

One, up and on glide slope . . . three-quarters of a mile, call the ball.'

'Five One One, Intruder ball, Five Point Six.'

Deep in the heart of the ship in Air Ops, a sailor wearing headphones wrote '5.6' in yellow grease pencil on the Plexiglas board in front of him and the time beside the notation that said 'Grafton, 511.' He wrote backward, so the letters and numbers read properly to the air officer, the air wing commander, and the other observers who were sitting silently on the other side of the board watching the television monitors and occasionally glancing at the board.

Just now the picture on the monitors was from a camera buried on the landing centerline of the flight deck, which pointed aft up the glide slope. As they watched the officers saw the lights of Jake's A-6 appear on the center of the screen, in the center of the crosshairs that indicated the proper glide slope and lineup. As the plane closed the ship the lights assumed more definition.

Up in the top of the carrier's island superstructure was Pri-Fly, the domain of the air boss. His little empire was pretty quiet just now since all the air traffic was being controlled via radar and radio from Air Ops, but two enlisted men behind the boss's chair were busy. One held a pair of binoculars focused up the glide slope. He saw the approaching Intruder, identified it, and chanted, 'Set Three Six Zero, A-6.' Regardless of a plane's fuel state, the arresting gear was always set at the maximum trap weight, in the case of the A-6, 36,000 pounds.

To his left, the other sailor made a note in his log and repeated into a sound-powered phone that hung from his chest, 'Set Three Six Zero, A-6.'

The air boss, a senior commander, sat in a raised easy chair surrounded by large bullet-proof glass windows. He could hear the radio transmissions and the litany of the sailors behind him, and noted subconsciously that they agreed with what his eyes, and the approach controller, were telling him, that there was an A-6 on the ball, an A-6 with a maximum trap weight of 36,000 pounds.

Under the after end of the flight deck in the arresting gear engine rooms, all four of them, sat sailors on the Pri-Fly sound-powered circuit. Each individually spun a wheel to mechanically set the metering orifice of his arresting gear engine to 36,000 pounds, then they sang out in turn, 'One set Three Six Zero A-6,' 'Two set Three Six Zero A-6,' and so on.

When the fourth and last engine operator had reported his engine set, the talker in Pri-Fly sang out, 'All engines set, Three Six Zero A-6,' and the air boss rogered.

On the fantail of the ship directly aft of the island, on the starboard side of the landing area in a catwalk on the edge of the deck, stood the sailor who retracted the arresting gear engines once they had been engaged. He too was on the Pri-Fly sound-powered circuit, and when the fourth engine reported set, he shouted to the arresting gear officer who stood above him on the deck, right on the starboard foul line, 'All engines set, Three Six Zero A-6.'

The gear officer looked up the glide slope. Yep, it was an A-6. He glanced forward up the deck. The landing area was clear. No aircraft protruded over the foul lines, there were no people in the landing area, so he squeezed a trigger switch on the pistol grip he held in his right hand.

This switch operated a stop-light affair arranged twenty feet or so aft of the landing signal officer's platform on the port side of the landing area. The LSO waving tonight, Hugh Skidmore, saw the red light go out and a green light appear.

'Clear deck,' he called, and the other LSOs on the platform echoed the call.

'Clear deck!'

This entire evolution had taken about fifteen seconds.

The ship was ready to recover the inbound A-6. Now if Jake Grafton could just fly his plane into that little sliver of sky that would give him a three wire . . .

He was trying. He was working the stick and throttles, playing them delicately, when he slammed into the burble of air disturbed by the ship's island. The plane jolted and he jammed on some power, then as quickly pulled it off as he cut through the turbulence into the calm air over the ramp. On he came, aiming for that eighteen-inches-thick window where the third wire waited, coming in at 118 knots in an eighteen-ton plane, the hook dangling down behind the main gear, coming in . . .

Hugh Skidmore strode about five feet into the landing area, inboard of the LSO's platform. Against his ear he held a telephonelike radio headset connected with the ship's radios by a long cord. Forward of the LSO's platform was a television monitor, the PLAT – pilot landing assistance television – which he checked occasionally to ensure the plane in the groove was properly lined up. He could hear the approach controller and he could hear and talk to Jake Grafton. Yet there was nothing to say. The A-6 was coming in like it was riding rails.

Then it was there, crossing the ramp.

Jake still had a steady centered yellow ball as the wheels smashed home. The ball shot off the top of the lens as he slammed the throttles to the stops and the hook caught seemingly all at the same time. The deceleration threw the pilot and bombardier forward into their harnesses.

The A-6 Intruder was jerked to a halt in a mere two hundred and sixty feet.

It hung quivering on the end of the arresting gear wire, then Jake got the engines back to idle and the rebound of the wire pulled the plane backward.

The gear runner was already twenty feet out into the landing area signaling the pilot with his wands: hook up. When he saw the aircraft's tailhook being retracted, the runner waved one of his wands in a huge circle, the signal to the arresting gear operator in the fantail catwalk to retract the engine.

Obediently the operator selected the lever for number-three engine and pulled it down. Since the lever was connected by a wire over three hundred feet long to a hydraulic actuating valve on the engine, this pull took some muscle. When he had the yard-long lever well away from the bulkhead, the sailor leaped on it with his feet and used the entire weight of his body to force the lever down to a ninety-degree angle.

By now the A-6 that had just landed was folding its wings as it taxied out of the landing area. By the time the tail crossed the foul line, the third engine operator said 'battery,' and the retract man got off the lever and let it come back to its rest position. As he did he heard the Pri-Fly talker sing out, 'Set Two Seven Zero A-7.'

On the LSO platform Hugh Skidmore leaned over to his writer, tonight the Real McCoy. 'Give him an OK three. Little lined up left at the start.'

McCoy scribbled the notation in his pocket logbook like this: 511 OK3 (LLATS).

Then both men turned their full attention to the A-7 in the groove as they waited for the clear-deck light to illuminate.

The second cat shot, into a sky as black as the ace of spades, went well. Jake leveled at 1,200 feet and turned downwind, as directed by the controller. He held 250 knots until the controller told him to dirty up, which he did at the same time he told Jake to turn base. So Grafton was turning as he changed configuration – slowing, retrimming and trying to maintain a precise altitude, all at the same time. He lost a hundred feet, a fact that Flap instantly commented upon.

Jake said nothing, merely kept flying his plane. *This is the big leagues. Gotta do it all here and do it well. Flap has a right to comment.*

A short, tight pattern left him still searching for a good steady start when he hit the glide slope. The secret to a good pass is a good start, and Jake didn't have it. He wasn't carrying enough power and that caused a settle. By the time he was back up to a centered ball he was fast, which he was working off when he hit the burble. He added power. Not quite enough. The ball was a tad low when the wheels hit the deck.

'A fair two-wire,' he told Flap as they rolled out.

Aviation Boatswain's Mate (Equipment) Third Class Johnny Arbogast enjoyed his work. He operated the number-three arresting gear engine, the one that got the most traps and therefore required the most maintenance. Still, Johnny Arbogast loved that engine.

During a slow, rainy day in port this past spring, the gear chief had worked out how much energy an engine absorbed while trapping an F-4 Phantom. The figure was nine million foot-pounds, as Johnny recalled. Nine million of anything is a lot, but *man!* Those planes make this engine sing.

Any way you cut it, an arresting gear engine was one hell of a fine piece of machinery. And Johnny Arbogast was the guy who ran *Columbia*'s number three, which was pretty darn good, he thought, for a plumber's kid from Cotulla, Texas, who had had to struggle for everything he ever got.

The engine consisted of a giant hydraulic piston inside a steel cylinder about thirty inches in diameter that was arranged parallel with the ship's beam. Almost fifty feet in length, the cylinder containing the piston sat inside a large steel frame. Around the piston were reeved two twelve-hundred-foot strands of arresting gear cable, one-and-five eighths-inch-thick wire rope made of woven steel threads. These two cables ran repeatedly around sheaves at the

76

head and foot of the main piston and squeezed it as the aircraft pulled out the flight deck pennant above Johnny's head. It was the metering of the fluid squeezed by the piston from the cylinder – pure ethylene glycol, or anti-freeze – through an adjustable orifice that controlled the rate at which the aircraft was arrested. Johnny set the size of this orifice for each arrestment as ordered by the talker in Pri-Fly.

To maintain proper tension on the engine cable as the aircraft on the flight deck was pulling it out, two anchor dampeners that held the bitter ends of each cable stroked simultaneously. These fifty-foot-long pistons inside cylinders about twelve inches in diameter pulled slack cable off the back, or idle, side of the engine, thereby keeping the wire taut throughout the system.

When he first reported aboard *Columbia*, the arresting gear chief had impressed Johnny with a story about an anchor dampener that sheared its restraining nut during an arrestment. The suddenly free dampener, as big as a telephone pole, was forcibly whipped through the aluminum bulkhead of the engine room into the 0-3-level passageway, where it cut a sailor on his way to chow sloppily in half. The running cable whipped the dampener like a scythe. It sliced through a dozen officers' stateroom bulkheads as if they were so much tissue paper. When the dampener had accomplished a 180-degree turn, it reentered the engine room and skewered the engine like a mighty spear, exploding sheaves and showering the room, and the operator, with sharp, molten-hot metal fragments. All this took place in about a second and a half. Fortunately the plane on the flight deck was successfully arrested before the now-unanchored cable could run completely off the engine, but the engine room was a shambles and the operator went to the hospital with critical injuries.

As a result of this little story, Johnny Arbogast developed a habit of running his eyes over the anchor dampeners after each arrestment. Tonight, after setting the engine to receive an A-6, he saw something that he had never before seen. As the anchor dampeners stroked back into battery after the last engagement, the steel cable on one of them had kinked about six inches out from the connecting socket that held the bitter end of the cable to the dampener piston.

A kink, like a kink in a garden hose.

Johnny Arbogast stared, not quite sure his eyes could be believed.

Yep, a kink.

If this engine takes a hit, that cable could *break*, right there at the kink!

Johnny fumbled with the mouthpiece of the sound-powered phone unit hanging on his chest. He pushed the talk button and blurted, 'Three's foul. Three's not ready.'

'*What?*' This from the deck-edge operator, who had already told the arresting gear officer that all the engines were set. And he had delivered this message over a half minute ago, maybe even a minute.

'*Three's not ready,*' Johnny Arbogast howled into his mouthpiece. '*Foul deck!*'

And then Johnny did what any sensible man would have done: he tore off the sound-powered headset and ran for his life.

Up on the fantail catwalk the deck-edge operator shouted at the arresting gear officer, 'Three's not ready.'

The gear officer was still standing on the starboard foul line on the flight deck and he didn't hear what the operator said. He eyed the A-6 in the groove and bent toward the sailor, who was also looking over his shoulder at the approaching plane, now almost at the ramp.

'Foul deck,' the sailor roared above the swelling whine of the engines of the approaching plane.

The gear officer's reaction was automatic. He released the trigger on the pistol grip he held in his hand and shouted, 'What the hell is wrong?'

Across the landing area on the LSO's platform the green 'ready deck' light went out and the red 'foul deck' light came on.

Hugh Skidmore was looking intently at the A-6 Intruder almost at the ramp when he saw the red light on the edge of his peripheral vision. He was faced with an instant decision. He had no way of knowing why the deck was foul – he only knew that it was. A plane may have rolled into the landing area, a man may have wandered into the unsafe zone . . . any one of a hundred things could have gone wrong and all one hundred were bad.

So Hugh Skidmore squeezed the red button on the pistol grip he held in his hand, triggering a bank of flashing red lights mounted above the meatball. At the same time he roared into his radio-telephone, 'Wave-off, wave-off.'

The flashing wave-off lights and the radio message imprinted themselves on Jake Grafton's brain at the same time. His reaction was automatic. The throttles went full forward as he thumbed in the speed brakes and the control stick came aft.

Unfortunately jet engines do not provide instantaneous power as piston engines do: the revs can build only as fast as the burners can handle the increasing fuel flow, which is metered through a fuel control unit to prevent flooding the engine and flaming it out. The power builds with revs. Tonight the back stick and the gradually increasing engine power flattened the A-6's descent, then stopped it . . . four feet above the deck.

The howling warplane crossed the third wire with its nose well up, boards in, engines winding to full screech, but with its tailhook dangling.

From his vantage point near the fantail the arresting gear officer watched in horror as the tailhook kissed the top of the third wire, then snagged the fourth. The plane continued forward for a heartbeat, then seemed to stop in midair.

It was a lopsided contest. An 18-ton airplane was trying to pull a 95,000-ton ship. The ship won. The airplane fell straight down.

As he took the wave-off, Jake Grafton instinctively knew that it had come too late. The ship was *right there*, filling the windscreen. He kept the angle-of-attack on the optimum indication – a centered doughnut – by feeding in back stick while he tried to bend the throttles over the stops.

Somehow he found the ICS switch with his left thumb and shouted to Flap, 'Hook up!' but the aircraft was already decelerating. The angle-of-attack indexer showed slow and his eye flicked to the AOA gauge on the panel, just in time to see the needle sweep counterclockwise to the peg as the G threw him forward into his harness straps.

Then they fell the four feet to the deck.

The impact snapped his head forward viciously and slammed him downward into the seat, stunning him.

He got his head up and tried to focus his eyes as cold fear enveloped him. Are we stopped? Or going off the angled deck? Dazed, scared clear through and unable to see his instruments, he instinctively placed the stick in the eight-degree-nose-up position and kept the engines at full power.

The air boss exploded over the radio: 'Jesus Christ, Paddles, why'd you wave him off in close?'

On the LSO platform Hugh Skidmore was having trouble finding the transmit button on his radio. He fumbled for it as he stared forward at the A-6 straining futilely against the fourth wire with its engines still at full power. Miraculously the airplane seemed to be all in one piece. Here a hundred yards behind those two jet exhausts without the protection of a sound-suppression helmet the noise was awesome, a thunder that numbed the ears and vibrated the soul.

Unwilling to wait for Skidmore's response, the air boss now roared over the radio at Jake Grafton : 'We got you, son. Kill those engines! You aren't going anywhere now.'

Long seconds ticked by before the pilot complied. When he did, finally, the air boss remembered Skidmore:

'*El Ss Oh*, if you ever, *ever*, wave off another airplane in close on this fucking boat I will personally come down there and throw your silly ass into the goddamn wake. Do you read me, you mindless bastard?'

Skidmore found his voice. 'The deck went foul, Boss.'

'We'll cut up the corpse later. Wave off the guy in the groove so we can get this squashed A-6 out of the gear and clean the shit out of the cockpit.'

The plane in the groove was still a half mile out, but Skidmore obediently triggered the wave-off lights. As he did so he heard the engines of the A-6 in the gear die as the pilot secured the fuel flow.

Already the arresting gear officer had his troops on deck stripping the pennant from number-three engine. The rest of the recovery would be accomplished with only three engines on line.

Skidmore turned to the Real McCoy. 'I guess I screwed the pooch on that one.'

McCoy was still looking at the A-6 up forward. The yellow shirts were hooking a tow tractor to the nose wheel. He turned his gaze on Skidmore, who was looking into his face.

He had to say something. 'Looks like the boss is safety-wired to the pissed-off position.'

Skidmore nodded toward the stern. 'I thought he could make it. I didn't think he was *that* close.'

'Well . . .'

'Oh, hell.'

Jake Grafton stood rubbing his neck in Flight Deck Control, the room in the base of the carrier's island

81

superstructure where the aircraft handler directs the movement of every plane on the ship. Flap Le Beau stood beside him. Someone was talking to the handler on the squawk box, apparently someone in Air Ops. The handler listened awhile, then leaned toward Jake and said, 'You need two more traps. The in-flight engagement was your fourth.'

'Yeah.'

'If you're feeling up to it, we'll give you another plane and send you out for your last two. Or you can wait until we get to Hawaii and we'll do the whole night bit again. It's up to you. How do you feel?'

Jake used a sleeve to swab the sweat from his forehead and eyes. 'What about tomorrow night?' he asked.

'The captain won't hold the ship in here against this coast just to qual one pilot. We have to transit to Hawaii.'

Jake nodded. That made sense. He flexed his shoulders and pivoted his head slowly.

The fear was gone. Okay, panic. But it was gone. He was still feeling the adrenaline aftershock, which was normal.

'I'm okay,' he told the handler, who turned to relay the message into the squawk box.

Flap pulled at Jake's sleeve. 'You don't have to do this tonight. There's no war on. It doesn't matter a whit whether you get qualled tonight or a week from now in Hawaii.'

Jake stared. The flippant, kiss-my-ass cool dude he had flown with all day was gone. The man there now was serious and in total control, with sharp, intelligent eyes. This must be the Flap Le Beau that was the legend.

'I can hack it. Are you okay?'

'I am if you are.'

'I am.'

'I gave you a load of shit today just to see if you could handle a little pressure. You can. You don't have anything to prove to anybody.'

82

Jake shook his head from side to side. 'I have to go now so the next time I'll know I can.'

A trace of a smile crossed Le Beau's face. He nodded, just the tiniest dip of the head, and turned toward the handler.

'What plane do they want us to aviate, Handler-man? Ask the grunts in Ready Four and have them send up the book.'

'Please, *sir!*'

'Of course, *sir*. Did I leave the please out? What's come over me? I must still be all shook up. You know, we came within two inches of being chocolate and vanilla pudding out there. If we'd fell another two inches you'd be cleaning us up with spoons. I'm gonna write a thank-you letter to Jesus. Praise *God*, that was a religious experience, Amen! I feel born again, Amen! The narrowness of our escape and my ecstasy must have made me the eensiest bit careless in my military manners. I apologize. You understand, don't you, sir?'

'Ecstasy! What crap! Go sit over there in that corner with your Amens and keep your mouth shut until your fellow jarheads get the maintenance book up here for your pilot to read. He can read, can't he?'

'Oh yes, sir. He's Navy, not Marine. He's got a good, solid, second-grade education. His mamma told me he did just fine in school until . . .'

Jake Grafton decided he was thirsty and needed to take a leak. He wandered away to attend to both problems.

He was slurping water from a fountain in the passageway outside the hatch to Flight Deck Control when he realized that Lieutenant Colonel Haldane was standing beside him. Haldane was wearing his uniform tonight, not his flight suit. His I-been-there decorations under his gold aviator wings made an impressive splotch of color on his left breast.

'What happened?' he asked Jake.

'They gave me a late wave-off, sir. I was almost at the ramp, or at it. Somebody said something about the deck going foul. Whatever, at the time all I knew was that the red lights were flashing and the LSO was shouting. So I did my thing. I was just too close.'

Haldane was watching his eyes as he spoke. When he finished speaking the colonel gave him another five seconds of intense scrutiny before he asked, 'Did you do everything right?'

Jake Grafton swallowed hard. This just wasn't his day. 'No, sir. I didn't. I knew we had passed the wave-off point, so I was concentrating on the ball and lineup. When the wave-off lights came on, I guess I was sorta stunned there for a tenth of a second. Then I reacted automatically – nose up, boards in, full power. I should have given her the gun and got the boards in, but I should have just held the nose attitude. Should have rode it into a bolter.'

Haldane's head bobbed a millimeter. 'Are you up to two more?' he asked.

'I think so, sir.'

'If you don't want to go I'll back you up. No questions asked.'

'I'd like to go now, sir, if we can get a bird.'

'How many carrier landings do you have?'

'Before today, sir, three hundred twenty-four.'

'How many at night?'

'One hundred twenty-seven, I believe.'

Haldane nodded. 'Whenever I have a close call,' he said, 'the first thing to go afterward is my instrument scan. I get way behind the plane, fixate on just one instrument. Really have to work to keep the eyeballs moving.'

'Yessir,' Jake said, and grinned. He liked the way Haldane used himself as an example. That was class. 'I'll keep it safe, Skipper,' Jake added.

'Fine,' said the colonel, and went into Flight Deck Control to see the handler.

'A thank-you letter to Jesus, huh?'

'That was the best I could do on the spur of the moment. Don't hold it against me.'

'Amen to that.' Jake sighed and tried to relax. They were sitting behind the jet-blast deflector for Cat One, waiting for the A-7 ahead to do his thing. Jake tugged at the VDI reflexively and wriggled to get his butt set in the seat.

He was still feeling the aftereffects of adrenaline shock, but he knew it, so he forced himself to look at everything carefully. Wings locked, flaps and slats out, stabilator shifted, roger the weight board, ease forward into the shuttle, throttles up and off brakes, cat grip up, wipe out the controls, check fuel flow, RPM, EGT . . . Lights on and bam! they were hurling down the catapult into the blackness.

Off the pointy end, nose up, gear up, climbing . . .

It went well until he got onto the ball, then he couldn't get stabilized. Too nervous. Every correction was too big, every countercorrection overdone. The plane wobbled up and down on the glide slope and went from fast to slow to fast again. He was waggling the wings trying to get properly lined up as he went across the ramp and that, coupled with not quite enough power, got him a settle into the two-wire.

The last one was more of the same. At this point Jake realized he was totally exhausted.

'Settle down,' Flap told him in the groove.

'I'm trying. Let's just get this fun over with, okay?' Crossing the ramp he lowered the nose and eased the power a smidgen to ensure he wouldn't bolter. He didn't. One wire.

He had to pry himself from the cockpit. He was so tired he had trouble plodding across the deck.

'Another day, another dollar,' Flap said cheerfully.

'Something like that,' Jake mumbled, but so quietly Flap didn't hear it. No matter.

'It was a late wave-off, and I'm sorry,' Hugh Skidmore told Jake in the ready room. The LSOs were waiting for Jake when he came in. The television monitor mounted high in the corner of the room was running the PLAT tape of the in-flight engagement, over and over and over. Colonel Haldane was there, but he stood silently without saying anything. Jake and the LSOs watched the PLAT tape twice.

'You owe me, Skidmore.'

'Other than that little debacle, your first one – the touch-and-go – was okay, the first trap okay, the second fair, the third okay. The fifth trap was a fair and the last one a no-grade. I almost waved you off. I don't want to see any more of that deck spotting—' After a glance at the skipper Skidmore ran out of words. He contented himself with adding, 'I think you were a little wrung out on the last one.'

Jake nodded. He had sinned there at the end and wasn't too proud to admit it. 'I spotted the deck on the last one. Sorry!' He tried to shrug but didn't have the energy. 'What about the in-flight?'

'Gave you a fair.'

'Fair? Now wait just a minute—' Jake knew the futility of arguing with the umpire, but that pass had cost him too much. 'I had a good pass going until everything went to hell.'

'Not all that good. You were carrying a little too much power in the middle and went fast. You made the correction but you overdid it. Approaching the ramp you were slow and settling into a two-wire when I waved you off.'

'How do you figure that?'

The Real McCoy spoke up. 'Jake, if you had been right on a centered ball when the wave-off came, you would have missed all the wires on the wave-off. Smacking on a big wad of power should have just carried you across the wires into a bolter. Hugh's right. You were a half ball low going lower when you gunned it. That pass would have been a fair two-wire. Look at that PLAT tape again. Carefully.'

Jake surrendered. 'I bow to the opinion of the experts.'

'Next time keep the ball centered, huh?'

Flap Le Beau spoke up. 'There had better not be a next time. If there is, you two asshole mechanics better swim for it before I get out of the plane.' He was apparently oblivious of the presence of Richard Haldane.

Jake glanced at the colonel to see how he was taking all this. Apparently without a flicker of emotion.

'No, I'm serious,' Skidmore said. 'If you ever get a wave-off in close like that, Jake, slam the throttles up and run the boards in, but don't rotate. Just ride her into a bolter.'

'But don't go into the water waiting for the wheels to hit,' the Real added.

Now Richard Haldane spoke. 'May I have a word with you gentlemen?'

Skidmore and McCoy went over to where the colonel was standing. Flap asked Jake, 'How are you supposed to know that it's an in-close wave-off if the LSOs can't figure it out?'

'The guy with the stick in his hand is always responsible,' Jake told the bombardier. 'He's the dummy who signed for the plane.'

After Jake and Flap debriefed both the planes they had flown that evening, Jake asked Flap if he wanted a drink.

'Yeah. You got any?'

'A little. In my stateroom. One drink and I'm into my rack. See you in a bit.'

Ten minutes later Flap asked, 'So Skidmore should not have waved us off, even though the cable might have parted on number three if we had caught it?'

'Yeah. That's right. The in-close position is defined as the point where a wave-off cannot be safely made. From that point on, in to touchdown, you are committed, like the pig. The LSO has to take you aboard no matter what. It's a practical application of the lesser of two evils theory.'

'Like the pig?'

'Yeah. A chicken lays eggs, she's dedicated. A pig gives his life, he's committed.'

'Where you from, anyway?'

'Virginia. Rural Virginia, down in the southwest corner. And you?'

'Brooklyn.'

'All that crap you gave me this morning about Louisiana and you're from Brooklyn?'

'Yep. Born in the ghetto to a woman who didn't know who my daddy was and raised on the streets. That's me.'

'So how did you get into the Corps?'

Flap Le Beau finished off his straight whiskey and grinned. He held up the glass. 'Got any more?'

'Help yourself.'

When he finished pouring, Flap said, 'Did you ever hear of a guy named Horowitz who funded scholarships for ghetto children?'

'No. Don't think so.'

'Well, it's sorta the in-thing for a millionaire to do these days. Publicly commit yourself to funding a college education for ten ghetto kids, or fifty, a hundred if you have the bucks. Sol Horowitz was the first. He promised to pay for the college education of a hundred first-graders in a public school in Brooklyn if they graduated from high school. I was one of the hundred. It's sort of amazing, but I actually got through high school. Then I got caught stealing some cars and the probation officer told the judge I had this college scholarship waiting, if I would only go. So the judge sentenced me to college. I kid you not.'

Flap sipped, remembering. Finally he continued. 'I screwed around at the university. Drank and came real close to flunking out, or getting thrown out. Miracle number two, I graduated. So somebody arranged for me to meet Horowitz. I don't know exactly what I expected. Some wizened old Jew with money sticking out of every pocket sitting in a mansion – I don't know. Well, Solomon Horowitz was none of that. He lived in a walk-up flat off Flatbush, a real dump. He looked me up and down and told me I was nothing.

' "You have learned nothing," he said. "You barely passed your courses – I hear you continued to steal cars. Oh yes, I have my sources. They tell me. I know." What could I say?

'Horowitz asked, "Who do you think gave you a chance to make something of yourself? Some oil baron? Some rich Jew asshole whose daddy left him ten million? I will tell you who."

'He rolled up his sleeve. He had a number tattooed on the inside of his wrist. He had been in Dachau. And you know something else? When he made the promise to send those kids to college, *he didn't have any money*. He made the promise because then he would have to work like hell to earn the money.'

'Why?' Jake asked.

'That was my question. I'll level with you, Jake. I was twenty-two years old and I'd never met anybody in my life who wasn't in it for himself. So I asked.

'Horowitz thought about it for a little bit and finally said he guessed I was entitled to know. The Nazis castrated him. He could never have any children. When he got out of Dachau after the war weighing ninety-one pounds, he came to America. He wanted his life to make a difference to somebody, he said, so he promised to send a hundred kids to college, blacks and Puerto Ricans who would never have a chance otherwise. He worked three jobs, seven days a week, saved his money, invested every dime. And he did it. Actually sent thirty-two, who were all of the hundred that finished high school and could read and write well enough to get into a college. Thirty-two. He paid board, room, books and tuition and sent a little allowance every month. Twenty-three of us graduated.'

Flap tossed off the last of the liquor and set the glass in the small metal sink jutting out from the wall.

'I thought long and hard about the interview. I decided I wanted my life to make a difference, to make Horowitz's life make a difference . . . you see what I mean. But I'm not Solomon Horowitz. All I knew how to do was drink, screw, do burglaries and fight. I wasn't so good at stealing cars – I got caught a lot. So I picked the fightin'est outfit of them all and joined up.

'They wouldn't send me to officer candidate school because of my record. I enlisted anyway. I was full of Horowitz's fire. I went to boot camp and finished first in my class, went to mortar school and came out first, so they made me an instructor. Got to be a pretty fair hand with a mortar and a rifle and led PT classes in my spare time. Finally they decided I might make a Marine after all, so they sent me to OCS.'

'How did you do there?' Jake asked, even though he thought he knew the answer.

'Number one,' Le Beau said flatly, without inflection. 'They gave me a presentation sword.'

'Going to stay in?'

'There's nothing for me in Brooklyn. My mother died of a drug overdose years ago. I've been in ten years now and I'm staying until they kick me out. The Corps is my home.'

'Don't you get tired of it sometimes?'

'Sometimes. Then I remember Horowitz and I'm not tired anymore. I've got his picture. Want to see it?' The Marine dug out his wallet.

Jake looked. Flap towered over Horowitz – a younger Flap togged out in the white dress uniform of a Marine officer. The old, old man had wispy white hair and stooped shoulders. His head was turned and he was looking up into the beaming face of the handsome black man. They were smiling at each other.

'Horowitz came to Parris Island for the graduation ceremony,' Flap explained. 'They gave me the sword and I walked over to where he was sitting and gave it to him.'

'He still alive?'

'On no. He died six months after this picture was taken. This is the only one of him I have.'

After Flap left, Jake slowly unlaced his flight boots and pulled them off. It took the last of his energy.

If the whole cruise goes like this day has, I'm not going to make it. Russian frigates, in-flight engagements . . . Jesus!

He eyed his bunk, the top one, and worked himself up to an effort. He didn't even pull off his flight suit. Sixty seconds after his head hit the pillow he was asleep.

CHAPTER SIX

The ships sailed across a restless, empty ocean. Jake saw no ships other than those of the task group whenever he went on deck, which he managed to do three or four times a day. Many sailors never went topside; they spent every minute of their day in their working spaces, their berthing areas, or on the mess deck, and saw sunlight only when the ship pulled into port. Jake Grafton thought he would go stir-crazy if he couldn't see the sea and sky and feel the wind on his face every few hours.

He would stroll around the deck, visit with Bosun Muldowski if he ran into him, chat with the catapult crews if they were on deck, and examine planes. His eyes seemed naturally drawn to airplanes. His destination on these excursions was usually the forward end of the flight deck, where he would stand between the catapults looking at the ocean. The wind was usually vigorous here. It played with his hair and tugged at his clothes and cleaned the below-decks smells from his nostrils.

The first morning he saw a school of whales to starboard. Knots of sailors gawked and pointed. The whales spouted occasionally and once one came soaring out of the water, then crashed down in a magnificent cloud of spray. Mostly the view was of black backs glistening amid the swells.

When he went below this first morning at sea, reentered the world of crowded passageways, tiny offices, and never-ending paperwork, the squadron maintenance officer cornered him. 'That plane you flew last night – well, we haven't found any airframe damage yet. Maybe we dodged the bullet.' If there was no damage there would be no official report assessing blame. 'The avionics took a helluva lot bigger lick than they're designed for, though. Radar and computer and VDI are screwed up.'

Jake threw himself into the problem assigned to him by Colonel Haldane. How would you attack a Soviet ship? Since the Soviets had all kinds of ships, he soon focused on the most capable, the guided missile cruisers that were the mainstay of their task forces, Kyndas and Krestas. After preliminary research of classified material in the Air Intelligence spaces, he paid a visit to the EA-6B Prowler squadron in their small ready room on the 0-3 level, near the number-four arresting gear room.

This squadron had only four aircraft, but they were Cadillacs. A stretched version of the A-6, the Prowler held a crew of four: one pilot and three electronic warfare specialists. The airplane's sole mission was to foil enemy radars. The electronic devices it used for this task were mounted in pods slung on the weapons stations. Other than the pilot's instruments, the panels of the cockpit were devoted to the displays and controls necessary to detect enemy radar transmissions and render the information they gave the enemy useless. Since it was a highly modified version of the A-6, the plane was popularly referred to as a Queer Six.

The Prowler crews in Ready Eight greeted Jake with open arms. They too were stationed on Whidbey Island when ashore, and two or three of the officers knew Jake. When he finally got around to explaining his errand, they were delighted to help. The capabilities of Soviet warships were their stock in trade.

Jake had already known that Soviet ships were heavily armed, but now he found out just how formidable they really were. Radar capabilities were evaluated, weapons envelopes examined. Finally Jake Grafton gave his conclusion:

'A single plane doesn't have much of a chance against one of these ships.' This comment drew sober nods from the two electronic warfare experts at his elbows.

Nor, he soon concluded, did a flight of planes have much of a chance if the weapons they had to use were free-falling bombs, technology left over from World War II. Oh, free-falling bombs had been adequate in Vietnam when attacking stationary targets ashore – barely adequate – but modern warships were another matter entirely. Ships would detect the aircraft on radar while they were still minutes away. Radar would allow antiaircraft missiles to be fired and guided long before the attacker reached the immediate vicinity of the ship. Then, in-close, radar-directed guns would pour forth a river of high explosives.

If our lucky attack pilot survived all that, he was ready to aim his free-fall weapons at a maneuvering, high-speed target. Even if he aimed his bombs perfectly, the bombs were unguided during their eight to ten seconds of fall, so if the ship's captain reversed the helm or tightened a turn, or if the pilot had miscalculated the wind, the bombs would miss.

And now our frustrated aerial warrior had to turn his fanny to the fire and successfully avoid on the way out all the hazards he had penetrated on the way in.

What the attack pilot desperately needed was a missile he could shoot at the ship, Jake concluded, the farther away the better. Alas, the US Navy's antiship missiles were still in the development stage, victims of Vietnam penny pinching, so the attack crews would have to make do with what they had. What they had were some short-range guided missiles like Bullpup, which unfortunately carried only a 250-pound warhead – enough to cripple a warship but not to sink it.

If the weather was good enough, the attacking planes could use laser-guided bombs, preferably two-thousand pounders. Although these weapons were unpowered, the laser seeker and guidance assembly on the nose of the weapon could steer it into the target if the attack pilot made a reasonably accurate delivery, and if the spot of laser light that the guidance system was seeking was indeed on the target. The weak point of the system was the beam of laser light, which was scattered by visible moisture in the air. Alas, over the ocean the sky was often cloudy.

With or without laser-guided bombs, the attackers were going to have to penetrate the enemy ship's radar-directed defenses. Here was where the EA-6B came in. The electronic warfare (EW) plane could shield the attack force electronically if it were in the middle of it or placed at the proper angle to the attack axis.

What about overloading the enemy's defenses with planes? Perhaps a coordinated attack with as many planes as we can launch, saturating the enemy's defenses with targets, one prays too many targets. Some would inevitably get through.

And our coordinated attack should come in high and low at the same time. Say A-6s at a hundred feet and A-7s and F-4s diving in from thirty thousand.

Jake made notes. The EA-6 crews had a lot of ideas, most of which Jake thought excellent. When he said his good-bye two hours after he came, he shook hands all around.

Back in his stateroom staring at his notes, Jake wondered what a war with the Soviets would be like. An exchange of intercontinental ballistic missiles would make for a loud, almighty short war, but Jake didn't think there would be much reason for the surviving warships to try to sink one another. Without countries to go back to, the sailors and the ships were all doomed anyway. Could there be a war without nuclear weapons, in 1973?

Really, when one is contemplating the end of civilization the whole problem becomes fantastic, something out of a sweaty nightmare. Could sane men push the button, thereby destroying themselves, their nations, most of the human race? He got bogged down at this point. The politicians would have to figure it out.

One thing he knew for sure – if there was a war without a nuclear Armageddon, the American admirals would go for the Soviet ships like bulldogs after raw meat.

It wouldn't be easy. He knew well that a strike on a single ship would be a fluke, an ambush of a straggler. Like every other navy, the Soviets would arrange their ships in groups for mutual support. Any attack would have to be against a task force.

Staring at his notes on detection ranges, missile and flak envelopes, Jake could envision how it would be. The ships would be rippling off missiles – the sky would be full of Mach 3 telephone poles. If that weren't enough, Soviet warships were covered with antiaircraft guns. American ships these days didn't have many, but then the Soviet Navy had no aircraft carriers to launch strikes against them. The flak from the Soviet ships would be fierce, would literally be a steel curtain the attacking planes would have to fly through.

An Alpha strike – everything the ship could launch, coming in high and low and in the middle, shielded by EA-6B Prowlers and coordinated as well as possible by an E-2 Hawkeye orbiting safely out of range a hundred miles away – that was the answer he would give Colonel Haldane.

Wouldn't ever happen, of course. America and Russia weren't about to fight a war. Planning an attack on a Soviet task force was just another peacetime military what-if exercise. Yet if it *did* happen, few of those planes would survive. And of those crews who successfully penetrated the cordon of missiles and flak, only the most fiercely determined would successfully drive the thrust home. For Jake Grafton knew that it was neither ships nor airplanes that won battles, but men.

Were there men like that aboard this ship? By reputation Flap Le Beau was one, but were there any more?

Disgusted with the whole problem, he began to think of home. He had visited his parents on their farm in southwestern Virginia this spring. In May, with the leaves on the trees coming out, the grass in the meadows growing green and tender, the cows nursing new-born calves.

His parents had been so glad to see him. Dad, well, his pride in his son had been visible, tangible. And Mother, smiling through her tears at her man-son come home.

He had helped his father with the cattle, once again felt the morning chill and smelled the aroma of warm bovine bodies, manure, sweet hay . . . Just the memory of it made him shiver here in his small stateroom aboard this giant steel ship. The dew in the grass that recorded every step, the sun slanting up over the low ridges and shining into the barn, his father's voice as he talked to the cattle, reassuring, steady . . . all of it came flooding back.

Why are you here, aboard this steel ship on this wilderness of ocean, worried about Russian flak and missiles, contemplating the ultimate obscenity? Why aren't you there, where you grew up, feeling the warmth of the sun on your back and helping your father in the timeless rituals that ensure life will go on, and on . . . as God intended? Why aren't you there to help your mother in her old age? Answer me that, Jake Grafton. You never hated the farm as your elder brother did — you loved it. Loved everything about it. Your parents — you love them. You are of them and they are of you. Why are you here?

Why?

Life aboard ship quickly assumed its natural rhythm, which was the rhythm dictated by two hundred years of naval tradition and regulations. Everyone worked, meals were served, the ship's laundry ran full blast, and every afternoon at precisely 13:30 the PA system came to life and announced a general quarters drill. 'This is a drill, this is a drill. General quarters, general quarters. All hands man your battle stations. Go up and forward on the starboard side and down and aft on the port side. General quarters.'

The aviators' battle stations were their ready rooms. While the damage control parties fought mock fires and coped with flooding, nuclear, chemical and biological attack, the aviators took NATOPS exams, listened to lectures, and generally bored one another. It was during these drills that Jake gave his lectures on shipboard operations. In addition to the material in the CV NATOPS, he added every tip he could recall from his two previous combat cruises. The lectures went well, he thought. The Marines were attentive and asked good questions. To his amazement, he found he actually enjoyed standing in front of the room and talking about his passion, flying.

After secure from general quarters the officers scattered to squadron spaces throughout the ship to do paperwork, to which there was no end in this life. The evening of the second day at sea Jake found an opportunity to discuss his Soviet ship project with the skipper, Colonel Haldane, who knew as much about the subject as Jake did. After they had spent an hour going over the problem, the colonel took him to the air wing spaces to meet the air wing ops officer, a lieutenant commander. Here the subject was aired again. The upshot of it was that Jake was assigned to help Wing Ops put together realistic exercises for the ship's air wing.

Officers could eat dinner in either of the two wardrooms aboard – the formal wardroom on the main deck, right beside Ready Four, where uniforms were required, or in the dirty-shirt wardroom up forward in the 0-3 level between the bow catapults where flight suits and flight deck jerseys were acceptable. In practice the formal wardroom was the turf of the ship's company officers who were not aviators, invaded only occasionally by aviation personnel on their best behavior. Here in the evening after dinner a movie was shown, one watched with proper decorum by congressionally certified gentlemen.

The aviators congregated in their ready rooms for their evening movies, here to whistle, shout, offer ribald suggestions to the characters, moan lustily at the female lead, and throw popcorn at the screen and each other. If a flyer didn't like the movie in his ready room, he could always wander off to another squadron's, where he would be welcome if he could find a seat.

And in the late evening somewhere in the junior officers' staterooms there was a card game under way, usually nickel-dime-quarter poker because no one had much money. Although alcohol was officially outlawed aboard ship, at a card game a thirsty fellow could usually find a drink. Or several. As long as one didn't appear in any of the ship's common spaces drunk or smelling of liquor, no one seemed to care very much.

Of course, a junior officer could skip the movie and card game and retire to his stateroom to listen to music or write letters. Since a lot of the junior officers were very much in love, a lot of them did this almost every night, Jake Grafton among them. Of course the lonely lovers had roommates, which sometimes presented problems.

'It's so damned unfair,' the Real McCoy lamented. 'I could get more information about the markets if I were sitting in a mud hut in some squalid village in the middle of India. Anywhere but here.' He turned his woeful gaze on his roommate. 'There are telephones everywhere on this planet except here. Everywhere.'

Jake Grafton tried to look sympathetic. He did reasonably well, he thought.

'It's the not knowing,' the LSO continued. 'I bought solid companies, with solid prospects, nothing speculative. But I am just completely *cut off*. Condemned to the outer darkness.' He gestured futilely. 'It's maddening.'

'Maybe you should put your investments in a trust or something. Give someone a power of attorney.'

'Who? Anyone who can do as well as I have in the market is doing it, not fooling around with someone else's portfolio for a fee.'

'We'll be in Hawaii in a week. I'll bet you'll find that you're doing great.'

The Real McCoy groaned and glanced at Jake Grafton with a look that told him he was hopeless. The LSO took a deep breath, then exhaled slowly. He looked so forlorn that Jake decided to try to get him talking.

A question. He should ask a question. After thinking about it for a moment, Jake said, 'Hey, what's the difference between stocks and shares? In the newspapers they talk about stockholders and shareholders and—'

He stopped because the Real gave him a withering look and stomped for the door. He slammed it shut behind him.

Dear Callie,

We are three days out of San Francisco on our way to Pearl Harbor. We are making about twenty knots. We tried to go faster but the escorts were taking a pounding in heavy swells, so we slowed down. The swells are being kicked up by a typhoon about fifteen hundred miles to the southwest. I got requalified on carrier landings, day and night, the first day out of port, but we haven't flown since.

My bombardier-navigator is a guy named Flap Le Beau. He's from Brooklyn and has been in the Marines for ten years. I'm still trying to figure him out. He appears to be a good BN and a fine officer. He wasn't too sure about me the first time we flew together and gave me a lot of gas to see if I could take it. What he didn't know is that I've learned to take gas from experts, so his little performance was just a minor irritation. I think he's a pretty neat guy, so I was lucky there. I think you'd like him too.

My roommate is a character, fellow called the Real McCoy. He is in a tizzy worrying about what is happening in the stock market while we are out of touch. He's made a lot of money in stocks and wants to make a lot more. If I knew anything about stocks I would too, but I don't. I couldn't make easy money if I owned the mint.

The skipper is a lieutenant colonel – same rank as a commander – named Richard Haldane. Don't know where he is from but he doesn't have an accent like I do. Neither does Flap, for that matter.

Jake didn't know he had an accent until Callie told him he did. She was a linguist, with a trained ear. Since she made that remark he was listening more carefully to how other people talked. Just now he said a few words to see if he could detect some flaw in his pronunciation. 'My name is Jake Grafton. I work for the government and am here to save you.'

Nope.

She wouldn't kid about a thing like that, would she?

Colonel Haldane has me giving lectures to the flight crews on flight operations around the ship. It's easy and sort of fun. It used to be that I didn't like standing in front of a crowd and saying anything, but now I don't mind it if I know the material I am going to talk about. I must have a little ham in me.

The colonel also has me doing some research on how to attack Soviet ships, just in case we ever have to. The research is difficult, especially when you realize that if the necessity ever arises, a lot of American lives are going to depend on how well you did your homework.

As I mentioned, the first day out of port I got requalified day and night. The day traps went okay, but the night ones were something else. On the fourth one I had an in-flight engagement, which means I caught a wire during a wave-off and the plane fell about four feet to the deck. The impact almost destroyed the airplane. It appears to have survived with only damage to the avionics, which is the electronic gear. Why a wheel didn't come off I'll never know.

Everyone says the in-flight wasn't my fault, but in a way it was. The LSO gave me a wave-off too late, and I shouldn't have rotated as much as I did when I poured the power to her. It's a technique thing. I did it by the book and got bitten, yet if I had deviated from approved wave-off procedure *in this particular case*, things would have probably worked out better.

All you can do is hope that when the challenge comes, you will do the right thing through instinct, training, or experience, or some combination of these. The one thing you know is that when the crunch comes you won't have time to think about how you should handle it. The hard, inescapable reality is that anyone who flies may die in an airplane.

I suppose I have accepted this reality on some level. Still, the in-flight shook me up pretty good. As the airplane decelerated, still in the air, we were thrown forward into the straps that hold us to the seat. At moments like that every perception is crystal clear, every thought arrives like a bell ringing. You are so totally alive that the events of seconds seem to happen so slowly that later you can recall every nuance. As I felt the plane decelerating, I knew what had happened.

In-flight!

I could feel her slowing, saw the needle of the angle-of-attack gauge swing toward a stall, saw the engine RPM still winding up . . . and knew that we were in for it. For an instant there we hung suspended above the deck. Then we fell.

The jolt of falling about four feet stunned me. I knew exactly what had happened, yet I didn't know whether or not we were safely arrested. I couldn't see too well. I didn't know if the hook had held, or if the cross-deck pennant had held together. Or if the airplane was in one piece — if the fuel tank had ruptured we were only seconds away from blowing up.

It was a bad scare.

I've had a few of those through the years and one more isn't headline stuff, but still, with the war over and all and me thinking about getting out, that moment was a hard, swift return to cold reality.

I have been thinking a lot about you these last few days. Our time together in Chicago was something very special. Although the visit didn't wind up quite the way I planned, everything else was super. Theron is a great guy and your folks seem like they would be very pleasant once I got to know them a little better.

He stopped and reread that last paragraph. That bit about the parents wasn't strictly true, but what could he say? *Your dad's a royal jerk but I like them like that.*

Diplomacy. This letter had some diplomacy in it.

When you stop and think about it, life is strange. Some people believe in preordination, although I don't. Still, you grow up knowing that somewhere out there is the person you are going to fall in love with. So you wonder what that person will be like, how she will look, how she will walk, talk, what she will think, how she will smile, how she will laugh. There's no way of knowing, of course, until you meet her. The realization that you have finally met her comes as a wondrous discovery, a peek into the works of life.

Maybe a guy could fall instantly in love, but I doubt it. I think love sort of creeps over you — like a warm feeling

103

on a clear blue fall day. This person is in your thoughts most of the time – all the time, actually. You see her when you close your eyes, when you look off into the distance, when you pause from what you are doing and take a deep breath. You remember how her eyes looked when she laughed, how she threw her head back, how her fingers felt when they touched you . . .

The loved one becomes a part of you, the most valuable part.

At least it is that way with me when I think of you.

As ever,
Jake

CHAPTER SEVEN

Visual dive-bombing really hadn't changed much since the 1930s, even though the top speeds of the aircraft had tripled and their ordnance-carrying capacity had increased fifteenfold. The techniques were still the same.

Jake Grafton thought about that as the flight of four A-6s threaded their way upward through a layer of scattered cumulus clouds. The four warplanes, spread in a loose finger-four formation, passed the tops at about 8,000 feet and continued to climb into the clear, open sky above.

Perhaps it was the touch of the romantic that he tried with varying degrees of success to keep hidden, but the link to the past was strong within him. On a morning like this in June 1942, US Navy dive bomber pilots from *Enterprise* and *Yorktown* topped the clouds and searched across the blue Pacific for the Japanese carriers then engaged in hammering Midway Island. They found them, four aircraft carriers plowing the broad surface of that great ocean, pushed over and dove. Their bombs smashed *Kaga*, *Akagi* and *Soryu*, set them fatally ablaze and turned the tide of World War II.

This morning thirty-one years later this group of bombers was on its way to bomb Hawaii, actually a small island in the Hawaiian archipelago named Kahoolawe.

The oxygen from the mask tasted cool and rubbery. Jake eyed the cockpit altimeter, steady at ten thousand feet, and unsnapped the left side of his mask. He let it dangle from the fitting on the other side as he devoted most of his attention to holding good formation. His position today was number three, which meant that he flew on the skipper's, Colonel Haldane's, right side. Number four was on Jake's right, number two on Haldane's left.

He glanced at his BN, Flap Le Beau, who had his head pressed against the radar hood. He was using both hands to twiddle knobs and flip switches, but he never took his eyes from the radar. Excellent. He knew the location and function of every knob, button and switch without looking. When the going got tough there would be no time to look, no time to fumble for this or that, no time to think.

The colonel's BN, Allen Bartow, was similarly engaged. From his vantage point twenty feet out from the colonel's wingtip, Jake could see every move Bartow made in the cockpit, could see him pull his head aft a few inches and eye the computer readouts on the panel just to the right of the radar screen, could see him glance down occasionally, referring to the notes on his kneeboard.

He had gotten to know Bartow fairly well the last few days. A major with twelve years in the Corps, Bartow was addicted to French novels. He read them in French. Just now he was working his way through everything that Georges Simenon had ever written. He had books stacked everywhere in his stateroom and carried one in his flight suit, which he pulled out whenever he had a few minutes to kill.

'I'm retiring as soon as I get my twenty years in,' he told Jake. 'On that very day. Then I'm going to get a doctorate in French literature and spend the rest of my life teaching.'

'Sounds dull,' Jake said, grinning, just to needle him.

To his surprise Bartow had considered that remark seriously. 'Maybe. Academic life won't be like the Corps, like life in a squadron. Yet we all have to give this up sooner or later. I enjoy it now, but when it's over I have something else I'll enjoy just as much. Something different. So now I've got the flying and the guys and the anticipation

106

of that something else. I'm a pretty rich man.' And he returned Jake's grin.

Bartow *was* rich, Jake reflected ruefully as he watched the bombardier sitting hunched over his scope. Richer than Jake, anyway. All Jake had was the flying and the cama- raderie. He didn't even have Callie – he had screwed that up.

Le Beau – he apparently didn't want anything else. Or did he?

'You got a gal waiting for you?' Jake asked his bombard- ier without taking his eyes off the lead plane.

'You can fly this thing and think about women too?'

'I always have time to think about women. You got one stashed somewhere?'

'Dozens.'

'A special one?'

'Naw. The ones I want to get serious about don't want me after they've had a good look. I'm just tempered, polished steel, a military instrument. How we doing on fuel, anyway?'

Jake glanced at the gauges. He punched the buttons to get a reading on his remaining wing fuel, then finally said, 'We're okay.'

'Umph. We're only fifty miles out.' Le Beau went back to the radar. 'Don't embarrass me. Try to get some decent hits.'

The bombs hanging under the wings were little blue twenty-five-pound practice bombs. Each one contained a small pyrotechnic cartridge in the nose that would produce a puff of smoke when the bomb struck, allowing the hit to be spotted. Each A-6 carried a dozen of these things on their bomb racks.

The planned drill was for the pilot of each plane to drop the first half-dozen manually, using the visual bomb sight à la World War II, then the second six using the aircraft's electronic system. Jake carefully set the optical sight to the

107

proper mil setting for a forty-degree dive with a six-thousand-foot release. Releasing six thousand feet above the target, the slant range was about nine thousand feet. To drop a bomb nine thousand feet from a target and hit it was difficult, of course – nearly impossible when you considered the fact that the wind would affect the bomb's trajectory throughout its fall. Yet *that* was the dive bomber's art.

Hitting the target was the payoff. Five thousand men at sea for months, the treasure spent on ships, planes and fuel, the blood spilled in training, all to set up that moment when the bomb struck the target. If the pilot could get it there.

Colonel Haldane expected his pilots to do their damnedest. Last night he taped a poster to the ready room bulkhead with the names of all his pilots on it. The poster was just as large, just as prominent as the one on the bulkhead that recorded each pilot's landing grades. You had to be able to get aboard ship safely to be a carrier pilot, but you weren't much use in combat unless you could hit the target when the chips were down. Haldane said as much. He went further:

'In this squadron, after the upcoming Hawaiian ops period, the pilots who are going to lead sections and flights are the pilots with the best bombing scores. I guarantee you, your bombing scores will appear on your fitness report. I expect each and every one of you to earn your pay on the bombing range.'

First Lieutenant Doug Harrison couldn't resist. 'Hey, Skipper. You can fly on my wing.'

'If you can out-bomb me, I will,' Haldane shot back.

Harrison was number four today, flying on Jake's right wing. You had to admire Harrison, for his chutzpah if nothing else. Haldane had spent years in Vietnam dive-bombing under fire and Harrison was just a year out of flight school. No fool, Harrison well knew how good the experienced professionals were and risked ignominy anyway.

Although he was less vocal about it, Jake Grafton took a backseat to no one when it came to pride in his own flying skills. He had seen his share of flak and dropped his share of bombs. His name would be at the top of that ready room poster if it were humanly possible to get it there.

Major Bartow pumped his fist at Jake, who scooted farther away from the lead plane. Number two, Captain Harry Digman, came under the lead, his canopy just a few feet below Haldane's exhausts, and surfaced where Jake had been. Now the formation was in right echelon.

Colonel Haldane did the talking on the radio. Cleared into the target area as a flight of F-4s were leaving, he led his echelon down in a gentle, sweeping left turn to 15,000 feet, then straightened out for the run up the bearing line. Over the target he broke to the left. Ten seconds later the second plane broke, and Jake ten seconds after that.

Around they came, now strung out, each pilot verifying his clearance from other airplanes, then concentrating on the target and flying his own plane.

The first essential for a successful run is to get to the proper roll-in point. This is that location in space from which you can roll in and arrive on the proper run-in heading at the preselected dive angle, today forty degrees. Practice targets, with run-in lines bulldozed into the earth and marks gouged out as reference points, help the pilots develop a feel for that correct, perfect place to roll in.

And 'roll in' describes the maneuver. Today Jake approached the bearing line obliquely, at about forty-five degrees off, waiting, watching the target get nearer and nearer as he ran the trim to one degree nose-down, the 500-knot setting, while he held the plane level with back stick.

Now!

He slaps the stick sideways and in a heartbeat has the

A-6 past the vertical, in 135 degrees of bank. Now the stick comes sharply back and the G's smash them into their seats as the pilot pulls the nose of the aircraft to just below the target while he adjusts the throttles. Since he is carrying low-drag practice bombs today, Jake sets the throttles at about eighty percent RPM.

G off, stick right to roll her hard to the upright position.

Flap flips on the master armament switch and makes the radio call: 'War Ace Three's in hot.'

If the pilot has rolled in properly, the plane is now in a forty-degree dive, the pipper in the bombsight below the target and tracking toward it. This is where Jake finds it now, although just a little too far right. He corrects this instantly by forcing the stick to the left, then jerking the wings back level. This is no place to try to be smooth – it is imperative that he quickly get the lane into the proper dive with the pipper tracking so that he will have as many seconds as possible to solve the drift problem. Jake flies his dives with both hands on the stick, muscling the plane to the position he wants.

A glance at the airspeed – over 400 and increasing – now the altimeter. Flap is calling the altitudes: 'Fourteen . . . thirteen . . . forty-one degrees . . . twelve . . .'

The wind is drifting the pipper leftward. Jake rolls right and forces the pipper back to the right. He wants the pipper to the right of the bearing line and drifting left toward it, yet at the moment of release it must still be slightly right of the bull's-eye. The bomb will continue to drift during its fall.

And he is steep. He must release with the pipper just a smidgen short of the target to compensate for that.

'. . . Ten . . . nine . . . eight . . .'

Coming down with the pipper tracking toward the bull's-eye, today a painted white spot in the middle of a white circle, he glances at the G-meter. Steady on one. He releases his death grip on the stick so that he can feel the

110

effect of the trim. Coming toward neutral, which means he is getting toward 500 knots true airspeed, 465 indicated. The briefest glance at the airspeed indicator – 445 and increasing . . .

'Seven . . .'

And since the target is several hundred feet above sea level and he has synchronized the movement of the pipper with the descent, he releases the bomb two hundred feet above six thousand feet with the pipper at a five o'clock position on the bull.

And pulls.

Wings level and throttles forward to the stops, pull until the G-meter needle hits four, then hold it there. He reaches for the master arm switch with his right hand – his arm weighs a ton with all this G on – and toggles it off.

Flap again on the radio: 'War Ace Three's off safe.'

With his nose passing the horizon Jake Grafton relaxes the G and scans the sky for the airplane in front of him. There! And farther around, the skipper. Okay. Nose on up and let her soar, converting that diving airspeed back into altitude.

The spotters on the ground are calling the hits. The skipper's first one was seventy-five feet at seven o'clock. His wingman gets a called score of a hundred-ten feet at twelve. Jack gets a score of fifty feet at five.

'Overcompensated for the wind,' he mutters to Flap, who has no comment.

Now they are back at 15,000 feet and he pulls the throttles back, steers a little wider as he makes his turn. He glimpses the flashing wings of the plane ahead as it rolls into its dive.

'War Ace Four, your hit seventy-five feet at nine o'clock.'

'Harrison's holding his own with the colonel,' Jake tells Flap, and chuckles.

He checks the drift of the puffs of smoke from the

practice bombs. He eyes the clouds, glances behind to see where Harrison is, checks his fuel, checks the annunciator panel for warning lights, then eyes the target to see where he should go to get to the roll-in.

Master Arm switch on, roll and pull!

'Don't you just love this shit?' Flap says between altitude calls on their second dive.

'Bull's-eye,' the target spotter says as Jake soars upward after release, and he reaches over and slaps Flap on the thigh.

'With a spoon, Flapjack!' He slams the stick sideways and the aircraft spins on its longitudinal axis. He stops it after precisely 360 degrees of roll.

'Okay, okay, you're the best in the west,' Flap says. 'Just keep popping them in there.'

After their sixth dive, it was Flap's turn. He had the radar and computer ready. This time as Jake rolled he had to point the fixed reticle of the bombsight exactly at the target. Then he squeezed the commit trigger on the stick and began to fly the steering commands on the vertical display indicator, the VDI, in the center of the instrument panel in front of him.

Squeezing the commit trigger told the computer where the target was and told the radar to track it. While Flap monitored the velocities the computer was getting from the inertial, the computer providing steering commands, wind-compensated of course, to guide Jake to the proper release point, which was that point in space where the bomb could be released to fall upon the target.

Jake concentrated upon the steering commands and followed them as precisely as he could. When the computer gave him a pull-up command he laid on the G while concentrating fiercely on keeping the wings level. The computer released the weapon and he kept the nose coming up.

'Seventy-five feet at six o'clock.'

He went around to do it again.

'You know,' he said to Flap, 'it's like they invented a machine to hit a baseball.'

'Just follow steering, Babe Ruth. This gizmo is smarter than you are.'

'Yeah, but I'm an *artiste!*'

'We ain't dodging flak today, Jake.'

This was the eternal war – the pilot wanted to drop them all visually and the bombardier wanted to use the system every time. Both men knew the system was better and they both knew Jake would never admit it. Today at this practice target the pilot had ideal conditions: a stationary target with a known elevation, a plowed run-in line, visual cues on the ground, no flak, the luxury of repeated runs that allowed him to properly dope the wind. The system of this A-6E was a first-time, every-time sure thing.

But a machine is hard to love.

The four A-6s rendezvoused off target and Harrison, the number-four man, slid under the other three checking them for hung bombs. Then Jake checked Harrison. Harrison and number two each had one little blue bomb still handing on the racks.

The skipper led them up to 20,000 feet and Flap dialed in the ships TACAN, a radio navigation aid. The mileage readout refused to lock – they were still too far out – but Flap soon had the ship on radar. One hundred thirty-two miles.

After checking the cockpit altitude – stable at 10,000 feet – Jake took his mask off and hung it on the left side mirror on the canopy rail. He swabbed the sweat off his face.

The planes were in parade formation, only about fifteen feet from the cockpit to the wing tip of the next man. Flying this close to another plane was work, but Jake

Grafton enjoyed it. The restless air always affected the planes differently as they sliced through it, so constant adjustments were required from the wingman. The lead just flew his own machine.

If you were the wingman, you kept the wing tip of the lead plane just below and behind the canopy. This look must be maintained with continuous small adjustments of stick and throttles, occasionally rudder. If you did it right, you could hang here no matter what the lead plane was doing – flying straight and level, banking, climbing, diving, executing wingovers, loops; whatever.

Jake settled in and concentrated. Doing this on a sunny morning in clear, fairly calm air was merely drill. Doing it on a stormy, filthy night with the planes bouncing in turbulence over an angry ocean demanded a high level of skill and confidence. With an emergency and a low reading on the fuel gauge, your ability to hang on someone's wing became your lifeline.

Bartow was motioning him out. A pushing motion.

'We're opening it up,' he told Flap, who glanced at Bartow, then gave the identical signal to Harrison, on Jake's right wing.

When he had opened the gap to about sixty or seventy feet, Jake stabilized and checked Harrison. He looked at the skipper's wingman, on the skipper's left wing. Everybody about right. Okay.

Flap had written down all the scores and now he was tallying them, figuring each crew's CEP – circular error probable. He did this by finding the sixth best hit. Half the bombs would hit within a circle with this radius.

In the skipper's cockpit Bartow was looking at his radar. Jake glanced at the mileage readout on the radar repeater between his legs: 126. Then his eyes flicked across the instrument panel. Airspeed 295 indicated, altitude 20,040 feet, warning lights out, hydraulic pressures okay. Fuel – about 7,600 pounds remaining.

He looked straight ahead, saw nothing, then glanced again across that gap toward Bartow.

He had his eyes focused on Bartow when an F-4 Phantom crossed his line of vision. Between him and the skipper. Flashed by going in the opposite direction, and at the same time another Phantom went by the skipper's left side, between him and his wingman.

They were there only long enough to register on Jake's brain, then they were gone. The A-6 jolted as it flew into the edges of the wash of the Phantom's wings.

'What was that?' Flap asking, raising his head and looking around.

Jake grabbed his oxygen mask and snapped it on. 'You won't believe this,' he said on the ICS, 'but a Phantom just went between us and the skipper. And another went down the skipper's left side, between him and Digman.'

'What?'

'Yeah, a flight of Phantoms just went through our flight. I shit you not. The skipper went between the lead and his wingman and one of them went between us and the skipper. We missed by *inches*.'

Jake stared across the gap that separated him from Bartow. Bartow was looking back at him. Had he seen the F-4s?

'If we had been still in parade formation,' Jake told Flap, 'you and me would be tapping on the pearly gates right now.'

Say the fighters were also going 300 indicated — that's a closing speed of 600 knots indicated, over 800 knots true. Almost a thousand miles per hour!

He had looked straight ahead just a second or two before they got here — and seen nothing.

But they were *there*, coming head-on, like guided missiles.

And he didn't see them. Of course the distance was over a half mile two seconds before they arrived, but still . . . He should have seen something!

He broke into a sweat. His mouth and lips were dry. He tried to swallow.

At those speeds, if his plane had collided with that Phantom . . .

He wouldn't have felt a thing. Not a single thing. He would have been just instantly dead, a spot of grease trapped in the exploding fireball.

'Well, Ace,' Flap said, 'you will be delighted to hear we have a fifty-foot CEP.'

Jake tried to reply but couldn't.

'If World War III comes, you and I will be among the very first to die,' Flap informed him. 'How about them apples? We've earned it.'

Those Phantoms – he wondered if the pilots of the fighters had even seen the A-6s.

'Gives you goose bumps, huh? Ain't life something else?'

'Did anybody see those Phantoms?' Jake asked.

Silence. Blank looks. They were debriefing the flight in the ready room. Seven blank faces.

'You mean I was the only one to see them?'

Later, in the solitude of his stateroom, he thought about miracles. About how close to the abyss he had come, how many times. What was that quote – something about if you stared into the abyss long enough, the abyss stared back.

That was true. He could feel it staring back just now.

No one doubted his word when he told them about the fighters. But no one else had seen them.

To be told later that you had a close call was like learning that your mother had difficulty when you were born. It meant nothing. You shrugged and went on.

The Phantoms must have been from this ship. That was easy enough to check. He examined the air plan and found the fighter squadron that had the target time immediately after the A-6 outfit, then paid a visit to their ready room.

'Hey, did any of you guys have a near midair today?

116

Anybody almost trade paint with four A-6s? On your way into the target?'

They stared at him like he was a grotesque apparition, a leering reminder of their own mortality. No one had seen anything. All must have been looking elsewhere, thinking of something else, because unless they were looking in exactly the right place, they would have missed it. Just as the other seven Intruder crewmen had.

Here in his stateroom he worked out the math. An F-4 was about fifty feet long. At a combined speed of 800 knots it would pass the eye in thirty-seven thousandths of a second. Less than an eye blink.

When death comes, she will come quick.

But you've always known that, Jake Grafton.

He got out of his chair and examined his face in the mirror over the sink. The face in the glass stared back blankly.

'A ship under way is a very difficult target,' Jake said.

Lieutenant Colonel Haldane didn't reply. He knew as well as Jake did that once free-falling bombs were released, a well-conned ship would turn sharply. Probably into the wind, although the attacker certainly couldn't count on that.

'Ideally we should drop as close to the ship as possible to minimize the time he has to turn,' Jake said. Such a choice would also minimize the effect of any errors in the computer, errors in velocity, drift angle, altitude, etc.

'That would be the ideal,' Haldane agreed, 'but it wouldn't be smart to get all our airplanes shot down trying for the perfect attack. We're going to have to pick an attack that maximizes our chances of hitting yet gives us a half-decent chance of getting to the drop point. Let's look again at the weapons envelopes we'll have to penetrate.'

Jake was briefing the skipper on the progress of the

planning efforts under way in the air wing offices. He had been attending these meetings for several days. Now he spread out several graphs he had constructed and explained them to his boss, Lieutenant Colonel Haldane.

As the attackers approached a Soviet task force, the first weapons that they would face would be SA-N-3 Goblet missiles, which could engage them up to twenty miles away at altitudes between 150 and 80,000 feet. These Mach 2.5 missiles would probably be fired in pairs, the second one following the first by a few seconds. Then the launcher would be reloaded and another pair fired – each launcher had the capacity to shoot thirty-six missiles. The number of launchers present would depend on the makeup of the task group, but for planning purposes figure there were ten. That's a possible 360 missiles in the air.

The next threat would be encountered at a range of nine or ten miles, when the attackers penetrated the envelope of the Mach 3.5 SA-N-1 Goa missiles. The weak point in the Goa system was the fire control director, which could engage only one target at a time. Yet since the missiles were carried on twin launchers, presumably two would be fired at the target, then a second target could be acquired while the launcher was reloaded. The magazine capacity for each launcher was sixteen missiles. Unfortunately the Soviets placed these weapons on destroyers as well as Kynda and Kresta cruisers, so one could expect a lot of launchers. Plan for twenty and we have another possible 320 missiles to evade.

If our harried attack crews were still alive seven miles from the target, they would enter the envelope of the Mach 2+ SA-N-4. This weapon was also fired from twin launchers, each with a magazine capacity of twenty missiles. Figure a task group with twenty launchers and we have a possible 400 missiles of this type.

Finally, after a weapons release, the attacker could expect surviving ships to fire a cloud of SA-N-5 Grail heat-seeking missiles, the naval version of the Soviet Army's Strela. Grail carried a one-kilogram warhead over a slant range of only 4.4 kilometers and needed a good hot tailpipe signature to guide, but just one up your tailpipe would ruin your day. Within the Grail envelope the attacker could expect to see dozens in the air.

Yet missiles were only half the story. There would also be flak, an extraordinary amount of it. Soviet ships bristled with guns. The larger guns would fire first, as soon as the attacking force came in range. As the distance between the attackers and the defenders closed, the smaller calibers would open fire.

The smaller the gun, the faster the rate of fire, so as the range closed, the sheer volume of high explosive in the air would increase exponentially. In close, that is within a mile and a quarter, the attacker would fly into range of six-barreled 30-mm Gatling guns, each capable of firing at a sustained rate of a thousand rounds per minute or squirting bursts of up to three times that volume.

'Since I started putting this data together,' Jake told the colonel, 'I've become a big fan of attack submarines.'

'Why don't you say what you really think?'

'Yes, sir. Attacking a Soviet task group with free-fall bombs will be a spectacular way to commit suicide.'

'If the balloon goes up, we'll go when we're told to go, suicide or not.'

'Yessir.'

'So we had better have a realistic plan, just in case.'

'The air wing is planning Alpha strikes. Two strikes, Blue and Gold, half the planes on each one.' An Alpha strike was a maximum effort, with fighters escorting the attackers and the entire gaggle diving the target in close order. The ideal was to get all the bombs on target and everyone exiting the area within sixty seconds.

'Okay,' Colonel Haldane said.

'That will only work on a daytime, good weather

119

launch,' Jake continued. 'In my opinion, skipper, we can figure on losing half our planes on each strike.'

Haldane didn't say anything.

'At night or in bad weather, they'll just send the A-6s. We're the only planes with the capability.'

CHAPTER EIGHT

Steam catapults make modern aircraft carriers possible. Invented by the British during World War II, catapults freed designers from the necessity of building naval aircraft that could rise from the deck under their own power after a run of only three hundred feet. So wings could shrink and be swept as the physics of high speed aerodynamics required, jet engines that were most efficient at high speeds could be installed, and airframes could be designed that would go supersonic or lift tremendous quantities of fuel and weapons. A luxury for most of the carrier planes of World War II, the catapult now was an absolute requirement.

The only part of the catapult that can be seen on the flight deck is the shuttle to which aircraft are attached. This shuttle sticks up from a slot in the deck that runs the length of the catapult. The catapult itself lies under the slot and consists of two tubes eighteen inches in diameter arranged side by side like the barrels of a double-barreled shotgun. Inside each tube – or barrel – is a piston. There is a gap at the top of each barrel through which a steel lattice mates the two pistons together, and to which the shuttle on deck attaches.

The pistons are hauled aft mechanically into battery by a little cart called a 'grab.' Once the pistons are in battery, the aircraft is attached to the shuttle, either by a linkage on the nose gear of the aircraft in the case of the A-6 and A-7, or by a bridle made of steel cable in the case of the F-4 and

RA-5. Then the slack in the bridle or nose-tow linkage is taken out by pushing the pistons forward hydraulically – this movement is called 'taking tension.'

Once the catapult is tensioned and the aircraft is at full power with its wheel brakes off, the firing circuit is enabled when the operator pushes the 'final ready' button.

Firing the catapult is then accomplished by opening the launch valves, one behind each tube, simultaneously, which allows superheated steam to enter the barrels behind the pistons.

The amount of acceleration given to each aircraft must be varied depending on the type of aircraft being launched, its weight, the amount of wind over the deck, and the outside air temperature. This is accomplished by one of two methods. Either the steam pressure is kept constant and the speed of opening of the launch valves is varied, or the launch valves are always opened at the same rate and the pressure of the steam in the accumulators is varied. Aboard *Columbia*, the steam pressure was varied and the launch valves were opened at a constant rate.

Although the launch valves open quickly, they don't open instantaneously. Consequently steam pressure rising on the back of the pistons must be resisted until it has built up sufficient pressure to move the pistons forward faster than the aircraft could accelerate on its own. This resistance is provided by a shear bolt installed in the nose gear of the aircraft to be launched, to which a steel hold-back bar is attached. One end of the bar fits into a slot in the deck. The bolt used in the A-6 was designed to break cleanly in half under a load of 48,000 pounds, only then allowing the pistons in the catapult, and the aircraft, to begin forward motion.

The superheated steam expanding behind the pistons drove them the length of the 258-foot catapults of the *Columbia* in about 2.5 seconds. Now up to flying speed, the aircraft left the deck behind and ran out into the air sixty feet above the ocean, where it then had to be rotated to the proper angle of attack to fly – in the A-6, about eight degrees nose-up.

Meanwhile, the pistons, at terminal velocity and quickly running out of barrels, had to be stopped. This was accomplished by means of water brakes, tubes welded onto the end of each of the catapult barrels and filled with water. The pistons each carried a tapered spear in front of them, and as the pistons reached the water brakes the spears penetrated the open ends, forcing water out around the spears. Water is incompressible, yet as the spears were inserted the escape openings for the water got smaller and smaller. Consequently the deeper the spears penetrated the higher the resistance to further entry. The brakes were so efficient that the pistons were brought to a complete stop after a full-power shot in only nine feet of travel.

The sexual symbolism of the tapered spears and the water-filled brakes always impressed aviators – they were young, lonely and horny – but the sound a cat made slamming into the brakes was visceral. The stupendous thud rattled compartments within a hundred feet of the brakes and could be felt throughout the ship.

Tonight as he sat in the cockpit of an A-6 tanker waiting for the cat crew to retract the shuttle, Jake Grafton ran through all the things that could go wrong with the cat.

The launching officer, Jumping Jack Bean, was wandering around near the hole in the deck that contained the valves and gauges that allowed him to drag steam from the ship's boilers to the catapult accumulators. The enlisted man who always sat on the edge of the hole wearing a sound-powered telephone headset that enabled him to talk to the men in the catapult machinery spaces was already in his place, staring aft at the two planes on the cats. The luminescent patches on his helmet and flight deck jersey were readily visible in the dim red glow of the lights from the ship's island superstructure, almost a hundred yards aft.

If anything goes wrong with the machinery below-decks, Jake Grafton knew, the probable result would be less end speed for the plane being launched. A perfect shot gave the launching aircraft a mere fifteen knots above stall speed. A couple knots less and the pilot would never notice. Five off, the plane would be sluggish. Ten off, a ham-handed pilot could stall it inadvertently. Fifteen or more off, the plane was doomed.

Bad, or 'cold,' cat shots were rare, thank God. The catapult was very reliable, more so than the aircraft that rode it. They could have an engine flame out under the intense acceleration, dump a gyro, lose a generator, spring a hydraulic or fuel leak . . . or the pilot could just become disoriented during the sudden, intense transition from sitting stationary on deck to instrument flight fifteen knots above a stall, at night. The blackness out there beyond the bow was total, a void so vast and bleak that one wanted to avert his eyes. Look at something else. Think about something else.

The hell of it was that there was nothing else to look at – nothing else to think about. Tonight Jake was flying a tanker, which was going to be flung off the pointy end of the boat in just a few minutes right into that black void, climb to 5,000 feet and tank a couple Phantoms, climb up to 20,000 and circle the ship for an hour and a half, then come back and trap. That was it, the whole damn mission. Go around and around the ship. Orbit. At max conserve airspeed. On autopilot. The challenge would be staying awake.

No, the challenge was this goddamn night cat shot. The worst part of the whole flight was right at the start – the blindfolded ride on the rabid pig . . .

The cat crewmen were now taking the rubber seal out of the catapult slot. Steam wisped skyward from the open slot, steam leaking from some fitting somewhere in the cat. They kept the slot seal in between launches, Jake knew, to help maintain the temperature of those eighteen-inch tubes.

The handler had parked the tanker here on the cat, probably so that the miserable peckerhead pilot would have to sit in the cockpit watching the steam wisp up from the cat against the backdrop of the black void while he thought about dying young.

And his life wasn't going so good just now. First Callie's jerk father, then Tiny Dick Donovan, the in-flight engagement, that near-midair . . .

Maybe God was trying to tell him something.

Or maybe those Phantoms this morning hadn't been there at all.

What if he had just imagined them? Of course the planes passed each other quickly, but there were at least two Phantoms and four A-6s, two guys in each plane. A total of twelve men, and *he* was the *only* one who had seen the varmint.

Really doesn't make sense.

Does it?

'What are you staring at through that windshield?' Flap Le Beau asked.

'There's a naked woman out there. If you look real careful you can see her nipples.'

'You look like you're mentally composing your will. That isn't good leadership. You are supposed to be impressing me with *your* self-confidence, calming *my* fears. The stick's on your side, remember?'

'What if those F-4s weren't really there this morning? What if I just imagined it?'

'Are you still on that? You saw 'em. They were there.'

'How come no one else is in a sweat?'

'What do you want me to do, fill my drawers? Slit my wrists? Fate fired a bullet and it missed.'

'You could have the common courtesy to look nervous, sweat it a little.'

'You're making me nervous.'

'That'll be the day,' Jake Grafton replied disgustedly.

'Okay, I'm sweating. It's dripping out of my armpits. Every jerk pilot I ever met has tried to kill me. I'm waiting for you to give it a whirl.'

'How come you got into aviation anyway?'

'Jungle rot. Pretty bad case. They tell me I'm now a paragraph and photo in a medical textbook. Little did I know when I signed up for this glamorous flying life how much jungle I still had to visit.'

The brown-shirt plane captain standing beside the aircraft waved his wands to get Jake's attention, then signaled for a start.

Time to do it.

'It could have been worse,' Flap told Jake as he started the left engine. 'I could have made medical history with a spectacular social disease. Wouldn't that have been a trip? For a hundred years every guy going overseas would have had to watch a movie featuring my diseased, ulcerated pecker.'

Six minutes later Jake rogered the weight board and eased the plane forward into the shuttle. He felt the nose-tow bar drop into the shuttle slot and came off the brakes and added power at the yellow-shirt's signal.

The engines began winding up. Another small jolt as the hydraulic arm shoved the cat pistons into tension, taking all the slack out of the hold-back bar. Now just the shear-bolt was holding them back.

Full power, wipe out the controls, check the gauges, cat grip up . . . 'You ready?' he asked Flap.

'I'm really really ready.'

He could feel the vibration as the engines sucked air and blasted it out the exhausts against the jet black deflector, feel rather than hear the ear-splitting roar. He swept his eyes across the annunciator panel – all warning lights out. The exterior light master switch was on the end of the cat grip, right beside his left thumb. He flicked it on.

126

The cat officer took a last look at the island, looked up the cat at the void, then swept his yellow wand down in a fencer's lunge until he touched the deck, then he came up to a point.

The catapult fired. The G's slammed him back . . . and both fire warning lights illuminated.

They were big red lights, one on each side of the bomb-sight on the top of the instrument panel. Labeled L FIRE and R FIRE, both lights shone into his eyes like spotlights as the acceleration pressed him deeper into the seat back.

Oh, God, he thought, trying to take it in as the adrenaline whacked him in the heart.

His eyes went to the engine instruments, white tapes arranged vertically in front of his left knee. They looked—

The acceleration stopped and the plane was off the cat, the nose coming up. A glance at the airspeed – not decaying. Angle-of-attack gauge agreed. He grabbed the stick and slapped the gear handle up. Wings level, check the nose . . .

His left hand rose automatically toward the emergency jettison button above the gear handle. If he pushed it and held it down for one second the five drop tanks, each containing two thousand pounds of fuel, would be jettisoned from the aircraft. She would instantly be five tons lighter and could then fly on one engine. He was sorely tempted but he didn't push it. His hands came back to the throttles.

Which engine was it?

Both lights were screaming at him!

Which fucking engine?

Engine tapes still okay . . . airspeed okay . . . eight degrees nose up. He was squinting against the glare of the red fire lights. He had let the left wing sag so he picked it up. Climbing through two hundred feet, 160 knots . . .

Both fire lights – the book said to pull the affected engine to idle, but he had *both* lights on!

Fire!

Was he on fire? If he was it was time to eject. Jettison this fucking airplane. Swim for it. He looked in the mirrors. Black. Nothing to see.

He became aware that Flap was on the radio. '. . . both fire lights . . . declaring an emergency . . . Boss, can you see any fire?'

The reply was clear in his ears. 'Off the bow, you look fine. You say you have both fire lights on?'

Jake cut in on Flap. 'Both of them. We'd like a dump charley.'

'Your signal dump. It'll be about eight more minutes until we have a ready deck. We'll call you.'

'Roger.'

His heart was slowing. She didn't seem to be on fire. Thank you, thank you, thank you.

Accelerating through 185 knots, he raised the flaps and slats, then toggled the switches for the wing and main dump valves. They were carrying 26,000 pounds of fuel and the max he could take aboard the ship was 6,000. He needed to dump ten tons of fuel into the atmosphere.

And as he reached for the switch that would isolate a portion of the combined hydraulic system, he looked at the hydraulic gauges. For the first time. He had forgotten to look at the hydraulic gauges before. Now, squinting against the glare of the fire lights, he saw the needle on the right combined system pump flickering.

Uh-oh. A fire could be melting hydraulic lines. Hydraulic fluid itself was nonflammable, but the lines could melt.

'We have hydraulic problems,' he told Flap.

'How come those fire lights are so bright?' Flap asked. 'I can barely see the gauges.'

'Dunno.' Jake was too busy to cuss out that comfortable, anonymous bureaucrat who had specified the wattage of the bulbs in the fire warning lights. They were certainly impossible to miss. You are about to die, they screamed.

128

'Maybe you better stop dumping the main tank.'

Flap was right. Jake secured the main tank dump. Still 8,500 pounds there.

By now he had the plane at 2,500 feet headed downwind, on the reciprocal of the launch bearing, steady at 250 knots. When he pulled the power back the fire lights stayed on.

Did they have a fire? Modern jet aircraft utilized every cubic inch of space inside the fuselage for fuel, engines, pumps, switches, hydraulic lines, electronic gear, wires, etc., and the spars and stringers that held the whole thing together. A fire anywhere within the plane had to be burning something critical. And if it got to the tanks . . . well, the explosion would be spectacular.

Jake again checked the rearview mirrors for a glow. Nothing.

'Get out the checklist,' he told Flap as he turned off the cabin pressurization system. Unfortunately the ducts carrying bleed air from the engines had failed on a half-dozen occasions in the past: the resulting fires had cost the Navy men and airplanes. Jake had no desire to add his name to that list. If there was a leak downstream of the valve that controlled cabin pressurization, closing the valve should isolate it.

'Got it right here. You ready?'

'Yeah.'

Flap read the comments and recommended procedure over the ICS. One of the comments read, If a fire warning light stays illuminated, secure the affected engine.

He only had two engines and both fire lights were lit. So much for that advice.

The right combined hydraulic system gauge read zero. The needle on the left one was sagging, twitching. And a hydraulic leak was a secondary indication of fire! But did he have one?

'Marine airplanes are shit,' he groused to Flap, who shot back:

'Yeah, the Navy gives us all the crap they don't want.'

Flap got busy on the radio and reported the hydraulic failure. Soon he was talking to Approach. The controller put them in an orbit ten miles aft of the ship. Jake slowed to 220 knots and checked the fuel quantity remaining in the wings. Still a few thousand. In the glow of the left wing-tip light he could just make out the stream from the dump pipe gushing away into the slipstream.

Well, he had it under control. Other than the nuisance glare of the fire lights, everything would be fairly normal. He would blow the gear down, lower the flaps electrically and just motor down the glide slope. He could hack it.

He released the left side of his oxygen mask. He sniffed carefully, then swabbed the sweat from his face. His heart rate was pretty much back to normal and the adrenaline was wearing off. There was no fire – he was fairly confident of that.

Wing fuel read zero. OK. He would leave the dump open a moment or two longer to purge the tank, then secure it. He reached down and punched the button to make the needle on the fuel gauge register main tank fuel. And stared, unable to believe his eyes. Only 3,500 pounds.

Holy . . . !

Yes, the main dump switch was off. But the valve never closed! All the fuel in the main tank had dumped, right down to the top of the standpipe, which prevented the last 3,600 pounds from going overboard. And he had already burned a hundred pounds of that 3,600.

He slapped on the mask and spoke to the controller. 'Uh, Approach, War Ace Five Two One has another problem out here. The main dump valve didn't close. We're down to Three Point Five. How soon can you give us a charley?'

'Standby, War Ace.'

Flap leaned across the center consol and stared at the offending fuel gauge for several seconds, then straightened up. He didn't say anything.

'How far is it to Hickam Field?' Jake asked.

Flap consulted the notes on his kneeboard. 'About a hundred fifty miles.'

'We're almost to bingo!' Jake exclaimed, his horror evident in his voice. 'We've got to have a tanker *right now!*'

Flap Le Beau keyed the radio: 'Approach, War Ace Five Two One, our state is Three Point Five. We're eight hundred pounds above bingo. Apparently the fuselage dump valve stuck open. Request a tanker ASAP.'

'Negative, War Ace. We'll take you aboard in about eight or ten more minutes.'

A sense of foreboding seized Jake Grafton. They were in deep and serious trouble. 'How's the spare tanker?' he asked.

'We're still trying to launch it,' was the reply. 'We should have it off in a few minutes.'

Jake couldn't help himself. 'Is there some problem with the spare?' He felt like a condemned man asking if he could have one more cigarette.

'Yes.' One word.

'They're digging us a hole,' Flap told Jake.

The pilot glumly examined the instruments. What else can go wrong? Bingo was the fuel state that required he depart for the shore divert field on a max range profile flight. Bingo was a low fuel emergency. And he was eight hundred pounds above that state. He had to leave for the shore field before his fuel reached that level or he would flame out before he got there.

Without additional fuel which only a tanker could provide, Jake had to trap or eject. Well, he still had some time. Right now he was burning four thousand pounds of fuel per hour. When he blew the gear down he would be unable to raise them again. And his fuel consumption would immediately jump to six thousand pounds per hour in level flight. More in a climb. At this moment he had three thousand four hundred.

Why had he switched the fuel gauge from the fuselage

131

tank to the wings? So he could monitor dumping. Of course, there was a totalizer there under the needle, but it was usually unreliable. Over the years he had developed a habit of ignoring it. What a fool he was! The lash stung and he laid it on hard.

He could stand the glare of the fire warning lights no longer. He took the L-shaped flashlight hanging on the webbing of his survival vest and pounded the offending lights until they shattered. The cockpit was darker, a lot darker, and that calmed him.

At least the weather was good tonight. Ceiling was high, maybe ten thousand feet, and the visibility underneath was ten miles or so. He could see the lights of the carrier eight miles away, just a little collection of red and white lights in the dark universe, and here and there, the little globs of light that were her escorts. At least he could fly alongside a destroyer or frigate when he had to eject. Then he and Flap wouldn't have to depend on the rescue helicopter to find them.

That was something. A straw to grasp.

Exasperated, his thoughts turned to Callie. It was four-thirty in the morning in Chicago; she was probably in bed asleep.

Thirty-one hundred pounds on the fuel gauge. A-6s had been known to flame out with as much as seven hundred pounds showing on the gauge. He could have as little as twenty-four hundred.

He got a pen from the sleeve pocket of his flight suit and did some figuring on the top card on his kneeboard, which as usual he wore strapped to his right thigh. The numbers told him he was burning sixty-seven pounds of fuel a minute, about ten gallons. Every six seconds a gallon of gas went into the engines. Twenty-four hundred divided by sixty seven – hell, he could dangle here twisting slowly in the wind for thirty-five more minutes. What's the problem? What's the sweat? Well, when he lowered the gear the power requirements would go up. He might bolter. The deck could stay fouled. The weather could go to hell. Something else could go wrong with the plane – like the gear might not come down or the hook might stay up. Or . . . He felt frustrated and outraged. The plane had betrayed him!

The second hand on the clock caught his eye. It swept around and around and around.

'Did I ever tell you about the time I stole a police car?' Flap asked.

'No, and I don't need to hear it now.'

'Stole a cruiser, with a bubble-gum machine on top, siren, police radio, even a shotgun on a rack in the front, the whole deal. Fellow in Jersey wanted it for a farm truck. He wanted to take the trunk lid off and weld up a pickup bed. Was gonna use it to haul manure. He was a retired Mafia soldier. Now I didn't know Mafia guys ever retired, but this one apparently had. He was out of the rackets and had him a little farm in north Jersey. A brother I knew told me there was five hundred bucks in it for me if I could come up with a police car. Luckily I knew another bro who was screwing a cop's daughter pretty regular, so I got to thinking. Five hundred bucks was real money to me back then. Anyway . . .'

Jake could hear pilots in other planes checking into marshal. It all sounded pretty normal. Well, the weather was good, no one was shooting . . .

'Ninety-nine planes in marshal, ninety-nine planes in marshal, this is Approach.' Ninety-nine meant 'all.' 'Your signal, max conserve. Add ten minutes to your commence times. Add ten minutes to push times.'

Now what?

Should he ask? He waited a minute, waited while another sixty-seven pounds of fuel went into the engines. Then he said, 'Approach, War Ace Five Two One. Does that ten minutes apply to me too?'

'Affirm.'

'Uh, what's the problem?'

Silence. Then, 'The nose gear collapsed on a Phantom on Cat Three. The deck is foul.' Cat Three was on the waist, in the landing area.

'War Ace Five Two One has Two Point Eight. Any word on Texaco?' Texaco was the tanker.

'We're working on it, War Ace.'

Flap left his story unfinished. Jake stared at the offending fuel gauge. Should he just say Bingo and go?

The ship was headed northwest, into the prevailing wind. Hickam was northeast. As the minutes passed they were getting no closer to Hickam, but on the other hand, they were getting no farther away. Without more fuel, what did it matter?

The minutes ticked by. Five, six, seven . . .

The needle on the fuel gauge passed twenty-four hundred pounds and kept descending. One pass – that was it. They would get one lousy pass at the deck. If he boltered for any reason, he and Flap were going to have to swim for it.

The crew fidgeted.

The hell of it was that they were betting everything on the emergency gear extension system. Compressed nitrogen would be used to blow the gear down since hydraulic fluid was no longer available to do the job. If any one of the three wheels failed to lock down, they could not trap aboard the ship. They would have to eject.

Betting your ass on any one system in an airplane with a variety of other problems is not the recommended path to a long and happy life.

Jake Grafton sat monitoring the instruments and thinking about the black ocean beneath him. At least the water was warm. With warm water came sharks. He hated sharks, feared them unreasonably. Sharks were his phobia. If he went into the water he would have to fight back the panic, have to keep functioning somehow.

He had never told anyone about the sharks. The thought of being down there with them made him nauseated. And at night, when he couldn't see. Of course he would be bleeding somewhere. Nobody ever ejected without getting cut somehow. Blood in the water, trying to keep from drowning . . .

'War Ace Five Two One, your signal charley.'

'Five Two One,' Jake acknowledged bitterly, then bit his lip. He should have told the brass to go to hell and bingoed.

First came ten degrees of flaps, which had to be lowered electrically. Linked to the flaps were the slats on the leading edge of the wing; they also came out. The flaps and slats changed the shape of the wings and allowed them to develop lift at lower airspeeds. They also added drag, slowing the plane.

Next came the hook. Jake merely pulled the handle and made sure the transition light disappeared.

The Intruder was slowing . . . 170 . . . 160 . . . 150 . . . 'Here goes nothing,' he told Flap as he lowered the gear handle to the gear down position, then rotated the knob on the end ninety degrees and pulled it out. The up-up-up indications on the panel barber-poled.

He waited. He could feel the drag increasing on the plane, could see his airspeed decreasing, and added power. The fuel-flow tapes surged upward.

C'mon, baby. Give me three down indications. Please!

The nose gear locked down first. Two seconds later the mains locked down. Seventeen hundred pounds of fuel left in the main bag.

'They're down' he announced to Flap and God and whoever else was listening.

Approach controller was giving him a steer.

'Hell!' Flap exclaimed disgustedly between calls from the controller, 'it wasn't even close. We don't even have a low fuel light.' The low fuel warning light would come on at about 1,360 pounds.

'We aren't down yet,' Jake pointed out.

'Oh ye of little faith, take note. We're almost down.'

Jake concentrated on flying the plane, staying on speed, smoothly intercepting the glide path. He was carrying less power than normal since the speed brakes were inoperative after the hydraulic failure, and while this saved a few gallons of gasoline, it caused its own problems. If he got high, retarding the throttles would be less effective than usual – the plane would tend to float.

He saw the ball two miles out. At a mile he called, 'Five Two One, Intruder ball, One Point Four.'

'Roger ball. Paddles has you. Looking good . . . fly the ball!'

The meatball began to rise above the datums and he pulled power aggressively while watching that angle-of-attack needle.

Paddles was talking to him. 'Power back on . . . too much, off a little . . . No, little more . . . lineup . . .'

Any second would come the burble, the swirl of air disturbed by the ship's island. He anticipated it just a smidgen on the power and didn't have to slam on too much, then he was quick to get it off.

Coming across the ramp the airspeed decayed a tad and the ball began to sink.

'Power!' shouted the LSO.

Slam! The wheels hit. Throttles to the stops . . . and the welcome, tremendous jerk as the hook snagged a wire.

'Two wire, I think,' Flap told him.

Jake didn't care. A huge sigh of relief flooded through him.

Here came the yellow-shirts. He raised the flaps and slats electrically while they chocked the plane, then cut the engines.

They were back.

Walking across the flight deck with their helmet bags in

their hands, with the warm sea wind on their wet hair, the firm steel deck beneath their flight boots, Flap repeated, 'It wasn't even close.'

No, Jake Grafton acknowledged to himself, it wasn't. Not tonight. But a man can't have luck all the time, and someday when he reached into that tiny little bag where he kept his luck, the bag would be empty. A hold-back bolt would break at the wrong time, a taxiing plane would skid into another, the airborne tanker would go sour, the weather would be bad . . . some combination of evil things would conspire against the man aloft and push him over the edge. Jake Grafton, veteran of more than 340 cat shots and arrested landings, knew that it could happen to him. He knew that as well as he knew his name.

The brass had taken the net from under the tightrope when they didn't let him bingo, and he was infuriated and disgusted with himself for letting them do it.

I think, Jake wrote to Callie that night, *that a man's fate is not in his control. We are under the illusion that we can control our destinies, that the choices we make do make a difference, but they don't. Chance rules our lives Chance, fate, fortune — whatever you wish to call it — sets the hook and pulls the string and we quiver and flail, jerk and fight. Maybe pray.*

I don't think praying helps very much. I do it anyway, just in case. I ask Him to be with me when I fall.

CHAPTER NINE

There are few things in life more satisfying than to be accepted as an equal in a fraternity of fighting men. Jake Grafton was so accepted now, and this morning when he entered the ready room he was greeted by name by the men there, who asked him about his adventures of the previous evening and listened carefully to his comments. They laughed, consoled him, and joked about the predicament he had found himself in last night. Several refused to believe, they said, that the main dump valve had failed: he had forgotten to secure it and was now trying to cover his sin by appealing to their naivete. All this was in good fun and was cheerfully accepted as such by Jake Grafton. He belonged. He was a full member of this aristocracy of merit, with impeccable credentials. His mood improved with each passing minute and soon he was his usual self.

He and his Marine colleagues inspected the board that recorded the pilots' landing grades. Jake's grades for his qualification landings were not displayed there, so like most of them, he had only two landings so far this cruise, an OK 3-wire and a fair 2-wire.

The bombing poster was more complicated, displaying the CEP of each crew, and to settle ties, the number of bull's-eyes. Jake ranked fourth in the squadron here. Today he was scheduled to go to the target with twelve five-hundred pounders, so perhaps he could better his standing.

He had a secret ambition to be the best pilot in the

squadron in landings and bombing and everything else, but he shared that ambition with everyone so it wasn't much of a secret. Still, it wasn't a thing that you talked about. You tried your very best at everything you did, glanced at the rankings, fiercely resolved to do better, and went on about your business. The rankings told you who was more skilled – 'more worthy' was the phrase used by the Real McCoy a day or two before – than you were.

The LSO regarded intrasquadron competition with good-natured contempt. 'Games for children,' he grumped. But Jake noticed now that McCoy's name was in the top half of the rankings on both boards.

This morning there was mail, the first in six days. A cargo plane brought it out from Hickam Field, trapped aboard, then left with full mail sacks from the ship's post office. Two hours later the mail was distributed throughout the ship.

Jake got three letters from Callie, one from his folks, and something from the commanding officer of Attack Squadron 128 in an official, unstamped envelope. He shuffled Tiny Dick Donovan's missive – probably some piece of official foolscap from a yeoman third in the Admin Office – to the bottom of the pile. Callie's letters came first.

She was taking classes at the University of Chicago, working on her master's degree. Her brother and her parents were fine. The weather was hot and muggy. She missed him.

I think that it is important for you to decide what you wish to do with your life. This is a decision that every man must make for himself, and every woman. To make this decision because you hope to please another is to make it for the wrong reason. We each owe duties to our families, when we acquire them, but we also owe a duty to ourselves to make our lives count for something. To love another person is not enough.

I have thought a great deal about this these last few weeks. Like every woman, I want to love. I feel as if I have this great gift to give – myself. I want to be a wife and mother. Oh, how I could love some man!

And I want the man I love to love me. To have a man who would return the love I have to give is my great ambition.

I have dated boys, known boys of all ages, and I do not want to marry one.

I want to marry a man. I want a man who believes in what he is doing, who goes out the door every day to make a contribution – in business, in academia, in government, somewhere. I want a man who will love not just me, but life itself. I want a man who will stand up to the gales of life, who won't bend with every squall, who will remain true to himself and those who believe in him, a man who can be counted on day after day, year after year.

An hour later, after he had reread Callie's letter three times and lingered over the one from his parents, he opened the official letter. In it he found a copy of his last fitness report, bearing Donovan's signature. In the text Donovan wrote:

> Lieutenant Grafton is one of the most gifted aviators I have ever met in my years in the naval service. In every facet of flying, he is the consummate professional. As a naval officer, Lieutenant Grafton shows extraordinary promise, yet he has not made the commitment to give of himself as he must if he is to fulfill that promise.

There was more, a lot more, most of it the usual bull-shit required by custom and instruction, such as a comment upon his support of the Navy's equal opportunity goals and programs. Jake merely skimmed this treacle, then returned to the meat: '. . . has not yet made the commitment to give of himself as he must if he is to fulfill that promise.'

A pat on the back immediately followed by a kick in the pants. His first reaction was anger, which quickly turned to cold fury. He stalked from the ready room and went to his stateroom, where he opened his desk and seized pen and paper. He began a letter to Commander Donovan. He would write a bullet that would skewer the sun of a bitch right through the heart.

What kind of half-assed crack was that? Not committed to being a good naval officer? Who the hell did that jerk Donovan think he was talking about anyway?

Even before he completed his first sentence, the anger began leaking from him. Donovan had said nothing about the Sea-Tac adventure, didn't even mention that the promising Lieutenant Grafton had punched out a windy blowhard and thrown him ass over tea kettle through a plate glass window, then spent a weekend in jail. Perhaps his comments dealt strictly with the performance of Jake's duties at the squadron. No, he *must* have meant that comment to cover the Sea-Tac debacle in addition to everything else. Worse, Donovan was right – a more committed, thinking officer would not have done it. A wiser man . . . well, he wouldn't have either.

Jake threw down the pen and rubbed his face in frustration.

Were Callie and Dick Donovan talking about the same thing?

'Man, you should have seen ol' Jake last night,' Flap Le Beau told his fellow Marines. 'Both the you're-gonna-die lights pop on bright as Christmas goin' down the cat, and this guy handled it like he was in a simulator. Cool as ice. Just sat there doin' his thing. Me – I was shakin' like a dog shittin' razor blades. I ain't been so scared since the teacher caught me with my hand up Susie Bulow's skirt back in the sixth grade.'

There were eight of them, four crews, and they had just finished a briefing for another flight to the Kahoolawe target. This time they were carrying real ordnance, twelve five-hundred-pound bombs on each plane. After they had reviewed how the fuses and arming wires should look on the bomb racks, the crews stood and stretched. That was when Flap took it on himself to praise his pilot to the heavens.

Jake was embarrassed. He had been frightened last night, truly scared, and Flap's ready room bull puckey struck a sour note. Still, Jake kept his mouth shut. This was neither the time nor place to brace Flap about his mouth.

He got out of his chair and went over in the corner to check his mailbox. Nothing. He gazed at the posters on the wall as if interested, trying to shut out Flap, who was expanding upon his theme: Jake Grafton was one cool dude.

One of the pilots, Rory Smith, came over and dug a sheet of official trash out of his mailbox, something he was supposed to read and initial. 'Flap gets on your nerves, does he?' he asked, his voice so soft it was barely audible. He scribbled his initials in the proper place and shoved the paper into someone else's box.

'Yeah.'

'Don't sweat it. To hear him tell it, every guy he flies with is the best who ever stroked a throttle. He was saying that in the ready room about his last stick five minutes before he was down in the skipper's stateroom complaining that the guy was dangerous. You just have to take him with a grain of salt.'

Jake grinned at Rory.

'Everybody else does,' the Marine said, then wandered off toward the desk where the maintenance logs on each aircraft were kept. Jake followed him.

Smith helped himself to the book for 511, the plane Jake had flown into an in-flight engagement.

'Gonna fly it today, huh?' Jake said.

'Yeah,' Smith said. 'The gunny says it's fixed. We'll see.'

'It'll probably go down on deck,' Jake pointed out. 'Down' in this context meant a maintenance problem that precluded flight. 'Since I bent it,' he continued, 'I'll fly it if you want to trade planes.'

'Well, I'm one of the maintenance check pilots and they gave it to me.'

'Sure.'

Meanwhile Flap had progressed to his favorite subject, women. Jake looked up from the maintenance book on his plane when Flap roared, 'Oh, my *God*, she was *ugly!*'

'*How* ugly?' three or four of his listeners wailed in unison.

'She was *so* ugly that paint peeled off the walls when she walked into a room.'

'*How* ugly?'

'So ugly that strong men fainted, children screamed, and horses ran away.'

'*How* ugly?' This refrain had become a chorus. Even Rory Smith joined in from the back of the room.

'Women tore their hair, the sky got black, and the earth trembled.'

'*That's* not ugly.'

'I'm telling you guys, she was *so* dingdong ugly that mirrors cracked, dogs went berserk, fire mains ruptured and one man who had smiled at her at night dropped stone cold dead when he saw her in the daylight. That, my friends, is the gospel truth.'

It was a typical afternoon in the tropics – scattered puffy clouds drifting on the balmy trade winds, sun shining through the gaps. Hawaii was going to be wonderful. Two more days, then Pearl Harbor! Oh boy.

Jake inspected the Mark 82 five-hundred-pounders

carefully. He hadn't seen deadly green sausages like this since the night he was shot down, seven months ago. Talk about a bad trip!

Well, the war was over, this was a peacetime cruise . . . He could probably spend another twenty years in the Navy and would never again have to drop one of these things for real. World War III? Get serious.

Up into the cockpit, into the comfortable seat, the familiar instruments arranged around him just so. The truth was he knew this cockpit better than he knew anything else on earth. Just the thought of never getting back into one bothered him. How do you turn your back on six years of your life?

Flap settled into the seat beside him as the plane captain climbed the ladder on Jake's side and reached in to help with the Koch fittings.

He had lived all this before – it was like living a memory.

And somehow that was good.

Rory Smith preflighted his aircraft, 511, very carefully indeed. That four- or five-foot fall couldn't have done this thing any good. The main concern was the landing gear. If anything cracked . . . Well, the airframes guys hadn't found a single crack. They had scraped the paint from the parts, fluoroscoped them and pronounced them perfect. What can a pilot doe? Just fly it.

The radar, computer and inertial were seriously messed up. All the component boxes of those systems had been replaced, as had the radar dish and drive unit in the nose. The vertical display indicator – the VDI – and the radio were also new.

When Smith and his BN – Hank Davis – were strapped in, they turned on each piece of gear and checked it carefully. The inertial was slow getting an alignment, but it did align. Make a note for the debrief.

They were the last A-6 to taxi toward a cat, number two

on the bow. The others were airborne and in a few minutes, Smith would join them at nine thousand feet. That altitude should be well above the tops of this cumulus, he thought, taking three seconds to scan the sky.

Roger the weight board, check the wing locks, flaps and slats down, stabilizer shifted, into the shuttle, off the brakes and power up. Check the controls.

'You ready?'

'Yep,' Hank Davis told him cheerfully.

Rory Smith saluted and placed his head back into the headrest. He watched the bow cat officer give his fencer's lunge into the wind as his arm came down to the deck. Out of the corner of his eye he saw the catapult deck edge operator lower both hands as he reached for the fire button.

In the space of a second the launching valves dropped open, 450 pounds of steam hit the back of the pistons, and the hold-back bolt broke. The G's slammed Smith back into his seat as War Ace Five One One leaped forward. And the VDI came sliding out of the center of the instrument panel.

Rory Smith reached for the black box with both hands, but too late. The front of it tilted down and came to rest in his lap. Jammed the stick back. All this in the first second and a half of the shot.

Desperately Smith heaved at the box against the G. He had to free to stick!

And then they were off the bow, the nose coming up. And up and up as he struggled to lift the fucking box!

With his right hand he reached under and tried to shove the stick forward. Like pushing against a building.

He felt the stall, felt the right wing go down. He was trying to lift the box with his left hand and push the stick forward with his right when Hank Davis ejected. The horizon was tilting and the nose was slewing right.

Oh, *damn!*

*

On the bridge of *Columbia* the captain saw the whole thing. The nose of the Intruder off of Cat Two rose and rose to almost thirty degrees nose up, then her right wing dropped precipitously. Passing thirty or forty degrees angle-of-bank he saw a man in an ejection seat come blasting out. The wing kept dropping past the vertical and the nose came right and the A-6 dove into the ocean. A mighty splash marked the spot.

Galvanized, the captain roared, 'Right full rudder, stop all engines.'

The officer of the deck immediately repeated the order and the helmsman echoed it.

The captain's eyes were on the ejection seat. The drogue streamed as the seat arched toward the sea. The seat was past the apogee when the captain saw a flash of white as the parachute began to deploy. He blossomed, but before the man on the end of the shrouds could complete a swing he hit the water. Splat.

This 95,000-ton ship was making twenty-five knots. The A-6 went in a little to the right of her course, and the survivor splashed a little right of that. All he could hope to do was swing the stern away. The stern with its thrashing screws.

There, the bow was starting to respond to the helm.

The rescue helicopter, the angel, was already coming into a hover over the survivor. His head was just visible bobbing in the water as the carrier swept by, still making at least twenty knots.

Missed him.

'War Ace Five Oh Five, Departure.'

'Go ahead, Departure.'

'Five Oh Five, your last playmate will not be joining you. Switch to Strike and proceed with your mission, over.'

'Roger that.' Major Sam Cooley gave the radio frequency change signal by hand to Jake on his left wing and the Real McCoy on his right. He waited until the formation came around to the on-course heading, then leveled his wings and added power for the climb. They were on top of the cumulus layer. Above them was sunny, deep blue open sky.

So Rory Smith didn't get that plane airborne, Jake thought. He should have accepted that offer to switch planes. It's a good day to fly.

'Rory Smith's dead.'

They heard the news in the ready room, after they landed.

'He never got out. When Hank Davis punched Rory was sitting there wrestling the VDI. Hank's okay. He said the VDI came out on the cat shot. Came clean out of the panel right into Rory's lap. Jammed the stick aft. They stalled and went in.'

'Aww . . . ,' Flap said.

When Jake found his voice he muttered, 'He must not have checked to see that it was screwed in there.'

'Huh?'

'Yeah,' he told Flap. 'You gotta tug on the thing to make sure the screws that hold it are properly screwed in. Doesn't matter except on a catapult shot. If the VDI isn't secured right on a cat shot, it can come back into your lap. The damn thing weighs seventy pounds.'

'I never knew that.'

'I thought *everybody* knew that.'

'*I* never knew that. I wonder if Smith did.'

Jake Grafton merely stared in horror at the BN. *He* was the one tasked to cover everything these Marines needed to know about shipboard operations. He had forgotten to mention checking the VDI before the shot. Flap didn't know. Maybe Rory didn't either. And now Rory Smith was *dead!*

He sagged into a nearby chair. He had forgotten to tell

them about the VDI on the cat! What else had he forgotten to tell them? *What else?*

The television camera on the ship's island super-structure had caught the whole accident on videotape. The tape was playing now on the ready room television. Jake stared at the screen, mesmerized.

The shot looked normal, but the horizontal stabilizer – the stabilator – was really nose up. Too much? Hard to tell. There he went, off the bow, nose up rapidly, way too high, the stall and departure from controlled flight, a spin de-veloping as the plane went in. One ejection. The whole thing happened very quickly. The A-6 was in the water twelve seconds after the catapult fired.

Just twelve seconds.

The show continued. The angel hovered, a swimmer leaped from about four feet into the water . . . lots of spray from the rotor wash . . .

Jake rose and walked out. In sick bay he asked the first corpsman he saw, 'Captain Hank Davis?'

'Second door on the left, sir.'

The skipper came out of Hank's room before Jake got to the door. He told Jake, 'He doesn't need any visitors just now. He swallowed a lot of seawater and he's pretty shook.'

'I need to ask him a question, sir.'

'What is it?'

Jake explained about the VDI, how the screws might not engage when the box was installed, how the pilot must check it. 'I need to know, Colonel, if Rory tugged on the VDI to check it before he got to the cat.'

The colonel said nothing. He listened to Jake, watched his eyes, and said nothing.

'I'll ask him,' Haldane said finally, then opened the door and passed through.

Minutes passed. Almost five. When Haldane reappeared, he closed the door firmly behind him and faced the pilot, who was leaning against the bulkhead on the other side of the passageway.

'He doesn't remember.'

'Did he know about the possibility of the VDI coming out?'

'No. He didn't.'

Jake turned and walked away without another word.

He was sitting in his stateroom at his desk when the Real McCoy came in. The only light was the ten-watt fluorescent tube above Jake's desk. McCoy seated himself on his bunk.

'Take a hike, will ya, Real? I need some time alone.'

McCoy thought about it for a few seconds. 'Sure,' he said, and left.

Summer in Virginia was his favorite time of year. Everything was growing, the deer were lazy and fat, the squirrels chattered in the trees. The sun there would be hot on your back, the sweat would dampen your shirt. You would feel good as you used your muscles, accomplished tangible work that stood as hard evidence of the effort that had been put into it. The folks up and down the road were solid, hard-working people, people to stand with in good times and bad. And he had given that up for this . . .

Sitting in his stateroom Jake Grafton could hear the creaks and groans of the ship, the noises made by the steel plates as she rode through the seaway. And man-made noises, lots of them, trapping and hammering, chipping, pinging, clicking, grinding . . . slamming as doors and hatches were opened and closed.

Responsibility – they give you a tiny little job and you fuck it up and someone dies. In twelve seconds. Twelve lousy seconds . . .

And he had tried hard. He had taken the time, made the effort to do it right. He had written point after point, gone through the CV NATOPS page by page, paragraph by paragraph. He had covered every facet of carrier operations that he knew about. And had forgotten one item, a scintilla of information that he had heard once, somewhere, about an improperly secured VDI that slid four inches out of the tray in which it sat when the plane went down the catapult. Probably there were messages about it, several years ago, but the Marines didn't take cat shots then and the info apparently went in one official grunt ear and out the other. Now, when they needed to know that tidbit, he had forgotten to tell them.

Luck is really a miserable bitch. Just when you desperately need her to behave she sticks the knife in and twists it, leering at you all the while.

Rory Smith was dead. No bringing him back. All the teeth gnashing, hair pulling, hand wringing and confessions in the world won't raise him from the Pacific and breathe life back into his shattered body. The cockpit of War Ace 511 was his coffin. He was in it now, down there on the sea floor. The sea will claim his body and the airplane molecule by molecule, until someday nothing remains. He will then be a part of this ocean, a part of the clouds and the trade winds and the restless blue water.

Jake opened his safe and got out a bottle of whiskey. He poured himself a drink, raised it to Rory Smith, and swallowed it down.

The liquor made him sleepy. He climbed into the top bunk.

This guilt trip was not good. Yet at least it gave him the proper perspective to view the flying, the ship, the Navy, and all those dead men. Morgan McPherson, the Boxman, Frank Allen, Rory Smith, all those guys. All good dead men. All good. All dead. All dead real damn good.

He was going to get out of the Navy, submit a letter of resignation.

Never again. I'm not going to stand in the ready room any more helplessly watching videotapes of crashes. I'm not going to any more memorial services. I'm not packing any more guys' personal posses-sions in steel footlockers and sending them off to the parents or widow with any more goddamn little notes telling them how sorry I am. I'm not going to keep lying to myself that I am a better pilot than they were and that is why they are dead and I'm not. I've done all that shit too much. The guys that still have the stomach for it can keep doing it until they are each and every one of them as dead as Rory Smith but I will not. I have had enough.

CHAPTER TEN

Jake and Flap flew a tanker hop the next afternoon, which was the last scheduled flying day before the ship entered Pearl Harbor. They were in the high orbit, flying the five-mile arc around the ship at 20,000 feet, when Flap said, 'I hear you are putting in a letter of resignation.'

Since it wasn't a question, Jake didn't reply. He had talked to the first-class yeoman in the air wing office this morning, and apparently the yeoman talked to the Marines.

'That right?' Flap demanded.

'Yeah.'

'You know, you are one amazing dude. Yesterday afternoon you dropped six five-hundred-pounders visually and got four bull's-eyes, then did six system bore-sights and got three more. Seven bull's-eyes out of twelve bombs. That performance put you first in the squadron, by the way.'

This comment stirred Jake Grafton. In the society of warriors to which he belonged it was very bad form to brag, to congratulate yourself or listen placidly while others congratulated you on your superb flying abilities. The fig leaf didn't have to cover much, but modesty required that he wave it. 'Pure luck,' Jake muttered. 'The wind was real steady, which is rare, and—'

Flap steamed on, uninterested in fig leaves. 'Then you motor back to the ship and go down the slide like you're riding a rail, snag an okay three-wire, find out a guy crashed, announce it's all your fault because you knew something he didn't, and submit a letter of resignation. Now is that weird or what?'

'I didn't announce anything was my fault.'

'Horse shit. You announced it to yourself.'

'I didn't—'

'I had a little talk with the Real McCoy last night,' Flap explained. 'You were moping down in your room. You sure as hell weren't crying over Rory Smith – you hardly knew the guy. You were feeling sorry for yourself.'

'What an extraordinary insight, Doctor Freud! I can see now why I'm so twisted – when I was a kid my parents wouldn't let me screw my kitty cat. Send me a bill for this consultation. In the meantime *shut the fuck up!*'

Silence followed Jake's roar. The two men sat staring into the infinity of the sky as the shadow cast by the canopy bow walked across their laps. This shadow was the only relief from the intense tropic sunshine which shone down from the deep, deep blue.

'Hard to believe that over half the earth's atmosphere is below us,' Flap said softly. 'Without supplemental oxygen, at this altitude, most fit men would pass out within thirty minutes. You know, you've flown so many times that flying has probably become routine with you. That's the trap we all fall into. Sometimes we forget that we are really small blobs of protoplasm journeying haphazardly through infinity. All we have to sustain us are our little lifelines. The oxygen will keep flowing, the engines will keep burning, the plane will hold together, the ship will be waiting . . . Well, listen to the news. The lifelines can break. We are like the man on the tightrope above Niagara Falls: the tiniest misstep, the smallest inattention, the most minuscule miscalculation, and disaster follows.'

Flap paused for a moment, then continued: 'A lot of people have it in their heads that God gave them a guarantee when they were born. At least seventy years of vigorous life, hard work will earn solid rewards, your wife

153

with be faithful, your sons courageous, your daughters virtuous, *justice* will be done, *love* will be enough – in the event of problems, the manufacturer will set things right. Like hell! The truth is that life, like flying, is fraught with hazards. We are all up on that tightrope trying to keep our balance. Inevitably, people fall off.'

In spite of himself Jake was listening to Flap. That was the problem with the bastard's monologues – you couldn't ignore them.

'I think you're worth saving, Grafton. You're the best pilot I've met in the service. You are very very good. And you want to throw it all away. That's pretty sad.'

Flap paused. If he was giving Jake a chance to reply, he was disappointed. After a bit he continued:

'I never had much respect for you Navy guys. You think the military is like a corporation – you do your job, collect your green government check, and you can leave any time you get the itch. Maybe the Navy *is* that way. Thank God, the Corps *isn't.*'

Stung, Jake broke his silence. 'During our short acquaintance, you haven't heard one snotty remark out of me about the Holy Corps. But if you want to start trading insults, I can probably think up a few.'

Flap ignored Jake. 'We Marines are all in this together,' he said, expanding on his thesis. 'When one man slips off the rope, we'll grab him on the way down. We'll all hang together and we'll do what we have to do to get the job done. The Corps is bigger than all of us, and once you are a part of it, you are a part of it forever. Semper Fidelis. If you die, when you die, the Corps goes on. It's sorta like a church . . .'

Flap fell silent, thinking. The Corps was very hard to explain to someone who wasn't a Marine. He had tried it a few times in the past and always gave up. His explanations usually sounded trite, maybe even a little silly. 'Male bonding bullshit,' one woman told him after he had delivered himself of a memorable attempt. He almost slapped her.

For you see, the Corps was *real*. The feelings the Corps aroused in Flap and his fellow Marines were as real, as tangible, as the uniforms they wore and the weapons they carried. They *would* be loyal, they *would* be faithful, even unto death. Semper Fi. They belonged to something larger than themselves that gave their lives a meaning, a purpose, that was denied to lesser men, like civilians worried about earning a living. To Marines like Flap civilians concerned with getting and spending, getting and spending, were beneath contempt. They were like flies, to be ignored or brushed away.

'I'm trying to explain,' he told Jake Grafton now, 'because I think you could understand. You're a real good aviator. You're gifted. You owe it to yourself, to us, to hang tough, hang in there, keep doing what you know so well how to do.'

'I've had enough,' Jake told him curtly. He had little patience for this sackcloth and ashes crap. He had fought in one war. He had seen its true face. If Flap wanted to wrap himself in the flag that was his business, but Jake Grafton had decided to get on with his life.

'Rory Smith knew,' Flap told him with conviction. 'He was one fine Marine. He knew the risks and did his job anyway. He was all Marine.'

'And he's dead.'

'So? You and I are gonna die too, you know. Nobody ever gets out of life alive. Smith died for the Corps, but you're gonna go be a civilian, live the soft life until you check out. Some disease or other is going to kill you someday – cancer, heart disease, maybe just plain old age. Then you'll be as dead as Rory Smith. Now I ask you, what contribution will you have made?'

'I already made it.'

'Oh no! Oh no! Smith made *his* contribution – he gave all

that he had. You've slipped one thin dime into the collection plate, Ace, and now you announce that dime is your fair share. Like hell!'

'I've had about two quarts more than enough from you today, Le Beau,' Jake spluttered furiously. 'I did two cruises to the Nam. I dropped my bombs and killed my gooks and left my friends over there in the mud to rot. For what? For not a single goddamn thing, that's for what. You think you're on some sort of holy mission to protect America? The idiot green knight. Get real – those pot-smoking flower-power hippies don't *want* protection. You'd risk your life for them? If they were dying of thirst I wouldn't piss in their mouths!'

Jake Grafton was snarling now. 'I've paid my dues in blood, Le Beau, *my* blood. Don't give me any more *shit* about *my fair share!*'

Silence reigned in the cockpit as the KA-6D tanker continued to orbit the ship 20,000 feet below, at max conserve airspeed, each engine sucking a ton of fuel per hour, under the clean white sun. Since the tanker had no radar, computer or inertial navigation system, there was nothing for Flap to do but sit. So he sat and stared at that distant, hazy horizon. With the plane on autopilot, there was also little for Jake to do except scan the instruments occasionally and alter angle-of-bank as required to stay on the five-mile arc. This required almost no effort. He too spent most of his time staring toward that distant, infinite place where the sky reached down to meet the sea.

The crazy thing was that the horizon looked the same in every direction. In all directions. Pick a direction, any direction, and that uniform gauzy junction of sea and sky obscured everything that lay beyond. Yet intelligence tells us that direction is critical – life itself is a journey *toward something, somewhere* . . .

Which way?

Jake Grafton sat silently, looking, wondering.

Hank Davis was still in a private room in sick bay when Jake dropped by to see him. He looked pale, an impression accentuated by his black-as-coal, pencil-thin mustache.

'Hey, Hank, when they gonna let you out of here?'

'I'm under observation. Whenever they get tired of observing. I dunno.'

'So how you doing?' Jake settled into the only chair and looked the bombardier over carefully.

Davis shrugged. 'Some days you eat the bear, some days the bear eats you. He got a big bite of my butt yesterday. A big bite.'

'Well, you made it. You pulled the handle while you still had time, so you're alive.'

'You ejected once, didn't you?'

'Yeah,' Jake Grafton told him. 'Over Laos. Got shot up over Hanoi.'

'Ever have second thoughts?'

'Like what?'

'Well, like maybe you were too worried about your own butt and not enough about the other guy's?'

'I thought the VDI came out on the shot? Went into Smith's lap?'

'Yeah.'

'Hank! What could you do? The damned thing weighs seventy pounds. Even with your help, Smith couldn't have got it back into its tray. No way. If you'd crawled across to help, you'd both be dead now. It's not like you guys had a half hour to dick with this problem.'

Davis didn't reply. He looked at a wall, swallowed hard.

Jake Grafton racked his brains for a way to reach out. *I should have told you guys about checking the VDI's security.* Although he felt that, he didn't say it.

Hank related the facts of his ejection in matter-of-fact tones. The chute had not completely opened when he hit the water. So he hit the water way too hard and had trouble getting out of his chute. The swimmer from the helicopter had been there in seconds and saved his bacon. Still, he swallowed a lot of seawater and almost drowned.

'I dunno, Jake. Sometimes life's pretty hard to figure. When you look at it close, the only thing that makes a difference is luck. Who lives or who dies is just luck. "The dead guy screwed up," everybody says. Of course he screwed up. Lady Luck crapped all over him. And if that's true, then everything else is a lie – religion, profession-alism, everything. We are all just minnows swimming in the sea and luck decides when it's your turn. Then the shark eats you and that's the fucking end of that.'

'If it's all luck, then these guilt trips don't make much sense, do they?' Jake observed.

'Right now the accident investigators are down in the avionics shop,' Hank Davis told him. 'They are looking for the simple bastard who didn't get the VDI screwed in right. All this *shit* is gonna get dumped right on that poor dumb son of a bitch! "Rory Smith is dead and it's *your* fault." Makes me want to puke some more.'

Squadron life revolves around the ready room, ashore or afloat. Since the A-6 squadrons always had the most flight crewmen, they always got the biggest ready room, in most ships Ready Five, but in *Columbia*, Ready Four. The ready room was never big enough. It was filled with comfortable, padded chairs that you could sink into and really relax in, even sleep in, but there weren't enough of them for all the officers.

In some squadrons when all the officers assembled for a meeting – an AOM – chairs were assigned by strict seniority. In other outfits the rule was first come, first served. How it was done depended on the skipper, who always got a chair up front by the duty desk, the best seat in the house. Lieutenant Colonel Haldane believed that rank had its privileges – at least when not airborne – so seniority reigned here. Jake Grafton ended up with a seat four rows back. The nuggets, first lieutenants on their first cruise, stood around the back of the room or sat on metal folding chairs.

AOMs were social and business events. Squadron business was thrashed out in these meetings, administrative matters dealing with the ship and the demands of the amorphous bureaucracies of the Navy and the Marine Corps were considered, lectures delivered on NATOPs and flying procedures, the 'word' passed, all manner of things.

At these soirees all the officers in the squadron got to know each other well. Here one got a close look at the department heads – the 'heavies' – watched junior officers in action, here the commanding officer exerted his leadership and molded the flight crews into a military unit.

In addition to the legal authority with which he was cloaked, the commanding officer was always the most experienced flyer there and the most senior. How he used these assets was the measure of the man, for truly, his responsibility was very great. In addition to the aircraft entrusted to him, he was responsible for about 350 enlisted men and three dozen officers. He was legally and morally responsible for every facet of their lives, from the adequacy of their living quarters to their health, professional development and performance. And he was responsible for the squadron as a military unit in combat, which meant the lives of his men were in his hands.

The responsibility crushed some men, but most commanding officers flourished under it. This was the professional zenith that they had spent their careers working to attain. By the time they reached it they had served under many commanding officers. The wise ones adopted the best of the leadership styles of their own former skippers and adapted it as necessary to suit their personalities. Leadership could not be learned from a book: it was the most intangible and the most human of the military skills.

In American naval aviation the best skippers led primarily by example and the force of their personalities – they intentionally kept the mood light as they gave orders, praised, cajoled, hinted, encouraged, scolded, ridiculed, laughed at and commented upon whatever and whomever they wished. The ideal that they seemed to instinctively strive for was a position as first among equals. Consequently AOMs were normally spirited affairs, occasionally raucous, full of good humor and camaraderie, with every speaker working hard to gain his audience's attention and cope with catcalls and advice – good, bad, indifferent and obscene. In this environment intelligence and good sense could flourish, here experience could be shared and everyone could learn from everyone else, here the bonds necessary to sustain fighting men could be forged.

This evening Rory Smith's death hung like a gloomy pall in the air.

Colonel Haldane spoke first. He told them what he knew of the accident, what Hank Davis had said. Then he got down to it:

'The war is over and still we have planes crashing and people dying. Hard to figure, isn't it? This time it wasn't the bad guys. The gomers didn't get Rory Smith in three hundred and twenty combat missions, although they tried and they tried damned hard. He had planes shot up so badly on three occasions that he was decorated for getting the planes back. What got him was a VDI that slid out of its tray in the instrument panel and jammed the stick.

'Did he think about ejecting? I don't know. I wish he had ejected. I wish to God we still had Rory Smith with us. Maybe he was worried about getting his legs cut off if he pulled the handle. Maybe he didn't have time to punch. Maybe he thought he could save it. Maybe he didn't realize

160

how quickly the plane was getting into extremis. Lots of maybes. We'll never know.'

He picked up the blue NATOPs manual lying on the podium and held it up. 'This book is the Bible. The engineers that built this plane and the test pilots that wrung it out put their hearts and souls into this book – for you. Telling you everything they knew. And the process didn't stop there – as new things are learned about the plane the book is continually updated. It's a living document. You should know every word in it. That is the best insurance you can get on this side of hell.

'But the book doesn't cover everything. Sooner or later you are going to run into something that isn't covered in the book. Whether you survive the experience will be determined by your skill, your experience, and your luck.

'There's been a lot of mumbling around here the last twenty-four hours about luck. Well, there is no such thing. You can't feel it, taste it, smell it, touch it, wear it, fuck it, or eat it. It doesn't exist!

'This thing we call luck is merely professionalism and attention to detail, it's your awareness of everything that is going on around you, it's how well you know and *understand* your airplane and your own limitations. We make our own luck. Each of us. None of us is Superman. Luck is the sum total of your abilities as an aviator. If you think your luck is running low, you'd better get busy and make some more. Work harder. Pay more attention. Study your NATOPs more. Do better preflights.

'A wise man once said, "Fortune favors the well prepared." He was right.

'Rory Smith is not with us here tonight because he didn't eject when he should have. Hank Davis is alive because he did.

'We're going to miss Rory. But every man here had better resolve to learn something from his death. If we do, he didn't die for nothing. Think about it.'

161

The best way to see Hawaii is the way the ancient Polynesians first saw it, the way it was revealed to whalers and missionaries, the way sailors have always seen it.

The islands first appear on the horizon like clouds, exactly the same as the other clouds. Only as the hours pass and your vessel gets closer does it become apparent that there is something different about these clouds. The first hints of green below the churning clouds imply mass, earth, land, an *island*, where at first there appeared to be only sea and sky.

Finally you see for sure – tawny green slopes, soon a surf line, definition and a crest for that ridge, that draw, that promontory.

Hawaii.

Jake Grafton stood amid the throng of off-duty sailors on the bow watching the island of Oahu draw closer and closer. She looked emerald green this morning under her cloud-wreath. The hotels and office buildings of Honolulu were quite plain there on the right. Farther right Diamond Head jutted from the sea haze, also wearing a cumulus buildup.

The sailors pointed out the landmarks to one another and talked excitedly. They were jovial, happy. To see Hawaii for the first time is one of life's great milestones, like your first kiss.

Jake had been here before – twice. On each of his first two cruises the ship had stopped in Pearl on its way to Vietnam. As he watched the carrier close the harbor channel, he thought again of those times, and of the men now dead whom he had shared them with. Little fish. Sharks.

He went below. Down in the stateroom the Real McCoy was poring over a copy of the *Wall Street Journal*. 'Are you rich enough to retire yet?'

'I'm making an honest dollar, Grafton. Working hard at it and taking big risks. We call the system capitalism.'

'Yeah. So how's capitalism treating you?'

'Think I'm up another grand as of the date of this paper, four days ago. I'll get something current as soon as I can get off base.'

'Uh-huh.'

'Arabs turned off the oil tap in the Mideast. That will send my domestic oil stocks soaring and melt the profits off my airline stocks. Some up, some down. You know, the crazy thing about investing – there's really no such thing as bad news. Whether an event is good or bad depends on where you've got your money.'

Jake eyed his roommate without affection. This worm's-eye view of life irritated him. The worms had placed bets on the little fish. Somehow that struck him as inevitable, though it didn't say much for the worms. Or the little fish.

'You going ashore?' McCoy asked.

'Like a shot out of a gun, the instant the gangway stops moving,' Jake Grafton replied. 'I have got to get off this tub for a while.'

'Liberty hounds don't go very high in this man's Navy,' McCoy reminded him, in a tone that Jake thought sounded a wee bit prissy.

'I really don't care if Haldane uses my fitness report for toilet paper' was Jake Grafton's edged retort. And he didn't care. Not one iota.

'Hello.'

'Hello, Mrs McKenzie? This is Jake Grafton. Is Callie there?'

'No, she isn't, Jake. Where are you?'

'Hawaii.'

'She's at school right now. She should be back around six this evening. Is there a number where she can reach you?'

'No. I'll call her. Please tell her I called.'

'I'll do that, Jake.'

The pilot hung up the phone and put the rest of the

quarters from his roll back into his trouser pocket. When he stepped out of the telephone booth, the next sailor in line took his place.

He trudged away looking neither right nor left, ignoring the sporadic salutes tossed his way. The palm trees and frangipani in bloom didn't interest him. The tropical breeze caressing his face didn't distract him. When a jet climbing away from Hickam thundered over, however, the pilot stopped and looked up. He watched the jet until the plane was out of sight and the sound had faded, then walked on.

About a ship's length from the carrier pier was a small square of grass complete with picnic table adjacent to the water. After brushing away pigeon droppings, Jake Grafton seated himself on the table and eased his fore-and-aft cap farther back onto his head. The view was across the harbor at the USS *Arizona* memorial, which he knew was constructed above the sunken battleship's superstructure. *Arizona* lay on the mud under that calm sheet of water, her hull blasted, holed, burned and twisted by Japanese bombs and torpedoes. Occasionally boats ferrying tourists to and from the memorial made wakes that disturbed the surface of the water. After the boats' passage, the disturbance would quickly dissipate. Just the faintest hint of a swell spoiled the mirror smoothness of that placid sheet, protected as it was from the sea's turbulence by the length and narrowness of the channel. The perfect water reflected sky and drifting cumulus clouds and, arranged around the edge of the harbor, the long gray warships that lay at the piers.

Jake Grafton smoked cigarettes while he sat looking. Time passed slowly and his mind wandered. Occasionally he glanced at his watch. When almost two hours had passed, he walked back toward the telephone booths at the head of the carrier pier and got back into line.

'Hey, Callie, it's me, Jake.'

'Well, hello, sailor! It's great to hear your voice.'

'Pretty nice hearing yours too, lady. So you're back in school?'

'Uh-huh. Graduate courses. I'm getting so educated I don't know what I'll do.'

'I like smart women.'

'I'll see if I can find one for you. So you're in Pearl Harbor?'

'Yep. Hawaii. Got in a while ago. Gonna be here a couple days, then maybe Japan or the Philippines or the IO.' Realizing that she probably wouldn't recognize the acronym, he added belatedly, 'That's the Indian Ocean. I don't know. Admirals somewhere figure it out and I go wherever the ship goes. But enough about me. Talk some so I can to listen to your voice.'

'I got your letter about the in-flight engagement. That sounded scary. And dangerous.'

'It was exciting all right, but we lost a plane yesterday on a day cat shot. An A-6. Went in off the cat. The pilot was killed.'

'I'm sorry, Jake.'

'I'm getting real tired of this, Callie. I've been here too long. I'm a civilian at heart and I think it's time I pulled the plug. I've submitted a letter of resignation.'

'Oh,' she said. After a pause, she added, 'When are you getting out?'

'Won't be until the cruise is over.'

'Are you sure about this?'

'Yeah.'

He twisted the telephone cord and wondered what to say. She wasn't saying anything on her end, so he plunged ahead. 'The plane that went in off the cat was the one I had the in-flight engagement in, ol' Five One One. The in-flight smacked the avionics around pretty good, and when they reinstalled the boxes one of the technicians didn't get the VDI properly secured. So the VDI box came out on the cat shot, jammed the stick. The BN punched and told us what happened, but the pilot didn't get out.'

'You're not blaming yourself, are you?'

'No.' He said that too quickly. 'Well, to tell the truth, I am a little bit responsible. With better technique I might have avoided the in-flight. That's spilled milk. Maybe it was unavoidable. But I was briefing these Marines on carrier ops — everything you need to know to be a carrier pilot in four two-hour sessions, and I forgot to mention that you have to check the security of the VDI.'

'I see.'

'Do you?'

'Not really. But aren't these risks a part of carrier aviation?'

'Not a part. This is the main course, the heart of it, the very essence. In spite of the very best of intentions, mistakes will be made, things will break. War or no war, people get killed doing this stuff. I'm getting sick of watching people bet their lives and losing, that's all.'

'Are you worried about your own safety?'

'No more than usual. You have to fret it some or you won't be long on this side of hell.'

'It seems to me that the dangers would become hard to live with—'

'I can handle it. I think. No one's shooting at me. But see, that's the crazy part. The war is over, yet as long as men keep flying off these ships there are going to be casualties.'

'So what will you do when you get out?'

'I don't know, Callie.'

Seconds passed before she spoke. 'Life isn't easy, Jake.'

'That isn't exactly news. I've done a year or two of hard living my own self.'

'I thought you liked the challenge.'

'Are you trying to tell me you want me to stay in?'

'No.' Her voice solidified. 'I am not suggesting that you do anything. I'm not even hinting. Stay in, get out, what-

166

ever, that's your choice and yours alone. You must live your own life.'

'Damn, woman! I'm trying.'

'I know,' she said gently.

'You know me,' he told her.

'I'm beginning to.'

'How are your folks?'

'Fine,' she said. They talked for several more minutes, then said good-bye.

The vast bulk of the ship loomed high over the bank of telephone booths. Jake glanced up at the ship, at the tails of the planes sticking over the edge of the flight deck, then lowered his gaze, stuffed his hands into his pockets and walked away.

The problem was that he had never been able to separate the flying from the rest of it – the killing, bombing, dying. Maybe it couldn't be separated. The My Lai massacre, Lieutenant William Calley, napalm on villages, burning children, American pilots nailed to trees and skinned alive, Viet Cong soldiers tortured for information while Americans watched, North Vietnamese soldiers given airborne interrogations – talk or we'll throw you from the helicopter without a parachute: all of this was tied up with the flying in a Gordian knot that Solomon couldn't unravel.

He thought he had cut the knot – well, Commander Camparelli and the Navy had cut it for him – last winter in Vietnam. He had picked an unauthorized target, the North Vietnamese capitol building in Hanoi, attacked and almost got it, then faced some very unhappy senior officers across a long green table. They knew what their duty was: *obey orders from the elected government.* What they couldn't fathom was how he, Lieutenant Jake Jackass from Possum Hollow, had lost sight of it.

We're all in this together. *We must keep the faith.* Wasn't that what you and your friends were always telling one another when the shit got thick and the blood started flowing?

We do what we must and die when we must *for each other*.

The faith was easier to understand then, easier to keep. Now the war was over. Although some people want to keep fighting it, by God, it's *over*.

Now the Navy was peacetime cruises, six- to eight-month voyages to nowhere, excruciating separations from loved ones, marriages going on the rocks under the strain, kids growing up with a father who's never there; it's getting scared out of your wits when Lady Luck kisses your ass good-bye; it's seeing people squashed into shark food; it's knowing – knowing all the time, every minute of every day – that you may be next. The life can be smashed out of you so quick that you'll inhale in this world and exhale in hell.

Lieutenant Jake Grafton, farmer's son and history major, was going to get on with his life. Do something safe, something sane. Something with tangible rewards. Something that allowed him to find a good woman, raise a family, be a father to his children. He would bequeath this flying life to dedicated half-wits like Flap Le Beau.

Yet he would miss the flying.

This afternoon as Jake Grafton walked along the boulevard that led into downtown Honolulu, huge, benign cumulus clouds were etched against the deep blue sky, seemingly fixed. He would like to fly right now – to strap on an airplane and leave behind the problems of the ground.

We are, he well knew, creatures of the earth. Its minerals compose our bodies and provide our nourishment. Our cells contain seawater, legacies of ancestors who lived in the oceans. Yet on the surface man evolved, here where there are other animals to kill and eat, edible plants, trees with nuts and fruits, streams and lakes teeming with life. Our bodies function best at the temperature ranges, atmospheric pressures and oxygen levels that have prevailed on the earth's surface throughout most of the age of mammals. We need the protection from the sun's radiation that the atmosphere provides. Our senses of smell and hearing use the atmosphere as the transmitting medium. The earth's gravity provides a reference point for our sense of balance and the resistance our muscles and circulatory systems need to function properly. The challenges of surviving on the dry surface provided the evolutionary stimulus to develop our brains.

Without the earth, we would not be the creatures we are. And yet we want to leave it, to soar through the atmosphere, to voyage through interplanetary space, to explore other worlds. And to someday leave the solar system and journey to another star. All this while we are still trapped by our physical and psychological limitations here on the surface of the mother planet.

Sometimes the contradictions inherent in our situation hit him hard. Last fall, while he was hunting targets in North Vietnam as he dodged the flak and SAMs, Americans again walked on the moon. Less than seventy years after the Wright brothers left the surface in powered flight, man stood on the moon and looked back at the home planet glistening amid the infinite black nothingness. They looked while war, hunger, pestilence and man's inhumanity to man continued unabated, continued as it had since the dawn of human history.

It was a curious thing, hard to comprehend, yet worth pondering on a balmy evening in the tropics with the air laden with fragrant aromas and the surf flopping rhythmically on the beach a few yards away.

Jake Grafton walked along the beach, stared at the hotels and the people and the relentless surf and thought of all these things.

An hour later, as he walked back toward the army base with traffic whizzing by, the tops of the lazy large clouds were shot with fire by the setting sun.

The problem, he decided, was keeping everything in proper perspective. That was hard to do. Impossible, really. To see man and his problems, the earth and the universe, as they really are one would have to be God.

The officers' club was full of people, music, light, laughter. Jake stood in the entrance for several seconds letting the sensations sink in. He tucked his hat under his belt, then strolled for the bar.

He heard them before he got to the door.

'How ugly was she?' three or four voices asked in a shaky unison.

'She was ugly as a tiger's hairball.' Flap's soaring baritone carried clearly. People here in the lounge waiting to be called for dinner looked at each other, startled.

'How ugly?'

'Ugly as a mud wrestler's navel.' Eyebrows soared.

'How ugly?' Eight or ten voices now.

'Ugly as a pickled pervert's promise.' Women giggled and whispered to each other. Several of the gentlemen frowned and turned to stare at the door to the bar. Jake saw one of the men, in his fifties, with short, iron gray hair, wink at his companion.

'*That's* not ugly!'

'She was so damn ugly that the earth tried to quake and couldn't – it just shivered. So ugly that five drunken sailors pretended they didn't see her. The city painted her red and put a number on her – two dogs relieved themselves on her shoes before I got to the rescue, that's how ugly she was. She was so desperately ugly that my zipper welded itself shut. And that, my gentle friends, is the gospel truth.'

Jake Grafton grinned, squared his shoulders, and walked into the bar.

CHAPTER ELEVEN

The air was opaque, the sun hidden by the moisture in the air. Two or three miles from the ship in all directions the gray sea and gray sky merged. *Columbia* was in the midst of an inverted bowl, three days northwest of Pearl laboring through fifteen-foot swells. The wind was brisk from the west.

From his vantage point in the cockpit of a KA-6D tanker spotted behind the jet blast deflector – the JBD – for Cat Three, Jake Grafton could see a frigate a mile or so off the port beam. Just ahead, barely visible on the edge of the known universe, he could make out the wake and super-structure of another.

Jake and Flap were standing the five-minute alert tanker duty, which meant that for two hours they had to sit in the cockpit of this bird strapped in, ready to fire up the engines and taxi onto the catapult as soon as the F-4 Phantom that was parked there – also on five-minute alert – launched. There was another fighter on five-minute status sitting just short of the hook-up area on Cat Four, and an airborne early warning aircraft, an E-2 Hawkeye, parked with its tail against the island. Sitting on the waist catapult tracks was a manned helicopter, the angel, which would have to launch before the catapults could be fired. A power unit with its engine running was pugged into each aircraft, instantly ready to deliver air to turn the engines. All five of the alert birds had been serviced and started, checked to make sure all their systems worked, then shut down.

The crews were strapped into the airplanes. The pilot of

the Phantom on Cat Four was reading a paperback novel, Jake could see, but he couldn't make out the title.

On the deck behind the waist catapults sat two more fighters and a tanker on alert-fifteen status, which meant that their crews were flaked out in their respective ready rooms wearing all their flight gear, ready to run for the flight deck if the alarm sounded.

Alert duty kept flight crews busy any time that planes were not aloft. Except in waters just off the shore of the United States, it was rare for a carrier to be below alert-thirty status. Alert-fifteen was the usual status for the high seas, with alert-five reserved for the South China Sea during the war just ended or other locations where a possible threat existed. Today a possible threat existed. Intelligence expected the Soviets to try to overfly the carrier task group as it transited to Japan with land-based naval bombers from Vladivostok or one of the fields on Sakhalin Island or the Kamchatka peninsula.

The Russkis were going to have their work cut out for them overflying the ship in this low visibility, Jake thought, if they came at all. He sat watching the frigate on the port beam labor into the swells, ride up and then bury her bow so deep that white spray was flung aft all the way to the bridge.

Columbia's ride was definitely more pleasant, but Jake could feel her pitching and see the leading edge of the angled deck rise and fall as she rode the restless sea.

To Jake's right, in the bombardier-navigator's seat, Flap Le Beau was reading a book by Malcolm X. Every time he got to the bottom of a page, he lowered the paperback and glanced around, his eyes scanning several times while he turned the page.

On one of Flap's periscope sweeps, Jake asked, 'That book any good?

'Guy sure is interesting,' Flap said, and resumed his reading.

'What's it about?'

'You don't know Malcolm X?'

'Uh-uh.'

'Hated honkeys. Believed the races should have their own enclaves, no mixing, that kind of stuff.'

'Do you believe that?' Jake asked tentatively. Flap was only the second or third black naval aviator Jake had ever met, and he had never discussed race with one.

'He had some good ideas,' Flap said, glancing at Jake. 'But no, I think the races should be integrated. America is for Americans – black, white, brown, yellow, green or purple. But what about you? You're from rural Virginia, nigger-hating redneck heaven, one-party bigot politics, pot-gutted klagel sheriffs – what d'ya think?'

'Ol' X should've had you writing his speeches.'

Jake Grafton wasn't stupid enough to proclaim himself a true believer in racial equality and brotherly love, certainly not to a black man probably capable of forcing him into the bigot cesspool with just a little effort.

'Who knows, if this Marine Corps gig goes sour, I might go into politics,' Flap allowed, then resumed reading his book.

His father had two black employees on his farm during the years Jake was growing up. They were both huge men, with hands like pie plates and upper arms larger than Jake's thighs. They were barely able to sign their names but they could work any four white men into the dirt. In their younger days they had worked on railroad track-repair gangs swinging sledge-hammers. 'Georgia niggers,' his father, Sam, had called them. How they came to end up on the Grafton farm Jake never quite understood, but Isaiah and Frank allowed from time to time that they had absolutely no intention of crossing the Virginia line south-bound. Then they would shake their heads and laugh at some private joke, creating the vision in the boy's mind of blood-thirsty southern sheriffs eager to avenge spectacular, unmentionable crimes.

His father treated the two blacks like the whites he hired occasionally, worked alongside them, shared food and smokes and jokes. Young Jake liked the men immensely.

Yet, like most of the boys of his generation in south-western rural Virginia, he accepted racial segregation as natural, as unremarkable and logical as the deference men showed women and the respect accorded the elderly. That is, he did until 1963, the year he turned eighteen. One evening while watching the network news show footage of Negro children in Birmingham being blasted with streams from high-pressure fire hoses, his father had let out an oath.

'I guess it's a damn good thing that I'm not colored,' Sam Grafton declared. 'If I were, I'd get me a gun and go to Birmingham and start shooting some of those sons of bitches. And I'd start with that bastard right there!' His finger shot out and Jake found himself staring at the porky visage of Bull Connor.

'Sam!' exclimed his mother disgustedly.

'Martha, what the hell do they have to do to get treated decent by whites? The colored people have put up with a hell of a lot more crap than any Christian should ever have to deal with. Those sons of bitches laying the wood to them aren't Christians. They're Nazis. It's a miracle the colored people haven't started shooting the damned swine.'

'Do you have to cuss like that?'

'It's high time some white people got mad at those bigots,' Sam Grafton thundered. 'I wish Jack Kennedy would get his ass out of his rocking chair and kick some butt. The President of the United States, saying there's nothing he can do when those rednecks attack children! By God, if Bull Connor was black and those kids were white he'd be singing a different tune. He's just another gutless politician scared of losing the bigot vote. Pfft!'

That evening had been an eye-opener for Jake. He started paying attention to the civil rights protests, listening to the arguments. His father had always been a bit different than his neighbors, marching to a different drummer. And he was usually right. He was that time, too, his son concluded.

Remembering that evening, he sighed, then glanced around the flight deck. People were lying on the deck beside their equipment, napping.

He was in the middle of a yawn when he heard the hiss of the flight deck loudspeaker system coming to life. 'Launch the alert-five. Launch the alert-five. We have bogies inbound.'

The lounging men on the flight deck sprang into action. Jake Grafton twirled his fingers at the plane captain, received a twirl in response. He turned on the left engine-fuel master switch and pushed the start button. With a low moan the engine began to turn. When the RPM was high enough he came around the horn with the throttle, then sat watching the temperatures and RPMs rise while he pulled his helmet on.

By the time he got the second engine started and the canopy closed, the chopper on the cat tracks was engaging its rotors. The ship was turning – Jake could see the list on the flight deck – coming about forty degrees left into the wind. Now the deck leveled out. The *Columbia*'s rudder was centered. Thirty seconds later the angel lifted off. It left the deck straight ahead. When it was safely past the bow the chopper pilot laid it into a right turn.

Now the catapult shuttles were dragged back out of the water brakes into battery while the final checkers inspected the two fighters and gave their thumbs-up. Red-shirted ordnancemen pulled the safety pins from the missile racks and showed them to the pilots. The yellow-shirted taxi director gave the pilot of the plane in front of Jake a come-ahead signal and let him inch the last two feet forward onto Cat Three while the green-shirted catapult hook-up men crawled underneath with the bridle and two more greenies installed the hold-back bar, on the Phantom a ten-foot-long hinged strap with the hold-back shear-bolt attaching to the airplane's belly and the other end going into a slot in the deck. The weight-board man flashed his board at the pilot and got a thumbs-up, then showed it to the cat officer, who also rogered. The whole performance was a ballet of multicolored shirts darting around, near and under the moving fighter, each man intent on doing his job perfectly.

As the taxiing fighter reached the maximum extent of the hold-back bar, the JBDs came up, three panels that would deflect the exhaust of the launching aircraft from the plane behind.

Now Jake saw the Phantom lower its tail – actually the nose-gear strut was extended eighteen inches to improve the angle-of-attack. He saw the cat officer twirl his fingers above his head for full power and heard the thunderous response from the Phantom, saw the river of black smoke blasted upward by the JBD, felt his plane tremble from the fury of those two engines. The fighter pilot checked his controls, and the stabilator and rudder waggled obediently. Thumbs-up flashed from the squadron final checkers.

The cat officer signaled for afterburners, an opening hand on an extended arm. The river of smoke pouring skyward off the JBDs cleared, leaving hot, clear shimmering gases. Incredibly, even here in the cockpit of the tanker the noise level rose. Jake got a good whiff of the acrid stench of jet exhaust.

My oxygen mask must not be on tight enough. Fix it when I'm airborne.

The last of the catapult crewmen came scurrying out from under the fighter. This was the man who swung on the bridle to ensure it was on firmly. He flashed a thumbs-up at the cat officer, the shooter.

The shooter saluted the F-4 pilot, glanced down the deck, and lunged. One potato, two potato, and wham, the fighter shot forward trailing plumes of fire from its twin exhausts. It hadn't gone a hundred feet down the track when the JBD started down and a taxi director gave Jake Grafton the come-ahead signal.

After he watched the Phantom clear the deck, the shooter turned his attention to the fighter on Cat Four, which was already at full power. He gave the burner sign. Fifteen seconds later this one ripped down the cat after the first one, which was out of burner now and trailing a plume of black smoke that showed quite distinctly against the gray haze wall.

Jake taxied forward and ran through his ritual as the wind over the deck swirled steam leaking from the catapult slot around the men on deck. Their clothes flapped in the wind.

Power up, control check, cat grip, engine instruments, warning lights, salute.

One potato, two pota – he felt just the tiniest jolt as the hold-back bolt broke, then the acceleration smashed him backward like the hand of God.

The strike controller told Jake to go on up to 20,000 feet. 'Texaco take high station.'

Flap rogered, then Jake said on the ICS, 'They must not be going to launch the alert-fifteen.'

'Why do you say that?'

'Surely they'll want us to tank the second section of fighters immediately after launch, if they launch them.'

'Maybe not.'

'Ours is not to reason why, our is but to do or die.'

'Noble sentiment. But let's *do* today, not die.'

'Aye aye, sir.'

'Don't get cute.'

Jake Grafton gave a couple of pig grunts.

177

'I thought you said you weren't going to insult the Corps?' Flap sounded shocked.

'I lied.'

The sea disappeared as they climbed through 3,000 feet. Jake was on the gauges. There was no horizon, no sky, no sea. Inside this formless, featureless void the plane handled as usual, but the only measure of its progress through space was movement of the altimeter, the TACAN needle, and the rotating numbers of the distance measuring equipment – DME.

Jake kept expecting to reach an altitude where the goo thinned perceptibly, but it was not to be. When he leveled at 20,000 feet he could see a blob of light above him that had to be the sun, yet the haze seemed as thick as ever. Just what the visibility might be was impossible to say without another object to focus upon.

Flap reported their arrival at high station. The controller rogered without apparent enthusiasm.

Jake set the power at max conserve and when the airspeed had stabilized, engaged the autopilot. He checked the cockpit altitude and loosened one side of his oxygen mask from his helmet. Flap sat silently for a moment or two, looking here and there, then he extracted his book from a pocket of his G-suit and opened it to a dog-eared page.

Jake busied himself with punching buttons to check that the fuel transfer was proceeding normally. The tanker carried five 2,000-pound drop tanks. The transfer of fuel from these drops was automatic. If transfer didn't occur, however, he wanted to know it as soon as possible because he would have that much less fuel available to give to other aircraft or burn himself. Today the transfer seemed to be progressing as advertised, so he had 26,000 pounds of fuel to burn or give away.

They were almost eight hundred miles northwest of Midway Island alone in an opaque sky. Other than flicking his eyes across the instruments and adjusting the angle-of-bank occasionally, he had nothing to do except scan the blank whiteness outside for other airplanes that never came.

The fighters were being vectored out to intercept the incoming Russians, the E-2 was proceeding away from the ship to a holding station – those were the only other airplanes aloft. There was nothing in this sky to see. Yet if an aircraft did appear out of the haze, it would be close, very close, on a collision course or nearly so, a rerun of the Phantom incident a week ago. He sure as hell didn't want to go through *that* again.

In spite of his resolution to keep a good lookout, boredom crept over him. His mind wandered.

He had signed the letter of resignation from the Navy yesterday and submitted it to Lieutenant Colonel Haldane. The skipper had taken the document without comment. Well, what was there to say?

Haldane wasn't about to try to argue him into staying – he barely knew Jake. If Jake wanted out, he wanted out. What he could expect was a form letter of appreciation, a handshake and a hearty 'Have a nice life.'

That *was* what he wanted, wasn't it?

Why not go back to Virginia and help Dad with the farm? Fishing in the spring and summer, hunting in the fall . . . He would end up joining the Lions Club, like his father. Lions meeting every Thursday evening, church two or three Sundays a month, high school football games on Friday nights in September and October . . .

It would be a chance to settle down, get a house of his own, some furniture, put down roots. He contemplated that future now, trying to visualize how it would be.

Dull. It would be damn dull.

Well, he had been complaining that the Navy was too challenging, the responsibility for the lives and welfare of other people too heavy to carry.

One life offered too much challenge, the other too little. Was there something, somewhere, more in the middle?

'Texaco, Strike.'

'Go ahead.'

'Take low station. Buster.' Buster meant hurry, bust your ass.

'We're on our way.'

Jake Grafton disengaged the autopilot and rolled the Intruder to ninety degrees angle-of-bank. The nose came down. Speed brakes out, throttles back, shallow the bank to about seventy degrees, put a couple G's on . . . the rate-of-descent needle pegged at 6,000 feet per minute down. That was all it would indicate. A spiral descent was his best maneuver because the tanker had a three-G limitation, mandated by higher authority to make the wings last longer. He was right at three G's now, the altimeter unwinding at a dizzying rate.

Low station was 5,000 feet, but it could be lowered if the visibility was better below this crud. Maybe he should ask. 'Ah, Strike, Texaco. How's the visibility and ceiling underneath?'

'A little worse than when you took off. Maybe a mile viz under an indefinite obscuration.'

'Who's our customer?'

'Snake-eye Two Oh Seven. He's got an emergency. Switch to button sixteen and rendezvous on him.'

Jake was passing ten thousand feet, still turning steeply with G on. Bracing himself against the G, Flap changed the radio channel and called.

'Snake-eye Two Oh Seven, this is Texaco. Say your posit, angels, and heading, over.'

'Texaco, I'm on the Three One Zero radial at nine miles, headed inbound at four grand. Better hurry.'

Jake keyed the radio transmitter. 'Just keep going in and we'll join on you.'

The fighter pilot gave him two clicks in reply.

Jake eyed the TACAN needle on the HSI, the horizontal situation indicator, a glorified gyroscopic compass. He had a problem here in three-dimensional space and the face of the instrument was an aid in helping him visualize it.

He rolled the wings level and stuffed the nose down more. His airspeed was at 400 knots and increasing.

'Snake-eye, Texaco, what's your problem?'

'We're venting fuel overboard and the pull-forward is going to take more time than we've got.'

'Posit again?'

'Three One Zero at five, angels four, speed three hundred, heading One Three Zero.'

'Are you in the clear?'

'Negative.'

'Let's go on down to three grand.'

Jake was passing six thousand feet, on the Three Three Zero radial at nine miles. He was indicating 420 knots and he was raising the nose to shallow his dive. He thumbed the speed brakes in and added some power. 'We're going to join fast,' he muttered at Flap, who didn't reply.

The problem was that he didn't know how much visibility he would have. If it was about a mile, like the controller on the ship said, and he missed the F-4 by more than that margin, he would never see him. Unlike the Phantom, the tanker had no radar to assist in the interception.

He was paying strick attention to the TACAN needle now. The seconds ticked by and the distance to the ship closed rapidly.

'There, at one o'clock.' Flap called it.

Now Jake saw the fighter. He was several hundred feet below Jake, which was good, at about a mile, trailing a plume of fuel. Grafton reduced power and deployed the speed brakes.

Uh-oh, he had a ton of closure. He stuffed the nose down to underrun the Phantom.

'*Look out!*'

The wingman! His tailpipes were *right there*, coming in the windscreen! Sweet Jesus!

He jammed the stick forward and the negative G lifted him and Flap away from their seats. In two heartbeats he was well under and jerked the stick back. He had forgotten about the wingman.

Still indicating 350, he ran under the Phantom in trouble and pulled the power to idle. 'At your one o'clock, Snake-eye. We'll tank at two seventy. Join on me.'

At 280 knots he got the power up and the speed brakes in. He quickly stabilized at 270 indicated. After checking to ensure that he was level headed directly for the ship, Jake turned in his seat to examine the Phantom closing in as Flap deployed the refueling drogue.

The three-thousand-pound belly tank the F-4 usually carried was gone. Fuel was pouring from the belly of the aircraft.

'Green light, you're cleared in,' Flap announced on the radio.

Jake turned back to his instruments. He wanted to provide a stable drogue for the fighter to plug. 'What's your problem, Snake-eye?'

'Belly tank wouldn't transfer. We jettisoned it and now we are pumping fuel out the belly. The check valve must be damaged. We're down to one point seven.'

'Strike, Texaco, how much does Two Oh Seven get?'

'All he needs, Texaco. We should have a ready deck in six or seven minutes. Pulling forward now.' This meant all the planes parked in the landing area were being pulled forward to the bow.

The green light on the refueling panel went out and the fuel counter began to click over. 'You're getting fuel,' Flap told the fighter.

They were crossing over the ship now. Jake Grafton eased the tanker into a descent. If he could get underneath

182

this haze he could drop the Phantom at the 180-degree position, only thirty seconds or so from the deck.

When the fuel-delivered counter registered two thousand pounds, Jake told the fighter pilot.

'Keep it coming. We're up a grand in the main bag. At least we're getting it faster than it's going over the side.'

At two thousand feet Jake saw the ocean. He kept descending. At fifteen hundred feet he spotted the carrier, on his left, turning hard. The ship was coming into the wind. From this distance Jake could only see a couple airplanes still to go forward. Very soon.

He leveled at twelve hundred feet and circled the ship in a left turn at about a mile.

Five thousand pounds transferred . . . six . . . seven . . . the ship was into the wind now and the wake was streaming straight behind her, white as snow against the gray sea as the four huge screws bit hard to drive her faster through the water.

'Snake-eye Two Oh Seven, this is Paddles. We're going to be ready in about two minutes. I want you to drop off the tanker on the downwind, dirty up and turn into the groove. Swells still running about fifteen feet, so the deck is pitching. Average out the ball and fly a nice smooth pass.'

'Two Oh Seven.'

Jake was crossing the bow now, the fuel counter still clicking. Eight thousand five hundred pounds transferred so far.

'Texaco, hawk the deck.'

'Roger.' Hawk the deck meant to fly alongside so that the plane on the bolter could rendezvous and tank.

This was going to work out, Jake told himself. This guy is going to get aboard.

The fuel-delivered counter stopped clicking over at 9,700 pounds. The fighter had backed out of the basket. Jake took a cut to the right, then turned back left and looked over his shoulder. The crippled fighter was descending and slowing, his hook down and gear coming out. And the fuel was still pouring from his belly in a steady, fire-hose stream. The wingman was well behind, still clean.

When the fighter pilot jettisoned the belly tank, Jake thought, the quick-disconnect fitting must have frozen and the plumbing tore loose inside the aircraft. There was a one-way check valve just upstream of the quick-disconnect; obviously it wasn't working. So the pressure in the main fuel cell was forcing fuel overboard through the broken pipe.

Jake slowed to 250 knots and cycled the refueling hose in and back out to reset the reel response. Now to scoot down by the ship, Jake thought, so that if he bolters, I'll be just ahead where he can quickly rendezvous.

He dropped to a thousand feet and turned hard at a mile to parallel the wake on the ship's port side.

The landing fighter was crossing the wake, turning into the groove, when Jake saw the fire.

The plume of fuel streaming behind the plane ignited. The tongue of flame was twice as long as the airplane and clearly visible.

'*You're on fire!*' someone shouted on the radio.

'*In the groove, eject, eject, eject!*'

Bang, bang, two seats came out. Before the first chute opened the flaming fighter went nose-first into the ship's wake. A splash, then it was gone.

'Two good chutes.' Another voice on the radio.

In seconds both the chutes went into the water. As Jake went over he spotted the angel coming up the wake.

'Boy, talk about luck! It's a wonder he didn't blow up,' Jake told Flap.

He was turning across the bow when the air boss came on the frequency. You always knew the boss's voice, a God-like booming from on high. 'Texaco, your signal, charley. We're going to hot spin you.'

Jake checked his fuel quantity. Nine thousand pounds left. He opened the main dump and dropped the hook, gear and flaps.

As advertised, the ball was moving up and down on the optical landing system, which was gyroscopically stabilized in roll and pitch, but not in heave, the up and down motion of the ship.

He managed to get aboard without difficulty and was taxied in against the island to refuel. He kept the engines running.

In moments the helicopter settled onto the deck abeam the island. Corpsmen with stretchers rushed out. The stretchers weren't needed. The two Phantom crewmen walked across the deck under their own power, wet as drenched rats, grinning broadly and flashing everyone in sight a thumbs-up.

Jake and Flap were still fueling five minutes later when two Soviet Bear bombers, huge, silver, four-engine turbo-props, came up the wake at five hundred feet. The bombers were about a thousand feet apart, and each had an F-4 tucked in alongside like a pilot fish.

The flight deck crew froze and watched the parade go by.

'We could have done a better job up there today,' Jake told Flap. 'We should have had the second radio tuned into Strike. Then we would have known what Two Oh Seven's problem was without asking. And we should have asked about that wingman. Phantoms always go around in pairs, like snakes.'

'Those tailpipes in our windscreen,' Flap said, sighing. 'Man, that was a leemer.'

Jake knew what a leemer was – a shot of cold urine to the heart. 'We gotta get with the program,' he told the BN.

'I guess so,' Flap said as he tucked Malcolm X into his G-suit pocket and zipped it shut.

The air wing commander was Commander Charles 'Chuck' Kall, a fighter pilot. He was known universally as CAG, an acronym that rhymed with *rag* and stood for Commander Air Group. This acronym had been in use in the US Navy since it acquired its first carrier.

CAG Kall made careful notes this evening as he listened to the air intelligence officer brief the threat envelopes that could be expected around a Soviet task force. Lieutenant Colonel Haldane, his operations officer Major Bartow, and Jake Grafton were the A-6 representatives at this planning session. Jake sat listening and looking at the projected graphics with a sense of relief — The AI's presentation sounded remarkably like his homemade presentation for Colonal Haldane several weeks ago. An attacking force could expect to see a *lot* of missiles and stupendous quantities of flak, according to the AI.

'They aren't gonna shoot all those missiles at the first American planes they see,' CAG said softly. He always spoke softly so you had to listen hard to catch his words. 'It wouldn't surprise me to find out that half those missile launchers are out of service for lack of maintenance. Be that as it may, these numbers should dispel any notions anybody might have that smacking the Russians is going to be easy. These people aren't rice farmers — they are a first-class blue-water Navy. Putting them under with conventional, free-fall bombs is going to be really tough. We're going to lose a lot of people and airplanes getting it done.'

'We'll probably never have to,' someone said, and three or four heads bobbed in agreement.

'That's right,' Kall said, almost whispering. 'But if the order comes, we're going to be ready. We're going to have a plan and we're going to have practiced our plan. We're not going to try to invent the wheel after war is declared.'

There were no more comments about the probability of war with the Soviet Union.

'We'll plan Alpha strikes,' CAG said. 'When we get to the Sea of Japan we'll schedule some and see how much training we need to make that option viable. At night and in bad weather, however, the A-6s are going to have to go it alone. I'd like to have the A-6 crews run night attacks against our own destroyers to develop a profile that gives them the best chance of hitting the target and surviving. Colonel Haldane and his people can work out a place to start and we'll go from there.'

'Aye aye, sir,' Haldane said.

CHAPTER TWELVE

One morning when Jake came into the ready room the duty officer, First Lieutenant Doug Harrison, motioned to him. 'Sir, the skipper wants to see you in his stateroom.'

'*Sir!* What is this, the Marines?'

'Well, we try.'

Jake sighed. 'You know what it's about?'

'No, sir.'

'For heaven's sake, my name is Jake.'

'Yes, sir.'

'You try too hard. Let your hair grow out to an inch. Take a day off from polishing your shoes. Do twenty-nine pushups instead of thirty. You can overdo this military stuff, Doug.'

The skipper's stateroom was on the third deck, the one below the ready room deck. Entry to the skipper's sub-division was gained by lowering yourself through a water-tight hatch, then going down a ladder.

Jake knocked. The old man opened the door. 'Come in and find a seat.'

The pilot did so. Colonel Haldane picked up a sheaf o: paper and waggled it, then tossed it back on his desk. 'You: letter of resignation. I have to put an endorsement on it What do you want me to say?'

Jake was perplexed. 'Whatever you usually say, sir.'

'Technically your letter is a request to transfer from th: regular Navy to the Naval Reserve and a request to b: ordered to inactive status. So I have to comment abou:

whether or not you would be a good candidate for a reserve commission. Why are you getting out?'

'Colonel, in my letter I said—'

'I read it. "To pursue a civilian career." Terrific. Why do you want out?'

'The war's over, sir. I went to AOCS because it was that or get drafted. I got a regular Navy commission in 1971 because it was offered and my skipper recommended me, but I've never had the desire to be a professional career officer. To be frank, I don't think I'd be a very good one. I like the flying, but I don't think I'm cut out for the rest of it. I'll be the first guy to volunteer to come back to fight if we have another war. I just don't want to be a peacetime sailor.'

'You want to fly for the airlines?'

'I don't know, sir. Haven't applied to any. I might, though.'

'Pretty boring, if you ask me. Take off from point A and fly to point B. Land. Taxi to the gate. Spend the night in a motel. The next day fly back to A. You have to be a good pilot, I know, but after a while, I think a man with your training and experience would go quietly nuts doing something like that. You'd be a glorified bus driver.'

'You're probably right, sir.'

'So what are you going to do?'

'I don't know, Skipper.'

'Hells bells, man, why resign if you don't have something to go to? Now if you had your heart set on going to grad school or into your dad's business or starting a whorehouse in Mexicali, I'd say *bon voyage* – you've done your bit. That doesn't appear to be the case, though. I'll send this in, but you can change your mind at any time up to your release date. Think it over.'

'Yessir.'

'Oh, by the way, the skipper of the Snake-eyes had some nice words for the way you tanked Two Oh Seven and

189

dropped him off on the downwind. A quick, expeditious rendezvous, he said, a professional job.'

'Too bad Two Oh Seven caught fire.'

'As soon as he slowed to landing speed the gas seeped into the engine bays around the edges of the engine-bay doors. The engines ignited the fuel. From the time the fire first appeared visually, it was a grand total of two and a half seconds before the hydraulic lines burned through. The pilot punched when the nose started down. He pulled back stick and there was nothing there.'

Jake Grafton just nodded.

'This is a man's game,' Haldane said. He shrugged. 'There's no glamour, no glory, the pay's mediocre, the hours are terrible and the stakes are human lives. You bet your life and your BN's every time you strap on an airplane.'

The carrier and her escorts sailed west day after day. *Columbia*'s airplanes remained on deck in alert status as her five thousand men maintained their machinery, coped with endless paperwork, and drilled. They drilled morning, afternoon, and evening: fire drills, general quarters, nuclear, biological and chemical attack, collision, flooding, engine casualty, and flight deck disasters. The damage control teams were drilled to the point of exhaustion and the fire fighting teams did their thing so many times they lost count.

The only breaks in the routine came in the wee hours of the night when underway replenishments – UNREPS – were conducted. The smaller escorts came alongside the carrier every third day to top their tanks with NSFO – Navy standard fuel oil – from the carrier's bunkers.

Nowhere was seamanship more on display than during the hours that two or three vastly dissimilar ships steamed side by side through the heavy northern Pacific night seas joined by hoses and cables.

The destroyers and frigates were the most fun to watch, and Jake Grafton was often on the starboard catwalk to look and marvel. The smaller warship would overtake the carrier from astern and slow to equal speed alongside. The huge carrier would be almost rock-steady in the sea, but the small ship would be pitching, rolling, and plunging up and down as she rode the sea's back. Occasionally the bow would bite so deep into the sea that spray and foam would cascade aft, hiding the forward gun mount from view and dousing everyone topside.

As the captain of the destroyer held his ship in formation, a line would be shot across the seventy-five-foot gap between the ships to be snagged by waiting sailors wearing hard hats and life jackets. This rope would go into sheaves and soon a cable would be pulled across the river of rushing water. When the cable was secured, a hose would go across and soon fuel oil would be pumping. Three hoses were the common rig to minimize the time required to transfer hundreds of tons of fuel. Through it all the captain of the small boy stood on the wing of the bridge where he could see everything and issue the necessary orders to the steersman and engine telegraph operator to hold his ship in formation.

One night a supply ship came alongside. While Jake watched, a frigate joined on the starboard side of the supply ship, which began transferring fuel through hoses and supplies by high-line to both ships at once. Now both the frigate and carrier had to hold formation on the supply ship. To speed the process a CH-46 helicopter belonging to the supply ship lifted pallets of supplies from the stern of the supply ship and deposited them on the carrier's flight deck, a VERTREP, or vertical replenishment.

Here in the darkness on the western edge of the world's greatest ocean American power was being nakedly exercised. The extraordinary produce of the world's most advanced economy was being passed to warships in stupendous quantity: fuel, oil, grease, bombs, bullets, missiles, toilet paper, movies, spare parts, test equipment, paper, medical supplies, canned soft drinks, candy, meat, vegetables, milk, flour, ketchup, sugar, coffee – the list went on and on. The supply ship had a trainload to deliver.

The social organization and hardware necessary to produce, acquire and transport this stupendous quantity of wealth to these powerful warships in the middle of nowhere could be matched by no other nation on earth. The ability to keep fleets supplied anywhere on the earth's oceans was the key ingredient in American sea power, power that could be projected to anyplace on the planet within a thousand miles of saltwater. For good or ill, these ships made Washington the most important city in the world; these ships made the US Congress the most important forum on earth and the President of the United States the most powerful, influential person alive; these ships enforced a global Pax Americana.

The whole thing was quite extraordinary when one thought about it, and Jake Grafton, attack pilot, history major and farmer's son, did think about it. He stood under a A-6's tail on the flight deck catwalk wearing his leather jacket with the collar turned up against the wind and chill, and marveled.

'I hear you're going to get out,' the Real McCoy said one evening in the stateroom.

'Yeah. At the end of the cruise.' Jake was in the top bunk reading his NATOPS manual.

McCoy had the stock listing pages of the *Wall Street Journal* spread across the floor, his cruise box, bunk and desk. He was sitting cross-legged on the floor with his notebook full of charts on his lap. He had fallen into the habit of annotating his charts each evening after the ship received a mail delivery. He leaned back against his locker, stretched out his legs, and sighed.

'I've thought about it,' he said. 'Getting exiled to the Marines got the wheels spinning. Being ten days behind the markets makes them spin faster. But no.' He shrugged. 'Maybe one of these days, but not now.'

Jake put down his book. 'What's keeping you in? I thought you really liked that investment stuff?'

'Yeah, makes a terrific hobby. I think my problem is I'm a compulsive gambler. Stocks are the best game around – the house percentage is next to nothing – just a brokerage fee when you trade. Yet it's just money. On the other hand, you take flying – that's the ultimate gamble: your life is the wager. And waving – every pass is a new game, a new challenge. All you have is your wits and skill and the stakes are human lives. There's nothing like that in civilian life – except maybe trauma medicine. If I got out I'd miss the flying and the waving too much.'

Jake was slightly stunned. He had never before heard flying described as a gamble, a game, like Russian roulette. Oh, he knew the risks, and he did everything in his power to minimize them, yet here was a man for whom the risks were what made it worth doing.

'If I were you,' Jake told the Real, 'I wouldn't make that crack about waving down in the ready rooms.'

'Oh, I don't. A lot of these guys are too uptight.'

'Yeah.'

'They think the LSO is always gonna save them. And that's what we want them to think, so they'll always do what we tell them, when we tell them. If they get the notion in their hard little heads that we might be wrong, they'll start second-guessing the calls. Can't have that now, can we?'

'Ummm.'

'But LSOs are human too. Knowing that you can make a mistake, that's what keeps you giving it everything you've got, all the time, every time.'

'What if you screw up, like the CAG LSO did with

me? Only somebody dies. How are you going to handle that?'

'I don't know. That's the bad thing about it. You do it for the challenge and you *know* that sooner or later the ax will fall and you're going to have to live with it. That's why flying is easier. If you screw up in the cockpit, you're just dead. There's a lot to be said for betting your own ass and not someone else's.'

'Aren't many things left anymore that don't affect someone else,' Jake muttered.

'I suppose,' said the Real McCoy, and went back to annotating his stock charts.

Columbia and her retinue of escorts entered the Sea of Japan one morning in late July through the Tsugaru Strait between the islands of Hokkaido and Honshu. Transiting the strait, the five-minute alert fighters were parked just short of the catapults with their crews strapped into the cockpits, but a mob of sailors stood and sat around the edge of the flight deck wherever there was room between the planes. Some were off-duty, others had received their supervisors' permission to go topside for a squint, many worked on the flight deck.

Land was visible to the north and south, blue, misty, exotic and mysterious to these young men from the cities, suburbs, small towns and farms of America. That was Japan out there – geisha girls, kimonos, rice and raw fish, strange temples and odd music and soft, lilting voices saying utterly incomprehensible things. And they were here looking at it!

Several large ferries passed within waving distance, and the Japanese aboard received the full treatment – hats and arms and a few shirts. Fishing vessels and small coasters rolling in the swells were similarly saluted as the gray warships passed at fifteen knots.

This was the first cruise beyond America's offshore

194

waters for many of these young men. More than a few sniffed the wet sea wind and thought they could detect a spicy, foreign flavor that they had never whiffed before in the nitrogen-oxygen mixture they had spent their lives inhaling back in the good ol' US of A. Even the homesick and lovelorn admitted this was one hell of a fine adventure. If the folks at home could only see this . . .

So steaming one behind the other, the gray ships transited the strait while the young men on deck soaked up impressions that would remain with them for as long as they lived.

Those men standing on the carrier's fantail saw something else: two thousand yards astern the thin sail of a nuclear-powered attack submarine made a modest bow wave. How long she had been there, running on the surface, no one on the flight deck was sure, but there she was. Those with binoculars could just make out a small American flag fluttering from the periscope.

Once through the strait, the ship went to flight quarters and the tourists cleared the flight deck. Except for the few pilots who had launched in the interception of the Russian Bears, most of the aviators had not flown for nine days. This layoff meant that they needed a day catapult shot and trap before they could legally fly at night. With this requirement in mind, the staff had laid on a series of surface surveillance missions in the Sea of Japan. These missions would also show the flag, would once again put carrier-borne warplanes over the merchantmen and warships that plied these waters just in case anyone had become bored listening to American ambassadors. By the time the carrier hurled her first planes down the catapults, the submarine had quietly slipped back into the depths.

Jake was not scheduled to fly today. He was, however, on the flight schedule – two watches in Pri-Fly and one after dark in the carrier air traffic control center, CATCC, pronounced cat-see. During these watches he was the squadron representative, to be called upon by the powers that be to offer expert advice on the A-6 should such advice become necessary. There was an A-6 NATOPS manual in each compartment for him to refer to, and before each watch he found it and checked it to make sure it was all there. Then he stood with observers from the other squadrons with the book in his hand, watching and listening.

In addition to ensuring the air boss and Air Ops officer had instant access to knowledgeable people, these watches were a learning experience for the observers. Here they could observe how the aircraft were controlled, why problems arose, and watch those problems being solved. In CATCC they could also watch the air wing commander, known as CAG, and their own skippers as they sat beside the Air Ops officer on his throne and answered queries and offered advice. Air Ops often conferred with the skipper of the ship via squawk box. Every facet of night carrier operations was closely scrutinized and heavily supervised. While the junior officer aloft in the night sweated in his cockpit, he was certainly not alone. Not as long as his radio worked.

During the day the seas became rougher and the velocity of the wind increased. By sunset the overcast was low and getting lower. Below the clouds visibility was decreasing. A warm front was coming into the area.

Jake watched the first night recovery on the ready room PLAT monitor as he did paperwork. The deck was moving and there were three bolters. The second night recovery Jake spent in CATCC with the NATOPS book in his hand. It was raining outside. Two pilots were waved off and four boltered, one of them twice. One of the tankers was sour and a flailex developed when the spare tanker slid on the wet catapult track during hook-up and had to be pushed back with a flight deck tractor. While this mess kept the deck foul, the LSOs waved off three planes into the already-full bolter pattern.

When the last plane was aboard – the recovery took thirty-eight minutes – Jake headed for his stateroom to work on a training report.

He was still at it half an hour later when the Real McCoy came in, threw his flight deck helmet and LSO logbook onto his desk and flopped into his bunk. 'Aye yei yei! What a night! They're using those sticks to kill rats in the cockpits and the weather is getting worse.'

'You were on the platform?' Jake meant the LSO's platform on the edge of the flight deck.

'Yep. I'm wavin' 'em. Another great Navy night, I can tell you. A real Chinese fire drill. Three miles visibility under a thousand-foot overcast, solid clag up to twenty-one grand, ten-foot swells – why didn't I have the sense to join the Air Force? The boys in blue would have closed up shop and gone to the club three hours ago.'

'The next war,' Jake muttered.

'Next war, Air Force,' McCoy agreed. 'So, wanna stand on the patform with me for the next act?'

Jake regarded his half-finished report with disgust, got out of his chair and stretched. 'Why not? I've listened to you wavers preach and moan for so long that I could probably do it myself.'

McCoy snorted. 'That'll be the day!'

Jake did a clumsy tap dance for several seconds, then struck a pose. 'He looked good going by me.'

McCoy groaned and closed his eyes. He was a self-proclaimed master of the short catnap, so Jake timed it. Sixty-five seconds after the LSO closed his eyes he was snoring gently.

They came out of the skin of the ship by climbing a short ladder to the catwalk that surrounded the flight deck, yet was about four feet below flight deck level.

The noise of twenty jet engines at idle on the flight deck was piercing, even through their ear protectors. Raindrops swirling in the strong wind displaced by the ship's structure came from every direction, seemingly almost at once, even up through the gridwork at their feet. The wind blew with strength, an ominous presence, coming from total darkness, blackness so complete that for a second or two Jake felt as if he had lost his vision. This dark universe of wind and water was permeated by the acrid stench of jet exhaust, which burned his nose and made his eyes water.

Gradually his eyes became accustomed to the red glow of the flight deck lights and he could see things – the outline of the catwalk, the rails, the round swelling shapes of the life raft canisters suspended outboard of the catwalk railing, and in the midst of that void beyond the rail, several fixed lights. The escorts. Above his head were tails of airplanes. He and McCoy crouched low as they proceeded aft toward the LSO platform to avoid those invisible rivers of hot exhaust that might be flowing just above their heads. Might be. The only sure way to find one was to walk into it.

Somewhere aloft in the night sky, high above the ship, were airplanes. With men in them. Men sitting strapped to ejection seats, studying dials and gauges, riding the turbulence, watching fuel gauges march mercilessly toward zero.

Jake and the Real McCoy climbed a ladder to the LSOs' platform as the first of the planes on deck rode a catapult into the night sky. Both men watched the plane's lights as it climbed straight ahead of the ship. There – they were getting fuzzy . . . And then they were gone, swallowed up by the night.

'Six or seven hundred feet, a couple of miles viz. That's it,' McCoy roared into Jake's ear.

The petty officer who assisted the LSOs was already on the platform getting out the radio handsets, plugging in cords, checking the PLAT monitor, donning his sound-powered headset and checking in with the enlisted talkers in Pri-Fly and Air Ops.

The platform was not large, maybe six feet by six feet, a wooden grid that jutted from the port side of the flight deck. To protect the signal officers from wind and jet blast, a piece of black canvas stretched on a steel frame was rigged on the forward edge of the platform, like a wall. So the platform was an open stage facing aft, toward the glide slope.

Under the edges of the platform, aft and on the seaward side, hung a safety net to catch anyone who inadvertently fell off the platform. Or jumped. Because if a pilot lost it on the glide slope in close and veered toward the platform, going into the net was the only way for the LSOs to save their lives.

Jake Grafton glanced down into the blackness. And saw nothing. 'Relax, shipmate,' McCoy told him. 'The net's there. Honest Injun.'

The platform was just aft of the first wire, about four hundred feet away from the ship's center of gravity, so it was moving. Up and down, up and down.

As McCoy checked the lights on the Fresnel lens, which was several hundred feet forward of the platform, Jake watched. McCoy triggered the wave-off lights, the cut lights, adjusted the intensity of the lens. The lights seemed to behave appropriately and soon he was satisfied.

The Fresnel lens was, in Jake's mind, one of the engineering triumphs that made carrier aviation in the jet age possible. In the earliest days, aboard the old *Langley*, pilots made approaches to the deck without help. One windy day one of the senior officers grabbed a couple signal flags and rushed to the fantail to signal to a young aviator who was having trouble with his approach. This innovation was so successful that an officer was soon stationed there to assist all the aviators with signal flags, or paddles. This officer helped the pilot with glide slope and lineup, and since the carriers all had straight decks, gave the vital engine 'cut' signal that required the aviator to pull his throttle to idle and flare.

When angled decks and jets with higher landing speeds came along, it became obvious that a new system was required. As usual, the British were the innovators. They rigged a mirror on one side of the deck and directed a high-intensity light at it. The light was reflected up the glide slope. By rigging a set of reference lights midway up on each side of the mirror, a datum was established. A pilot making his approach would see the light reflected on the mirror – the ball – rise above the datum lights when he was above glide slope, or high, and descend below it when he was low. The landing signal officer was retained to assist the pilot with radio calls, and to give mandatory wave-offs if an approach became unsafe.

The Fresnel lens was the mirror idea carried one step further. The light source was now contained within five boxes, stacked one on top of the other. The datum lights were beside the middle, or third, box. Due to the way the lens on each light was designed, a horizontally wide but vertically narrow beam of light was directed up the glide slope by each box. Crossing the fantail, the beam from the middle box, the 'centered ball,' was a mere eighteen inches in height.

This was the challenge: a pilot must fly his jet airplane through turbulent air into an eighteen-inch-thick window in the sky. At night, with the deck moving as the ship rode a seaway, hitting this window became extraordinarily difficult, without argument the most difficult challenge in aviation. That anyone other than highly skilled, experienced test pilots could do it on a regular basis was a tribute to the training the Navy gave its aviators, and was the reason those who didn't measure up were ruthlessly weeded out.

You could do it or you couldn't – there was no in between. And yet, no one could do it consistently every time. The task was too difficult, the skills involved too perishable. So night after night, in fair weather and foul, they practiced, like they were doing on this miserable night in the Sea of Japan, eighty miles west of Honshu.

As Jake Grafton stood on the platform staring into the darkness as the wind swirled rain over him, he was glad that tonight was not his night. It felt so good to be *here*, not up *there* sweating bullets aa the plane bounced around, trying to keep the needles steady, watching the fuel, knowing that you were going to have to fly that instrument approach to the ball, then thread the needle to get safely back aboard. To return to the world of the living, to friends, to food, to letters from loved ones, to a bunk to sleep in, to a world with a past *and* a future. There in that cockpit when you were flying the ball there was only the present, only the airplane, only the stick in your right hand and the throttles in your left and the rudder beneath your feet. There was only the *now*, *this* moment for which you had lived your whole life, *this* instant during which you called upon everything within you to do this thing.

Oh, yes. He was glad.

Other LSOs were climbing to the platform now, so Jake moved as far back as he could to stay out of the way. All these specialists were here to observe, to see another dozen landings, to polish their skills, to learn. This was normal. The platform was packed with LSOs on every recovery.

The last airplane to be launched was upon the catapult at full power when the lights of the first plane on the glide slope appeared out of the gloomy darkness astern. In secopnds the catapult fired and the deck became unnaturally silent.

The Real was already three feet out onto the deck holding the radio headset against his ear with his left hand while he held the Fresnel lens control handle in his right over his head, a signal to his colleagues that he was aware the deck was foul. Jake leaned sideways and looked forward around the edge of the canvas screen. The waist catapult crewmen were working furiously to put the protector plate over Cat Three's shuttle and clear the launching gear from the flight deck. Until they were out of the landing area, the deck would remain foul.

'Come on, people,' the air boss roared over the flight deck loudspeaker. He seemed to believe that his troops worked best when properly stimulated. In any event, he didn't hesitate to stimulate them. 'We've got a Phantom in the groove. Let's clear the deck.'

The last flight deck tractor zipped across the foul line near the island, yet three cat crewmen were still struggling with the protector plate.

Jake lifted one side of his mouse ears away from his head. He heard McCoy roger the ball call.

The air boss on the loudspeaker again: 'He's called the ball. Let's get this deck clear *now*, people!'

There, the cat crewmen were running for the catwalk. Jake looked aft. The Phantom was within a half mile, about two hundred feet high, coming fast. On his nose-gear door was a stop-light arrangement of little lights, red, yellow and green, that was operated by the angle-of-attack instrument in the cockpit. Red for slow, yellow for on speed, and green for fast. The yellow light was lit, but even as Jake saw it, the red light flickered.

'You're going to go slow,' Real told the pilot. 'Little power.'

The red foul deck light went out and the green light came on.

'Clear deck,' shouted the LSO talker.

'Clear deck,' McCoy echoed, and lowered his right arm.

The jet was slamming through the burble causd by the island, his engines winding up, then decelerating. In seconds the Phantom crossed the ramp with its engines wailing, its hook reaching for a wire. Then the hook struck in a shower of sparks and the main gear thumped down. The

202

hook snagged the second wire as the engines wound up to their full fury – a futile roar, because the big fighter was quickly dragged to a quivering halt. The exterior lights went out. The hook runner raced across the foul line with his wands signaling 'hook up.' Seconds later the Phantom was taxiing out of the landing area and the wings were folding.

Meanwhile McCoy was giving the grade to another LSO, who was writing in the log. 'Little slow in the middle, OK Two.'

McCoy glanced at Jake. 'Nice pass. Pitching deck and reduced visbility and he handled it real well. I bet I couldn't do as well on a shitty night like this.'

Then he was back out into the landing area listening to the radio. In seconds another set of lights came out of the goo. Another Phantom. This guy had more difficulty with the pass than the first fighter, but he too successfully trapped. The third Phantom boltered and McCoy waved off the fourth one. It was going to be a long recovery.

One of the LSOs handed Jake his radio. He put it to his ear in time to hear the RA-5C Vigilante call the ball.

The Vigilante was the most beautiful airplane the Navy owned, in Jake's opinion. It was designed as a supersonic nuclear bomber back when nuclear bombs were big. The weapon was carried in an internal bay and was ejected out a door in the rear of the plane between the tailpipes. The Navy soon discovered this method of delivery didn't work: the bomb was trapped in the airplane's slipstream and trailed along behind – sometimes for seconds at a time before it fell free. The weapon's impact point could not be predicted and there was a serious danger that the bomb would strike the aircrft while it was tagging along behind, damaging the plane and the weapon. So the Vigilantes were converted to reconnaissance aircraft. Fuel tanks were installed in the bomb bays and camera packages on the bellies.

With highly swept wings and empennage, a needle nose, and two huge engines with afterburners, the plane was extraordinarily fast, capable of ripping through the heavens at an honest Mach 2+. And it was a bitch to get aboard the ship. Jake thought the Vigie pilots were supermen, the best of the best.

Yet it was the guys in back who had the biggest *cojónes*, for they rode the beast with no control over their fate. Even worse, they rode in a separate cockpit behind the pilot that had only two tiny windows, one on each side of the fuselage. They could not see forward or aft and their view to either side was highly restricted. A-6 BNs with their seats beside the pilot and excellent view in all quadrants regarded the Vigie backseaters with awe. 'It's like flying in your own coffin,' they whispered to one another, and shuddered.

Tonight the Vigie pilot was having his troubles. 'I got vertigo,' he told McCoy on the platform.

'Fly the ball and keep it coming,' the LSO said. 'Your wings are level, the deck is moving, average out the ball. You're slightly high drifting left . . . Watch your lineup!' The Vigilante was a big plane, with a 60-foot wingspan – the foul lines were 115 feet apart.

'Pick up your left wing, little power . . . right for lineup.'

Now the Vigie was crossing the ramp, and the right wing dropped.

'*Level your wings,*' McCoy roared into the radio.

The Vigilante's left wing sagged and the nose rose. Jake shot a glance at the PLAT monitor: the RA-5 was way too far right, his right wingtip almost against the foul line.

His gaze flipped back to the airplane, just in time to hear the engines roar and see the fire leap from the afterburners two white-hot blowtorches fifteen feet long. The light ripped the night open, casting a garish light on the parked planes, the men standing along the right foul line, and the ship's superstructure.

With her hook riding five feet above the wires and her left wing slightly down, the big swept-wing jet crossed the deck and rose back into the night sky. Only then did the fire from the afterburners go out. The rolling thunder continued to wash over the men on the ship's deck, then it too dissipated.

An encounter with an angry dragon, Jake thought, slightly awed by the scene he had just witnessed.

'A nugget on his first cruise,' McCoy told his colleagues, then dictated his comments to the logbook writer.

The motion of the ship was becoming more pronounced, Jake thought, especially here on the platform. When the deck reached the top of its stroke, he felt slightly light on his feet.

McCoy noticed the increased deck motion too, and he switched the lens to a four-degree glide slope, up from the normal three and one half. The talker informed the controllers in Air Ops.

In seconds there was another plane on the ball, this time an A-7 Corsair. 'Three One Zero, Corsair ball, Three Point Two.'

'Roger ball, four-degree glide slope. Pitching deck.'

This guy was an old pro. McCoy gave him one call, a little too much power, and that was all it took. He snagged a three.

The next plane was the Phantom that boltered, and this time he was steadier. Yet the steeper glide slope fooled him and he was fast all the way, flattened out at the ramp and boltered again.

The next plane, a A-7, took more coaching, but he too caught a wire. So did the Phantom that followed him, the one that had waved off originally. The next A-7 had to be waved off, however, because the deck was going down just before he got to the in-close position, while he was working off a high and slightly fast. If he had overdone his power reduction he would have been descending through the glide slope just as the deck rose to meet him: a situation not conducive to a long life.

An A-6 successfully trapped, then the Phantom came around for his third pass. Clear sky and the tanker were twenty-one thousand feet above, so the pressure was on. McCoy looked tense as a coiled spring as he stood staring up the glide slope waiting for the F-4's lights to appear out of the overcast.

There!

'One Zero Two, Phantom ball, Four Point Two, trick or treat.' Trick or treat meant that he had to trap on this pass or be sent to tank.

'Roger ball, four-degree glide slope, it'll look steep so fly the ball.'

A dark night, a pitching deck, rain . . . these were the ingredients of fear, cold, clutching, icy as death. A carrier pilot who denied he ever experienced it was a liar. Tonight, on this pass, this fighter pilot felt the slimy tentacles of fear play across his backbone. As he crossed the ramp he reduced power and raised the nose. The heavy jet instantly increased its rate of descent.

'No,' screamed McCoy.

The hook slapped down and the main mounts hit and the number one wire screamed from its sheaves.

'There's one lucky mother,' McCoy told the writer and the observing signal officers when the blast of the Phantom's two engines had died to an idling whine. 'Spotted the deck and should have busted his ass, but the deck was falling away. Another military miracle. Who says Jesus ain't on our side?'

More A-7s came down the chute. The first one got aboard without difficulty but the second announced he had vertigo.

'Roger that. Your wings are level and you're fast. Going high. Steep glide slope, catch it with power. More power.'

206

He was getting close and the red light on his nose gear door winked on. He was slow. 'Power. Power! *Power!*

At the third power call the Real McCoy triggered the wave-off lights, but it was too late. Even as the Corsair's engine wound up, the wheels hit the very end of the flight deck and there was a bright flash. With the engine winding up to full screech the plane roared up the deck, across all the wires, and rotated to climb away. McCoy shouted 'Bolter, bolter, bolter,' on the radio.

Now McCoy handed the radio and Fresnel lens pickle to the nearest LSO. He began running toward the fantail. Jake Grafton followed.

The dim light made seeing difficult. The deck was really moving here, 550 feet aft of the ship's center of gravity. The ship was like a giant seesaw. Keeping your knees bent helped absorb the thrusts of the deck.

McCoy took a flashlight from his hip pocket and played it on the ramp, the sloping end of the flight deck. The ramp dropped away at about a thirty-degree angle, went down ten or twelve feet, then ended. That was the back end of the ship. The flashlight beam stopped three feet right of the centerline stripe, at the deep dent.

'Hook strike,' Jake shouted.

'No, that's where his main mount hit.' Real scanned with the flashlight and stopped at another dent, the twin of the first. 'There's where the other wheel hit. His hook hit below the ramp.' Then McCoy turned and ran for the LSO platform, with Jake following.

Back on the LSO platform McCoy told the sailor wearing the sound-powered phones, 'His hook hit the back end of the ship and disintegrated. He doesn't have a hook now. Tell Air Ops.'

Without a hook, the plane could be trapped aboard only with the barricade, a huge nylon net that was rigged across the landing area like a giant badminton net. Or it could be sent to an airfield in Japan.

Air Ops elected to send the crippled plane to Japan.

McCoy got back to the business of waving airplanes. He had the Vigilante on the ball, with an A-6 and EA-6B behind him, then the E-2 Hawkeye and KA-6 tanker to follow.

This time the Vigie pilot drifted right of centerline and corrected back toward the left. He leveled his wings momentarily, so McCoy let him keep coming. Then, passing in close, the left wing dropped. The Vigilante slewed toward the LSOs' platform as McCoy screamed 'Wave-off' and dived to the right.

Jake had his eyes on the approaching plane, but McCoy was taking everyone on the platform with him. Jake was almost to the edge when the RA-5 swept overhead in burner, his hook almost close enough to touch. Instinctively Jake ducked.

That was close! Too close. Now Jake realized that he and McCoy were the only two people still on the platform. He looked down to his right. Two hands reached up out of the darkness and grabbed the edge by Jake's foot. *Everyone else went into the net.*

They clambered back up, one by one. The talker picked up his sound-powered headset where he had dropped it and put it back on.

McCoy leaned toward the talker. 'Tell Air Ops that I recommend he send the Vigie to the beach for fuel and a turnaround. Give that guy some time to calm down.'

And that is what Air Ops did.

The last plane was still two miles out when a sailor brought a lump of metal to the platform and gave it to McCoy. 'We found this down on the fantail. There's a lot of metal shards down there but this was the biggest piece. I think it's a piece of hook point.'

McCoy examined it by flashlight, then passed it to Jake.

It was a piece of the A-7's hook point, all right. About a

pound of it. The point must have shattered against the structure of the ship and the remnants rained down on the fantail.

When the last plane was aboard, Jake followed McCoy down the ladder to the catwalk, then down another flight into the ship.

'That was exciting,' Jake Grafton told the LSO.

'You dum ass. You should have gone into the net.'

'Well, I didn't think—'

'That Vigie about got us. No shit.'

'Hell of a recovery.'

'That's no lie. Did you hear about the A-7 that had the ramp strike?'

'No.'

'The talker told me. The guy had a total hydraulic failure on the way to the beach and ejected. He's in the water right now.'

'You're kidding.'

'The rebound of the hook shank probably severed his hydraulic lines. He's swimming for it. Just another great Navy night.'

The pilot of the RA-5C Vigilante who had so much trouble with lineup on this recovery landed in Japan and refueled. He returned to the ship for the last recovery of the evening and flew a fair pass into a three-wire.

The A-7 pilot with the hydraulic failure wasn't rescued until ten o'clock the next morning. He spent the night in his life raft, buffeted by heavy seas, overturned four times, though each time he regained the safety of the raft. He swallowed a lot of seawater and did a lot of vomiting. He vomited and retched until blood came up. Still retching when the helicopter deposited him back on the carrier, he had to be sedated and given an IV to rehydrate him. He was also suffering from a serious case of hypothermia. But he was alive, with no bones broken. His shipmates trooped to sick bay in a steady procession to welcome him back to the company of living men.

CHAPTER THIRTEEN

The Soviet intelligence ship *Reduktor* joined the task group during the night and fell in line astern. At dawn she was two miles behind the carrier wallowing heavily. When the sun came up she held her position even though the task group raised its speed to twelve knots. When the sea state eased somewhat the Soviet ship rode steadier.

Jake came up on deck for the first launch of the day only to find that the AGI was dropping steadily astern. Her captain knew the drill. The carrier had been running steadily downwind, but to launch she would turn into the wind, toward the AGI. So now the Soviet ship was slowing to one or two knots, just enough to maintain steerageway.

At the brief the air intelligence officers showed the flight crews file photos of this Okean-class intelligence collector. She was a small converted trawler. Had she not been festooned with a dazzling array of radio antennas that rose from her superstructure and masts, one would assume her crew was still looking for fish.

So there they were. Russians. In *Reduktor*'s compartments they were busy with their reel-to-reel tape drives – probably all made in Japan – recording every word, peep or chirp on every radio frequency that the US Navy had ever been known to use. Doubtlessly they monitored other frequencies occasionally as well, just in case. These tapes would be examined by experts who would construct from them detailed analyses of how the US Navy operated and what its capabilities were. Encrypted transmissions would be turned over to specialists who would try to break the codes.

In short, the crew of *Reduktor* were spies. They were going about their business in a lawful manner, however, in plain sight upon the high seas, so there was nothing anyone in the US Navy could do about it. In fact, the American captains and watch officers had to make sure that their ships didn't accidentally collide with the Soviet ship.

There was one other possibility, not very probable, but possible. *Reduktor* might be a beacon ship marking the position of the American task group for Soviet forces. Just in case, American experts aboard the US ships monitored, recorded and analysed every transmission that *Reduktor* made.

Anticipating the coming of a Soviet AGI, the US task group had already reduced its own radio transmissions as much as possible. During the day the aircrews from *Columbia* operated 'zip-lip,' speaking on the radio only when required. Specialists from the Communications Security Group – COMSEGRU – had visited every ready room to brief the crews.

This morning Jake Grafton spent a moment watching the old trawler, then went on with his preflight. He would, he suspected, see a lot of that ship in the next few months.

After four days of operations in the Sea of Japan, *Columbia* and her escorts called at Sasebo and stayed for a week. *Reduktor* was waiting when they came out of port.

The first week of August was spent operating off the southern coast of Korea, then the task group steamed south and spent a week flying in the South China Sea. The Soviet AGI was never far away.

Here, for the first time, the air wing began flying the Alpha strikes that Jake had helped plan with CAG Ops. Jake didn't get to go on the first one, when Skipper Haldane led the A-6s. Due to his bombing scores, however, he was scheduled to lead the A-6s the next day. He and Flap spent half the night in Strike Planning with the other element leaders making sure they had it right.

CAG Kall sat in a corner and sipped coffee during the entire session. He didn't say much, yet when he did you listened carefully because he had something to say worth listening to. He also smiled a lot and picked up names easily. After an hour you thought you had known the man all your life. That night in his bunk the thought tripped through Jake Grafton's mind that he would like to lead the way Chuck Kall did.

Well, tomorrow he would get his chance. Six Intruders were scheduled to fly and the maintenance gunny said he would have them. The target was an abandoned ship on a reef a few miles off the western coast of Luzon, the northernmost of the Philippine Islands. Today's strike had pretty well pulverized the ship, but there were enough pieces sticking out of the water to make an aiming point. The water was pretty shallow there. To make sure there were no native fishing boats in the target area tomorrow before live bombs rained down, an RA-5C was scheduled to make a prestrike low pass.

Jake had so many things on his mind that he had trouble falling asleep. He took the hop minute by minute, the climb-out, the rendezvous, frequency changes, formation, airplane problems, no-radio procedures, the letdown to roll-in altitude . . . he drifted off to sleep and dreamed about it.

The morning was perfect, a few puffy low clouds but widely scattered. The brisk trade wind speckled the sea with whitecaps and washed away the haze.

After a quick cup of coffee and check of the weather, Jake met with the element leaders for two hours. Then he went to the ready room for the crew briefs, briefed the A-6's portion of the mission, read the maintenance logbook on his assigned plane and donned his flight gear. By the time he walked out onto the flight deck with Flap Le Beau he had been working hard for four hours.

The escort ships looked crisp and clean upon a living blue sea. The wind – he inhaled deeply.

He and Flap took the time to inspect the weapons carefully. For today's mock attack they had live bombs, four Mark-84 two-thousand-pounders. A hit with one of these bombs would break the back of any warship that was cruiser-size or smaller. The multiple ejector racks that normally carried smaller bombs had been downloaded so the one-ton general purpose bombs could be mated to the parent bomb racks. There were two of these on each wing. As usual, the centerline belly station carried a two-thousand-pound drop tank. One of the bombs, the last one to be dropped, had a laser-seeker in the nose. The other three were fused with a mechanical nose fuse and an electrical tail fuse.

The mechanical nose fuse was the most reliable fuse the Navy possessed, which made it the preferred way to fuse bombs. A bare copper wire ran from a solenoid in the parent rack forward across the weapon to the nose, where it went through a machined hole in the fuse housing and then through the little propeller at the very front of the fuse. The wire physically prevented the propeller from turning until the weapon was ejected from the rack. The wire then pulled out of the fuse and stayed on the rack, which freed the propeller. As the bomb fell the wind spun the propeller for a preset number of seconds and armed the fuse. When the nose of the bomb struck its target, the fuse was triggered. After a small delay – one hundredth of a second to allow the weapon to penetrate the target – the fuse detonated the high explosive in the bomb.

If the mechanical fuse was defective, the electric tail fuse would set the bomb off. That fuse was armed by a jolt of electricity in the first two feet of travel as the bomb fell away from the parent rack, then its arming wire, an insulated electrical cable, pulled loose.

The BN's job on preflight was to check to ensure the ordnancemen had rigged bombs, fuses and arming wires correctly. Since any error here could ruin the mission, Jake Grafton always checked too. Today he and Flap stood side by side as they examined each weapon. Everything was fine.

The bomb with the laser-seeker in the nose was the technology of the future, the technology that had already made unguided free-fall bombs obsolete and would itself be made obsolete by guided missiles. One had to aim a laser-light generator at the target and hold the light on it as the bomb fell. If the bomb was dropped into the proper cone above the target, the seeker would guide it to the reflected spot of laser light by manipulating small canards on the body of the device.

In two or three years the A-6 would have its own laser-light generator in the nose of the aircraft. Now the generators, or 'designators,' were hand-held. Today a radar-intercept officer in the backseat of an F-4 orbiting high above the target would aim the designator while Intruders, Corsairs and other Phantoms dropped the bombs. This system worked. Navy and Air Force crews used it with devastating effect on North Vietnamese bridges in the last year of the war.

Due to the cost of the seekers, each plane had only one for today's training mission. Dropping three unguided weapons in addition to the guided one had an additional benefit – the pilot had to try for a perfect dive to put all four on the target. If one bomb was a bull's-eye and the other three went awry, he screwed up.

The plane looked good. Strapped in waiting for the engine start, Jake Grafton arranged his charts in the cockpit, then paused for a few seconds to savor the warmth of the sun and the wind playing with his hair. The moment was over too soon. Helmet on, canopy closed, crank engines.

The cat shot was a hoot, an exhilarating ride into a perfect morning. His airplane flew well, all the gear worked as advertised, none of the other A-6s had maintenance problems and all launched normally.

The A-6s rendezvoused at 9,000 feet. When Jake had his gaggle together, he led them upward to 13,000 feet and slowly eased into position on the right of the lead division, today four Corsairs. When all the other divisions were aboard, the strike leader, the CO of one of the A-7 squadrons, rolled out on course to the target and initiated a climb to 23,000 feet.

The climb took longer than usual. The bombers were heavily loaded. At ninety-eight percent RPM all Jake could coax out of his plane was 280 knots indicated. He concentrated on flying smoothly so his wingmen would not have to sweat bullets to stay with him.

The six-plane division was broken up into two flights of three. Jake had one wingman on each side. Out farther to the right flew another three-plane flight, but its leader was also flying formation on Grafton. Just before the time came to dive, the man on each leader's left would cross over, then the two flights would join so that there were six airplanes in right echelon. The plan was for Jake to roll in and the others to follow two seconds apart, so that all six were diving with just enough separation between the planes that each pilot could aim his own bombs. If they did it right, all six would be in the enemy's threat envelope together and divide the enemy's antiaircraft fire. And all would leave together. That was the plan, anyway.

Flap had the radar and computer fired up, so Jake was getting steering to the target. He was merely comparing it to the course the strike leader was flying, however.

The radio frequency was crowded. The strike leader was talking to the E-2 Hawkeye, the RA-5C was chattering about a fishing boat that he had chased away from the target and the cloud cover, someone had a hydraulic problem, the tankers wanted to change the poststrike rendezvous position because the carrier wasn't where it was supposed to be when this evolution was put together, and one of the EA-6s was late getting launched and was going to be late getting to its assigned position. Situation normal, Jake thought.

He checked the position of his wingmen regularly, yet he spent most of his time scanning the sky and staying in proper position in relation to the strike leader. When he had a spare second he brought his eyes back into the cockpit to check his engine instruments and fuel.

The cumulus clouds below thickened as the strike group approached the coast of Luzon. The bases were at 4,000 feet, but the tops were building. From 23,000 feet the clouds seemed to cover about fifty percent of the sea below.

Would there be holes over the target big enough to bomb through?

The twenty-six bombers and their two EA-6 escorts began their descent toward their roll-in altitude of 15,000 feet. The leader left his throttle alone, so the airspeed began to increase. The faster the strike could close a Soviet task group, the fewer missiles and less flak it would encounter. In aerial warfare, speed is life.

Now CAG was on the radio. He was at 30,000 feet over the target in an F-4. 'Where are the Flashlights?'

Flashlight was the F-4 that would illuminate the target with the laser designator. Actually there were two F-4s, both carrying hand-held laser designators. The pilots would have to find a hole in the clouds so the RIOs – radar intercept officers – could aim the designators, then they would have to maneuver to keep the target in sight and avoid colliding with one another. In a real attack on Soviet ships, the pilots would also be dodging missiles and flak.

'Uh, Flashlight is trying to find the target.'

The F-4's electronic system was designed to find and

track other airborne targets, not find the remnants of a wrecked ship resting on a reef. The A-6s' systems, however, were working fine. Flap had the target and Jake was getting steering and distance. In the planning sessions he had argued that A-6s should carry the designators but had been overruled.

'Ten miles to roll-in,' Flap told Jake. The strike was passing 20,000 feet. Now the strike leader dropped his nose farther, giving the group about 4,000 feet a minute down. Three hundred twenty knots indicated and increasing.

Passing 18,000 feet Jake pumped his arm at the A-6 on his left side. Flap did the same to the man on his right. The Intruder formation shifted to echelon.

The tops of the clouds were closer. Still some holes, but the target wasn't visible through them.

The situation was deteriorating fast. Without holes in the clouds, the F-4s carrying bombs could not find the target. The A-7s might be able to, but not in formation since the pilots could not fly formation and work their radars and computers too. The A-6s could break off at any point and make a system attack on the target, individually or in pairs. This was the edge an all-weather, two-man airplane gave you.

The strike leader, Gold One, knew all this. He had only seconds to decide.

'This is Gold One. Let's go to Plan Bravo. Plan Bravo.'

Jake Grafton lowered his nose still farther. Now he wanted to descend below the formation. The A-7s were shallowing their dive, which helped.

Flap was on the ICS: 'Target's twenty degrees left. Master Arm on.'

'Kiss off,' Jake told him, and Flap took a few seconds to splay his fingers at the wingman on his right as Jake turned left to center steering and dropped his nose still more. Fifteen degrees down now, going faster than a raped ape, the plane pushing against the sonic shock wave and vibrating slightly, nothing but clouds visible in the windscreen dead ahead. The other A-6s would continue on course for four seconds each, then turn toward the target. All six would run the target individually.

'We're in attack,' Flap announced, and sure enough, the attack symbology apeared on the VDI in front of Jake.

'War Ace One's in hot,' he announced on the radio.

He took one more quick look around to ensure the other airplanes in this gaggle were clear.

Something on his left wing caught his eye. His eyes focused.

The bomb on Station One, the station nearest the left wing tip – *the propeller on the mechanical fuse was spinning!* The fuse was arming.

He gaped for half a second, unwilling to believe his eyes.

The propeller was spinning.

One bomb in a thousand, they say, will detonate at the end of arming time. The propeller will spin for 8.5 seconds to line up the firing circuit.

He could drop it now!

His thumb moved toward the pickle. The master armament switch was already on. All he had to do was squeeze the commit trigger and push the pickle. The bomb would fall away and be clear of the plane when the fuse finished arming. If it blew then . . .

He would still be within the blast envelope.

All these thoughts shot through his mind in less than a second. Even while he was considering he scanned the instruments to ensure he was tracking steering with his wings level.

He looked outside again. The propeller was stopped.

The bomb was armed! And it hadn't exploded. Okay, we've dodged the first bullet.

He pushed the radio transmit button as he retarded the throttles and raised the nose. 'War Ace One has an armed bomb on the rack. Breaking off the attack and turning north at . . .' He looked at the altimeter. He was descending through 12,000 feet. '. . . At twelve thousand.'

He grabbed the stick with his left hand and used his right to move the Master Arm switch to the safe position.

Everyone was talking on the radio – A-6s calling in hot, and A-7s breaking up for dives, F-4s looking for holes – probably no one heard Jake's transmission.

'Station One,' he told Flap on the ICS when he had his left hand back on the throttles, talking over the gabble on the radio. 'The bomb is armed.'

He concentrated on flying the plane, on getting the nose up and turning to the north. He was in the clouds now, bouncing around in turbulence. A northerly heading should take him out from under the strike gaggle, which was circling the target to the south.

'The arming wire pulled out of the fuse somehow,' he told Flap. 'I saw the propeller spinning. The fucking thing is armed.'

He looked again at the offending weapon. Now he saw that the thermal protective coating was peeled back some-what. The Navy sprayed all its weapons with a plastic thermal coating after experiencing several major flight-deck fires in which bombs cooked off. The coating must have had a flaw in it, something for the slipstream to work on. The slipstream peeled the coating, which pulled the arming wire.

A two-thousand-pound bomb . . . if it detonated under the wing, the airplane would be instantly obliterated. The fuel in the plane would probably explode. So would the other three weapons hanging on the plane. Not that he or Flap would care. They would already be dead, their bodies crushed by the initial blast and torn into a thousand pieces.

And this turbulence . . . it could set off that fuse.

He retarded the throttles. Almost to idle. Cracked the speed brakes to help slow down.

'Let's climb out of this crap,' Flap suggested.

Jake slipped the speed brakes back in and raised the nose. He added power.

Finally he stabilized at an indicated 250 knots.

'Cubi?' Flap asked.

'Yeah.'

Flap hit a switch and the computer steering went right. Jake looked at the repeater between his legs. The steering bug was at One Six Zero degrees, eighty miles. Flap dialed in the Cubi TACAN station.

'It could go at any time,' Jake said.

'I know.'

'Let's get off this freq and talk to Black Eagle.'

Flap got on the radio as they climbed free of the clouds. The turbulence ceased.

Left turn. Fly around the target and the strike group to seaward.

No. Right turn. Go around on the land side. The other planes would be leaving the garget to seaward. Maybe at this altitude. No sense taking any more chances than—

An F-4 shot across the windscreen going from right to left. Before Jake could react the A-6 flew into his wash. Wham! The plane shook fiercely, then it was through.

'If that didn't set the damned thing off, nothing will,' Flap said.

Like hell. The jolts and bumps might well be cumulative.

Jake concentrated on flying the plane. He was sweating profusely. Sweat stung his eyes. He stuck the fingers of his left hand under his visor and swabbed it away.

Black Eagle suggested a frequency switch to Cubi Point Approach. Flap rogered and dialed the radio.

They were at 18,000 feet now and well above the cloud tops.

Jake glanced at the armed bomb from time to time. If he pickled it the shock of the ejector foot smacking into the weapon to push it away from the rack might set it off.

If the bomb detonated he and Flap would never even know it.

One second they would be alive and the next they would be standing in line to see St Peter.

What a way to make a living!

Just fly the airplane, Jake. Do what you can and let God worry about the other stuff.

'Cubi Approach, War Ace Five Oh Seven. We have an armed Mark Eighty-Four hanging on Station One. We're carrying three more Mark Eighty-Fours, but they are unarmed. After we land we want to park as far away from everything as possible. And could you have EOD meet us?' EOD stood for explosive ordnance disposal.

'Roger live weapon. We'll roll the equipment and call EOD.'

Cubi Point was the US naval air station on the shore of Subic Bay, the finest deep-water port in the western Pacific. It had one concrete runway 9,000 feet long. Today Jake Grafton flew a straight-in approach over the water, landing to the northeast.

He flared the Intruder like he was flying an Air Force jet. He retarded the engines to idle, pulled the nose up and greased the main mounts on. He held the nose wheel off the runway until the airspeed read 80 knots, then he lowered it as gently as possible. Only then did he realize that he had been holding his breath.

The tower directed him to taxi back to the south end of the runway and park on the taxiway. As he taxied he raised his flaps and slats and shut down his left engine. Then he opened the canopy and removed his oxygen mask. He wiped his face with the sleeve of his flight suit.

A fire truck was waiting when Jake turned off the runway. He made sure he was across the hold-short line, then eased the plane to a stop. One of the sailors on the truck came over to the plane with a fire bottle, a fire extinguisher on wheels. Jake chopped the right engine. On shutdown the fuel control unit dumped the fuel it contained overboard, and this fuel fell down beside the right main wheel. If the brake was hot the fuel could ignite, hence the fire bottle. The danger was nonexistent if you shut down an engine while taxiing because you were moving away from the jettisoned fuel. But there was no fire today.

One of the firemen lowered the pilot's boarding ladder. Jake safetied his ejection seat and unstrapped. He left the helmet and mask in the plane when he climbed down.

The thermal casing on the armed bomb had indeed been peeled back by the blast of the slipstream, pulling the arming wire and freeing the fuse propeller.

Jake Grafton was standing there looking at it when he realized that a chief petty officer in khakis was standing beside him.

'I'm Chief Mendoza, EOD.'

Jake nodded at the weapon. 'We were running an attack. I just happened to look outside for other planes just before we went into a cloud and saw the propeller spinning.'

Flap came over while Jake was speaking. His put his hands on his hips and stood silently examining the bomb.

'If you'd dropped it like that, sir, it might have gone off when the ejector foot hit it,' the chief said.

Neither airman had anything to say.

'Guess you guys were lucky.'

'Yeah.'

'Well, I gotta screw that fuse out. We'll snap a few photos first because we'll have to do a bunch of paperwork and the powers that be will want photos. I suggest you two fellows ride on the fire truck. You don't want to be anywhere around when I start screwing that fuse out.'

'I'll walk,' Jake said.

Flap Le Beau headed for the fire truck.

The chief turned his back on the weapon while the

firemen took photos. He was facing out to sea, looking at the sky and the clouds and the shadows playing on the water when Jake Grafton turned away and began walking.

The pilot loosened his flight gear. He was suddenly very thirsty, so he got out his water bottle and took a drink. The water was warm, but he drank all of it. His hands were shaking, trembling like an old man's.

The heat radiated from the concrete in waves.

He wiped his face again with his sleeve, then half turned and looked back at the plane. The chief was still standing with his arms folded, facing out to sea.

As he walked Jake got a cigarette from the pack in his left sleeve pocket and lit it. The smoke tasted foul.

CHAPTER FOURTEEN

A week after Jake and Flap visited Cubi Point for three whole hours, *Columbia* maneuvered herself against the carrier pier.

Subic Bay, Olongapo City across the Shit River, the BOQ pool, the Cubi O Club with its banks of telephone booths and the Ready Room Bar out back – Jake Grafton had seen it all too recently and it bruoght back too many memories.

He got a roll of quarters and sat in a vacant telephone booth with a gin and tonic, but he didn't make a call. Callie wasn't in Hong Kong – she was in Chicago. Mail was arriving regularly but there were no letters from her; in fact, she hadn't written since he called her from Hawaii.

Somehow he had screwed it up. He sat in the phone booth smoking a cigarette and sipping the drink and wondered where it had gone wrong.

Well, you can't go back. That's one of life's hard truths. The song only goes in one direction and you can't run it backward.

Morgan McPherson, Corey Ford and the Boxman were gone, gone forever. Tiger Cole was undergoing rehab at the Naval Aeromedical Institute in Pensacola and working out each day in the gym where the AOCS classes did their thing, in that converted seaplane hangar on the wharf. Sammy Lundeen was writing orders at the Bureau of Naval Personnel in Washington, Skipper Camparelli was on an admiral's staff at Oceana. Both the Augies had gotten out of the Navy – Big was going to grad school someplace and Little was in dental school in Philadelphia.

And he was here, sitting in fucking Cubi Point in a fucking phone booth with the door open, listening to a new crop of flyers get drunk and talk about going across the bridge tonight and argue about whether the whores of Po City were worth the risk.

They're up there now near the bar, roaring that old song:

> *'Here I sit in Ready Room Four,*
> *Just dreaming of Cubi and my Olongapo whore,*
> *Oh Lupe, dear Lupe's the gal I adore,*
> *She's my hot-fucking, cock-sucking Olongapo whore . . .*

All his friends were getting on with their lives and he was stuck in this shithole at the edge of the known universe. The war was over and he had no place to go. The woman he wanted didn't want him and the flying wasn't fun anymore. It was just dangerous. That might be enough for the Real McCoy, but it wasn't for Jake Grafton.

He finished his first drink and began on his second – he always ordered his drinks two at a time in this place – and lit another cigarette.

He was just flat tired of it – tired of all of it. He was tired of the flying, tired of the flyers, tired of the stink of the ship, the stink of the sailors, the stink of his flight suit. He was tired of Navy showers, tired of floating around on a fucking gray boat, tired of sitting in saloons like this one, tired of being twenty-eight years old with not prospect one.

'Hey, whatcha doin' in there?' Flap Le Beau.

'What's it look like, dumb ass? I'm waiting for a phone call.'

'From who?'

'Miss June. The Pentagon. Hollywood. Walter Crank-case. The commissioner of baseball. Whoever.'

'Hmmm.'

'I'm getting drunk.'

'You look pretty sober to me.'

'Just got started.'

'Want any company, or is this a solo drunk?'

'Are you waiting for a call?'

'No. The only one who could conceivably want to talk to me would be the Lord, and I ain't sure about Him. But He knows where to find me if and when.'

'That's comforting, if true. But you say you're not sure?'

'No, I'm not.'

'Life's like that.'

'Come on up to the bar. I'll buy the next round.'

'Some of that Marine money would be welcome,' Jake admitted. He pried himself from the booth and followed Flap along the hallway and up the short flight of stairs into the bar room.

Flap ordered a beer and Jake acquired two more gin and tonics. 'Only drink for the tropics,' he told Flap, who cheerfully paid the seventy-five-cent tab and tossed an extra dime on the counter for the bartender. These Americans were high rollers.

'Miss June, huh?'

'Yeah,' said Jake Grafton. 'I wrote her a fan letter about her tits. Gave her the number of that booth. Told her when I was gonna be in Cubi. She'll call anytime.'

'Let's go play golf. We got enough time before dark.'

'Golf's a lot of work. Whacking that ball around in this heat and humidity . . .'

'Come on,' Flap said. 'Bring your drinks. You can drive the golf cart.'

> '*Oh Lupe, dear Lupe's the gal I adore,*
> *She's my hot-fucking, cock-sucking Olongapo whore . . .*'

There was a line of taxis in front of the club. Jake and Flap went to the one at the head of the line. Jake took huge slurps of both his drinks before he maneuvered himself into the tiny backseat, so he would be less likely to spill any.

And away they went in a cloud of blue smoke, the little engine in the tiny car revving mightily, the Filipino driver hunched over the wheel and punching the clutch and slamming the shift lever around like Mario Andretti.

The golf course was in a valley. Hacked out of the jungle were long, rolling fairways and manicured greens with sand traps and fluttering hole flags. Somewhere up there in the lush tropical foliage beyond the rough was the base fence, a ten-foot-high chain-link affair topped by barbed wire. Beyond the base fence were some of the world's poorest people, kept in line by a Third World military establishment and ruled by a corrupt, piss-pot tyrant. The native laborers who maintained this golf course, and were of course not allowed to play on it, were paid the magnificent sum of one US dollar a day as wages.

The whole damned scene was ludicrous, especially if you were working on your forth drink of the hour. The best thing was not to think about it, not to contemplate that vast social chasm between the men running lawnmowers and raking sand traps and the half-tanked fool driving this shiny little made-in-Japan golf cart. Best not to dwell on the shared humanity or the Grand Canyon that sepraated their dreams and yours.

The heat and humidity made the air thick, oppressive, but it was tolerable here in the golf cart with the faded canvas top providing shade. Jake stuck to piloting the cart while Flap drove, chipped and putted.

'Hotter than hell,' Jake told Flap.

'Yeah. Fucking tropical rain forest.'

'Jungle.'

'Rain forest. Nobody gives a shit about jungle, but they bleed copious dollars over rain forest.'

'Why is that?'

'I dunno. I got a seven on that last hole.'

'That's a lot of strokes. You aren't very good at this.'

'When I play golf, I play a *lot* of it. The object of the game is whacking the ball.'

'Keep your own score. I"m just driving.'

'Driver has to keep score. That's the way it's done at all the top clubs. Pebble Beach, Inverness, everywhere. Gimme a six on the first hole and a seven on this one.'

'You wouldn't cheat, would you?'

'Who? Me? Of course I'd cheat. I'm a nigger, remember?'

Jake wrote down the numbers and put the cart in motion. 'You shouldn't call yourself a nigger. It isn't right.'

'What do you know about it? I'm the black man.'

'Yeah, but I have to listen to it. And I don't like the word.'

'Bet you used it some yourself.'

'When I was a kid, yeah. But I don't like it.'

'Just drink and drive. It's too damn hot to think.'

'Don't use that word. I mean it.'

'If it'll make you happy.'

'I'm out of booze.'

'Well, you can get drunk tonight. Right now you can sit half-tanked and enjoy the pleasure of watching the world's greatest black colored Negro African-American golfer while you contemplate your many heinous sins.'

'It seemed like a good day for a drunk.'

'I've had days like that.'

The problem was, Jake finally admitted to himself, somewhere along the fourth fairway, that he had no dreams. Everyone needs dreams, goals to work toward, and he didn't have any. That fact, and the gin, depressed him profoundly.

He didn't want to be skipper of a squadron, or an admiral, or a farmer. Nor did he want to be an executive vice president in charge of something or other for some grand, important corporation, luxuriating in his new Buick and his generous expense account and his comfortable semi-custom house in an upscale real estate development and his blond wife with the big smile, big tits and purse full of supermarket coupons. He didn't want a stock portfolio and he didn't want to spend his mornings poring over the *Wall Street Journal* to see how rich he was. Just for the record, he also didn't give a damn about French novels and doubted if he ever could.

He didn't want *anything*. And he didn't want to *be* anything.

What in hell do people do who don't have any dreams?

True, he had once wanted to be a good attack pilot. To walk into the ready room and be accepted as an equal by the best aerial warriors in the world. He had achieved that ambition. And found it wasn't worth a mouthful of warm spit.

He had worked awful hard to get there, though.

That was something. He had wanted something and worked hard enough to earn it. And he was still alive. So many of them weren't. He was.

That was something, wasn't it?

He was still thinking about that two holes later when Flap dropped into the right seat of the cart after a tee shot and said, 'There's somebody in the jungle up by the next hole.'

'How do you know?'

'Two big birds flew out of there while I was in the tee box.'

'Birds fly all the time,' Jake pointed out. 'That's the jungle. There's zillions of 'em.'

'Not like that.'

Jake Grafton looked around. He and Flap were the only people in sight. There weren't even any Filipino grounds-keepers. 'So?'

'So I'm going to hit this next one over into the jungle on that side, then go in there to look for the ball. You just sit in the cart and look stupid.'

'I've heard that some locals like to crawl under the fence and rob people on this course.'

'I've heard that too.'

'Let's get outta here. You don't need to play hero.'

'Naw. I'll check 'em out.'

'I hear they carry guns.'

'I'll be careful. Just stop up there by my ball and let me slap it over into the jungle.'

'Don't go killing anybody.'

'They're probably just groundskeepers working on the perimeter fence or something.'

'I mean it, Le Beau, you simple green machine shit. Don't kill anybody.'

'Sure, Jake. Sure.'

So Flap addressed his ball in the fairway and shanked it off into the rough. He said a cuss word and flopped into the cart. Jake motored over to the spot where the ball had disappeared into the foliage and stopped the cart. They were still sixty yards or so short of the green.

'I think this is the spot.'

'Yeah.'

Flap Le Beau climbed out and headed for the jungle, his wedge in his left hand.

Jake examined his watch – 5:35 P.M. The shadows were getting longer and the heat seemed to be easing. That was something, anyhow. Damned Le Beau! Off chasing stickup guys in this green shit – if there were any stickup guys. Probably just a couple of birds that saw a snake or something.

He waited. Swatted at a few bugs that decided he might provide a meal. Amazing that there weren't more bugs, when you thought about it. After all, this was the jungle, the real genuine article with snakes and lizards and rain by the mile and insects the size of birds that drank blood instead of water.

Jake had seen enough jungle to last a lifetime in jungle

survival school in 1971, on the way to Vietnam that first time. They held the course in the jungle somewhere around here. He ate a snake and did all that Tarzan shit, back when he was on his way to being a good attack pilot.

For what?

That had been a stupid goal.

It had been a stupid war, and he had been stupid. Just stupid.

He was still sitting in the cart five minutes later trying to remember why he had wanted to be an attack pilot all those years ago when Flap came out of the jungle up by the green and waved at him to come on up. He was carrying something. As Jake got nearer he saw that Flap had a sub-machine gun in his right hand and his golf club in his left. The shaft of the club was bent at about a sixty-degree angle six inches or so up from the head.

He pulled the cart alongside Flap and stopped. 'Is that a Thompson?'

'Yeah. There were two guys. One had a machete and one had this.' Flap tossed the bent club in the bin in back of the cart.

'Is it loaded?'

Flap eased the bolt back until he saw brass, then released it. 'Yep.'

'Did you kill them?'

'Nope. They're sleeping like babies.'

Jake got out of the cart. 'Show me.'

'What do you want to see?'

'Come on, Le Beau, you moron. I want to see that these dumb little geeks are still alive and that you didn't kill them just for the fucking fun of it.'

Jake took three steps and entered the foliage. Flap trailed along behind.

The vegetation was extraordinarily thick for the first five or six feet, then it thinned out somewhat and you could see. For about ten feet.

'Well, where are they?'

Flap elbowed by him and led the way. One man lay on his face and the other lay sprawled ten feet away, on his back.

Jake rolled the first man over and checked his pulse. A machete lay a yard away. Well, his heart was still beating.

Jake picked up the machete and went over to the second man. He was obviously breathing. As Jake stood there staring down at him, taking in the sandals, the thin cotton shirt and dirty gray trousers, the short hair and brown skin and broken teeth, the man's eyes opened. Wide. In terror. He tried to sit up.

'Hey. You doing okay?'

His eyes left Jake and went behind him. Jake glanced that way. Flap was standing nonchalantly with the Thompson cradled in his left arm, peering lazily around. Yet his right hand was grasping the stock and his forefinger was on the trigger.

The man slowly got to his feet. He almost fell, then caught himself by grabbing a tree.

'Grab your buddy and get back across the fence.'

The Filipino worked on his friend for almost a minute before he stirred. When he had him sitting up, he looked at the two Americans. Jake jerked his head at the fence, then turned and headed for the fairway. Flap followed him.,

Jake tossed the machete into the bin beside Flap's rented golf bag and the bent club. Flap dumped the Tommy gun there too and sat down in the passenger seat.

'You're really something else, Grafton.'

'What do you want to do? Play golf or discuss philosophy?'

'I've heard it said that golf is philosophy.'

'It's hot and I'm thirsty and a little of your company goes a hell of a long way.'

'Yeah. Tell you what, let's go see what the rest of this course looks like. Drive on.' He flipped his fingers and Jake pressed the accelerator. The cart hummed and moved. 'Just drive the holes and we'll ride along like Stanley and Dr Livingston touring Africa. Nothing like an evening drive to settle a man's nerves and put everything into perspective. When we get back to the clubhouse, I'll buy you a drink. Maybe later we can go find two ugly women.'

'How ugly?'

'Ugly enough to set your nose hair on fire.'

'That's not ugly.10

'Maybe not,' Flap said agreeably. 'Maybe not.

CHAPTER FIFTEEN

The days at sea quickly became routine. The only variables were the weather and the flight schedule, but even so, the possible permutations of light and darkness, storms and clouds and clear sky and the places your name could appear on the flight schedule were finally exhausted. At some point you'd seen it all, done it all, and tomorrow would be a repetition of some past day. So, you suspected, would all the tomorrows to come.

Not that the pilots of the air wing flew every day, because they didn't. The postwar budget crunch did not permit that luxury. Every third day was an off day, sprinkled with boring paperwork, tedious lectures on safety or some aspect of the carrier aviator's craft, or – snore! – another NATOPS quiz. Unfortunately, on flying days there were not enough sorties to allow every pilot to fly one, so Jake and the rest of them took what they could get and solaced themselves with an occasional ugly remark to the schedules officer, as if that harried individual could conjure up money and flight time by snapping his fingers.

On those too-rare occasions when bombs were the main course – usually Mark 76 practice bombs, but every now and then the real thing – Jake Grafton managed to turn in respectable scores. Consequently he was a section leader now, which meant that when two A-6s were sent to some uninhabited island in the sea's middle to fly by, avoid the birds, and take photographs, he got to lead. He led unless Colonel Haldane was flying on that launch, then he got to fly the colonel's wing. Haldane *was* the skipper, even if his CEP was not as good as Jake's. Rank has its privileges.

Of course Doug Harrison reminded the skipper of his earlier commitment to letting the best bomber lead. Haldane's response was to point to the score chart on the bulkhead. 'When *you* get a better CEP than *mine*, son, I'll fly your wing. By then my eyes will be so bad I'll need someone to lead me around. Until that day . . .'

'Yessir,' Harrison said as his squadron mates hooted.

Jake had been spending at least half his time in the squadron maintenance department, and now the skipper made it official. Jake was to assist the maintenance officer with supply problems.

The squadron certainly had supply problems. Spare parts for the planes were almighty slow coming out of the Navy supply system. The first thing Jake did was to sit down with the book and check to see if the requisitions were correctly filled out. He found a few errors but concluded finally that the supply sergeant knew what he was doing. Then he sat down for a long talk with the sergeant.

Armed with a list of all the parts that were on back order, he went to see the ship's aviation supply officer, a lieutenant commander in the Supply Corps, a staff corps that ranked with law and medicine. Together they went over Jake's list, a computer printout, then sorted through the reams of printouts that cluttered up the supply office. Finally they went to the storerooms, cubbyholes all over the ship crammed with parts, and compared numbers.

When Jake went to see Colonel Haldane after three days of this, he had several answers. The erroneous requisitions were easily explained – there were actually fewer than one might expect. Yet the Marine sergeant was the odd man out with the Navy supply clerks, who were giving him no help. The system would not work if the people involved were not cooperating fully and trying to help each other.

The most serious problem, Jake told the colonel, was the shortages on the load-out manifest when the ship put to sea. Parts that should be aboard the ship weren't. Related to this problem was the fact that the supply department had stored some of its inventory in the wrong compartments, effectively losing a substantial portion of the inventory that was aboard. This, he explained, was one reason the clerks were less than helpful with the squadron supply sergeant – they didn't want to admit that they couldn't find spare parts that their own records showed they had.

Lieutenant Colonel Haldane went to see CAG, the air wing commander, and together they visited the ship's supply officer, then the executive officer. Jake didn't attend these meetings but he read one of the messages the captain of the ship sent out about shortages in the load-out manifest. Sparks were flying somewhere. Two chief petty officers in the supply department were given orders back to the States. Soon parts began to flow more freely into the squadron's maintenance department. One evening the supply sergeant stopped Jake in the passageway and thanked him.

It was a pleasant moment.

One day the flight schedule held a surprise. From the distant top branches of the Pentagon aviary came tasking for flights to photograph estuaries along the coast of North Vietnam. Told to stay just outside the three-mile limit, the aircrews marveled at these orders. They knew, even if the senior admirals did not, that even if the North Viets were preparing a mighty fleet to invade Hawaii and they managed to get photographs of the ships, with soldiers marching aboard carrying signs saying WAIKIKI OR BUST, the politicians in Washington would not, could not renew hostilities with the Communists in Hanoi. Still, orders were orders. In Ready Four the A-6 crews loaded 35-mm cameras with film, hung them around the BNs' necks, and went flying.

There were no enemy warships lurking in the estuaries. Just a few fishing boats.

It was weird seeing North Vietnam again, Jake told himself as he flew along at 3,000 feet, 420 knots, dividing his attention between the coast and his electronic counter-measures – ECM – alarms as Flap Le Beau busied himself with a hand-held 35-mm camera. The gomers were perfectly capable of squirting an SA-2 antiaircraft missile out this way, even if he was over international waters. Or two or three missiles. He kept an eye on the ECM and listened carefully for the telltale sounds of radar beams painting his aircraft.

And heard nothing. Not even a search radar. The air was dead.

The land over there on his right was partially obscured by haze, which was normal for this time of year. Yet there it was in all its pristine squalor – gomer country, low, flat and half-flooded. The browns and greens and blues were washed out by the haze. The place wasn't worth a dollar an acre, and certainly not anybody's life. That was the irony that made it what it was, a miserable land reeking of doom and pointless death.

Looking at it from this angle four miles off the coast, from the questionable safety of a cockpit, he could feel the horror, could almost see it, as if it were as real and tangible as fog. All those shattered lives, all those terrible memories . . .

They had fuel enough for thirty minutes of this fast cruising, then they planned to turn away from the coast and slow down drastically to save fuel. First Lieutenant Doug Harrison was somewhere up north just now, taking a peek into Haiphong Harbor. Grafton would meet him over the ship.

They were fifteen minutes into their mission when Jake first heard it – three different notes in his ears, notes with a funny rhythm. Da-de-duh . . . da-de-duh . . .

He reached for the volume knob on the ECM panel. Yes, but now there were four notes.

'Hear that?' he asked Flap.

'Yeah. What is it?'

'Sounds like a raster scan.'

'It's a MiG or F-4, man. Look, the A1 light is illumin—'

He got no more out because Jake Grafton had rolled the plane ninety degrees left and slapped on five G's as he punched out some chaff.

When the heading change was about ninety degrees, Jake rolled out some of the bank and relaxed the G somewhat. The coast was behind him and he was headed out to sea. The Air Intercept light remained illuminated and the tone continued in their ears, although it was back to three notes, a pause, then the three notes again.

'We're on the edge of his scan, but he sees us all right,' Flap said.

'Hang on.'

Throttles forward to the stops, Jake lowered the left wing and pulled hard until he had turned another ninety degrees. Now he was heading north. He let the nose drop and they slanted down toward the ocean. Meanwhile Flap was craning his head to see behind. Jake was looking too, then coming back inside to scan the instruments. Outside again . . . too many puffy clouds. He saw nothing.

The adrenaline was really pumping now.

'See anything?' he demanded of Flap.

'You'll be the first to hear if I do. I promise.'

Probably a Phantom, but it could be a MiG! Out over the ocean, in international waters. If it shot them down, who would know?

Or care?

Goddamn!

This A-6 was unarmed. Sidewinders could be fitted but Jake had never carried one, not even in training. This was an *attack* plane, not a fighter. And there was no gun. For reasons known only to God and Pentagon cost efficiency experts, the Navy had bought the A-6 without any internal guns. Against an enemy fighter it was defenseless.

The raster beat was tattooing their eardrums. Now they had a two-ring-strength strobe on the small Threat Direction Indicator – TDI. Almost directly aft.

He did another square corner, turning east again, then retarded the throttles to idle to lower the engines' heat signature and kept the plane in a gentle descent to maintain its speed. The enemy plane extended north, then turned, not as sharply. Now it was at five o'clock behind them.

Jake looked aft. Clouds. Oh, sweet Jesus! Dit-da-de-duh, dit-da-de-duh, dit-da-de-duh . . . the sound was maddening.

He was running out of sky. Passing eleven hundred feet. The ocean was down here.

He slammed the throttles full forward. As the engines wound up he pushed the nose over to convert what altitude he had into airspeed. He bottomed out at four hundred feet on the altimeter with 500 knots on the airplane. He pulled, a nice steady four-G pull.

He was climbing vertically, straight up, when he entered the clouds. Concentrating on the gauges, trying to ignore the insane beat of the enemy radar, he kept the stick back but eased out most of the G. Still in the clouds with the nose up ten degrees, he rolled upright and continued to climb.

The sound of the enemy's radar stopped. The MiG must have sliced off to one side or the other, be making a turn to reacquire him. But which way? He had been concentrating so hard on flying the plane that he hadn't had time to watch the TDI.

'Right or left?' he asked Flap.

'I dunno.'

The clouds were thinning. Lots more sunlight. Then the A-6 popped out on top.

Jake looked left, Flap right.

The pilot saw him first, three or four thousand feet above, turning toward them. An F-4.

'It's a fucking Phantom,' he roared over the ICS to Flap.

Flap spun and craned over Jake's shoulder. Then he flopped back in his seat and held up middle fingers to the world.

Jake raised his visor and swabbed his face. Now the strobe reappeared on the TDI and the music sounded in his ears. He reached with his right hand and turned the ECM equipment off.

The plane was climbing nicely. He engaged the auto-pilot, then turned to watch the F-4. It tracked inbound for several seconds, then turned away while it was still a half mile or so out.

Jake took off his oxygen mask and helmet and used his sleeve to swab the perspiration from his face. He was wearing his flight gloves, so he used them to wipe his hair. The sweat made black stains on his gloves and sleeve. Then he took off one glove and used his fingers to clean the stinging, salty solution from his eyes.

'Think he did that on purpose?' Flap demanded when he had his helmet back on and could again hear the ICS.

'How would I know?'

One evening as Jake entered the stateroom, his room-mate, the financier, glanced at him and groaned. 'Not another haircut! For heaven's sake, Jake, why don't you just shave your head and be done with it?'

Grafton surveyed his locks in the mirror over the sink. 'What are you quacking about? Looks okay to me.'

'Is this the third haircut this week?'

'Well, I admit, watching these Marines parade off to the barbershop on an hourly basis has had a corrosive effect on my morals. I feel like a scuz bucket if I don't go along. What are you caterwauling about? It's my head and it'll all grow out, sooner or later.'

'You're ruining my image, Grafton. Already they are giving me the evil eye. I feel like a spy in the house of love.'

'You've been reading Anaïs Nin, haven't you?'

'Bartow loaned me an edition in English. Wow, you ought to read some of that stuff! Ooh la la. It's broadening my horizons.'

'What are you working on this evening?' The Real had paper strewn all over his desk, but there wasn't a stock market listing in sight.

McCoy frowned and flipped some of the pages upside down so that Jake couldn't see them. Then he apparently thought better of his actions and sat back in his chair surveying Grafton. The frown faded. In a moment he grinned. 'We're going to cross the line in two days.'

The line – the equator. The task group was heading south-east, intending to sail around the island of Java and reenter the China Sea through the Sunda Strait. Of necessity the ship would cross the equator twice.

'So?'

'I'm the only officer shellback in the squadron. Everyone else is a pollywog, including you.'

A pollywog was a sailor who had never crossed the equator. A shellback was one who had previously crossed and been duly initiated into the Solemn Mysteries of the Ancient Order of Shellbacks. It was easy enough to find out who was and who wasn't. In accordance with naval regulations, all shellbacks had the particulars of their initiation recorded in their service records – ship, date and longitude.

'Too bad you'll miss out on all the fun,' Jake said carelessly.

McCoy chuckled. 'I ain't gonna miss a thing, shipmate, believe you me. I'm coming to the festivities as Davy Jones. But if you're willing, I could use a little help.'

Jake was aghast. 'Help from a lowly pollywog?'

'We'll have to keep this under our hats. Can't have scandalous things like this whispered around, can we? This would be help on the sly, for the greater glory of King Neptune.' He picked up the documents on his desk that he had turned over to keep Jake from seeing and passed them to his roommate.

The next two days passed quickly and pleasantly. Then the great day arrived. There was, of course, no flying scheduled. All morning people – presumably shellbacks – bustled around the ship on mysterious errands, with lots of giggling.

The pollywogs were given strict orders over the ship's loudspeaker system. They were to go to their staterooms or berthing compartments after the noon meal and remain there until summoned into the august presence of Neptunus Rex, Ruler of the Raging Main. Actually there were over two dozen Neptunes, selected strictly on seniority, i.e., the number of times they had crossed the line. Initiation ceremonies would be held simultaneously in ready rooms, berthing areas and mess decks throughout the ship, and each ceremony would be presided over by Neptunus Rex.

In his stateroom, Jake took off his uniform and pulled on a pair of civilian shorts. He donned a T-shirt and slid his feet into shower thongs. Then he settled back to wait for his summons.

It wasn't long in coming. The telephone rang. The duty officer. 'Pollywog Grafton, come to the ready room.'

'Aye aye, sir.'

Jake took off his watch and dog tags. After he checked to ensure that his stateroom key was in his pocket, he went out and locked the door behind him.

The ready room was rapidly filling with his fellow wogs. Jake slipped into his regular seat. Colonel Haldane was lounging in his seat near the duty officer's desk, chatting quietly with the executive officer. Alas, both officers were also wogs and were decked out for the festivities to come in jeans and Marine Corps green T-shirts. Standing everywhere around the bulkheads were officers from the air wing and other squadrons in uniform. Shellbacks. They immediately began to heckle the Marines, and Grafton.

'You're in for it now, wogs . . . Just you wait until King Neptune arrives . . . You slimy wogs are in deep and serious . . .'

The public address system crackled to life. Ding ding, ding ding, ding ding, ding ding, ding ding. Ten bells. 'Ruler of the Raging Main, arriving.'

A howl of glee arose from the onlookers, who laughed and pointed at the assembled victims, many of whom were making faces at their tormentors. Now Flap Le Beau stood in his chair, his arms folded across his chest. He was wearing a pillowcase on top of his head, held on with a band. His face was streaked with paint. As the onlookers hooted, he explained that he was an African king, ruler of the ancient kingdom of Boogalala, and he demanded deferential treatment from this Rex guy.

The shellbacks successfully shouted him down. Finally he sat, promising that he would renew his demands when the barnacled one arrived. One row behind him, Jake Grafton grinned broadly.

They didn't have long to wait. The door was flung open and the Real McCoy stalked in. 'Attention on deck,' he roared. The Marines snapped to attention like they were on parade. When everyone was erect and rigid, McCoy continued, 'All hail, Neptunus Rex, Ruler of the Ragin' Main.'

'Hail,' the assembled shellbacks shouted lustily.

Here they came, the royal party, led by the air wing commander, the CAG, who was decked out in a bedsheet. Behind him came Neptunus Rex, wearing a gold crown that looked suspiciously like it had been crafted of cardboard and spray painted. He wore swimming trunks and tennis shoes, but no shirt. His upper arms each bore a tattoo

244

of a well-endowed, totally naked woman and on his chest was a screaming eagle in flight. A bedsheet cape flowed behind him. In his hand he carried a cardboard trident. As he seated himself on his throne – a chair on a platform so that everyone had a good view – Jake recognized him, as did half the men in the room. Bosun Muldowski.

The Real McCoy – Davy Jones – took his place at the podium and adjusted the microphone. He was wearing long underwear, which he and Jake had decorated with a bottle of iodine last night in a vain attempt to paint fish, octopi and other sea creatures. Alas, the outfit just looked like a bloody mess, Jake decided now. McCoy was enjoying himself immensely, and it showed on his face.

Flap Le Beau stood up again in his chair. 'Hey, King! How's it going?'

McCoy frowned, CAG frowned, Neptune frowned.

'Sit down, wog! Show some respect in the royal presence.'

'Uh, Davy, you don't seem to understand. I'm King Flap of Boogalala. Being a king my very own self, I shouldn't be here in the company of these slimy pollywogs. I should be up there on a throne beside ol' Neptune discussing the many mind-boggling mysteries of the deep and how he's making out these days with the mermaids.'

'Well pleaded, King Flap.' The onlookers seemed to disagree, and hooted their displeasure. Davy looked over at Neptune. 'What say you, oh mighty windy one?'

Neptune scowled fiercely at the upstart Le Beau. 'Have you wogs no respect? The dominions of the land are irrelevant here upon the briny deep, where I am sovereign. I suggest, Davy, that the loud-mouth pretender kiss the royal baby three times.'

'Wog Le Beau, you heard the royal wish. Thrice you shall kiss the royal baby. Now sit and assume a becoming humility or you will again face the awesome wrath of mighty Neptune.'

Le Beau sat. He screwed up his face and tried to cry. And almost made it. A gale of laughter swept the room.

It was good to be a part of this foolishness, Jake Grafton thought, good to have a hearty laugh with your shipmates, fellow voyagers on this journey through life. He and the Real had worked hard to get some laughs, and they succeeded. Many of the wogs were hailed individually before the royal court and their sins set forth in lurid detail. Major Allen Bartow was confronted with a book labeled *S'il Vous Plaît* really a NATOPS manual with a suitable cover − from which spilled a dozen Playmate-of-the-Month foldouts.

'Reading dirty books, slobbering over dirty pictures . . . shame, shame!' intoned Davy Jones, and King Neptune pronounced the sentence: three trips through the tunnel of love.

After about an hour of this nonsense the wogs were led up to the hangar deck, then across it to an aircraft elevator, which lifted the entire Ready Four pollywog/shellback mob to the flight deck. There the remainder of the initiation ceremonies, and all of Neptune's verdicts, were carried out.

The tunnel of love was a canvas chute filled with garbage from the mess decks. All the wogs crawled through it at least once, the more spectacular sinners several times. At the exit of the tunnel were shellbacks with saltwater hoses to rinse off the garbage, but the wogs were only beginning their odyssey.

Next was the royal baby, the fattest shellback aboard, who sat on a throne without a shirt. His tummy was liberally coated with arresting gear grease. Victims were thrust forward to kiss his belly button. He enthusiastically assisted the unwilling, grabbing ears and smearing handfuls of grease in the supplicants' hair. After kisses from every three or four victims, able assistants regreased his gut from a fifty-five-gallon drum that sat nearby. A messy business from any angle . . .

A visit to the royal dentist was next on the list. This worthy squirted a dollop of a pepper concoction into his victim's mouths from a plastic ketchup dispenser. Expectoration usually followed immediately.

After a visit to the royal barber – more grease – and the royal gymnasium, the wogs ended their journey with a swim across the royal lagoon, a canvas pool six inches deep in water. No, Jake learned as he looked at the victims splashing along, the water was only about one inch deep. It floated on at least five inches of something green, something with a terrible smell. Shellbacks arranged around the lagoon busily offered opinions about what the noisome stuff might be. The wogs slithered through this mess to the other side, where shellbacks helped them out, wiped them down, and congratulated them heartily. Without hesitation Jake flopped down and squirmed his way through the goo while his squadron-mates on the other side – the ones who had beat him over – cheered and offered impractical advice.

Jake joined Flap Le Beau on the fantail, where they stood watching the proceedings and comparing experiences as they wiped away the worst of the grease with paper towels.

The ship wasn't moving, Jake noticed. She lay dead in the water on a placid, gently heaving sea. Around her at distances ranging from one to three miles her escorts were similarly still. All the ships were conducting crossing-the-line initiation ceremonies. Painted ships upon a painted ocean, Jake thought.

With a last glance at the sea and the sky and the merry group still cavorting on the flight deck, he headed below for the showers.

'Getting shot down was a real bad scene,' Flap le Beau told Jake. They were on a surface surveillance mission along the southern coast of Java, photographing ships. To their right was the mountainous island with its summits wreathed in clouds, to the left was the endless blue water. They had just descended to 500 feet to snap three or four shots of a small coaster bucking the swells westward and were back at 3,000 feet, cruising at 300 knots. The conversation had drifted to Vietnam.

Perhaps it was inevitable, since both men had been shot down in that war, but neither liked to talk about their experiences, so the subject rarely came up. If it did, it was in an oblique reference. Somehow today, in a cockpit in a tropic sky, the subject seemed safe.

'It was just another mission, another day at the office, and the gomers got the lead right and let us have it. I hadn't even seen flak that morning until we collected a packet. Goose was killed instantly – one round blew his head clean off, the left engine was hit, the left wing caught fire. All in about the time it takes to snap your fingers.'

'What were you doing?'

'Dive-bombing, near the Laotian border. We were the second plane in a two-plane formation, working with a Nail FAC.' A FAC was a forward air controller, who flew a small propeller-driven plane.

'We were on our second run. Oh, I know, we shouldn't have been making more than one, but the FAC hadn't seen any shit in the air and everything was cool during our first run. Then whap! They shot us into dog meat going down the chute. I grabbed the stick, pickled the bombs and pulled out, but the left engine was doing weird things and the wing was burning like a blowtorch and Goose was smeared all over everything, including me. Wind howling through the cockpit – all the glass on his side was mashed out. Real bad scene. So I steered it away from the target a little and watched the wing burn and told Goose good-bye, then I boogied.'

'How long did you wait before you ejected?'

'Seemed like an hour or so, but our flight leader told me

later it was about a minute. All the time he was screaming for me to eject because he could see the fire. But we were at about six thousand feet at that point and I wanted a little distance from the gomers and I wanted the plane slowed down so I wouldn't get tore up going out. There was so much noise I never heard anything on the radio.'

Jake remembered his own ejection, at night, over Laos. Just thinking about it brought back the sweats. He didn't say anything.

'When I got on the ground,' Flap continued, 'I got out my little radio and started talking. Now I'd checked the battery in that jewel before we took off, but I could barely hear the FAC. I found a place to settle in where I could keep an eye on the chute. Then the rescue turned to shit. The gomers were squirting flak everywhere and it was late in the afternoon and darkness was coming. What I didn't know until way afterward was that the guy flying the rescue chopper got a case of cold feet and decided his engine wasn't right or something. Anyway, he never came. It got dark and started raining and I decided I was on my own.'

'So how'd you feel?'

'Well, I felt real bad about Goose. He was a good guy, y'know? Tough getting it like that.'

'I mean how did *you* feel?'

'Like I had never left Marine recon. At least my jungle rot wasn't itching. That was something. I skinned out of all that survival gear and kept only what I needed and decided to set up an ambush. What I really wanted was a rifle. All I had was the forty-five. And my knife.'

'Didn't you think they might catch you?'

'No way, man. I knew they wouldn't. Couldn't. Not unless they shot me or something. I was on the ground for two weeks and had people walk by within six feet of me and they never saw me.'

'So what did you do?'

'Do? Well, I found a guy who had a rifle and took it, and his food. Ball of rice, with a lot of sand mixed in. You sort of have to develop a taste for it.'

'Uh-huh.'

'Checked in on the emergency freq about once a day, when the gomers weren't close. Didn't want to overwork the batteries in that radio. But they never heard me. A patrol found me on the fourteenth day. It was a good thing, because my jungle rot was starting to itch by then. You can never really cure that shit, you know.'

'So how many gomers did you kill?'

'A dozen that I know about.'

'Know about?'

'Yeah. I kept busy building booby traps and such. With a little luck the traps got a few more of 'em. In a way, it sort of made up for losing Goose. Not really, I guess. But it helped.'

'Uh-huh.'

'A fucked-up war, that's what it was. A hell of a mess.'

'Yeah,' Jake said, and checked the fuel and the clock on the instrument panel. 'I think we're going to have to turn around.'

'Okay,' Flap Le Beau said. 'Boy, it sure is pretty out here today.'

'There's a decision point for every career officer,' Lieutenant Colonel Haldane said, 'one day when you wake up and decide that you want to make a contribution. And for pilots, that doesn't mean driving an airplane through the sky every day.'

He and Jake were sitting in the ready room. Jake had the duty and sat at the duty desk and Haldane was in his chair just behind it. There was only one other officer in the room, doing paperwork near the mailboxes. Haldane's voice was low so that only Jake could hear it.

'True, some officers merely decide to stay until retirement, and I suppose that's okay. We need those people too. But the people we want are those who dedicate themselves to making the service better, to being leaders, people who try to grow personally and professionally every day. Those folks are few and far between but we need them desperately.'

Jake merely nodded. Haldane had read the latest classified messages and handed the board back to Jake just before he began this monologue. Apparently Jake's letter of resignation was on his mind, although he hadn't mentioned it.

Haldane went on, almost thinking out loud: 'In every war America fought before Vietnam, the people who led the military to victory were never the people in charge when the shooting started. US Grant and William T. Sherman weren't even in the army when the Civil War started. Phil Sheridan was a captain. Eisenhower and George Patton were colonels at the start of World War II, Halsey and Nimitz were captains. Curious, don't you think?'

Before Jake could reply, he continued, 'In peacetime the top jobs go to politicians, men who can stroke the civilians and oil the wheels of the bureaucracy. During a war the system works the way it is supposed to – men who can lead other men in combat are pulled to the top and given command. In Vietnam this natural selection process was stymied by the politicians. It was a political war all the way and the last thing they wanted was to relinquish the controls to war fighters. So we lost. And you know something funny? We could afford to lose because we didn't have anything important at stake in the first place.

'Someday America is going to get into a fight it has to win. I don't know when it will come or who the fight will be with. That war may come next year, or twenty years from now, or fifty. Or a hundred. But it *will* come. It always has in the past and evolution doesn't seem to be improving the human species anywhere near fast enough.

251

'The question is, who will be in the military when that war comes? Will the officer corps be full of glorified clerks, efficiency experts and computer operators putting in their time to earn a comfortable retirement? Or will there be some military leaders in that mix, men who can lead other men to victory, men like Grant, Patton, Halsey?'

Haldane rose from his chair and adjusted his trousers. 'Interesting question, isn't it, Mr Grafton?'

'Yessir.'

'The quality of the people in uniform – such a little thing. And that may make all the difference.'

Haldane turned and walked out. The officer doing paperwork had already left. Jake pulled out the top drawer of the desk and propped his feet up on it.

That Haldane – a romantic. Blood, thunder, destiny . . . If he thought that kind of talk cut any ice anymore he was deluding himself. Not in this post-Vietnam era. Not with the draft dodgers who didn't want to go and not with the veterans who weren't so quick.

Jake Grafton snorted. He had had his fill of this holy military crap! His turn expired when this boat got back to the States in February. Then somebody else could do it.

And if the United States goes down the slop chute someday because no one wants to fight for it, so be it. No doubt the Americans alive then will get precisely what they deserve, ounce for ounce and measure for measure.

What was that quote about the mills of the gods? They grind slowly?

CHAPTER SIXTEEN

Singapore lies at the southern end of the Malay peninsula, a degree and a half north of the equator. This city is the maritime crossroads of the earth. Ships from Europe by way of Suez and the Red Sea, India, Pakistan, Africa and the Middle East transit the Strait of Malacca and call here before entering the South China Sea. Ships from America, Japan, China, Taiwan, Korea and the Soviet Far East call here on their way west. The city-state is close enough to the Sunda Strait that it makes a natural port call for ships from the Orient bound for South Africa or South America via the Cape of Good Hope.

Although it is one of the world's great seaports, Singapore doesn't have a harbor. The open roadstead is always crammed with ships riding their anchors, except on those rare occasions when a typhoon threatens. There are few piers large enough for an oceangoing vessel, so the majority of the cargo being off- or on-loaded in Singapore travels to and from the ships in lighters. The squadrons of these busy little boats weaving their way through the anchored ships from the four corners of the earth and all the places in between make Singapore unique.

As befits a great seaport, the city is a racial melting pot. The human stew is composed mostly of Malay, Chinese, Thai, Hindu, Moslem, and Filipino, with some Japanese added for seasoning, but there are whites there too. British, primarily, because Singapore was one of those outposts of empire upon which the sun never set, but also people from most of the countries of Europe, Australia, New Zealand, and, inevitably, America.

Visitors who have always considered their place, their nation, as the zenith of civilization here receive a shock. Vibrant, cosmopolitan Singapore is a major vortex, one of those rare places where the major strains of the human experience come crashing together and swirl madly around until something new is created.

To the delight of visiting American sailors, the British still had a military base there, Changi, and shared it with those stout lads from Down Under, the Australians, who naturally came supplied with Down Under lassies. Australian women were the glory of Singapore. These tall, lithe creatures with tanned, muscular legs and striking white teeth that were forever being displayed in dazzling smiles somehow completed the picture, made it whole. You ran into them at Raffles, the old hotel downtown with ceiling fans and rattan chairs and doddery old gentlemen in white suits sipping gin. You ran into them in the lobbies and restaurants of the new western hotels and in the bazaars and emporiums. You saw them strolling the boulevards and haggling with small Chinese women in baggy trousers for sapphires and opals. You saw them everywhere, young, tan, enjoying life, the center of attention wherever they were. It helped that their colorful tropical frocks contrasted so vividly with the drab trousers and white shirts that seemed to be the Singaporean national costume. They were like songbirds surrounded by sparrows.

'If Qantas didn't bring them here, the United Nations should supply them as a gesture of good will to all human kind.'

Flap Le Beau stated this conclusion positively to Jake Grafton and the Real McCoy as they stood outside Raffle Hotel surveying the human parade on the sidewalk.

'I think I'm in love,' the Real McCoy told his companions. 'I want one of those for my very own.'

254

The three of them had ridden the liberty boat two miles across the anchorage an hour ago. They had walked for an hour, taking it all in and had developed a terrible thirst. Just now they were contemplating going into Raffles to see if their need could be quenched somewhat.

'After forty-five days at sea, everything female looks mighty good to me,' Flap Le Beau said, then smiled broadly at an elderly British lady coming out of the hotel. She nodded graciously in reply and seated herself in a waiting taxi.

'Well, gentlemen,' Jake Grafton said, and turned to face the white antique structure, 'shall we?'

'Let's.'

The temperature inside was at least ten degrees cooler. The dark interior and the ceiling fans apparently had a lot to do with that, but the very Britishness of the place undoubtedly helped. The heat and humidity could stay outside – it wouldn't dare intrude.

The American aviators went to the bar and ordered – of all things – Singapore slings. The waiter, a Chinese, didn't bat an eye. He nodded and moved on. He had long ago come to terms with the curious taste of liquor that seemed to afflict most Americans.

'You sort of expect to see Humphrey Bogart or Sidney Greenstreet sitting around under a potted palm,' the Real commented as he tilted his chair back and crossed his legs.

Jake Grafton sipped his drink in silence. Forty-five days at sea riding the catapults, night rendezvouses above the clouds, instrument approaches to the ball, mid-rats sliders, ready room high jinks, lying in his bunk while the ship moved ever so gently in the sea as he listened to the creaks and groans . . . then to be baptized with a total immersion in *this*. Cultural shock didn't begin to describe it. The sights and sounds and smells of Singapore were sensory overload for a young man from a floating monastery.

He sat now trying to take it all in, to adjust his frame of reference. He had been here once before, on one of his cruises to Vietnam. He tried to recall some details of that visit, but the memories were vague, blurred scenes just beyond the limits of complete recall. He had sat here in this room with Morgan McPherson . . . at which table? He couldn't remember. Morgan's face, laughing, he could see that, but the room . . . Who else had been there?

Oh, Morg! If you could only be here again. To sit here and share a few moments of life. We wouldn't waste it like we did then. If only . . .

So many of those guys were dead. And he had forgotten. That the moments he had spent with them were fuzzy and blurred seemed a betrayal of what they had been, what they had given. Life goes on, but still . . . All that any man can leave behind are the memories that this friends carry. He isn't really gone until they are. But if the living quickly forget, it is as if the dead man never was.

'. . . we oughta go buy some souvenirs,' the Real was saying. 'The folks at home would really like . . .'

Jake polished off the last of his drink and stood. He threw some Singapore dollars on the table, money he had acquired this morning from the money changers aboard ship. 'See you guys later.'

'Where are you going?'

He was going back to the ship, but he didn't want to say that. 'Oh, I dunno. Gonna just walk. See you later.'

Outside on the street he stuffed his hands into his pockets and turned toward the wharves. He walked along staring at the sidewalk in front of him, oblivious of the traffic and the sights and the human stream that parted to let him past, then immediately closed in behind him.

The next day Jake stood an eight-hour duty officer watch in the ready room. About two in the afternoon the Real McCoy came breezing in.

'Today's your lucky day, Grafton. You are blessed to have Flap and me for friends. Truly blessed.'

'I know,' Jake told him dryly.

'We met some Brits. What a bunch they are! How we ever kicked them out of the good ol' US of A is a mystery I'll never understand.'

'A military miracle.'

'These are *good* guys.'

'I'm sure.'

'They've invited us to a party at Changi this evening. A party! And they swore that some Aussie women would be there! Quantas stews. Can you beat that?' Without pausing to let Jake wrestle with that question, he steamed on. 'When do you get off?'

'Uh, two hours from now.'

The Real consulted his watch. 'I'll wait. Flap is taking the next boat in, but I'll wait for you. I've got directions. We'll grab a cab and tootle on over to *party hearty*. Maybe, just maybe, we'll get a glorious opportunity to lower the white count. Oooh boy!'

McCoy strode up the aisle between the huge, soft chairs, past the silent 16-mm movie projector, and blasted through the door into the passageway.

Jake sat back in his chair and opened the letter from his parents yet again. It had been two weeks since the last mail delivery, via a cargo plane out of Cubi Point, and this was the current crop, delivered this morning – one letter from his mother. She signed it 'Mom and Dad,' but she wrote every word. Nothing from Callie McKenzie.

Maybe that was for the best. It had been a hell of a romance, but now it was over. She was from one world, he was from a completely different one. Presumably she was doing her own thing there in Chicago, going to class and dating some long-haired hippie intellectual who liked French novels. What was it about French novels?

But he desperately wished she had written. Even a Dear

John letter would be preferable to this vast silence, he told himself, wanting to believe it but not quite sure that he did.

Oh well. Like most of the things in his life, this relationship was out of his control. Have a nice life, Callie McKenzie. Have a nice life.

Darkness comes quickly in the tropics. Twilight is an almost instantaneous transition from daylight to darkness. Jake, Flap and the Real had just arrived at Changi by taxi and found the outdoor pavilion when the transition occurred. Whoom, and the lanterns in the pavilion were flickering bravely against the mighty darkness.

The Brit and Aussie soldiers had indeed not forgotten their invitation of the afternoon. They led the three Americans around and introduced them, but Flap was the only surefire hit with the ladies. Soon he had all five of the women gathered around him.

'The Aussies aren't used to black men wearing pants,' the Real whispered to Jake. 'Those stews will get over the novelty in a while and we'll get a chance to cut a couple out.'

Jake wasn't so sure. The soldiers seemed to be eyeing the crowd around Flap with a faint trace of dismay. Nothing obvious, of course, but Jake thought he could see it.

'Hey, mate. How about a beer?' The Australian who asked held out a couple of cold bottles of Fosters.

'Thanks. Real hard duty you guys got here.'

'Beats the outback. Beats that scummy little war you Yanks gave in the Nam, too. Saigon was a bit of all right but the rest of it wasn't so cheery. This is mighty sweet after that busman's holiday, I can tell you.'

'It was the only war we had,' the Real explained, then poured beer down his throat. Jake Grafton did the same.

Two beers later Jake Grafton was sitting at a table in the corner listening to Vietnam War stories from a couple of the Aussies when one of the stews came over to join them. 'Mind if I join you chaps?'

'Not at all, not at all. Brighten up the party. How long are you in for this time, Nell?'

'Off to Brisbane and Sydney tomorrow. Then back here via Tokyo the following day.' Nell winked at Jake. 'Girl has to keep herself busy now, doesn't she?'

Grafton nodded and grinned. Nell returned it. She was a little above medium height, with fair hair and a dynamite tan. Several gold bracelets encircled each of her wrists and made tiny tinkly noises when she moved her arms.

'My name's Jake,' he told her.

'Nell Douglas,' she said, and stuck out her hand. Jake shook it. Cool and firm. And then he looked around and realized the Aussies had drifted and he and Nell were alone.

'So what do you do for the Yanks?'

'I'm a pilot.'

'Oh, God!' Not another one. I've sworn off pilots for at least three months.' She smiled again. He liked the way her eyes smiled when she did.

'Better tell me about it. Nothing like a sympathetic listener to ease a broken heart.'

'You don't look like the sympathetic type.'

'Don't be fooled by appearances. I'm sensitive, sympathetic, charming, warm, witty, wonderful.' He shrugged. 'Well, part of that's true, anyway. I'm warm.'

Now her whole face lit up. Her bracelets tinkled.

'How long have you been flying with Qantas?'

'Five years. My father has a station in Queensland. One day I said to myself, Nell old girl, if you stay here very much longer one of these jackeroos will drag you to the altar and you'll never see any more of the world than you've seen already, which wasn't very much, I can tell you. So I applied to Qantas. And here I am, flying around the globe with my little stew bag and makeup kit, serving whiskey to Japanese businessmen, slapping pilots, giving lonely soldiers the hots, and wondering if I'm ever going back to Queensland.'

'What's a jackeroo?'

'You Yanks call them cowboys.'

This could be something nice, Jake thought, looking at the marvelous, open, tanned female face and feeling himself warmed by her glow. There are a lot of pebbles on the beach and some of them are nuggets, like this one.

'So a station's a ranch?'

'Yes. Sheep and cattle.'

'I was raised on a farm myself. Dad ran a few steers, but mainly he raised corn.'

'Ever going back?' Nell asked.

'I dunno. Never say never. I might.'

She told him about the station in Queensland, about living so far from anything that the world outside seemed a fantasy, a shimmering legend amid the heat and dust and thunderstorms. As she talked he glanced past the lanterns into the darkness beyond, at that place where the mown grass and the velvet blackness met. The night was out there as usual, but here, at least, there was light.

An hour or so later someone turned on the radio and several of the women wanted to dance. To Jake's surprise Flap 'Go Ugly Early' Le Beau proved good at dancing, slow or fast, so good that he did only what his partner could do. You had to watch him with three or four of the sheilas before you realized that he sensed their skill level almost instantaneously and asked of them only what they had to give. Nell pointed that out to Jake, who saw it then. She danced a fast number with Flap – she was very good – as the Aussies and Brits watched appreciatively. They applauded when the number ended.

Nell rejoined Jake and led him out onto the floor for the next slow number. 'I don't dance very well,' he told her.

'That's not the point,' she said, and settled in against him to the beat of the languid music.

It was then that Jake Grafton realized he was in over his head. The supple body of the woman against his chest, the caress of her hair on his cheek, the faint scent of a cologne he didn't recognize, the touch of her hands against his – all this was having a profound effect and he wasn't ready.

'Relax,' she whispered.

He couldn't.

The memory of his morning in bed with Callie four months ago came flooding back. He could see the sun coming through the windows, feel the clean sheets and the sensuous touch of her skin . . .

'You're stiff as a board.'

'Not quite.'

'Oops. Didn't mean it quite that way, love.'

'I'm not a very good dancer.'

She moved away a foot or so and looked searchingly into his face. 'You're not a very good liar either.'

'I'm working on it.'

She led him by the hand through the crowd and out of the pavilion into the darkness. 'Why is it all the good ones come with complications?'

'At our age virgins are hard to find,' Jake told her.

'I quit looking for virgins years and years ago. I just want a man who isn't too scarred up.'

She led him to a wall and hopped up on it. 'Okay, love. Tell Ol' Nell all about it.'

Jake Grafton grinned. 'How is it that a fine woman like you isn't married?'

'You want the truth?'

'If you feel like it.'

'Well, the truth is that I didn't want the ones who proposed and the ones I wanted didn't propose. Propose marriage, that is. They had a lot of things in mind but a trek to the altar wasn't on the list.'

'That sounds like truth.'

'It is that, ducky.'

The music floating across the lawn was muted but clearly audible. And she was right there, sitting on the wall. Instinctively he moved closer and she put an arm around his shoulder. Their heads came together.

Before very long they were kissing. She had good, firm lips, a lot like Callie's. Of course Callie was . . .

His heart was thudding like a drum when they finally parted for air. After a few deep breaths, he said, 'There's another woman.'

'Amazing.'

'I'm not married or anything like that. And I haven't asked her to marry me, but I wanted to.'

'Uh-huh.'

'I think she gave up on me. Hasn't written in a couple months.'

'You like your women dumb, then?' she asked softly, and put her lips back on his.

Somehow she was off the wall and they were entwined in each other's arms, their bodies pressed together. When their lips parted this time, a ragged breath escaped her. 'Whew and double whew. You Yanks! Sex-starved maniacs, that's what you are.'

She eased away from him. 'Well, that was my good deed for today. I've given another rejected, love-starved pilot hope for a brighter future. Now I think it's time for this Sheila to trek off to her lonely little bed. Must fly tomorrow, you know.'

'Going to be back in Singapore day after tomorrow?'

'Yes.'

'What hotel? Maybe I can stop by and take you to dinner.'

'The Intercontinental.'

'I'll walk inside with you.'

'No, just stay where you are, mate. I've had quite enough

tonight. One more good look at you in the light and I might drag you off to my lonely little bed for a night of sport. Can't have that, can we, not with you pining your heart out for that other silly girl.'

'With that she was gone. Across the lawn and into the crowd.

Jake Grafton leaned on the wall and lit a cigarette. His hands were trembling slightly.

He didn't know quite what to think, so he didn't think anything. Just inhaled the cut-grass smell and looked into the darkness and let his heart rate subside to its normal plodding pace.

At least half an hour passed before Jake went back into the pavilion. Three half-potted Aussies were huddled around the piano watching Flap dance with the three stews who were still there. Le Beau had them in a line and was teaching them new steps to the wailing of a Japanese music machine. Everyone else had left, including the Real McCoy. Tomorrow was a working day for most of them.

Jake decided one more beer for the road wouldn't hurt, so he picked a bottle out of the icy water of the tub and joined the piano crowd.

'Hey, mate.'

'How you guys doing tonight?'

'Great.'

'Sure nice of you fellows to invite us to your wing ding. Makes a good break after forty-five days at sea.'

'Don't know how you blokes manage.'

'Prayer,' Jake told them, and they laughed.

The biggest of them was a brawny man three or four inches taller than Jake and at least forty pounds heavier. Most of his bulk was in his chest, shoulders and arms. He hadn't said anything yet, but now he gestured to Flap. 'Wish your bleedin' nigger mate would pick his bird and let us at the other two.'

Jake Grafton carefully set his beer on the piano. This was getting to be a habit. The last time they had sent him to the Marines.

Wonder where they'll send me this time?

He stepped in front of the big Aussie, who still had one giant mitt wrapped around a bottle of beer.

'What did you say?'

'I said, I wish your bleedin' nigger mate would—'

As Jake drew back his right fist for a roundhouse punch he jabbed the Aussie in the nose with his left. This set the man momentarily off balance, so when the right arrived on his chin with all Jake's weight behind it, it connected solidly with a meaty thunk that rocked Jake clear to the shoulder. The Aussie went backward onto the floor like he was pole-axed. And he stayed there.

'Nice punch, mate, but you—' said the one to the left, but his words stopped when Jake's fist arrived. The man took it solidly on the side of the head and sent a right at Jake that connected and shook him badly.

Stars swam before Grafton's eyes. He waded in swinging furiously. Some of his punches missed, some hit. That was the lesson he had learned as a boy on the grade school playground – keep swinging and going forward. Most boys don't really like to fight, so when you keep swinging they will fall back, and ultimately quit. Of course, these soldiers weren't boys and worse, they *liked* to fight.

His attack worked for several seconds, then the third Aussie, who was now behind him, grabbed him and spun him around. Before Jake could get set he took a shot on the cheekbone that put him down.

Dazed, he struggled to rise. When he got to his feet it was too late. All three of the Aussies were asleep on the floor and Flap Le Beau was standing there calmly scrutinizing him.

'What was that all about?'

Jake swayed and caught himself by grabbing the piano.

'They insulted Elvis.'

Flap sighed. 'I guess we've worn out our welcome.' He took Jake's arm and got him started for the door. 'Ladies,' he said, addressing the three stews gaping at them, 'it's been a real treat. The pleasure of your company was sweeter than you will ever know.'

He beamed benignly at them and steered Jake out into the night.

The base was quiet. No taxi at the main gate. They waved at the sentry and kept walking. Jake's right hand throbbed and so did his head. The hand was the important thing, though. He rubbed it as he walked.

'What really happened back there?' Flap asked.

'The big stud called you a nigger.'

'You hit him for *that*?'

'Yeah. The asshole deserved it.'

Flap Le Beau threw back his head and laughed. 'Damn, Jake, you are really something else.'

'He was peeved because you were monopolizing the women.'

Flap thought this was hilarious. He roared with laughter.

'Want to tell me what's so damn funny?'

'You are. You nitwit! All of them are bigots. Even the women. I wasn't getting anywhere with them. Not a one of those women would have gone to bed with me, not even if I was the richest nigger in America and had a cock eighteen inches long. They'll go back to Australia and tell all about their big adventure, talking to and dancing with an American *nigger*. "Oh, Matilda, you won't believe this, but I even let him *touch* me." '

Jake didn't know what to say, so he said nothing.

After a bit Flap asked, 'Think you broke your hand?'

'Dunno. Don't think so. Maybe stoved it. Man, I got that big guy with a perfect shot. Had everything behind it and drove it right through his chin.'

'He never moved after you hit him. Bet it's the first time anybody ever knocked him out.'

'Thanks for coming to the rescue, Kemo Sabe.'

'Any time, Tonto. Any time. But you could have broken your hand hitting that guy that hard.'

'Had to. He outweighed me by forty pounds. If I had just given him a you-piss-me-off social punch he would have killed me.'

'You're a violent man, Jake.'

'I had a lot of trouble with potty training.'

The next morning he realized the dimensions of the quandary he faced. Nell Douglas was a fine woman, passionate, level-headed, intelligent, thoughtful ... And Callie McKenzie was one fine woman, also passionate and level-headed, intelligent, educated, well spoken ... He was in love with one and could easily fall in love with the other. But the woman he loved hadn't written in two months and had made it clear that he wasn't measuring up.

The woman he could love wasn't being quite so picky. No doubt when he knew her better she would get more picky – women were like that. But she wasn't being picky *now!* And if you couldn't take the heat there was always celibacy to fall back on.

Alas, celibacy didn't seem very attractive to Jake Grafton. Not when you are in your twenties, in perfect health, when the sight, smell and touch of a woman make the blood pound in your temples and your knees turn to jelly.

He sat in his chair in his stateroom savoring the memories of last night. Of how her lips had felt against his, how her hot, wet tongue had speared between his teeth and stroked his tongue, how her breasts had heaved against his chest, how her thighs had pressed against his while her hands stroked his back. Gawd Almighty!

He liked the way she talked, too. That flat Australia

266

wang was sexy as hell. Just made shivers run up your spine when you recalled how the words sounded as she said them. '. . . I might drag you off to my lonely little bed for a night of sport.' Well, lady, I wish . . .

I don't know what I wish! Damnation.

He was writhing on the horns of this dilemma when the door opened and the Real McCoy staggered through. He flopped into his bunk and groaned. 'Wake me up next week. I am spent. Wrung out like a sponge. That woman turned me every way but loose. There are hot women and there are *hot* women. That one was a thermonuclear.'

'Tough night, huh?'

'She was after me every hour! I didn't sleep a wink. Every *hour!* I'm so sore I can hardly walk.'

'Lucky you escaped her evil clutches.'

'Never in my born days, Jake, did I even contemplate that there might be women like *that* walking the surface of the earth. Australia is merely the greatest nation on the planet, that's all. That they breed women like *that* down there is the best-kept secret of our time.'

Jake nodded thoughtfully and flexed his right fist. It was sore and a little swollen.

'I'm getting out of the Nav, arranging to have my subscription to the *Wall Street Journal* sent to me Down Under, and I am going south. May the cold, blue light of Paris never again meet my weary gaze. It's the Southern Cross for me, Laddie Buck. I'm going to Australia to see if I can fuck myself to death before I'm forty.'

With that pronouncement the Real McCoy turned on his side and curled his pillow under his head. Jake looked at his watch. The first gentle snore came seventy-seven seconds later.

Were the women bigots? Well, Flap should know. If he and those three stews were prejudiced, they probably were. But what about Nell?

And what about you, Jake? Are you?

Aaugh! To waste a morning in port fretting about crap like this.

He pulled a table around and started a letter to his parents.

The liberty boat for the enlisted men was an LCI – landing craft infantry – a flat-bottomed rectangular-shaped boat with a bow door that flopped down to let troops run through the surf onto the beach. Jake often rode it from the beach to the ship. This evening, however, he was dressed in a sports coat and a tie and didn't want to get soaked with salt spray, so he headed for the officers' brow near Elevator Two. The captain's gig and admiral's barge had been lowered into the water from their cradles in the rear of the hangar bay. In ten minutes he was descending the ladder onto the float, then he stepped into the gig.

Jake knew the boat officer, a jaygee from a fighter squadron, so he asked if he could stand beside the coxswain on the little midships bridge. Permission was granted with a grin and a nod. The rest of the officers went below in either the fore or aft cabin.

With the stupendous bulk of the carrier looming like a cliff above them, the sailors threw the lines aboard and the coxswain put the boat in motion. It stood out from the ship and swung in a wide circle until it was on course for fleet landing.

The water was calm this evening, with merely a low, low swell stirring the oily surface. The red of the western sky stained the water between the ships, gave it the look of diluted blood.

The roadstead was full of ships: freighters, coasters, tankers, all riding on their anchors. Lighters circled around a few of the ships, but only a few. Most of them motionless like massive steel statues in a huge park lake.

But there were people visible on most of the ships. As the gig threaded its way through the anchorage Jake co see them sitting under awnings on the fantails, sometimes cooking on barbecue grills, talking and smoking on after-decks crowded with ship's gear. Most of the sailors were men, but on one Russian ship he saw three women, hefty specimens in dresses that reached below their knees.

'Pretty evening,' the jaygee said to Jake, who agreed.

Yes, another gorgeous evening, the close of another good day to be alive. It was easy to forget the point of it all sometimes, easy to lose sight of the fact that the name of the game was to stay alive, to savor life, to live it day to day at the pace that God intended.

One of Jake Grafton's talents was to imagine himself living other lives. He hadn't been doing much of that lately, but riding the gig through the anchorage, looking at the ships, he could visualize sitting on one of those fantails, smoking and chatting and watching the sun sink closer and closer to the sea's rim. To go to sea and work the ship and spend quiet evenings in port in the company of friends – it would be very good. *I could live that way*, he reflected.

Maybe in my next incarnation.

The Intercontinental was a huge, modern hotel built on a slight hill. The lobby was a cavern seven or eight stories high. Marble floors accented with giant potted plants, a raised bar with easy chairs in the middle, all the accents a lush burgundy, polyester fabric glued to the walls – yuck!

Jake settled into one of the bar's overstuffed polyester chairs and tilted his head back. You could almost get dizzy looking up at the balconies, which were stacked closer and closer together until they met at the ceiling. Tropical plants hung from planters along each balcony, so the view upward was green. Dark green, because the lighting up here was very poor.

'Grotesque, isn't it?'

He dropped his gaze from the green canopy above to the young woman walking toward him. he stood and grinned.

ep.'

'The interior designer was obviously demented.' Nell Douglas settled into the chair opposite. A waiter appeared and hovered.

'Something to drink?' Jake asked her politely.

'A glass of white wine, please.'

'Scotch on the rocks.'

The waiter broke hover and disappeared behind a large potted leafy green thing.

'So how was your flight in?'

'Bumpy. Storms over the South China Sea. How's your hand?'

'You heard about that, huh?'

'The other girls were all atwitter. Your black friend really impressed them.'

'Flap can move pretty fast when he wants to. He's handy to have around.'

'If the necessity arises to knock people senseless. Is he lurking nearby now, just in case?'

Vaguely uneasy, Jake flashed a polite smile. 'No, I think he came ashore earlier today hoping to cheat some opal merchants. And my hand's fine.' He wiggled his fingers at her, pretending she cared.

Their drinks came and they sat sipping them in silence, both man and woman trying to sense the mood of the other.

After a bit Nell said, 'He's some kind of trained killer, isn't he?'

That comment was like glass shattering. Amazingly, Jake Grafton felt a tremendous sense of relief. It had been a nice fantasy, but this woman was not Callie.

'I guess everyone in combat arms is,' he said slowly, 'you want to look at it that way. I deal in high explosive myself. I fly attack planes, not airliners.'

He took the plastic stir stick from his drink and chewed at it. Why do they put these damn things in a drink that's nothing but whiskey and ice? He took it out of his mouth and broke it between his fingers as he examined her face.

'I started the fight,' he continued, now in a hurry to end it. 'One of the soldiers referred to Captain Le Beau as a nigger. He happens to be my BN and a personal friend. He is also a fine human being. The fact that his skin is black is about as important as the fact that my eyes are gray. That word is an insult in America and here. The man who said it knew that.'

'The only black people in Australia are aborigines.'

'I guess you have to be an American to understand.'

'Perhaps.'

The waiter reappeared with his credit card and the invoice. Jake added a tip, signed it and pocketed the card and his copy.

Her face was too placid. Blank. Time to get this over with. 'Would you like to go to dinner?'

Nell Douglas looked this way and that, apparently searching for something to say.

Finally she sat her wineglass on the table and leaned forward slightly. She looked him in the eye. 'It was wonderful the other night, and I am sure you are a fine person, but let's leave it at that.'

He nodded and finished his drink.

'We grew up on opposite sides of the world.' She stood and held out her hand. 'Thanks for the drink.'

'Sure.'

Jake stood and shook. She threaded her way through the potted jungle and made for the elevators.

'Did you get laid?' the Real McCoy asked late that night in their stateroom aboard ship.

'She said we grew up on opposite sides of the world.'

'You idiot. You're suppose to fuck 'em, not discuss philosophy.'

'Well, it probably turned out for the best,' Jake said,

thinking of Callie. He desperately wished she would write. She could write anything – if she would just put *something* in an envelope and stick a stamp on it.

He decided to write her.

He got a legal pad, climbed into the top bunk and adjusted the light just so. Then he began. He went through their relationship episode by episode, almost thought by thought, pouring out his heart. After eight pages he ground to a halt.

Every word was true, but he wasn't going to send it. He wasn't going to take the chance that he cared more than she did.

You aren't going to get very far with the fairer sex if you aren't willing to take some risks.

I'm tired of taking risks. Someone else can take a few.

Faint heart never won—

If she cared, she'd write. End of story.

The night before the ship weighed anchor Lieutenant Colonel Haldane asked Jake to come to his stateroom. According to the duty officer. Jake went.

Flap was already there sitting in the only chair. Jake sat on the colonel's bed and Flap passed him a sheet of paper. It was a letter from the commander at Changi. Fight in the pavilion. Jake scanned it quickly and passed it back to Flap, who handed it to Haldane, who tossed it on his desk.

'The skipper of the ship got this. He wants me to investigate, take action, and draft a reply for his signature. What can you tell me?'

Jake told the colonel about the incident, withholding nothing.

'Any comments, Captain Le Beau?'

'No, sir. I think Mr Grafton covered it.'

Haldane made a face. 'Okay. That's all. We're having a

back-in-the-saddle NATOPS do in the ready room at zero seven-thirty. See you there.'

Both the junior officers left. Jake closed the door behind him.

Twenty frames down the passageway he asked Flap, 'Was that it? We aren't in hack or candidates for keelhauling?'

'Naw. Haldane will apologize profusely to our allies, tell them that he's ripped us a new one, and that's that. It was just a friendly little social fight. What more could there be?'

Jake shrugged. 'My hand's still sore.'

'Next time kick 'em in the balls.'

CHAPTER SEVENTEEN

At dawn one morning the task group weighed anchor and entered the Strait of Malacca. With Sumatra on the left and the Malay peninsula on the right, the ships steamed at 20 knots for the Indian Ocean, or the IO as the sailors called it, pronouncing each letter.

In the narrows the strait was a broad watery highway with land on each horizon. The channel was dotted with fishing boats and heavily traversed by tankers and freighters. As many as a half dozen of the large ocean-going ships were visible at any one time.

As usual in narrow waterways, the carrier's flight deck and island superstructure were crowded with sightseeing sailors. Typically, Jake Grafton was among them, standing on the bow facing forward. With all of the great ship behind him the sensation was unique, almost as if one were a seabird soaring along at sixty feet above the water into the teeth of a 20-knot wind.

This morning Jake watched the steady stream of civilian ships and marveled. He had flown enough surface surveillance missions over the open ocean to appreciate how empty the oceans of the earth truly were. Often he and Flap flew a two-hour flight and saw not a single ship, just endless vistas of empty sea and sky. Yet here the ships plowed the brown water like trucks thundering along an interstate highway.

A hundred years ago these waters hosted sailing ships. As he stood on the bow watching the ships and boats this

274

morning he thought about those sailing ships, for Jake
Grafton had a streak of romance in him about a foot wide.
Clipper ships bound for China for a load of tea left England
and the eastern ports of the United States and sailed south
to round the Cape of Good Hope on the southern tip of
Africa. The sailors would have gotten close enough to land
for a glimpse of Africa only in good weather. Then they
crossed the vast Indian Ocean and entered this strait, where
they saw land for the first time since leaving England or
America. Months at sea working the ship, making sail,
reefing in storms, watching the officers shoot the sun at
noon and the stars at night when the weather allowed, then
to hit this strait after circumnavigating half the globe –
it was a great thing, a thing to be proud of, a thing to
remember for the rest of their lives. Exotic China still lay
ahead, but here the sailors probably saw junks for the first
time, those flat-bottomed Chinese sailing ships that carried
the commerce of the Orient. Here two worlds touched.

Jake looked at the freighters and tankers with new
interest. Perhaps he should look into getting a mate's
license, consider the merchant marine after the Navy. It
was a thing to think on.

Standing on the bow with the moist wind in his hair and
the smell of the land filling his nostrils as the task group
transited this narrow passage between two great oceans, he
was struck by how large the earth really was, how diverse
the human life, how many truths there must be. The US
Navy was a tiny part of it, surely, but only a tiny part. He
had been confined long enough. He needed to reach out
and embrace the whole.

The Indian Ocean lay ahead, beyond that watery horizon. The flying there would be blue water ops, without the
safety net of a divert field ashore. The ship would be
hundreds of miles from land, so when the planes burned
enough fuel to get down to landing weight there would
be no dry spot on earth they could reach with the fuel

remaining in their tanks. They had to get abroad. Airborne tankers could provide fuel for another handful of attempts, but their presence would not change the scenario – every pilot would have to successfully trap or eject into the ocean.

Carrier aviation never gets easier. The challenge is to develop and maintain skills that are just good enough. In this war without bullets the stakes were human lives. Each pilot would have only his skill and knowledge to keep him alive in the struggle against the weather, chance, the vagaries of fate. Some would lose. Jake Grafton knew that as well as he knew his name. He might be one of them.

Thinking about that possibility as he stood here on the bow, he took a deep breath of the moist sea air and savored it.

A man never knows.

Well, he would do his best. That was all he could do. God had the dice, He would make the casts.

Jake was standing the squadron duty officer watch in the ready room one night when first Lieutenant Doug Harrison came in from a flight. He gave Jake his flight time figure and handed him the batteries from his emergency radio – the batteries were recharged in a unit above the duty officer's desk – then dropped into the skipper's empty chair as Jake annotated the flight schedule. Only then did Grafton turn and take a good look at the first-cruise pilot. His face was pasty and covered with a sheen of perspiration.

'Tough flight, huh?'

Harrison dropped his eyes and massaged his forehead with a hand. 'No . . . Got a cigarette?'

'Sure.' Jake passed him one, then held out a light.

After Harrison had taken three or four puffs, he took the cigarette from his mouth and said softly, 'After we landed, I almost taxied over the edge.'

'It's dark out there.'

'I've never seen anything like it. No light at all, the deck greasy, rain on top of the grease . . . it was like trying to taxi on snot.'

'What happened?'

'Taxi director took me up to the bow on Cat One, then turned me. Wanted me to taxi aft on Cat Two. It was that turn on the bow. Sticking out over the fucking black ocean. I was *sure* I was going right off the bow, Jake. I about shit myself. I kid you not. Pure, unadulterated terror, two-hundred proof. I have *never* had a feeling like that in an airplane before.'

'Uh-huh.'

'I was turning tight, I could feel the nose wheel sliding, the yellow-shirt was giving me the come-ahead signal with the wands, and the edge was *right there!* And there isn't even a protective lip. You know how the bow just turns down, same as the stern?'

'So what did you do?'

'Locked the left wheel and goosed the right engine. The plane moved about a foot. I could feel the left wheel sliding. To make things perfect I could also feel the deck going up and down, up and down. Every time it started down the vomit came up my throat. Then the yellow-shirt crossed his wands and had the blue-shirts chock it right where it sat. When I climbed down from the cockpit I couldn't believe it – the nose wheel was like *six inches* from the edge! It was so dark up there that I had to use my flashlight to make sure. There was *no way* the nose wheel was going around that corner. Even if it had, the right main wouldn't have made the turn – it would have dropped off the edge.'

Harrison took a greedy drag on his cigarette, then continued: 'My BN couldn't even get out of the cockpit. The plane captain didn't have room to drop his ladder. He had to stay in the cockpit until they towed the plane to a decent parking place.'

'Why'd you keep taxiing when you knew you were that close to the edge?'

Harrison closed his eyes for a second, then shook his head. 'I dunno.'

'I know,' Jake Grafton told him positively. 'You jarheads are spring-loaded to the yessir position. Doug, if it doesn't feel right, don't do it. You have only one ass to lose.'

Harrison nodded and sucked on the cigarette. The color was slowly coming back to his face. After a bit he said, 'Did you ever watch those RA-5 pilots taxi at night? The nose wheel is way aft of the cockpit. They are sitting out over the ocean when they taxi that Vigilante to the deck edge and turn it. I couldn't do that. Not in a million years. Just watching them gives me the shivers.'

'Don't obey a yellow-shirt if it doesn't look right,' Jake said, emphasizing the point. 'It isn't the fall that kills you, Doug, or the stop at the bottom – it's the sudden realization that, indeed, you *are* this fucking stupid.'

When Doug wandered off Jake went back to the notes of his talks on carrier operations. He was expanding and refining them so he could have them typed. He thought he would send them back to the senior LSO at the West Coast A-6 training squadron, VA-128 at Whidbey Island. Maybe there was something in there that the LSOs could use for their lectures.

Boy, if he wasn't getting out, it would sure be nice to go back to VA-128 when this cruise was over. Rent a little place on a beach or a bluff overlooking the sound, fly, teach some classes, kick back and let life flow along. If he wasn't getting out . . . If Tiny Dick Donovan was willing to take him back. Forgive and forget.

But he was getting out! No more long lonely months at sea, no more night cat shots, no more floating around the IO quietly rotting, no more of this—

Allen Bartow came up to the desk. 'When you get off

278

here tonight, we're having a little game down in my room. We need some squid money in the pot.'

'I've still got a lot of jarhead quarters from the last game. I'll bring those.'

'The last of the high rollers . . .'

He wasn't going to miss it, he assured himself, for the hundredth time. Not a bit.

One of the most difficult tasks in military aviation is a night rendezvous. On a dark night under an overcast the plane you are joining is merely a tiny blob of lights, flashing weakly in the empty black universe. Without a horizon or other visual reference, the only way the trick can be done is to keep your instrument scan going inside your cockpit while you sneak peeks at the target aircraft. The temptation is to look too long at the target, to get too engrossed in the angles and closure rate, and if that happens, you are in big trouble.

On this particular night Jake Grafton thought he had it wired. He was rendezvousing on the off-going tanker at low station, 5,000 feet over the ship on the five-mile arc. There it was, its lights winking weakly.

'Ten o'clock,' Flap said.

'Roge, I got it.'

'He'll be doing two-fifty.'

Jake glanced at his airspeed. Three hundred knots indicated. He would have to work that off as he closed. But not quite yet.

The tanker would be in a left-hand turn. Jake cranked his plane around until he had his nose in front of it and was looking at it through the right quarter panel, across the top of the radar scope-hood. He eased in a little left rudder and right flaperon to help keep his plane in a position where he could see the tanker.

With the target plane on the right side the A-6 was difficult to rendezvous because the cockpit was too wide – the BN sat on the pilot's right. This meant that the right glareshield and canopy rail were too high and, as the planes closed, would block the pilot's vision of the target aircraft if he allowed himself to get just a little behind the bearing line or get a tad high. Jake knew all this. He had accomplished several hundred night rendezvous and knew the problems involved and the proper techniques to use without even thinking about it. Tonight he was busy applying that knowledge.

Yet something was wrong. Jake checked his instruments. All okay. Why was the tanker moving to the right? Instinctively he rolled more wings level, rechecked his attitude gyro, the altimeter, the airspeed . . . All okay. And still the sucker is moving right!

'Texaco, say your heading.'

'Zero Two Zero.'

Hell! Now Jake understood. He was still on the outside of the tanker's turning radius, not on the inside as he had assumed. He leveled his wings and flew straight ahead to cross behind the tanker, feeling slightly ridiculous. He had *assumed* that he was on the inside . . .

Now, indeed, he was on the inside of the tanker's turn. He turned to put the nose in the proper position and started inbound. Checking the gauges, watching the bearing, slowing gently . . . 280 knots would be perfect, would give him 30 knots of closure . . .

And the tanker was . . . Jesus! Coming in awful fast – *way too fast!* Power back, boards out, and . . .

'Look at your altitude.' Flap.

Jake looked. He was at ninety-degrees angle-of-bank, passing 4,500 feet, descending.

He leveled the wings and got the nose up. The tanker shot off to the left.

'I'm really screwed up tonight,' he told the BN.

'Turn hard and get inside of him, then close.'

Jake did. He felt embarrassed, like a neophyte on his first night formation hop. Yet only when he got to within two hundred yards and could make out the tanker's position lights clearly was he sure of the tanker's direction of flight. Only then was he comfortable.

He wasn't concentrating hard enough. Attempting to rendezvous on a single, flashing light, in a dark universe devoid of any other feature . . . it was difficult at best and impossible if you weren't completely focused.

Flap extended the drogue as Jake crossed behind the tanker and surfaced on his right side. 'You got the lead,' said the tanker pilot, Chance Malzahn. Jake clicked his mike twice in reply as Chance slid aft. He dropped slightly and disappeared from sight behind. Jake concentrated on flying his own plane, staying in this steady, twenty-degree angle-of-bank turn, keeping on the five-mile arc, holding altitude perfectly.

In seconds the green ready light on the refueling panel went out and the counter began to click off the pounds delivered. The refueling package worked.

'Five Twenty-Three is sweet,' Flap told the ship.

The green ready light appeared again. Malzahn had backed out of the drogue. Now he came up on Jake's left side.

'You got the lead,' Jake told him as Malzahn's drogue streamed aft.

The drogue looked like a three-foot-wide badminton birdie. It dangled on the end of a fifty-foot-long hose aft and slightly below the wash of the tanker. To get fuel, Jake would have to insert his fuel probe, which was permanently mounted on the nose in front of his windscreen, into the drogue and push it in about five feet. When the take-up reel on the tanker had turned the proper amount, electrical switches would mate and begin pumping fuel down the hose into the receiver aircraft.

The trick was getting the probe into the drogue, the basket. If the basket was new, with all the feathers in good shape, it was usually almost stationary and fairly easy to plug. If it was slightly damaged, however, it tended to weave back and forth in the windstream and present a moving target. Turbulence that bounced the tanker and receiver aircraft added to the level of difficulty. And, of course, there was the 'pucker factor' – extensive experience has proven that the tension of a pilot's sphincter is directly proportional to the level of his anxiety, ie, higher makes tighter, etc.

Tonight, needing only to hit the tanker to 'sponge' the excess fuel, Jake's anxiety level was normal, or even slightly below. He was fat, had plenty of fuel. And the air was fairly smooth. The only fly in the ointment was the condition of that Marine Corps drogue. Tonight it weaved in a small, erratic figure-eight pattern.

Jake stabilized his plane about ten feet behind the drogue and watched it bob and weave for a moment. Flap Le Beau kept his flashlight pointed at it.

'Little Marine bastard is bent.'

'Yeah.' Flap was full of sympathy.

Flopping drogues had cracked bullet-proof windscreens, shattered Plexiglas and fodded engines. Tonight Jake Grafton eyed this one warily, waited for his moment, then smartly added power and drove his probe in. Drove it at that spot where the drogue would be when he got there. He hoped.

Miraculously he timed it right. The probe captured the drogue and locked in. He kept pushing until the green light above the hose chute in the tanker came on. Now he was riding about fifteen feet below the tanker's tail and ten feet aft. As long as he stayed right here, held that picture, he would get fuel.

'You get twelve hundred pounds,' Chance Malzahn told him.

Two clicks in acknowledgement.

'Nice,' Flap said, referring to the plug, the flashlight never wavering.

When the last of the gas was aboard Jake backed out. He came up on Malzahn's left side and took the lead as Malzahn reeled in his hose. After a word with Tanker Control, Malzahn cut his power and turned away, headed down on a vector for an approach.

Jake and Flap were now Texaco. Soon two F-4s came to take a ton of fuel each, then they turned away and disappeared in the vast darkness.

Jake took the tanker on up to high station, 20,000 feet, and settled it on autopilot at 220 knots. Around and around the ship, orbiting. Flap got out a paperback book and adjusted his kneeboard light. Jake loosened one side of his oxygen mask and let it dangle.

'Do you ever see the faces of the men you killed?' Jake asked. They had been orbiting the ship at high station for almost half an hour.

'What do you mean?'

Jake Grafton took his time before he answered. 'I got shot down last December. We ended up in Laos. Had to shoot three guys before they got us out. They were trying to kill us – me and my BN – and one of them shot me. That's how I ended up with this scar on my temple.'

'Uh-huh.'

'Had to do it, of course, or they would have killed us. Still, I see them sometimes in dreams. Wake up feeling rotten.'

Flap Le Beau didn't say anything.

'Dropping bombs, now, I did that for a couple cruises. Bound to have killed a lot of people. Oh, most of the time we bombed suspected truck parks and crap like that – probably killed some ants and lizards and turned a lot of trees into toothpicks. That's what we called them, toothpick missions – but occasionally we went after better targets. Stuff where there would be people. Not just trees in the jungle and mud roads crossing a creek.'

'Yeah.'

'Toward the end there we were really pounding the north, hitting all the shit that Johnson and McNamara didn't have the brains or balls to hit six years before.'

'It was fucked up, all right.'

'One mission, close air support of some ARVN, they told me I killed forty-seven of 'em. Forty-seven. That bothered me for a while, but I don't see them at night. Forty-seven men with one load of bombs . . . it's like reading about it in a newspaper or history book . . . doesn't seem real now. I still see those three NVA though.'

'I still see faces too.'

Below them an unbroken cloud deck stretched away in all directions. The sliver of moon was fuzzy and there weren't many stars – they were trying to shine through a gauzy layer of high cirrus.

'Wonder if it'll ever stop? If they'll just fade out or something.'

'I don't know.'

'Doesn't seem right somehow, to lose fifty-eight thou sand Americans, to kill all those Vietnamese, all for nothing.'

Flap didn't reply.

'I don't like seeing those faces and waking up in a cold sweat. I had to do it. But damn . . .'

He wanted to forget the past, forget all of it. The present was okay, the flying and the ship and the men he shared it with. Yet the future was waiting out there, somewhere hidden in the mists and haze. He was reaching out for *something*, something that lay ahead along that road into the unknown. Just what it would be he didn't know. He was ready to make the journey though.

Under the overcast it was raining. At five thousand feet visibility was down to two or three miles and the oncoming tanker had trouble finding them, even with vectors from tanker control. It was that kind of night, with nothing going right. Once he was there Jake slipped in behind, eyed the basket, and went for it. He got it with only a little rudder kick in close and pushed it in.

Nothing. The green light over the hose hole did not illuminate.

'Are we getting any?' Flap asked the other crew.

'No. Back out and let us recycle.'

Jake retarded the power levers a smidgen and let his plane drift aft. The basket came off the probe. He moved out to the right and Flap told the other crew to recycle. They pulled the hose all the way in, then ran it out again.

This time Jake missed the basket on the first try. He stabilized and slipped in on his second attempt.

'Still no gas.'

'Tanker Control, this is Five Two Two, we're sour.'

'Roger, Two Two. Your signal is dump. Steer Two Two Zero and descend to One Point Two, over.'

'Five Two Two, Two Two Zero and down to One Point Two.'

'Texaco, Tanker Control, you steer Two Zero Zero and descend to One Point Two, over.'

Jake slid left and the other tanker went right. It was already streaming fuel from the main and wing-tip dumps. Nine tons of fuel would have to be dumped into the atmosphere. Too bad, but there it was.

Jake settled onto his desired course and popped his speed brakes. The nose went over. When he stabilized he looked to the right for the other A-6, which was already fading into the rain and darkness. He came back into the cockpit and concentrated on his instruments.

This little world of needles and dials illuminated by red lights had always fascinated him. Making the needles behave didn't seem all that difficult, until you tried it. And on nights like this, when he felt about half in the bag, when he was having trouble concentrating, then it was exquisite torture. Everything he did was either too little or too much. It was maddening.

The perverse needles taunted him. *You are too high*, they whispered, *too fast, off course, now you are low* . . . He had to work extremely hard to make them behave, had to pay strict attention to their message. The slightest inattention, the most minute easing of his concentration would allow the needles to escape his grasp.

The controller worked him into a hole in the bolter pattern, which was rapidly filling up. The voices on the radio told him the story as he struggled to make the needles behave. The weather was worse than forecast. Rain was ruining the visibility, the sea was freshening, and one of the F-4s had already boltered twice. Nearest land was 542 miles to the northwest. There were no sweet tankers in the air.

'Ain't peace wonderful?' Flap muttered.

'Landing checklist,' Jake said, and they went through it. They were too heavy so they dumped fifteen hundred pounds of fuel to get to landing weight. Crazy, that the only good tanker was dumping to land instead of hawking the deck to help that Phantom crew, but ours is not to reason why, ours is but to do or . . .

At a mile and a half he saw the ship, a tiny smear of red light enlivening the dead universe.

Flap called the ball at Six Point Oh.

'Roger Ball.'

Jake recognized the Real McCoy's voice, but just in case he didn't the Real continued. 'Deck's dancing, Jake. Watch your lineup.'

He had the ball centered, nailed there, and with just a little dip of the wings he chased the landing centerline to the right, working the throttles individually so as not to over-control. The rain flowed around the canopy in a continuous sheet, but the engine bleed air kept the pilot's windscreen clear.

There was an art to throttle-work on the ball, moving each individual lever ever so slightly, yet knowing when to move them both. Tonight Jake got it just right. He deck got closer and closer, the ball stayed centered, the lineup was good, the angle-of-attack needle behaved . . . and they caught a three-wire.

'Luck,' Jake told Flap as they rolled out of the landing area.

They taxied him to a stop abeam the island where a half-dozen purple-shirts – grapes – waited with a fuel hose. Jake opened the canopy as the squadron's senior troubleshooter climbed the ladder. The wind felt raw and the rain cold against his skin.

'We're going to hot pump you and shoot you again,' the sergeant shouted over the whine of the engines. 'This is the only up tanker.'

Jake stuck his thumb up to signify his understanding.

The sergeant went back down the ladder and raised it as Jake closed the canopy. Might as well keep the rain out. The sergeant flashed a thumbs-up and went around to the BN's side of the plane to watch the refueling operation. Jake moved the switch to depressurize the tanks.

Refueling took a while. They needed twenty thousand pounds for a full load and the ship's pumps could only deliver it at about a ton a minute.

He was tired and his butt felt like dead meat, yet it was very pleasant sitting here in the warm, comfortable cockpit. From their vantage point here beside the foul line they had a grandstand seat. The planes came out of the rain and darkness and slammed into the deck. The first two trapped, then a Phantom boltered, his hook ripping a shower of sparks the length of the landing area. This was the guy who had already boltered twice before.

Ah yes, this comfortable cockpit, with everything working just the way it was supposed to, the rain pattering on the Plexiglas and collecting into rivulets that smeared the light.

He was tired, but not too much so. Just pleasantly tired.

Jake unhooked his oxygen mask and laid it in his lap. He took off his helmet and massaged his face and head. He used his sleeves and gloves to swab away the perspiration, then pulled the helmet back on.

The minutes ticked by as the fuel gauges faithfully reported the fuel coming aboard.

They were still fueling when the errant F-4 came out of the gloom and snagged a two-wire. The pilot stroked the afterburners on the roll out. The white-hot focused flames poured from the tailpipes for about a second, then went out, leaving everyone on deck half-blinded.

Two minutes later an A-7 carrying a buddy store, a tanking package hung on a weapon's station under one wing, was taxied from the pack up to Cat Two and launched. Apparently the brain trust in Air Ops wanted more gas aloft.

At last Jake and Flap were ready. Pressurize the tanks. Boarding ladders up, refueling panel closed, seats armed, and they were taxiing toward Cat Two, the left bow catapult.

Spread the wings, flaps to takeoff, slats out, wipe out the cockpit, ease into the shuttle. There, the jolt as the hold-back reached full extension, then another jolt as the shuttle went forward into tension. Off the brakes, throttles up.

He watched the engines come up to full power as he pulled up the catapult grip and arranged the heel of his hand behind the throttles, felt the airplane tremble as the engines sucked in vast quantities of that rainy air and slammed it out the tailpipes into the jet blast deflector – the JBD. Fuel flow normal, temperatures coming up nicely, RPM at 100 percent on the left engine, a fraction over on the right. Hydraulics normal, everything okay.

Jake wiped out the cockpit, glanced at the panel, ensured Flap had his flashlight on the standby gyro . . . 'You ready?'

'Let it rip.'

He flipped on the exterior light master switch on the end of the cat grip with his left thumb.

The hold-back bolt broke. *He felt it break.* Then came the shot, a stiff jolt of terrific acceleration, which lasted about a quarter of a second. Then it ceased. *Sweet Jesus fucking Christ the airplane was still accelerating but way too god-damn slow!*

He was doing maybe 30 knots when he released the cat grip and closed the throttles. Automatically he extended the wing-tip speed brakes. He jammed his feet down on the top of the rudder pedals, locking both brakes.

They were still going forward, sliding on the wet, greasy deck. Thundering toward the bow, the round-down, the edge of the cliff . . .

Jake pulled the left throttle around the horn to idle cutoff, stopping the flow of fuel to that engine.

He released the left brake and engaged nose-wheel steering. Slammed the rudders to neutral, then hard right. That should capture the nose wheel and turn it right, if the shuttle wasn't holding it. But the nose wheel refused to respond.

Still going forward, but slower. The edge was there, coming toward them . . . only seconds left.

He released both brakes, and engaged nose-wheel steering and slammed the rudder full left. He felt something give. The nose started to swing left.

On the brakes hard. *Is there enough deck left, enough—?*

An explosion beside him. Flap had ejected. The air was filled with shards of flying Plexiglas.

Sliding, turning left and still sliding forward . . . he felt the left wheel slam into the deck-edge combing, then the nose, now the tail spun toward the bow, the whole plane still sliding . . .

And he stopped.

Out the right he could see nothing, just blackness. The right wheel must be almost at the very edge of the flight deck.

He took a deep breath and exhaled explosively.

His left hand was holding the alternate ejection handle between his legs. He couldn't remember reaching for it, but obviously he had. He gingerly released his grip.

The Plexiglas was gone on the right side of the canopy. Flap had ejected through it. Where his seat had been there was just an empty place.

Was Flap alive?

Jake closed the speed brakes and raised the flaps and slats, watched the indicator to make sure they were coming in properly, exterior lights off. Out of the corner of his eye he saw people, a mob, running toward him. He ignored them.

When he had the flaps and slats up, he unlocked the wings, then folded them. The wind was puffing through the top of the broken canopy . . . rain coming in. He could feel the drops on the few inches of exposed skin on his neck.

Was the plane moving? He didn't think so. Yet if he opened the canopy he couldn't eject. The seat was designed to go through the glass – if the canopy was open, the steel bow would be right above the seat and would kill him if he tried to eject. And if this plane slid off the deck he would have to eject or ride it into that black sea.

Now the reaction hit him. He began to shake.

A yellow-shirt was trying to get his attention. He kept giving Jake the cut sign, the slash across the throat.

But should he open the canopy?

Unable to decide, he chopped the right throttle and sat listening as that engine died.

Someone opened the canopy from outside. Now a sergeant was leaning in. 'You can get out now, sir. Safe your seat.'

'Have they got it tied down?'

'Yes.'

He had to force himself to move. He safetied the top and bottom ejection handles on the seat and fumbled with the

Koch fittings that held him to the seat. Reached down and fumbled in the darkness with the fittings that attached to his leg restraints. There. He was loose.

He started to get out, then remembered his oxygen mask and helmet leads. He disconnected all that, then tried to stand.

He was still shaking too badly. He grabbed a handhold and eased a leg out onto the ladder, all the while trying to ignore the blackness yawning on the right side, and ahead. Here he was, ten feet above the deck, right against the edge. He felt like he was going to vomit.

Hands reached up and steadied him as he descended the boarding ladder.

With his feet on deck, he looked at the right main wheel. Maybe a foot from the edge. The nose-wheel was jammed against the deck-edge combing and the nose-tow bar was twisted.

Jake asked the yellow-shirt, 'Where's my BN?'

The sailor pointed down the deck, toward the fantail. Jake looked. He saw a flash of white, the parachute, draped over the tail of an A-7. So Flap had landed on deck. Didn't go into the ocean.

Now the relief hit him like a hammer. His legs wobbled. Two people grabbed him.

His mask was dangling from the side of his helmet, and he swept it out of the way just in time to avoid the hot raw vomit coming up his throat.

He started walking aft, toward the island and the parachute draped over that Corsair a hundred fifty yards aft. He shook off two sailors who tried to assist him. 'I'm all right, all right, okay.'

An A-7 came out of the rain and trapped.

There was Flap, walking this way. Now he saw Grafton, spread his arms, kept walking.

The two men met and hugged fiercely.

*

Lieutenant Colonel Richard Haldane watched the PLAT tape of the cat shot gone awry five or six times as he listened to Jake Grafton and Flap Le Beau recount their experience in the ready room.

They were euphoric – they had spit in the devil's eye and escaped to tell the tale. In the ready room they went through every facet of their adventure for their listeners, who shared their infectious glee.

Isn't life grand? Isn't it great to still be walking and talking and laughing after a trip to the naked edge of life itself?

After a half hour or so, Haldane slipped away to find the maintenance experts. He listened carefully to their explanations, asked some questions, then went to the hangar deck for a personal examination of 523's nose-tow bar.

Apparently the hold-back bolt had failed prematurely, a fraction of a second before the launch valves fully opened, perhaps just as they began to open. The KA-6D at full power had begun to move forward, creating a space – perhaps just an inch or two – between the T-fitting of the nose-tow bar and the catapult shuttle. Then the shuttle shot forward as steam slammed into the back of the catapult pistons. At this impact of shuttle and nose-tow bar, the nose-tow bar probably cracked. It held together for perhaps thirty feet of travel down the catapult, then failed completely.

Now free of the twenty-seven-ton weight of the aircraft, the pistons accelerated through the twin catapult barrels like two guided missiles chained together. Superheated steam drove them through the chronograph brushes five feet short of the water brakes at 207 knots.

With a stupendous crash that was felt the length of the ship, the pistons' spears entered the water brakes, squeezed out *all* the water and welded themselves into the brakes. Brakes, spears, and pistons were instantly transformed into one large lump of smoking, twisted, deformed steel. Cat Two was out of action for the rest of the cruise.

Colonel Haldane was less interested in what happened to the catapult than the sequence of events that took place inside 523 after the catapult fired. Careful analysis of the PLAT tape showed that the plane came to a halt just 6.1 seconds later. Total length of the catapult was 260 feet, and it ended twenty feet short of the bow. The plane had used all 280 feet to get stopped. The bombardier ejected 3.8 seconds into that ride.

That Jake Grafton had managed to get the plane halted before it went into the ocean was, Colonel Haldane decided, nothing less than a miracle.

Seated at his desk in his stateroom, he thought about Jake Grafton, about what it must have felt like trying to get that airplane stopped as it stampeded toward the bow and the black void beyond. Oh, he had heard Grafton recount the experience, but already, while it was still fresh and immediate, Grafton had automatically donned the de rigueur cloak of humility: 'In spite of everything I did wrong, miraculously I survived. I was shot with luck. All you sinners take note that when the chips are down clean living and prayer pays off.'

Most pilots would have ejected. Haldane thought it through very carefully and came to the conclusion that he would have been one of them. He would have grabbed that alternate ejection handle between his legs and pulled hard.

Yet Grafton hadn't done that, and he had saved the plane. Luck, Haldane well knew in spite of Grafton's ready room bullshit, had played a very small part.

Should he have ejected? After all, the Navy Department could just order another A-6 from Grumman for $8 million, but it couldn't buy another highly trained, experienced pilot. It took millions of dollars and years of training to produce one of those; if you wanted one combat experienced, you had to have a war, which was impractical to do on a regular basis since a high percentage of the liberal upper crust frowned upon wars for training purposes.

Yep, Grafton should have punched. Just like Le Beau.

Sitting here in the warmth, safety, and comfort of a well-lit stateroom nursing a cup of coffee, any sane person would reach that obvious conclusion. Hindsight is so wonderful.

And the same person would be wrong.

Great pilots always find a way to survive. Almost by instinct they manage to choose a course of action – sometimes in blatant violation of the rules – that results in their survival.

The most obvious fact here was probably the most important: Jake Grafton was still alive and uninjured.

Had he ejected . . . well, who can say how that would have turned out? The seat might have malfunctioned, he might have gone into the ocean and drowned, he might have broken his neck being slammed down upon the flight deck or into the side of an airplane. Le Beau had been very lucky, and he freely admitted it, proclaimed it even, in the ready room afterward: 'I'd rather be lucky than good.'

Grafton was good. He had saved himself and the plane. Yet there was more. In the ready room afterward he hadn't been the least bit defensive, had stated why he did what he did clearly and cogently, then listened carefully to torrents of free advice – the what-you-should-have-done variety. He wasn't embarrassed that Flap ejected. He blamed no one and expressed no regrets.

Haldane liked that, had enjoyed watching and listening to a man whose rock-solid self-confidence could not be shaken. Grafton believed in himself, and the feeling was contagious. One wondered if there were anything this man couldn't handle.

Now the colonel dug into the bottom drawer of his desk. In a moment he found what he was looking for. It was a personal letter from the commanding officer of VA-128, Commander Dick Donovan. Haldane removed the letter from its envelope and read it, carefully, for the fourth or fifth time.

I am sending you the most promising junior officer in the squadron, Lieutenant Jake Grafton. He is one of the two or three best pilots I have met in the Navy. He seems to have an instinct for the proper thing to do in a cockpit, something beyond the level that we can teach.

As an officer, he is typical for his age and rank. Keep your eye on him. He has a temper and isn't afraid of anything on this earth. That is good and bad, as I am sure you will agree. I hope time and experience will season him. You may not agree with my assessment, but the more I see of him, the more I am convinced that he is capable of great things, that someday he will be able to handle great responsibilities.

I want him back when your cruise is over.

Colonel Haldane folded the letter and put it back into its envelope. Then he pulled a pad of paper around and got out his pen. He hadn't answered this letter yet, and now seemed like a good time.

Donovan wasn't going to be happy to hear that Grafton was resigning, but there wasn't anything he or Donovan could do about it. That decision was up to Grafton. Still, it was a shame. Donovan was right – Grafton was a rare talent of unusual promise.

When the adrenaline rush had faded and the ready room crowd had calmed down, Jake and Flap went up to the forward – 'dirty shirt' – wardroom between the bow cats. Flap had already been to sick bay and had several minor Plexiglas cuts dressed. 'Iodine and Band-Aids,' he told Jake with a grin. 'I've been hurt worse shaving. Man, talk about luck!'

In the serving line each man ordered a slider, a large

cheeseburger so greasy that it would slide right down your throat. With a glass of milk and a handful of potato chips, they sat on opposite sides of a long table with a food-stained tablecloth.

'I didn't think you could get it stopped,' Flap said between bites.

'You did the right thing,' Jake told him, referring to Flap's decision to eject. 'If I hadn't managed to get it sliding sideways I would have had to punch too.'

'Well, we're still alive, in one piece. We did all right.'

Jake just nodded and drank more milk. The adrenaline had left his stomach feeling queasy, but the milk and slider settled it. He leaned back in his chair and belched. Yep, there's a lot to be said for staying alive.

Down in his stateroom he stood looking around at the ordinary things, the things he saw every day yet didn't pay much attention to. After a glimpse into the abyss, the ordinary looks fresh and new. He sat in his chair and savored the fit, looked at how the light from his desk lamp cast stark shadows into the corners of the room, listened to the creaks and groans of the ship, examined with new eyes the photos of his folks and Callie that sat on his desk.

He twiddled the dial of the desk safe, then pulled it open. The ring was there, the engagement ring he had purchased for her last December aboard *Shiloh*. He took it from the safe and held it so the light shone on the small diamond. Finally he put it back. Without conscious thought, he removed his revolver from a pocket of his flight suit and put that in the safe too, then locked it.

He was going to have to do something about that woman.

But what?

It wasn't like he had her hooked and all he had to do was reel her in. The truth of the matter was that she had him hooked, and she hadn't decided whether or not he was a keeper.

So what is a guy to do? Write and pledge undying love? Promise to make her happy? Worm your way into her heart with intimate letters revealing your innermost thoughts?

No. What he had to do was speak to her softly, tell her of his dreams . . . if only he had any dreams to tell.

He felt hollow. Everyone else had a destination in mind: they were going at different speeds to get there, but they were on their way.

It was infuriating. Was there something wrong with him, some defect in him as a person? Was that what Callie saw?

Why couldn't she understand?

He thought about Callie for a while as he listened to the sounds of the ship working in a seaway, then finally reached for a pad and pen. He dated the letter and began:

'Dear Mom and Dad . . .'

When he finished the letter he didn't feel sleepy, so he took a hot shower and dressed in fresh, highly starched khakis and locked the door behind him. There weren't many people about. The last recovery was complete. The enlisted troops were headed for their bunks and the die-hard aviators were watching movies. He peered into various ready rooms to see who was still up that he knew. No one he wanted to talk to. He stopped in the arresting gear rooms and watched a first-class and two greenies pulling maintenance on an engine. He stopped by the PLAT office and watched his aborted takeoff several more times, wandered through the catapult spaces, where greenies supervised by petty officers were also working on equipment. In CATCC the graveyard shift had a radar consol torn apart.

In the Aviation Intermediate Maintenance avionics shop the night shift was hard at repairing aircraft radars and computers. This space was heavily air-conditioned and the lights burned around the clock. The technicians who worked here never saw the sun, or the world of wind and sea and sky where this equipment performed.

Finally, on a whim, Jake opened the door to the Air Department office. Warrant Officer Muldowski was the only person there. He saw Jake and boomed, 'Hey, shipmate. Come in and drop anchor.'

Jake helped himself to a cup of coffee and planted his elbows on the table across from the bosun, who had a pile of paper spread before him.

'You did good up there on that cat.'

'Thanks.'

'Kept waiting for you to punch. Thought you had waited too long.'

'For a second there I did too.'

They chewed the fat for a while, then when the conversation lagged Jake asked, 'Why did you stay in the Navy, Bosun?'

The bosun leaned back in his chair and reached for his tobacco pouch. When he had his pipe fired off and drawing well, he said, 'Civilians' worlds are too small.'

'What do you mean?'

'They get a job, live in a neighborhood, shop in the same stores all their lives. They live in a little world of friends, work, family. Those worlds looked too small to me.'

'That's something to think about.' Jake finished his coffee and tossed the Styrofoam cup in a wastebasket.

'Don't you go riding one of those pigs into the water, Mr Grafton. When you gotta go, you go.'

'Sure, Bosun.'

CHAPTER EIGHTEEN

A Soviet task group came over the horizon one Sunday in late November. *Columbia* had no flying scheduled that day, so gawkers packed the flight deck when Jake Grafton came up for a first-hand look. A strong wind from the south-west was ripping the tops off the twelve- to fifteen-foot swells. Spindrift covered the sea, all under a clear blue sky. *Columbia* was pitching noticeably. The nearest destroyer was occasionally taking white water over the bow.

Up on deck Jake ran into the Real McCoy. 'Where are they?'

McCoy pointed. Jake saw six gray warships in close formation, closing the American formation at an angle from the port side, still four or five miles away. The US ships were only making ten knots or so due to the sea state, but the Soviets were doing at least twice that. Even from this distance the rearing and plunging of the Soviet ships was quite obvious. Their bows were rising clear of the water, then plunging deeply as white water cascaded across the main decks and smashed against the gun mounts.

On they came, seemingly aiming straight for *Columbia*, which, as usual, was in the middle of the American formation.

Gidrograf, the Soviet Pamir-class AGI that had been shadowing the Americans' for the last month, was trailing along behind the Americans, at least two miles astern. Her speed matched the Americans' and she made no move to join the oncoming Soviet ships.

'What do you think?' McCoy asked.

'Unless Ivan changes course, he's going to run his ships smack through the middle of our formation.'

'I think that is exactly what he intends to do,' McCoy said after a bit, when the Russians were at least a mile closer.

'Sure looks like it,' Jake agreed. The angle-of-bearing hadn't changed noticeably, which was the clue that the ships were on collision courses. He glanced up at *Columbia*'s bridge. Reflections on the glass prevented him from seeing anyone, but he imagined that the captain and the admiral were conferring just now.

'Under the rules of the road, we have the right of way,' McCoy said.

'Yeah.' Somehow Jake suspected that paper rules didn't count for much with the Russian admiral, who was probably on the bridge of his flagship with one eye on the compass and the other on the Americans.

The Soviet ships were gorgeous, with sleek, raked hulls and superstructures bristling with weapons and topped with radar dishes of various types. The biggest one was apparently a cruiser. A couple were frigates, and the other three looked like destroyers. All were armed to the teeth.

The American destroyer on the edge of the formation gave way to the Russians. On they came. Now you could see the red flags at their mastheads as dots of color and tiny figures on the upper decks, like ants.

'Big storm coming,' McCoy said, never taking his eyes off the Russians. 'Up from the southwest. Be here this evening.'

Jake looked aft, at the carrier's wake. It was partially obscured by parked aircraft, but he saw enough. The wake was straight as a string. He turned his attention back to the Soviet ships. About that time the collision alarm sounded on *Columbia*'s loudspeaker system. Then came th announcement: 'This is not a drill. Rig for collision port-side.'

The Soviet destroyers veered to pass ahead and behind *Columbia* but the cruiser stayed on a collision course. Now you could plainly see the sailors on the upper decks, see the red flag stiff in the wind, see the cruiser's bow rise out of the water as white and green seawater surged aft along her decks, see that she was also rolling maybe fifteen degrees with every swell.

But she was a lot smaller than the carrier. The American sailors on the flight deck were well above the Russians' bridge. In fact, they could see the faces of the Russian sailors at the base of the mast quite plainly. The Russians were hanging on for dear life.

The Russian captain was going to veer off. He had to. Jake jumped into the catwalk so he could see better as the cruiser crossed the last fifty yards and the carrier's loud-speaker boomed, 'Stand by for collision portside. All hands brace for collision.'

The Soviet captain misjudged it. He swung his helm too late and the sea carried his ship in under the carrier's flight deck overhang. The closest the two hulls came was maybe fifteen feet, but as the cruiser heeled her motion in the sea pushed her mast and several of the radar antennae into the underside of the flight deck overhang. The Russian sailors clustered around the base of the mast saw that the collision was inevitable only seconds in advance and tried to flee. Two didn't make it. One fell to the cruiser's main deck, but the other man fell into that narrow river of white water between the two ships and instantly disappeared from view.

The top of the mast hit the catwalk forward of the Fresnel lens and ripped open three of the sixty-man life raft containers. The rafts dropped away. One ended up on the cruiser and the others went into the sea. The Russians' mast and several radar antennae were wiped off the super-structure and her stack was partially smashed.

Then the cruiser was past, surging ahead of *Columbia* with her mast trailing in the water on her portside.

Jake bent down and stuck his head through the railing under the life raft containers so that he could keep the cruiser in sight. If the Russian captain cut across *Columbia*'s bow he was going to get his ship cut in half.

He did cut across, but only when he was at least six or seven hundred yards ahead, still making twenty knots.

The Soviet ships rejoined their tight formation and continued on course, pulling steadily away.

An American destroyer dropped aft to look for the lost Soviet sailor as the air boss ordered the flight deck cleared so he could launch the alert helo.

The helo searched for half an hour. The destroyer stayed on the scene for several hours, yet the Russian sailor wasn't found.

By evening a line of thunderstorms formed a solid wall to the southwest, a wall that seemed to stretch from horizon to horizon. As the dusk deepened lightning flashed in the storms continually. Jake was on deck watching the approaching storms and savoring the sea wind when the carrier and her escorts slowly came about and pointed their bows at the lightning.

The ships rode better on the new course. Apparently the heavies had decided to sail through the storm line, thereby minimizing their time in it. Unfortunately the weather on the back side of the front was supposed to be bad; heavy seas, low ceilings and lots of rain. Oh well, no flying tomorrow either.

When the darkness was complete and the storms were within a few miles, Jake went below. This was going to be a good night to sleep.

The ringing telephone woke Jake. The Real McCoy usually answered it since all he had to do was roll over in his bunk and reach, and he did this time. The motion of the ship was less pronounced than it had been when Jake and Real went to bed about 10 P.M., during the height of the storm.

'McCoy, sir.'

Jake looked at his watch. A little after 2 A.M.

After a bit, he heard his roommate growl, 'This had better not be your idea of a joke, Harrison, or your ass is a grape . . . Yeah, yeah, I'll tell him . . . In a minute, okay?'

Then McCoy slammed the receiver back on the hook.

'You awake up there?'

'Yeah.'

'They want us both in the ready room in five minutes, ready to fly.'

'Get serious.'

'That's what the man said. Must be World War III.'

'Awww . . .'

'If Harrison is jerking our chains he'll never have another OK pass as long as he lives. I promise.'

But Harrison wasn't kidding, as Jake and the Real found out when they went through the ready room door. The skipper and Allen Bartow were standing near the duty desk talking to CAG Kall. Flap Le Beau was listening and sipping a cup of coffee. All of them were in flight suits.

'Good morning, gentlemen,' CAG said. He looked like he had had a great eight hours sleep and a fine breakfast. He couldn't have had, Jake knew. Things didn't work like that in this Navy.

''Morning, CAG,' McCoy responded. 'So it's war, huh?'

'Not quite. Pull up a chair and we'll sort this out.'

Apparently the admiral and CINCPACFLT had been burning the airways with flash messages. The Soviet ambassador in Washington had delivered a stiff note to the State Department protesting the previous day's naval incident in the Indian Ocean, which he called 'a provocation.'

The powers that be had concluded that the US Navy had to serve notice on the Russians that it couldn't be bullied.

'The upshot is,' CAG said, 'that we have been ordered to make an aerial demonstration over the Soviet task group, tonight if possible.'

'What kind of demonstration, sir?'

'At least two airplanes, high-speed passes, masthead height if possible.'

Eyebrows went up. McCoy got out of his chair and went to the television, which he turned to the continuous weather display. Current weather was three to four hundred feet broken to overcast, three-quarters of a mile visibility in rain. Wind out of the northwest at twenty-five knots.

CAG was still talking. '. . . it occurred to me that this would be a good time to try our foul weather attack scheme on the Russians. I thought we could send two A-6s and three EA-6Bs. We'd put a Hummer up to keep it safe. The admiral concurred. The Prowler crews and Hummer crews will be here in a few minutes for the brief. What do you think?'

'Sir, where are the Russians?'

'Two hundred miles to the east. Apparently the line of thunderstorms went over them several hours ago and they are also under this system.'

As he finished speaking the ship's loudspeaker, the 1-MC, came to life: 'Flight quarters, flight quarters, all hands man your flight quarters stations.'

In minutes the Prowler and Hawkeye crews came in and found seats and the brief began. CAG did the briefing, even though he wouldn't be flying. Forget the masthead rhetoric from Washington – the lowest any of the crews could go was five hundred feet.

The three senior pilots of the Prowler squadron would fly their planes, and the CO of the E-2 squadron would be in the left seat of the Hawkeye. Lieutenant Colonel Haldane and the Real McCoy would fly the go A-6s and Jake Grafton would man the spare.

'Uh, skipper,' Flap said, 'if I may ask, why McCoy?'

'He's got the best landing grades in the squadron. Grafton is second. As it happens, they have more traps than anyone else in the outfit and getting back aboard is going to be the trick. As for me, this is my squadron.'

'Yessir, but I was wondering about McCoy. Let's face facts, sir. When the landing signal officer has the best landing scores – well, it's like an umpire having the top batting average. There's just a wee bit of an odor, sir.'

Laughter swept the room as McCoy grinned broadly. He winked at Jake.

'What say you and I flip for the go bird,' Jake suggested to McCoy.

'Forget it, shipmate. If my plane's up, I'm flying it. Tonight or any other night.'

'Come on! Be a sport.'

The Real was having none of it. And Jake understood. Naval aviation was their profession. Given the weather and sea state, this would be a very tough mission. When you began ducking the tough ones, you were finished in this business. Maybe no one else would know, but *you* would.

In flight deck control Jake looked at the airplane planform cutouts on the model ship to see where his plane was spotted. Watching the handler check the weight chits as rain splattered against the one round, bomb-proof window and the wind moaned, Jake Grafton admitted to himself that he was glad he had the spare. He wasn't ducking anything – this was the bird the system gave him and he wasn't squawking.

All he had to do was preflight, strap in and start the engines, then sit and watch Haldane and McCoy ride the catapult into the black goo. After that he could shut down and go below for coffee. If he went to the forward mess deck galley he could probably snag a couple doughnuts hot from the oven.

The handler was a lieutenant commander pilot who had left the Navy for two years, then changed his mind. The only billet available when he came back was this one – two years as the aircraft handler on *Columbia*. He took it, resigning himself to two years of shuffling airplane cutouts around this model, two years of listening to squadron maintenance people complain that their airplanes weren't where they could properly maintain them, two years listening to the air boss grouse that the go birds were spotted wrong, two years checking tie-down chains and weight chits, two years listening to the hopes, dreams and fears of young, homesick sailors while trying to train them to do dangerous, difficult jobs, two years in purgatory with no flying . . . yet the handler seemed to be weathering it okay. True, his fuse was getting almighty short and he wasn't getting enough sleep, but his job performance was first-rate, from everything Jake had seen and heard. And behind the tired face with the bleary eyes was a gentle human being who liked to laugh at a good joke in the dirty-shirt wardroom. Here in Flight Deck Control, however, he was all business.

'Forty-six thousand five hundred pounds? That right, Grafton?' The handler was reading from Jake's weight chit. This would be his weight if he launched.

'Yessir.'

Savoring the hubbub in Flight Deck Control while surreptitiously watching the handler, Jake Grafton felt doubt creep over him. Was getting out a mistake? It had been for the handler. An eight-to-five job somewhere, the same routine day after day . . .

He turned for the hatch that led to the flight deck. The first blast of cool air laden with rain wiped the future from his mind and left only the present, this moment, this wild, windy night, this airplane that awaited him under the dim red island floodlights.

His bird was sitting on Elevator Four. The tail was sticking out over the water, so he checked every step with his flash-light before he moved his feet. If you tripped over the three-inch-high combing, you would go straight into the ocean to join that Russian sailor who went in yesterday. Poor devil – his shipmates didn't even stop to look for him. How would you like to go to sea in that man's navy?

Going around the nose he and Flap passed each other. 'What a night,' Flap muttered.

Both men were wearing their helmets. They had the clear visors down to keep the rain and salt spray out of their eyes. The wind made the raindrops hurt as they splattered against exposed flesh.

Jake took his time preflighting the ejection seat. He was tempted to hurry at this point so he could sit down and the plane captain could close the canopy, but he was too old a dog. He checked everything carefully, methodically while he used his left hand to hang tightly to the airplane. The motion of the ship seemed magnified out here on this elevator. The fact he was eight or nine feet above the deck perched on this boarding ladder and buffeted by the wind and rain didn't help. He pulled the safety pins, inspected, counted and stowed them, then he sat.

The plane captain climbed the ladder to help him hook up the mask, don the leg restraints, and snap the four Koch fittings into place. Then the plane captain went around to help Flap. When both men were completely strapped in, he closed the canopy.

Now Jake checked the gear handle, armament switches, circuit breakers, and arranged the switches for engine start. He had done all these things so many times that he had to concentrate to make sure he was seeing what was there and not just what he expected to see.

When he had the engines started, Flap fired up the

computer while Jake checked the radio and TACAN frequencies.

'Good alignment,' Flap reported, and signaled to the plane captain to pull the cable that connected the plane to the ship's inertial navigation system.

They were ready. Now to sit here warm and reasonably dry and watch the launch.

The E-2 taxied toward Cat Three on the waist. A cloud of water lifted from the deck by the wash of the two turbo-props blasted everything. The plane went onto the cat, the JBD rose, then the engines began to moan. Finally the wing-tip lights came on. The Hawkeye accelerated down the catapult and rose steadily into the night. The lights faded quickly, then the goo swallowed them.

'Uh-oh,' Flap said. 'Look over there at Real's plane.'

A crowd of maintenance people had the left engine access door open. Someone was up on the ladder talking to McCoy. In less than a minute a figure left the group and headed for Jake's plane.

The man on the deck lowered the pilot's boarding ladder while Jake ran the canopy open. Then he climbed up. The squadron's senior troubleshooter. 'Mr McCoy can't get his left generator to come on the line,' he shouted. 'Jake had to hold his helmet away from his left ear to hear. 'You're going in his place.'

'His tough luck, huh?'

'Right.'

'The breaks of Naval Air . . .'

'Be careless.' The sergeant reached for Jake's hand and shook it, then shook Flap's. He went down the boarding ladder and Flap closed the canopy.

'We're going,' Jake said on the ICS. 'In McCoy's place.'

'I figured. By God, when they said all-weather attack, they meant all-weather. Have you ever flown before on a night this bad?'

'No.'

'Me either. Just to send a message to the Russians, like the Navy was an FTD florist. Roses are red, violets are blue, you hit our ships and we'll fuck you. The peacetime military ain't what it was advertised to be. No way, man.'

The yellow-shirted taxi director was signaling for the blue-shirts to break down the tie-downs. Jake put his feet on the brakes. 'Here we go.'

It never gets any easier. In the darkness the rain streaming over the windshield blurred what little light there was and the slick deck and wind made taxiing difficult. Just beyond the bow the abyss gaped at him.

He ran through possible emergencies as he eased the plane toward the cat.

Total electrical failure while taking the cat shot was the emergency he feared the most. It wasn't that he didn't know what to do – he did. The doing of it in a cockpit lit only by Flap's flashlight as adrenaline surged through you like a lightning bolt would be the trick. You had just one chance, in an envelope of opportunity that would be open for only a few seconds. You had to do it right regardless or you would be instantly, totally dead.

'Why do we do this shit?' he muttered at Flap as they taxied toward the cat.

'Because we're too lazy for honest work and too stupid to steal.'

The truth of the matter was that he feared and loathed night cat shots. And flying at night, especially night instrument flight. There was nothing fun about it, no beauty, no glamour, no appeal to his sense of adventure, no sense that this was a thing worth doing. The needles and gauges were perverse gadgets that demanded his total concentration to make behave. Then the night flight was topped off with a night carrier landing – he once described a night carrier hop as sort of like eating an old tennis shoe for dinner, then choking down a sock for dessert.

Tonight as he ran through the launch procedures and

ran the engines up to full power, rancid fear occupied a portion of his attention. A small portion, it is true, but it was there.

He tried to fight it back, to wrestle the beast back into its cage deep in his subconscious, but without success.

Wipe out the cockpit with the controls, check the engine instruments . . . all okay.

Jumping Jack Bean was the shooter. When Jake turned on his exterior lights, he saluted the cockpit perfunctorily with his right hand while he kept giving the 'full power' signal with the wand in his left hand. Jake could see he was looking up the deck, waiting for the bow to reach the bottom of its plunge into a trough between the swells.

Now Bean lunged forward and touched the wand to the deck. The bow must be rising.

The plane shot forward.

Jake's eyes settled on the altitude instruments.

The forward edge of the flight deck swept under the nose.

Warning lights out, rotate to eight degrees, airspeed okay, gear up.

'Positive rate of climb,' Flap reported, then keyed the radio and reported to Departure Control.

The climb went quickly because the plane was carrying only a two-thousand-pound belly tank and four empty bomb racks. But they had a long way to climb. They finally cleared the clouds at 21,000 feet and found the night sky filled with stars.

An EA-6B Prowler was already there, waiting for them. It was level at 22,000 feet, on the five-mile arc around the ship. Its exterior lights seemed weak, almost lonely as they flickered in the starry night.

The Prowler was a single-purpose aircraft, designed solely to wage electronic war. Grumman had lengthened the basic A-6 airframe enough to accept two side-by-side cockpits, so in addition to the pilot the plane carried three electronic warfare specialists known as ECMOs, or electronic counter-measures officers. Special antennae high on the tail and at various other places on the plane allowed the specialists to detect enemy radar transmissions, which they then jammed or deceived by the use of countermeasures pods that hung on the wing weapons stations. Tonight, in addition to the pods, this Prowler carried a two-thousand-pound fuel tank on its belly station. Although the EA-6B was capable of carrying a couple missiles to defend itself, Jake had never seen one armed.

As expensive as Boeing 747s, these state-of-the-art aircraft had not been allowed to cross into North Vietnam after they joined the fleet, which degraded their effectiveness but ensured that if one were lost, the Communists would not get a peek at the technology. Here, again, America traded airplanes and lives in a meaningless war rather than risk compromising the technological edge it had to have to win a war with the Soviets, a war for national survival.

Jake thought about that now – about trading lives to keep the secrets – as he flew in formation with the Prowler and looked at the telltale outline of helmeted heads in the cockpits looking back at him. Then the Prowler pilot passed Jake the lead, killed his exterior lights, slid aft and crossed under to take up a position on Jake's right wing.

The Prowler pilot was Commander Reese, the skipper of the squadron. He was about five and a half feet tall, wore a pencil-thin mustache, and delighted in practical jokes. Inevitably, given his stature, he had acquired the nickname of Pee Wee.

Jake retarded the throttles and lowered the nose. In seconds the clouds closed in around the descending planes and blotted out the stars.

'Departure, War Ace Five Oh Two and company headed southeast, descending.'

'Roger, War Ace. Switch to Strike.'

'Switching.'

Flap twirled the radio channelization knob and waited for the Prowler to check in on frequency. Then he called Strike.

Flying in this goo, at night, wasn't really flying at all. It was like a simulator. The world ended at the windshield. Oh, if you turned your head you could see the fuzzy glow of the wing-tip lights, and if you looked back right you could see your right wing-tip light reflecting off the skin of the Prowler that hung there, but there was no sense of speed or movement. Occasional little turbulence jolts were the only reminder that this box decorated with dim red lights, gauges and switches wasn't welded to the earth.

The big plan was for each bomber and its accompanying Prowler to run a mock attack on the Soviet task group as close to simultaneously as possible. Jake would approach from the southwest, Colonel Haldane from the northwest. The E-2 Hawkeye, the Hummer, would monitor their progress and coordinate the attack. However, each A-6 BN had to find the task group on radar before they sank below the radar horizon. Then the bombers would run in at five hundred feet. In an actual attack they would come in lower, perhaps as low as two hundred, but not at night, not in this weather, for drill. The risks of flying that close to the sea were too great.

Flap started the video recorder, a device that the A-6A never had. This device would record everything seen on the radar screen, all the computer and inertial data, as well as the conversation on the radio and in the cockpit.

'Recorder's on,' he told Jake. 'Keep it clean.'

This electronic record of the attack could be used for poststrike analysis, or, as CAG had hinted in the brief, sent to Washington to show to any bigwigs or congressmen who wanted to know what, exactly, the Navy had done in response to the collision at sea.

Had the Soviet skipper intended to bump the carrier?

Did he tell the truth to his superiors? These imponderables had of course been weighed in Washington, and orders had been sent to the other side of the earth.

It was midafternoon in Washington. The city would be humming with the usual mix of tourists, government workers anxious to begin their afternoon trek to the suburbs, the latest tunes coming over the radios, soap operas on television . . .

Jake wondered about the weather there. Late November. Was it cold, rainy, overcast?

All those people in America, finishing up another Monday, and he and Flap were here, over the Indian Ocean, passing ten thousand feet with a Prowler on their wing and a Soviet task group somewhere in the night ahead.

'See it yet?'

'No. Stop at eight thousand and hold there.'

As they flew eastward the turbulence increased. Jake had Flap arrange his rearview mirror so he could keep tabs on the Prowler. Pee Wee Reese seemed to be hanging in there pretty well. He had to. If he lost sight of the bomber, he would have to break off. Two planes feeling for each other in this soup would be a fine way to arrange a midair collision.

'The Commies aren't where they're supposed to be,' Flap said finally.

'You sure?'

'All I know is that the radar screen is empty. Rocket scientist that I am, I deduce the Reds aren't where the spies said they would be. Or *Columbia*'s inertial was all screwed up and this is the wrong ocean. Or all the Reds have sunk. Those are the possibilities.'

'Better ask Black Eagle.'

It turned out the E-2 was also looking for the Soviets at the maximum range of its radar. It soon found them, teaming hard to the northeast, directly away from Jake and Flap and directly toward the line of thunderstorms that had just passed over them.

'They know something's up,' Jake said.

'Terrific. They're at general quarters expecting us and we'll have to go under thunderstorms to get to them. And to think we almost didn't get a date for this party.'

'Man, we're having fun now.'

Flap didn't reply. He was busy.

After a bit he said, 'Okay, I got 'em. Give me a few moments to get a course and speed and then we'll go down.'

While he was talking the electronic warfare (EW) panel chirped. A Soviet search radar was painting them. In addition to the flashing light on the panel when the beam swept them, Jake heard a baritone chirp in his headset.

So much for surprise.

The turbulence was getting worse. The bouncing was constant now. Rain coursed around the windscreen and across the canopy. 'Radar is getting degraded,' Flap muttered. 'Rain. I got them though, course Zero Five Zero at fifteen. Lots of sea return. Swells are big down there, my man.'

'Can we go down?'

'Yeah.'

Jake glanced over at the reflection of the Prowler in the mirror. Pee Wee was riding fairly steadily, cycling up and down as the planes bounced, but never slipping too far out of position. Jake carefully eased the throttle back and let the nose go down a half a degree. When he was sure the EA-6B pilot was still with him, he lowered the nose some more.

A pale green light caught his eye, and he glanced at the windscreen. Dancing tendrils of green fire were playing across it.

'Look at this,' he told Flap. 'Saint Elmo's fire.'

'This makes my night,' the BN said. 'All we need is fo

the Russians to squirt a missile at us and this will be a complete entertainment experience.'

'Will a lightning bolt do?'

'Don't say stuff like that. God's listening. You're passing five thousand.'

'Radar's altimeter's set.'

'Roger. Station one selected, master arm to go.'

They were up to four hundred knots indicated now. The EA-6B was right there, hanging on. Eighty miles to go.

Wasn't Saint Elmo's fire an indicator that lightning might strike? Wasn't that what the old sailors said? Even as he wondered the flickering green fire faded, then disappeared completely.

Black Eagle gave them a turn. Jake banked gently to the new heading. The steering to the target was forty degrees left, but the controller in the E-2 was trying to coordinate the attack. When he had one of the formations four miles farther from the target than the other, he would have them turn inbound and accelerate to five hundred knots. The pilots would call their distance to go on the radio every ten miles. The plan was for the bombers and their EA-6B escorts to pass over the Soviet task group thirty seconds apart. Neither formation would see the other, so this separation was required for safety reasons.

Jake eased his descent passing twenty-five hundred feet. He shallowed it still more passing a thousand and drifted slowly down to five hundred, keeping one eye on the radar altimeter. He adjusted the barometric pressure on the pressure altimeter so it matched the radar altimeter's reading exactly.

The turbulence had not let up, nor had it increased. The rain was heavier, though. The high airspeed kept the windscreen clear but the water ran across the top and sides of the canopy in sheets.

'War Aces, turn inbound.'

Jake came left to center the steering and fed the throttles

forward until they were at ninety-eight percent RPM. Pee Wee stayed right with him.

'Five Oh Two, seventy miles.'

Fifteen seconds later he heard Haldane's voice: 'Five Oh Five, sixty miles.'

Each plane was inbound on a bomb run at eight and a third nautical miles per minute. They were a little over thirty seconds apart, but the extra margin was an added safety cushion.

'I should get them at about thirty miles, I think,' Flap said.

And when we can see them, they can see us.

Jake reached down and flipped the IFF, the transponder, to standby. No use giving the Reds an easy problem.

He glanced at the EW panel. Still quiet. When they rose above the Russians' radar horizon it would light up like a Christmas tree.

'Five Oh Two, sixty miles.'

The turbulence was getting vicious. The radar altimeter beeped once when Jake inadvertently dropped to four hundred feet. He concentrated on the instruments, on the altitude indicator on the VDI, on the needle of the rate-of-climb indicator, cross-checking the radar and pressure altimeters, all the while working to keep his wings level and steering centered. Every moment or two he glanced in the mirror to check on Pee Wee Reese, who was sticking like glue. No question, the guy was good.

'Five Oh Two, fifty miles.'

Rain poured over the plane, so much that a film of water developed on the windscreen even though they were doing five hundred knots.

'Five Oh Two, forty miles.'

A lightning flash ahead distracted him for several seconds from the instruments. When he came back to the he had lost fifty feet. He struggled to get it back as wondered if Haldane had seen the lightning flash. Shou they go under a thunderstorm? It was Haldane's call. Jake wasn't breaking off the run unless the skipper did.

'Five Oh Two, thirty miles.'

Twenty-nine, twenty-eight . . .

'They've turned,' Flap said. 'They're heading southeast. Follow steering.'

Even as Jake eased right to center the bug, the EW panel lit up and the tones assailed him. X-band, Y-band – the Russians had every radar they had turned on and probing, looking for a target.

Now the tones of the radars became a buzz. The bomber was so close to the EA-6B, which was jamming the Russian radar, that the bomber's EW gear was overwhelmed.

'Five Oh Two, twenty miles.'

'Master Arm on, we're in attack,' Flap reported.

The attack symbology came alive on the VDI.

Another lightning flash. Closer. Lots of rain.

'Five Oh Five, ten miles.' That was Haldane.

Fifteen miles . . . fourteen . . . thirteen . . .

'They're jamming me. Keep on this heading.'

Now Flap flipped on frequency agility, trying to change his radar's frequency to an unjammed wavelength long enough to get a look.

'Five Oh Two, ten miles.'

Three lightning flashes in a couple seconds. They were flying right under a boomer. The turbulence was so bad Jake had trouble concentrating on the instruments. Pee Wee was still hanging on, though.

Five miles.

Four.

Three.

Symbols marching down toward weapons release.

Lights. The Russian ships should be lit up. He should pass over them just after weapons' release. *But don't look!* No distractions. *Concentrate!*

Two.

One.

Release marker coming down. Steering centered. Commit trigger pulled.

Click. Flag drop on the ordnance panel and the attack light on the VDI went out.

If there had been a bomb, it would now be falling.

A searchlight split the night. Three or four, weaving.

Instantly he had vertigo. He stared at the VDI, forced himself to keep his wings level as he tugged the stick slightly aft to begin a climb.

And then the lights were behind. That quick.

More lightning ahead. Jake eased into a left turn, toward the north. The skipper went out to the southeast, so this direction should be clear.

He would climb away from this ocean, turn west to head for the carrier, get out of this rain and turbulence and lightning, and to hell with the Ivans!

Message delivered: fuck you very much, stiff letter to follow.

He had the power back to ninety percent and was up to two thousand feet, in a ten-degree angle-of-bank left turn passing north on the HSI when the lightning bolt struck. There was a stupendous flash of light and a sound like a hammer striking, then nothing.

He was blind. Everything was white. Flash blindness. He knew it.

He keyed the ICS and told Flap, 'Flashlight—' but there was no feedback in his headset. A total electrical failure And he was blind as a bat, two thousand feet over the water in a turn.

He *had* to see.

He blinked furiously, trying by sheer force of will to see the instrument panel.

But there was no light, no electricity.

He reached behind him with his left hand, found th

handle for the ram-air turbine – the RAT – and pulled hard. Real hard.

The handle came out.

Perhaps four seconds had passed, not more.

The white was fading. He reached for his oxygen mask with both hands and unfastened the right side.

What the plane was doing he had no way of knowing, although he knew whatever it was, it wasn't good. But he couldn't fly blind. His seat-of-the-pants instincts were worthless. Oh, he knew *that*, had had it drummed into him and had experienced it on so many night carrier landings that he wasn't even tempted to try to level the wings.

The white was fading into darkness. He blinked furiously, then remembered his L-shaped flashlight, hanging by a hook on the front of his survival vest. He found it and pushed the switch on.

In the growing darkness he saw the spot the beam made on the instrument panel. Another few seconds . . .

But there was already a spot of light on the needle-ball turn indicator! *Flap!* He must have had his head in the scope when the lightning hit.

He could see. The VDI was blank. The standby gyro showed a thirty-degree left turn. Ten degrees nose-down.

Cross-check with the turn indicator!

Turn needle pegged left. He rolled right to center it, overdid it and came back left some. The standby gyro responded.

The altimeter! Going down.

Back stick. Stop the needle. Gently now. Coming down on eleven hundred feet. Stop it there, center that turn needle. Standby gyro disagrees by five degrees. *Ignore it!*

Flap was shouting and he caught the muffled words: 'Reese is still with us. He has his lights on. I think he wants to take the lead.'

Jake could see now. His vision was back to normal. How many seconds had it been?

He risked a glance in the rearview mirror. There was Reese, with his exterior lights on, bobbing like a cork on Jake's right wing. Reese must be the world's finest formation pilot, to hang on through that gyration.

Should he chance it? Should he pull the power and try to ease back onto Reese's wing without a radio call or signal?

Even as the thought shot through his mind, he was retarding the throttles. Reese's plane began to move forward.

Okay! Flap was flipping his flashlight at Reese in the EA-6B's cockpit.

Pee Wee knows. He wants me to fly on him. It's our only chance if the TACAN and radar are screwed up. We'll never find the ship on our own.

Now Reese was abeam him, the two planes flying wing tip to wing tip and bouncing out of sync in the turbulence.

Be smooth, Jake. Don't lose him. Don't let him slip away into this black shit or you'll be swimming for it.

He stabilized in parade position on Reese's left side, so that he was looking straight up the leading edge of the swept wing into the cockpit. Reese was just a dark shape limned by red light, the glow from his instrument panel.

No comforting red glow in this cockpit. This place was dark as a tomb.

The bouncing was getting worse. He had to cross under, get on Reese's right side so he wouldn't be looking across the cockpit at the other plane.

He tucked the nose down gently and pulled a smidgen of power. Now power back on and a little right bank while he wrestled the stick in the chop.

Right under the tail, crossing, surfacing on Pee Wee's right wing. Okay. Now hang here.

Another flash of lightning. He flinched.

Flap was shouting something. He concentrated, trying to make sense of the words. '. . . must've zapped us with a zillion volts. Every circuit breaker we got is popped. I'm going to try to reset some, so if you smell smoke, let me know.'

'Okay,' he shouted, and found reassurance in the sound of his own voice.

All he had to do was hang on to Reese. Hang on and hang on and hang on, and someday, sometime, Reese would drop him onto the ball. The ball would be out there in the rain and black goo, and the drop lights, and the centerline lights, and the wires, strung across that pitching, heaving deck.

All he had to do was hang on . . .

As Flap pushed in circuit breakers and the cockpit lights glowed, then went out, then glowed again, the planes flew into and out of deluges. The torrents of rain were worse than they had been coming in. Several times the rain coursing over the canopy caused Reese's plane to fade until just the exterior lights could be seen.

Jake concentrated fiercely upon those lights. Each time the rain would eventually slacken and the fuselage of the EA-6B would reappear, a ghostly gray presence in the blacker gloom.

Finally the clouds dissipated and a blacker night spread out before them. Far above tiny, cold stars shown steadily. They were on top, above the clouds. Behind them lightning strobed almost continually.

Jake eased away from Reese and put his mask to his face. The oxygen was flowing, cool and rubbery tasting. He lowered it again, then swabbed the sweat from his eyes and face with the fingers of his left hand.

When he had his mask fixed back in place he glanced at the instruments. The instrument lights were on – well, some of them. It was still dark on Flap's side. The VDI was still blank, but the standby gyro was working. The TACAN needle swung lazily, steadily, around and around the dial.

He pushed the button to check the warning lights on the annunciator panel. The panel stayed dark. Both generators were probably fried. Maybe the battery. He recycled each of the generator switches, but nothing happened. Finally he just turned them off.

Fuel – he checked the gauge. Nine thousand pounds. He pushed the buttons on the fuel panel to check the quantity in each tank. The needle and totalizer never moved. They were frozen.

Flap was still examining the circuit breaker panel with his flashlight.

'Hey, shipmate, you there?' Flap – on the ICS.

'Yeah.'

'A whole bunch of these CBs won't stay in.'

'Forget it.'

'We're gonna need—'

'We'll worry about it later.'

Later. Let's sit up here in the night above the storms and savor this moment. Savor life. For we are alive. Still alive. Let's sit silently and look at the stars and Reese's beautiful Prowler and breathe deeply and listen to our hearts beating.

CHAPTER NINETEEN

The radome on the nose of the aircraft had a hole in it. Jake and Flap examined it with their flashlights. It was about the size of a quarter and had black edges where the Plexiglas or whatever it was had melted. They had shut down on Elevator Two so the plane could be dropped below to the hangar deck.

Now they stood looking at the hole in the radome as the sea wind dried the sweat from their faces and hair and the overcast began to lighten toward the east.

Dawn was coming. Another day at sea.

The hole was there and that was that.

'Grafton, you're jinxed,' Flap Le Beau said.

'What do you mean?' Jake asked, suddenly defensive.

'Man, things happen to you.'

'I was doing fine until I started flying with you,' Jake shot back, then instantly regretted it.

Flap didn't reply. Both men turned off their flashlights and headed for the island.

Lieutenant Colonel Haldane had rendezvoused with Pee Wee Reese and Jake had transferred over to his wing. An approach with a similar aircraft was easier to fly. Fortunately the weather had cleared somewhat around the ship, so when the two A-6s came out of the overcast with their gear, flaps and hooks down they were still a thousand feet above the water. There wasn't much rain. The ship's lights were clear and bright.

Jake boltered his first pass and made a climbing left turn

off the angle. He and Flap had been unable to get the radio working again, so he few a close downwind leg and turned into the groove as if he were flying a day pass. He snagged a one-wire.

The debrief took two hours. After telling the duty officer to take him off the schedule for the rest of the day, Jake went to breakfast, then back to his bunk. The Real McCoy woke him in time for dinner.

Jake and Flap didn't fly again for four days. The skipper must have told the schedules officer to give them some time off, but Jake didn't ask. He did paperwork, visited the maintenance office to hear about the electrical woes of 502, did more paperwork, ate, slept, and watched three movies.

The maintenance troops found another lightning hole in the tail of 502. Jake went to the hangar deck for a look.

'Apparently the bolt went in the front and went clear through the plane, then out the tail,' the sergeant said. 'Or maybe it went in the tail and out the front.'

'Uh-huh.' The hole in the tail was also about quarter size, up high above the rudder.

'Was the noise loud?'

'Not that I recall.'

'Thought it must be like sitting beside a howitzer when it went off.'

'Just a metallic noise,' Jake said, trying to remember. Funny, but he didn't remember a real loud noise.

'You guys were sure lucky.'

'Like hell,' Jake told him. He was thoroughly sick of these philosophical discussions. 'Pee Wee Reese was on my wing and the lightning didn't hit him. It hit me. He didn't get a volt. *He* had the luck.'

'You were lucky you didn't blow up,' the sergeant insisted. 'I've heard of planes hit by lightning that just blew up. You were lucky.'

'Planes full of avgas, maybe, but not jet fuel.'

The sergeant wasn't taking no for an answer. 'Jets too,' he said.

Thanksgiving came and went, then another page was ripped off the ready room calendar and it was December.

Jake had that feeling again that his life was out of control. 'You just got to go with the flow,' the Real McCoy said when Jake tried to talk to him about it.

'It's a reaction to the lightning strike,' Flap said when Jake mentioned it to him. Jake didn't bother telling him he had had it off and on for years.

Yet gradually the feeling faded and he felt better. Once again he laughed in the ready room and tried to remember jokes. But he refused to think about the future. I'm going to take life one day at a time, he decided. If a guy does that there will never be a future to worry about. Just the present. That makes sense, doesn't it?

'What does it feel like to die?' Flap Le Beau asked.

He and Jake were motoring along at 350 knots at five thousand feet just under a layer of cumulus puffballs. Beneath them the empty blue sea spread away to the horizon in every direction. This afternoon they were flying another surface surveillance mission, this time a wedge-shaped pattern to the east of the task group. They were still on the outbound leg. They had not seen a single ship, visually or on radar. The ocean was empty.

All those ships crossing the Indian Ocean, hundreds of them at any one time, yet the ocean was so big . . .

'Did you ever think about it?' Flap prompted.

'I passed out once,' Jake replied. 'Fainted. When I was about fourteen. Nurse was taking blood, jabbing me over and over again trying to get the needle into a vein. One second I was there, then I was waking up on the floor after some nightmare, which I forgot fifteen seconds after I woke up. Dying is like that, I suspect. Not the nightmare part. Just like someone turned out the light.'

'Maybe,' Flap said.

'Like going to sleep,' Jake offered.

'Ummm . . .'

'What got you thinking about that, anyway?'

'Oh, you know . . .'

The conversation dribbled out there. Flap idly checked the radar, as usual saw nothing, then rearranged his fanny in his seat. Grafton yawned and rubbed his face.

The radio squawked to life. The words were partially garbled: the aircraft was a long way from the ship – over two hundred miles – and low.

'This is War Ace Five Oh Eight,' Flap said into his mask. 'Say again.'

'Five Oh Eight, this is Black Eagle. We'll relay. The ship wants you to investigate an SOS signal. Stand by for the coordinates.'

Flap glanced at Jake, shrugged, then got a ballpoint pen from the left-shoulder pocket of his flight suit and inspected the point. He scribbled on the corner of his top kneeboard card to make sure the pen worked, then said, 'War Ace is ready to copy.'

When he had read back the coordinates to the controller in the E-2 Hawkeye to ensure he had copied them correctly, Flap tapped them into the computer and cycled it. 'Uh-oh,' he muttered to Jake. 'It's over four hundred miles from here.'

'Better talk to the controller.'

Flap clicked his oxygen mask into place. 'Black Eagle, Five Oh Eight. That ship looks to be four hundred twenty-nine miles from our present position, which is' – he pushed another button on the computer – 'two hundred forty-two miles from the ship. We don't have the gas and we can't make the recovery.'

Grafton was punching the buttons, checking the wing fuel. They launched with a total of 18,000 pounds, and now had 11,200.

'Roger, War Ace. They know that. We're talking to them on another frequency. They want you to go look anyway. They only got about fifteen seconds of an SOS broadcast, which had the lat-long position as a part of it. The ship thinks you can get there, give it a quick look-over, then rendezvous with a tanker on the inbound leg on this frequency.'

Already Jake had swung the plane fifteen degrees to the right to follow the computer's steering command to the ship in distress. Now he added power and began to climb.

'Set up a no-rad rendezvous, just in case,' Jake told Flap.

He wanted to know where to find the tanker even if the radio failed. The only way to fix positions in this world of sea and sky was electronically, in bearings and distances away from ships that were radiating electronic signals that the plane's nav aids could receive. Unfortunately the A-6s radar could not detect other airplanes. And the tanker had no radar at all. Of course, Flap could find the carrier on radar if he were within 150 miles of it and the radar worked, and they could use the distance and bearing to locate themselves in relation to the tanker. If the radar kept working.

There were a lot of ifs.

The ifs made your stomach feel hollow.

Seventeen days had passed since their night adventure in the thunderstorm and here they were again, letting it all hang out.

Jake Grafton swore softly under his breath. It just isn't fair! *And the ship in distress might not even be there.* A fifteen-second SOS with the position. Sounded like an electronic program, one that could have easily broadcast the wrong position information. The ship could be hundreds of miles from the position they were winging they way to, and they would never find it.

The emergency broadcast might have been an error — a radioman on some civilian freighter might have

327

inadvertently flipped the wrong switch. There might not be any emergency at all.

No doubt the bigwigs on the carrier had considered all that. Then, safe and comfortable, they had sent Jake and Flap to take a look. And to take the risks.

Finding the tanker would be critical. Jake eyed the fuel gauge without optimism. He would go high, to forty thousand feet, stay there until he could make an idle descent to the ship in distress, make a quick pass while Flap snapped photographs, then climb back to forty thousand headed toward the carrier. The tanker would be at 150 miles, on the Zero Nine Five radial, at forty grand. If it were not sweet, or this plane couldn't take fuel, they wouldn't be able to make it to the ship. They would have to eject.

At least it was daytime. Good weather. No night sweats. No need to do that needle-ball shit by flashlight. That was something.

Now Jake turned in his seat to look behind him at the sun. He looked at his watch. There should be at least a half hour of daylight left when they reached the SOS ship, but the sun would be down by the time they got to the tanker. Still, there would probably be some light left in the sky. Perhaps it would be better if the sky were completely dark, then they could spot the tanker's flashing anticollision light from a long distance away. But it would not be dark. A high twilight, that was the card the gods of fate had dealt.

One of these fine Navy days we're gonna use up all our luck. Then we two fools are gonna be sucking the big one. That's what everyone is trying to tell us.

'We won't descend unless you have a target on the radar,' Jake told Flap.

'Uh-huh.'

That was a good decision. No use squandering all that fuel descending to sea level unless there was a ship down

328

there to look at. And if there was a ship, it would show on radar.

What if the ship had gone under and the crew was in lifeboats? Lifeboats wouldn't show on radar, not from a long distance.

'How far can you see a lifeboat on that thing?' he asked Flap, who had his head pressed against the scope hood.

'I dunno. Never looked for one.'

'Guess.'

'You were right the first time. We don't go down unless we see something.'

He leveled at forty thousand feet and retarded the throttles. Twenty-two hundred pounds per hour of fuel to each engine would give him .72 Mach. Only they had used four thousand pounds climbing up here. Seven thousand eight hundred pounds of fuel remaining. It's going to be tight. He retarded the throttles still farther, until he had only eighteen hundred pounds of fuel flowing to each engine. The airspeed indicator finally settled around 220 knots, which would work out to about 460 knots true.

Flap unfolded a chart and studied it. Finally he said, 'That position is in the channel between the islands off the southern coast of Sumatra.'

'At least it isn't on top of a mountain.'

'True.'

'Wonder if the brain trust aboard the boat plotted the position before they sent us on this goose chase.'

'I dunno. Those Navy guys . . . You never can tell.'

After much effort, Flap got the chart folded the way he wanted it. He wedged it between the panel and the Plexiglas so he could easily refer to it, then settled his head against the scope hood. After a bit he muttered, 'I see some islands.'

Land. Jake hadn't seen land in over a month, not since the ship exited the Malay Strait. *Columbia* was scheduled to spend three more weeks in the Indian Ocean, then head for Australia.

Rumors had been circulating for weeks. Yesterday they were confirmed. Australia, the Land Down Under, the Last Frontier, New California, where everyone spoke English – sort of – and everyone was your mate and they drank strong, cold beer and they liked Yanks . . . oooh boy! The crew was buzzing. *This* was what they joined the Navy for.

Those few old salts who claimed they had been to Australia before were surrounded by rapt audiences ready for just about any tale.

'The women,' the young sailors invariably demanded. 'Tell us about the women. Are they really fantastic? Can we really get dates?'

Tall, leggy, gorgeous, and they *like* American men, actually prefer them over the home-grown variety. And their morals, while not exactly loose, are very very *modern*. One story making the rounds had it that during a carrier's visit to Sydney several years ago the captain had to set up a telephone desk ashore to handle all the calls from Australian women wanting a date with an American sailor! Any sailor! *Send me a sailor!* These extraordinary females gave the term 'international relations' a whole new dimension.

That was the scuttlebutt, solemnly confirmed and embellished by Those Who Had Been There, once upon a time Before the Earth Cooled. The kids listening were on their first cruise, their first extended stay away from home and Mom and the girl next door. They fervently prayed that the scuttlebutt prove true.

The Marines in the A-6 outfit were as excited as the swab jockeys. They knew that, given a choice, every sane female on the planet would of course prefer a Marine to a Dixie cup. Australia would be liberty heaven. As someone said in the dirty-shirt wardroom last night, *Columbia* had rendezvous with destiny.

All this flitted through Jake Grafton's mind as he flew eastward at forty thousand feet. He too wanted to be off the ship, to escape from the eat-sleep-fly cycle, to get a respite from the same old faces and the same old jokes. And Australia, big, exotic, peopled by a hardy race of warriors – Australia would be fun. He hummed a few bars of 'Waltzing Matilda,' then glanced guiltily at Flap. He hadn't heard.

Jake's mind returned to the business at hand. Hitting the tanker on the way back to the ship was the dicey part . . . Why did fate keep dealing him these crummy cards?

The fiercely bright sun shone down from a deep, rich, dark blue sky. At this altitude the horizon made a perfect line, oh so far away. It seemed as if you could see forever. The sea far below was visible in little irregular patches through the low layer of scattered cumulus, which seemed to float upon the water like white cotton balls . . . hundreds of miles of cotton balls. To the northeast were the mountains of Sumatra, quite plain now. Clouds hung around the rocky spine of the huge island, but here and there a deep green jungle-covered ridge could be glimpsed, far away and fuzzy. The late afternoon sun was causing those clouds to cast dark shadows. Soon it would shoot their tops with fire.

'There's something screwy about this,' Flap said.

'What do you mean?'

'Ships don't sink in fifteen seconds. Not unless they explode. How likely is that?'

'Probably a mistake. Radio operator hit the wrong switch or something. I'll bet he thought no one heard the SOS.'

'Wonder if the ship tried to call him back.'

'Probably.'

'Well, I say it's screwy.'

'You'd better hope we find that tanker on the way home. Worry about that if you want to worry about something.

Extended immersion in saltwater is bad for your complexion.'

'Think it might lighten me up?'

'Never can tell.'

'Life as a white man . . . I never even considered the possibility. Don't think it would work, though. You white guys have to go without ass for horribly long periods. I need it a lot more regular.'

'Might cure your jungle rot too.'

'You're always looking for the silver lining, Grafton. That's a personality defect. You oughta work on that.'

The minutes ticked by. The mountains seemed closer, but maybe he was just kidding himself. Perspective varies with altitude and speed. He had noticed this phenomenon years ago and never ceased to marvel at it. At just a few thousand feet you see every ravine, every hillock, every twist in the creeks. At the middle altitudes on a clear day you see half of a state. And from up here, well, from up here, at these speeds, you leap mountain ranges and vast deserts in minutes, see whole weather systems . . . In orbit the Earth would be a huge ball that occupied most of the sky. You would circle it in ninety minutes. Continents and oceans would cease to be extraordinarily large things and appear merely as features on the Earth. The concept of geographical location would cease to apply.

At this altitude he and Flap were halfway to heaven. On his kneeboard Jake jotted the phrase.

He was checking the fuel, again, when Flap said, 'We're a hundred twenty miles out. I can see the area.' The area where the ship in distress should be, he meant, if it were really there.

Odd day for an emergency at sea. Most ships got in trouble in bad weather, when heavy seas or low temperatures stressed their systems. On a day like this . . .

'I got something on the radar. A target.'

'The ship?'

'The INS says it's about four or five miles from the position Black Eagle gave us. Of course, the inertial could have drifted that much.'

'Big ship?'

'Well, it ain't a rowboat. Not at this distance. Can't tell much more than that about the size. A blip is a blip.'

'Course and speed?'

'She's DIW.' Dead in the water, drifting.

He would pull the power at eighty miles, descend with the engines at eighty percent RPM initially to ensure the generators stayed on the line.

'It's about fifteen miles from the coast of Sumatra, which runs northwest to southeast. Islands to seaward, west and southeast. Big islands.'

'Any other ships around?'

'No. Nothing.'

'On a coast like that . . .'

'Maybe we'll see some fishing boats or something when we get closer.'

'Yeah.'

'I'll tell Black Eagle.' Flap keyed the radio.

They arrived over the ship at seven thousand feet, the engines at idle. Peering down between cumulus clouds, Jake saw her clearly. She was a small freighter, with her super-structure amidships and cranes fore and aft. Rather like an old Liberty ship. No visible smoke, so she wasn't obviously on fire. No smoke from the funnel either, which was amidships, and no wake. There was a smaller ship, or rather a large boat, alongside, right against the starboard side.

Jake put the plane into a right circle so Flap could get pictures with the hand-held camera and picked a gap in the clouds to descend through. The engines were still at idle.

They dropped under the clouds at 5,500 feet. 'Shoot the whole roll of film,' Jake told Flap. 'From every angle. We'll circle and make one low pass down the rail so you can get a closeup shot of the ship and that boat alongside, then we're out of here.'

'Okay.' He focused and snapped.

'Looks like the crew has been rescued.'

'Swing wide at the stern so I can get a shot of her name.'

Jake was passing three thousand feet now, swinging a wide lazy circle around the ship, which seemed to be floating on an even keel. Wonder what her problem was?

'Can you read the name?'

'You're still too high. It'll be in the photos though.'

'Fuel? Sixty-two hundred pounds, over six hundred miles to *Columbia*. He shivered as he surveyed the drifting freighter and the small ship alongside. That small one looked to be maybe eighty or ninety feet long, a small superstructure just forward of amidships, one stack, splotchy paint, a few people visible on deck.

'There's people on the freighter's bridge.'

'About finished?'

'Yeah.'

'Here we go, down past them both.' Jake dumped the nose. He dropped quickly to about two hundred feet above the water and leveled, pointing his plane so that they would pass the two stationary vessels from bow to stern. Jake adjusted the throttles. If he went by too fast Flap's photos would end up blurred. He steadied at 250 knots.

'They aren't waving or anything.'

Jake Grafton saw the flashes on the bow of the small ship and knew instinctively what they were. He jammed the throttles forward to the stops, rolled forty degrees or so and pulled hard. He felt the thumps, glimpsed the fiery tracers streaming past the canopy, felt more thumps, then they were out of it.

'*Flak!*' Now Flap Le Beau found his voice.

'Fucker's got a twenty-millimeter!'

They were tail on to the ships, twisting and rolling and

334

climbing. The primary hydraulic pressure needles flickered. So did the secondary needles. The BACK-UP HYD
light illuminated on the annunciator panel.

'Oh sweet fucking Jesus!'

Jake leveled the wings, trimmed carefully for a climb.

The plane began to roll right. The stick was sloppy. Jake
used a touch of left rudder to bring it back.

Heading almost south. He jockeyed the rudder and stick,
trying to swing the plane to a westerly heading. The plane
threatened to fall off on the right wing.

It was all he could do to keep the wings level using the
stick and rudder. Nose still a degree or so above the
horizon, so they were still climbing, slowly, passing two-
thousand feet, doing 350 knots.

'Get on the radio,' Jake told Flap. 'Talk to Black Eagle.
Those guys must be pirates.'

He retarded the throttles experimentally, instinctively
wanting to get down to about 250 knots so the emergency
hydraulic pump would not have to work so hard to move
the control surfaces. He trimmed a little more nose up. The
nose rose a tad. Good.

'Black Eagle, Black Eagle, this is War Ace, over.'

They were in real trouble. The emergency hydraulic
pump was designed to allow just enough control to exit a
combat situation, just enough to allow the crew to get to a
safe place to eject.

'Black Eagle, this is War Ace Five Oh Eight with a red
hot emergency, over.'

And the emergency pump was carrying the full load. All
four of the hydraulic pressure indicator needles pointed at
the floor of the airplane, indicating no pressure at all in any
of their systems.

'Black Eagle, War Ace Five Oh Eight in the blind. We
cannot hear your answers. We have been shot up by pirates
on this SOS contact. May have to eject shortly. We are
exiting the area to the south.'

Just fucking terrific! Shot down by a bunch of fucking pirates! On the high fucking seas in *1973!* On a low, slow pass in an unarmed airplane. Of all the shitty luck!

'Squawk seventy-seven hundred,' Jake said.

Flap's hand descended to the IFF box on the consol between them and turned the mode switch to emergency. Just to be sure he dialed 7700 into the windows. Mayday.

'There's an island twenty miles ahead,' Flap said. 'Go for it. We'll jump there.'

The only problem was controlling the plane. It kept wanting to drop one wing or the other. Jake was using full rudder to keep it upright, first right, then left. The stick was almost useless.

He reached out and flipped the spin assist switch on. This would give him more rudder authority, if the loss of hydraulic pressure hadn't already made that switch. It must have. The spin assist didn't help.

When the left wing didn't want to come back with full right rudder, he added power on the left engine. Shoved the power lever forward to the stop. That brought it back, but the roll continued to the right. Full left rudder, left engine back, right engine up . . . and catch it wings level . . .

'Seventeen miles.'

'We aren't gonna make it.'

'Keep trying. I don't want to swim.'

'Those fuckers!'

Three thousand feet now. Now if he could just maintain that altitude when the wings rolled . . .

They were covering about four and a half nautical miles per minute. How many minutes until they got there? The math was too much and he gave up. And he could see the island ahead. There it was, green and covered with foliage, right there in the middle of the windscreen.

'Fifteen miles.'

The roll was left. Full right rudder, left engine up. The

roll stopped but the nose came down. Full back stick didn't help. He ran the trim nose-up as he pulled the right engine to idle.

The nose was coming up. Yes, coming, so he started the trim nose-down. The wing was slowly rising, oh so slowly, rising . . .

They bottomed out at fifteen hundred but the plane began a very slow roll to the right, the nose still climbing.

He reversed the engines and rudder, played with the trim.

Slowly, agonizingly, the wings responded to the pilot's inputs. Now the nose fell to the horizon and kept going down.

Full nose-up trim! He held the button and glanced at the trim indicator on the bottom of the stick. Still nose-down! Come on!

They bottomed out this time at one thousand feet and the entire cycle began again.

'We won't make it the next time,' Jake told Flap.

'Let's jump at the top, when the wings and nose are level.'

'You first and I'll be right behind you.'

Nose coming down, right wing coming down, soaring up, up, to . . . to twenty-three hundred feet.

'Now,' Jake shouted.

An explosion and Flap was gone. Jake automatically centered the rudder as he pulled the alternate firing handle. Instantly a tremendous force hit him in the ass. The cockpit disappeared. The acceleration lasted for only an instant, then he began to fall.

CHAPTER TWENTY

The parachute opened with a shock. As Jake Grafton turned slowly in the shrouds the airplane caught his eye, diving toward the ocean like a wounded gull. The nose rose and it skimmed the sea, then began to climb. It soared skyward in a climbing turn, its right wing hanging low, then the wing fell and the nose went through and it dove straight into the sea. There was a large splash. When the spray cleared only a swirl of foam marked the spot.

The pirates! Where were they?

He got his oxygen mask off and tossed it away, then craned his head. He saw the other parachute, lower and intact with Flap swinging from it, but he couldn't see the pirate ship or its victim.

Oh, what a fool he'd been. To fly right over a drifting ship with another craft tied to it – and to never once think about the possibility of pirates! These waters were infamous . . . and the possibility never even crossed his mind. Son of a bitch!

The sea coming toward him brought him back to the business at hand. There was enough of a swell that the height was easy to judge – and he didn't have much time. He reached down and pulled the handle on the right side of his seat pan. It opened. The raft fell away and inflated when it reached the end of its lanyard. He felt around for the toggles to the CO_2 cartridges that would inflate his life vest. He found them and pulled. The vest puffed up reassuringly.

Good! Now to ditch this chute when I hit the water.

Amazingly, the thoughts shot through his mind without conscious effort. This was the result of training. Every time the ship left port the squadron held a safety training day, and part of that exercise involved each flight crewman hanging from a harness in the ready room while wearing full flight gear. Blindfolded, each man had to touch and identify every piece of gear he wore, then run through the proper procedure for ejections over land and sea. Consequently Jake didn't have to devote much thought to what he needed to do: the actions were almost automatic.

The wind seemed to be blowing from the west. He was unsure of directions. The way he wanted to go was toward that island – yes, that was south – and the wind was drifting him east. Somehow he also knew this without having to puzzle it out.

The raft touched the water. He felt for the Koch fittings near his collar bones that attached his parachute harness to the shroud lines and waited. Ready, here it comes, and . . . He went under. Closing his mouth and eyes automatically as the surge of cold seawater engulfed him, he toggled the fittings as he bobbed toward the surface. He broke water gasping for air.

The parachute was drifting away downwind. Now, where was that line attached to the raft?

He fumbled for it and finally realized it was wrapped around his legs or something. He began pulling toward the raft with his arms and finally grabbed the line. In seconds he had the raft in front of him.

All he had to do was get in.

The first time he slipped off the raft and went under on his back. Kicking and gasping, he managed to get upright and swing the raft so it was in front of him again.

This time he tried to force the raft under him. And almost made it before it squirted out and his head went under again.

339

The swells weren't helping. Just when he had the raft figured out, a swell broke over him and he swallowed saltwater.

Finally, after three or four tries, he got into the raft. He gingerly rolled so that he was on his back and lay there exhausted and gasping.

A minute or two passed before he realized he was still wearing his helmet. He removed it and looked for a lanyard to tie it to. He might need it again and everything not tied to him was going to be lost overboard sooner or later. He used a piece of parachute shroud line that he had tucked into his survival vest months ago.

Only then did he remember Flap and start sweeping the horizon for him.

The radio! He got out his survival radio, checked it, then turned it on. 'Flap, this is Jake.'

No answer.

Jake lay in his bobbing, corkscrewing raft looking at clouds and thinking about pirates and cursing himself. In a rather extraordinary display of sheer stupidity he had managed to get himself and Flap Le Beau shot out of the sky by a bunch of pirates. Yo ho ho and a bottle of rum. After the war was over! Not just any Tom, Dick or Harry can put an almost-new, squawk-free A-6E into the god-damn drink! Is that talent or what? The guys at the O Clubs were going to be shaking their heads over this one for a long long time.

Colonel Haldane was going to shit nails when he heard the happy news.

He looked at his watch. The damn thing was full of water. It had stopped. Perfect!

And his ass was six inches deep in water. Occasionally more water slopped in, but since the doughnut hole in which he sat was already full, the overflow merely drained out. Useless to try to bail it.

Luckily the water wasn't too cold. Sort of lukewarm.

The tropics. And to think real people pay real money to swim in water like this.

He tried to radio again. This time he got an answer. 'Yo, Jake. You in your raft?'

'Yep. And you?'

'Nope. It's like trying to fuck a greased pig.'

'You hurt?'

'No. You?'

'No.'

'Well, nice talking to you. Now I gotta get into this sonuvabitching raft.'

'Pull the damn thing under you. Don't try to climb into it. Pull it under you.'

'Call you back after a while.'

A cigarette. He could sure use a cigarette. He made sure the radio was firmly tied to his survival vest, then laid it in his lap. The cigarettes and lighter were in his left sleeve pocket. He got them out. The cigarettes were sodden. The lighter still worked though, after he blew repeatedly on the flint wheel and dried it off somewhat. It was one of those butane jobs. He extracted a wet cigarette, put it to his lips and lit the lighter. The cigarette refused to burn.

He put the cigarette back into the pack and stowed the pack away. If he ever managed to get ashore he could dry these things out and smoke them.

Wait! He had an unopened pack in his survival vest. Still wrapped in cellophane, an unopened pack would be watertight.

He wanted a cigarette now more than anything else he could think of. He got the left chest pocket of the vest open and felt around inside, trying not to let the rest of the contents spill.

He found it. Thirty seconds later he had a cigarette lit and was exhaling smoke. Aaah!

Bobbing up and down, puffing away, he decided he was thirsty. He had two plastic baby bottles full of water in his survival vest. He got one out and opened it, intending to drink only a little. He drained it in two long gulps.

He almost tossed the empty away, but thought better of it and slipped it back into the vest pocket.

Something on top of a swell to his left caught his eye, then it was gone. He waited. Flap, sitting in his raft, visible for a second or two before the out-of-sync swells lowered Jake or Flap.

He checked the radio. He had turned it off. He turned it on again and immediately it squawked to life. 'Jake, Flap.'

'Hey, I saw you.'

'I've seen you twice. How far apart do you think we are?'

'A hundred yards?'

'At least. We've got to do some thinking, Jake. We're going to be out here all night. The ship won't be close enough to launch a chopper until dawn.'

Jake looked longingly at the island, the one he and Flap had been trying to reach when they ejected. He saw flashes of green occasionally, but it was miles away. And the wind was blowing at a ninety-degree angle to it.

'Let's try to paddle toward each other. If we could get together, tie our rafts together, we'd have a better chance.'

A better chance. The words sprang to his lips without conscious thought, and now that he had said them he considered their import. A night at sea in one of these pissy little rafts was risky at best. The sea could get a lot rougher, a raft could spring a leak, the pirates might come looking, sharks . . .

Sharks!

A wave of pure terror washed over him.

'Okay,' Flap said. 'You paddle my way and I'll paddle toward you. I don't think we can make it before dark but we can try. I'm going to turn my radio off now to save the battery.'

Jake inspected himself to see if he was injured, if he was bleeding. Adrenaline was like a local anesthetic; he had

342

been far too pumped to feel small cuts and abrasions. If he were bleeding . . . well, sharks can smell blood in the water for miles and miles.

He felt his face and neck. Tender place on his neck. He held out his gloved right hand and stared at it: red stain. Blood!

For the love of God!

Must be a shroud burn or Plexiglas cut.

He got up on his knees in the raft. This was an inherently unstable position and he took great pains to ensure he didn't capsize. Crouching as low as he could, he began paddling with his hands, making great sweeping motions. Then he realized he didn't know where Flap was, so he forced himself to stop and look. There, just a glimpse, but enough. He turned the raft about sixty degrees and resumed paddling.

It was hard work. Every thread Jake wore was of course soaked, so even though the air was warm and humid, he stayed cool. Stroke for a while, pause to look for Flap, stroke some more, the cycle went on and on.

Finally he became aware that the sun was down and the light was fading. He got out his survival light, triggered the flash, and stuck it onto the Velcro that was glued to a spot on the right rear of his helmet. Then he put the helmet on. Three minutes later he saw that Flap had done the same thing. They were, at this point, maybe fifty yards apart.

Jake paused for a moment to rest.

What a mess! And if he had had a lick of sense, used an ounce of caution, they wouldn't be floating around out here in the middle of the ocean, at the ends of the earth.

He cussed awhile, then went back to work.

It was completely dark when they got the rafts together. Lengths of parachute shroud from their survival vests were quickly tied so the two rafts lay side by side. They arranged themselves so that Jake's feet were adjacent to Flap's head, and vice versa.

The two men lay inert in the rafts for minutes, resting. Then Flap said, 'This is a fine mess you got us into, Grafton. A very fine how-do-you-do.'

'I'm sorry.'

Flap was silent for several seconds. 'You really think this is your fault? I'm sorry I said that. It ain't. It's the fault of that asshole son of a bitch over there that smacked us with that twenty mike-mike. Talk about a cheap shot! I'd like to cut his nuts off and make him eat 'em.'

'Think Black Eagle heard any of our transmissions?'

'I don't know.'

'Boy, I hope so. I'd hate to think that that chicken-shit pirate cocksucker might get a free shot at somebody else tomorrow.'

'Turn off that flashing light on your helmet. Makes my eyes hurt.'

Jake did so. He took off the helmet. Then he got out his second baby bottle of drinking water and took a big slug. He held it out for Flap. 'Here.' Flap had to feel for it. The darkness was total. There were some stars visible, but the moon wouldn't be up for some hours yet.

'Shit. This is water.'

'What did you expect? Jack Daniel's?'

Flap drained the bottle and handed it back. Jake carefully screwed the top back on and stowed it.

'Want to try mine?'

Jake felt in the darkness. Another baby bottle. He sipped it. Brandy. The liquor burned all the way down. He passed it back. 'Thanks.'

'So what's for supper?'

'I got a candy bar in my vest someplace,' Jake told the Marine. 'Stuck it in here while we were in the Philippines, so it's only three months old.'

'I'll wait. I got one from Singapore. Maybe for breakfast, huh?'

'Yeah. You hurt any?'

'Scratched up in a couple places. Nothing bad.'

'I did a little bleeding from a cut on my neck. Maybe the sharks will come.'

Flap had nothing more to say, so Jake sat thinking about sharks. He hated the whole idea. An unseen terror that stalked and *ate* you – it was something from a horror movie, some poorly animated, low-budget monstrosity designed to make kids scream at the Saturday afternoon matinee.

But it was *real.*

Real sharks lived in these waters and they would come – of that he was absolutely certain.

Lying there in the darkness in this rubberized canvas raft with your butt in the water, shivering because the water kept wicking up your flight suit and evaporating, bobbing up and down, up and down, endlessly, up and down and up and down, your mind fixated upon sharks, on the giant predators with row upon row of huge, sharp teeth that even now were following the blood trail, coming closer, coming up from deep deep down towards this flimsy little raft that their teeth could slash through as if it were tissue paper, coming to rip and tear your flesh and *eat you!*

At some point he realized that he had his Colt automatic in his hand. He hadn't thumbed off the safety, thank God, but it was there in his hand and he couldn't remember pulling it from his shoulder holster.

He hefted it.

He had always liked the bulk of it, the thirty-nine ounces of smooth blued steel and oiled wood that promised deadly power if he ever needed it. Tiger Cole had given it to him. It held eight big .45 caliber slugs, any one of which would kill anything from a mouse to a moose. If he shot a shark with this thing, it was going to die quick.

The problem was that the sharks were under water and bullets don't go very far when fired into water. Certainly not these big slow lead slugs. It would be better if he had

345

his .357, but life wasn't like that. If the shark would only stick his head out of the water and hold still . . .

His survival knife! It wasn't all that sharp and, to tell the truth, wasn't really much of a knife, but he could stick a shark with it. And probably get his hand ripped off.

He transferred the automatic to his left hand and got the knife from his survival vest.

The first thing the sharks would do was bump the raft. He would feel that, he hoped. They would bump it and rub it with their sandpaper hide and sniff the blood and finally use their teeth. If they punctured the raft he would go into the water. Then he was doomed. Sooner or later they would get a leg or foot and even if he killed the bastard that did it, the blood would draw more sharks that would finish the job, if he hadn't already bled to death.

He was living a nightmare. If only he could wake up.

He sat in the darkness listening to the slop of the water and waiting for the bump and shivering from the cold. Every sense was alert, straining.

How long he sat like that, half-frozen with fear, listening, he didn't know, but eventually the moon rose and a sliver of light came through a gap in the clouds. Flap saw him then.

'Hey, what's the knife and gun for?'

He was so hoarse that he had trouble with the word and had to clear his throat before he got it out. 'Sharks.'

'You stick that knife into your raft and you'll be swimming.'

Jake just sat shivering.

'Throw out some shark repellent. You got some in your vest, don't ya?'

'It don't work. Ain't worth shit.'

'Won't hurt. Throw it out.'

Now he had the problem of what to do with the gun and knife. 'Hold the gun, will ya?'

'Holster it. The knife too. Believe me, there'll be plenty of time if you need 'em.'

When he had tossed the shark repellent packets into the water, Jake felt better. It was crazy. The repellent – allegedly a mixture of noxious chemicals and ground-up shark gonads – was worthless: someone had done a study and said it had no noticeable effect on sharks and was a waste of government money to acquire. Even though Jake knew all that, throwing the repellent into the water still gave him a sense that he was doing *something*, so he felt better. Less terrorized and more able to cope.

The moonlight helped too. At least if he got a glimpse he could shoot or stab.

'Sorry I got you into this,' he told Flap.

'If this moonlight cruise causes me to miss Australia, Grafton, I'm going to kick your ass up between your shoulder blades. I've been sitting here thinking about Australia and those chocolate aborigine women who will think I'm Sidney fucking Poitier, and believe you me, this buck nigger is really really ready.'

'Those aborigine men may show you how to use a boomerang for a suppository if you mess with their women.'

Flap dismissed that possibility with an airy wave. He was shivering too, Jake noticed.

'Actually I ought to charge you a travel agent's fee,' Jake told the BN. 'You'll cadge free drinks on this tale for years. A silver moon, a tropical lagoon—'

'And you. I wouldn't pay ten cents Hong Kong money to go on a moonlight cruise with you. You got all the romance of a . . .'

They bantered back and forth for a while, then talked seriously about their situation. The US Navy would search until Jake and Flap were rescued or the heavies were convinced they were dead, no matter how long it took. Right this very moment the ships of the task group were

347

making their best speed eastward, eating up the sea miles, their screws thrashing the black water into long foamy ribbons that stretched back under that pale slice of moon to the horizon. At dawn the carrier would pause in her eastward charge only long enough to veer into the wind and launch her planes.

Just in case someone was up there right now, Flap got out his radio and made a few calls. There was no answer, which didn't upset them.

In the morning. The carrier's planes would come in the morning. And if that pirate was anywhere around when the sun came up, he was going to Davy Jones's locker faster than the *Arizona* went to the bottom of Pearl Harbor.

Eventually the conversation petered out and exhaustion caught up with them. Both men dozed as their tiny rafts rocked in the long swells.

Jake woke up to vomit. The equilibrium of the raft was too precarious to stick his head over the side, so he heaved down his chest. He slopped some water over himself to wash the worst of it away.

Seasick. Fuck it all to hell!

He heaved until his stomach was empty, then retched helplessly as his stomach convulsed.

Flap was philosophical. He wasn't sick. 'These things happen in the best of families, even to swab jockeys. It won't kill you. You're tough.'

'Shut up.'

'Wait until I tell the guys in the ready room about this Sailor Grafton, puking his guts like a kid on the Staten Island ferry.'

'Could you please—'

'It'll get worse. You'll see. You'll think you're gonna die. You're really in for it now.'

The convulsions had subsided somewhat when Jake felt the first nudge, just an irregularity in the motion of the raft. He almost missed it.

His seasickness was forgotten. He was reaching for the automatic when Flap said, 'Uh-oh. I think a shark bumped me.'

Now he scanned the water. His eyes were well adjusted to the moonlight. He glimpsed a fin break water, for maybe two seconds. Then it was gone.

'Shark,' he told Flap. 'I saw one!'

'See what you caused! All that moaning about sharks and you attracted the sons of bitches.'

Another bump, more aggressive this time. Jake thought he could feel the grinding from the rough hide rubbing against the fabric of the raft. They didn't have to bite it – if they rubbed it enough they would rub a hole through it.

Fear coursed through him, fear as cold as ice water in his veins. Automatically he had drawn his feet into the raft and tucked his elbows in, which drove his butt deeper into the water. And there was nothing between his butt and those teeth but a very thin layer of rubberized canvas.

He tried to see downward, into the depths where the predators were. Not enough light. It was like looking into a pot of ink.

'See anything?'

'If I scream,' Flap said, 'you'll know they got me.'

'You asshole! You stupid perverted Marine asshole!'

'They're just curious.'

Another nudge. Jake thought he saw something pass out to his right that was darker than the surrounding blackness, but he wasn't sure.

'You hope,' Jake muttered. 'Maybe they're hungry too.'

A fin broke water fifty feet or so away, slightly to the right of the way Jake was facing. He thumbed off the pistol's safety, leveled it and couldn't see the sights clearly! He squeezed off the shot anyway. The muzzle flash temporarily blinded him.

The report was strangely flat. There was nothing to echo

or concentrate the noise. The recoil of the weapon in his hand felt reassuring though.

He blinked his eyes clear and looked at Flap. He had some kind of knife in his right hand and was watching the water intently. It wasn't a government-issue survival knife.

'What kind of knife is that?'

'Throwing knife. For stabbing.'

'What if you want to cut something?'

'Got another knife for that.'

'What are you, a walking cutlery shop?'

'Just look for sharks, will ya? Try not to shoot me or either of the rafts. If they get you I may need your boat.'

'Maybe they like dark meat. Can I have your stereo?'

'My roommate has first dibs.'

They sat staring intently at the water near them. Occasionally a shark nudged them, but the level of aggression didn't seem to increase.

Maybe they would get out of this with whole hides. Then again . . .

A fin broke water just ten feet to Jake's immediate right. He swung the pistol and squeezed the trigger in almost the same motion. The water seemed to explode.

Dimly he saw a tail slashing furiously and spray cascaded over them. The rafts rocked dangerously.

In seconds it was over. The shark sounded.

'Think that was the only one?' Flap asked, his voice betraying his tension for the first time.

'We'll see.'

For some reason the terror that had gripped Jake earlier was gone. He still had enough adrenaline coursing through his veins to fuel a marathon and his heart was thudding like a drum, but for the first time he felt ready to face whatever came.

Nothing came.

If there were any more sharks out there, they stayed away from the raft. After a while Flap tried his radio again.

This time he got an answer. One of the E-2 Hawkeye *Columbia* was up there somewhere far above, the warm, dry and comfortable.

Flap told them of the pirates, of being shot down, of flying south trying to keep the A-6 airborne on the backup hydraulic system and finally ejecting into the sea.

'We're all right. Both of us are in our rafts, uninjured, and the rafts are lashed together.'

Jake had his radio out by this time and heard a calm voice say, 'We'll get planes off at dawn to look for you. You guys check in after sunrise about every fifteen minutes, okay?'

'Roger that. Keep the coffee hot.'

Jake Grafton spoke up. 'Black Eagle, tell the Ops guys that they need to arm the planes. If anybody shoots at them, they need to defend themselves vigorously.'

'I'll pass that along. Wait one while I talk to the ship on the other radio.'

They sat in the darkness with their radios in their hands. Finally the radio came back to life. 'Five Zero Eight Alpha, just how sure are you that you were actually shot at? Is there any way the hydraulic failure could have been a coincidence?'

The question infuriated Grafton. 'I've been shot at before,' he roared into the radio. 'I've been shot at and missed and shot at and hit. You tell those stupid bastards on the ship that we were *shot down*.'

'Roger. You guys hang tough. Talk to you again fifteen minutes after sunrise.'

His anger kept Jake warm for about five minutes. Then he was just cold and tired. With every stitch they wore sopping wet, Jake and Flap huddled in their rafts and shivered. After a time their thirst got the better of them and Flap broke out his two baby bottles full of water. He passed one to Jake, who drank it quickly, afraid he might spill it.

The moon rose higher and gave more light, when it wasn't obscured by clouds.

Eventually, despite the conditions, exhaustion claimed them and they dozed. Jake's mind wandered feverishly. Faces from the past talked to him – Callie, his parents, Tiger Cole, Morgan McPherson – yet he couldn't understand what they were saying. Just when he thought he was getting the message, the faces faded and he was half-asleep in a bobbing raft, wet and cold and very miserable.

Occasionally they talked. Once Jake asked Flap, 'If that attack last month against the Russians had been real, do you think we would have made it?'

'I dunno.'

'Think we would have hit the cruiser?'

'Maybe.'

'They said it was eighty percent probable.'

'I say maybe. I don't do numbers.'

'I think we would be dead.'

'Maybe,' Flap said.

Time passed too slowly, every minute seemed like an hour. The temptation to call Black Eagle to see if he was still up there was very strong and hard to resist. Jake got his radio out twice. Each time he stowed it without turning it on. He might need all the juice in those batteries tomorrow. Wasting battery power now would be stupid.

The worsening sea state brought them fully and completely awake. The swells were bigger and the wind was stronger.

At the top of each swell the rafts pitched dangerously, forcing each man to hang on tightly to keep from being thrown out. They made sure they still had a lanyard attached to each raft.

They had been hanging on to their seats in their frail craft for an eternity when Flap said, 'You shouldn't have called the heavies stupid bastards.'

'I know.'

'Someone will ream you out when we get back.'

'Give me something to look forward to.'

Gradually they became aware that the sky was lightening up. Dawn. It was coming.

Incredibly, the wind strengthened and began to rip spindrift from the swells. Jake reeled in his helmet – it had fallen overboard at some point during the night – dumped out the water and put it on. He ran the clear visor down to keep the salt spray out of his eyes.

It worked. Incredibly, his head was also warmer. He should have been wearing this thing all night!

'Put on your helmet,' he shouted at Flap, who had his tucked under his thighs.

The clouds were just beginning to show pink when they saw the ship. It was almost bows on and coming this way. A little ship, one stack, coming with a bone in its teeth.

Jake pointed.

'Of all the fucking luck!' Flap Le Beau swore.

It was the pirate ship.

CHAPTER TWENTY-ONE

'They've seen us,' Flap shouted over the wind. 'They're coming this way.'

'Better ditch the guns and radios,' Jake told him. He drew the Colt .45 from its holster under his life jacket and survival vest and slipped it over the side. In a holster sewn inside a pocket of his survival vest he had a five-shot Smith & Wesson .38 with a two-inch barrel that he kept loaded with flares. He ditched that too.

The radio – he held on to the radio for a moment as he watched the bow wave of the oncoming small ship subside. They were stopping.

Son of a . . .

He used his survival knife to cut the parachute shroud line that tied him to the radio and lowered it to the water, then released it. Out of the corner of his eye he saw Flap slip his .45 over the side.

'The knife,' Flap told him. 'Dump it too. They'll just take them away from us.' Jake opened his hand and the knife made a tiny splash.

The small ship drifted to a stop on the windward side of the two rafts, about fifteen feet away. Her bulk created a sheltered lee. It was a nice display of seamanship, but Jake and Flap were in no mood to appreciate it.

Staring down from the rail were eight brown faces. Malays, from the look of them. They held assault rifles in their hands.

The sides of this little ship had once been blue, but now

the blue was heavily spotted with rust. Where some of paint had peeled glimpses of gray were visible. Apparently she had once been a patrol boat. Forward of the bow was a gun mount, now empty. That was where they had had the twenty millimeter. It must be stowed below.

The men on deck lowered a net and made gestures with their rifles. Jake and Flap slowly paddled over. Flap went up the net first. Jake followed him. The ship was rocking heavily in the swells. The net was wet, hard to grasp firmly. His foot slipped on the wet cordage and he almost went into the sea. When he was clear of the raft the people on deck began shooting bursts of fully automatic fire. He looked down. Holes popped everywhere on the inflated portions of the rafts and spray flew.

By the time he pulled himself up enough to grasp the rail, the rafts were completely deflated and sinking.

Hands grabbed him and pulled. He scrambled on up the net. As he was coming over the rail, someone hit him in the helmet with a rifle butt and he sprawled onto the deck. Flap was already lying there on his back looking upward.

Most of the crew were barefoot. A couple of them looked like teenagers. Their clothes were ragged and dirty. There was nothing half-assed about their weapons however, worn AK-47s without a fleck of rust. Several of them had pistols stuck into their belts or the tops of their pants.

One of them gestured toward a ladder with the barrel of his weapon. Up. Jake glanced at Flap. His face was expressionless. Grafton prayed that he looked at least half that calm.

At the top of the ladder was the bridge.

The man working the helm and engine was a bit larger than medium height, apparently fit, and had a wicked scar on his chin. The ship was already gathering speed and heeling in a turn. The captain, if captain he was, glanced at them, then concentrated on putting the ship on the course he wanted. When he had the helm amidships and had checked the compass, he said, 'Gentlemen, welcome aboard.'

Jake looked around. Two of the crew were behind them and the rifles were leveled at his and Flap's backs. He turned back to the captain.

'Take off all that . . .' He gestured toward their life jackets and survival vests. 'And the helmets. You look very silly in those helmets.'

Jake and Flap unsnapped their torso harnesses and let them fall into the puddle that was spreading away from each man. They got rid of the G-suits and helmets. Jake took off his empty shoulder holster and dropped it into the pile.

'Where's the pistol?'

Jake shrugged.

The captain took one step and slapped him, quickly and lightly. He stood with his hands on his hips in front of Jake, looking up at him. 'I think you will answer my questions. Where is the pistol?'

'In the ocean.'

The captain went back to the wheel and checked the compass. 'And your survival radios? Where are they?'

'Same place.'

'Where did you fly from?'

'USS *Columbia.*'

'Where is she?'

'West of here.' He toyed with the idea of lying for less than a heartbeat. 'Maybe two or three hundred miles now.'

'When will the planes come looking for you?'

'Shortly.'

'When?'

'I don't know. Sometime soon. After the sun comes up.'

'My men must learn to shoot better. Now we have this complication.'

'Must be a tough way to make a living.'

The captain continued as if he hadn't heard. 'The question is, do we need you alive? You disposed of your radios so you cannot talk to the airplanes on UHF. You could have warned them that you would die if they attacked us. Alas, we have only a marine band radio. It's a pity.'

'You speak English pretty well.'

The captain was scanning the ocean and glancing occasionally at the sky. He didn't bother looking at the two Americans. 'But I do not think they will attack. They will look us over and take many pictures. That is all.' His eyes flicked to their faces. 'What do you think?'

Unfortunately Jake thought he was right. He tried to keep his face deadpan but his turmoil probably showed. The captain apparently thought so. He said something to the guards and waved his hands. They prodded the aviators in the back and turned them around. As they left the bridge, Jake saw one of the crewmen opening the pockets of the survival vest and dumping the contents on the deck.

They were shoved into a tiny compartment below the main deck. There was a large hasp on the door.

'Can we have some water?' Jake asked the three men who pushed him inside right behind Flap. They ignored him.

The door swung shut and they heard the padlock snapping closed. The compartment was only slightly larger than a bedroom closet and had apparently been used for storage. There was no light and no electrical sockets, although there was one small, filthy porthole that admitted subdued light.

Flap leaned against the door and listened. After a bit he shrugged. 'They've gone, I think.'

'Maybe there's a bug.'

'Go ahead and look for it, James Bond.'

Jake sat against a wall and began taking off his boots. He took off his socks and wrung the water out, then put them back on. 'They'll probably shoot us after a while,' he said.

'Probably,' Flap agreed. He also sat. 'The captain ain't

357

sure if he'll need us or not. The bastard has it figured pretty good. I'll bet he can get this thing to port before the US Navy can get a surface ship here to board him. He thinks so too. But he's saving us just in case.'

'What do you think they did with the freighter?'

'Sank her would be my bet. They were probably off-loading high-value items when we showed up.'

'And the crew?'

Flap shrugged.

'Then why in hell did these guys shoot at us?'

'Perhaps someone panicked. Or they didn't want their picture taken. The airplane overhead was a problem they hadn't figured on.'

'So you think this is some kind of local industry?'

'Don't you?'

'I don't know.'

'Well, look at it. Here we are on the southern coast of Sumatra, about the most out-of-the-way corner of the earth it's possible to imagine. In among these islands we're well off the shipping lanes, which go through the Sunda Strait or the Strait of Malacca. So these dudes from a local village sail out into the shipping lanes, board a ship – probably at night when only one or two people are on watch on the bridge – then bring it here and loot it. They probably kill everyone aboard and scuttle the ship. The high-value items from the cargo that can't be traced eventually end up in the bazaars in Singapore or Rangoon or even Mombassa. The ship never shows up at its destination and no one knows what happened to it. Say they knock off one ship a year, or one every two years. Be a nice little racket if they don't pull it too often and get the insurance companies in a tizzy.'

'But someone got off fifteen seconds of an SOS and we came to look.'

'To look and take pictures. They probably thought they had killed everyone on that ship, then the SOS burned their eardrums. They should have disabled the radio but they didn't. One mistake led to another. So instead of waiting to loot the ship after dark, they decided to try it in daylight. Then we showed up. You know as well as I do that a good photo interpreter could identify this ship sooner or later. The captain knows that too. So he fired when we gave him a golden opportunity. I'll bet he was the bastard at the trigger.'

'He's going to get photographed again today.'

'But the victim isn't tied up alongside. Now this is just a little ship going about its business in a great big ocean.'

Jake merely grunted. After a bit he said, 'It doesn't figure.'

'What doesn't?'

'That ship they stopped is an old freighter. Looked to me like a Liberty ship. Eight to ten thousand tons, no more than that. Why didn't these guys stop a big container ship? All the valuable electronic stuff gets shipped in sealed containers these days.'

'Beats me.' Flap sat and removed his boots and socks. After a while he said, 'The bastards could at least have given us water. I'm really thirsty.'

He had his boots back on when he said, 'Did you notice the captain's hands? The calluses on the edges of his palms? He's a karate expert. If you had even flinched when he slapped you he might have broken your neck.'

'Now you tell me.'

'You did fine. Handled it well. Be submissive and don't give them the slightest reason to think you might fight back.'

'I'm certainly not going to strap on a karate expert.'

Flap snorted. 'They're the easiest to beat. They're too self-confident.'

Jake didn't think that comment worth a reply. He retrieved his cigarettes from his flight suit shoulder pocket and carefully removed each one from the pack, trying not to tear the wet paper. He laid them out to dry. Then he rolled onto his side and tried to stretch out. The compartment was too small. At least his ass wasn't submerged.

A bullet in the head or chest wasn't a cheery prospect. All these months of planning for the future and now it looked as if there would be no future. Strange how life works, how precarious it is. Right now he wanted water, food and a cigarette. If he got those, then he would want a hot bath and dry clothes. Then a bunk. The wants would keep multiplying, and sooner or later he would be staring at a bulkhead and fretting about insubstantial things, like what the next ready room movie was going to be, his brush with death shoved back into some dark corner in the attic of his mind.

He had faced death before in the air and on the ground, so he knew how it worked. If you survived you had to keep on living – that was a law, like gravity. If you died – well, that was that. Those left behind had to keep on living.

Maybe in the great scheme of things it really didn't matter very much whether these two blobs of living tissue called Jake Grafton and Flap Le Beau died here or someplace else, died today or next week or in thirty or fifty years. The world would keep on turning, life for everyone else would go on, human history would run exactly the same course either way.

It mattered to Jake, of course. He didn't want to die. Now or any other time. Presumably Flap felt the same way.

Fuck these pirates! Fuck these assholes! Murdering and stealing without a thought or care for anyone else. If they get theirs, life is good.

As he thought about the pirates Jake Grafton was swept by a cold fury that drove the lethargy from him.

He sat up and looked at Flap, who had also curled up on the deck. He wasn't asleep either. 'We gotta figure out a way to screw these guys good.'

Flap didn't smile. 'Any suggestions?'

'Well, if they shoot us, we sure as hell ought to take a

couple of them with us. I don't think they'll shoot us in here. Blood and bullet holes would be hard to explain if this ship were ever searched. I figure they'll take us topside, tie a chain around us and put us over the side. Maybe shoot us first.'

'And . . . ?'

'If we could kill a couple of the bastards we ought to give it a try.'

'Why?'

'Don't give me that shit!'

'What's a couple more or less?'

'You'd let them shoot you without a struggle?'

'Not if I have a choice. I'm going to take a lot of killing. But if they want us dead we're going to end up dead, sooner or later.

'That's my point. When I go to meet the devil I want to go in a crowd.'

Flap chuckled. It was a chuckle without mirth. 'What I can't figure out, Grafton, is why the hell you joined the Navy instead of the Marines.'

'The Navy is more high-toned.'

They sat talking for most of an hour, trying to plan a course of action that would kill at least one and hopefully two pirates.

Flap could kill two men in two seconds with his bare hands, Jake assumed, so it seemed that the only real chance they had was for him to cause enough commotion to give Flap those two seconds. He didn't state this premise, however Flap let it go unchallenged. They hadn't a chance of surviving, not against assault weapons. But if their captors relaxed, if only for an instant . . .

When they finally ceased talking, both men were so tired they were almost instantly asleep, curled around each other on the deck because there was no room to stretch out and rocked by the motion of the ship.

About an hour later a jet going over woke them. The

thunder of the engines faded, then increased in volume. Then it faded completely and they were left with just the sounds of the ship. The plane did not come back.

The pirates came for Flap and Jake after the sun set. Both men stood when they heard the padlock rattle and assumed positions on opposite sides of the door. When the door opened two men were there with their weapons leveled, ready to fire.

One man motioned with the barrel of his rifle.

Jake went first, with Flap behind. They had discussed it and concluded a fight in the confined interior passageways was too risky. They shuffled along with their heads down, going willingly in the direction indicated.

When they came out on deck they saw land close aboard, just visible in the twilight. The shore was rocky, but the dark jungle began just inland from the rocks. Maybe three hundred yards. The water was flat, without swells. The ship was inside the mouth of a river headed upstream.

The two pirates wanted them to go aft. The deck here was probably only six feet wide. Flap was looking scared and had his hands up about head high. Two men stood on the dark fantail watching them come, their rifles cradled in their arms.

'Four,' Jake muttered. 'Jesus . . .'

They had just reached the fantail when they heard a jet running high. They looked up.

'Point,' Flap said, and Jake did, enthusiastically, as Flap shot a quick glance back over his shoulder.

What happened next happened so quickly Jake almost didn't react. Flap half-turned and his right arm swept down. The blade of a knife buried itself in the solar plexus of the gunman just behind him. This man staggered and looked down in stupefied amazement at the knife handle sticking out of his chest.

The man behind him had been looking up, trying to see

the jet. He dropped his gaze in time to see Flap Le Beau hurtling across the ten feet of space that separated them. He swung the rifle, but too late.

With one vicious, backhand swipe, Flap cut his throat from ear to ear. Blood spouted from severed arteries as the man collapsed. In a continuation of his motion, Flap spun and rammed the knife into the left kidney of the first man, who was somehow still on his feet and trying to turn to bring his rifle to bear.

Meanwhile Jake Grafton had launched himself at the two spectators standing with their rifles cradled in their arms. They too had been looking up, which gave him just the break he needed. He took them both down in a flying tackle.

He got his hands on one of the rifles and used it as a club. He smashed the butt into one man's Adam's apple.

The other man had retained his rifle and now it fired, the muzzle just inches from Jake's ear. Deafened, with the strength born of terror, Jake dropped the weapon in his hands and seized the barrel of the other man's AK-47 as he drove a punch at his face. The blow glanced off his forehead, but the man struggled to hold on to the rifle, so Jake let fly again. This time his fist connected solidly and the man went to the deck, still holding on to the rifle. Jake ripped it from his hands and slammed the butt down on his throat with all his strength.

With the rifle coming up, he turned in time to see Flap inserting his throwing knife back into the sheath that hung down his back, inside his flight suit. The fighting knife had a triangular blade about four inches long – it went into the sheath worn on his left forearm, under the sleeve of his flight suit.

Le Beau picked up an AK-47, glanced at the action, then fired one round into each of the four men lying on the deck. Then he flashed a grin at Jake. 'Still alive, by God!'

Jake grabbed the rifle on the deck at his feet and

removed the magazine. He stuck it into a chest pocket of his flight suit. 'I thought you ditched your knives.'

'I haven't been without a knife since I was thirteen.'

'Let's see if we can get to the bridge.'

'If it gets too hot we'll go over the side and swim for shore.'

'Okay.'

With his rifle at the ready, Flap went forward on the starboard side. Jake took the port.

The bridge stuck out over the deck. Someone appeared in the window and Jake snapped off a shot. The window shattered and the head disappeared. A miss.

An open hatch revealed a ladder that probably gave access to the engine room. Jake pulled the hatch shut and rotated the lever that dogged it shut. He looked around for something to block the lever so it couldn't be opened. Nothing.

He came to another open hatchway, a short passage-way across the superstructure to the starboard side of the ship.

He paused, trying to decide what to do. Sweat was running into his eyes. And he was thirsty as holy hell. What he wouldn't give for one drink of water!

Flap's head popped around the corner on the starboard side. He saw Jake and came his way. 'What did ya shoot at?'

'Someone on the bridge.'

'There's at least five more guys on this tub, probably more.'

'How come they aren't coming after us?'

'We're probably pretty near their base. When they pull in, someone on the pier will take care of us.'

'We gotta get off this bucket.'

'They'll gun us in the water.'

Jake wiped the sweat from his eyes and tried to think. 'Somebody is probably in the engine room,' he said. 'The ladder down is here on the port side. What say you go up to the bridge and keep them occupied. I'll go to the engine room and try to disable this tub. Then we go over the side.'

'Which way?'

'Port side. In five minutes.'

'My watch isn't working.'

'*About* five minutes. Or if the engines stop.'

'Okay.'

Jake checked to make sure no one was in sight, then he moved back to the engine room hatch, opened it and latched it open. The ladder down was actually a steep stair.

Uh-oh. He wished he hadn't volunteered to do this.

What the hell! They were dead this morning when this pirate ship came over the horizon.

With the rifle at the ready and the safety off, he eased down the ladder, waiting for the inevitable bullet.

This is like committing suicide slowly.

The area at the bottom of the ladder was shielded by a large condenser. Jake paused behind it, wiped the sweat from his hands and gripped the rifle carefully. He eased his head out, so that he could look with one eye. He was looking aft along a narrow passageway between the ship's two diesel engines. He saw a leg, the back of a leg. He pulled his head back and turned so he could see forward. Ease the head out and peek. No one.

Okay. Someone aft, no one visible forward. He would step out, shoot the guy aft, then swing so he could shoot forward.

That was a good plan.

He was going to get shot. Sure as shit.

He took a deep breath, and exhaled slowly. His heart was pounding a mile a minute.

Now!

He leaped out and squeezed the trigger.

The man was using a pipe wrench on a valve. The bullets slammed him down. Jake spun. A man coming through the door shooting as Jake's bullets caught him, hammered him.

Something slammed into Jake's side, turning him half around.

He staggered, leaned back against the starboard engine and looked aft.

The man there wasn't moving. The man forward had taken at least three in the chest.

Jake dug the extra magazine out of his chest pocket and substituted it for the magazine in his weapon. His left side was numb. Shock. He staggered aft. The magazine of the AK-47 on the floor looked like it still held ten shells or so. He pocketed it.

Now he heard a racket from topside that he knew were shots. Flap. He peered through the open hatch that led forward.

Fuel valves. This guy had been opening or closing these valves. The main tank must be on the other side of this bulkhead.

Which ones were the feed lines? He picked two that looked like they went up over the engines to the fuel injectors. Holding the rifle in his left hand, he began screwing the starboard engine valve shut. Then he closed the one to the port engine.

The engines would take a minute or so to die. If he had picked the right valves.

Unwilling to wait, he spied a large red valve at the bottom of the bulkhead with a pipe that wasn't connected to anything. The valve had a rusty padlock on it. Must be the tank drain valve. He put one bullet into the lock. The lock broke, and diesel fuel began running out of the bullet hole.

Jake twisted the valve. It was rusty.

Desperate to be out of here, he laid down the rifle and used both hands. It opened. Fuel began running out, at first a trickle, then a steady stream. He kept twisting.

The steady throb of the diesels took on a new note. Several cylinders missed. The starboard engine died. By the time the port engine stopped he had the drain valve full open. He was getting splashed with diesel fuel.

The lights died to a dim glow when the port engine quit. With the generators off, the lights were using battery juice.

He grabbed the rifle and started aft through the engine room for the ladder. He heard more shots, quite clearly now that the engines were silent.

His left side was pretty bloody and the pain was fierce.

Well, if he was going to fuck these guys, he should do the job right. He went back to the second man he shot and ripped his shirt off. It was cotton. He went back to the drain valve and let some diesel fuel run onto the shirt. He squeezed the shirt to get rid of the excess and dug his lighter out of his pocket.

The plastic butane piece of shit refused to light. He blew several times on the flint wheel. Come on, goddamnit!

There. He held the flame under a corner of the shirt. It took. He waited until the shirt was going pretty well, then dropped it into the gap between the catwalk and one engine. The diesel fuel was running into the bilges there.

The fire lit with a whoof.

Jake eased his head around the corner of the ladder, and jerked it back just in time. Bullets spanged into the condenser.

The fire was spreading in the bilges. Already the smoke was dense, the lights barely visible.

This couldn't be the only ladder topside. The other ladder must be on the starboard side. Trying not to breathe the smoke, he hurried that way.

Coughing and gagging, he found the ladder.

Was there someone up here waiting for him?

'Come on, Jake.' Flap's voice.

He was having trouble breathing and his feet were getting damned hot. Somehow he lost the rifle. He

367

scrambled up the ladder on all fours, slipped and slammed his head against a step and slid a couple steps before he caught himself.

Hands grabbed him and pulled. He kept scrambling and somehow they made the deck.

'I've been shot.'

'Let's get over the side or you'll get shot again. There's at least four of them forward.'

'Where?'

'We go off the fantail. Ship's sideways in the river.'

They went that way, Jake barely able to walk. He took deep breaths, trying to get enough oxygen. Spots swam before his eyes. 'They'll shoot us in the water.'

'It's our only chance. Come on.'

Flap tossed his AK-47 into the water, then jumped after it. Jake followed.

The darkness was almost total now. Jake was only able to swim with his right arm. His left side felt like it was on fire. Several times he got mouthfuls of water, so he swallowed them. It tasted good.

He was struggling. More water in his mouth and nose. He gagged.

'Just float. I've got you.' And Flap did have him, by the collar of his flight suit.

Jake concentrated on staying afloat and breathing against the pain in his side.

Flap was pulling him backward, so he could see the fore-shortened outline of the ship, and smoke black as coal oozing out amidships. He could also see the glow of fire coming from a ladder well, apparently the one on the port side, since he could now see the top of the bow. All this registered without his thinking about it, which was good, since he needed desperately to concentrate on breathing and keeping his head above water.

They were maybe fifty yards from the ship when he saw muzzle flashes from the bow.

'They're shooting,' he tried to say, but he swallowed more water.

'Relax,' Flap whispered. 'Quit trying to help. Let me do this.'

Somehow they must have swum out of the main channel, Jake realized, because the ship was pulling away from them. The current must be taking her downstream.

The current and the darkness saved them. When the twenty-millimeter cannon on the bow opened up, the bullets hit downstream, abeam the ship. Bursts split the night for almost a minute, but none of the shells even came close.

CHAPTER TWENTY-TWO

'I never saw a knife like that before.'

'Designed it myself,' Flap said. 'Call it a slasher.'

Of course Jake couldn't see the knife now, since they were sitting in absolute total darkness under a tree in the jungle, but Flap had borrowed his lighter and gone looking for tree moss. Now he was back and was cutting up his and Jake's T-shirts to use as a bandage. He had inspected the wound in the glow of the lighter when they first got ashore. 'It's nasty but not deep. You are one lucky white boy. I think maybe one rib broke, and it ain't too bad.'

'Feels like one of your knives is stuck in there.'

Jake sat now holding the moss in place while Flap cut up the shirts. The moss was slowing the bleeding, apparently. He heard a motorboat coming down the river. They sat silently while it passed. When the sound had faded, Jake asked, 'So what are we going to do?'

'Not much we can do tonight. There's an overcast so there wouldn't be much light when the moon comes up. The jungle canopy will keep it dark down here. We're going to have to just sit tight until morning.'

'Think they'll come looking for us tonight?'

'In the morning maybe. Maybe not. I hope they come. We need some weapons. All we have are my knives. Be easier to ambush them here than around their village, wherever that is.'

'The stabber and the slasher.'

'Yep.'

'Where did you learn to throw a knife like that?'

'Taught myself,' Flap told him. 'It's a skill that comes in handy occasionally.'

Jake moved experimentally. He tried to stretch out and relax to ease the pain. After a bit he said, 'I don't think their village is far upriver. It was narrowing when we left that ship.'

'We'll work our way upriver in the morning. We need a boat to get out to sea.'

'Tell you what, Tarzan, is there any way you could rustle us up some grub? My stomach thinks my throat is cut.'

'Tomorrow. You like snake?'

'No.'

'Tastes like—'

'Chicken. I've heard that crap before. I ate my share at survival school.'

'Naw. Tastes like lizard.'

'I don't like them either.'

'Sit up and hold up your arms and let me wrap this thing around you.'

Jake obeyed. When Flap finished he eased his arms back into his flight suit and zipped it up. 'What about bugs?'

'They're okay as an appetizer, but you expend about as many calories gathering them as—'

'How are we gonna keep 'em from bleeding us dry tonight?'

'Smear your skin with mud.'

Jake was already encased in mud almost to his waist from wading through the goo to get ashore. He scraped some from his legs and ankles and applied it to his face and neck.

After a bit, Flap asked, 'How many guys were in the engine room?'

'Two. What happened topside?'

'They pinned me down. I needed a couple grenades and didn't have them. Got one of them, though.'

'We're lucky to be alive.'

'Grafton, you are the luckiest SOB I know. If that bullet had been an inch farther right you'd be lying dead in that engine room. It's scary – we're using up oodles of luck and we're still young men. We're gonna be high and dry and clean out of the good stuff before we're very much older.'

They lay down on the jungle floor and tried to relax. Lying in the darkness in the muck, swatting at mosquitoes as the creepy-crawlies examined them – Kee-rist! Well, at least they weren't sitting in seawater to their waist or huddled in a steel compartment waiting for an executioner to come for them.

After a while Jake said, 'Are you ever going to get married?'

'You read my mind. I was lying here hungry and thirsty and miserable as hell contemplating that very subject. And you?'

'Smart ass!'

'No, seriously – why don't you tell the Great Le Beau all about it. After all, before a man commits holy matrimony he should have the benefit of unbiased, expert counsel. Even if he plans on ignoring the pithy wisdom he will undoubtedly receive, as you most certainly will.'

'I *might* get married. If she'll say yes.'

'Ahh – you haven't queried your intended victim. Or you have and she refused in a rare fit of eminent good sense. Which is it?'

'Haven't asked.'

'Uh-huh.'

'Met her last year in Hong Kong.'

'I met a girl in Hong Kong once upon a time,' Flap replied. 'Her name was . . . damn! It was right on the tip of my tongue. Anyway, she worked at the Susy Wong whorehouse, a couple of blocks from the China Fleet Club. You know it? She was maybe sixteen and had long black hair that hung almost to her waist and exquisite little breasts that—'

'I met an American girl.'

'Umph.'

'I knew you'd be interested, seeing how we fly together and all, so I'll tell you. Since you aren't sleepy and we got nothing else to do.' And he did. He told about meeting Callie, what she looked like, sounded like, how he felt when he was with her. He told Flap about her parents and about Chicago, about getting out of the Navy and what she said. He had been talking for at least half an hour when he finally realized that Le Beau was asleep.

His side throbbed badly. He changed positions in the detritus of the jungle floor, trying to find one that would cause the least stress on his wound. The sharpness of the pain drove his mind back to the pirate ship, to the prospect of death in a few moments by execution.

Flap threw that knife into that one guy and sliced the other's throat in what – three seconds? Jake had never seen a man move so fast, nor had he ever seen a man butchered with a knife. Shot, yes. But not slashed to death with one swipe of the arm, his throat ripped from ear to ear, blood spurting as horror seared the victim's face.

Life is so fragile, so tenuous.

Luckily he had gotten into motion before the surprise wore off the other two.

And the engine room, the horror as that man came around the engine shooting and the bullet struck him. Now the scene ran through his mind over and over, every emotion pungent and powerful, again and again and again.

Finally he let it go.

He felt like he had that sticker of Flap's stuck in his side right now.

So those other guys died and he and Flap lived. For a few more hours.

It was crazy. Those men, he and Flap – they were like

fish in the sea, eating other fish to sustain life before they too were eaten in their turn. Kill, kill, kill.

Man's plight is a terribly bad joke.

He was dozing when the sound of a motorboat going upriver brought him fully awake. Flap woke up too. They lay listening until the noise dissipated completely.

'Wonder what happened to the pirate ship?'

'Maybe it sank.'

'Maybe.'

After the sun came up the foliage was so thick that Jake had to keep his hand on Flap's shoulder so that he wouldn't lose him. Flap moved slowly, confidently and almost without noise. Without him Jake would have been hopelessly lost in five minutes.

Flap caught a snake an hour or so after dawn and they skinned it and ate it raw. They drank water trapped in fallen leaves if there weren't too many insects in it. Once they came to a tiny stream and both men lay on their stomachs and drank their fill.

Other than the noises they made, the jungle was silent. If anyone was looking for them, they were being remarkably quiet.

Jake and Flap heard the noises of small engines and voices for a half hour before they reached the village, which as luck would have it, turned out to be on their side of the river. It was about noon as near as they could tell when they hit the village about a hundred yards inland. Thatched huts and kids, a few rusty jeep-type vehicles. They could smell food cooking. The aroma made Jake's stomach growl. A dog barked somewhere.

They stayed well back and worked their way slowly down to the riverbank to see what boats there might be.

There were several. Two or three boats with outboard engines and one elderly cabin cruiser lay moored to a shor pier just a couple of dozen yards from where Jake and Flap crouched in the jungle. Beyond the boats was a much larger pier that jutted almost to midstream. Resting against the T-shaped end of it was the hijacked ship. Above the ship numerous ropes made a latticework from bank to bank. Leafy branches of trees dangled from the ropes – camouflage. The freighter seemed to be held in place against the current mainly by taut hawsers from the bow and stern that stretched across the dark water to the river's edge, where they were wrapped numerous times around large trees.

From where they lay they could just see the ship's name and home port: *Che Guevara, Habana.*

Flap began to laugh.

'What's so funny?' Jake whispered.

'A Cuban freighter. We got shot down and almost killed over a Commie freighter. If that doesn't take the cake!'

'My heart bleeds for Fidel.'

'Ain't it a shame.'

The ship's cranes were in motion and at least a dozen men were visible. A large crate was lowered to the pier and six or eight men with axes began chopping it open. Apparently they didn't have a forklift.

Inside the box were other, smaller boxes. Pairs of men hoisted these and carried them off the pier toward the village.

'Weapons,' Flap said. 'They hijacked a ship full of weapons.'

'What do you think was in those little boxes just now?'

'Machine guns, I think. Look, aren't those ammo boxes?'

'Could be.'

'They are. I've seen boxes like that before. One time up on the Cambodian border.'

'Maybe this ship wasn't hijacked. Maybe those guys met it in midocean to put aboard a pilot.'

'Then why the SOS?'

Jake shrugged, or tried to. The pain in his side was down

to a dull throb, as long as he held his shoulder still and didn't take any deep breaths.

'These dudes are ripping off a Commie weapons shipment,' Flap said slowly. 'Maybe one bound for Haiphong. Guns and ammo are worth their weight in gold.'

'That little cabin cruiser is our ticket out of here, if it isn't a trap.'

'Maybe,' Flap said shortly. 'We can't do anything until tonight anyhow, so let's make ourselves comfortable and see what we can see. I don't see any floodlights anywhere; these people won't be working at night. But that little boat is just too good to be true. The captain we met yesterday didn't impress me as the type of careless soul who would leave a boat where we could swipe it at our convenience.'

After a few minutes Jake muttered, 'I haven't seen the captain yet on the dock.'

'He's around someplace. You can bet your ass on that.'

'That ship we set fire to isn't here either.'

'Maybe they abandoned it. But remember that boat that went down the river last night, then came back hours later? It was probably that cruiser there, and it probably rescued everyone left alive. The captain is here. I can feel him.'

'Okay.'

'See that shack just up there on the left? From there a fellow would have a good view of the boat and the dock. Keep your eyes on that. I'm going to slip around and see what they're doing with all these weapons they're taking off that ship.'

'Leave me one of your knives.'

'Which one?'

'The sticker.'

Flap drew it from the sheath hanging down his back and handed it to Jake butt-first. Then he took two steps and disappeared into the jungle.

A throwing knife with a needle-sharp point and a slick

376

handle, the weapon was perhaps ten inches long. Jake slipped it into his boot top, leaving just enough of the hilt exposed so that he could get it out quickly. He hadn't the foggiest idea how to throw it, but he had no qualms about jabbing it into somebody to defend himself. His throbbing side was a constant reminder that these people wanted him dead.

Lying under a tangle of vegetation, he rolled on his good side and gingerly unzipped his flight suit. The bandage was encrusted with old blood. Nothing fresh. He zipped the flight suit back up and rolled on his belly. He wormed his way forward until he could just see the shack and the pier beyond, then checked to ensure that he was completely hidden. He decided he was.

At least two hours had passed when Flap returned. It was hard to judge. Time passed slowly when you were lying in a jungle with bugs crawling around and flying critters gnawing at your hide. If you were short of sleep, so hungry that your stomach seemed knotted, suffering from a raging thirst and had diarrhea, every minute was agony. Jake dared not leave his post, so he shit where he lay.

Once he heard a jet. It was far away, the sound of its engines just a low hum.

'Jesus H. Christ!' Flap whispered when he crawled up beside Jake, startling him half out of his skin. 'What died?'

'That's shit, you bastard. Never smelled it before, huh?'

'For crying out loud, you could at least have dropped your flight suit.'

'There's someone over there in that shack. He stuck his head out twice and looked around. Seen smoke a couple times too, just a whiff, like he's standing right inside the door smoking a cigarette.'

'There's two of them in there. I looked in the back window.'

Jake had kept his eyes glued on that shack and hadn't once glimpsed Flap. For the first time he realized just how terrifically good Le Beau was in the jungle.

'Here, this is for you.'

Flap passed over an AK-47. 'It's loaded with a full clip. Safety is on.'

'Found this lying around, did you?'

'Relax. They won't find the guy who had it for quite a while. Maybe never. Gimme my sticker back. I feel kinda naked without it.'

Jake got the knife from his boot and handed it over.

'Lotta good that would have done you in your boot. You should have stabbed it into the dirt right by your hand, so you could grab it quick.'

'Next time. Until then I'll just stick to ol' Betsy here. Appreciate the gift. So what's the setup?'

The bad guys were stacking the weapons back in the jungle, out of sight from the air. Most of the stuff was still in crates. 'They got a hell of a pile out there but I don't think they got it all. Certainly not a shipload. There's no way of telling what's left on the ship.'

'I've been figuring,' Jake said. 'Seems to me that the first thing we have to do after dark is take out those two guys in the shack and check out that cabin cruiser.'

'It may be booby trapped.'

'I don't think so. That was the boat we heard last night. The guys in the shack are supposed to kill us if we try for it.'

'Can't start the engine here.'

'I know. We'll have to cast off and drift downriver. We can use one of your knives to cut us some poles to keep it off the banks. Then when we're a couple miles downriver, we'll start the engine and motor out to sea.'

'What if the engine won't start?'

'We just drift on out.'

'They'll follow.'

'Not if we blow up the ammo dump and sink all these little boats.'

Flap gave a soft whistle of amazement. 'You don't want much, do you?'

'So what's your plan?' Jake asked.

'Kill the guys in the shack and steal the boat. The Navy can come back any old time and bomb these dudes to hell.'

Jake snorted. 'Your faith in the system is truly amazing. Here we are in a foreign country – Indonesia, I think. Whatever. Assuming we manage to get rescued and tell our tale, the only thing the US Navy can do is send a polite note to the State Department. State is going to pass this hot tip to the National Security Council, which will probably staff the shit out of it. The fact that these weapons are going to be sold to revolutionary zealots in Asia, the Mideast or Africa who will use them to cause as much hell as humanly possible and murder everyone who disagrees with them won't cause one of those comfortable bureaucrats to miss a minute's sleep. When the nincompoops who brought you Vietnam get through scratching their butts, they'll give the US ambassador to Indonesia a note to give to whoever is running this country this week. That whoever may or may not do anything. After all, he's probably getting a cut of this operation. There's a whale of a lot of money to be made here: your karate expert captain friend is probably smart enough to spread it around a little.'

'A lot of the weapons are still on Fidel's freighter,' Flap pointed out.

'We'll have to blow it up too.'

'Just out of curiosity, what little army is going to do all this blowing up you envision?'

'You and me.'

Le Beau rolled over on his back and threw an arm across his face. In a moment he said, 'You got gall, Grafton, I'll give you that. You lay there with a bullet hole in your side, wearing your own shit and tell me that 'you and me' are going to blow up a weapons cache and a ship! My ass. They'll smell you fifty feet away. *You* want *me* to go do the hero bit and probably get myself killed.'

'We'll both go. But this is a volunteer deal. You're senior to me and we aren't in the airplane anymore. It's your call.'

'Thank you from the bottom of my teensy little heart. Ah me . . . My second command – I used to lead a whole platoon, you know. Now it's just me and one wounded flyboy with the shits. My military career is going up like a rocket.'

'Oh, cork it. What do you want to do?'

'You think you're up for this?'

'Yeah.'

'Well, you asked for it. Here's the plan.'

As Jake Grafton listened the thought occurred to him that Flap Le Beau had been thinking about screwing these pirates all afternoon. He got a warm feeling. Flap had let him suggest it. Flap Le Beau was one hell of a good guy.

'Not right after dark,' Flap said. 'They'll expect us then. After midnight, in the wee hours.'

'The moon will be up sometime after midnight,' Jake pointed out. 'The clouds will probably obscure it though.'

'It would be good if the clouds let the moonlight through. They'll relax and maybe sleep.'

They pulled back into the jungle to a small stream. Jake undressed and sat in it. The diarrhea was drying up, a little anyway, leaving him very thirsty. He drank and drank from the stream. Then he washed out his flight suit and under-wear and put them back on.

Finally he and Flap stretched out in the damp, rotting leaves. The bugs were bad, but they were very tired and the muffled noise from the village and the pier lulled them to sleep. They were both emotionally wrung out from their experiences of the last two days and nights, so their sleep was dreamless. When they awoke the light was fading rapidly and the noise from the ship had ceased. They drank again from the stream, Jake relieved himself, then they crawled back to the vantage point where they could see the shack and the small boats.

The waiting was hard.

When you have finally crossed the threshold, left behind good meals, a comfortable bed, clean clothes and the relaxed company of friends, life becomes a mere battle for survival. The nonessential sinks out of sight.

They lay in the foliage, one man on his stomach watching, the other on his side or back napping. Fortunately there was a small electric light mounted on a pole near the boat dock.

The hours dragged. With nothing to look forward to but battle, and perhaps death, delay was painful. Yet they waited.

The guards in the shack were changed several hours into the night. Two new men came, the two inside left. All of them carried rifles.

No one approached the boats. Even when the rain came. At first it was gentle, then it increased in intensity. Still no one came to cover the boats or check their moorings.

All activity on the dark freighter ceased. From their vantage point the watchers caught occasional glimpses of cigarettes flaring, but the ship was just a blacker spot in the black night.

Finally activity in the village ceased.

The rain continued to fall.

Jake slept again.

When Flap shook him awake, the rain had slowed to a drizzle.

'Look,' he whispered so softly that at first Jake didn't understand. He had to inch around to see what Flap was pointing at. After several seconds he realized he was looking at the two men standing by the boat dock smoking. They were away from the light, but there they were, quite plain.

'They came out of the shack. I'm going now.'

'Okay.' Jake fumbled with the AK-47, made sure the action was clear of leaves, then eased it through the foliage in front of him and spread his feet. Only then did he realize Flap had disappeared.

Minutes passed as he watched the figures by the boat dock. He could hear the murmur of voices. They stood smoking and talking.

Jake waited. If Flap were discovered now, they had no choice but to try for the cabin cruiser.

Finally the men turned and ambled uphill for the shack. One of them paused while the other went on ahead. He was facing in this direction. Only when he turned toward the shack did Jake realize that he was zipping up his pants. He had relieved himself.

The first man was already inside. The second man paused in the doorway. Flap was inside. Jake stopped breathing and blinked rapidly, trying to see in the almost nonexistent light. If the man shouted or fired his weapon . . .

Then he turned for the door and merged with another shadow coming out. Now he disappeared within.

In less than a minute Flap Le Beau came across the open ground toward Jake's position. He was walking calmly, with a rifle in each hand. When he approached Jake's position he said softly, 'Come on. Let's look at the boat.'

Jake wormed his way straight ahead out of the brush, then struggled to his feet. Flap was already at the boat dock. Jake followed along, trying to look as nonchalant as the two guards had.

Flap got into the cabin cruiser. 'The battery works,' he reported.

'Any fuel?'

'There's a can here. Let me see.' A half minute passed. 'Well, it's gasoline. A couple of gallons. I'm going to pour it into the tank.'

382

This cabin cruiser – what if it were sabotaged? Maybe they should take one of the little boats. Jake looked in them for oars. Each of them had a set. They had outboard engines too, but the presence of oars seemed to indicate that the owners of the boats weren't brimming with confidence over the reliability of those engines. Or maybe they were just careful.

It was going to be a big gamble.

Jake turned his back on the cabin cruiser and stood looking at the village. A faint glow from three or four lights showed through the foliage.

Flap joined him on the dock. 'Decision time, shipmate. We can untie this scow and get out of here right now with a chance and maybe a future. They won't know this tub's gone until morning.'

'You're senior,' Jake told him. 'You make the decision and you live with it.'

'I'm giving you a choice.'

'This is ridiculous.' They couldn't stand here in plain sight arguing like two New York bankers waiting for a taxi. 'Lead the way, Le Beau. I'll be right behind you.'

Flap took one of the AKs and lowered it into the water, then released it. With the other rifle in his left hand, he turned and walked off the dock. Jake followed him.

They circled the village through the jungle. The weapons cache was on the side away from the sea, a hundred yards from the long pier. At least two guards were on duty.

Flap picked a vantage point and watched for a while with Jake beside him. The guards walked the perimeter alertly. After the second one passed, Flap told Jake, 'They're too alert. They know something's up.'

'Maybe they missed that guy you killed this afternoon.'

'Maybe.'

'What if there's someone inside the pile?'

'There is. Believe it.'

'Let's go around to the other side and get a look before we go in.'

Flap led the way with Jake behind him. Jake concentrated on following Flap, afraid that he might lose him, and let Flap worry about avoiding the opposition.

Flap halted on a little hill halfway between the ship and the cache. The village was directly opposite them. To get to the boat landing, however, they would have to either pass the village or retrace the route they had just traveled, circling both the weapons cache and the village.

'Has to be here,' Flap said. 'It's shitty, I know. But we'll need a side shot at the ship. From the boat landing we're looking at the stern.' After a bit he asked, 'Think you can get here on your own if you have to?'

'Yeah. Unless they turn off that streetlight across the way.'

'They won't. Let's go.'

They went back toward the cache and settled in fifty feet away, hidden in waist-high foliage. Flap waited until a guard went by and turned the corner, then he flitted across the gap like a shadow and disappeared into an aisle between stacks of boxes. He left his rifle with Jake.

One minute passed, then another.

The second guard came around the corner and walked by.

Flap had to find the man inside amid the aisles, if there was one, kill him, then come back to dispose of the guards outside. It was a tall order, yet these men had to be down before Jake and Flap could rip into the boxes, which could not be done noiselessly.

Several more minutes ticked by. Jake fingered his flooded, useless watch. Perhaps he should have thrown it away.

Okay, Flap. Where are you, shipmate?

Come on! Come on, Flap!

Oh, Jesus, don't let anything happen to Le Beau.

384

Little late to think about that, isn't it, Jake? You two could be on a boat going down the river right this very moment if you hadn't insisted on going through with this.

Well, something had gone wrong. Flap was in trouble.

Jake was torn by indecision. If he went inside looking he could blow this whole deal. Yet if Le Beau were injured he might die without assistance.

Here comes one of the guards. Walking and looking, his rifle held carelessly in the crook of his arm.

As the guard went by the aisle where Flap had disappeared, he hesitated. Jake stared at him across the sights of the AK. Now the guard took a step back and peered into the gloom as Jake's finger tightened on the trigger. *If he points his weapon he's dead.*

Hands reached for the guard and jerked him forward off his feet, into the aisle.

What were you worried about, Jake? Flap's the best, the absolute best, a fucking super-Marine.

More time passed.

Waiting was the hard part. If you didn't know what was happening.

Jake lifted his head and took a long, careful scan of the area. No one moving.

The other guard came around the corner. He was more alert than the first one. He held his rifle in both hands, the muzzle up. He looked puzzled.

Uh-oh, he didn't pass the other guy and now he's wondering where he is.

He stopped and looked about carefully, then turned and went back the way he had come. When he reached the corner an arm shot forward. The guard jerked away.

Even from this distance Jake could see the hilt of the knife protruding just below his chin. The rifle fell harmlessly as the man staggered, grabbing at his throat. Le Beau was right there, an arm coiling around the man's mouth to ensure he didn't scream. When he went down Jake hobbled forward.

Le Beau was bent over holding his side. Blood splotched his flight suit everywhere. The Marine jerked the knife from the man's throat and wiped it on his leg, leaving yet another streak on his filthy flight suit, then slipped it into his sleeve sheath.

'What happened?'

'Guy inside had a knife. He got me good.'

'Let's saddle up and get the fuck outta here.'

'No. They bought us tickets and we're taking the ride. Quick, let's drag this guy out of sight. Grab hold.'

They each took an arm.

'How bad is it?' Jake wanted to know.

'I don't know. Burns like fire.'

'Can you keep going?'

'We'll see.' As they dropped the body in a dark aisle, Flap muttered, 'Always knew I'd get it with a knife.'

He led the way down a gloomy aisle, almost feeling his way along. 'The stuff we want is down here. Fuses and wire. Found it this afternoon.'

They attacked the side of a box with Flap's throwing knife. The nails ripping loose sounded loud as gunshots.

'How do you know what's in each box?'

'Seen crates like these before, in Cambodia. This is all Russian stuff. The crates got symbols on them for the comrades who can't read Russian. Like me.'

The side of the crate came loose. Flap dug into it. He came out with a handful of primers and wire. After a little more digging they extracted a timer.

'Now all we gotta do is find the plastique.'

Jake was horrified. 'You don't know where it is?'

'Couldn't find it this afternoon.'

'Maybe it's still on the ship.'

'Maybe. Get out your lighter and look.'

They found a crate with the lid already open. Grenades. Each man stuffed four or five into his chest pocket, then they went on.

Time was dragging. The lighter got hot and flickered. It was about out of butane. Someone was going to come check on the guards any minute now.

Jake was about to give in to despair when they found the plastique. There were at least five crates of it, piled one on top of the other.

'Boost me up,' Flap said.

Lying on top of the crates, Flap pried at the lid of the topmost one with his knife. More groaning noises, as loud as fire sirens. Finally he said, 'Okay, pass up the primers and stuff.'

'How long do you want on the timer?'

'Thirty minutes.'

The timer was mechanical. Jake began winding it up as fast as he could. When the spring would go no tighter, he used the lighter. The clock face would take up to a twelve-hour delay. He set thirty minutes, then passed it up to Flap.

Two minutes passed before Flap asked for help to get down. His side was wet with warm blood.

'Those anti-tank rockets are down this way,' he murmured. He took four steps and fell.

Jake helped him up. 'Let's try to get a bandage on that.'

'With what?'

'Shirt off one of the corpses.'

'We don't have time. Come on!

They took four of the rockets, two for each man. Flap was visibly weaker now, but in the spluttering light of the butane lighter he took the time to explain how to arm, aim and shoot. The lighter died for the last time before they were through and couldn't be relit. Jake dropped it and slung his rifle over his back. Then he hoisted two of the rockets.

He had to help Flap to his feet. Flap hoisted his two and let the rifle lay. He turned and led the way.

Two steps out of the aisle Flap froze. A figure stood in front of him with a rifle leveled.

The captain!

'You two! I knew you weren't dead.'

He took a step closer. 'You have caused me a great deal of trouble. Now I'm going to cause you a great deal of pain.'

Quick as thought he moved forward and smashed Flap in the head with the butt of his rifle. Flap collapsed.

The captain drove a kick at Jake Grafton that caught him right where his rib was broken. He almost passed out from the pain.

When he came to his senses he was lying almost across Flap. The captain was talking. 'Been into the weapons, I see. What else have you done?' He kicked Jake again, but he took the blow mostly on his shoulder.

Jake felt for Flap's left arm. He found it. The sleeve was loose. The knife came free in his hand.

Another kick. 'What have you done in there? Answer me!'

As the foot flashed out again Jake grabbed it and pulled. Off balance, the captain fell. Jake scrambled to his knees and went for him but the man was too quick. He was coming off the ground so Jake slashed with the knife, a vicious, desperate backhand.

The captain staggered back. Through all the kicks he had kept his rifle in his left hand. Now he dropped it and grabbed his stomach with both hands as a shriek of agony escaped him.

His guts spilled out.

The captain fell to the ground. Jake crawled toward him and stabbed, again and again and again.

When the captain went limp Jake slashed at this throat for good measure, then rolled over moaning. He couldn't breathe. His side!

The captain quivered. In a haze of pain, Jake stabbed the knife into his chest and left it there.

Somehow he got to his feet.

Le Beau seemed only partially conscious. Jake grabbed

him by the back of the neck of his flight suit and heaved. The Marine slid about two feet.

Jake needed both hands.

The boat dock. He had to get Flap to the boat.

No way but to drag him.

In a haze of pain, struggling to breathe, he pulled. He paused occasionally to glance over his shoulder, because he was dragging him backward. Right by the lights of the village.

Someone would see him and shoot him.

He didn't care.

How he made the journey he didn't know. Flap stirred several times but he didn't come to.

Finally he had the Marine on the boards of the dock. In a supreme effort he got him over the side of the cabin cruiser onto its deck.

He paused, breathing raggedly, not getting enough air but sucking hard anyway.

Cast off. He had to cast off.

Somehow he remembered the other boats. He got out on the dock and fumbled with their ropes.

The knife! Damn, he had left it sticking in the captain.

He managed to untie all of the ropes except one, which was knotted too tight for his fingers. In his pain and anxiety he forgot all about the second knife that Flap carried.

The ropes for the cabin cruiser came loose easily.

Jake got aboard just as the current began to ease it away from the dock. Those other boats that were free from their moorings were already drifting.

The grenades.

He fumbled in his chest pocket for one. He pulled the pin and held it as the distance increased.

Now.

He let the spoon fly, gritted his teeth and heaved. It hit on the dock, bounced once, then rolled into the moored boat.

Jake sagged down just as it went off.

The noise would bring the pirates. Maybe this would be a good time to see if the engine in this boat can be started.

Fumbling with the switches by the helm, he found the one for the battery. A little light came on. There was a button just beside it. Here goes nothing!

Please, God.

The engine turned over.

He jabbed the button in and held it. Grind, grind, grind as he played with the throttle.

A choke. Maybe there was a choke. Desperately he felt around the panel.

He found it and pulled it out. The engine ground several more times, then caught. He inched the throttle forward from idle and spun the helm.

He had the boat headed downriver when the first bullets thudded in.

One man shooting. No, two.

He hunkered by the wheel and fed in full throttle.

The boat accelerated nicely. He slewed it and craned his head to see. The banks of the river were even darker than the water.

Stay in the middle.

More bullets whapping in. The windshield in front of Jake shattered. Then something hit him in the shoulder, drove him forward into the panel. Somehow he kept his feet under him.

The shooting stopped. He was rounding a bend. He got himself into the seat behind the wheel.

How far to the sea? Would the pirates follow?

He was worrying about that when he heard the explosion, a roar that grew and grew and grew, then died abruptly.

His head swam and he worked desperately hard to breathe. Somehow he stayed conscious and kept the boat in the channel.

Eventually the darkness of the trees on the riversides merged with the night and the boat began to pitch and roll. The ocean. They were out of the river.

There was a bungee cord dangling from the wheel. With the last of his strength Jake managed to hook the free end to the bottom of the chair where he had been sitting.

He rolled Flap over to check on him. He had a terrible knot on his forehead and the pupil of one eye was completely dilated. Concussion.'

'Hey, Flap. It's me, Jake.'

The Marine moved. His lips worked. Jake put his head down to hear. 'Horowitz had a brother. Tell him . . . Tell him . . .'

Just what Jake was to tell him Flap didn't say.

Jake was so tired. He lay down beside Flap.

The boat ran out of fuel an hour later. It was rolling amid the swells of a sun-flecked blue sea when a pilot of an A-7 from *Columbia* spotted it. The crewman of the helicopter lowered found Jake Grafton and Flap Le Beau lying side by side in the cockpit.

CHAPTER TWENTY-THREE

Jake woke up in a room with cream-colored walls and ceiling, in a bed with crisp white sheets. A sunbeam shown like a spotlight through a window. An IV was dripping into a vein in his left arm.

Hospital.

His curiosity satisfied, he drifted off to sleep again. When he next awoke a nurse was there taking his pulse. 'Welcome back to the land of the living,' she said, and lowered his wrist back to the bed. She annotated a clipboard, then gave him a grin.

'Where am I?'

'Honolulu. Trippler Army Hospital.'

'Hawaii?'

'Yes. You've been here almost a day now. You're just coming out of the recovery room.'

'Le Beau? Marine captain. He here too?'

'Yes. He's still in recovery.'

'How is he?'

'Still asleep. He's had an operation. You've had one too but yours didn't take quite as long.'

'When he wakes up, I want to talk to him. Okay?'

'We'll see. You take that up with the doctor when he comes around. He should be here in about thirty minutes. Is there anything I can do for you?'

'No.'

She busied herself arranging the sheets and checkin

that he had fresh water in a glass by the bed. He lay taking it in, enjoying the brightness and the cleanliness.

After a bit curiosity stirred him. 'What day is it?'

'This is Wednesday.'

'We got shot down . . . December nine. What day . . . is it now?'

'The sixteenth of December.'

'We missed Australia.'

'What was that?'

'Nothing,' he murmured, and closed his eyes again. He was very tired.

He was still pretty foggy when he talked to the doctor, either later that morning or that afternoon. The sunbeam had moved. He noticed that.

.'We operated on your left side. Your lung collapsed. Lucky you didn't bleed to death. And of course you were shot in the shoulder. By some miracle the bullet missed your collarbone. Went clean through.'

'Uh-huh.'

'You're also fighting a raging infection. You aren't out of the woods yet, sailor.'

'Le Beau, how's he doing?'

'He's critical. He lost a lot of blood.'

'He gonna make it?'

'We think so.'

'When he wakes up, I want to see him.'

'We'll see.'

'Bring him in here. This room's big enough. Or take me nto his room.'

'We'll see.'

'How'd we get here, anyway?'

'The ship medevaced you two to Clark and the Air 'orce flew you here.'

'I may not be out of the woods, but I'm out of the jungle.'

The next day Flap was wheeled into the room. His bed 'as placed beside Jake's. A bandage covered half his head.

But he grinned when he saw Jake out of his one unob-structed eye.

'Hey, shipmate.'

'As I live and breathe,' said Flap Le Beau as the nurses hovered around hooking up everything. 'The neighbor-hood is integrating. Better put the house up for sale while you still can.'

'If you don't stop that racist stuff I'm gonna start calling you Chocolate.'

'Chocolate Le Beau,' he said, savoring it. 'I like it. They hung that Flap tag on me because I talk a lot. My real name is Clarence.'

'I know. Middle initial O. What's that stand for?'

'Odysseus. I picked it out in college after I read the *Odyssey*. Clarence O. Le Beau. Got a ring to it, don't it?' He directed the question to one of the nurses, who looked sort of sweet.

'It *is* very nice,' she said, and smiled.

'So how you feeling?' Jake asked.

'Like a week-old dog turd that's been run over by a truck. And you?'

'Not quite that chipper.'

When the nurses were leaving Flap told the sweet one, 'Come back and see us anytime, dearest.'

'I will, Clarence O.'

When they were gone, Flap told Jake, 'Don't worry. I'll get you one too. Trust me.'

'So what's wrong with your head?'

'Concussion and blood clot. They had to drill a hole to relieve the pressure. Another hole in my head – just what needed, eh?'

'The captain laid you out with a butt stroke. I killed him.'

'I figured that or we wouldn't be here. But some other time, huh? I don't want to even think about that shit.'

'Yeah.'

'What's for lunch? Have they told you?'

'No.'

'I am really ready for some good grits.'

'Guess we missed Australia.'

'These things happen. Don't sweat it. You can make it up to me somehow.'

The following day they were visited by a Navy commander, an officer on the staff of Commander In Chief Pacific – CINCPAC. He interviewed both men, recorded their stories, then when they tired, left while they napped. He came back for another hour just before dinner and asked questions.'

'If I can do anything for you gentlemen, give me a call.'

He left a card with his name and telephone number on the stands beside each of their beds.

They had lost a lot of weight. When the nurses first sat Jake up he was amazed at how skinny his legs and arms were.

Improvement was slow at first, then quicker. By the fifth day Jake was walking to the bathroom. He bragged, so Flap got himself out of bed and went when the nurses weren't there. He had trouble with his balance but he made it to the john and back by holding on to things.

On the eighth day they went for a hike, holding on to each other, to see what they could see. A nurse caught them and made them retrace their steps.

The hospital was half-empty. 'Not like it used to be. You were the first gunshot victim we saw in two months,' one nurse told Jake.

'Not like the good old days,' he replied.

'They weren't good days,' he was told. 'Thank God the war is over.'

On the day after Christmas they demanded clothes. That afternoon an orderly brought them cardboard boxes containing some of their clothes that the guys on the ship had packed and sent. The orderly helped Jake open his. Inside he found underwear, uniforms, shoes, insignia.

As he was inspecting a set of khakis, the thought went through his head that he should discard this shirt and buy another.

Where had that thought come from? He was getting out – *out* of the Navy!

He sat on the edge of the bed holding the shirt, looking at it but not seeing it. *Out*. To do what? What could he conceivably do as a civilian that would mean as much to him as what he had spent the last six years of his life doing?

He was a naval officer. Lieutenant, United States Navy.

That meant something.

He was digging in the box when he found a letter. It was from the Real McCoy.

Hey Shipmate,

When you read this you will probably be getting spruced up to go to the club or chase women. Some guys will do about anything to get out of a little work.

This boat was like a damn funeral parlor the night you and Flap didn't come back. The mood improved a thousand percent when they announced that the chopper was inbound with both of you aboard. The captain and CAG and Skipper Haldane were there on the flight deck with the medicos when the chopper landed, along with a couple hundred other guys.

After the docs got you guys stabilized and you left in the COD, the captain got on the 1-MC and said some real nice things about you. It was pretty maudlin. I forgot most of it so I won't try to repeat it here, but suffice it to say that every swinging dick on this boat is glad you two clowns made it.

Australia is on. TS for you. We'll party on without you, but you'll be missed.

Your friend,
Real

Two days later Jake decked himself out in a white uniform and Flap selected a set of khakis. They strolled the grounds. The days were Hawaii balmy with clouds every afternoon. One day they took a taxi to the golf course and rented a golf cart.

Out on the fairways they went over the whole adventure again, little by little, a scene here, a scene there. Gradually they dropped it and went on to other subjects, like women and politics and flying.

One day Flap brought the subject up again, for what proved to be the last time. 'So *where* is my slasher?'

'I think I left it sticking in the captain. But I might have just dropped it somewhere. It's a little hazy.'

'That was my best knife.'

'Tough.'

'I designed it. It was custom-made for me. Cost me *two hundred* bucks.'

'Order another.'

Flap laughed. 'I can see you are oozing remorse over my loss.'

'To be frank, I don't give a shit about your knife.'

'You're as full of tact as ever. That's one of the qualities that will take you far, Grafton. Ol' Mister Smooth.'

'And the horse you rode in on, Clarence O.'

'It's my turn to drive this friggin' cart. You're always hoggin' the drivin'.'

'That's because *I'm* the pilot. Why don't you tell me about some of the ugly women you've run across in your adventures?'

'Well, by God, I just will.' And he did.

In the evenings there was little to do, so Jake wrote letters. His first was to his former roommate, Sammy Lundeen. He hit the highlights of this last cruise and devoted a whole page to crossing the line. In the finest traditions of naval aviation, he seriously downplayed his and Flap's role in the pirate adventure. Luck, luck, luck – he and Flap had survived due to the grotesque ineptitude of the villains and despite their own extraordinarily stupid mistakes, mistakes that would have wrung tears from the eyes of any competent aviator. All in all, the letter was quite a literary effort, first class fiction. That thought didn't occur to Jake, of course, when he reread it before stuffing it into an envelope. His buddy Lundeen would chuckle, Jake knew, and shake his head sadly. Good ol' Sammy.

Instinctively he adopted a completely different tone when he wrote to Tiger Cole, his last BN during the Vietnam War. There was no bullshit in Tiger Cole, and no one who knew him would try to lay the smelly stuff on him. You gave it to that grim warrior straight and un-adorned.

He ended the letter this way:

> I have never thought of myself as professional. Never. I've been a guy who went into the service because there was a war and I've merely tried to do my best until the time came for me to go back to the real world. Still I have watched so many pros since I have been in the Navy – you included – that I think I'm beginning to see how the thing is done. And why. I hope so, anyway. So I've decided to stay in.
>
> The decision hasn't been easy. I guess no important commitment is.
>
> Whenever I get back to the mainland, I'll give you a call. I'll probably take some leave. Maybe swing by Pensacola if you're still there and we can swill a beer at the club.
>
> Hang tough, shipmate.
>
> Your friend,
> Jake

One day Jake penned a letter to Callie. Then he put it in

the drawer beside his bed. Each day he got it out, read it through and debated whether or not he should mail it.

She probably had another boyfriend. There was always that possibility. Jake Grafton had no intention of playing the fool, with this or any other woman. So he kept the letter formal, as if he were writing to a great-aunt. He omitted any reference to his adventure with the pirates or the fact that he was just now residing in a hospital room. But on the second page he said this:

> I've decided to stay in the Navy. It has been a tough decision and I've had to really wrestle with it. The arguments for getting out are many and you know most of them. The Navy is a large bureaucracy; anyone who thinks the bureaucracy will miss them when they are gone is kidding himself.
>
> Still, this is where I belong. I like the people, I can do the work, I believe the work is important. Of course the Navy is not for everyone, but it is, I believe, the best place for me. I know full well that there is nothing that I can do here that others cannot do better, but here I *can* make a contribution.

He closed with a few pleasantries and the hope that all was fine with her.

On New Year's Eve he got it out again to read it through carefully.

The tone was wrong, all wrong.

He added a PS.

> As I reread this letter it occurs to me that I've made a very stupid mistake. The last few months I've been so busy worrying that you might not love me as much as I love you that I lost sight of what love is. Love by its very nature opens you up to getting burned.
>
> I love you, Callie. You were a rock to hang on to the

last year of the war, the one sane person in an insane world. And you've been a rock to hang on to these last six months. You've been in my thoughts and in my dreams.

If I love you more than you love me, so be it. I'm tough enough to love and lose. But I just wanted you to know how much I care.

As ever,
Jake

In the third week of January he and Flap moved to the BOQ. They continued to visit the hospital on an outpatient basis. Flap took daily physical therapy to overcome the effects of his head injury. The knife wound in his side drained slowly and healed stubbornly. Eventually it did heal, leaving a bad scar.

Jake merely needed a checkup occasionally. His collapsed lung and the resultant infection had been more serious than the bullet hole in his shoulder, which healed quickly, yet by now he was well on his way to a complete recovery. He went with Flap every morning anyway and kibitzed as the Marine went through his exercises. Then they went to the golf course and rode around in a golf cart.

One day they rented clubs. They merely slapped at the balls, since neither man could swing a club with any vigor. Slap the ball a hundred feet, using mostly arms and wrists, get in the cart and drive over to it, slap the thing again. It was crazy, but it felt fine.

After that they played daily. Gradually the shoulders and ribs loosened up and they swung more freely, but neither man had ever played much golf and neither was very good.

They were standing on the carrier pier at Pearl Harbor when *Columbia* arrived in early February.

'Look who has returned!' the Real McCoy shouted when they walked into the ready room. 'The prodigal sons are *back!*'

'We only came aboard for a change of underwear. It's been hell, golf every day, hot women every night . . .'

They were surrounded by people shaking their hands and welcoming them back. When the mob scene had subsided to a low roar, the Real asked Jake, 'By any chance did you bring a copy of the *Wall Street Journal?*'

'I hate to give you the bad news, roomie, but the market is down a thousand points this morning. They're talking about a depression.'

'Aah . . . ,' said the Real, searching Jake's face.

'Millionaires are leaping out of windows even as we speak.'

'You're kidding, right?'

After lunch Jake went to his stateroom with McCoy. He crawled into the top bunk and let out a long sigh. 'Feels so good.'

'Got something to show you,' the Real said. From his desk he brought forth a series of aerial photos. 'We took these before we smacked that hijacked Cuban freighter. See that big blast area – that's where the pile was that you and Flap blew up.'

'You guys bombed the Cuban ship?'

'Oh yes. The government of Indonesia thought those weapons might go to some of their own indigenous revolutionaries, so they asked for our help before we even offered it.'

'I never saw anything about it in the papers.'

'They never told the press.'

'I'll be darned.'

That night the entire squadron went to the O Club en masse. It was an epic party, complete with a letter the next day from the CO of the base to the captain of *Columbia* complaining about rowdy behavior and demanding

401

damages. That night Jake and Flap slept in their bunks aboard ship.

Before the ship sailed, Jake spent a quiet moment with Lieutenant Colonel Haldane. 'I'd like to stay in the Navy, Skipper. I want to withdraw my resignation.'

Haldane smiled and offered his hand. Jake shook it.

'There's one other thing,' Jake said slowly. 'I hear that some of the guys are going to get some traps the first day out of port just in case they need to fly during the transit to the States. I'd need too many to get current, but I'd take it as a personal favor if you'd let me and Flap get one.'

'I need up chits from the flight surgeon.'

'That's the rub. I think I can get one but I don't think they'll give Flap an up. The doctors at Trippler want him to do more physical therapy. He still has some balance problems.'

'According to that report we received from CINCPAC, he took a rifle butt in the head.'

'Yessir. One hell of a butt stroke. He had lost a lot of blood by the that time and didn't have the reflexes to minimize the impact.'

'Well, you and Flap take your medical files to the flight surgeon and have him look you over. Then have him call me.'

'Aye aye, sir.'

Somehow it worked out. Jake and Flap rode the catapult two hours after *Columbia* cleared Pearl. By some miracle he didn't question he got a plane full of gas, so he had to burn down or dump before he could come back into the pattern.

They yanked and banked and shouted over the ICS as they did tight turns around the tops of cumulus clouds. Jake managed a loop and a Cuban eight before Flap begged for mercy. He was dizzy.

Jake smoked into the break at five hundred knots. The air boss never peeped. Better yet, Jake snagged a three-wire.

On the morning of the fly-off Jake took the Pri-Fly duty. All the planes of the air wing were to be launched: the crews were selected strictly on the basis of seniority. Tonight they would be home with wives and children and sweethearts. Jake and Flap were, of course, not flying off. They were riding the ship into port. Flap had an appointment at the Oakland Naval Hospital and Jake was catching a commercial flight to Oak Harbor via Seattle to pick up his car, then he was taking a month's leave. He thought he would head for Virginia by way of Chicago. Maybe look Callie up, see what she was up to. At the end of the month he would report again to Tiny Dick Donovan at VA-128.

The fly-off went well. One by one every plane on the ship taxied to the catapults and was shot aloft. They rendezvoused in divisions over the ship and headed east.

When the last plane was gone and the angel helicopter had settled onto the angle and shut down, the ship secured from flight quarters. Jake went down to the strangely empty flight deck and walked around one last time.

Not really. He would be back. If not this ship, then another. Once again he savored the oily aroma of steam seeping up from the catapults, felt the heat as it mixed with the salty sea breeze.

He was wandering the deck when Bosun Muldowski approached. He stunned Jake with a salute. Jake returned it.

'Hear you're staying in, Mr Grafton.'

'Yep. Your example shamed me into it.'

Muldowski laughed. 'It's a good life,' he said 'Beats eight to five anywhere. Maybe if I had found the right woman and had some kids . . . But you can't live on maybes. Didn't work out that way. You gotta live your life one day at a time. That's the way God fixed it up. Today do what you do best and let tomorrow take care of tomorrow.'

Jake was packing in his stateroom when the ship docked at the Alameda carrier pier. The Real McCoy had flown off with the Marines – he had earned it. McCoy's steel footlockers sporting new padlocks sat one atop the other by the door. His desk was clean and nothing hung in his closet. His bunk was stripped and the sheets turned in.

Jake had also turned in his sheets and blankets. Last night he had packed the suitcase he was taking on leave – now he was stuffing everything else into the parachute bags. The suitcase he had purchased in Hawaii. The padlocks for the bags lay on the desk. Net gain after one eight-month cruise: one suitcase and some new scars.

The engagement ring he had purchased for Callie oh those many months ago was the last item left in his desk safe. He held it in his hand and wondered what to do with it. The suitcase might get stolen or lost by the airline, shuffled off to Buffalo or Pago Pago or Timbuktu. For lack of a better option, he put the ring in his shirt pocket and buttoned the pocket.

The telephone rang. 'Lieutenant Grafton, sir.'

'Mr Grafton, this is the duty officer at the officers' brow. You have a visitor.'

'Me?'

'Yes, sir. You need to come sign her in and escort her.'

'Okay, but who is this pers—?' He stopped because he was talking to a dead phone. The duty officer had hung up.

There was obviously some mistake. He didn't know a soul in the San Francisco Bay area. He glanced at his new watch, guaranteed to be waterproof to a depth of three hundred feet or his money back. He had four hours to catch the plane from the Oakland airport. Plenty of time.

He grabbed his ball cap and headed for the ceremonial quarterdeck at the head of the officers' brow. It was on the hangar deck, which was the scene of hundreds of sailors coming and going on a variety of errands, most of them frivolous. Crowds of sailors stood on the aircraft elevators shouting to people on the pier below. Near the enlisted brow a band was tooting merrily.

He saw her standing, looking curiously around when he was still a hundred feet away.

Callie McKenzie!

As he walked toward her she spotted him. She beamed.

'Hello, Jake.'

He couldn't think of anything to say.

'You've lost some weight,' she said.

'Been sick.'

'Oh. Well, aren't you glad to see me?'

'Thunderstruck. I'm speechless.'

She looked even better than he remembered. As he stared her eyes danced with amusement and a smile grew on her face.

'I *never* expected to see you here,' he told her. 'Not in a million years.'

'Life is full of surprises.'

'Isn't it, though?'

He was rooted where he stood, unable to take his eyes off her and unsure what to do next. Why was she here? Why hadn't she written in five months? Then a thought struck him: 'Did you come with someone?' he asked, and glanced around, half expecting to see her mother, or even some man.

'No.' She reached out and touched his arm. 'All these sailors are staring at us. Can you sign me in so we can go somewhere and talk?'

Jake flushed. 'Oh, yes, sure.'

The officer of the deck and quartermaster of the watch grinned shamelessly, enjoying Jake's obvious discomfort. Jake scribbled his name beside Callie's in the visitors' log, then steered her away with two fingers on her elbow.

'Let's go up to the flight deck. Fine view of the bay area from up there.'

Indeed, the view from the flight deck was spectacular. The San Francisco skyline, Treasure Island, airliners coming and going at San Francisco International and Oakland – the panorama would have frozen most people who had spent the largest part of the last eight months looking at empty ocean dead in their tracks. However Jake Grafton was too acutely aware of the presence of Callie McKenzie to give the scene more than a glance.

'How are your folks?' he asked finally, breaking the silence.

'They're fine. And yours?'

'Okay. Almost called you a time or two.'

'And I almost wrote you. I should have. And you should have called.'

'Why didn't you write?'

'I didn't want to influence your decision. To stay in or get out, what to do with your life. This was your decision, Jake, not mine.'

'Well, I made it. I'm staying in.'

'Why?'

Jake Grafton ran his fingers through his hair. 'I was looking for something. Turns out I had it all along and just didn't realize it.'

'What were you looking for?'

'Something worth doing. Something that made a difference. The war was such a mess . . . I guess that I lost sight of what we're all about here. It's more than ships and planes and cats and traps. I realized that finally.'

'I always thought that what you did was important.'

'Your dad didn't.'

'Dad? I love him dearly but this is my life, not his.'

'So what are you going to do with your life?'

She didn't answer. She lowered her head and began walking slowly. Jake stayed with her. When she got to the bow of the ship she stood looking across the water at San Francisco with the wind playing in her hair.

'I guess I'm like most modern women. I want a family and a career. Languages have always fascinated me, and I have found I love to teach. That's the big plan, but some of it is contingent.'

'On what?'

'On you.'

'Well, I don't think that's very fair. After all, lady, you shoved me out into the cold to make up my own mind.'

'You were never out in the cold, Jake. There hasn't been an hour in the last eight months that I wasn't thinking about you. I've read and reread your letters until I almost wore out the paper. Especially that last letter. I think I was wondering too, wondering if you loved me as much as I loved you.'

'You were always with me too,' he confessed, and grinned. 'Maybe an hour or two now and then you slipped away, but most of the time you were there.'

Her hand found his. They began strolling along the deck. The breeze was fresh and crisp.

'So why did you come here?' he asked.

'I came to get married.'

He gaped. It was like a kick in the stomach. He had thought . . . He jerked his hand from her grasp.

'Who's the lucky guy?' he managed.

'You,' she said, her head cocked slightly to one side, her lips twisting into a grin.

'*Me?*'

'Who else could it be? I love you more than words can tell, Jacob Lee Grafton.'

'You want to marry *me?*'

She laughed. He had always liked her laugh. 'Do you want me to get down on one knee and propose?'

'I accept,' he told her, and seized both her hands. 'Where and when?'

'This afternoon. Anywhere.'

'My God, woman! This is sudden. Are you sure?'

'I've been thinking about this for a year,' she told him. 'I'm absolutely certain.'

'Well, I'll be . . .' He took off his cap and ran his fingers through his hair. Then he remembered the ring. He pulled it from his shirt pocket, looked at it, then put it on her finger.

Now she was surprised. 'You knew I was coming?'

'No. I bought that for you over a year ago. Been carrying it ever since.'

'Oh, Jake,' she said, and wrapped her arms around his neck. Her lips found his.

He finally broke the embrace and seized her hand. 'Come on. We'll need a best man. My BN is still aboard. He and I were going to have lunch together.'

The quickest way to Flap's stateroom was into the catwalk behind the island, then into the 0-3 level and down. On the catwalk Jake happened to glance at the pier. There was a pink Cadillac convertible parked at the foot of the officers' brow with four women in it.

Muldowski was walking across the brow. Now he turned and saluted the American flag on the fantail.

Jake cupped his hand to his mouth and shouted, '*Muldowski! Hey, Bosun!*'

The warrant officer looked up. He pointed.

'I'm getting *married*,' Jake Grafton roared. 'Will you give the bride away?'

'When?' Muldowski boomed.

'This afternoon. Wait for us. We'll be down in ten minutes.'

'Is that the bride?'

'Yes.'

'I may keep her my—' The rest of the bosun's comment was drowned by music as the band launched into another tune.

The women in the convertible were on their feet applauding. The bosun started clapping too, as did dozens of people on the pier.

Callie was grinning broadly. She looked so happy. What the heck! In full view of the world Jake swept her into his arms.